McAdam's Women

•

Pebbles On The Beach

EVELYN HOOD
OMNIBUS

McAdam's Women

•

Pebbles On The Beach

LITTLE, BROWN AND COMPANY

A Little, Brown Book
This edition first published in Great Britain by Little, Brown in 2001
The Evelyn Hood Omnibus Copyright © Evelyn Hood 2001

Previously published separately:
McAdam's Women first published in Great Britain by
Little, Brown and Company 1994
Published by Warner Books 1995
Copyright © Evelyn Hood 1994
Pebbles On The Beach first published in Great Britain by
Little, Brownand Company 1995
Published by Warner Books 1996
Copyright © Evelyn Hood 1996

The moral right of the author has been asserted.

A CIP catalogue record for this book
is available from the British Library.

ISBN 0 316 85889 7

Printed and bound in Italy

Little, Brown and Company (UK)
Brettenham House
Lancaster Place
London WC2E 7EN

McAdam's Women

1

Although she had been watching the doorway intently for the past five minutes, Isla felt a sense of shock, like a fist slamming into her breastbone, when the girl she had been expecting arrived. They had never set eyes on each other before, but she would have known immediately who the newcomer was, even if they had only glanced at each other in a crowded street in passing.

From beneath a black cloche hat clear blue eyes swept the busy tearoom, halting as they reached the table in the corner, and Isla's tentative, half-raised hand.

They flared, just as Kenneth's did whenever he was astonished. Black-gloved fingers reached out to grasp the door-frame for a moment, and then, wiping the shock from her face with a deliberate effort, the girl came across the room, skirting tables, side-stepping waitresses.

Isla had intended to rise to meet her, but instead she stayed where she was, pinned to the small chair by this reminder of her recent loss. The paralysing agony had hit her several times since Kenneth's death; just as she thought that she had accepted it and come to terms with it, sudden realisation and a wave of desolation swept anew through her.

1

Now her first sight of Kenneth's daughter – his older daughter – had revived it.

The girl had his clear, steady, somewhat pale blue eyes, though in her case they were fringed with gold, instead of Kenneth's more stubby lashes. She had his strongly marked brows, his mouth – without, of course, the red-gold moustache above it – his straight neat nose. Beneath the black velvet hat she wore, Isla glimpsed hair the vibrant glowing bronze of autumn leaves. The colour Kenneth's had been. Her face was oval, her chin neatly rounded where his had been square. Slim and straight, dressed in a high-necked black knitted suit, black stockings, black shoes, she even had Kenneth's walk, lithe and quick and easy, though constricted at that moment by the tables in the room.

Isla's throat tightened, and for a moment tears prickled behind her eyes. She fought them back, telling herself sternly that she was not going to let herself weep in this public place, in front of this young woman who looked so familiar to her, yet was a stranger.

Swallowing hard, she regained her own self-control as the girl arrived beside her table, suddenly hesitant and unsure. 'You can't be—' she began, then stopped, folding her mouth round the next two words as though to hold them back.

Isla got to her feet. 'I'm Isla Mc—' She hesitated, then said clearly, 'Isla McAdam.'

The girl's eyes flared again, this time with arrogant anger, and she ignored the hand that was held out to her. 'You've got no right to that name!'

'Please believe me when I say that I thought I had,'

2

Isla said steadily, letting her hand fall back to her side.
'And you're Ainslie.'

'But you're so young!'

'I'm twenty-six.' Twenty-six for the past week. Her
birthday had come one short week after hearing of
Kenneth's death.

'My God!' There was anger in Ainslie's voice.
'You're only five years older than I am – and he was
forty-six!' She swayed slightly, groped for the back of a
chair, found it, and sank into it.

'I knew Kenneth's age, but I never felt that it mattered.' Isla took her own seat again, still fighting to
keep her voice level. She had made up her mind that
she wasn't going to be afraid of this girl, but despite
herself, the fear was there. Without knowing it, she had
been part of a terrible wrong committed against Ainslie
McAdam and her mother and brother.

Colour rose to Ainslie's cheeks and contempt honed
her voice. 'How could he do this to – to us?'

It was numbing to look into eyes so like Kenneth's,
yet cold in a way his had never been. Under his daughter's antagonistic stare Isla might well have given way to
her grief and her terror of the unknown future, but it
was the contemptuous note in the girl's voice that saved
her from possible weakness. She wasn't to blame for
what had happened, she had nothing to be ashamed of.
She would not allow this young woman to make her feel
like a criminal.

'Ainslie – Miss McAdam, it was you who suggested
this meeting. If you've changed your mind, you're free
to go, though I've ordered tea for us both.'

It arrived just at that moment, brought to them by a

middle-aged woman so plump that her small white frilled apron looked like a postage stamp stuck on to her black dress. She deftly transferred the cups and saucers and the nickel-plated teapot and sugar bowl and milk jug to the spotless white table-cloth, then scurried to a huge sideboard and brought back a tiered plate-stand filled with plates of cakes and biscuits. Her eyebrows rose and she looked hurt when Ainslie McAdam impatiently flapped a hand at her and said, 'Take these away!'

'Madam? The cakes've just come up fresh from the bakery below . . .'

Isla forced the corners of her lips into a placating smile. 'They look delicious, but I don't think we're in the mood for them today.'

The woman's eyes swept from one to the other, taking in Ainslie's black suit and the black armband on the sleeve of Isla's grey woollen coat. Her own face fell into solemn lines.

'Of course, madam,' she murmured, and went off, leaving them alone and silent in a roomful of chattering, brightly dressed women.

Ainslie McAdam watched, her brows drawn together in a straight line above brooding eyes, as Isla drew off her gloves and began to pour tea. She shook her head when Isla lifted the milk jug, and pulled her own gloves off, lifting a hand to flick the flowing end of the black silk scarf that served as a hatband back from her shoulder.

Carefully, aware of the unblinking gaze opposite, Isla poured her own tea, added milk and more sugar than she would normally have taken, and stirred the liquid. The hot sweet tea helped to steady her nerves.

4

'This is very difficult for us both,' she said as she returned the cup to its saucer.

'I asked you to meet me here because I won't have you calling on my mother. She's never been strong, and now she's ill with worry and shame over this – this business. I'll not have her upset any further!'

'I've no intention of forcing myself on your mother, or on any other member of your family.'

Ainslie's eyes said that she didn't believe that. 'Why would you come here to Paisley if you weren't out to make trouble for us?'

'I came at my—' Isla stopped herself just in time from saying, 'my husband's,' and changed it to, 'your father's lawyer's invitation. There are matters we have to discuss.'

'You – talk to his lawyer?' Ainslie's voice rose, and one or two people at neighbouring tables turned to look at the two sombrely dressed young women. She noticed the curious glances, and lowered her tone. 'But there's nothing to talk about. You weren't his wife!'

The words stung against Isla's cheeks like small stones, raising spots of colour. 'I thought I was.'

'You thought wrong!'

'I know that now. And I didn't ask Mr Forbes for this meeting – as I said, I'm in Paisley at his invitation.'

'I don't see why,' Ainslie McAdam said with open hostility.

'Nor do I, until I see him.'

Ainslie's right hand, having dealt with the troublesome hat-ribbon, was rubbing nervously at the third finger of her left hand. Her gaze dipped to the gold band on Isla's wedding finger, and her mouth tightened.

'Mr Forbes said' – she hesitated, then went on as though the words were wrenched out of her throat, 'he told me that there were – children.'

'We – I have a four-year-old daughter and a baby son.'

The girl's eyes darkened. She drew in her breath sharply, then said in a burst of anguished rage, 'I wish he knew how much misery he's caused with his selfishness! I wish I could tell him! He's ruined everything for me – for us!'

Tears sparkled among her lashes, diamonds in a mesh of gold, and Isla automatically stretched a comforting hand across the table towards her. Ainslie jerked back, rising to her feet with an awkward motion that set the china on the table jangling and the tea slopping in the cups.

'Don't touch me!'

'My dear—'

'Keep away from my mother! Keep out of Paisley!' Ainslie McAdam blurted the words, her face crumpling, then almost ran out of the room, heedless of the faces that turned to watch her go then swung back to where Isla sat, alone, at the table.

She reached for her cup and discovered that she was trembling so much that she had to use both hands to lift it from the saucer. Head bowed, she sipped at the tea again, but now its warmth held no comfort for her. The waitress appeared as she put the cup down, her face creased with concern.

'Is something wrong, madam? Isn't your friend coming back? She's scarcely touched her tea.'

'No, she's not coming back.'

'Oh dear, your saucer's wet. I'll fetch a clean one.'

Her fussing was irritating, yet comforting. Nobody had fussed over Isla, until Kenneth came into her life. She smiled her thanks at the woman when the clean cup and saucer arrived, and after she had poured out more tea she opened her envelope handbag and drew out a single, folded sheet of paper. The letter had been handed to her by the solicitor when he came to her home to break the news of Kenneth's death – and the news about his other wife and children, living in Paisley.

Although she knew the few words off by heart, Isla smoothed the sheet out and read them slowly, carefully, one by one.

'My darling Isla,

By the time you read this you will know the truth about me. Please, my dearest, forgive me for what I have done, and what I must now do. I can see no other way. You have given me more happiness in the past few years than I have ever known before, though you will know now what I always knew – that I had no right to it. Kiss the children for me, and I hope that you can find it in your heart to let them think kindly of me.

I love you all, Kenneth.'

The letter had been in her possession for only fourteen days, but already the creases where she had folded and refolded it were beginning to bite into the paper, and the fainter lines, where she had impetuously crumpled the page up and thrown it away in the first angry throes of her grief, were fading.

7

She smoothed it yet again, carefully, before tucking it away in the small pocket that held her return train ticket to Gourock, the Clydeside town where she lived. Then she signalled to the waitress to bring the bill.

After fumbling in her purse for the necessary coins to pay the smart, aloof cashier in her raised box by the entrance, she went into the ladies' room, unable as yet to face the busy pavements. The mirror, lit discreetly, reflected a thin face, normally with a smooth olive glow to the skin, inherited from her Italian mother. Since Kenneth's death, the glow had gone, leaving her skin almost sallow. Her brown eyes, tilted slightly at the outer corners in an almond shape, were large and expressive, and her surprisingly full mouth, her best feature, was pale. She stared intently into the glassy depths, noting that grief ill became her, thinking of Ainslie McAdam's creamy skin and blue eyes against the unrelieved black clothes she wore.

Fumbling in her bag, she found a pale pink lipstick that Kenneth had bought for her. Isla had never made her face up until she met him, but he had persuaded her to try some lipstick, and she had to admit that it enhanced the colour of her skin and improved the mouth that she had always considered to be too large, but Kenneth had described as beautiful, and eminently kissable.

The memory of his words almost brought tears to the surface again. She forced them back and applied the lip colouring lightly, but it didn't do as much for her as it had in the days when she had been happy and fulfilled, a woman in love, a woman who knew that she was loved in return.

After tidying an errant strand of black hair away beneath her plain woollen cloche hat, she went downstairs and through the bakery on the ground floor, wondering, as she stepped out on to the pavement, how the May sun could shine, the small fluffy clouds drift calmly across the sky, the people around her go about their business as though nothing had happened. How could a world suddenly robbed of her beloved husband's presence – for to Isla he was still her husband, despite what she now knew of him – continue to function?

Even the discovery that she was not his legal wife couldn't dull the edge of her love for him, her need of him. She felt like a widow. She was a widow, no matter how the law stood in the matter.

A clock chimed. She looked up and saw it atop the imposing Town Hall on the other side of the wide bridge spanning the river that ran through the town centre on its way to the Clyde. It was a quarter to three, and her appointment with the lawyer was at three o'clock. She had already ascertained that Moss Street, where he had his office, was only a short distance away. A few minutes would take her there.

Taking advantage of a break in the traffic, she made her way to the other side of the bridge, mildly curious as to what lay beyond the stone balustrade edging the opposite pavement. The Town Hall was to her left, rising from the river bank; on the opposite bank, to Isla's right, people walked through well-laid-out public gardens, or sat on the wooden slatted benches facing the bright flower beds. A handsome statue of Queen Victoria stood on a plinth in the middle of the gardens, her back to Isla.

She smiled faintly at the stone figure, thinking that it was little wonder that even the likeness of the dead Queen should be turned away from her. She was a fallen woman now, with no right to the gold band that Kenneth had put on her finger. She briefly touched her left hand with her right, and, under the material of her glove, felt the ring's outline. She wasn't going to take it off; she had decided that almost as soon as she heard that their marriage had been bigamous. Even the thought of that word, harsh and ugly, made her wince.

Below, a stick, once part of a tree or a bush, circled lazily in the water and was almost caught in the long grasses fringing the river. It broke free at the last moment, disappearing beneath the bridge, drifting with no will of its own. Isla sympathised with that stick. She too was drifting, alone and with no power, it seemed, to control her own life.

She would have liked to go down the stone steps further along the pavement and into the gardens, moving among the flowers, perhaps sitting on a bench, defying Queen Victoria's stony disapproval, but there was no time for such luxuries. Instead, she turned away from the water and re-crossed the road.

Thin strands of music met her as she neared the handsome war memorial on open paved ground. A handful of men stood below it, faces hollowed by lack of nourishment. One played a penny whistle, one had an accordion, another beat on a child's toy drum with a stick. A fourth man jigged from foot to foot in a pale imitation of a dance as he played the fiddle. Lying upside-down on the ground at their feet was a well-worn cloth cap. They were almost certainly ex-servicemen, learning the hard way that their country's gratitude for their service during the most appalling war the world had ever experienced didn't stretch as far as guaranteeing them the right to earn their own livings once they returned home.

Pausing to search in her purse, Isla thought of her own adored father, who had been killed in action in April 1915, shortly before her twelfth birthday. Her mother had died three years later, an early victim of the great influenza epidemic that shadowed the ending of the war.

She tossed a coin into the cap and the man with the drum said hoarsely, 'Thanks, missus.'

It might well be the last time she would be able to help poor souls such as these, Isla thought as she went on her way, passing another group, this time idling on a street corner, hands in pockets. A grim smile twisted her mouth as she pictured herself entertaining people in the streets in order to feed and clothe her children. She had no musical talent at all, unlike her father, with his rich baritone voice, or Aunt Lally, his sister, who had taken her into her Edinburgh home after she was orphaned.

It struck her that while it had become commonplace in the 1920s to see men playing musical instruments or singing in the streets in the hope of making a few pence, she had never seen women taking it up. Surely there must be many women in the position she now found herself, alone and destitute, with small children to care for. They tended to work for their more fortunate sisters, taking in washing or sewing, or scrubbing stairs and other women's houses.

11

Isla wondered if that was what she would have to do. If so – she drew a deep breath and squared her shoulders – she would do it. She would do anything, rather than lose her children, all that was left to her of the happy years she had spent with Kenneth.

The words 'Forbes and Son Limited' glinted at her from a polished brass nameplate on the wall of the building she was passing. She walked through the close and up the spotlessly clean stairs, whitewashed in two broad strips down the sides, to find out what lay in store for her.

2

The woman in the reception area looked at Isla with more than passing interest when she introduced herself.

'Take a seat, Mrs – er . . .' she said, a sudden flush coming to her face as she stumbled over the name. 'I'll tell Mr Forbes you're here.'

She disappeared into one of the rooms flanking the square hall. The door closed quietly behind her, then opened again a moment later. A fair-haired young man came out, looked at Isla with unexpected hostility, then walked past her without a word and disappeared into another room. She was still staring after him, puzzled by his attitude, when the receptionist said, 'Mr Forbes will see you now.'

After the hostility she had encountered from Ainslie McAdam – and from the young man who had recently left this office – Isla felt that Gilchrist Forbes, coming round his large desk to meet her, hand outstretched, was an old friend. He had been remote and stilted early in their first meeting, but once he had realised that she was completely unaware of her husband's other life he had mellowed, treating her with a comforting courtesy that was still evident in his manner as

13

he seated her, then went back to his own place behind the desk.

'You found your way here with no trouble?' As before, the well-educated voice brought a lump to her throat. He spoke just like Kenneth. Kenneth's voice had attracted her the very first time they had met in the ward of an Edinburgh hospital, where he had been admitted with appendicitis after being taken ill on a business trip to the city, and she had been undergoing her nursing training. 'It's fortunate that we're only a short distance from the station.'

'I arrived by an earlier train. Kenneth's daughter had written, asking me to meet her first.'

His thick brows, dark and speckled with grey, rose sharply. 'Ainslie contacted you?' His voice was disapproving.

'I presume she got my address from you.'

'Yes, she did wheedle it out of me.' Gilchrist Forbes frowned down at the papers on his desk. 'But I advised her to leave matters be, and I thought she had agreed. I should have known better where Ainslie's concerned.'

'I imagine that her curiosity got the better of her,' Isla remarked dryly, drawing off her gloves. 'She'd got it into her head that I might call on her mother and cause trouble.'

He glanced up with a quick motion of the head, concern in his eyes. 'You'd not do that, surely.'

His reaction, coming on top of Ainslie's attitude, suddenly angered Isla. 'I assured her, and I can assure you, Mr Forbes, that I have no intention of doing such a cruel thing,' she said sharply. 'I may not have been legally married to Kenneth, but I believed that I was. I love—'

her voice broke and she brought it under control at once, digging her fingernails into the palms of her hands. 'I loved him,' she corrected herself, and saw embarrassment in his eyes. This man didn't belong to a generation that spoke of love. Neither had Kenneth, though with her he had managed to overcome his reservations. 'I would do nothing to harm him or his family. I even stayed away from his funeral, though that was very hard. I shall always regret not being able to see him laid to rest.'

'I'm sorry, my dear, but, like you, I'm in a very difficult situation. Kenneth McAdam was one of my closest friends. Our two wi— our families know each other well, and it came as a great shock to me to learn first of his death, then of your existence.'

Isla nodded, smoothing her gloves out on her lap. The fingers of her right hand stole across to touch her gold wedding band for comfort. She was reminded of much the same movement made by Ainslie a short while earlier.

'Would you like some tea?'

'I'd rather attend to our business, then get back to my children.'

'Of course.' He cleared his throat, and rustled the papers on the desk. 'I'm afraid that I can give you nothing but bad news.'

'I expect little else, these days,' said Isla, then listened intently while he explained that Kenneth had taken an overdose of laudanum because the hitherto comfortable Glasgow-based business he had inherited from his father had crashed due to financial problems. She had already been given that information, on his earlier visit to her home, but then she had been too distraught to take it all in.

'Why?' she asked now. 'Why should he have been in such distress that he could see suicide as the only way out? It wasn't like Kenneth. At least, not the Kenneth I knew.'

Gilchrist Forbes paused, compressing his lips tightly together, reluctant to betray his dead friend.

He had glossed over the situation when talking to Catherine McAdam, and she, wrapped up in her own thoughts, had accepted what he said without question.

Ainslie, however, had come to his office later and insisted on hearing in detail about her father's financial troubles. Forbes found himself thinking that Ainslie and the young woman now facing him had a lot in common. They both had a way of looking directly at him, of wanting to know everything, no matter how much it might hurt them. They even shared the same expression in their eyes, one of deep loss, and a determination to survive. Neither would turn away from the truth, however hard it might be. He wondered if Kenneth himself had ever noticed the similarity between daughter and consort.

Isla's brows tucked down in a slight frown as the silence lengthened. 'Mr Forbes?' she prompted, and the solicitor was jerked back to the present.

'I'm sorry – I was trying to think of how best to explain matters to you.'

'I believe that the time to soften blows is long past, Mr Forbes. I know very little about business, but I'm sure I can deal with a straightforward explanation. I understand that my husband was an insurance broker, though he never spoke of his work.'

'He was well thought of in the city, but to be frank,

16

it would seem that he had taken to speculating somewhat rashly with his clients' money.'

'It can't have been easy, running two families. I
wish,' Isla said, 'that he had confided in me. It's hard
for me to know now that he was so worried, and I did
nothing to help because I was in ignorance.'

Forbes blinked at her. Her attitude was so unlike
Catherine McAdam's that for a moment he floundered.
Catherine had turned her head away when he tried to
explain about Kenneth's financial problems, had flatly
refused to accept a word of it.

'Under the circumstances,' he said at last, 'he could
scarcely have confided in you, of all people.'

'If he had, I would surely have tried to understand,'
Isla told him steadily. At least she would have heard the
truth from Kenneth's own lips of why he had drawn her
into an illegal marriage, and how he had managed for
five years to live a lie. Now she would never know the
answers.

She said aloud, 'I imagine that there is very little
money for anyone to inherit. And of course his legal
family will have first right to anything he left – including the house my children and I inhabit.'

'That, like most of his estate, will be sold and the
proceeds will go to his creditors. Catherine, his . . .'

The man's voice faltered, and Isla said clearly, 'His
wife.'

The papers rustled sharply. 'As you say. Catherine
has money of her own, enough, perhaps, to cushion the
worst of the blow. Do you yourself have private means?'

'I have nothing. I was training to be a nurse when I
met Kenneth.'

'Is there no family to assist you?'

'I was an only child, and my parents both died several years ago. I have an aunt, but I'm quite certain that she only has enough to support herself.'

She was relieved that Aunt Lally, in Edinburgh, was too far away to know anything of the situation. Not that she had ever been interested in Isla's problems. 'If I'd wanted a man and children you can be sure I'd have got them,' she had said often during the few years Isla had lived with her. 'But I'd no intention of tying myself down. Life's for living, not for fretting about others.' It was quite impossible to imagine Aunt Lally, who loved spending money, having any savings.

'There's a tenement block here in Paisley, in George Street, that Kenneth owned. I handled the purchase for him, years ago, and the rent collector's a man I use myself for other properties. It seems that Kenneth signed the building over to you several months ago. Did he not tell you?'

Isla looked at him in astonishment. 'Not a word.' Then, with sudden hope, 'Does that mean that the rent it has made since he signed it over will come to me?'

He cleared his throat, and a slight flush appeared over his cheekbones. 'Kenneth re-invested the proceeds in his company – I assume that he did it on your behalf, to make the money work for you.'

Isla saw her hopes of a nest-egg fade away. 'But it would have been lost when the company folded.'

'Sadly, yes. The rent it has made in the past few weeks is yours, of course, but it amounts to very little, because it's an old property and the tenants don't necessarily pay promptly, though I can assure you that the collector we use is very conscientious.' Gilchrist Forbes riffled through the papers before him until he found the right one. He studied it, stroking his chin. 'One of the dwelling-houses is lying vacant at the moment, but I'm sure that we can find tenants for it. I could put the building on the market on your behalf.'

'How soon would you expect to find a buyer?'

His brows lifted slightly at her forthright question and she knew with grim amusement that because of her youth and her accent, more broad than his own prim, educated speech, he had instantly assumed that she was no businesswoman.

'Frankly,' he said after a slight pause, 'I wouldn't be too optimistic. Businessmen are finding these times hard, and it is, as I said, an old building. But there's no harm in searching for a buyer.'

'Then we must do so,' said Isla briskly, adding as an afterthought, 'that empty flat – I could live there in the meantime.'

Concern flashed into Gilchrist Forbes' eyes. 'I scarcely think that it would be the most suitable place for your children.'

'There's nothing wrong with tenements, Mr Forbes. I was raised in a Glasgow tenement, and I survived the experience.'

'But – but this is an old building—' Consternation made the man stammer over his words. 'And with Catherine and her children already living in this town—'

'How much time do I have before I must move from the house we're in now?'

'No more than another month, I'm afraid. If I can manage to sell the tenement for you in that time you could use the money to buy somewhere else to live – perhaps in the area where you live at the moment.'

'And if not, I've no option but to move into the empty flat. I'd be grateful if you would retain it for me, just in case. I must keep a roof over my children's heads somehow,' she reminded him as he opened his mouth to argue.

The Town Hall clock could be heard chiming the half hour, and he automatically consulted the watch pinned across his waistcoat. Isla, suddenly feeling stifled, got to her feet. 'I must go.'

'But there are still some matters to discuss.'

'Perhaps we can meet again. Next week?'

'Certainly. I'll call on you – shall we say Wednesday, at three o'clock? I'm sorry, my dear,' he went on, going ahead to open the office door for her. 'This must be extremely difficult for you.'

'I shall manage.' Then, as they crossed the hall, she asked, 'That young man who was in your office when I arrived – who is he?'

'My son, Colin. He and Ainslie McAdam are' – he paused, then said – 'were to be married.'

Recalling the way Ainslie had touched the third finger of her left hand, feeling for the consolation of a ring that was no longer there, and the girl's bitter, 'He's ruined everything for me!' Isla felt a flash of contempt for the young man who had cared so little for his fiancée that he had abandoned her at the first whisper of scandal.

'Indeed? I take it that he ended the engagement because of her father's shameful death?'

Something of her condemnation must have sounded

in her voice, because Gilchrist Forbes was cool when he retorted, 'Indeed not. It was Ainslie who ended it, very much against my son's wishes.'

The rapport that had been growing between them had vanished with her criticism of his son, and his voice was formal when he wished her good day and closed the door behind her, leaving her to walk alone down the stairs to the street.

Emerging from the tearoom after her disastrous confrontation with her father's secret 'wife', Ainslie McAdam walked aimlessly along the street, weaving her way around pedestrians without seeing any of them. Someone called her name, and she looked up to see a former schoolfriend, her round, rosy face suitably solemn, but her eyes bright with curiosity. Clearly she had heard the rumours that had begun circulating despite all Gilchrist Forbes' attempts to keep the details of Kenneth's suicide quiet.

'Ainslie, I meant to write to you. I was so sorry to hear about your father.'

'Thank you, Christine. I'm – I'm in a terrible rush,' Ainslie said, and hurried on, knowing full well that Christine was gaping after her, taken aback by her coldness. But she couldn't talk to anyone while her mind was filled with pictures of the woman she had just left. She had expected – had hoped – to see someone much older, a plain elderly spinster, perhaps, who had somehow embroiled Kenneth McAdam in her clutches. Instead she had been confronted by a young woman only a few years older than herself. At that moment, for the first time in her life, she hated her father with all her heart.

She was glad that he was dead, she told herself fiercely, swinging round a corner and almost bumping into a great crowd of women straggling along the pavement, moving in the opposite direction from Ainslie herself. Young, old, fat, thin, all dressed in working clothes with scarves wound round their heads, they talked and laughed and called to each other loudly as they poured along the pavements past her. Drifts of cotton clustered on a coatsleeve here, a mop of hair there, and Ainslie realised that she had walked right through the town and was nearing Ferguslie Mills as it was disgorging its workers at the end of a shift.

She glanced at her watch and discovered to her astonishment that, somehow, the afternoon had passed, and she should have been home an hour earlier. She turned the next corner and kept walking, this time with purpose, past the cricket ground and the neat double row of back-to-back housing built to accommodate some of the mill workers, then under the railway bridge and up the hill to where a row of comfortably large houses stood back from the road, separated from it by their neat gardens.

Her heart sank when she saw the small car; its chocolate-brown paintwork and chrome gleaming in the late-afternoon sun, standing in the driveway of her own home. Letting herself in quietly at the front door, she tried to escape upstairs to her room, but her mother's voice called her name as she passed the drawing-room's closed door. Ainslie hesitated, then decided to pretend she hadn't heard the summons. Just as she gained the staircase the drawing-room door opened.

'Ainslie?'

She stopped, turning towards the man she had once promised to marry. 'Hello, Colin.'

'Your mother wants to see you.' His voice was gruff, and his hazel eyes, when she met them, still carried the hurt of her rejection.

There was nothing else for it. Ainslie stepped back down into the hall and walked past him and into the room.

'Ainslie, where have you been?' Catherine McAdam wanted to know as soon as her daughter appeared. She lay on a chaise longue, a rug over her legs and cushions piled behind her back. The windows were curtained against the daylight, and fringed standard lamps glowed feebly in the twilight within the room.

'I went out for a walk. I thought you were resting in your room, Mother.'

'I was, but I had to come downstairs to see to some business.' The rings on Catherine's limp hand sparkled in the electric light as she indicated the open desk. Colin moved to it and began to gather the spilled papers together neatly, his back towards mother and daughter. 'I could have done with your help,' Catherine went on reproachfully.

'What d'you want me to do?'

'It's too late now, I had to see to it all myself, with Colin's help. Now I'm trying to persuade him to stay for tea.' A warm note crept into Catherine's voice. She had been delighted when her daughter and Colin Forbes became engaged, and furious when, only days after her father's death, Ainslie had taken it upon herself to return the handsome diamond and emerald ring that had been specially made for her.

'I expect he has to get back home.'

'I've already explained that to your mother,' Colin said stiffly, turning away from the desk. 'Goodbye, Mrs McAdam.' He took Catherine's hand in his for a moment. 'Remember that you only need to telephone myself or my father if you need help. Goodbye, Ainslie.'

'Goodbye.' She opened the door for him, and her mother said sharply, strength coming into her voice, 'Ainslie, have your manners deserted you entirely? You might at least see Colin to his car, since I'm not fit to do so.'

'I expect he remembers where he left it.'

'Ainslie!' A cushion tumbled softly to the floor as Catherine, outraged, struggled to sit upright.

Colin's face had gone quite white. 'I can find my own way out, Mrs McAdam. I know this house well,' he said, looking at Ainslie, who glanced away. Still shocked by her meeting with the woman who had been part of her father's secret life, she didn't feel strong enough to deal with Colin's pain as well as her own.

'Nonsense, Colin, I hope that we've not entirely forgotten our manners in this house, despite all that's happened.'

Catherine put a hand on the rug over her legs as though about to throw it back and escort her guest to the door personally, and Ainslie said, 'Stay where you are, Mother. I'll see Colin to his car.'

24

3

They walked through the square hall and down the stone steps in silence, blinking as they emerged into the sunny garden. The familiar scent of petrol and sunwarmed leather upholstery filled Ainslie's nostrils as Colin opened the car door; his car was so familiar to her that she knew just how hot the leather passenger seat would feel against her calves on such a day.

He tossed the brief-case into the car then straightened and said, his hand on the door-frame, 'Something's troubling you.'

'My father's killed himself and left us with the shame of knowing that he had another wife and family hidden away,' she retorted tartly. 'Is it any wonder that I'm troubled?'

He reddened under the sting of her sarcasm. His fair colouring and his tendency to flush easily was a great burden to him, Ainslie knew. It was one of the qualities that had once endeared him to her. 'I mean that something else is troubling you. I was at the window, I saw you charging in the gate and up the drive as though you were about to do battle with some poor soul. Your eyes' – he hesitated, then swallowed and said, 'Your eyes are very bright, and that means that you're angry.'

She bit her lip and scuffled the toe of one of her smart black strapped shoes in the gravel, heedless of scratch marks. 'I met her this afternoon.'

'Who?' The question was automatic, followed immediately by, 'You don't mean your father's—'

'His *woman*!' Ainslie spat the word out. 'Colin, she's quite pretty. And she's young, not much older than I am!'

'I know. I saw her outside my father's office. That's why I had to come here, instead of him. He'd arranged to meet with her.'

'You didn't tell Mother that, did you?'

'Of course not – d'you take me for an utter fool? I said he'd had to call on a very old client who needed his advice urgently.'

Ainslie gave a bark of harsh laughter. 'Scarcely a very old client. How could he? How could he take up with someone not much older than I am?'

'How did you happen to meet her?'

'I wrote to her, when I heard that she was coming to Paisley to see him. We had tea together.'

His jaw tightened. 'You shouldn't have done that, Ainslie.'

'I had to see her for myself.' She rushed on, her voice suddenly choked, tears gathering behind her eyes, 'They even had children together, Colin! A girl and a boy, just like Mother had. Only they're still very s-small—'

His hand closed over her arm. 'Come for a spin – we can talk about it, away from here.' He looked beyond her bent head to the drawing-room window, worried that her mother might see them and assume that he was upsetting her daughter. But there was no movement in the narrow space between the curtains.

Ainslie drew away from him, shaking her head. 'Mother would only think that we were making up. She'd start expecting me to wear your ring again.'

'Would that be so terrible?' His voice was low, but vehement. 'Ainslie—'

'The past is past, Colin. Nothing can ever be the same again. Everything's changed!'

'I see no reason why we should change too. I love you, Ainslie, yet you've not even given me the chance to—'

'Hello, Colin,' Ainslie's young brother called cheerfully from the gate, and Colin, inwardly cursing, turned to smile at the boy as he and his closest friend, both in the neat blue blazer and striped blue and silver tie of Paisley Grammar School, came up the short gravelled drive.

'Hullo, Innes – Gordon.' He hoped that the boys would continue on round the side of the house to the back door to coax something to eat from the cook, but instead they stopped, letting their schoolbags drop to the ground, their hands and eyes hungrily reaching out to the car.

'I'm going to get one just like this when I'm old enough,' Innes announced, and Gordon gave him a scornful look.

'You're only eleven! By the time you're old enough to drive, this'll be out of date. I've got a cigarette card of the new Delage sports car. That's the sort of car I'm going to get when I'm old enough.'

'You didn't tell me! Why didn't you bring it to school?'

'And let everyone put their grubby fingers on it? I'm keeping it at home, in my album.'

Ainslie, who could have kissed the boys for arriving at just the right moment, saw that her young brother's eyes were bright with avarice.

'What would you swop for it? I'll give you my Swift open tourer card.'

'And your Alvis?'

The boys began wrangling, and Colin, with a resigned shrug, got into the car.

'You couldn't take us for a run, could you?' Innes asked at once. Colin started to shake his head, but Ainslie cut in.

'Go on, just a short spin.'

'Your mother—'

'I'll explain to Mother,' she said, and with whoops of glee the boys jostled their way, schoolbags and all, into the rear seat.

Colin shot an angry look at her and then, resigned to his fate, started the engine. Ainslie waved as the car reversed down the short drive, then went back indoors to where her mother was still lying on the sofa.

'You took your time – the two of you must have had quite a lot to talk about.'

'Innes arrived, with Gordon. Colin's taken them both out for a short drive. We didn't think you'd mind.'

Catherine shifted restlessly. 'He's such a nice young man. I can't think why you gave him back his ring.'

'I told you, Mother – this isn't the time to think of marriage.'

A sharp note came into the older woman's voice. 'Don't be so silly, girl, it's the perfect time. The Forbeses are comfortably off, and one day Colin will take over the business. A connection with them just now would put us in better standing with the town than we are at the moment, after what your father did. Anyway, I can't afford to keep you indefinitely, you know that. Not now that I've got Innes's school fees to see to.'

'You won't have to keep me. I shall find a job.'

'You're not trained for anything other than marriage!' Catherine said irritably.

'I'll find something.'

'You sound more like your Grandmama McAdam every day! She was always a difficult, stubborn woman. I can't think why your grandfather married her.'

It was a chant that Ainslie had heard over and over again. 'Won't you let me open the curtains? It's such a lovely day—'

'Leave them!'

'Very well.' Her hands dropped from the curtains. 'I'll take the tray to the kitchen, and find out how dinner's coming along.'

'Tell Cook not to make anything for me. I don't feel like eating.'

'But you must eat, Mother.' Ainslie regarded the older woman with concern. Catherine's greying fair hair was drawn back tightly, accentuating the harsh lines of her face and the droop of her mouth. Her cheekbones jutted sharply beneath her pale skin. 'You have to keep your strength up.'

'I can't think why,' Catherine said bleakly. 'There seems to be little point, now.'

As Ainslie carried the tray out of the room, she marvelled that her mother hadn't realised why she had given her engagement ring back to Colin. After what her father had done, she herself no longer had any desire to marry, to become tied to a man, dependent on him, open to the humiliation and hurt her mother was suffering. She had loved her father, almost worshipped him, despite the fact that he showed little interest in her. Now, she would never trust men again.

Although she had told the lawyer that she had to hurry back home, Isla turned away from the station when she left his office. She walked back towards the Cross, where she asked a passerby for directions to the cemetery, and was directed to one of the tram-stops. The ex-servicemen were still playing their reedy music as she passed the war memorial. Only a few coins lay in the pathetic cap.

Paisley, she realised as the tram rocked along, was built on three terraces. The High Street ran along one of them, with all the streets on Isla's left swooping downhill, and the streets on her right running uphill. She glimpsed a handsome church with a great broad sweep of steps leading from the pavement to the arched doors; it was very like a church she had seen in Paris, where she and Kenneth had spent their honeymoon.

And all the time, a small voice whispered in her ear, Ainslie and her mother and brother had been going about their lives here in Paisley, no doubt believing that Kenneth was away on business. Was that what he had told them? She tried to close her mind to the malice in the voice, not wanting her precious memories to become soured and blackened.

The conductress tapped her on the shoulder. 'This is the cemetery, hen,' she said cheerfully, pointing. 'Just across the road there.'

Inside Woodside Cemetery's stone gates Isla made enquiries at the small office, then walked up the wide driveway between the gravestones, some of them so elaborate that they were like miniature war memorials. Kenneth's grave had yet to be marked by a headstone; the earth was still raw above him but the dead funeral flowers had been cleared away and someone – Ainslie? The real Mrs McAdam? – had recently put some carnations into an urn at the foot of the grave.

Isla stood for a long time looking at the mound. She had expected to weep, had wanted to weep, to ease the pain that had been gnawing at her ever since Gilchrist Forbes, hat in hand, face sombre, had come into her comfortable home to tell her that Kenneth had left her for ever. But her eyes remained obstinately dry. The man she had loved, still loved, wasn't really here, in this quiet, green graveyard where the dead slept in peace beneath the trees. He was still with her – and yet not with her.

She turned away, and started on her journey home.

After their quiet marriage in Edinburgh, Isla and Kenneth McAdam had settled in a comfortable little house in Gourock, by the River Clyde. Isla had come to the place as a stranger, and had not made many friends. For one thing, she wasn't used to having friends and therefore didn't feel the need of them, and, for another,

Kenneth didn't care to see people when he was at home, claiming that he had enough contact with others in his office.

Isla had been happy to go along with his wishes. During her training she had lived in the nurses' quarters and spent her off-duty time with Aunt Lally, a garrulous woman who usually had her tenement flat filled with people. At times Isla had ached for peace and quiet, and at last, in Gourock, she had found it.

Although Kenneth was often away – on business, he had told Isla, and she had had no reason to doubt him – she had never felt lonely. She enjoyed gardening and sewing and reading, and when first Barbara and then Ross were born, she had had more than enough to do.

Grace, the maid, opened the door as her mistress went up the front path between the hydrangea bushes. 'How are the children?' Isla asked as soon as she got indoors.

'Miss Barbara was frettin' for ye, but she got over it. Pearl took them both out for a walk this afternoon. I'll make ye a nice cup of tea.'

'I don't want—' Isla began, but Grace had already vanished into the little kitchen at the rear of the house. Wondering why it was that the Scots felt that everything could be cured by tea, Isla hung up her coat and went upstairs, towards the sound of splashing and squealing. Barbara loved bathtime.

Before going in to see her daughter she opened the door of the small nursery. The room was quiet and smelled of baby powder and clean clothes airing before the guarded fire. The coverings were folded back invitingly in Barbara's small bed in the corner, and Ross was

32

already in his cot, clean and contented, almost asleep. She bent over the cot, resisting the temptation to lift him into her arms and bury her face in him, and he lifted heavy lids to smile drowsily at his mother, his lips parting to reveal four pearly little teeth, then slid back into sleep.

He was his father's child, fair-skinned and red-haired and blue-eyed. And very like his grown half-sister, Isla thought, as she straightened up from the cot. Kenneth had taken such delight in his children, claiming that it was because he was so much older than the average father, and had had longer to wait.

Isla wondered if he had been as devoted to Ainslie and her brother as he was to his second family. Part of her mind told her that she should hate him for deceiving her, trapping her into a tissue of lies, then leaving her with two children who were, in the eyes of the law, illegitimate. One day, perhaps, when she could look back over the years to this time in her life, she would feel anger against him, but not now, not yet. Now, she knew only terrible loss.

The bathroom was steamy and smelled of the floral soap Barbara loved. Pearl, who had come to help Isla after Barbara's birth, was lifting the little girl out of the water.

'Mummy!'

Barbara wriggled with excitement, reaching dripping hands out to her mother, and Pearl shrieked, 'For any favour, bairn, will ye stay still. Mind yer mammy's nice clothes, ye'll get her all wet!'

'Never mind about my clothes, they'll dry.' Isla dropped to her knees and gathered the plump, towel-

33

swathed body close. Water trickling from Barbara's hair, making it look much darker than its usual fiery bronze, ran down beneath the collar of Isla's blouse, but she paid no heed to it.

'Did you bring Daddy back with you?'

'Not this time, darling. He'll be away for – for a long time,' Isla said, and over her daughter's wet head she saw Pearl's eyes fill with sympathetic tears.

'I missed you,' Barbara said into her ear. 'I cried for you.'

'You knew I'd come back, surely.' Isla squeezed her eyes shut to fight back her own tears. She didn't want her own grief to touch her children. 'You know I'd not leave you and Ross,' she said. 'Not ever, whatever happens.'

4

At the end of June Isla's home was repossessed to pay Kenneth McAdam's debts, and as nobody had bought the tenement building he had left her, she had no option but to move herself and her children to its empty ground floor flat.

She left her home without looking back. Although the house was small, it had been the grandest she had ever lived in. She had loved having a garden, and a front door that opened on to a path, instead of a landing or a close. Now she was returning to tenement life.

Mr Forbes had warned her that the building she now owned was old, but even so, she hadn't realised just how old, or how small and cramped it would be. Her parents and Aunt Lally had lived in modern tenements, with tiled closes and stairs that were scrubbed down each week then carefully edged with white pipeclay to give them a smart appearance, but this building was small and sad and neglected.

The outer wall, facing on to the street, looked dark and damp, and when Isla ventured in, Ross clutched in one arm, her free hand holding Barbara's, she saw that the stone floor of the narrow close was cracked and broken and uneven. The centre of each of the steps rising into the darkness of the upper floor was hollowed almost to the level of the step below, and she was thankful that she lived on the ground floor, and didn't have to climb into that unfriendly darkness above. The paintwork on the door of her new home was faded and scratched, the wood itself furrowed with deep ravines, as though some predatory beast had once clawed at it in a frenzy. The entire building smelled of damp and stale food and too many years of human habitation. A child wailed from somewhere at the back of the close, and Isla felt that the misery in the sound matched her own feelings.

The empty flat was situated at the front of the building. When Isla released Barbara's hand to search for the large clumsy key the lawyer had given her, the little girl stayed by her side instead of running off to explore as she usually did.

The door had to be pushed hard before it creaked open. Isla, peering into the gloom before her, almost lost her nerve and scurried back to the street; she had to force herself to move forward instead, the floorboards squeaking underfoot.

The door opened straight into a small empty room. Isla went towards the only window with a sense of purpose that was put on for the children's benefit, and pulled aside the dingy curtain stretched across the window. The very touch of the material, stiff and clammy, sent a shiver down her spine, and she found herself rubbing her hand against her skirt afterwards.

The window was filthy. A cool breeze from the gaps in the frame brushed her face and she breathed it in with relief. A small sink leaned against the wall below the window as though tired out, its single tap weeping slowly and sadly. Barbara, clutching a brightly coloured rubber ball that had been Kenneth's last present to her, stood in the middle of the floor and stared round at the mottled walls.

'Where's the bedroom?' she wanted to know. There were two narrow doors, one on either side of the small fireplace. Isla opened them to reveal cobwebbed shelves, only a few inches in depth. Glancing round she saw that half of the wall opposite the window was covered by wooden folding doors. The hinges complained as the doors were pulled open, and dust showered down on her. The bed was there, a high metal frame supporting a solid wooden platform. The space below it was dark and forbidding.

'There isn't a bedroom, love. This is called a wall-bed. You'll sleep here with me.'

Barbara scampered over to stand by her mother, going on tiptoe to inspect the dark space. 'It looks dirty.'

It did. Isla remembered wall-beds as clean, comfortable places, with piled pillows and soft quilts. Her parents hadn't had much money, but they had been thrifty, and her mother had always kept a clean house and had taken great care of the possessions bought, one by one, when they could be afforded. Even Aunt Lally, who was more of a 'feast and famine' person, enjoying money when she had it, and coping cheerfully with spells of enforced poverty, took a pride in her small home.

'We can clean it,' Isla said with a cheeriness she

didn't feel. 'And we'll wash the window to let more light in, and once our furniture arrives it'll look fine.'

Barbara gave her one of her direct looks. 'There isn't a bathroom.'

'The water closet's outside, but that doesn't matter. When I was a little girl we didn't have a bathroom inside. We used a tin bath, all cosy in front of the fire.'

Now that her eyes were growing accustomed to the gloom she could make out the handle of a chamber-pot that was lurking beneath the bed. 'Look, we can use this at night if we have to, then empty it into the privy in the morning.'

With difficulty, because Ross was squirming in her arms, she bent and pulled the chipped, stained delft pot out from under the bed. A little puddle of gritty dust lay on the bottom, and Isla only just managed to smother a scream when a long-legged spider scuttled into the interior from under the rim. She set the pot down hastily on the wooden bed so that Barbara, shorter than the bed, couldn't see into it. Her daughter, head tilted back, doubtfully surveyed the bulge of the pot from below, then announced, 'We're going to have to clean that, too. We'll have to clean everything,' she added, glancing over at the filthy little gas-cooker beside the sink.

'It'll all look better when the furniture arrives,' Isla said hopefully, giving in to Ross's noisy demands and putting him down to ease the strain on her aching arm. He took two steps away from her, then fell over on to cracked linoleum that was so faded that it was impossible to see what the pattern had been. He broke into an angry roar and as Isla picked him up again, Barbara put down her ball. It rolled across the floor to disappear under the cobwebby gloom beneath the sink.

'See? It was the floor that pushed him over,' she said accusingly. Then she clutched at her mother's skirt with one hand and added, her voice suddenly uncertain, 'I want Pearl.'

'Barbara, you know that Pearl couldn't come with us,' Isla coaxed, doing her best to keep a cheerful note in her voice. 'We're going to be all by ourselves now, just you and me and Ross, all cosy in our new little house.'

Barbara stuck the thumb of her free hand in her mouth. 'I still want Pearl,' she said around it, indistinctly. 'I want to go home.'

Isla, bouncing Ross in her tired arms to calm him, looking round the small, bleak single room, agreed wholeheartedly with her daughter. But she couldn't say so, or give way to the tears that were building up in her throat. For the children's sakes, she had to be strong. She had to manage, though at that moment she didn't know how she was going to do it.

The furniture arrived a few minutes later, trundled along the street from the station on a cart. The man and the boy in charge of the cart edged the pieces one by one along the narrow stone close and into Isla's new home, beneath the interested stares of the women and children lounging around in the street outside. She had let almost all of the handsome furniture that she and Kenneth had chosen between them go with the house, and kept only what she considered to be essential. But the room was so small that when the cart was finally unloaded it was crammed.

'Ye'll have tae sell most o' it, missus,' the man observed as Isla fumbled in her purse for the money to pay him. When he had left she tucked Ross, who had fallen asleep in her arms, into the only armchair that she had brought with her, then searched the jumble of boxes until she found bedding for the cot, which was wedged into a corner beside the wall-bed. The little boy tumbled into the cot bonelessly, without waking, and she drew the blanket over him, deciding that it was better to leave him undisturbed than to try to change his napkin and wash him. It was only then that she discovered that Barbara had gone.

'Barbara?' she said hopefully, peering at the clutter around her. There was no answer, nor had she expected there to be. It was difficult to miss Barbara when she was around; almost from birth she had made her presence felt, first with a cheerful babbling, then, as she grew older, with words that swiftly became sentences, sentences that became paragraphs, paragraphs that became great spiels of continuous chatter.

Isla racked her brains, and recalled that she had last seen her daughter while the last pieces of furniture were being delivered, standing nose to nose outside the close with a ragged little girl of about the same age. They had been studying each other intently, silently, as children did when they first met.

She ran out to the close-mouth, careful to leave the door on the latch so that she could get back in, and gazed up and down the street. Groups of children played in the gutter, and the women who had come to close-mouths and windows to stare openly at the furniture being carried in from the cart had gone back to their gossiping. There was no sign of the familiar bronze curly head.

Panic-stricken now, Isla ran back through the close and burst out into the back court, a gloomy and overgrown walled-in area. The section nearest the tenement was paved with broken slabs, weeds thrusting up between them, edged on one side by a row of shaky-looking dustbins and coalsheds with sagging doors. A small outhouse opposite the bins probably housed the water closet, and just beyond it stood the washhouse. Then came two broken steps leading to what looked like a very small neglected field.

'Barbara?'

'Is it yer wean yer lookin' for?' a voice said, almost at her elbow. The window beside the back door was open and a young woman sat just inside the room, her head bound up in a scarf knotted at the top. Her blouse was unbuttoned and a small bald baby was fastened to one breast, sucking steadily and noisily. A cigarette smouldered in the woman's free hand.

'My – my little girl.'

The turbanned head nodded towards the steps. 'She's behind the washhoose there with oor Greta. She's fine,' she called after Isla as she hurried up the steps and peered round the outhouse.

Barbara was sitting on a sagging, slimy, wooden bench, her favourite doll on her knee. Beside her sat the child Isla had seen earlier, a thin little waif dressed in a frayed jersey that had been made for someone larger, and almost covered the skimpy little skirt beneath it. The two children were undressing the doll, their heads close together.

'Barbara! I was worried about you!'

Barbara looked up, unrepentant. 'Greta wanted to see Bella's frilly knickers coming off. I didn't go far away,' she added defensively, after another look at her mother's anxious face. Greta, tossing a disinterested glance over her shoulder, went back to the doll.

'Ach, leave them alone, they're no' doin' any harm – for once,' the woman's voice called from the open window, and Isla hesitated, then went slowly back to the close. As she walked past the open door of the water closet, the smell from the interior hit her.

'I suppose she's as well there as under my feet,' she said, as she reached the window.

'Ye'll have enough tae dae, with just movin' in,' the other woman agreed, hauling the baby away from her breast. It came free with a loud sucking noise, eyes and milk-flecked mouth opening wide with indignation. Before it could utter a yell, the small mouth was clamped against the other breast.

'That'll keep ye quiet,' the woman said, then, to Isla, 'Ye'll be ready for a cup of tea? Come on in an' I'll make one.'

'I'll have to get back to the baby.'

'On ye go, then, an' I'll bring the tea through in a wee minute. It's no bother,' the woman said airily when Isla tried to protest.

In the tiny room that was now their home, Ross was still asleep. Isla started trying to tidy the place, but hadn't got far when knuckles rapped at the door. Seen in her entirety, her new neighbour was small and broad, with button-bright black eyes set on either side of a button nose. She walked into the room with a rolling gait that reminded Isla of a sailor accustomed to the moving deck of a ship, and looked round with open curiosity. A mug of steaming tea was clutched in each fist and the baby, asleep now, was fastened against her breast by a shawl deftly wound round her shoulders and hips, and formed into a snug little hammock.

'Ye've got some bonnie furniture.' She settled herself in the armchair and thrust a mug at Isla. 'I put condensed milk intae it, an' two spoonfuls of sugar. Ye'll be needin' yer strength.'

Isla sipped at the tea, and tried not to wrinkle her nose. The liquid was strong and very sweet, with an underlying flavour of grease, as though the mug had been washed in dirty water.

'I'm Magret,' said her first caller.

'I'm Isla Moffatt.' Isla had decided to revert to her maiden name. She had no legal right to Kenneth's name, and neither did the children.

'Isla? That's nice. I wish I'd heard it afore we named her Daisy.' Magret indicated the bald-headed baby with a dip of the chin. 'She's cried after a flower. Have ye ever seen a daisy? Bonny, isn't it?' she went on when Isla nodded. 'Oor Greta's cried after a flower tae, her real name's Magret like mine, with a Rita added on to it. We cry her Greta because he' – she jerked her chin in the general direction of her own home – 'says her real name's too much of a mouthful for a wee skelf like her.' She hesitated, then said delicately, 'I saw ye were wearing a mournin' band when ye arrived.'

'My husband died recently.' Isla spoke with difficulty round a lump that had suddenly come to her throat.

Magret sucked in her breath. 'Ach, that's a shame, so it is. Where did ye used tae live?'

'Ayrshire.'

'I thought ye sounded different from most of us here. More posh.' Isla, who had been raised in Glasgow and didn't have an Ayrshire accent, said nothing. 'Don't fret, hen, ye'll be all right here. The folks is decent enough – most of them. He –' her chin gave another spasmodic jerk towards the back of the building – 'works at the mills. How'll ye keep yersel' and the bairns? Widows don't get much – the folk that pay out the money seem tae think women an' bairns can live on air,' she added, with a sniff.

'I'll need to think of something.' Isla decided to say nothing about the few pieces of jewellery she possessed, some inherited from her mother, some given to her by Kenneth. She planned to sell them to raise money for food for herself and the children. She wasn't entitled to any widow's pension because strictly speaking she had never been married in the first place. The responsibility for seeing that her children survived rested solely on her own shoulders.

'Ye could start by pawnin' some o' this,' Magret suggested, looking round the room. 'There's a pawn-shop not far from here, in Canal Street. He's a fair man tae deal with, no' like some.' She reached out a rough red hand and stroked a handsome chest of drawers. 'That's bonny, but it's out o' place here. The more furniture ye've got, the more corners for the weans tae hurt themselves on. Better tae ask at the grocer's shop for orange boxes – they're grand for keepin' stuff in. Anyway' – she lowered her voice and narrowed her eyes – 'if the rent man sees this lot on top of the posh way ye talk, he'll think ye're a toff and mebbe put up yer rent. Ye'd not want that. The rent's high enough for a flea-pit like this.'

Isla, recalling that she herself was the landlady, felt a guilty pang. Her face warmed and she bent it over her tea. She had discovered that once she got used to the taste, the hot sweet liquid was comforting.

Magret chattered on, thankfully more interested in telling Isla about the other tenants than in asking questions. Isla learned that old Granny Thomson lived alone 'through the wall', and that the McNabs occupied the flat directly across the close from hers.

'He's younger than she is. Her husband drank himself tae death last year an' left her tae run their wee baker's shop, three doors down,' Magret confided, adding, 'they make good pies and she's a clean woman, and fair wi' the prices. Her new man started as the message boy in the shop, and she wed him just months after her man died. He was a bad-tempered pig, so he was. At least she never carries bruises now. There's three lots live up the stair, and it'll be your turn tae use the clothes-lines on Wednesday mornings. Don't hang anythin' out there on a Tuesday or Mrs Leach'll have the nose off ye. She's awful snappy, thinks she's above the rest of us.' She gave a sudden bellow of laughter, and Ross jumped and muttered in his sleep, though the baby on Magret's breast didn't stir.

'She does live above us, come tae think of it! I meant that she's awful snooty, but she's got more bark than bite. Here, I'd better be going, or he'll be in looking for his dinner, and me with the tatties not even peeled.'

She drained her mug, and, after a struggle, levered herself and her baby out of the chair, easing her way round the table to peep at Ross, still sound asleep. 'My, look at that head of hair! Ye could warm yer hands at it!'

When she had gone, Isla studied the furniture, knowing that Magret was right – most of it would have to go. She decided to call on the pawnbroker in the morning.

Barbara arrived, looking more cheerful now that she had found a friend, and announced that she was hungry. After a search, Isla found the food that she had carefully packed that morning in Gourock. She filled the kettle, trying in vain to turn the tap off hard enough to stop its persistent dripping, and lit the tiny gas cooker, making a mental note to start scrubbing the layers of grease off it first thing in the morning. It looked as though the previous tenant had never even attempted to clean it.

Ross was irritable when she roused him, and after feeding him and washing him sketchily, she put him back into his cot then cut the string that held the mattress firmly in a roll, and found pillows and blankets. She attacked the wall-bed vigorously with a stiff-bristled handbrush, raising clouds of dust, then made it up, and she and Barbara climbed in. It was still early, but Isla was bone-weary, and there was no reason to stay up.

'It's cosy here, isn't it?' she said when the two of them were snuggled together in the bed.

'You won't close the doors and leave us in the dark, will you?' Barbara asked anxiously.

'Of course not.' A chill crept up Isla's spine at the very thought. Heaven alone knew what might be lurking in the shadows below. She tried not to let her mind dwell on it.

Exhausted though they both were, they were kept awake by footsteps and voices and laughter as people went up and down the street outside. In the building itself, doors banged, people scuffed their way along the close, and feet tramped back and forth above their heads. Something scuttled behind the skirting board, and Barbara clutched at her mother fearfully.

'What's that?'

'Nothing, pet, nothing at all,' Isla comforted her, while the skin at the back of her neck crawled.

The two of them waited, holding their breaths, but the sound wasn't repeated. Gradually, Barbara's fingers eased their tight grip on Isla's arm.

'I like Greta,' she said, her voice drowsy. 'She's going to teach me to play peevers.' Then, mercifully, she fell asleep.

Isla, too, slept, and dreamed of Kenneth; of walking with him along the shore at Gourock, sitting by the fire with him, lying in his arms in their marriage bed. A drunken voice raised in song startled her awake during the night, to darkness, Barbara's knees digging painfully into her side, and the realisation that Kenneth was gone for ever.

She turned over and wept her loneliness into her pillow, until it and her face and her hair were all soaked with tears.

5

'I think it was most unwise of you to move to Paisley, Mrs – er—' Gilchrist Forbes paused uncomfortably.

'I'm calling myself Mrs Moffatt now. I have a right to the name, I was born to it,' Isla assured him tartly. 'And I wouldn't dream of raising my children in that tenement if I'd any other option, I can assure you of that.' She was tired after a night's broken sleep, depressed at the prospect of having to live in the old tenement. The lawyer's cool disapproval was more than she could take.

'Did my – did Kenneth know what the place was like? Did he know the conditions his tenants have to live in?'

The man looked offended. 'George Street is in an old part of the town, and the tenements there have been standing for some time. I understand that they now enjoy gas lighting and running water, and of course the rents are very low, to compensate for the lack of other amenities.'

'I'd hardly call life there enjoyable, even with gas lighting and water that sometimes won't stop running,' Isla told him, tightening her grip on Ross, who was struggling to get down from her lap. 'Barbara, don't touch!'

'I was only looking,' Barbara said at once from the desk, folding her hands behind her back. 'Not touching.'

There had been nobody for Isla to leave the children with. Now, realising the impossibility of carrying on a conversation with the lawyer while trying to cope with them both, she gave in and got to her feet, putting the little boy down, but keeping a tight hold of his hand. 'I only came to let you know that I was installed, and to make arrangements about the rent.'

'It's collected every Friday evening. I can arrange to have it delivered to you on Monday mornings.'

'I think it would be best for me to call here for it. And as I don't want anyone to know that I'm the landlady, I suggest that your collector knows me only as an ordinary tenant, and collects rent from me every week as well as from the others. You can leave the money in the outer office on Monday mornings, then I won't have to trouble you. Good day, Mr Forbes.'

'My dear—' Gilchrist Forbes reached the door before her, almost falling over Barbara in the process. Although it was clear to Isla that her presence in his office – in Paisley, come to that – made the man feel most uncomfortable, he nevertheless seemed to be genuinely concerned about her well-being. 'It's a difficult business, collecting rents from that type of building. Many of the tenants tend to be in arrears, and I can't guarantee a fixed sum every week. How will you manage?'

'I shall have to do the best I can – like my fellow tenants,' Isla told him, and he bit his lip. Barbara, impatient to be out in the street again, scurried out of the door as soon as he opened it, and ran across the hall to the outer door. As she reached up for the handle, the door opened almost in her face, and she recoiled with a squeak of surprise, tripping over the edge of the carpet and landing, with a thud, on the floor.

The newcomer, the fair-haired young man Isla had seen on her first visit to the office, dropped to his knees beside her.

'Are you all right?'

'I'm fine.' Barbara sat up and beamed at him. 'I bounced like a ball.'

He laughed, and took her hands in his. 'Let's see if you can bounce back up again, then. Up you come – one, two th—' His voice trailed away as the little girl got to her feet and he looked beyond her to see Isla.

'This is my son, Colin. Colin, this is Mrs . . .'

Gilchrist Forbes hesitated, and it was left to Isla to say shortly, 'Mrs Moffatt. I've decided to return to my own name.'

The laughter had gone from Colin Forbes' face, and as he let go of Barbara's hands Isla was fixed, once again, by an unfriendly look. She returned it as their hands touched briefly, then fell apart.

'I like the one that knocked me down,' Barbara said as they went down the stairs to the street, 'but I don't like the old man, 'cos he doesn't like us, much, does he?' Then as they emerged on to Paisley Cross again, she asked hopefully, 'Can we go back now? Greta's waiting to teach me how to play peevers.'

Before returning to George Street they called in at the pawnbroker's in Canal Street, where Isla arranged for someone to come and have a look at her furniture. She then spent most of the money she had left, buying food and cleaning materials, and when they got back to the tenement she settled Ross in his cot with his toys while Barbara scampered out to play. Isla rolled her sleeves up, put on an apron, tied her hair up in a scarf, and tackled the gas stove.

The pawnbroker arrived two hours later and arranged to take most of the furniture off her hands for what seemed to be a very small amount of money. Half an hour after that, two boys arrived with a handcart and almost all the furniture left from the Gourock house was taken away.

The women standing round the entrances to the closes watched, their sharp eyes appraising every item and judging its value, probably to the penny, Isla thought. She smiled nervously at one or two of them, and received blank stares in return. Someone made a remark about snobby folks who liked to show off their possessions, and there was a general snigger of agreement.

'Pay no heed, missus,' the man with the cart muttered. 'Some folks is just jealous of everyone else.'

Isla bit her lip, and tried to ignore the stares.

'Folk never take kindly tae new neighbours,' Magret told her when she called in, Daisy tied to her by the shawl, and a cigarette – the same cigarette as yesterday, for all Isla knew – in her free hand. 'They'll come round in their own good time. Just don't be snobby with them when they dae talk tae ye. Ye'll need tae try tae redeem yer furniture when the ticket falls due, then just leave it in and take out another ticket. That way it stays yours. That's what we do with a bonny clock his auntie gave us when we got married.'

By now Isla had realised that the mysterious 'he'

Magret kept referring to was her husband. Magret sighed, then said wistfully, 'I'd like fine to see that clock on our mantelshelf just one time, but it's never been there, for we can never afford tae bring it out. The money's always needed for somethin' else.'

. Daisy was less flower-like than any baby Isla had ever seen. Beneath her bald little pate she studied the room with close-set black eyes, clearly inherited, along with the snub nose, from her mother.

Magret puffed at her cigarette and looked on while Isla scraped at the stove with a broken knife she had found lying near the dustbins in the back court. Ribbons of solid grease peeled off and fell on to the newspaper she had spread out on the floor.

'I don't know why ye're botherin', hen. It'll only get dirty again. That's what I hate about housework – it always has tae be done again.'

Daisy whimpered, and Magret settled herself in the armchair and opened her blouse, chattering on over the baby's head about the time when she had worked in Coats' mill, not far from George Street.

'It was nice, the way we all worked taegether. That's where I met him. It was noisy, right enough, and the fluff went for some of the women's lungs, but everyone was pally and we all had a good laugh. I'll mebbe get back there some day, when Daisy's older.'

'You might have another baby by then,' Isla ventured, and Magret gave a husky laugh.

'No' me, hen, not after the time I had with these two. I'd tae stay in the Infirmary for a week when I was carrying Daisy, and I near lost her the way I lost the two that came after our Greta. It's the rickets, ye see.

The nurse said the rickets was making it awful difficult for me tae carry weans.'

She hauled up her skirt unselfconsciously to reveal curved, vein-clustered legs, and Isla realised that the young woman's rolling walk and solid stocky body were due to the cruel disease, brought on by malnutrition, that distorted growing young bones.

'They said there'd be no more weans for me,' Magret explained, pushing her skirt down again.

'I'm sorry.'

'Ach, it suits us fine, for weans cost money and we've scarce got enough for the two we have already. He doesnae get a big pay. See my sister Agnes? Six weans she's got – and there'll be more afore she gets too old for it. She's never done carrying an' birthing weans, and worryin' about where their next meal's comin' from.' Magret shook her head and took another puff at her cigarette. 'I'd not want tae be her, poor soul. Anyway, I'd not want tae go back into that Infirmary – there was a terrible smell stingin' at my nose all the time from all that disinfectant they used. Cleaning like dafties day and night, so they were!'

'How could you agree to such a thing?'

It had been a long day. At the end of days like this, Gilchrist Forbes wondered if the time had come to hand over the business to his son and retire to the soothing pleasures of his books and his garden.

'I didn't agree to it,' he said wearily. 'There was no question of that. The woman owns the building and she has a right to live there if she wishes.'

Colin glared at his father across the over-furnished

drawing-room. 'But here in Paisley – scarcely more than a mile from the McAdams' home! She could have chosen to live anywhere in Scotland – why settle so close to Ainslie and her mother?'

'It takes money to buy or rent a place to live, and Kenneth McAdam left nothing but debts.'

'Surely she has money of her own – or family she can turn to?'

'Apparently not.' Gilchrist filled his glass almost to the brim, then tilted the decanter enquiringly. When Colin shook his head, his father set down the decanter and sipped at his own whisky.

'I find it hard to believe that she's entirely alone in the world.' The younger man's normally cheerful face was set in hard lines, his eyes stormy.

'There's an aunt in Edinburgh—'

'Well, there you are, then!'

'But Mrs – Mrs Moffatt tells me that she has no wish to throw herself and her children on this woman's mercy.'

Colin snorted. 'No doubt she'll have no hesitation in throwing herself on Mrs McAdam's mercy.'

'She claims that she has no intention of doing so.'

'And you believe her?'

Gilchrist took another swallow of whisky and tried to keep his own temper under control. 'Colin, I don't know what she has in mind. Nor do I have the power to order her out of her own property.'

'You must reason with her, Father! Point out that it's wrong for her to—' Colin stopped abruptly as his mother came into the room.

'What's wrong for who?' Phemie Forbes asked at once. She loved gossip and had ears as sharp as a bat's, particularly when it came to things she wasn't supposed to hear.

'Nobody, my dear,' Gilchrist started to say, but Colin blurted out, 'We were talking about Kenneth McAdam's . . .' Under his father's suddenly hard gaze he paused, biting back the words he had been about to utter, then said sullenly 'Kenneth McAdam's other woman.'

Phemie's round, good-natured face wrinkled with concern. 'Poor Catherine, all those years as a good wife to the man, and now this terrible shock on top of his death. It's changed her beyond recognition, Gilchrist. She's refusing to put a foot over her own doorstep, convinced that the whole town's whispering and pointing.' She sat down in her usual armchair by the fire and reached for her embroidery. 'I keep telling her that folk forget quickly, but she'll not listen to me.'

'I'm wondering if they really will forget, with the woman moving to Paisley,' Colin said.

'Moving to—' Phemie, about to plunge her needle into the heart of a half-stitched rosebud, plunged it into her own finger instead, and gave a choked shriek of pain. 'Look what you've made me do!'

She held her hand well away from the material in the embroidery ring and her husband hurriedly set down his glass and dropped to his knees beside her, whipping a crisp white handkerchief from his breast pocket to mop the bead of blood from her finger.

'Gilchrist, you'll ruin your handkerchief!' Phemie pulled her hand back and sucked at the injured finger. Round it she said, 'In Paisley? In this town?'

'In a tenement building in George Street that Mr McAdam left to her,' Colin confirmed.

'But surely the property should pass to Catherine?'

Gilchrist Forbes' knees cracked like winter twigs as he straightened up. 'Kenneth signed it over to her legally some time before his death. I can't force her to give it up, or to move away from the town.'

'But what'll happen if poor Catherine gets to hear of it?'

'The young woman's calling herself by her own name – Moffatt. I don't think she intends to make life difficult for Catherine.'

'I'd not be so sure about that,' Colin put in, and his father glared at him.

'She has two children to support, Phemie. It's my belief that she merely wants a roof over their heads until such time as she can make other plans.'

'There are children?'

'A boy and a girl.'

Tears came into Phemie's eyes. She loved children, and had always mourned the fact that she herself had had only one. She had been looking forward to Colin's marriage to Ainslie McAdam, and the hope of having many grandchildren in the future. 'The poor wee souls, what a start to have in life!'

'She seems to be a caring mother, I'm sure she'll do her best for them.' Gilchrist Forbes stared down at his handkerchief, then, guiltily, started refolding it to hide the bloody stain.

'I think you're being altogether too kindly in your attitude, Father,' Colin told him shortly. 'The woman may well be more ruthless than you think. Ainslie's very concerned about it all.'

'If Catherine hears that this woman and her children

are here, in Paisley, it may well be the final straw,' his
mother agreed. 'She's in quite a state of depression as it
is over Ainslie's latest news.'

'What news?' Colin came across the room towards his
mother, bumping into an occasional table in his haste.
'What about Ainslie?'

'Did you not know? She's found work for herself.'

'Where? What's she doing?'

'Let me see that handkerchief, Gilchrist.' Phemie
held out a hand and her husband reluctantly relinquished the folded square. She shook it out and tutted.
'Just as I thought – you've managed to get blood on it.
It must be soaked in salt and cold water at once.'

'Mother, what sort of work has Ainslie found?' Colin
persisted.

'She's taken on a position at Blayne's the auctioneers
in MacDowall Street. Catherine's most upset about it,
but Ainslie's not trained for anything, after all, and
with Innes's school fees to find, not to mention the
house to run, there's little Catherine can do about it.
You know Ainslie, she can be very deter— Colin, where
are you going?'

'Out.' Her son threw the word over his shoulder.

'Colin,' Phemie began, but he had already gone. She
sighed, crumpling the handkerchief in her hand. 'Poor
boy, he's still very upset about Ainslie returning his
ring.'

Gilchrist Forbes picked up his glass of whisky. 'No
point in fretting about it, my dear. They must work out
their own problems, as we had to do at their age.'

'We didn't have such bad problems, though, Gil.'
Phemie's voice was wretched. 'Who'd have thought of a

level-headed man like Kenneth McAdam killing himself, then turning out to be a bigamist?'

Her husband shook his head. 'I wish he'd come to me when his business started going wrong. I would have done all I could to help. It should never have come to this.'

'What's this other woman like, Gil?'

The sound of his son's car starting up took Forbes to the window. He watched the vehicle roaring out of the gate, scattering gravel to left and right. 'Young, much younger than Kenneth. She has dignity, I'll give her that. I don't think she's out to cause more trouble for Catherine. I can't understand why he did it – took her through a marriage ceremony, I mean. I'd never dream of doing such a thing.'

Phemie, setting aside the handkerchief and picking up her embroidery, smiled fondly at him. 'I don't think you would, my dear. But this whole business has just proved that we never know what's going on behind other people's walls, hasn't it?'

He swung round from the window. 'Are you telling me that the McAdams weren't happy in their marriage?'

Phemie sighed. 'Even though she's a friend I'll admit that I've always sensed a coldness in Catherine. I think she put appearance before anything else. Kenneth, now – I'm not sure that he was strong enough for her. From what Catherine's said about her father-in-law, I get the impression that he was a much stronger man than poor Kenneth. She seemed to admire him greatly. What was he like, Gil? I never knew him well – he died not long after I became friendly with Catherine.'

'I remember him as being very able, in every way. Kenneth worshipped him.'

'Perhaps,' said Phemie shrewdly, 'he lived in his father's shadow.'

'Surely not.' Then, tiring of the turn the conversation was taking, Gilchrist Forbes said, 'As to Ainslie, I think she may well rue the day she decided to earn her own living. She could come running back to Colin yet.'

'I'd not be too sure of that, she's a very determined girl. Stubborn, Catherine says, like her grandmother.'

'In that case,' her husband returned to his chair and reached for the evening newspaper, 'we can only hope he gets over her quickly, and finds someone more suitable.'

6

Within two weeks Isla let her few remaining pieces of furniture go to the pawnshop, realising that the room was too small for them. She bought an old fireside chair from the pawnbroker, scrubbing it well before covering its slippery, worn seat and back with remnant material bought cheaply from a draper's shop. She bought more cloth to make curtains for the window, and another curtain to stretch on string across the storage space below the bed. She crawled reluctantly into the space first, poking a long-handled brush ahead gingerly, and found a dirty tin hip-bath which served herself and the children very well, once it was scrubbed out with disinfectant.

An orange box obtained from the local greengrocer made a serviceable cupboard for their few dishes, turned on its side and with a scrap of bright material hung on a string along the top to curtain it off. Searching the waste-ground at the back of the building, she found two bricks of the same size and used a piece of wood to scrape off the slimy creatures adhering beneath them, holding the bricks at arm's length as she worked, her face twisted with disgust. When she was satisfied that the bricks were free of pests, she scrubbed them with Jeyes Fluid and sat the orange-box on top of them to keep it clear of the floor.

Her own clothes and the children's clothes were hung from nails hammered into the walls, and another curtain on a string beneath the sink closed off an area for the cleaning utensils. She scrubbed the shallow wall-cupboards and lined their shelves with an unwanted roll of wall-paper bought for two pence from a paint-shop, and after finding a spider in the flour crock, made sure that all the food kept in the cupboards was well covered.

The rent money, which she collected every Monday morning from Mr Forbes' front office, was spasmodic, and barely enough, at times, to see her through the week and pay her own rent on a Friday evening, but as soon as she could, she bought paint to brighten up the warped woodwork round the window. Gradually the room began to look cleaner and brighter.

It was impossible to get rid of the smell of sweat and urine and stale cooking that had soaked into the fabric of the entire tenement, but Isla did her best, blocking up mouse-holes in the skirting and swabbing Jeyes Fluid into the cracks in the floorboards to deter the cockroaches that emerged at night and sometimes were to be found during the day, wandering across the hearth. Once, she and Barbara collapsed shrieking into each other's arms after a particularly large cockroach marched across the table before their horrified eyes during a meal.

She worked from morning to night on the small room, falling into bed bone-weary after each day's efforts. The work helped to ease her deep sense of loss;

Kenneth was never far from her mind and she cried herself to sleep most nights, longing for the warmth of his arms, and the security that his love and strength had given her. She talked about him to the children, determined that they wouldn't be allowed to forget him. But there was nobody she herself could talk to about him, and about what he had meant, and still meant, to her. So she worked instead, driving herself on.

'This place smells like the Infirmary,' Magret complained one day, fanning the air before her. Isla, on her knees in a corner of the room, brushing disinfectant into a particularly bad crack, straightened her aching back and rubbed a hand across her forehead.

'If I don't get rid of those insects I'll go mad.'

'Ach, ye'll never get rid of them,' Magret told her. 'They was here before us, and they'll be here long after we've gone. 'Sides, they don't do any harm.'

That same evening, noticing Barbara scratching furiously, fingers buried in her thick bronze hair, Isla investigated, and recoiled in horror as she saw tiny lice scurrying over her daughter's scalp, weaving through the hair like natives bustling through a jungle. She snatched Ross up from the floor, where he was placidly playing with a toy motor car, and saw that his scalp, too, was alive with vermin.

'What's the matter?' Barbara asked apprehensively, eyeing her mother's face.

'N-nothing.' Isla put Ross down and filled the kettle at the sink with shaking hands. 'I think it's time you both got your hair washed, that's all.'

'You washed it yesterday.'

'I know that.' Isla suddenly realised to her horror that

she had absent-mindedly raised her hand to scratch her own head, and snatched it back. She could have burst into tears. She had done her best to make sure that the children were clean, but now it seemed that she was fighting a losing battle. It would have done no good to insist that they stayed away from the other children. Thanks to Greta, Barbara had settled into her new life and had been accepted by the other children in spite of the fact that she 'talked posh' and wore better clothes than they did. She had learned to play peevers and spent most of her day hopping and skipping and jumping over chalked squares and symbols on the pavement.

A natural mimic, she had fallen quickly into her new friends' speech patterns, and although Isla did her best to make sure that she spoke properly in the house, she knew that Barbara had to be free to talk to the other children in their own language. The little girl had, fortunately, adjusted to the sudden changes in her life, and it would be cruel to isolate her from the rest of the youngsters in the street.

The children yelled their protests when she scrubbed hard at their heads that night. The next day she went out and bought a fine-toothed comb and a large cake of coal tar soap, which added its own pungent aroma to the strong smell of disinfectant.

Magret sniffed at the air on her next visit, and said knowledgeably, 'Nits?'

Isla stared at her in horror. 'How did you know?'

'It's the smell of the soap. No need tae look so worried, hen – all the kids has got nits round here. Some worse than others – have ye not seen the poor wee souls with the shaved heads? It doesnae mean ye're dirty,' she hurried to assure her stricken friend. 'I've heard that nits can be found in grand houses tae.'

As the weeks went by, Isla got to know the other people in the building – old Granny Thomson, a tiny wizened creature, bent and twisted with arthritis, who crept in and out of her own door like a mouse and never spoke to anyone; Lena McNab, a striking-looking woman who ran the tiny baker's shop a short distance along the road, and her husband and former messenger-boy Peter, thin and clearly younger than Lena, peering at life through a pair of thick wire-framed spectacles. Lena had a warm heart, and sometimes gave her neighbours pastries and loaves that had become too stale to sell. Broken up and soaked in a mixture of milk and water, then covered with a scattering of sugar, the stale bread and pastries made a nourishing meal for the children.

Two of the flats upstairs were tenanted by the Kellys, a shy young couple, and Mrs Brown and her son, recently out of school and apprenticed to a joiner's shop. There was no sign of Mr Brown – Magret said that he had run away with 'the woman from the Co-op'. The third flat, a single room sandwiched between the others, which both had two rooms, was the residence of the formidable Mrs Leach, a gaunt widow who wore her grey hair twisted into a small tight bun at the back of her head, and made it her business to see that the other inhabitants behaved themselves.

The first time Isla hung out clothes to dry Mrs Leach came forging her way up the steps from the close to inspect them.

'Ye're not used tae hangin' out a washin', are ye?' she said with a disparaging sniff.

'I know fine how to do it,' Isla snapped back, aware that it would be fatal to give in to a bully.

To her astonishment, Mrs Leach reached up, unpinned a garment from the line, and flipped it about. 'Ye shouldnae hang yer bairn's trousers from the waist like that,' she said, her hands re-pinning the small garment so rapidly that they were blurred. 'Ye hang them from the legs, then the waistband can blow in the wind an' get dry. Here, I'll give ye a hand.'

She delved into the basket and proceeded to hang the clothes on the line, driving the wooden pegs into place so strongly that Isla expected them to snap in two.

'Ye've got some bonny things,' the woman commented as she worked. 'It's nice tae see things like that hangin' on our lines.' She wiped her hands on her wrap-around pinny and bent to Ross, who was watching, wide-eyed, clutching at his mother's skirt.

'How old is he?'

'Fourteen months.'

'He's a bonny wean.' Mrs Leach bared her yellowed teeth in a smile at Ross, who retreated further into Isla's skirt, pushing a thumb into his mouth.

'An' ye don't want him doin' that,' Mrs Leach snapped, straightening. 'His teeth'll grow in crooked.'

When Isla told Magret about the encounter her friend nodded sagely. 'If she helped ye tae hang yer washing, it means that she approves o' ye,' she announced.

It was a surprise to find that young Mrs Kelly was Mrs Leach's only child.

'That's why the wee soul never opens her mouth – she's never had the chance,' Magret said. 'They came down in the world after Mr Leach was killed in an accident at his work, and they'd nowhere else tae go but here. The lassie worked in an office, and when she insisted on gettin' married tae one of the lads she worked with, no matter what her mother had to say aboot it, Mrs Leach got them the house through the wall from her, so's she could keep an eye on them.'

She drew her breath in sharply through pursed lips and shook her head. 'Poor souls – the old woman gave them a right hard time when he lost his job last year – not that it was his fault that the place where he worked closed down. Ye'd have thought he'd done it just tae spite her, the way she went on. I think that's why they've no' got any weans yet – he must be scared tae touch the lassie, with her mother only the thickness of a wall away from their bed. If ever I treat my lassies the way she treats hers, I hope they've got the sense tae push me under a tram.'

Gradually, Isla began to settle into her new home. She managed to clear the lice from the children's heads and also managed, by dint of careful budgeting, to keep the three of them nourished and still have enough left over to pay the rent-collector when he called every Friday. He was a tall, sour-faced man who spread the coins out over his palm and counted every one carefully before stowing them away in his leather pouch and writing the date and the amount down in a large book, licking his pencil before he began. He had the look of a man who wouldn't take kindly to people being behind with the rent.

Magret had confirmed Isla's instincts from the beginning. 'Ye don't want tae get intae his bad books, hen.

He'd no' care about you being on yer lone with the weans tae look after – he'd take yer last penny out of yer hand and think nothin' of it.'

Isla grew to hate her Monday morning trip to Gilchrist Forbes' office to collect the rent-money, because she was taking money from people she knew, people who had little enough to spare and found it difficult at times to raise the rent. But she had no option, for she had her own children to care for. The little she made by keeping her furniture in pawn helped, but not much, and as the summer crept along she had to pawn first one piece of jewellery, then another, to make ends meet.

A previous tenant had left a rusty old garden fork by the bins. Seeing it lying there, Isla thought of saving money by growing vegetables. She already knew that a patch of the weedy stretch of ground at the back of the tenement officially belonged to the single room she and the children now lived in; she marked it off carefully with rows of stones so that nobody, particularly Mrs Leach, could accuse her of taking over anyone else's weeds, and carefully went over it, picking up stones and rubbish, which she piled neatly in one corner before fetching the fork.

The ground hadn't been dug for years, and it was as hard as the mysterious bits of iron she kept finding in it. Stopping to catch her breath, she saw that several people were at their windows, watching her, and even the dingy net curtain at Granny Thomson's window was twitching. Soon there was a row of children peering over the wall at her.

'Heh, missus,' one of them shouted. 'Are ye buryin' some'dy?'

'I'm going to grow things,' she told him, and the children howled with laughter, as though she had said something very funny.

After struggling for an entire afternoon Isla had made very little impact on the ground. Nevertheless, she went back to it again and again whenever time and weather permitted. Magret watched, fascinated, Daisy straddled across her hip.

'Ye'll never dae it.'

'I'm doing it now.' Isla proudly indicated a square foot of exposed earth. Magret peered at it, and sniffed.

'Even if ye dae manage tae get somethin' planted, it'll vanish as soon as it appears,' she argued, nodding towards the next tenement, where a large, rowdy fatherless family was known to survive mainly on the proceeds of the children's thefts. 'That lot'd steal a dead cat out of a gutter, so they would.'

'I'd like to see them try,' Isla said grimly, plunging the fork into the ground and leaning her weight on it. 'I've got my children to feed, and nobody's going to stop me!'

At the beginning of August Barbara celebrated her fifth birthday. When she and Kenneth had talked about the forthcoming event, not long before his death, Isla had suggested buying a doll's house for their daughter.

'I used to have one when I was a little girl – a lovely house, with stairs to the bedrooms and a cook in the kitchen,' she recalled, the pleasure of playing with the dolls' house flooding back to her. 'I wish I'd been able to keep it, for my own little girl.'

Kenneth had put his arm about her. 'She shall have a new one all to herself,' he promised. 'We'll choose it between us, and you can have the enjoyment of decorating and furnishing it for her.'

Remembering, Isla blinked back tears and looked round the shabby home she now shared with her children.

There was no room for a fine doll's house here, nor the money to buy one. She must find some other gift for Barbara, something she could make herself, for she couldn't afford to buy presents.

She was working on her gift a week before Barbara's birthday when someone rapped on the door. Isla, assuming that it was Magret, called out, 'The door's on the latch,' then jumped to her feet, showering clothes-pegs and scraps of cloth on to the floor, as Ainslie McAdam walked in.

'What are you doing here?'

Ainslie's mouth tightened as she looked at the mourning band on Isla's arm, then her gaze travelled on around the room. She was clearly shocked by what she saw. 'So it's true – you are living here!'

'I am – not that it's any business of yours.' Isla was stung by the look on the other girl's face as she took in the shabby room. At their last meeting she had felt herself to be in the wrong, ignorant though she had been of Kenneth's other family. This time, though, she wasn't going to allow Ainslie McAdam to dominate her. 'Who told you we were here?'

'Colin Forbes.'

'I might have known. He'd no business to tell you anything about me.' Isla stooped to gather up the clothes-pegs and the scraps of material she had been working on.

'It is my business, if you're living in Paisley. I told you already that—'

Isla straightened up. Ainslie was the same height as herself and she met the girl's blue eyes unblinkingly. 'This was the only place we could come to. I had to get out of the house I was in, and I've no money of my own. Ken— your father,' she amended, seeing the way the other girl winced at her familiar use of his first name, 'left me this building. We were lucky one of the rooms was lying empty.'

Ainslie's curl of the lip intimated that nobody living in such a place could consider themselves to be lucky. 'You could have sold it and used the money to find somewhere further away,' she said aloud.

'And starved my children under some hedge while we waited to find out if anyone wanted it?' Isla's voice was scathing. 'It's for sale now, but not a soul's made an offer.' She saw that her hands were shaking, and busied them in smoothing out the pieces of cloth she had laid on the table.

Ainslie moved forward, and her foot caught against something. She bent and picked it up, her brows wrinkling as she studied the clothes-peg in her hand. A piece of white rag had been tied round the knob at the top of the peg and a face stitched on to the cloth. Round blue eyes stared back at her, and there was the suggestion of a neat nose and a smiling rosebud of a mouth.

Isla, reddening, almost snatched the peg from Ainslie's hand. 'Don't worry,' she said dryly, 'I'm not a witch, making effigies of you and your mother. It's a doll for my daughter's birthday.'

'Is that the red-haired child I saw playing in the str—' Ainslie flinched as Ross, disturbed from his sleep, shifted and whimpered from his cot in a shadowy corner of the room. Isla went to soothe him, then, when the whimpering rose to a wail, she lifted him from the cot.

'You haven't told me yet why you've called,' she said as she turned. A shaft of light from the window turned the baby's sweat-damp curls to flame as she carried him over to the chair by the fire.

'You know fine why I called. You'll have to find somewhere else to live!' Ainslie's voice was harsh and loud, and Ross, still half asleep, clutched at his mother and cringed away from this angry stranger, pushing his hot face into Isla's neck. The smell of ammonia from his wet napkin soured the air.

'It's all right, love, Mummy's got you safe.' Isla soothed him, then over his head she asked Ainslie McAdam, 'Where d'you suggest we go?'

'Anywhere but Paisley! I'll not have you upsetting my mother . . .'

'I've already told you that I've no intention of going anywhere near your mother.'

'But she might hear about you. Someone might tell her.'

'I doubt if we move in the same social circles,' Isla pointed out, and the younger girl flushed at the contempt in her voice.

'I'm working now – I don't earn much but I could probably give you some money in a few weeks' time if you—'

'Miss McAdam, you may not think much of my

71

home, but at least it's mine and I'm not beholden to anyone. I wouldn't take a penny of your money, not even if you were the wealthiest woman in the country and I was starving.'

'You took my father's money. You had his children.'

If she hadn't been holding Ross, Isla would have launched herself at the girl and known the satisfaction of bundling her out of the room by force. Instead, she said, her voice shaking, 'At the time, I thought I had the right, as his legal wife. Now, will you please get out of my house?'

Ainslie's fists clenched by her sides. 'Don't you care about how terrible it's been for us, for my mother, with the whole town talking about what my father did? Isn't that bad enough, without having his – his—' she choked, then rushed on, 'you living right here in Paisley!'

Her selfishness infuriated Isla. 'D'you never give a thought to the suffering he must have gone through, to be driven to do what he did?'

'Why should I? He made sure that he was well out of it, well away from the whispering and the glances!' the girl said bitterly.

'It seems to me that it must take a great deal of misery to cause any human being to put an end to his life. As to my presence here in Paisley' – Isla's voice was as sharp and as cold as an icicle as she got to her feet, holding Ross close, and swept past Ainslie to the door – 'I'm here only because my bairns and I have nowhere else to go. I'm using my own name, not your father's. I've said nothing to anyone about my past life, and I don't intend to.' She lifted the latch and the door swung creakily open. 'Now – I'd be grateful if you would just go away and let me and my children be.'

Ainslie hesitated, then walked past her and into the close. Isla closed the door at once, then waited, clutching Ross, her ears straining for the sound of the young woman walking out of the close. Eventually it came, the tap of well-shod feet moving out into the street and away.

Isla went slowly back to the fireside chair, Ross weighing heavily in her arms, and collapsed into it. The baby, frightened by something he couldn't understand, clutched at her and burst into tears.

'It's all right, pet,' Isla tried to reassure him. Then her own tears came, and the two of them wept together.

7

Ainslie McAdam was in turmoil as she left the old tenement. She had gone there with the intention of talking things out once and for all with the woman who had brought such shame down on her family, making it clear to Isla how impossible it was for her to stay in Paisley.

But as she stepped out on to the pavement she felt that she had failed miserably, and had only succeeded in making herself look foolish.

A gaggle of toddlers played contentedly in the sun-splashed gutter, most of them barefoot and wearing dirty, ragged clothing. One or two were naked from the waist down. Ainslie shuddered and averted her eyes – and found herself looking at the little red-haired girl she had seen on her way in. The child, better dressed than most of her companions, was energetically swinging one end of a rope, her brown eyes sparkling with enjoyment. Another little girl held the other end, while a third child, in the middle, leapt high with both feet clamped together to allow the rope to swing beneath her. As Ainslie watched, she mistimed a leap, and was sent sprawling on the pavement as the rope tangled her ankles, bouncing up again almost at once.

'My turn!' Isla's daughter – and her own half-sister, Ainslie realised with sudden horror – pushed her end of the rope into the defeated child's hands and took her place. 'Ready? One, two, three, a-leary,' she chanted, feet together, skirt flying as she leapt into the air, up and down, her feet scarcely brushing the pavement before she was airborne again, the rope smacking against the stone slabs beneath her.

Ainslie turned and almost ran from the place.

When she got home her mother was in her usual place, on the sofa in the drawing-room, a glass and a half-empty bottle of tonic wine on a table close to hand.

'You're late,' she said as soon as her daughter went in.

'I had some work to finish,' Ainslie lied. Crossing the carpet to kiss Catherine, she realised that compared to the small room she had recently visited, the drawing-room was enormous. She had always taken her home, with its large, high-ceilinged, carpeted rooms and its comfortable furnishings, for granted, and had never been in any other type of house, until today.

'How are you feeling, Mother?'

'Oh . . .' Catherine shrugged one shoulder, and let her voice drift into silence.

'Did anyone call?'

'Don't be silly, Ainslie, who would call on us now?'

'Mrs Forbes, for one.' Ainslie tried to keep her voice cheerful.

'She did look in,' Catherine acknowledged, reaching

for her glass, then, 'what do you mean, you had work to finish?'

'Some items that came in this afternoon had to be catalogued.' It was the truth, she had had to work very hard to make time to visit George Street, but she had managed it.

'See to the fire, will you? Your father would turn in his grave,' Catherine went on as her daughter obeyed, 'if he knew that you were working as an ordinary clerkess, after all the money he spent on your education.'

'I don't know how to do anything else. I can't type, or sew, or cook.'

'You were brought up to be a lady, and to run your own house efficiently when the time came.'

Ainslie, poking at the coals in the grate, gave a soft sigh, recognising the build-up to a spate of reproaches over her broken engagement. 'It's a lovely day, Mother – too warm for a fire. Why don't you go into the garden and sit in the sun for a little while?'

'I prefer to be indoors,' Catherine McAdam said flatly. 'That reminds me – Innes is in the garden and he should be working at his homework now. Fetch him in, will you?'

Ainslie did as she was asked, glad of the chance to escape from the stuffy drawing-room. The garden at the rear of the house was brilliant with colour from the rose-bushes her father had planted. They massed the flower-beds, filled a small circular bed in the middle of the lawn like a jewelled brooch set against green velvet, and swarmed up the red brick wall that hid the vegetable garden from sight.

Innes was crouched down by the wall, studying a

butterfly that had settled on his hand. 'Look,' he said as his sister approached. 'Isn't it beautiful?'

She bent down, steadying herself with one hand on his back, careful to avoid letting her shadow fall on the insect and startling it. The rich colour of its spread wings glowed in the sunlight.

'Beautiful,' she agreed.

'It's a Red Admiral. Look, its wings are the same colour as your hair. I wish mine wasn't so gingery.'

'There's nothing wrong with your hair.' Ainslie ruffled it affectionately, recalling that the baby she had seen that afternoon in George Street had the same fiery red head. 'Mother says it's time for homework.'

He groaned. 'Already?'

'You'd better go in.' She watched as he coaxed the butterfly on to a cluster of yellow nasturtiums fronting the flower border, then followed him as he made for the back door.

'I suppose I should let her know I'm in.' Innes trotted into the drawing-room while Ainslie went upstairs to change out of the black skirt and jacket she had worn to the auction house.

A large portrait of the first Innes McAdam, her grandfather, hung on the half-landing beside the bathroom door. He had been a handsome man, with piercing eyes below a thatch of crisp white hair, a neatly trimmed moustache and beard hiding the lower part of his face. He had died when Ainslie was only a month old, leaving the successful business he had started as an ambitious young man to his only child, her father.

'He was so disappointed to have a granddaughter instead of a grandson,' Catherine had told Ainslie so frequently that, as a child, she had believed that her arrival in the world had been the sole cause of her grandfather's departure from it. 'I wish he had lived to see Innes.'

In her room, Ainslie stripped to her petticoat and poured water from the flowered china ewer into the matching basin. As she washed she heard Innes come upstairs and go into his own room, then her mother's bedroom door opened and closed. Ainslie put on a black crêpe de Chine dress and brushed her curly hair until it crackled. The house was hushed, as always, and she found herself missing the bustle and excitement of the auction house.

To her surprise, she had discovered that she enjoyed working in the auction house. She liked the bustle of the place, and the continual coming and going. She found satisfaction in neatly listing the goods that came in and noting the possible value of each item.

She sat on the bed and picked up a fashion magazine, then tossed it down almost at once, rising to wander listlessly about the room. She was in mourning – there was no sense in looking at bright-coloured clothes that she couldn't wear.

Almost an entire wall of the bedroom was taken up by a long low bookcase topped with ornaments and toys that had been dearly loved in their day. Every book she had ever owned was on the shelves, from her first picture book to handsomely bound editions of favourites such as *The Wind in the Willows*, and the works of Dickens and Jane Austen. Most of them had been gifts from her father, who had himself been a keen reader.

Looking at them now, Ainslie wondered if the books

proved his love for her, or merely his desire that she should understand literature. She had wanted so much to be able to love her parents openly, and had always envied those school friends who talked about cosy chats with their mothers, and hugs from their fathers. Her parents' desire that she should be well fed and well dressed, their concern over her childhood ailments, showed that they cared about her, but neither of them had been demonstratively affectionate.

It embarrassed her now to remember how she had followed Colin Forbes around as a small child, desperate for any sign of kindness, grateful for it. Deep down, she knew that she had become engaged to Colin because he was the only person who had ever said that he loved her. Because of that – and because their engagement had pleased her parents.

Then, just when she had begun to hope that she could change her world, setting up a home with Colin, having children who would grow up knowing that they were loved and cherished, her father had ruined everything. And Ainslie, crushed beyond belief by his final desertion, his final betrayal, had decided that it only proved that no man, not even Colin, could be trusted.

She thought of the dark little room she had been in earlier that day, the tiny scraps of cloth on the table and the clothes-peg with a face drawn on to a piece of rag, the young woman who had criticised her sharply for not giving any thought to her father's misery. She wished now that she had kept away from George Street.

She turned from the bookcase with a swift twist of the body, and sat down again on the bed, thinking now about her mother. Catherine McAdam had always seemed to be such a strong character, a woman more than capable of standing alone. She had run her home with great competence, taken her rightful place in local society, known just what to do and what to say in any situation.

She had turned to nobody for help when her husband died, arranging immediately after the funeral for all his clothes to be sent to a charitable organisation, and packing his personal possessions away until such time as Innes was old enough to inherit them. She had had his bedroom door locked, and then, with everything seen to, she had become an invalid.

'Let your mother work through her grief in her own time,' the doctor had told Ainslie when she voiced her concern about Catherine's listlessness. 'She'll come to terms with her loss when she's ready.'

But as the weeks passed Catherine hadn't shown any signs of recovery. Sometimes Ainslie wondered if she was genuinely grieving, if she had perhaps been closer to her husband than Ainslie had thought. That possibility didn't comfort her at all, but merely added to her growing terror with the fear that her mother, too, might kill herself rather than go on alone.

She jumped up from the bed and smoothed the coverlet briskly, trying to smooth her worries away at the same time, then went into her mother's room. Catherine, in a long-skirted black evening dress and a light wrap over her shoulders, sat at the dressing-table, staring blankly into the mirror. Even in the midst of mourning, even in her depression, she insisted on dressing for dinner, although only her children were there to see her.

'Mother, would you like me to brush your hair?'

Catherine's body rippled as though a shiver had run through it. Her mirrored eyes lifted to stare at Ainslie blankly, then blinked, recognition drifting into them.

'Very well.' She sat straight-backed as Ainslie carefully removed the pins from her hair and let it drop over her shoulders, then began to draw the brush through it. The room was immaculate, as usual, with Catherine's silver-backed brushes and mirror neatly laid out on the dressing-table. The small studio portrait of Catherine and Kenneth McAdam that had always stood on the dressing-table was gone, replaced by a photograph of Ainslie's grandfather Innes and his wife, a woman with character in her features rather than beauty. Looking from the portrait in its elaborate silver frame to her own mirrored reflection, Ainslie had to acknowledge that her mother was right – there was a look of Grandmother McAdam about her features.

'Perhaps you should have a change, Mother – go away for a few weeks,' she suggested as she worked.

'Why should I want to do that?'

'It might do you good. Helensburgh, maybe. There are some pleasant hotels there, and the sea air can be very bracing.'

Catherine shook her head impatiently, almost tangling her fine greying hair in the brush. 'How can I go away just as Innes is about to start the new school year?'

'I can see to him.'

'You?' Catherine gave a short, bitter laugh. 'You've got your work to attend to now.'

'I'm not there all the time. And the servants are very

well trained, they can be trusted to look after him when I'm not at home.'

'No.' Catherine snapped the word out, then folded her lips tightly. Ainslie, who knew better than to argue, said nothing more.

When her mother's hair was pinned into its usual twisted plait at the back of her head, she went downstairs to see that the table was set for dinner and the meal ready on time. As the clock chimed seven Catherine came in to take her place at the foot of the table. Innes, his face shining from a recent bout with his face-flannel, scampered into the dining-room a few minutes later.

'Sorry, Mother, I had to finish the sentence before I forgot what I was writing about,' he said breathlessly, his bright hair introducing light and movement into the room.

Catherine smiled, and held her arms out to him. 'Come and give Mother a kiss, darling.'

As he smacked a kiss on her pale cheek, her arms encircled him tightly. Watching, remembering how Isla had comforted her own red-haired son earlier that day, Ainslie suddenly felt very lonely.

Isla made two dolls out of clothes-pegs, wrapping pipe-cleaners round them to make arms, clothing them in long dresses and giving them mob caps. She bought a small orange box from the greengrocer's and hid it beneath the wall-bed. In the evenings, while the children slept, she covered its interior with scraps of wall-paper, drawing a large kitchen range on the back wall and a dresser on one of the side walls. A circle of cardboard nailed on to an empty wooden bobbin made a table, and other bobbins covered with cloth served as stools. With Plasticine, she made some plates for the table, finishing the single-roomed house off with a curtain stretched across the front on string.

Barbara was delighted with her gift. 'It's a house just the same size as ours, isn't it?' she said in wonder, kneeling before the orange box house. 'This is the mummy and this is the little girl.'

'She's a big little girl.'

'Not as big as her mummy.' Barbara stood the two peg dolls side by side and sure enough, one was a fraction smaller than the other. 'Where's the daddy?'

'You don't get daddy dolls,' Isla told her, and the little girl's lower lip trembled.

'Yes you do,' she insisted. 'Of course you do! Where is he?'

'At work?' Isla suggested, her mind on her sewing box. There was still some white material left that would do for a shirt, and a scrap of black that could be turned into trousers, and perhaps some kind of cap.

Barbara's face cleared, and she nodded. 'All right, but he'll be coming home. He'll be coming home soon.'

'Tomorrow.' Isla hugged her daughter. Barbara scarcely ever asked about Kenneth's whereabouts now, but clearly he was still in her mind.

Magret, invited with her children to share the small dumpling Isla had made for the occasion, was enthralled by the little house.

'Who'd've thought ye could turn an old orange box intae a house, and a clothes-peg intae a dolly?' she marvelled, studying one of the dolls closely. 'It's bonny, Isla.'

'It's not difficult.'

'Not for you, mebbe, but I'd never manage it.' Magret handed the doll back to her elder daughter, who bustled importantly over to the orange box and knelt down, pushing the top half of her body into it as she replaced the doll. Catching a glimpse of skinny little buttocks, Isla realised that Greta didn't wear drawers.

When Barbara woke up the next morning the daddy doll was in residence, much to her delight. The next day, over a mug of tea, Magret asked Isla to make a peg doll for Greta.

'She's been on at me for one ever since she saw Barbara's.'

Isla sipped the tea, realising that she was now used to its strength and sweetness, and to the mingled taste of condensed milk and grease.

'I could show you how to make it,' she offered, but Magret shook her head.

'I'm not good with my hands, like you,' she coaxed, and beamed her delight when Isla gave in.

8

Isla had begun to admit to herself that in trying to wrest a vegetable patch from the weedy backyard she was fighting a losing battle, but her pride wouldn't let her give in. She well knew that almost everyone living within sight of the back court was watching her progress, and, like Magret, none of them thought that she would succeed. So she battled on, glancing up one evening to see a young lad watching her from beside the wash-house.

Isla smiled at him, recognising Mrs Brown's son Drew, and he looked away in embarrassment, then looked back at her.

'What're ye growin'?'

'Potatoes, if I ever manage to clear enough land.'

He spat on his hands, then held them out. 'I'll give ye a hand. See's the fork.'

She handed it over, stepping back to let him get to the pitifully small amount of earth she had won from the grasses. He drove the tines of the fork deep into the ground with more force than she had thought possible from his slight frame, then leaned on the handle, lifting a solid clod of earth free. It had been bound into place by generations of grass roots that stubbornly held on to

it, and he had the sense to work patiently at it until all
the roots had snapped. He dumped the clod on the
ground and smashed at it with the side of the fork, then
drove the tines into the ground again.

Isla left him to it and went into the building. When
she came back with a mug of tea in each hand, he had
got into the rhythm of it, and had learned the sense of
trying to gain only a little ground at a time.

He straightened up and accepted the tea with mumbled thanks. Together they sipped in silence. 'It might
not work,' Isla said at last, 'but I don't think there's any
harm in failing as long as you've tried.'

'Aye.' The lad drained the last of the tea, his Adam's
apple bobbing in his thin throat, then handed the mug
back and got on with his work, digging steadily until a
cloud of midges, those tiny maddening flies that perse-
cuted Scotland, arrived and made further work
impossible.

'I could do more for ye, if ye want,' he said diffidently as the two of them retired to the close.

Isla hesitated, then decided that frankness was the
only way. 'I can't afford to pay you.'

'Doesnae matter. I like diggin'.'

'What'll your mother say?'

'It was her that sent me down. I'd nothin' tae dae.'

'I tell you what – if you want to help, I'll share the
potatoes with you and your mother.'

For the first time, he looked fully at her, and
grinned. 'Aye. That'd be fine.'

By the time Barbara started school, Isla and young
Drew Brown had dug over more than half the patch of

ground between them, and a succession of women up and down George Street had asked Isla to make peg dolls for their daughters, just like the dolls Barbara and Greta had been showing off to the other children.

Isla, aware of the importance of building up a good relationship with her neighbours, refused nobody, and soon almost every little girl playing out on the pavement had become the proud owner of a peg doll. Some of the women offered her money in exchange for her work, while others brought half a dozen home-made scones, or a fruit loaf, or a good soup-bone with fragments of meat still attached, or a piece of material.

By the time she started attending the West School, only ten minutes' walk away from George Street, Barbara had made a number of friends, though Greta was her closest confidante. Barbara admired Greta; in her eyes, the child could do no wrong. This led to some conflict between mother and daughter, especially over the business of underwear.

'Greta doesn't need to wear drawers,' Barbara protested after being caught playing in the street with nothing on underneath her skirt. Her rolled-up knickers were substituting for a pillow in a battered dolls' pram that Greta had inherited from an older cousin.

'She would if she was my little girl.'

Barbara's lower lip slid forward mutinously. 'Drawers just get in the way when you want to pee in the yard.'

'When you want to – *what?*' Horrified, Isla stared at her daughter. 'But you always use the privy, like a good girl. Don't you?' she added, as Barbara shrugged her shoulders and scuffed the toe of one shoe over the floor.

'Sometimes someone's in the privy and I can't wait,

87

and anyway, every time I use it that old Mrs Leach comes running down to make sure I didn't make a mess,' Barbara muttered, adding, 'anyway, the grass is nicer, it's not all dark and smelly like the privy, and it tickles.'

'Barbara!' It was all that Isla could do not to shake the child. 'You must never ever use the yard as a privy, d'you hear me? No matter what anyone else does. If you do, I'll – I'll give you such a smacking!'

Barbara stared up at her, wide-eyed. Isla rarely hit her, and never hard.

'D'you hear me?' Isla insisted, and the child finally gave a sullen nod. When she had been sent out to play, with firm instructions to keep all her clothes on, Isla went back to her ironing, gnawing at her lower lip, aware that it was going to be hard to continue to insist on certain standards when the children Barbara played with had their own way of looking at life. The little girl had settled in well, even accepting her new surname without question, and as far as she was concerned the future would be like the present, living in one small room playing out on the pavement or in the rubbish-strewn backyard.

Isla still hoped that one day she and her children would be able to move out of George Street and back into the sort of home Kenneth had once provided for them. It was a hope that had begun to turn into a dream, for not one person had made an offer so far for the tenement building. But she refused to accept that she and her children were going to remain in George Street for ever.

Ross, playing on the hearth-rug with a wooden toy, lost interest in it and grabbed the leg of the fireside

chair for support while he hauled himself upright. He
toddled across the floor, moving from one piece of furniture to the other, until he got to the door, then
banged on it, whimpering.

'You're too wee to go out and play,' Isla told him. As
he continued to grizzle, she fetched the bag of clothes-
pegs and offered it to him. He snatched at it and sat
down on the floor, turning the bag upside down and
emptying its contents out.

'Whatever would we do without pegs?' Isla wondered
aloud, lifting the flat-iron from the gas ring and putting
her finger in her mouth to damp it so that she could
test the iron's heat. Barbara had started walking at an
earlier age than Ross, but Magret had assured Isla that
boys usually took longer than girls to get on their feet.
Isla saw it as a blessing. All too soon Ross would be
insisting on going out to play in the street like his sister, and then there would be two of them to deal with.

She thought of the little boys who played in the gutter, naked from the waist down, and the older boys, up
to all sorts of mischief, from knocking on doors then
running away to stealing from the local shops. Would
Ross grow up to be like that? The responsibility of raising her children on her own weighed heavily on her
shoulders, reviving the aching misery of Kenneth's
death. At times like this, she would have sacrificed
everything in the world, except Barbara and Ross, to
bring Kenneth back again.

On the first day of the school term Magret and Isla saw
their daughters settled in a large classroom noisy with
the wails of children thrown into panic at the thought of

being abandoned by their mothers. Barbara and Greta had no such qualms. Seated side by side, they were both enchanted with the double bench and the two desks with lids that could be raised to reveal an inviting space within, waiting to be filled.

'Thank God,' Magret said with all her heart as the two women made their way home. 'I made such a fuss the first day I started school that my mammy had tae take me home again. I got a right hammerin' when we got there, too. Black affronted, she was. I never liked the school. See the very smell of the place? When I went in there today I nearly turned and ran out again, the memories of my own time were that strong.'

Isla nodded. 'It helps when they've got each other. I was sorry for that woman whose wee boy wouldn't let go of her legs.'

Their smug pleasure at having such well-behaved children didn't last long. At half-past ten that morning, when Isla answered an imperious thumping at the door, Barbara marched past her into the room. 'I'm back,' she announced, tossing the shabby little school-bag that Isla had bought from the pawn-shop on to the floor.

'What are you doing here? You're supposed to be at school!'

'I've been,' said Barbara. 'We played with boxes of sand and sang a song, then they let us out, so me and Greta came home.'

Magret burst in just then without waiting to knock, towing a puzzled Greta by the wrist. 'Isla—'

'I know.'

'What would ye make of them?' Magret asked in exasperation, while Isla explained to her daughter, 'You

90

were only let out to play for a wee while. Then you were supposed to go back in again until I came to take you home for your dinner.'

'Back again?' Barbara asked in astonishment.

'Aye, my lass, and tomorrow tae. Isla, we'll need tae take them back, an' me with the wean sleepin' in her cot . . .'

'Tomorrow?' Barbara and Greta squeaked in unison.

'You didn't say about tomorrow too,' Barbara accused her mother.

'Hen, ye've got years o' it ahead o' ye,' Magret said with heart-felt sympathy, adding to her own daughter, 'and you too, wee imp that ye are, what's yer daddy goin' tae say about this?'

'He'll have a good laugh about it.' Isla was beginning to see the funny side of the situation herself. 'You look after Ross, Magret, and I'll take them back. You'll come with me, won't you, Greta?'

'Uhuh,' Greta said round the thumb she had stuck into her mouth, while Barbara gave a huge sigh of irritation over the contrary ways of adults.

'You didn't say anything about going back in,' she pointed out as she and Greta were shepherded out of the room and through the close. 'You should have said!'

Ainslie McAdam had never been happier in her life. Charlie Blayne, her employer, was a broad-shouldered middle-aged man with twinkling blue eyes and a head of thick curly hair that had once been rich brown and was now well sprinkled with grey.

'I see myself as a working man's auctioneer, lass,' he told Ainslie when she applied for the post as his office

91

clerkess. 'Folk die, an' their relatives want to get rid of a houseful of stuff, some of it pure rubbish. So they send for me, and if it can be sold, I'll sell it for them. Or mebbe they need a bit o' money, so they bring their granda's clock, or ornaments they never liked anyway – stuff they don't want back, or else they'd pawn it.'

He tipped his chair back and looked with satisfaction round his small office. It was filled with papers and ledgers and boxes crammed with books and spoons and pipe racks and pots and pans. A rag doll stared blankly at Ainslie over the top of one box.

'Folk all want different things. A picture frame or a nice wee ornament for the mantelpiece – or a toy for the wean,' Charlie went on, nodding at the doll. 'An' mebbe they're looking for a bit of a gamble. In a shop they must pay the price asked, but here, they might get just what they want for less, or have a bit of fun out-biddin' the next man.' He beamed at Ainslie. 'D'ye see what I mean?'

'I think so.'

'Ye never get bored in this job, lass. Ye never know from one day to the next what'll come in – or who. Now . . .' He swung his feet down from the desk and became more businesslike. 'What I need is someone to keep the paperwork tidy. There's lists to be sorted out and valuations to record, and letters to write and books to keep. There's not much to it, but I'd as soon be free to get on with the business of seein' to the sales and the stores and going out and about, valuing stuff. D'ye think ye could manage it?'

'I was good at arithmetic at school, and I can deal with lists,' she said cautiously.

'Can ye use a telephone?'

'Yes.'

'What about a typewriter?'

'I'm willing to try it.'

'Aye, well, that suits me. We'll see how things go for a week or two, will we? If ye don't like it, say so, an' if I don't think ye'll fit in, I'll have to tell ye, lass. No point in either of us wasting our time over something that won't work. I can start ye off at six shillin's a week.'

It wasn't much, but Ainslie had never worked before, and beggars couldn't be choosers. She nodded, and he ran a thoughtful eye over her neat black skirt and jacket. 'Ye'll be in the store-rooms sometimes, lass, an' it's awful mucky there. It's mucky in the offices, come to that,' he added frankly. 'That's somethin' else ye could mebbe try to see to. It's not easy keeping a place like this clean. Ye'll get into a mess.'

'I'll bring an overall.'

'Aye, that'd be wise,' said Charlie Blayne.

The offices, Charlie's and Ainslie's, both small and both cramped, stood at the end of a long gallery that ran the length of the auction-room below and was connected to it by a stair at the far end. The gallery was crammed with items, particularly before a sale, and at times there was little more than a narrow passageway between the offices and the stairs, between high walls of tea-chests and crates and tables and roped sets of chairs. Double wooden doors with a smaller door set in one of them led from the auction rooms to the cobbled yard and the street, and two other doors at the opposite side opened into the large store-rooms where the goods were kept. Before each sale it was Ainslie's job to see that the goods on offer were clearly listed and marked, so that they could be brought into the saleroom in the correct order.

A narrow door and dark wooden stairway led directly from her office to the street outside, so that she could come and go each day without having to enter through the saleroom. Each morning, as soon as she arrived, she wrapped herself in an overall she had bought for work. The old building seemed to ooze dust through every chink and crack, and a number of women were specially employed just to keep the furniture for sale dusted and polished. Ainslie saw to the two offices, sweeping and dusting and cleaning out the fireplaces every morning before clambering up on to a high stool to work at the sloping desk. When the day was done, she had to wash her hands and often her face before leaving, because of the dust.

Charlie Blayne was an easy-going employer, with the knack of turning the men and women who worked for him into a second family. From the first day, Ainslie loved her work, and after a few weeks it seemed to her that she only truly came alive while she was busy in the tiny office, or down in the rooms, lists in hand.

While she was working there was little time to think of anything else, but as soon as she stepped out on to the narrow dreary street and set off homewards she started fretting about Catherine, who was still refusing to go out or to take an interest in life again. She also refused to let Ainslie tell her anything about her work.

'If your father knew – and your poor grandfather . . .' She gave a shudder of disgust. 'Auction rooms!'

'Auction houses can be very respectable, Mother,'

Ainslie protested, more hurt for Charlie Blayne's sake than her own.

'Yes, they can. Christie's, for one, or Sotheby's – but you're not employed by them, are you?'

'I doubt if they'd want me, since I have no qualifications.'

'You have to work in some nasty little place, when you could have done so much better for yourself!' Catherine ranted on, and Ainslie held her tongue, knowing that her mother would never change her views.

Innes, who was at the adaptable age where life always goes on, was doing well at school, and clearly relieved to be back there after a summer spent in a house in mourning.

'Will Mother ever get better?' he asked his sister once, wistfully.

She hugged him. 'Of course she will.'

Innes inspected his large-knuckled bony hands. 'She says she wants me to be just like grandfather McAdam when I'm old enough. Does that mean dying, too?'

Ainslie felt a chill creep up her spine. 'Of course not. She means she would like you to go into business.'

'Work in an office?' He wrinkled his freckled nose. 'I'd rather do something with cars. Or p'raps go to Africa to collect creatures for a zoo.'

'Best not to tell Mother that. There's plenty of time yet, you might think of all sorts of things you want to do before the time comes.'

'I won't ever want to be in business,' Innes said firmly, then added, 'but whatever it turns out to be, it'll be something that makes a lot of money for us all, so you and Mother needn't worry about that.'

9

In October an Indian summer, an unexpected spell of golden warm weather, descended on the west of Scotland, and one of Ainslie's former schoolfriends invited her to a tennis-party. The invitation was waiting on the drawing-room mantelpiece when she returned from the auction rooms; she read it and stuffed it back into the envelope without comment, but her mother, watching her, asked with studied casualness, 'What was that?'

'Lena Gillespie's having some people in for tennis on Saturday.'

'I think you should go,' Catherine said at once.

'But we're still in mourning, Mother.'

'Even so, you've not been anywhere this year, and it's not right for young people to shut themselves away for too long. It would do you good to see your friends again.'

'I don't really think I want to play tennis. For one thing, I'm out of practice.'

'Nonsense.' Catherine sipped at her tonic wine – the bottle, Ainslie noticed, was almost empty. It had been full that morning when she left. 'Phemie Forbes was here this afternoon, and she recognised the envelope, because Colin got one this morning. Phemie says he's going, and she's sure he'll be happy to drive you.' A smile brushed her lips briefly. 'She and I were just recalling the tennis parties we went to when we were your age. We enjoyed them so much.'

For the moment, her interest in the forthcoming social event had brought colour to her cheeks, and a lilt to her voice. For her sake, Ainslie agreed to go.

When the day came, her tennis dress felt very light and flimsy after the sombre black clothes she had been wearing. Surveying herself in the mirror, smoothing the crisp snowy skirt over her hips, Ainslie realised with surprise that the dress was loose. She must have lost weight since her father's death. The grandfather clock in the hall – a longpiece, auctioneers called it – chimed the hour, and immediately afterwards Catherine called up from the hall, 'Ainslie, Colin's here.'

As she went downstairs, Ainslie felt rather as though she had forgotten to put on her outer clothes and had come from her room in her petticoat. But her mother, waiting in the hall with Colin Forbes, nodded approval as she reached the bottom step.

'You look very nice, dear. Don't you think so, Colin?'

Colin cleared his throat and muttered something, and Catherine picked up her daughter's racquet, waiting in its press on the hall table, as Innes appeared from the kitchen.

'Can I come?' he asked hopefully. He had been taking lessons the year before, and showed promise, but the lessons had been cancelled after his father's death.

'No you can't, this party is for grown-ups. You can

stay here, with me. We'll have a lovely afternoon together.'

Innes's face fell, and Ainslie wished that she could have sent him in her place. She had borrowed a book on furniture from Charlie Blayne, and would have enjoyed an afternoon with it.

Catherine accompanied them as far as the steps, and stood in the doorway, waving, as the car went down the short drive. Ainslie, glancing back, noticed with concern that she wasn't the only member of the household to lose weight. Her mother, who had always been slender, was now almost stick-like.

'I wish Mother would start going out again,' she said, settling herself in the familiar bucket seat. 'She badly needs fresh air and company.'

'My mother's done her best to coax her, but it doesn't seem to be any good.' Colin steered round a car parked too near a corner, then added levelly, 'It's not easy to get the McAdams to co-operate.'

Ainslie opened her mouth to argue, then closed it again. They drove the rest of the way in silence.

Lena's father owned a local engineering firm, and the family lived in one of the largest houses in Paisley. There were almost twenty young people gathered round the tennis court, and Ainslie, on her first social outing since her father's death, was greeted with squeals of pleasure from the girls she had grown up with.

Lena hugged her. 'You poor darling – has it all been terrible?' Her large brown eyes were soft with concern.

'Not too bad.'

'I heard you'd had to find employment,' someone else chimed in, a girl who had been one of Ainslie's closest friends in their final year at school. 'I can't imagine how I would manage if I had to do such a thing!' She gave an exaggerated shiver, and lifted a hand delicately to her cheek in order to show off her new engagement ring. Her fiancé, the son of a man who owned a chain of successful groceries throughout Scotland, put a protective arm about her shoulders, and she snuggled back against him – just like a kitten in a basket, Ainslie thought, wondering why she had ever admired the girl.

The afternoon dragged by. She took her turn on the court, and found that although her skill swiftly returned, her heart wasn't in the game at all. She drank tea on the flagged terrace, ate tiny sandwiches and creamy cakes, went with the others to admire the new lily-pond, then played tennis again. And at last, to her relief, it was time to go home.

Most of the others were changing in the house before driving to Glasgow to attend the theatre, but since Ainslie was still in mourning, it was not possible for her to join them. For that, she thought as they all walked round to the front of the house, she was grateful.

'There's no reason why you shouldn't go to the theatre,' she pointed out to Colin.

'Yes, why not?' Lena chirped. 'The chauffeur can drive Ainslie home.'

He shook his fair head. 'I brought her here and I'll see her home again,' he said, ushering Ainslie to where the car waited on a wide sweep of gravel.

As the others went into the house, a group of carefree moths in their white tennis outfits, he tucked her into the bucket seat then went round to the driver's door. 'Did you enjoy yourself?' he asked as he got in and switched on the engine.

'Oh yes,' Ainslie lied.

Colin eased the car between huge gateposts and turned on to the road. 'So – tell me about this place where you work.'

She described it all in an impersonal way, reluctant to let her enthusiasm show, or to let him know that walking into her cramped little office was like pulling on a cosy, much-loved dressing-gown on a winter's night. She had a superstitious notion that if she let the two very different areas of her existence get too close to each other, they might collide, and cause some sort of damage to themselves, and to her.

Colin listened in silence, his square capable hands steady on the wheel. When she glanced at him she saw that his face was expressionless, and that he was staring straight ahead, never glancing sideways at her as he had so often done in the old days.

'I'm beginning to get a grasp of the ledgers, though the first time I saw them it was like reading Greek— I didn't think I would ever be able to make sense of them. I'm very slow when it comes to using the typewriter, but Cha— Mr Blayne doesn't seem to mind, and the letters do look more official when they've been typed.'

She caught at the dashboard as the car suddenly swerved round a corner and she was thrown against Colin. He had tossed their jackets on to the back seats, and for a moment, as their shoulders touched, she felt his arm hard and warm against hers, bringing back sudden memories of another time, another life, when being with Colin had been the most exciting thing that had ever happened to her.

'What are you doing?'

'Taking another route.'

She glanced at the small wristwatch her parents had given her on her twenty-first birthday. 'Mother will be wondering where I've got to.'

'She knows you're with me. She knows you're safe,' he shot back at her, his voice abrupt. They were driving out into the country now, instead of continuing through the town. The car swerved again, this time towards a layby, then stopped.

Colin killed the engine, then turned in his seat and said, without any preamble, 'Ainslie, will you marry me?'

She stared into his eyes, only inches away from hers. They were best described as hazel, but they changed colours according to his mood. Today, they were grey, the colour of the River Cart on a stormy day. 'Colin, we've been through this before—'

'There's no harm in going through it again. I'm asking you, in all seriousness, to become my wife. And don't answer without taking time to think about it,' he added swiftly as her lips parted. 'You owe me that, at least.'

She did, but at the same time she knew already what her answer must be. She had ended their engagement, and she had no intention of changing her mind. He must have known that himself, for he slammed a hand on the wheel and said, the words pouring out, 'I hoped you'd hate that job, hate having to earn your own living. I hoped that you'd have realised by now that your future lies with me. It always has, Ainslie. I want nothing more than to look after you, and give you everything you want and deserve, and make you happy. And if you're worried about your mother and brother, there's no need, for I'll gladly take them on, too. Look . . .' He turned in his seat, fumbling in the pocket of the jacket in the back seat, withdrawing a small white box. 'I brought this with me today. It's rightfully yours.'

His hands, Ainslie noticed, were trembling as he snapped the box open. 'I love you – did I forget to say that?' Colin asked huskily. 'I love you, and I want you to take this back, because it's yours, and so am I.'

The engagement ring blazed against its white satin bed. She remembered how snugly that ring had fitted on her finger, how happy she had been to see it there. But it belonged to another world, a world that could never be brought back. Afraid that the jewels might draw her down into their depths and drown her senses until she was unable to think clearly, she looked away, to the tumble of bushes edging the road. Other jewels gleamed back at her – glossy red rosehips, fat blackberries, ripe and bursting with their sweet purple juices, set among emerald green leaves. She stared at them until they blurred and merged and she realised that there were tears in her eyes. She still loved the man by her side, but as a very dear friend, not as a future husband.

'Colin, I'm very fond of you, but I'm not going to marry you.'

'But I thought . . .' he began, then stopped, finally saying angrily, 'where's the sense in punishing us both because of what your father did?'

'I'm not punishing anyone. It's just that everything's changed.'

'It needn't.'

'But it has. There's no sense in pretending otherwise.'

'It's that damned woman's fault – the one who's come to live in George Street. If she'd kept away from the town everything would have been over and forgotten by now!'

'I don't need her presence to remind me of what my father did,' Ainslie shot back at him. Then, seeing the bleak look in his eyes, she added lamely, 'I'm – I'm sorry, Colin.'

'So am I.' He snapped the box shut, tossed it into the glove compartment. 'I've made a fool of myself, haven't I?'

'No!' She reached out to him, but he drew his hand back sharply.

'For God's sake, Ainslie, don't start pitying me now!'

She wished that she could be anywhere but where she was. 'You've always been my best friend, Colin. I'd hate it if you turned your back on me.' Then, as he sat mute, staring through the driver's window at the other side of the road, she added, 'If you'd rather, I'll walk the rest of the way home. It's not far.'

'Don't be daft!' Colin snapped, and started the car. He said nothing more until they drew up in the McAdam drive. Then, leaving her to open her own door, he said, his voice still clipped, 'I promise I won't propose to you again. I'll not make a nuisance of myself.'

She shut the door and stepped back, watching as he turned the wheel to take the car past her along the short stretch of driveway in front of the house, then reversed noisily until the rear bumpers almost touched the locked doors of the garage where her father had once kept his own car. It had been sold immediately after the funeral, despite Innes's protests that one day he himself would need it.

Throwing up a spray of gravel, Colin went off down the drive, stopping the car with a jerk at the gate, then taking off into the road to a scream of protest from the tyres.

As Ainslie turned towards the front door she glimpsed a movement at the small gap between the drawing-room curtains, and realised that her mother had been watching for their arrival. Catherine came into the hall as she closed the front door. 'Well? Did you have a lovely afternoon?'

'Yes, thank you.' Ainslie made for the stairs and started to ascend.

'Why didn't you bring Colin in for tea? You know he'd have been very welcome.'

'He was in a hurry.' Ainslie threw the words over her shoulder and kept climbing. She had just laid the racquet down when the bedroom door opened and her mother walked into the room without knocking.

'What happened?'

'We played tennis, we had afternoon tea, then I came home.'

'Ainslie, don't be annoying! Why didn't Colin come in with you?'

Suddenly Ainslie, standing before the mirror, taking off the ribbon she had used to tie her hair back, remembered Colin's reaction to her refusal, remembered him saying, 'But I thought . . .', then choking the words back. Suddenly, she knew. She turned to face her mother, tossing the ribbon down on to the bed. 'It was all planned, wasn't it?'

'What was?'

'You and Mrs Forbes decided that this would be the perfect opportunity for Colin to ask me to change my mind about marrying him, didn't you?'

A slender hand went up to Catherine's throat. Her eyes widened, and Ainslie saw that her cheeks had gone quite pink. 'He proposed? Oh, Ainslie, how wonderful!'

'No need to pretend, Mother – you knew. That's why you urged me to go to the tennis party with him.'

'Well, I – Phemie did say when she was here the other day that Colin's been pining ever since you gave his ring back.'

Ainslie felt quite sick with shame and pity as the full realisation of the situation hit her. 'Did his mother hint to him that I'd changed my mind? How could you? How could you be so cruel?'

'I don't know what you're—' Catherine's eyes fell on her daughter's left hand, bare of rings. She whimpered faintly, and sat down suddenly on the bed. 'You turned him down? Again?'

'I told him what I had told him before. What I've told you, again and again. I don't want to marry anyone.'

There was a short silence, during which Ainslie could almost hear her mother's fury crackling in the air between them, then, 'I spent the entire afternoon praying – praying!' Catherine burst out. 'Hoping that you would come to your senses and accept him. How many men have the courage to face humiliation twice? Do you realise what you've done to that poor boy – to me?'

'What *I*'ve done? I didn't lead him to believe that I had changed my mind. You did that – you and that scheming mother of his!'

'How dare you talk about my friend like that! How dare you presume to know better than your elders and betters—'

'Mother, I will not marry in order to please anyone, even you.'

'If your father could hear you!' Catherine's hand, which had gone to her throat, now moved to her mouth, as though pressing back a sob. Round her slim fingers she said, 'He was so pleased when you and Colin announced your engagement. What do you think he would make of you now?'

Ainslie linked her own fingers behind her back and took a deep breath. 'My father didn't stop to wonder how I might feel about it before he took his own life – or before he became husband to another woman and father to another family. Why should I concern myself with him?'

The colour drained from Catherine's face. 'How dare you?' she said again, in a harsh whisper.

'I'm sorry to vex you, Mother, but I'm only trying to make you understand about my own feelings.'

'Your feelings? That's been the trouble all along. You're selfish, Ainslie, you always have been, from the moment you were born. Selfish and obstinate and uncaring, just like your Grandmother McAdam. She ruined her husband's life, and now you're ruining mine. You're no better than she was.'

'Then perhaps it's as well that I've turned Colin down. I might have ruined his life as well, and I care for him too much to do that.'

Catherine gave a bitter little laugh. 'You flatter yourself, my dear. You don't care for anybody but yourself, do you? You don't care that people in this town are wondering what sort of mother I am, letting my daughter go out to work in some nasty little auction room. Or what sort of wife I must have been, for my husband to take another woman behind my back—' Her voice broke, then changed to an eerie banshee wailing. Her hands went up to clutch at her head, fingers digging into her scalp. Ainslie went to her, alarmed by such behaviour from her normally emotionless mother, but Catherine pulled away from her touch.

'Leave me be! The only one who truly cares is Innes,' she said with sudden, almost frightening dignity. 'One day he'll make up to me for everything you and your father did.'

She rose from the bed and walked, straight-backed, out of the room, leaving Ainslie shaken and confused. She and her mother had had disagreements for as long as she could remember. She recalled, frequently, occasions when she stood obstinately silent, taking the sting of her mother's sarcastic tongue, refusing to let herself weep. But they had never had such an ugly, venomous quarrel before. And never, until now, had Catherine lost control.

Guilt welled up. She had allowed herself to hit back, had behaved very badly towards her mother at a time when Catherine wasn't herself. Although Ainslie's anger was justified by the fact that Colin had been cruelly deceived by his mother and hers, she would have to apologise.

She leaned forward until her forehead was resting against the cool mirror, closing her eyes. There seemed to be no way to please her mother, other than by giving up her job and agreeing to marry Colin. But if she did that, she would betray herself. It was too high a price for anyone to pay for other people's happiness.

With a flash of insight, Ainslie realised that she had spent the first twenty-one years of her life betraying herself. She had tried, really tried, to do what others wanted – her parents, her teachers, her friends, even Colin – but she had always fallen short of their expectations, because pleasing them meant displeasing herself.

Her father's death had put an end to it. Torn from the life she had always known, cast into an uncertain future, she had changed far more than even she herself had suspected before that moment. She had become a different person, a woman who was learning, slowly and painfully, how to make her own way in the world. Independence was beckoning, and she had started the long journey towards it. Having started, she must continue, and that meant never again allowing herself to be hurt simply in order to make others happy.

Nor, she realised, did she have the right to interfere in other people's lives. She had been no better than Catherine when she went to George Street and tried to order Isla out of the town and out of their lives. Isla had been her father's business, not hers.

When the maid came to remind her that dinner was on the table, Ainslie, still in her tennis dress, sent word downstairs that she wasn't hungry. She stripped, washed, and brushed out her curly red hair until it crackled. During the day she restrained it in a long plait hanging down her back, but when she was at home she liked to leave it loose. After changing into her nightdress and dressing-gown, she took *The Wind in the Willows* from the shelves, and turning to her favourite chapter, the one about Mole and Rat seeking shelter far from home on a cold winter's night, she settled down to read.

Almost at once she fell asleep, tired out by fresh air and exercise, followed by the stress of the scenes with Colin and then her mother, then wakened with a start to find Innes standing beside her, a tray in his hands.

'I got you this from the kitchen.'

He had brought a roast beef sandwich and a glass of milk. Ainslie still wasn't hungry, but, touched by his concern, she nibbled at the sandwich and sipped the milk while Innes sat on the side of the bed and watched. 'How was the tennis party?'

'All right. I'll probably be stiff tomorrow, not having played all summer.'

'I miss it,' he said. 'I miss everything. D'you think we'll ever get back to normal again?'

'Of course we will, next year.' She put down her sandwich, unable to take another bite. 'I ate too many sandwiches this afternoon. I'm still full up.'

'I'll finish it if you like,' he offered, and ate the food as though he hadn't had any dinner at all. Innes had always had a huge appetite.

'Mother sat with a face like thunder all through dinner, then went to bed with a headache,' he said round a mouthful of bread and meat. 'I might as well be honest,

109

I heard you both rowing after you came back from the tennis party.'

'She's still angry because I won't marry Colin.'

'I thought you liked Colin.'

'I do, but I don't want to spend the rest of my life married to him.'

'If you did marry him, he'd probably teach you to drive his car. He'll probably give you a car of your own.'

'Marriage is about more than cars, Innes.'

'I wonder if it'll happen to me one day.' Innes licked his fingers then lay back on the bed beside her and linked his fingers behind his head. 'Marrying, I mean, not learning to drive. I'm definitely going to do that as soon as I'm old enough.'

'Time you were in bed.'

'In a minute.' He yawned, then said, 'I don't like you and Mother quarrelling, Ainslie. We've only got each other now, the three of us.'

She put her arm around him. 'I'll apologise to her in the morning. It'll be all right.'

'That's good.' There was a pause, then he said sleepily, 'Tell me again about the place you work in.' His red hair was soft against her chin and his body solid and comforting within the circle of her arm. Ainslie was tempted to drop a kiss on his cheek, but held back, knowing that he would hate it.

'Outside my tiny office there's this long wide gallery, stacked with all sorts of furniture . . .' she began.

10

Once she realised that school was a five-days-a-week occurrence, Barbara took to it like a duck to water. She loved the sand trays, where the children used their fingers to write out figures and letters, and the importance of having a desk of her own. She loved the games in the school-yard at playtime, the chanted multiplication tables, the stories and songs and poems. She and Greta played schools in their spare time, commandeering Ross and Daisy and any other small child they could get hold of as pupils.

With Drew Brown's help, Isla cleared the patch of earth in the backyard, but the soil was poor, soured by years of neglect, smoke and soot from the chimneys, and by the cats and dogs who roamed the area, using the backyards as lavatories. Every weekday morning, after she had watched Barbara and Greta run in through the school gates to mingle with the other children in the playground, Isla, pushing Ross in the little perambulator she had brought to Paisley with her, walked on past the huge bulk of the Ferguslie Mills, where the machinery gave out a continual muffled roar, towards the open moors on the outskirts of the town.

Here, while Ross toddled around, she hunted out molehills, carefully scraping them up with a battered tablespoon and stowing the rich soil away in an old shopping bag kept specially for the purpose.

'It's dung ye want tae feed the earth,' Drew said when he found Isla emptying the battered old bag over the newly dug patch, shaking it vigorously to make sure that not a speck of good soil was lost.

'Where can I get it?'

The boy shot a surprised look at her, as though wondering if she was pulling his leg. 'From the horses that go up an' down the street, of course. It's the best thing ye can use for growin' things. I'll get some for ye after work if ye want, or ye could ask any of the laddies round here tae gather it for ye in a bucket, for a ha'penny, or one or two empty bottles tae take tae the wee shop.'

Isla felt colour rise to her face. She was well used by now to the sight and sound of the great cart-horses pulling wagons and carts along George Street, but even so she had never thought of using their droppings for her vegetable bed. She gave the bag a final vicious shake, cursing her own stupidity. What sort of example could she set her own children when she didn't even remember that manure was good for growing things, she chided herself, then a giggle bubbled to her lips as she realised that not knowing about manure was scarcely likely to damage their young lives.

She followed Drew's advice the next morning, impatient to get on with planting the old potatoes she had been carefully hoarding under the bed for weeks. As soon as she stepped tentatively out of the close, bucket in one hand and shovel in the other, a grubby little boy arrived at her side.

'Is it dung ye're after, missus? I'll see tae it for ye!' He grabbed the bucket and shovel, and was off before she could say anything. Isla looked after him helplessly, convinced that she had seen the last of her precious possessions. Thieving was rife in the street, and she had been well warned by Magret never to leave Ross's little perambulator outside on its own.

'It's not all badness, it's just that some poor souls have nothin' at all, except what the weans can lay their hands on,' Magret had said. 'Folks has got tae live.'

Ten minutes later, the boy thumped on the door and handed Isla her shovel and a steaming bucket, filled to the brim with richly smelling manure. 'I kenned there was a cuddy just turned intae Castle Street,' he explained. 'I had tae run tae catch up wi' it.'

She gave him a halfpenny, which he folded tightly into his fist as he followed her through the close and into the yard. The bucket was heavy, and she marvelled at such a small boy being able to carry it all the way from Castle Street on his own.

'What're ye doin', missus?' He gave a huge sniff and swatted at his nose with the back of his hand.

'Growing potatoes.'

'Tatties? When'll they be ready, then?'

'Mind yer own business,' Magret snapped from behind him. 'Get back tae yer own close – go on, now! Ye don't want tae tell the likes of him too much,' she went on when he had gone, his bare feet slapping hard against the steps and along the close, the hems of his ragged trousers flapping about his knees. 'He'd be wantin' tae know when

113

the tatties'd be ready for him tae steal.' She wrinkled her nose as Isla, after a struggle, managed to upend the bucket, and a solid lump of manure thumped out on to the turned earth. 'God bless us, what a reek!'

'I'll soon have it dug in.' Isla sniffed the air then said thoughtfully, 'It's a good healthy natural smell.'

Magret, used to the stink of blocked drains and broken sewage pipes and human beings crowded together in old, unsanitary housing, gave her new friend a puzzled look.

'I don't know how ye can say that – it's chokin' me,' she complained, waving her hand before her nose while Isla seized her fork and began spreading the manure over the earth.

Over the next few days Drew obtained several more bucketsful of manure for her, and helped to dig it in. 'I think it's as ready as it can be,' she said at last, and went to the house. When she brought the old tin tray out from under the wall-bed, she saw that the potatoes she had saved for the garden were already sprouting. Putting the vegetable knife into the pocket of her pinny, she carried the tray out.

'Now we need to cut each potato in half, and plant each half with the sprouting side up.'

Drew took a penknife from his pocket and reached for a potato. When they had all been cut and planted in rows, Isla fetched her bucket and Drew found an abandoned tin can, and together they carried water from the wash-house to give the soil a good soaking. Then, side by side, they surveyed the smooth weed-free bed with satisfaction.

'With any luck, we'll have good new potatoes to eat next spring,' Isla said.

Drew, now comfortable in her presence, beamed and said, 'Aye!' just as Barbara, playing in the wash-house with Greta and the peg dolls, came hurrying up the steps, her face screwed up.

'Mummy, my dolly's lost her face!' She brandished the little doll, now with an ordinary peg-head atop her dressed body.

'Bring the cloth here and I'll fasten it back on.'

'But I don't know where it went,' Barbara wailed. 'I want her face back. I don't want her to have an old peg-face!'

'Give it here.' Drew, who had struck up a friendship with the children, took the peg from her and sat down on one of the steps beyond the wash-house. 'I'll do a new face for her, if you like. I've got some wee tins of paint upstairs that'll finish her off nicely.'

Barbara sat beside him, fascinated, as he started working at the peg with the tip of his knife. 'Two eyes – and a nose – and a nice smiley mouth,' he said as he worked. 'And curly hair, too, with a bit of a fringe at the front, like yours.' The knifepoint moved deftly, the peg twirling about in his fingers, then he gave the doll back to Barbara, said, 'Back in a tick,' and hurried into the close, whistling tunelessly.

'Look at what Drew's done, Mummy.' Barbara handed the peg to Isla, who took it and was still studying the neat little bland face and the swirl of curly hair that the lad had carved from the plain wooden knob when he came back, some tiny paint tins and a brush and an old bit of rag in his hands.

'Now then,' he said, taking the peg doll back and opening one of the tins. In a few minutes the little face had sprung to life, with blue eyes, tilted up at the corners, a neat little rosebud mouth, and brown curly hair.

'Careful,' Drew cautioned as he handed it to Barbara. 'Let her get dry, or she'll smudge into all the colours of the rainbow.'

'I didn't know you were so clever, Drew,' Isla said, astonished, and he blushed, then shrugged.

'Och, it's nothing. I like making wee things out of old bits of wood. It gives me something to do with my hands.'

There had been no further visits from Ainslie McAdam, and Isla, greatly relieved, allowed herself to hope that the girl had decided to leave her alone. She hadn't seen Gilchrist Forbes or his disapproving son either, and that suited her. Each Monday morning she went to the lawyer's office, where she received a sealed envelope from his receptionist. She signed for it, and left the office as quickly as she could, feeling very like Judas as she pushed the envelope, with its ill-gotten gains, deep into her pocket.

Back home, spreading the money out on the table, she felt as though she was stealing it from them, particularly from Mrs Brown, after all Drew's help with the potato bed. But she had no option. One day, she kept promising herself, she would make amends. One day when – if – she ever had money she would do all she could to improve their living conditions, although for the life of her she couldn't see what could be done. The entire row of tenements was old and should have been pulled down long since. What these people needed was rehousing.

Often there was a brief note with the money, recording

a tenant's inability to pay the full amount, or any money at all, and informing her that if she wanted action to be taken against the non-payer she should notify Mr Forbes. She threw the notes on the fire, feeling as though she was prying on her neighbours. She had no intention of taking action against anyone simply because they were too poor to pay the rent on time. Poverty wasn't a crime, although people like Gilchrist Forbes seemed to think it was.

Often, it was Granny Thomson who hadn't paid her rent. Old as she was, the woman did some cleaning in one of the shops to augment her tiny pension, but she suffered from rheumatism and bronchitis, and often she couldn't get out of bed, let alone work. When that happened, Isla and Magret took it in turns to see that the old woman didn't starve, taking a bowl of soup or a cup of tea and a bit of bread and butter in to her stuffy, cold, dark little room until she was on her feet again. It hurt Isla to know that Granny Thomson lived in constant fear of someone else being given her job while she was unable to do it, and of ending her days in the poorhouse. Her mingled gratitude and choking shame at 'being a burden' to her neighbours almost broke Isla's heart. She wished that she could tell the old woman the truth, and assure her that as long as she owned the building, Granny wouldn't be put out. But she had to stay silent.

Sometimes the Browns were unable to pay all the rent, and once the Kellys were defaulters, because there had been a strike at the factory that employed Mr Kelly and he had been laid off. Both he and his wife aged with worry over the two-week strike, and so did Isla, on their behalf, then to their mutual relief the strike was settled and the rent money slowly made up during the following week.

It was a hand-to-mouth existence, and she often wondered if Kenneth had had any knowledge of the struggle his tenants went through simply to survive, or about the conditions they had to live in. It disturbed her to think that he might have known, and yet not cared enough to do anything about it.

November came raging in with strong, bitterly cold winds that found every chink and crack in the old tenement. Rags and newspaper had to be stuffed round windows and below doors, and at night the flames within Isla's fragile gas mantles often flickered in the draught. It rained all the time, which meant that the washing had to be dried indoors, the smell of wet wool and the steam of its drying adding to the stuffiness and humidity of the single room. It became difficult to get close to the fire, because the washing had to take priority.

'I wish I was a vest,' Barbara grumbled more than once. 'Then I'd get to be nice and cosy in front of the fire.'

All Isla's energies were concentrated on keeping the children as healthy as possible. She fed them plates of thick porridge morning and night, because it was a cheap and nourishing way of filling their stomachs. Scattering precious sugar as thickly as she dared over it, she remembered her own childhood, when her mother had poured generous spoonfuls of honey or golden syrup over her porridge, then added cream. Her father, a true Scotsman, salted his porridge, but Isla and her mother liked theirs sweet and rich.

She learned from Magret that it was best to delay a visit to the greengrocer's until it was almost closing time, when he was anxious to sell off any vegetables that might not be fit for sale the next morning. Carrots and potatoes and turnips, chopped up and simmered with a handful of lentils and barley and a bone, made a nourishing broth that lasted for a few days. If there was meat on the bone, it was carefully pared off to add a savoury flavour to platefuls of potatoes.

Survival became the centre of Isla's existence. She lay awake at night listening to the rain sloshing down the gutters at the side of the street, worrying about the cost of calling in the doctor and paying for medication if one or both of the children took ill. She didn't even dare to contemplate the thought of any illness touching her, making her too weak to care for Barbara and Ross. But the porridge and home-made soup, with fish whenever Isla could afford it, kept the three of them well.

Poor little Greta wasn't so fortunate. In mid-November she took a sore throat and had to miss school and stay at home, one of her father's socks, filled with hot salt, tied around her small neck. Isla took Ross to fetch Barbara from school, keeping an eye on the clouds racing overhead as she hurried the children out of the school gates, anxious to get them indoors before the rain started to fall again. Her clothes-horse was already groaning under the weight of drying clothes; she didn't want to have wet coats and shoes to deal with as well.

'Come on, Barbara – don't pull at me like that!'

Barbara, undeterred, gave another tug on her mother's hand. 'Mummy, that lady over there looks funny.'

Isla's eyes followed her daughter's pointing finger.

The school stood opposite West Station, and in her rush to get the children home she hadn't noticed the black-clad figure leaning against the station wall, head bowed. The woman's unfashionably long skirt hung down below her coat, and on the ground by her booted feet stood a basket. One or two neatly wrapped parcels had spilled from it.

Nobody else seemed to have noticed her. Isla pushed Ross's perambulator across the road and bumped it up on to the pavement, turning it with its back against the bitter wind.

'Are you all right?' She put a hand tentatively on the woman's shoulder and a paper-white face swung towards her.

'So silly,' the woman whispered. 'Came over faint. I'll be – all right in a minute.'

Isla looked up and down the street, but it was almost empty. Nobody wanted to loiter on such a day.

'D'you think she's going to die?' Barbara asked in her clear voice, staring up into the old lady's face.

'Sshh! Of course not!' Beneath her hand Isla felt the bony shoulder ripple in a half-laugh.

'At least I'll die with – my boots on!' the frail voice commented.

'Can you tell me where you live?'

' 'Course I can. Not stupid, just a bit – breathless. It's just round the – corner there. I'll go on in a minute, when – when I've caught my breath.'

Isla stooped and scooped the parcels into the basket, then straightened and put an arm about the woman. 'Barbara, can you manage to push Ross's chair for me while I help this lady?'

'Of course I can.' Barbara stooped in her turn, picking up a folded umbrella that Isla hadn't noticed. 'Here, Ross,' she told her brother, 'you can carry that.' She swung the chair round with a bit of an effort and began to push it towards the corner.

'Put your arm over my shoulders, and I'll put my arm around your waist.' Isla organised the old lady, who was taller than she was, and drooped over her. Slowly, they made their way round the corner, past the entrance to the West Station, then followed the road in a gentle downhill curve towards the large houses opposite the cricket ground. Barbara had difficulty in manoeuvring the push-chair, especially as the furled umbrella clutched in Ross's chubby little hands stuck out on either side and tended to hit off the wall, but she managed it, concentration making her tongue protrude beyond her teeth.

'Round here,' the woman said feebly, and Isla saw to her dismay that the road they had turned into led uphill. There were high walls on either side, and no sign of a house, and she doubted whether Barbara, or she herself, burdened as she was, could manage to keep going to the top of the hill. But there was nothing else for it but to grit their teeth and forge on. To her surprise, the old lady stopped only a matter of yards further along, outside a small faded green wooden door set in the high wall.

'Here we are. I can take the basket, my dear, if you'll open the door.'

Barbara, forsaking the pram, squeezed past her mother's legs to stare through the opened gate. 'It's a magic place!' she said with delight, and the woman laughed, a wheezy, rusty sound ending in a fit of coughing.

121

'That's what I used to think when I was your age,' she said when she had caught her breath again. 'I'd forgotten that.'

The gate opened on to a small quiet road. On their left, flanked by tall trees, stood the high wall that divided this road from the main road, and on the right a series of gates led to gardens and houses. Even the wind had lost some of its power in this sheltered place; while it buffeted and howled against the other side of the wall, the little road seemed untouched, only the tops of the highest trees swaying before it.

'Just a few gates along, dear – not far to go.'

When they reached the right gate, Barbara wrestled with the latch, finally managing to open it. 'Use the umbrella for the – children, or they'll be soaked – by the bushes,' the elderly woman advised Isla. 'I'm much better now, I can manage.' Isla opened the large black umbrella and put it into Ross's hands. He held it high as Barbara, her head ducked forward beneath its shelter, pushed him up the flagged path, edged on either side by dripping bushes. Between the bare twigs, Isla, taking up the rear, could see small leaf-strewn lawns on either side.

'Now I'm for it,' the woman said gloomily, edging round the pram to mount the two steps into the small, open, glass-sided porch. Her legs, impossibly thin and looking like saplings planted in the sturdy boots she wore, just managed the climb. She tugged at a brass bell-pull set by the side of the front door and the bell jangled in the depths of the house.

'Will your mummy be angry?' Barbara asked, wide-eyed, deserting the pram and skipping up into the porch, which had a bench running down each side. The woman chuckled again, and again ended up coughing and spluttering. She dug into her coat pocket and produced a handkerchief, which she held to her mouth.

'I've not got a mummy,' she said through the folds. 'I've got an Annie, and she's far worse.'

As she spoke, the door opened to reveal a stout woman with iron-grey hair curling out from under a frilly white cap. Her sturdy body was clothed in a black dress and white apron, and her round, ruddy face was wrinkled with concern.

'Miss Flora, where have you—' She stopped, her gaze travelling down to Barbara, then to where Isla wrestled with the umbrella, trying to get it down, hampered by the basket and the push chair. 'What's happened?'

'Nothing, nothing. I took a little turn in the – the street, that's all, and these young people - kindly helped me back home.'

'I told you, didn't I, Miss Flora? I told you that you weren't strong enough to go out on your own. But would you list—'

'You were right, Annie, as usual. Now,' said Miss Flora, 'are we going to stand here – all day, or are we going to get indoors out of the cold and – offer these kind people some refreshments?'

Isla had succeeded in closing the umbrella, showering herself with rainwater in the process. 'No, really, we must get home before the rain starts,' she began, but Miss Flora interrupted.

'Nonsense, my dear, you've saved my life and I insist – on giving you a cup of tea, at least.' Stronger now that she was back home, she swept into the hall, Barbara scampering after her.

11

Isla, realising that there was no help for it, began to unfasten the straps that held Ross into the chair.

'Here – I'll get it,' Annie said as she lifted the little boy out and began to wrestle one-handedly with the push-chair. She surged down the steps and lifted the chair, muttering as she did so, 'Never pays a blind bit of notice to what I say. Oh no – off she goes and what happens? She very near kills herself!'

'Come in here, my dear,' the elderly woman called from beyond an open door to the right as Isla followed Annie into the hall, 'There's a nice fire.'

Barbara stood in the middle of the room, turning slowly, her eyes and mouth open as she took in every detail of the polished furniture and the pictures on the walls.

'You should go straight to your bed,' the maid told her employer sternly. 'You'll make yourself ill again. She's just getting over a bout of bronchitis,' she explained to Isla. 'She should never have gone out on a day like this, but try telling her that.'

'I was bored. I needed the fresh air. And now I'd like a cup of tea – if you don't mind. And some bread to toast, and whatever you think the children would like to drink.' Now that she was safely home, Miss Flora's breathing was easier. 'Take off your coat, my dear, and sit down here, by the fire.'

Annie, muttering under her breath, peeled her employer and then the two children efficiently out of their coats, while Isla took her own off.

'I don't know what I'd do without her, but she fusses,' the old lady said as Annie, arms piled high with coats, went out of the room. 'I'm Flora Currie, by the way.' A large bony hand was thrust out towards Isla. She shook it and introduced herself and the children, then allowed herself to be coaxed into a cushioned chair by the fire.

Ross, intimidated by the strange room, pulled at her skirt and she lifted him on to her lap, saying automatically, 'Barbara, don't touch anything.'

'Nonsense, children need to touch things. She'll be sensible, I'm sure.' Miss Currie – Isla had noticed that both hands were free of rings – sat down in the chair opposite. She had kept her hat on; it was a woollen black turban, and its slightly Eastern look suited her hawk-like nose and angular features. The colour had come back into her face. 'D'ye see that large, pink shell, little girl? Fetch it over here, will you?'

When Barbara did as she was told, carrying the shell carefully in both hands, Miss Currie took it and held it to the child's ear. 'If you listen, you can hear the sea. Hear it?'

Barbara concentrated, frowning, then the frown faded and her brown eyes widened in astonishment. 'I can! I can hear the sea, Mummy!' She brought the shell over and held it first to Isla's ear, then to Ross's, then to her own again.

'My father brought that home for me when I was about your age,' Flora Currie told her. 'He was a sea captain, sailing out of Greenock.'

'My daddy's going to bring one just like it for me when he comes back to us,' Barbara said at once.

Miss Currie's eyes flicked swiftly to Isla's face, a mute question in them. She read the answer, then said calmly, 'I expect he will. Until then, you're welcome to come and listen to my shell now and again. It likes people to listen to it.'

Annie came in with a large tray and set out the tea things on a low table between both women. She had included sturdy mugs of milk for the children, and piled a plate with slices of bread. While Miss Currie showed Barbara how to spear the slices on a brass toasting fork and hold them close to the bars of the fire until they were browned, Isla drank the hot tea gratefully, and ate buttered toast and Madeira cake, feeding Ross, still perched on her knee, mouth open like a little fledgling.

As they ate, Flora Currie talked about her childhood, spent in the house where she still lived, and about her father and mother and two older brothers.

'I'm all that's left now – apart from some nephews and nieces scattered about Scotland and too busy to visit me.'

She asked few questions, only enough to learn that they lived not far away, in George Street.

'But it seems like a hundred miles away,' Isla told her. 'I'd no idea that this road existed so close to where we live.'

Ross, growing bolder, wriggled to get down, and she handed him over to Barbara with instructions to behave themselves.

'Oh, let them explore a little, I'm sure they won't hurt anything. My brothers and I and the other children who lived here when we were young enjoyed popping in and out through that gate,' Flora Currie said. 'After I read *Alice in Wonderland* I felt that the gate would have fitted well into the story. I'd forgotten all about that until your little girl reminded me. The road opens out at the other end, of course, so that vehicles can get through. My papa had a carriage – the double gate just a little bit along from where we came in leads into our drive and up to the carriage-house, but the gates haven't been opened in years, and the carriage-house is filled with rubbish.' She leaned forward, her eyes on Isla. 'You don't speak like the people round here.'

'I was brought up in Glasgow, then I lived in Edinburgh for several years, then on the Clyde coast. We've only been in Paisley for a few months.'

'You've still got a trace of that pretty East coast lilt to your voice. I used to love excursions to Edinburgh – it has such an air of timelessness about it.'

As though on cue, the clock on the mantelshelf chimed softly and Isla said, 'We must go . . .' just as rain spattered on the bay window behind Miss Currie.

'Better stay here until this shower passes,' she advised, just as Barbara's clear little voice called from the hall, 'Mummy, come and see this!'

'Barbara, what are you up to?' Isla jumped up and hurried towards the sound of her daughter's voice. The children were standing at an open door on the other side of the hall, towards the back of the house.

'Look!' Barbara disappeared into the room, towing Ross behind her.

'Barbara!'

'They've found my secret vice,' Flora Currie said, moving past Isla to the open door. 'We all have our failings, I suppose.' She gave Isla a lop-sided, shamefaced smile. 'This used to be my mother's sewing room, but since my parents died and my brothers married and moved away, I've taken it over as my own. Come and see.'

Isla stopped on the threshold, staring. The room was filled with dolls' houses, sitting on counters that had been built around the walls. Large elaborate houses and smaller modest dwellings jostling together, some wide, some narrow, some high, some single-storey. Barbara was moving along the counters, hands clasped behind her back, the tension in the curled fingers and small shoulders indicating a repressed urge to open each house front and look inside.

For a long moment Isla gaped, then she said huskily, 'How wonderful.'

'So you don't think I'm a stupid old woman who's never properly grown up?'

Isla turned, and realised that Miss Currie's eyes were green. 'I think you're very lucky.'

A gust of wind hurled rain against the window, but nobody noticed as, one by one, Miss Currie opened the fronts of the houses, revealing doll families in parlours and nurseries and kitchens and studies. Ross, too small to see, found a box half filled with miniature furniture and dolls and tiny animals tucked away beneath one of the counters, and squatted happily on the floor to empty it.

'I've got a dolls' house,' Barbara told Miss Currie proudly. 'My mummy made it out of a box. And she made clothes-peg dollies for me and Greta and some of the other wee girls in our street.'

'Indeed? You've got a very clever mummy.' The old woman smiled at Isla.

The grandfather clock in the hall chimed the hour, and Isla, suddenly noticing the mess Ross was making, stooped to put everything back into the box. 'We must go – I have to get to the shops.'

It was still raining, with no sign of an improvement now, and Miss Currie offered her the large black umbrella. 'You can hand it in some time,' she said, and waved from the porch as they set off into the November gloom, Isla negotiating the push-chair with one hand and holding the umbrella with the other.

'I like that lady,' Barbara said as Isla filled the tin bath before the fire that evening. 'When I'm old like her I'm going to live in a big house.' Her brows wrinkled in thought, then she said, 'We had a house like that once.'

'Something like it.' Isla refilled the kettle at the tap and put it on to the stove, then caught Ross up as he toddled past her and settled into her chair to take his clothes off. 'Come on, young man, time for your bath.'

'When can we go back to our house?' Barbara persisted. Isla looked at her over the top of Ross's red head.

'I don't know, love,' she said, and the longing that swept over her for Kenneth was so great that she had to blink back tears.

*

She returned the umbrella on the following day, intending to hand it in and then hurry away. But Flora Currie herself opened the door, the knitted turban still pulled firmly down over her ears, and insisted on giving her a cup of tea.

'Annie's doing the shopping today, so we'll have to manage on our own,' she said, leading the way through the hall to a door hidden in the shadows behind the stairs. It opened into a kitchen fragrant with the smell of baking and warmed by a large range.

'How are you, Miss Currie?'

'Oh, completely recovered from that silly nonsense yesterday. Annie's quite right, of course, I should never have ventured so far after being in bed for two weeks. But sometimes I feel the need to defy her, just to prove to myself that I'm still alive. Sit down there,' Flora ordered, and Isla obediently sat at the white-scrubbed table that took up most of the room. Ross wandered about fingering the knobs on the cupboard doors.

'Can I help?'

'No need, my dear, I know how to fend for myself.'

Flora measured tea into a small teapot then eyed the huge kettle simmering on the range, and added, 'Though I'd be grateful if you could see to that monster for me.' She held out her large bony hands to reveal swollen knuckles and some slightly twisted fingers. 'Rheumatics,' she explained, scowling at her hands. 'I might tip the kettle too far and scald myself, and then I'd never hear the end of it from Annie. She insists on being the servant, and wearing that ridiculous uniform,' she went on, setting out cups and half filling a mug with milk for Ross while Isla poured boiling water into the teapot. 'I've tried to get her to settle for a skirt and cardigan like mine, but she never will.'

She produced a plate of spiced scones, still warm from the oven. 'I have to do my baking when Annie's out at the shops. She won't admit that I've got a lighter hand than hers when it comes to pastry, in spite of the rheumatism. My mother, bless her, believed in her children learning how to cook and bake.' She slit the scones and spread them generously with butter. 'Being a seaman, my father agreed with her. My brothers could cook and sew – not that their wives allowed it, for the very thought shocked them. My brother Arnold did that.' She nodded at a framed sampler on the wall, the words, 'The Heart of A House Is The Kitchen', surrounded by neatly stitched forget-me-nots. 'In secret, when his wife wasn't around, just to prove to himself that he could still manage it.'

She poured the tea and sat down. 'I take it that you're a widow.'

'My husband died six months ago.'

Flora nodded. 'I thought as much, the way your little girl talked about her daddy. How d'you cope, with two children to look after on your own?'

'I manage.'

'I'm sure you do.' Flora Currie pushed the plate of scones towards Isla and poured out more tea for them both. 'Tell me about the dolls' house you made for your daughter.'

'It's just a wee orange box with a curtain over the front.'

'I'd like to hear all about it all the same – what you did for furniture, and how you made the dolls.'

She listened with interest, breaking in with an occasional question, as Isla described the making of the orange-box house. 'I used to try to make houses myself,' she recalled. 'But I wasn't good at it. I lack your imagination.'

Then, planting her hands flat on the table, she levered herself to her feet. 'Come and have another look at my collection. It's not often I get to show them off. Annie complains about the dust they collect, and thinks I'm a stupid old woman. It's good to meet someone who understands.'

In the room that held the dolls' houses, Ross made for the box he had been playing with on the previous day. 'Leave him be,' Flora said when Isla tried to stop him. 'It's only broken furniture and dolls that were never repaired. I'm no good at throwing things out. I'd some notion of giving the houses to my nieces, but my brothers tended towards sons, and the only two girls were given handsome dolls' houses by their parents before I got round to making the offer.' She looked round the room, and sighed. 'They should really be given to a hospital or something. They'll just be a nuisance to my heirs one day, and they're meant to be played with, after all.'

'Not that one.' Isla pointed to the grandest house, a Victorian mansion complete with a butler's pantry, and servants' quarters in the attic. 'That's a collector's item.'

'That was my own, when I was small. My grandmama gave it to me, and I was only allowed to play with it when my nurse or my mother were there to see that I didn't do any damage. I used to long to be allowed to spend just ten minutes with it on my own; I think that's why I was so determined to do as I pleased once I had the freedom.' She sighed, touching the house lovingly. 'Poor thing, it's been neglected. It was put away in the attic when I got older, and not brought out until long after my parents died. I kept meaning to have it renovated, but I never got around to it.'

The front door opened and closed. 'We're in here, Annie,' Flora Currie called, and the maid, in her outer clothes, glanced in at the door, sniffing when she saw Isla.

'You're here again, are you?'

'Mind your own business,' her mistress snapped back at her, while Isla, suddenly afraid that she was outstaying her welcome, knelt to replace the toys that Ross had taken out of the box.

'We must go.'

'Would you like to choose one of the houses as a Christmas gift for your little girl?' Miss Currie asked abruptly as they were about to leave the room. Isla was taken aback by the suddenness of the offer, but rallied.

'It's very kind of you, but she's fine with the one she's got.'

'You said it was made from a box, and I thought she might like . . .'

Isla felt hot colour surge into her face. 'She's fine,' she repeated, and regretted the sharpness in her voice as soon as she saw the stricken look on Miss Currie's face.

'My dear, I'm so sorry if I offended you.'

'You didn't. It's just that . . .' Isla's voice trailed away and they surveyed each other in an awkward silence. Ross, between them, looked up at their faces, puzzled by the sudden tension in the little room. Miss

Currie bent and scrabbled in a corner beneath one of the tables, bringing out a shabby little dolls' house.

'This is the one I had in mind, it seemed to me to be the right size for a child of your daughter's age. It needs doing up, but from what you've told me, I'm sure that you could do it very well.'

Isla wished that she had never come back to the house. 'I don't mean to be rude, Miss Currie, but,' she bit her lip, then said in a rush of words, 'it's just that I'll not take anything from anyone unless I can pay for it. And I can't afford to buy a dolls' house just now, not even a wee one.'

The older woman's flush deepened. 'Oh my dear, I should have realised.'

'It was kind of you to think of Barbara. No, Ross!' Isla seized his hand, which was reaching out hopefully towards the box. 'We have to go now, pet.' She escaped thankfully to the hall to collect her coat and Ross's small jacket, hating herself for depriving Barbara and for hurting the old lady, but knowing that she couldn't, wouldn't, accept charity.

To her astonishment, Annie, still hanging up her own outdoor clothing, muttered out of the side of her mouth, 'For any favour, let her give the lassie the wee house.'

'What?'

'Go on,' the woman hissed, putting a large cold hand on Isla's. 'She's got nob'dy of her own, and she's fair desperate to do somethin' for somebody. It surely couldnae do any harm to give in to her just this once!'

Isla's resolve faded as she looked into Annie's round face and saw the pleading look in her eyes. She swallowed hard, her hand falling away from the hook that held her coat, then turned and went back into the room, where Flora Currie stood, looking lost and alone, still clutching the little dolls' house.

'Miss Currie – if you're sure that you really mean it—'

The green eyes lit up. 'I do! You'll accept it, then?'

'Yes, but I'll not take it without paying for it. I can't afford to pay in money,' she added hurriedly as she saw the older woman open her mouth to protest, 'but I could do some renovation work on your Victorian house in return, if you want me to.'

'Oh my dear, that would be so kind of you. I accept.'

'I'll need to work on the wee house here, for there's no room in my own place.'

'Och, that's no trouble at all. I'm sure there are some wee pots of paint around that you could use – and there's the furniture in the box. You're welcome to it, if you can do anything with it,' Flora Currie enthused.

From the doorway, Annie said heavily, 'I suppose that'll mean a mess for me to clear up.'

But the faintest of smiles tugged at the corners of her mouth.

12

Because their year of mourning still had five months to run, there could be no Christmas or New Year celebrations in the McAdam household. Christmas trees, becoming more fashionable now, could be seen here and there in their neighbours' bay windows as December matured, and Ainslie, alighting from the bus each night, liked to look at the trees with their pretty decorations as she walked home.

It was a custom that the McAdams had never taken up, but Colin's family had a tree each year, and she recalled with pleasure the fresh pine smell that had pervaded their large drawing-room the year before, and the way the light from the tall red candles on their dinner table had gleamed on green pine needles. She and her mother and brother had had dinner with the Forbeses last Christmas Day, and she had become engaged to Colin on New Year's Day, at a dinner party in the McAdam house.

Her father had been present at the engagement celebration, but not at the Forbeses' dinner table, because he was always busy at Christmas. Now, Ainslie knew where he had been.

136

Although they didn't make much of Christmas Day themselves, the family did give gifts to each other, and it was Catherine McAdam's custom to present small gifts to the servants. Ainslie had had a generous allowance since leaving school, but that had stopped with her father's death, and it occurred to her that she might buy presents for her mother and brother from the auction house. Nervously, she approached Charlie at the beginning of December and asked if she could purchase a pair of china figures for her mother, and a boxed set of model cars that she knew Innes would love.

He squinted up at her from his desk. 'This is an auction room, lass, not a shop.'

'I know that, but I thought that if I paid the reserve price . . .'

He tutted and shook his head. 'They might go for more than the reserve price if they're auctioned, and if I sold to you instead, I could be depriving my clients of money – and myself of commission. If you want 'em, lass, you must go into the auction room at the right time and bid for 'em.'

Her mouth went dry at the prospect, and a gleam of amusement came into the eyes surveying her. 'Scared, are you? No need to be – I'll not let you buy a wardrobe by mistake. Go on and bid for 'em – it'll be good experience for you. When it's your turn to run an auction you'll know what the other folk in the room feel like.'

'When I—? I'm not going to be an auctioneer. I'm office staff.'

'Think so?' Charlie Blayne tilted his chair back, openly grinning now. 'Everyone turns their hands to

everything here, and I think ye'd do well as an auctioneer, once ye learn the ropes.'

The thought of Catherine McAdam's reaction if her
daughter was ever to run an auction made Ainslie feel
faint. 'I'll maybe just have a look round the shops.'

'That's the coward's way out, and ye never struck me
as a coward, Ainslie McAdam. Go on,' Charlie urged,
'I'll be auctioning the items ye want later this week, and
the office can look after itself for an hour. I'll expect ye
to be there – and that's an order, young lady.'

Ainslie scarcely slept on the night before the auction.
She told herself a dozen times that she couldn't go
through with it, and her stomach started churning
when, looking down from the interior office windows
the next day, she saw the public surging in through the
street doors. Still unsure as to her final decision, she
finished the work she was doing, blotted and closed the
big ledger, then took a deep sustaining breath and went
down the outer stairs, into the street, and into the auction room via the public door.

She had watched a few sales from the safety of the
gallery, and had been aware of the surge of excitement
wafting up from the floor below, but being in among it
all was quite different. There was a tingle in the air, a
sense of anticipation. Some people stood about in
groups, heads together, arguing, dissenting, sometimes
agreeing, all the time eyeing each other slyly, measuring
up the opposition. Others drifted in ones and twos
around the room, examining the stacked furniture and
rolled carpets, running their fingers over the china or
through drawers of cutlery, making notes on scraps of
paper. Ainslie, too, walked about, studying items she

had no intention of buying, carefully ignoring the pieces she was interested in, trying to look as though she was an old hand when it came to attending auctions.

There was a buzz of excitement as Charlie swept down the stairs from the gallery, dressed in his usual auction-day clothes, a smart lounge suit with a bow-tie at the collar of his crisply starched shirt. Leonard, his clerk, was in close attendance, his arms filled with ledgers and lists.

Some people moved to the rows of chairs below the platform, but Ainslie remained on her feet at the rear of the room, ready to slip out through the street door if her nerve failed her. To her horror, Charlie, after casting a quick glance round the room, saw her lurking in the background and rapped his gavel on the lectern, booming, 'Order now, ladies and gentlemen – and make way for the young lady at the back there. Come forward, madam, and take a seat. Don't worry, we won't expect ye to bid for it.'

A ripple of appreciative laughter ran through the crowd, and there were hearty guffaws from the furniture movers as they recognised Ainslie. The bidders standing in front of her looked over their shoulders, then stepped aside. Blushing, she had no option but to walk through their midst like Moses moving between the parted waves, to take a seat. Charlie gave her the ghost of a wink, then rapped again on the lectern, and the auction began.

He was good at his profession, taking his audience neatly through the lots, occasionally tossing out a joke to set them at their ease. His eyes seemed to be everywhere, and no bid, no matter how unobtrusive, went unnoticed. Beside him, Leonard scribbled furiously, keeping pace with each and every bid and the names of the successful bidders, while the aproned men responsible for putting each lot on view without any time-wasting worked smoothly and efficiently.

Ainslie's terror ebbed away as she watched the proceedings, fascinated, then her mouth went dry when Charlie, giving her a meaningful look, announced, 'Lot twenty-six, ladies and gentlemen – a handsomely boxed set of model cars, every detail correct. An excellent buy for the car enthusiast. What am I bid?'

Ainslie put a hand up and called out an amount that she knew to be well below the reserve. Charlie's eyebrows rose.

'The young lady knows a good bargain when she sees one,' he told his audience smoothly. 'Any other bids?'

Somebody at the back of the room put in a bid. Ainslie topped it, then had to top it again, and again. They were over the reserve price and approaching her limit when, to her astonishment, the other bidder dropped out, and Charlie slammed the gavel down once, twice, and said, 'Sold to the young lady in the front row.'

The unexpected success boosted her confidence, and when the china figures she wanted for her mother were brought out half an hour later, she bid with more confidence, again starting below the reserve price. This time, though, the bidding was rapid, quickly going beyond her limit, and she had to concede the figures to a plump woman further down the row. During her look around before the auction, she had noticed a set of china wall plates, so she waited, and managed to buy them when their turn came. Then, flushed with success, she escaped back to the office.

'That was a dirty trick to play on me – starting the bidding below the reserve price,' Charlie said when he came up to the office later. Ainslie shot him a quick sidelong glance, and was relieved to see that though the words were grim, he was smiling.

'I thought that that was what bidding was all about, Mr Blayne,' she told him demurely. 'If I'd started at the reserve price, I might not have got the cars.'

He laughed. 'Ye're quite right. Well done, lassie, ye got a bargain both times, and my clients still got a price they'll be happy with. D'ye see now what I meant about not selling at the reserve price?'

Ainslie nodded. 'I didn't know an auction could be such a challenge.'

'It can be enjoyable, but it can be like gambling, too. It's amazing the folk who come in and buy stuff they don't need, just for the fun of bidding.'

'And the folk who bid, then can't pay,' chipped in Leonard, a small, elderly man who, with his large hooked nose and sharp eyes, looked like the picture of Punch in one of Ainslie's childhood books. He put the plates and the box of model cars down on a table, and gave her a broad wink as Charlie continued on into his own office. 'Ye did all right, hen,' he whispered. 'Good for you!'

Ainslie and Innes attended the midnight church service on Christmas Eve, debating over the following day's routine as they walked home. It had always been the family custom to take their presents downstairs and put them on the dining-room sideboard to be opened after breakfast, but this year everything was different.

'I think we should,' Ainslie said firmly.

'But if Mother stays in bed we can't open the presents.'

'Then we'll leave them there until dinner. She'll be at the dinner table.'

'But that means that I'll have to wait all day to open them!' Innes's voice was anguished.

'That can't be helped. We should do as we've always done.'

To their surprise, Catherine was already seated at the breakfast table when they went into the dining-room in the morning, and there were two wrapped parcels on the sideboard. Ainslie and Innes, who had met on the stairs and entered the room together, exchanged glances.

'Merry Christmas, Mother.' Ainslie kissed Catherine's cheek. 'It's good to see you downstairs at this time of day.'

'One must make an effort, I suppose, on special occasions.'

When they had finished eating and the dishes – Catherine's scarcely touched – had been cleared away, the servants were summoned to the dining-room to receive a sealed envelope each from their mistress. They curtsied and scurried out, then it was the family's turn. Innes tore at his parcels and exclaimed with delight over the model cars and the *Boys' Own Annual* he received from his mother. Catherine unwrapped the parcel he had given her to reveal a wooden teapot stand.

'I made it in school,' Innes said proudly. 'Yours too,

Ainslie, but I didn't have time to finish the other one.
I should have it done by February.'

Ainslie put the book-end down and went round to
his side of the table to give him a hug. 'Thank you,
Innes, it's beautiful.'

He wriggled out of her embrace. 'Aren't you going to
open your other presents?'

Catherine had given Ainslie a pair of leather gloves.
She herself glanced at the decorated plates and said
vaguely, 'They're very pretty,' then put them aside,
and excused herself, saying that she had a headache
and must go upstairs to lie down.

Unlike the English, the Scots worked through
Christmas and holidayed on New Year's Day, their own
special celebration. There was an air of excitement about
the auction rooms when Ainslie went in that day, a
holiday feeling. Charlie Blayne presented a small box of
chocolates to each of the women on his staff, and a
miniature bottle of whisky to each of the men, and as
the day drew to a close he summoned them all together
in the auction room, where a table covered with a white
cloth held trays bearing small glasses of whisky and
ginger wine, and plates filled with thick slices of dark
fruit-cake.

When they had all taken a glass, Charlie raised his.
'A good year it's been, and a better one to come. My
thanks to all of ye,' he said, beaming round at them.
'Drink up, now, and eat up too. My missus made the
cake and she'll have something to say if I take any of it
back home.'

Going home at the end of the day, Ainslie could still

taste the sharp tang of the ginger wine on her tongue, and feel its fire in her stomach. Her spirits sank as she let herself into the house and breathed in the usual funereal atmosphere. It was as though Christmas had been shut out, left on the doormat.

As soon as she went into the dining-room she saw that Innes's teapot stand had gone, but the plates she had given her mother still stood untouched on the sideboard. They ate in the usual silence, broken only by Innes as the dessert was cleared away.

'Mother, may I go to the matinee in the Glen Cinema on New Year's Eve?'

'Certainly not,' Catherine said at once. 'Cinemas are dirty, unhygienic places. You don't know who you'll be sitting next to.'

His face fell. 'But it's Tom Mix! You let me go last year, and I'm a whole year older now.'

'I said no, Innes.'

'But Douglas is going, his parents said he could.'

'Douglas isn't in mourning,' Catherine snapped, and he flushed scarlet and said no more, excusing himself a few minutes later and going up to his room.

'He's still a little boy, Mother,' Ainslie ventured when they were alone. 'It's hard on him, keeping a whole year of mourning.'

Catherine gave her an icy look. 'It's hard on us all, and it has been much harder on me than it should have been. When are you going to stop this foolish nonsense?'

Ainslie kept her eyes on the table-cloth. She had made herself apologise abjectly to her mother after their bitter quarrel on the day of the tennis party; Catherine

144

had acknowledged the apology stiffly, but ever since then the wall that had always stood between them had been noticeably stronger. 'I'm not going to tie myself to marriage for the sake of living a comfortable life, Mother,' she said doggedly, for what seemed like the hundredth time.

'It's what you were raised to do!'

'It's what you were raised to do as well, and it's brought you nothing but grief. Why try to make me follow in your footsteps?'

As soon as the words were out she regretted them. Catherine's face went bone-white. She got to her feet so abruptly that for a moment Ainslie thought her mother was going to come round the table and strike her. Instead, Catherine walked to the sideboard, reaching out to clutch at its dark solidity for support.

'That,' she said in a low voice, 'was a cruel thing to say.'

'Yes, it was. I'm sorry.' Was she going to spend the rest of her life apologising for speaking her own mind? Ainslie wondered wearily. 'But we've already been over it all, Mother, and we'll never agree.' She heard the pleading in her own voice. 'Even if I did change my mind, Colin has his pride. He wouldn't marry me now.'

'There are other eligible young men, but none of them will want you either, if you don't pull yourself together soon.' Catherine's voice was tight with anger. 'Do you want to become an old maid? Do you want to lose what looks you have and skivvy away in that stupid auction house until they decide they don't want you any more? And you needn't think I'll support you then, for Innes and I will have better things to do!'

Her hand swept out in a strange groping motion, catching the three plates Ainslie had bought for her, sweeping them on to the floor. One bounced on the thick carpet, but the other two crashed against the chair Catherine had just vacated, and fell to the floor in a shower of fragments. For the space of a breath mother and daughter stared at each other, then Ainslie got up and walked out of the room, brushing past the maid, who had come running at the sound of breaking china.

After the maid had swept up the pieces of china Catherine McAdam sent both servants to bed and sat huddled in the drawing-room, staring into the fire while the house settled around her for the night.

Through no fault of her own, everything in her life had gone wrong. Catherine had been raised to be a good wife, and was quite certain that she had fulfilled her purpose in life admirably. She had never enjoyed Kenneth's attentions in the privacy of their marriage bed – it had always been her belief that no well-bred woman could ever go through such a business without feeling disgust and repugnance – but the thought of him sharing a bed with another woman while she herself wore his ring was more than she could bear. He had dealt her the final humiliation by killing himself, making her the object of vulgar gossip in the town and among her neighbours.

And as if that wasn't enough, she was now cursed with a daughter who might as well have been born into a working-class family for all the gratitude she ever showed. An ungrateful, uncaring girl with no sense of duty, no feeling for anyone else but herself.

She took the brandy decanter from the cupboard and poured a generous measure into a glass. The doctor had prescribed brandy with a raw egg whipped into it to keep her strength up, but in recent months Catherine had found that she preferred the brandy on its own. It soothed the bitterness and dulled the memories of Kenneth's and Ainslie's faults. She refilled the glass, and by the time she had emptied it again the fire was a silver-rose glow in the grate, and the room was chilly. Stiffly, she got to her feet and went into the hall and went up the stairs, holding tightly to the banisters, halting as she neared the top to study her father-in-law's portrait.

It, like the brandy, always soothed and calmed her. The landing light had been left on, and its glow brought his painted face to life, picking out the twinkle in his blue eyes, the crispness of his snowy hair, the firm planes of his face. Catherine stood motionless for some time, drinking in each detail, then went up another few carpeted stairs and reached out to the cool glass, running the tips of her fingers over the outline of his mouth, then up to touch his cheek.

Innes McAdam had been able to transform a room simply by walking into it, she thought, her stiff, ageing limbs becoming fluid at the memory, just as they had each time she saw him, all those years ago, when she was sixteen and he twenty-five years her senior. Her father's friend, quite unaware of her, other than as one of Kenneth's friends; unaware that she only came to his home whenever she could in the hope of seeing him. Even if he was away from the house she was content just to be there, touching door-knobs he had touched, books his hands had held.

His wife, Kenneth's mother, had never been worthy of him in Catherine's opinion. She was generally acknowledged to be a woman of strong character, an intellectual who sat on committees, raised funds, and was known for her work among the poor. Catherine had merely seen her as a bad wife, content to spend her time with others instead of devoting it to her husband's comforts, and spoiling her only son when she should have encouraged him to grow up to be as strong and as noble as his father.

Catherine's smile faded, and her hand stilled on the glass. Marrying Kenneth had been the closest she could get to marrying Innes McAdam himself. At least it gave her his name, made her part of his family. But he had died just over a year after the marriage, shortly after Ainslie's birth. And tragically, Ainslie had inherited her grandmother's nature rather than her grandfather's. Her mother-in-law, Catherine thought bitterly, would probably have approved of the girl's stubborn foolishness.

But at least there was another Innes, young and now hers alone, who would be raised to be a worthy successor to his grandfather. At the thought, Catherine's smile returned. Her Innes would carry on the family name and make it mean something in Paisley again. He would atone for all the mistakes his father had made.

Soothed, she let her hand fall away from the portrait and continued on to the upper landing. As long as she had Innes, nothing else mattered.

13

In the weeks before Christmas, Isla went along to Flora Currie's house every day to work on the little dolls' house. She had decided to turn it into a country cottage, painting the roof to resemble thatch and giving the exterior walls the look of rough white-washed stonework.

She added mock timbering, and climbing roses all round the walls. Then, using scraps of wallpaper and linoleum and carpet that Flora provided, she papered the interior and covered the floors.

Digging about in the box, she found furniture that could be adapted, cutting out rockers for the chairs from strong cardboard then glueing them on and painting them, making tiny cushions, curtains that tied back with ribbon, frills for dressing-tables and stools.

Flora was overcome with admiration. 'Where did you learn to do all that?'

Isla, making a cradle from a matchbox, cardboard, and glue, smiled up at her. 'I enjoy finding ways of making things.'

Flora raked through drawers and cupboards, finding broken necklaces, bits of ribbon, scraps of material for

Isla to use. She insisted on contributing a family of little china dolls, and Isla dressed them – a dress and
apron for the mother, smocks for the two little girls,
overalls and a work shirt for the 'daddy doll' she knew
Barbara would insist on. Strands from an old summer
hat of Flora's were deftly woven into straw hats for the
family, and in the cradle lay a tiny baby wearing a white
lacy gown.

The work took time, and Magret soon wanted to
know where she got to in the mornings. Isla, knowing
instinctively that it was best to keep her two lives apart,
said that she had managed to find some cleaning work
in one of the houses at Castlehead.

Barbara, too, was fully occupied. With Christmas
approaching, her class was rehearsing for its part in the
school Christmas concert, and Barbara, who had always
loved singing, was in her element, warbling carols in her
clear, sweet little voice all the time she was at home.
Ross, not to be outdone, sang along with her, much to
her annoyance.

'He keeps getting it wrong,' she protested.

'But he's learning the words quite well. Aren't you,
my clever lad?'

Ross beamed up at his mother from where he sat on
the fireside rug. 'Oil city,' he agreed.

'It's Royal – David's – City, not oil city,' his exasperated sister snapped, and flounced out to practise her
carols with Greta in the wash-house.

Isla finished the little doll's house in good time, and was
able to spend the last few days before Christmas studying the Victorian house and planning the renovation

work. She was nervous about undertaking it, but Flora Currie was adamant. 'You said you would do it, and I have every faith in your ability. In fact, I insist!'

On the last day of the school term, Isla and Magret, dressed in their best, attended the concert, which was staged in the large gym hall. They went alone, because Tommy was on the late shift at the mill.

'Not that he'd have gone anyway,' Magret said as they walked to the school. 'The men always leave that sort of thing tae their womenfolk. Ye'll mebbe get some grandads, though.'

Sure enough, the few men among the crowd flocking into the large hall tended to be older – retired men, bored and looking for any diversion that might brighten the monotonous days. A lot of the women had brought small children with them, for there was nobody to look after them at home. Ross clung to Isla's hand while Magret carried Daisy, bound snugly to her by a shawl, as usual.

The large echoing hall was decorated for the occasion: Ross stared about, enchanted, while Daisy reached grasping fingers up towards the brightly coloured paper streamers criss-crossing over the ceiling and walls. A small decorated Christmas tree stood at one side of the stage, and there was a vase of paper flowers on the piano at the opposite side. As the hands on the clock above the stage reached the time announced for the beginning of the concert a self-conscious young teacher in a low-waisted wool stockinette grey dress, her hair plaited into braids curling like shells around her ears, crept out of the wings to take her seat on the piano stool and flutter through the sheets of music before her.

'That's Miss Wilson,' a hoarse voice said from behind Isla. 'She taught our Myra last year. Awful nice lassie, but awful shy.'

'She looks as if she's wearing her mother's dress,' Magret whispered loudly into Isla's ear just then. 'She'd be pretty if she just wore something more modern.'

Miss Wilson, uncomfortably aware that the entire audience was staring at her, cast an imploring look into the wings, and then, at a hidden signal, raised her hands high and crashed them down on to the piano. Daisy, now slumbering contentedly against her mother's soft pillowy breasts, jerked violently, while Ross, on Isla's lap, clutched at her sleeve for reassurance. A small child somewhere near the front of the hall let out a wail of fright. The hall lights went out, the curtain opened to reveal a row of carol singers clutching paper candles with scarlet crayoned flames, and the concert was under way.

When the 'babies' ' turn came, Greta lurked shyly in the back row, while Barbara was right at the front, singing lustily and beaming down at the audience, her cheeks pink with excitement. Ignoring her teacher's frowns, she waved happily at her mother and brother when she spotted them, and her voice soared above the others as they launched into, 'Once in Royal David's City'. Ross, kicking his heels painfully against Isla's shins, joined in with great enthusiasm.

'I told you not to sing, it was just the schoolchildren that were supposed to sing,' Barbara nagged huffily when she joined her mother and brother later for tea and mince-pies in one of the classrooms which, like the hall, was decorated with paper streamers. Ross bit into a mince pie, ignoring her.

'Nobody could hear him,' Isla said in his defence.

'I could, all the way up on the stage,' said Barbara, then, hopefully, 'Could you hear me? Was I good? Was I the best?'

Filled with mince-pies, they walked home in the dark, the lights going off one by one in the school behind them. It was long past the children's bedtime, and Ross grizzled to be carried. He fell asleep almost at once, his sticky little face nuzzling into Isla's neck, and his breath, sweet with mincemeat, puffing warmly against her chin. Barbara and Greta ran hand in hand ahead of their mothers, singing snatches of carols, shrieking with laughter, then suddenly falling silent as a drunk man lurched out of a pub and towered over them, telling them in a slurred voice that they were bonny wee lassies, so they were.

Isla felt her stomach tighten. She often heard intoxicated men lurching home past her window at night, sometimes singing, sometimes quarrelling, their voices loud and their words ugly and menacing. She had seen them in the street now and then during the day, but she had never before had to confront one.

Magret had no such qualms. 'Now you leave the lassies be,' she ordered sharply as the man reached out a hand towards Barbara's bright hair.

He jerked round towards her voice. 'Who d'ye think ye're . . .' he started to say, then the tone of his voice changed. 'Is it yersel', Maggie? How are ye, hen?'

The light from the pub window caught his face, gaunt and stubbly. Hair stuck in tufts from under a peaked cap, and he stank of drink.

'I'm fine, Willie, and so will you be, when ye've slept

153

it off. Away home, now, for I've got more tae dae at this time of night than stand in the cold talking tae ye.'

'Aye, right ye are, pet. Nae harm done, eh?' the man said, and lurched off along the road. Barbara, subdued now, came hurrying back to Isla's side and took a firm grip on her coat.

'I didn't like that man.'

'Ach, there's no harm in him, pet,' Magret assured her. 'But it's as well no' tae talk tae men that smell of drink, eh?' To Isla she added, as they hurried towards their own close, 'Poor soul – he was a gaffer in the mills when I worked there. A good, sober man he was too, then his wee boy died of the diphtheria and his wife went off with someone else. Look at him now. It's a shame, so it is.'

'Drunk men scare me,' Isla admitted.

'Ach, they're all right, most of them. They drink for comfort, but the pity of it is that some of them don't have the sense tae settle for one or two glasses. My own father was drunk more often than he was sober, and my poor mother had a time of it tryin' tae keep us from starvin' tae death.' Magret huffed air angrily out of her nostrils. 'The publicans never have that worry, though! They're happy tae line their pockets with other folks' hard-earned money. I'm fortunate that my own man knows how tae take a sociable drink then call it a day.'

The dolls' house was smuggled into the George Street flat on Christmas Eve and hidden beneath the bed. On Christmas Day, Barbara's astonishment and delight made Isla feel that her hard work had been well worth while.

Greta was summoned at once to admire it. 'You can

have my other house,' Barbara announced graciously, and Greta's thin little face lit up.

'She must be a real nice lady ye're workin' for, Isla, tae give ye a house like that for the wean,' Magret marvelled. Then, as Ross charged across the space between them, towing his Christmas present, a brightly painted, jointed wooden dog that nodded its head and moved its legs when pulled along on a string, 'He'll wear your oilcloth out by New Year.'

'It's already worn out. I doubt if it'll last another six months,' Isla said in despair. Small though the room was, there always seemed to be something that needed replacing.

Daisy, allowed down on to the floor more often now that she was two months from her first birthday, squirmed after the wooden dog on her stomach, with no hope of catching it. Magret scooped her up and planted a loud kiss on her head, now covered with fine downy brown hair, then sniffed the air appreciatively. 'That smells good.'

'It's a boiling fowl I put on to simmer on the stove for our Christmas dinner. I made a dumpling, too.'

'We always have our special dinner at New Year.' Magret's bright little eyes twinkled with anticipation. 'Wait till the New Year, Isla – that's a grand occasion here. Everyone gets the day off work, an' there's parties in just about every house, with dancing and singing – out in the street tae, if the weather's no' too bad.' Her twinkle broadened into a grin. 'Ye'll not get much sleep on Hogmanay, for the noise.'

Kenneth had always claimed to prefer celebrating Christmas, and Isla was keeping the custom alive for his

155

children, although now she realised that Kenneth must have established the custom because his other family had naturally expected him to be with them for New Year – a time, he had told her, when his office was at its busiest. Staring absently at the two little girls down on their knees by the dolls' houses, she wondered why she had always believed every word he said, never questioned him about those busy times when he had to be away from home for days and occasionally weeks. She supposed that it was because she had loved him too deeply to do otherwise.

'Magret, why don't you and the children have your dinner with us today?' she suggested, anxious for company on a day that held so many memories for her.

'That'd be grand – if ye're sure there's enough for us all.'

'Of course there is. That's what Christmas is about – sharing.'

Even with Magret's cheerful company to dull the edge of her memories, Isla was glad to see Christmas Day past and eager to get to work on Flora Currie's Victorian dolls' house on Boxing Day. She felt a tingle of anticipation as she unhooked the catch and the front of the house swung open like double doors, to expose the rooms within.

Ross, used to Miss Currie's house by now, went happily to the kitchen with Annie, who shrugged Isla's protests aside with, 'Ach, I'd plenty wee brothers and sisters when I was a lassie. I can surely manage tae see tae just the one.'

Fired by enthusiasm after the school concert, Barbara

had decided to organise her own carol concert, and was too busy coaxing some of the street children to form a choir to accompany her mother to Castlehead. Magret had agreed to keep a watchful eye on her.

'She's got quite bossy since she started school,' Isla told Flora as her fingers worked confidently at glueing a length of fringing round the canopy of a double bed for the master bedroom. The original canopy had come unstuck in several places, and it was easier to renew it than replace it. 'To think that I was worried when we first moved to George Street in case the other children ostracised her and broke her heart! But it was never easy to keep Barbara down. I can't think where she gets her determination from.'

Flora, a willing assistant, was sifting through a box of old costume jewellery, sorting beads into sizes and laying aside lengths of chain. Isla had earlier discovered part of a necklace which included tiny crystal drops, and had decided to try her hand at making a chandelier, if she could find enough fine chain.

'She gets it from you, my dear. It takes determination and courage to face life with no money to speak of, and two small children to care for.'

Isla arranged fringing on a sheet of paper and brushed glue carefully along its length. 'That's not courage, it's necessity. I was such a timid child – nothing like Barbara. I'm sure she's got her strength of mind from her fath—'

She stopped abruptly, and Flora Currie flicked a sidelong glance at her, then said casually, 'I wonder what the thirties will bring. It seems no time at all since we were approaching 1920. I used to think when I was young that time would slow down as I got older, but it doesn't. It gets faster and faster.'

'I've found the years rushing by since the children were born,' Isla said, relieved that they had moved on to a safer subject. 'A few years ago they didn't even exist, yet in no time at all they'll be into their teens, and thinking of what they want to make of their own lives. What's that wee box you've got there?'

Flora held it up. 'I remember keeping bits and pieces in it as a child. I can't think where it came from – my father may well have brought it back from one of his trips.'

Isla wiped her fingers on a cloth, then took the little box from her and studied it. 'You know that nice laquered chest you've got in your front hall? I could paint this up to look just like it for the dolls' house hall. And I could make a nice vase to put on it, with a spray of flowers . . .'

In return for the shared Christmas dinner, Magret had invited Isla and the children to eat their New Year's Day dinner with her and Tommy and their children.

'It'll be steak pie, same as we always have, with tatties and carrots. That's what we like best,' she said, her eyes bright with happy anticipation. 'There'll probably be some folks comin' in after – my mam and my sister, and her lot. I love New Year, so I dae, we always have such a good time!'

New Year's Eve was always a busy day for Scottish housewives, for tradition demanded that every house had to be rid of the old year's dirt and dust, ready to start a new year afresh.

As well as cleaning out every nook and cranny, the womenfolk also had to make sure that there was food for the flood of visitors they might expect. The children, roped in to help, were sent to the shops with long lists wrapped round the money to pay the shopkeepers, or set to minding smaller brothers and sisters or beating carpets and rugs in the backyards and helping their mothers to shift furniture so that every corner of every room could be cleaned thoroughly.

Wash-houses were in great demand for the final few days of the old year, and the clothes-lines in every yard were crammed, as were clothes-horses indoors. Smaller items of clothing bubbled and steamed in metal pails and tubs on top of stoves and ranges, cheek by jowl with 'clootie' dumplings, tied in clean dish-cloths or pillow-cases, simmering in pans of water. Flat irons were fitted in among the pots and tubs wherever room could be found for them, so that they would be hot enough for use once the clothes were dry. There was scarcely an oven in the town that didn't hold at least one steak pie in the making.

It was the men's task to see that there was enough drink available in the house for all who might call in after the bells rang to welcome the new year. Those men with dark hair were expected to 'first foot' other houses, arriving as soon as possible after the bells rang, armed with a bottle of whisky, a large wedge of black bun – a rich cake crammed with fruit – and a lump of coal to bring plenty and good fortune to the household for the coming year.

The Hogmanay cleaning usually brought a rich harvest to the children, as empty bottles and jam-jars that had lain forgotten in cupboards came to light, some to be borne off to the nearest shop and exchanged for halfpennies and farthings, some carefully set aside for the penny matinee at the Glen Cinema, down at the Cross, a welcome haven from parental tyranny on Saturday afternoons, and every Hogmanay.

By early afternoon on that final day of 1929, many of the mothers were beginning to lose patience with their offspring, and deciding that they could probably manage to get on with the work faster on their own. Gradually, the children returned to their play, banished to the street with thick wads of bread and jam and instructed not to come in again until summoned for the obligatory bath, hair-washing, and change into clean clothes. The lucky ones were despatched to the cinema, some of the older girls carrying the baby of the family, a dummy stuck in his or her mouth.

One of Greta's older cousins, an eight-year-old girl, called to take her to the cinema, and Barbara, who had heard of the delights of the moving pictures from the older children in the street, begged to be allowed to go too. When Isla refused permission, Barbara flew into a tantrum and, on being smacked, climbed on to the box bed, drew the curtains shut, and sulked. Isla left her to it, wondering if she was being over-protective, yet uneasy about letting the little girl go.

'Mebbe next year, when you're six,' she opened the curtains to tell Barbara, who flounced round in the bed so that her back was to her mother. Sighing, Isla got on with her work.

She was on her knees by the cooker, trying to reach right under it with a brush to coax every bit of fluff out of hiding, when Magret burst into the room, her face white and strained, Daisy in her arms.

'Take the bairn for me,' she gasped, 'There's somethin' happened at the Glen – I'm away tae look for our Greta!'

Isla scrambled to her feet. 'What do you mean—?' she began, but Magret bundled the baby into her arms, and with a wail of, 'Oh God – my wee lassie!' she was out of the house, through the close and out into George Street, running as fast as her curved legs and stocky body would allow.

14

Ross, who had been put into his cot to play and had fallen asleep, woke in fright. With her free arm Isla scooped him out on to the floor, and he staggered drowsily after her, still grizzling, as she carried Daisy outside.

Women had come to the close-mouths all up and down the street, and some had started running in the direction of the Cross, still carrying dusters or floor brushes. Others hung out of windows, loudly demanding to know what had happened.

'It's the Glen!' The news was passed from mouth to mouth along the street. 'It's on fire!'

A woman who had appeared at the next close dropped her metal bucket with a clatter as the words reached her, giving a cry of pure anguish. She started to run, kicking off shabby down-at-heel slippers and running on in her bare feet, lurching clumsily from side to side, sawing her clenched fists through the air. 'My bairns!' she screamed as she went. 'My bairns are in there!'

'Mummy, what is it? What's happened?' Barbara arrived on the pavement. Just as Isla opened her mouth to reassure her, a boy came hurtling past, yelling, 'The Glen's burnin'! The bairns is all killed!'

'Greta?' Barbara's eyes filled with tears. 'Where's Greta? I want to see her . . .' Her voice was an anguished wail that set Ross to crying again and started Daisy off. Up and down the street people were weeping, and more and more of them were taking to their heels. Mrs Leach and her thin, pale daughter joined Isla on the pavement, along with Mrs Brown and Granny Thomson. Drew Brown was there too, clutching a carpet beater. His mother put a hand on his arm when she heard the news.

'Thank God you didnae go this year, son. These poor, poor bairns!'

'Greta was there – Magret's gone to look for her.'

'Mebbe they all got out in time,' young Mrs Kelly ventured, and her mother sniffed.

'That's no' likely, is it? Now ye know,' she nagged at the young woman, 'why I would never let ye go. If it's no' fleas, it's fire!'

Men began to appear round the corner of Maxwellton Street, earlier than usual, come from the mill as word of the fire spread. One or two stopped to question the women at the close-mouths before hurrying on to the Cross in search of their children, or to see if they could help.

Numbly, Isla shepherded her three tearful charges back into the tenement. There was no sense in standing out on the pavement, and Daisy was heavier than she looked. She sat the little girl down on the rug, and Daisy promptly fell over and lay there, breaking her heart. Isla picked her up and sat down so that she could hold Ross as well. Barbara insisted on burrowing into her arms too, and the four of them huddled together, cramped in the small armchair, waiting for news.

An hour dragged by before Magret came back, her husband Tommy with her, carrying Greta, her face streaked with dirt and dried tears, a bruise purpling one cheekbone. At sight of her, Barbara burst into tears, setting off Greta and Ross and Daisy.

'If ye'd seen it, Isla,' Magret choked against the background of wailing children. 'All the folk screamin' and shoutin' for their bairns, an' the firemen an' the polismen carryin' these poor wee souls out, some of them just lyin' there and not movin'. Not even cryin' . . .'

Tommy clumsily patted her shoulder with his free hand. They were both ashen.

'Was the whole place on fire?'

Tommy shook his head. 'We never seen any flames. They'd stopped the trams, an' we found her on one of them.'

'A polisman wanted tae take her tae the Infirmary, but she's all right – not like some of those other poor wee pets. She just needs tae be safe with her mammy and daddy, don't ye, my wee hen?' Magret reached up and stroked her daughter's face gently.

'What about Greta's cousin?'

'She's – she's all right.' Tommy's voice was husky, and choked on the first word. 'They was both lucky. Come on, pet, we'd best get her tae her bed,' he urged, and Magret nodded and held out her arms for Daisy.

'I'll see ye later, Isla.'

'You're wet, Mummy,' Barbara said when they had

gone. She sniffed tears back and pointed to the large damp patch on Isla's skirt, then looked down at her own skirt. 'I'm wet too – so's Ross.'

For the first time Isla noticed the sharp smell of urine hanging in the air. 'Poor wee Daisy, I never thought to change her.'

More washing to do if she wanted everything to be clean for the new year, she thought. But at least Greta was safe, and so were her own two. She knelt and gathered them both into her arms. If she had let Barbara go – if she had lost her in the same year she had lost Kenneth –

The thought was more than she could bear.

Contrary to rumour, the cinema had not caught fire. A reel had started to smoulder in the projection room and the smell of burning celluloid had permeated the packed cinema. Before anything could be done to reassure them, the children had panicked, rushing to the exits only to find that they couldn't open the doors. Those who reached them first were the victims – crushed and smothered as the frantic children behind them struggled to escape from the building forcing them to the ground, clambering over them in search of safety.

Sixty-nine children died needlessly, and at midnight the bells that rang in 1930 tolled, too, for the lost children, and a town in mourning.

Magret insisted on her Ne'erday dinner going ahead as planned. 'We've still got tae eat,' she said, and so Isla and Barbara and Ross, together with Granny Thomson, who had no relatives of her own, crowded into the small one-roomed flat. With the resilience found only in children, Greta had recovered from the previous day's ordeal, though it would be at least a week before the bruising on her face disappeared. The children ate heartily, while the adults picked at their food, still numbed by what had happened.

'It's a terrible way tae start a new year, losin' a bairn,' Magret voiced all their thoughts as she carefully mashed potatoes for Granny Thomson then ladled gravy over them. 'More than one for some folk – I heard that four were lost from the one family, an' one of them a bairn just about the same age as your Ross, Isla.' Her voice shook on the last few words, and Isla noticed that she and Tommy kept glancing at Greta, as though reassuring themselves that she was still with them.

'There ye are, Granny,' Magret went on with determined cheerfulness, 'you eat that up. The poor soul's no' got a tooth left in her jaw,' she mouthed to Isla across the old woman's head. 'Cannae manage the meat.' Aloud, she said, 'I did custard an' stewed apple for after, ye'll enjoy that, won't ye?'

Granny Thomson nodded, loudly sucking the purée of potatoes and gravy from a spoon, her face almost touching her plate, her back hunched and the bones of her spine pushing against the material of her dress. She left not long after the meal was finished, her thin colourless lips stretched in a toothless smile of gratitude, and Isla made her own excuses a little later, when members of Magret's and Tommy's families began to arrive. The small room was becoming unbearably crowded, and the talk was all about the cinema disaster. Isla felt that she couldn't bear to hear about it any more.

Not that it could be avoided. Everywhere she went, people were talking about the tragedy. Early in January the pavements were thronged to see the small coffins go by on their way to Hawkhead Cemetery for burial in a communal grave, some of them children who had been in Barbara's class at school. Many of those who had survived were still receiving treatment in Paisley Alexandra Infirmary. Funds were set up to help the bereaved families and the victims, and the cinema manager was arrested in connection with the closed exits that denied safety and life to so many small victims.

Even Flora Currie talked about the tragedy when Isla went back to her house to work on the Victorian dolls' house.

'I heard that there were riots outside the Infirmary, with people wanting to get in to see what had happened to their children, and the police trying to hold them back. Those poor, poor souls. In my childhood a little girl we played with was killed in the street when a cart ran over her – I can still remember the shock of hearing the news. I'd been so sure until then that only old people died. It was dreadful – and it still is – to realise that it can happen to little children too. I recall my mama trying to write to that child's parents and saying to my papa, what comfort can one give to people who have lost a child?' She sighed. 'And now I must find the right words myself.'

'You knew one of the children?'

Flora nodded. 'Innes McAdam, the son of people I used to know.'

They were taking tea in the parlour. Isla, about to sip from her cup, set it back in the saucer with a faint clash

167

of china. For a moment the room seemed to shift around her, then to her relief it steadied. Flora Currie didn't notice.

'I only knew the boy slightly. Such a nice child, and so polite, even as a little tot. His father was very friendly with one of my brothers at one time. They grew apart after they left school, long before Arnold left Paisley. Arnold was a bit of a perfectionist, and I believe that eventually Kenneth McAdam just didn't match up to his standards, though I thought him a very pleasant youth. As it turned out, my brother's judgement may have been correct.'

Her voice rattled on and Isla, quite unable to stop her, had no option but to listen.

'Kenneth's problem was that he grew up in his father's shadow. His father was a fine man, very well thought of in the town, but I always pity children who have to follow perfection. After all, we're all as God made us, for better or worse. Unfortunately, Kenneth didn't inherit his father's strength of character as well as his father's business. I remember Arnold saying that Kenneth tended to take the easy way out of a dilemma instead of facing up to it.'

She paused, and Isla frantically sought for some way of changing the subject. Before anything came to mind, Flora went on, every word a spear plunging into Isla. 'Poor man, I'm not so sure that he did take the easy way out in the end. Apparently his business began to fail, and he speculated foolishly with clients' money in a bid to save it. Instead, inevitably, he lost good money after bad, then took his own life. It was a terrible blow to his wife. She's a very proud woman.'

'Miss Currie—'

But the old lady was well into her subject now, her eyes cloudy as she looked into the past. 'As if she didn't have enough to bear, she discovered that he had set up a second wife somewhere else, a woman much younger than himself, and had two children by her. So poor Kenneth ruined the lives of another three people when he decided to put an end to it all. Such a tragedy, and now his own son's gone as well. He looked like his father, too. Kenneth was a handsome young man, with vivid blue eyes and red hair that seemed to light up any room he was in. I can see it yet – like autumn leaves on a sunny—'

Ross was playing on the carpet, in a patch of January sunlight that made his downbent head glow. Flora's eyes had been resting absently on the little boy as she spoke. Now her voice stopped abruptly, her eyes clearing and widening, flying up to meet Isla's frightened gaze.

'Oh, my dear,' she said on a breath of sound. 'What a very stupid old woman I am, talking about Kenneth's other wife and two children, never stopping to wonder where they might be, or what they might be doing . . .'

'It's—' Isla choked and tried again. 'I—' But the words wouldn't come. She put down the cup and saucer, blundered to her feet, and ran from the room.

The dolls'-house room was comforting and familiar, a haven where nothing bad could happen. Isla picked up the four-poster bed she had been working on before the New Year, blinking hard to clear the mist from her eyes. The new canopy was firm and straight now; she found the curtains that had been hemmed for it, then began to glue each one into place so that it could be gathered back later and tied to the bedposts. Her mind was numb and she left it in peace, concentrating on her fingers, shutting the rest of the world out.

Half an hour passed before Flora Currie tapped on the door and came in, cup and saucer in hand.

'I made some fresh tea. Annie's taken the children out for a walk. I hope you don't mind.'

Isla stared at her, startled. For once, she had forgotten about her children. 'I'm sorry, I shouldn't have just walked out and left them like that.'

'You needed time on your own – and Annie loves being with them,' Flora said timidly, then, 'Oh, Isla! Oh, my dear, I wish someone had broken into the house and cut my tongue out while I was asleep last night. My mama always said that I spoke before I thought, but the things I said today were quite inexcusable!'

'You weren't to know.'

'But I should have guessed!'

'I was hoping that nobody would guess. A lot of Scots have red hair, and you wouldn't have expected to find us right here, in Paisley.'

Now that her secret was out and she had got over the first shock of it, it was a relief to tell someone about it all. Once she started, though, she couldn't stop; the words poured out, and Flora Currie had the sense to let her talk without interruption.

'My dear child, what a hard time you've been having – and nobody to turn to,' she said when Isla had at last come to a stop.

'I'm managing, and the children are thriving. And I've good memories of the time I had with Kenneth.'

'You don't resent what he did to you?'

'Resentment doesn't come into it. I loved him.'

'I really didn't think I'd missed out on anything, staying single,' Flora said after a moment. 'Now I'm beginning to wonder.' Then her tentative smile faded. 'Now that I know, I hope that you'll continue to come here, and go on working on my little house.'

'Are you so sure that you want me to? It could be embarrassing for you, having me around,' Isla explained, when the older woman looked puzzled. 'After all, you know the McAdams.'

'Scarcely at all, now, and anyway, why should I let the past hinder a good friendship? Annie and I would miss you and the little ones sorely if you stopped coming, so I hope we'll hear nothing more about that,' Flora said firmly. 'And I give you my word that nobody, not even Annie, shall know what you've just told me.'

She beamed at Isla, who summoned a wavering smile in return. Then Flora rubbed her bony hands together vigorously.

'I do hate sentiment,' she announced. 'It embarrasses me. Now then – what plans do you have for today's work?'

Charlie Blayne called at the McAdam house on New Year's Day to tell Ainslie to take as much time off as she wanted. Standing on the step, twisting his cap round and round in his big hands, he said, 'We'll manage fine till you get back, lass. Your poor ma'll be needin' you.'

She stared at him through the cotton-wool haze that

had wrapped itself around her since Innes's death. 'I'm sorry I can't ask you in,' she heard herself saying.

'I'd not expect it – not at a time like this.' He stumbled backwards down the steps to the gravel drive. 'I just wanted you to know – for as long as your ma needs you.'

But Catherine McAdam didn't need anyone but Innes. She didn't want anyone but Innes. Time after time, as she served tea to the few people allowed into the house, or tried to coax Catherine to eat, Ainslie caught her mother looking at her with eyes that told her, clearly and coldly, that the wrong one had died.

'She could have borne my death better than his,' she said through frozen lips to Colin when he called at the house. Her mother, who couldn't sleep at night, had fallen into one of her sudden, exhausted dozes on the drawing-room sofa, and the two of them sat in the dining-room, at either side of the polished table.

'Don't say that.' He reached across the table and covered her hand with his. His fingers were warm and real; Ainslie, who had had the eerie feeling since Innes's death that she wasn't really there, and that her own flesh had become transparent, half expected his hand to sink through hers on to the surface of the table, but it didn't.

'It's the truth. She never cared for me, it was always Innes – and I didn't blame her, because he was such a – such a nice little boy, wasn't he?' She hadn't cried before, not even when she saw her brother in the Infirmary, pale and calm, looking as though he was asleep, the only sign of the violence that had ended his life a large bruise at his temple, flaring up into the red hair that someone had carefully combed. But now the tears spilled down her face, and Colin came round the table and held her, not as a would-be lover, but as a friend, someone she could lean against, a support and a comfort.

'Why did he do it?' she wept into his jacket. 'Why did he defy Mother and go to that beastly cinema?'

'Because he was young, and restless, and because he'd had enough mourning.' His hand was gentle on her hair. 'Ainslie, kids always do impetuous things. Innes wasn't to know what was going to happen any more than anyone else.'

By the time he left, she felt as though she had been completely emptied of tears. She looked in on her mother, who still slept, then went quietly into Innes's room, feeling a need to sit among his possessions for a while.

Catherine McAdam's eyelids fluttered and lifted, and she was wide awake. Since Innes's death, she only knew that she had been sleeping when she woke, for there was no drifting, no drowsiness or sense of letting the day go and slipping into rest. She was either asleep in a deep black pit filled with nothing, or awake with unbearable anguish tearing at her, sharp-toothed and bloody-clawed.

She sat up slowly and lowered her feet to the floor, then stood up carefully, holding on to a nearby occasional table, feeling very old and very frail.

'You must eat, Catherine,' Phemie Forbes had coaxed that morning. 'You must keep your strength up.' She had visited every day since the cinema disaster, bringing beef tea and calves' foot jelly and urging the red-eyed servants to make nourishing broths that Catherine could scarcely touch. 'You have to keep going, dear, for Ainslie's sake.'

She was like an irritating housefly, buzzing and droning and refusing to go away. She didn't understand, Catherine thought impatiently as she made her way across the room, moving from one piece of furniture to another, testing the carpet with each step as though it was a marsh. None of them understood. The pain she felt had nothing to do with lack of food. In any case, why keep going for Ainslie's sake, when Ainslie had done nothing for her?

She groped across the precarious, furniture-free desert of the hall, finally clamping a hand tightly on the newel post with a grunt of relief. After a pause to gather her strength, she started to climb the stairs one step at a time, the beast inside her snapping at her heart as she recalled Innes going upstairs in exactly the same way when he was learning to walk, his nurse by his side. She remembered the way he swatted the woman's protective hand aside and insisted on climbing on his own. So determined, so like his grandfather!

She paused for breath, clinging to the banister, misery washing over her in fresh waves as she looked up at the portrait. Now there would be no McAdam to carry on the name and make amends for Kenneth's sins.

As she opened the door of Innes's room Ainslie looked up, startled, from where she sat on the bed, her eyes swollen. The two women stared at each other, then Catherine said harshly, 'How dare you come into his room!'

'Mother—'

'Get out!' She stepped aside, holding the door open, and the girl went without another word. Closing the door behind her, Catherine erased her presence from the bedcover with swift, angry movements of her hands, muttering angrily to herself as she worked.

When she was satisfied that the covering was free of Ainslie's presence, she moved about the room, touching Innes's possessions to calm herself. The model cars Ainslie had given him at Christmas annoyed her, so she swept them off the top of the bookcase and into the waste-paper basket. Finally she settled in an armchair and closed her eyes, soaking in the atmosphere of the place.

Innes was still very much a part of this room. It didn't know that he was dead, and while it waited for his return, he was still alive.

15

Most of the small victims of the New Year tragedy were buried together in Hawkhead Cemetery, but Innes McAdam was laid to rest beside his father in Woodside Cemetery. Catherine refused to attend the funeral service, and it was left to Ainslie to travel with her young brother on his last journey, Gilchrist Forbes and his son by her side.

There was a great throng of people around the open grave, some of them friends of the McAdam family, many of them strangers from all over the town, united in their sorrow. As the minister's voice droned on, Ainslie remembered the last time she had stood by this grave. Then, she had been filled with shock and bitterness, but now there was only a deep, aching grief.

Glancing up, she saw Charlie Blayne among the throng, unusually sombre and serious in black. The sight of him brought a little warmth to her heart. He was a reminder that although her past had been shattered beyond repair, she still had some sort of future.

A small reception was held for close friends in the McAdam house after the funeral. Catherine, with Phemie Forbes hovering protectively by her side, received her guests in the drawing-room, a bleak-eyed ghost of the gracious hostess she had once been. They stood around in uncomfortable groups, eating sandwiches, drinking tea, trying to make conversation in hushed voices. The funeral of a child was so much more harrowing than that of an adult. Ainslie, moving among them, trying to make sure that everyone present was thanked for their attendance, bent over her mother's chair.

'Can I get you anything, Mother?'

Catherine shook her head without looking at her.

'At least, dear,' Ainslie heard someone say to her mother as she moved on, 'you still have Ainslie. She must be such a comfort.'

'So one would have thought.' Catherine's voice, strengthened with bitterness and contempt, rang out. 'But it seems that my daughter cares far more for her place of employment than her home, or her family.'

There was a sudden, uncomfortable silence. Heads turned, and all eyes fixed on Catherine, who gazed back at them arrogantly, then on Ainslie, who looked as though she had just been slapped hard in the face. Colin Forbes stepped forward to put a hand on her arm, his fingers tightening; she looked up at the mingled anger and pity in his gaze, forcing her lips into a smile, then moved on, away from him, saying something banal to one of the staring faces. The woman blinked, answered, and the soft hum of voices started up again, with an undertone of relief.

Ainslie went back to the auction rooms two days later. There was no sense in staying at home. It was clear that her mother had no need of her presence.

*

177

Isla had become so involved in working on the Victorian house that even when the snow came she made a point of struggling along to Castlehead, wrestling Ross's push-chair over frozen, slippery humps of snow, glad of its support as her shoes skidded on the ice. He was almost two years old now, and well able to walk, but not for long distances.

She had been working hard since Christmas and the dolls' house was almost finished. A cook in a volumi-nous white apron ruled over a little scullery maid in the well-stocked kitchen, the master sat in his armchair in the library, while his wife, in plum-coloured silk, occu-pied the drawing-room, busy with her embroidery, which was stretched over a curtain ring Isla had found in one of Flora's boxes of odds and ends. There were two children and a baby in a lacy cradle in the nursery, under their nurse's watchful eye.

In the hall stood the small wooden box Isla had noticed several months before, painted to make a pass-able copy of the inlaid chest in Flora's hall. She was still working on the chandelier, which was proving to be a long-drawn-out, difficult task.

'We could hang it in the dining-room,' she suggested one Monday afternoon. She had come on to Castlehead after collecting Barbara from school; Greta was at home nursing toothache, so Isla had taken advantage of her absence to spend some extra time on the dolls' house. Both children were in the kitchen with Annie, who had become a firm favourite.

'You'll have finished that house in a few more weeks.'

'Yes.' Isla had enjoyed every minute of the task. It

had given purpose to her days, and the thought of being without it saddened her. They were having tea in the drawing-room; glancing at the window, she saw that the snow had stopped falling.

'We'd better go, before it comes on again.'

Someone tugged at the bell-pull just then, and they heard Annie bustling along the hall, then after a moment the parlour door opened and Ainslie McAdam walked into the room. She stopped in her tracks as she recognised Isla, the rosy glow that the cold weather had brought to her face deepening.

Isla, as horrified as the other girl by this unexpected encounter, struggled to her feet as Flora said, 'Ainslie, my dear, how good of you to call. This is my friend, Isla Moffatt; Isla, this is Ainslie McAdam.'

'How do you do?' Ainslie came further into the room reluctantly, unable to do anything else, short of turning on her heel and leaving the house she had just entered. She pulled her glove off and held a hand out. Isla took it and they exchanged a brief clasp of fingers, Isla's warm, Ainslie's icy.

'You'll have some tea?'

'I – I think not, Miss Currie, I must get home. I just called to thank you for sending the basket of fruit to my mother.'

'My dear girl, of course you must have tea – I'll not have you going back out into that snow without something warm to drink.' Flora put her hand to the bell-pull just as Annie came in with fresh tea and an extra cup.

'Sit down, both of you,' Flora instructed, pouring tea. Watching her, admiring the calm, unhurried way in which she guided the conversation, bringing first one of her guests in, then the other, making it seem that they were conversing with each other when, in fact, she herself was acting as go-between all the time, Isla admired her fluent ability, recognising the years of training Flora had undergone while growing up in her mother's house. She would have made a grand wife for some ambitious businessman.

But not even Flora's skill could bridge the gap between herself and Ainslie McAdam; unable to bear the tension in the room a moment longer, Isla shook her head when Flora went to fill her cup, and stood up.

'I must go, Miss Currie – please, stay where you are,' she added as Flora began to get up. 'I'll collect the children and Annie can see me to the door.'

'Very well, my dear. I'll see you soon.'

'I came at a bad time,' Ainslie said when the door closed.

'Not at all, Isla was about to go home anyway. She brings the children to visit me often.'

'Really?' Ainslie couldn't hide her surprise.

'Oh yes. She saved my life one day – helped me home when I'd gone out too soon after a bout of illness, and wasn't able to get back under my own steam. She's a considerate young woman, and I admire her very much,' Flora said calmly, giving her visitor a swift sidelong glance. 'Life's extremely difficult for her, poor girl. It can't be easy for a young widow, raising two wee ones on her own like that, with hardly any money, but she never complains.'

Ainslie remained silent, staring at her fingers, which

were crumbling a piece of Annie's excellent fruit loaf. Flora took pity on her.

'How is your mother, my dear? I thought of calling, then I decided that it might be best to leave it for a while. She probably has more visitors than she can cope with.'

Ainslie looked up, her face shadowed. 'She's started eating again, though scarcely enough to feed a bird.'

'It's a terrible thing, losing a child,' Flora agreed.

Ainslie nodded, then said, as though unable to stop herself, 'I'm worried about her, Miss Currie. She sits in Innes's room for hours at a time, and she insists on making the servants lay a place for him at the table at every meal. She keeps looking at his chair all the time we're at the table, as if she's listening to something he's saying.' Her lower lip trembled, and was brought under control. 'The housemaid's given notice – when I asked her to reconsider, she said that my mother frightens her.'

'Have you spoken to her doctor?'

'I tried, but he just says it's her way of dealing with her loss, and she'll come out of it in time. I'm not so sure.'

'We can only hope that he's right. It must be a terrible thing, losing a son.' Flora paused, then went on gently, 'Losing a brother's a terrible thing, too, though sometimes other folk forget that. But once the edge of the grieving dulls, my dear, you'll have all the years of knowing him to sustain and comfort you.' After letting silence hang between them for just the right amount of time, she asked briskly, 'Would you like to have a look at my collection of dolls' houses?'

'Dolls' houses?' Astonishment swept away the tears
that threatened to spill from Ainslie's eyes.

'It's a daft hobby for an old woman like me, I know,
but I like to show them off now and again – when I
meet someone I think will understand. This way . . .'

The girl's amazement turned to admiration when
Flora unlatched the front of the big Victorian house.

'This is perfect!'

'You should have seen it before Isla started on it.'

'Isla?'

'Oh yes indeed, she's been working very hard. She's
making a chandelier just now, and look at the family
portraits she cut out of magazines. She made the frames
herself, and this rocking chair,' Flora told her proudly.
'The thing is – what do I do with it when it's finished?'

'Oh, you must keep it and enjoy it.'

'Nothing's enjoyable, my dear, when there's nobody
to share it with. Besides, I have so many.'

'Not like this one. It's a collector's item.'

'Then perhaps some collector should have it. I feel
that all Isla's hard work should be seen, and admired.'

'If you ever think of selling it, let me know,' Ainslie
said earnestly. 'I'm sure my employer would like to
have a look at it – he's a good valuator.'

'Really?' A light came into Flora's eyes. 'Ainslie, I've
just had an idea – what about asking your employer to
auction it for me, then the amount raised can be handed
over to the Glen Cinema fund?'

'You mean that you'd give away that beautiful wee
house?'

'Why not? I've had my pleasure in watching it come
to life again, and I intended to make a donation to the

fund in any case. This seems to be a fitting way to do it.'

'If you're quite sure . . .'

'Oh I am,' said Flora. 'Quite sure. The more I think of the idea, the more I like it. Would you ask your employer to call? And come with him – I'd like to see you again, my dear.'

Later, when she had seen her guest out, Flora returned to the back room to study the Victorian house.

'A very fitting contribution,' she said to herself, well satisfied.

Isla finished the Victorian house a few weeks later, but refused to be present when Ainslie brought Charlie Blayne to see it.

'But, Isla, you must be here! After all, you've made such a wonderful job of renovating it, and I'm sure Mr Blayne'll want to meet you.'

'It's your house, and your idea. I think it's a very generous idea, but I'd as soon not be involved,' Isla insisted, and wouldn't be swayed. She did, however, agree to go along the day after the auctioneer's visit to find out what had happened.

Flora met her at the door, glowing with excitement. 'My dear, Mr Blayne was very impressed indeed, and most disappointed not to meet you. He came back this morning in person to pack the house up and take it away. It's to be auctioned next week, and I've been invited to attend.' She drew Isla and Ross into the hall, talking all the time. 'Apparently they fix what's called a reserve price on things that are auctioned, and they won't sell below it—'

When she named the reserve price Isla gasped, then said faintly, 'Well, it is an old house, and very well made.'

Flora brushed the words aside with a wave of the hand. 'It was the work you put into restoring it that's brought the value up.'

Annie brought a tea-tray into the drawing-room, heavy-footed as usual. 'I don't know,' she grumbled as she set it down. 'Strangers tramping in and out the place, auctioneers carrying things out to a van – the neighbours'll think you're having to sell everything you own to make ends meet.'

'Away with you,' Flora retorted. 'You're enjoying the excitement as much as I am. We've been a pair of old fogies for too long – we need a bit of a stir in our lives.'

'We don't need footprints all over my newly scrubbed doorstep,' Annie shot back, and held a hand out to Ross. 'Come on with me, son – there's still some sanity in my kitchen, thank goodness.'

'I'm going to miss the pleasure of bringing that wee house back to life,' Isla said later as they gazed at the gap left by the Victorian house.

'I haven't had such a good time for years,' Flora admitted. 'Of course, there are the other houses.'

'Miss Currie, I doubt if Annie could stand any more of our nonsense.'

'Och, away with you, lassie, she's had the time of her life. There's nothing she likes more than a reason to grumble. Besides, she's taken to your wee ones. She'd miss them as much as I would.'

'And I'll miss coming here. I've enjoyed having

something to do apart from housework, and looking after the children.'

'We all need some sort of interest in life. I feel ten years younger myself, and you look better. When you first came here you were worn down by worries. Now there's colour in your face, and a sparkle to your eye. You've filled out a bit, too.'

'It's all Annie's home baking.'

'I think it's a sense of fulfilment. And it's not all one-sided, you know. Look at me – not a sniffle or an ache have I had since that day you had to half carry me home. We're good for each other – we mustn't give up now.'

Flora looked around the room, then pointed to a modest little house. 'That one could do with a bit of cheering up.'

'D'you know what that one always reminds me of?' Isla asked. 'Have you read *Little Women?*'

'Many times.' The older woman looked puzzled, then understanding dawned. 'Are you talking about the house that Jo and Beth and their sisters lived in? An American dolls' house? Could you do that?'

A tingle of excited anticipation ran through Isla. 'I'd like to try.'

Flora beamed at her. 'I've got the book somewhere – come and help me to look for it.'

The Victorian house fetched a very good price at the auction rooms, and resulted in considerable publicity for Flora Currie. She came straight from the auction to George Street, throwing Isla into a panic when she arrived on the doorstep. Flora swept into the small room and beamed at Magret, who was sitting by the fire.

'How d'you do?'

'This is Miss Currie, Magret, my . . .' Isla swallowed hard, then said, 'My employer, the one I've told you about. This is my neighbour, Mrs McDougall.'

With the merest hint of a raised eyebrow in Isla's direction, Flora shook Magret's hand while with her free hand she patted Ross's head when he came to throw his arms affectionately about her knees.

'I'll be going, then.' Magret gathered Daisy up and edged towards the door, and Isla, completely thrown by Flora Currie's arrival, nodded.

'I'll see you later. I'm sorry,' she added as soon as the door had closed. 'I had to tell her that I was working for someone at Castlehead. She was wondering where I got to every day, and I didn't want to say about the dolls' houses.'

Flora, more interested in the room than in Isla's dealings with her neighbours, was at the orange-box cupboard, fingering the curtain across it. 'What a sensible idea. Isla, I just had to come and tell you . . .' She launched into a description of the auction, and the interest the Victorian dolls' house had attracted before finally going to a collector who had paid an amazingly large sum of money for it.

'Everyone wanted to know who had restored it, but I didn't give them your name,' she said reassuringly. 'I merely said that it had been done by a very talented young friend. A young man from the Paisley *Daily Express* spoke to me, he's going to put something in the newspaper about it.' Her eyes were shining and her voice rattled on; Isla had never seen her so animated.

Almost as soon as she had gone, Magret returned, her face concerned. 'She didnae come tae turn ye off, did she?'

'No, nothing like that.'

'That's all right, then. She seems tae be a decent woman, for all her posh talk,' Magret said. 'It's good tae be appreciated, isn't it?'

16

In March, Barbara and her friends presented their concert in the wash-house to an invited audience of mothers and little brothers and sisters. Heedless of the fact that Christmas was long over, the gathering of little girls, many with dirty faces and bare feet and runny noses, bawled their way through a selection of Christmas carols, followed by some Great War songs, most of them sung by Barbara herself.

The women enjoyed every minute of it, clapping loudly at the end, while the little girls curtsied low, the smallest falling over and being hauled to her feet by those on either side.

'That Barbara's a right clever wee lassie,' Magret enthused afterwards. 'She'll mebbe go on the music halls when she's old enough.'

Barbara had wanted to invite Flora Currie, but Isla managed to dissuade her. Instead, Barbara ran through the entire repertoire on her own before Flora and Annie in the drawing-room at Low Road. Drunk on their praise, she then danced along the pavement all the way home, clutching a silver sixpence and a bag of sweets she had been given as a reward for her hard work.

Flora Currie's donation of the entire amount raised by the auction of the Victorian house to the Glen Cinema fund had created quite a stir in the town. Both local newspapers, the *Express* and the *Gazette*, had written articles about it, and Mr Leckie, owner of a big toyshop in New Street, had called.

'He did all he could to get your name out of me, but he didn't succeed,' Flora told Isla later. 'However, I did tell him about your plans to make a *Little Women* house, and he's shown an interest in buying it when it's finished. If he does, you must overcome your shyness and start charging for your work. In fact, I could advance some of the money to you now.'

'No! If he buys it you can pay me part of the money – but not until it's finished and paid for,' Isla said warily. She could have done with some extra money, but she couldn't take payment for work that hadn't been done. Secretly, she didn't believe that the sale to Mr Leckie would ever go through. The man would have lost interest, surely, long before the house was finished.

In April, when work was under way on the *Little Women* dolls' house, Ross had his second birthday. Isla bought him a toy delivery van, and baked a cake for the occasion, inviting Magret and her daughters in for tea.

A few days after the little birthday party, Isla lost the rent money. There were few hiding places in the single-roomed flat, and she felt safer with the little money she had tucked into her bag. On that particular Friday, she had spent an hour or two window-shopping along the High Street and through the Cross, the busiest area of the town, returning home via St Mirrin Brae and Causeyside Street. Barbara and Greta were old enough now to make their own way home from school, so they didn't have to be fetched.

When they got back to George Street Ross ran ahead of her into the close and out into the backyard. Isla fetched the old hoe that Flora Currie had given her and went to work on her little garden, where the first potato shoots were beginning to show. When Barbara arrived home, she put the hoe away and went into the house to make tea. It was then, going into her bag to get the packet of tea she had bought on her outing, she realised that her shabby purse had gone.

Panic blossomed as she checked her coat pockets, then the pocket of the pinny she wore in the house, then looked under the cushion on the chair and even, futile though it was, in the cot that was getting too small for Ross, and on and under the wall-bed.

'My purse – it's not here—'

'Have we been burgled?' Barbara asked, wide-eyed.

'No, pet, but your mummy's been very careless.' Isla fought back panic. 'Run and ask Mrs McDougall if she'll keep an eye on you and Ross while I go out to look for my purse.'

Barbara did as she was told, and returned with Magret, whose expression mirrored Isla's sick fear. Nobody in George Street could afford to lose money, that scarcest of commodities. 'How much was in yer purse?'

'Everything I had. I'll need to go back along the

street – mebbe I left it in the shop where I bought some tea.'

Isla ran all the way back to St Mirren Brae, but the grocer and his assistant shook their heads when she asked breathlessly if a purse had been handed in.

'I mind ye comin' in earlier, hen,' the grocer said, 'but I never saw what ye did with yer purse after ye paid me.'

Isla retraced her steps along the High Street and down Castle Street, peering into the gutter and along the foot of the house walls, returning to George Street empty handed.

'I'll just have to tell the rent man I'll pay him next week,' she told Magret, who retorted, 'He'll not like that.'

'He'll just have to like it. I've never been behind with the rent before.'

'Can ye not ask that woman ye work for tae pay ye next week's wages in advance?'

Isla shook her head, appalled at the thought of asking anyone, particularly Miss Currie, for financial help.

'I couldn't do that.'

Magret sniffed. 'See these rich buggers? They'd not give a crust tae a dyin' dog, most of them. I wish I could help ye, Isla, but we've not got much more than our own rent.'

'Don't worry about it, I'm sure Mr Reid'll be willing to wait for one week.' It would be hard to make up two weeks' rent next Friday, but she would do it somehow. The thought of explaining the situation to Gilchrist Forbes and asking him to have a word with the rent collector came to her, and was dismissed. For one thing, she couldn't rid herself of the feeling that it was wrong to be treated differently from the other people in the tenement, and for another, the older Forbes might not be in the office, and she couldn't, wouldn't, ask for favours from that cold-eyed son of his.

The children were both asleep when the rent collector arrived that night. He scowled and pushed his lower lip out when Isla explained the situation, taking a step into the room so that she had no option but to retreat before him.

'My employers'll no' like that.'

'I told you, I'll make it up next week.'

He continued to move forward until he was in the middle of the room. 'An' how dae I know that? How dae I know ye'll no' do a moonlight flit and be out of here by next week?'

'I've no intention of leaving.'

'Have ye got nothin' ye could pay on account? Somethin's better than nothin'.'

'Every penny I had was in my purse.'

His eyes travelled over her, then he said, 'I could mebbe put it in the book that ye'd paid somethin'.'

'I'm not asking you to lie for me, Mr Reid, or to use your own money. I'm just asking you to wait for a week.'

The man blinked rapidly, then said, 'That'd be fine with me, hen, but ye see, it's the man that owns this place that's not very patient. He likes tae get his rent in time, and it's me that'll get intae trouble if it's not. So . . .' his tongue moistened his lower lip and he noted something in his book, ignoring her protest.

'That's the entry made, all nice and tidy like,' he

announced, stuffing the book into his pocket. 'The thing is, hen, what can ye dae for me in return?'

'I didn't ask you to lie, Mr Reid. I don't owe you anything.'

'Aye ye dae . . .' He stepped towards her again and Isla, suddenly realising what he meant, retreated behind the fireside chair.

'I've said I'll pay you double next week.'

'Mebbe so, hen, but it seems tae me that there's still that wee bit on account tae be settled.'

'Mr Reid, if you don't get out of here, I'll—'

'Ye'll what?' The chair was scooped aside, then the man was crowding Isla against the wall, his hand on her arm, the stubby fingers squeezing into the soft flesh. 'There's always another way for lassies tae pay their debts. It suits them – an' it suits me.'

Isla tried to drag back on the grip that was drawing her towards him. The smell of the man was thick in her nostrils, a mixture of tobacco and spirits and hair-oil and clothes in sore need of washing. 'Let go of me!'

'I will, hen – in my own time.'

'I'll scream,' she warned, knowing even as she said it that she couldn't shout for help, couldn't waken the children.

He laughed, moving in on her, confident of himself now. 'Go ahead, hen, scream all ye want. Folk round here know how tae mind their own business.'

Isla, caught between his body and the wall, tried to bring her knee up sharply, but he was too close. Instead, she managed to stamp hard on his instep, causing just enough pain to make him step back for a moment. He swung in towards her almost immediately, but she had

gained enough time to slide sideways along the wall
and reach the poker, which she had propped up against
the fireplace before going to answer his knock at the
door. She gripped it between both hands, forcing it up
towards his face. 'If you don't get out of my house, I'll
use this on you. I mean it!'

He stepped back, his gaze flicking between her face
and the poker. 'There's no need to be like—' A whine
came into his voice as Isla took the advantage and followed him, still clutching the poker. 'I only wanted tae
help ye.'

'And to help yourself,' she said between her teeth. At
that moment, she would have swung the heavy poker
without hesitation, would have done anything she had to
do in order to rid herself of him. 'Get out of my house,
Mr Reid.'

'It's you that'll be gettin' out, ye wee bitch. I'll see
tae that. I'll see you and yer brats out on the street!'

She pulled her arm back as though to swing the
poker, and he ducked instinctively, then ran for the
door, his nerve broken. Isla slammed it shut behind him
and leaned on the panels, her heart pounding so hard
that she thought it would burst out through her ribs.

'Mummy?' Barbara, startled awake by the slamming
door, sat up in bed, knuckling her eyes. Ross, a heavy
sleeper, didn't stir.

'It's all right, pet, I – I opened the door to shoo a fly
out and the wind slammed it.'

'Did the fly get hurt?' Barbara asked drowsily. The
thought of her daughter's concern for a fly after what
had almost happened brought a sudden spurt of laughter to Isla's throat.

'No,' she said on a giggle. 'The fly's fine.'

'Good.' Barbara slid back into sleep as Isla groped her way to the chair by the fire and sank into it, the poker still clutched tightly in her hand.

'He'll complain about ye. Ye'll mebbe be put out,' Magret fretted the next morning.

'Put out for refusing to let him molest me? It's me that'll be complaining about him.'

Magret's eyes darkened with alarm. 'Don't go makin' trouble, Isla, they'll no' listen tae ye. They always believe their own.' She twisted the dish towel between her hands into a rope. 'I was that worried about ye last night. I'd've asked Tommy tae sit with ye till the man had gone, but . . .' She stopped, and looked away, embarrassed. Isla understood. Magret couldn't risk losing her own home, even for a friend.

'Has this happened before?'

'Of course. It happens all the time.'

'Has it happened to you?'

Again, Magret's eyes slid away. 'There was one time, when he was laid off and there wasnae enough money.' She shivered, then said, 'I made sure after that that the rent was paid, even if it meant us goin' without.'

'Does Tommy know?'

'Of course not!' Magret was shocked at the very idea. 'Men have their pride, the shame of it would've near killed him. Either that or he'd've killed Geordie Reid, then we'd've lost the room for sure.'

'I wish now that I'd hit him with the poker, instead of just threatening him,' Isla said between her teeth. 'A

195

man like that shouldn't be allowed to go round bullying women and – using them.'

'Ach, it's just life, hen. Plenty women have tae face worse than that, day in and day out.'

'Your envelope's not ready yet. You'll have to wait, or come back later,' the receptionist told Isla when she presented herself at the offices in Moss Street first thing on Monday morning.

'I'm not here for the envelope, I'm here to speak to Mr Gilchrist Forbes.'

'Mr Forbes isn't in the office this morning.'

'What about his son?'

'He's here, but—'

'Then I'll see him,' Isla said. Since the father wasn't available, the son would have to do. She wasn't going to leave the office until she had had her say.

The woman hesitated, then shrugged and went away.

A few minutes later she reappeared, and Isla, clutching Ross by the hand, followed her into an office smaller than Gilchrist Forbes', but just as cluttered.

Colin Forbes' expression showed it clear that he, too, deplored this meeting. 'Mrs – Moffatt. Won't you sit down?' He made no move to shake hands, but stayed on his feet until she was seated.

Isla drew Ross to her side, taking some comfort in his nearness, and instructed him in a whisper to be a good boy. Then over his red curls she told Colin Forbes, clearly and calmly, exactly what had happened on the previous Friday evening. The event was burned into her mind – she had thought of little else all weekend – and

she repeated everything George Reid had said, every
move he had made, in detail.

Colin Forbes listened with growing distaste. 'I find it
hard to believe that one of our employees . . .' he began
when she had finished.

'I'm sure you do. I'm also aware that you're more
concerned with protecting your employee's interest than
mine.'

Colour rose beneath his fair skin. 'I assure you—'

'And I assure you, Mr Forbes, that every word I've
told you is the truth. Not only that – I've been making
enquiries over the weekend, and it seems that I'm not
the only woman in the street to have had this experience.'

'Nobody has ever complained to us before about Mr
Reid.'

Isla gave a short laugh. 'Tell me, Mr Forbes, would
you complain if it meant being thrown out of your
home? I've heard of one poor young woman who was
left with three children to feed after her husband had to
go into the Infirmary. She didn't pay any money at all
to Mr Reid for a few weeks, but I'm quite sure that his
book says differently. Mr Reid puts in the money himself, then claims his reward for keeping a roof over
their heads. When – or if – the tenants can afford to pay
back-rent he makes them repay to the last penny. That
way, he gets his enjoyment without having to pay for it.'

The young man was almost crimson now, one hand
fiddling with a pencil. 'Mrs Moffatt, all you had to do
was to let my father or me know that you were unable
to pay the rent this week, and we would have had a
word with Reid.'

'Why should I seek favours that my own tenants can't have? I believe that every landlord should try living in their own property now and again, Mr Forbes. They may well learn something to their own disadvantage.'

They glared at each other across the desk, openly hostile now, then he asked, 'You realise that this may well mean that George Reid will lose his job?'

'In my opinion, he deserves to.'

'Very well. My father will be in the office this afternoon,' he said stiffly. 'I'll tell him about your visit.'

'Please do.' Isla got to her feet. 'And you can also tell him that if Mr Reid should call for the rent in future, I'll not be opening my door to him. Nor will my neighbours, if I have my way of it.'

17

In spite of her brave words, Isla grew more and more nervous as the week passed, and on Friday evening she kept the poker close at hand.

She was breaking stale bread into a bowl for the children's supper when someone knocked at the door, and Barbara, washed and in her nightdress, scampered to open it before Isla could stop her.

'Come in,' she said hospitably, and stepped back. Isla's fingers, reaching frantically for the poker, fell to her side as Colin Forbes walked in.

'Good evening, Mrs Moffatt. I came to assure you that Reid won't be troubling you again.'

Relief flooded over her, but, stubbornly, she didn't want to reveal it to young Forbes and let him think that she was being pathetically grateful. So she went on with her work, picking up the kettle and pouring warm water from it into the bowl. 'You mean he'll be troubling the poor souls in another area?'

His voice sharpened. 'My father and I looked into your complaint very thoroughly, and as a result of our investigations the man no longer works for us. Until we find someone more trustworthy, I'll collect the rents.'

Isla added milk to the bowl, then divided the mixture between two smaller bowls and put them on to the table. 'Barbara, stir these for me – carefully, mind, no splashing.' As the little girl scrambled importantly on to a chair, she bent to lift the tin bath to the side.

'Let me do that for you.' The young man put the rent book on the table and hoisted the bathtub up, moving towards the sink.

'Not there,' Barbara told him sharply. 'Mummy empties it in the backyard, over the potatoes, 'cos it's not been raining and they need water.'

He put the tub down by the sink then straightened. 'You're growing potatoes?'

'It's cheaper than buying them,' Isla said dryly, fetching her purse.

'Mummy's mixed a lot of dung into the earth,' Barbara told him blithely as she stirred at the bread and milk. 'It smells, but it's good for the potatoes. Would you give me the sugar, please?' She indicated the paper bag on a shelf by the cooker, and he handed it to her.

'Thank you. Dung comes out of horses,' Barbara explained as she dipped a dry spoon into the bag.

'So I've heard,' he agreed solemnly.

'Here you are.' Isla tipped coins on to the table and sorted them out, pushing most of them over towards him.

'There's too much here.'

'I wasn't able to pay last week's rent,' she reminded him, 'so I must pay it this week.'

He coloured. 'Aren't you being unnecessarily exact, Mrs Moffatt? How much have you left yourself to live on?'

'We'll manage.' She had had to pawn Kenneth's last Christmas gift to her, a bracelet that she had been hoping to keep. Even so, the next week was going to be difficult, but she had no intention of admitting it to this well-dressed man who had never in his life known what it was like to have to do without.

He glanced at Barbara, dribbling sugar, grain by grain, into one of the bowls, then at Ross, who stood by her side, craning up to watch the procedure, his blue eyes bright with anticipation, and said, low-voiced, 'D'you think you're being fair to your children?'

Isla fisted her hands on the table.

'We'll manage,' she repeated. Overhead, someone walked across the floor, and the ceiling gave out a series of creaks. Colin Forbes glanced up involuntarily, then looked round the room. Isla bridled as she saw that, unlike Miss Currie, who had noted only the attempts to improve it, all he saw was the shabbiness, the cracks in the ceiling, the damp patch in the corner.

'It's not much of a place, is it?' Isla asked, watching his face. 'It doesn't seem fair to me to take rent from the folk that have to live here.'

'People must pay their way.'

'Did my – did Kenneth McAdam own many other properties like this one?'

He had opened the rent book and was noting the amount she had paid. His hand faltered, then moved on. 'A few.'

'D'you think he ever visited them, and looked at the leaking windows and the draughts and the water running down from the backyard and into the close when it's been raining?'

201

'I'm sure my father could find something better for you.'

'I doubt if I could afford it. And as you just said yourself, Mr Forbes, people must pay their way.'

'Good night, Mrs Moffatt.' He snapped the book shut and swept the coins up, then turned on his heel.

As he opened the door, Barbara said cheerfully, 'Bye!'

'Bye,' Ross sounded like an echo.

Colin Forbes's face softened into a smile. 'Bye,' he said, and left.

She followed him into the close, closing the door behind her so that the children couldn't hear. She must have been left to the last, for he was on his way out of the close. 'Mr Forbes, why do you dislike me so much?' she asked his departing back bluntly.

He swung round. 'I beg your pardon?'

'I asked why you dislike me so much. I think I have a right to know.'

The close was only dimly illuminated by a gas lamp in the street, and Colin Forbes was a vast black shadow blocking out most of the feeble light. 'I get the distinct impression that the feeling's mutual, Mrs Moffatt.'

'Only because you made it very plain that you disliked me intensely from the first moment you saw me, at your father's office. If you have a reason, I can't think what it is.'

There was a pause, then he said bitterly, 'Ainslie McAdam and I were engaged to be married.'

'So your father told me. I understand that she ended the engagement.'

'She did – because she was ashamed over the way her father had betrayed his family with you.'

Isla stared, then began to laugh. She was shocked by
her own reaction, but the laughter bubbled up of its
own accord, filling the space between them, before she
could stop it.

'I'm glad someone's amused,' she heard Colin Forbes
say coldly above her mirth. 'At least the whole sorry
business hasn't been wasted entirely.'

'I'm – I'm sorry.' Isla pressed her fingertips against
her mouth to quell further laughter. She swallowed
hard, then said, 'It's just that I've never been held
responsible for so many crimes in my life. All I did
was marry the man I loved in the belief that he was
free to marry me. Yet Ainslie's convinced that I plot-
ted to tear Kenneth from his family, you're certain that
somehow I forced her to end your engagement – and
now Mr Reid's lost his job because of me. I'm beginning to wonder if I started the Great War without
realising it.'

'You're being ridiculous, Mrs Moffatt,' the shadow
looming against the street light told her coldly.
'Ridiculous and childish.'

'Possibly, but I'm not the only one, Mr Forbes.
From what I know of Ainslie McAdam, I'd say that
she's an intelligent young woman, with a mind of her
own. You make her sound like a lassie with a powder
puff for a brain, someone who could be easily pushed
into ending her engagement.' Anger began to replace
the amusement. 'If she gave your ring back to you, Mr
Forbes, it wasn't just because of me. She must have had
her own reasons, and perhaps it's time you began to ask
yourself what they might be.'

She heard him draw his breath in sharply, then

without another word he strode out of the close and along the street.

Isla sagged against the clammy, peeling wall for a moment, then pulled herself clear and stood upright. She had been cruel – but he had asked for it. 'Him and his disapproval!' she said aloud, the words echoing through the dim close, then with a quick, decisive gesture she spun round and went back into the house.

'For goodness' sake, Barbara!'

'What?' Barbara asked blankly, looking up from her bowl. Ross had clambered up on to a chair and the two of them were relishing their bread and milk. No wonder, Isla thought, peering into the sugar bag as she put it away. In her absence, Barbara had used up almost the entire week's supply.

'Did you have to talk like that to Mr Forbes?'

'I said please when I asked for the sugar, and thank-you when he gave it to me.'

Isla wiped milk from Ross's chin. 'I meant, did you have to chatter on about dung?'

Barbara, unperturbed, dug her spoon into her bowl and scraped up the last of the mush. 'Oh, that. I thought he might want to know about how to grow potatoes,' she said.

On the first anniversary of Kenneth McAdam's death, Isla didn't go to Flora Currie's house. Instead, she stayed at home, cleaning the room from top to bottom, throwing herself into hard work in a bid to keep her memories at bay. When the children were asleep that night and the tenement had creaked into silence, she wept into her pillow. The edges of her grief had dulled, but she still missed and wanted him.

The next morning Barbara, visiting the privy before going off to school, came hurrying back. 'Mummy, someone's dug your garden up!'

It was Mrs Leach's turn for the wash-house, and her washing was already on the line. Isla ducked beneath it and went to the far corner, where the tumbled earth was draped with stripped plants; when she picked one up it lay limply across her fingers, already dead. The thief must have struck the night before, after dark. Looking up at the building, she glimpsed Drew at a window, watching her, and a moment later he came hurrying out in shirt and trousers, thumbing his braces over his shoulders. Mrs Brown and Magret arrived at his back, with Greta and Daisy in tow.

'After all your hard work – it's a shame, so it is.' It was the first time Mrs Brown had directly addressed Isla.

'And after your Drew's digging, too.'

'I hope they were all bad,' Barbara announced. 'I hope that whoever ate them got a sore tummy.'

'Barbara! What's done's done, so we might as well hope that whoever took them was in real need of them.'

'The shaws were still small,' Drew mourned. 'The potatoes must have been like wee marbles.'

Isla nodded. 'I know. Could they not at least have left them until they could steal a decent meal?'

'Ach, most of the folks round here would never think of that.' Magret glanced up at the surrounding windows. 'It could have been anyb'dy.'

Mrs Leach came out of the wash-house with another basket of washing, her daughter at her back. 'I knew it wouldnae be worth the bother,' she said without sympathy as she began to peg out the clothes. 'Ye were askin' for trouble.'

'It was nice to see things growing, though,' Mrs Kelly ventured, and her mother gave a snort.

'It was a waste of time, that's what it was.'

Isla pounced on Ross, who had scampered into the yard dressed only in vest and trousers, and, Daisy at his heels, was approaching the looted bed with the clear intention of plunging his bare feet into the soft earth. As she pulled him away, struggling and protesting, she heard Mrs Leach say, 'Catch me workin' my fingers tae the bone just tae give some thief a meal!'

A few weeks later Isla was putting a batch of scones into the oven when the door, on the latch, was pushed open and Ross, now old enough to play outside with the other children, came hurrying in and made straight for her. His free hand locked on to her apron and his fiery head butted at her thigh as he attempted to get as close to her as possible.

She dusted flour off her hands. 'What's wrong, pet?' Ross was still learning to cope with the rough and tumble of street life, and often came running to her for comfort when things got too much for him.

'Lady . . .' he whined as someone rapped on the door. Isla moved to open it, but the little boy was like an anchor, holding her back, and she had to gather him into her arms before she could get to the door.

Despite the mildness of the day, the woman who stood in the close wore a heavy black coat reaching almost to her ankles. As soon as the door opened she moved forward imperiously, so that Isla had no option but to step back and let her into the room.

'What d'you want?'

The newcomer's head tilted back slightly, the brim of her hat lifting to reveal a pale, haggard face dominated by cold grey eyes.

'I am Mrs McAdam – Mrs Kenneth McAdam. And this' – the grey gaze moved to Ross – 'must be Kenneth's son. I saw him out on the pavement.' She was well spoken, but her voice was harsh, the words falling like stones from her thin mouth.

Icy water seemed to trickle down Isla's spine. 'What do you want?'

'The boy, of course.'

'The—?'

'I've come for the boy,' Catherine McAdam said slowly and clearly, as though talking to an idiot. 'He's my husband's son—'

'He's my son!'

'—and naturally, he must be raised in my husband's house,' the woman went on as though Isla had not spoken. 'Not in this' – she looked round the room, her lip curling in disgust – 'this hovel.'

'Mrs McAdam.' It was strange, addressing another woman by the name she had once thought to be hers. 'This is my son, mine! And you and I have nothing to discuss.'

Catherine McAdam surveyed her dispassionately, then dismissed her, looking back at Ross. The pale lips shaped a slight smile. 'He's a true McAdam. He's going to grow up to look just like his grandfather.'

Isla began to have the eerie feeling that the woman

who had invaded her home wasn't even aware of her as a human being, only some sort of mechanism that had produced Kenneth's son. His second son, she thought, and knew why Catherine McAdam was there. She had lost her own child, and she was looking for a replacement.

'Nobody's going to take my bairn away from me.' As Ross tightened his grip on her neck she put a hand up to his curly head, over one ear, wondering if he understood what was being said.

Catherine looked surprised. 'But he's a McAdam, with the McAdam blood in his veins. I can give him everything – a comfortable home, a good education. His room's waiting for him, with toys and books in it. I can teach him to follow in his grandfather's footsteps.'

'No!'

'Would you deny him all that, when you yourself can give him nothing?'

'Mrs McAdam,' Isla fought to keep the growing fear from her voice, 'I have every sympathy with you in the loss of your own son, but you can't walk into my home and demand mine to take his place.'

In answer Catherine took an impatient step towards her, coming close enough for Isla to catch the faint scent of brandy on her breath. She held her arms out towards Ross, and Isla backed away. This woman represented a threat far more terrifying than the blundering, lustful rent collector had. She could scarcely take a poker to her supposed husband's legal wife, she thought wildly.

'You're – you're not yourself, Mrs McAdam. You should be at home.'

Ross began to whimper and struggle; his weight was

almost too much, but she daren't even shift his position lest Catherine McAdam took the opportunity to lunge at her while she was off balance, and snatch him from her arms.

The woman's hands fell back to her sides. 'If it's money you want, you can have it,' her harsh voice said. 'I have no objection to paying you for the time you've spent caring for him.'

'I don't want a penny of your money, I just want you to get out of my house!'

'My dear, your sort of woman always needs money,' Catherine told her with sweeping contempt. 'I shall instruct my lawyer to have a legal agreement drawn up and delivered to you tomorrow. As for now . . .' she held her thin arms out again. 'Give him to me.'

'No!' Isla's voice rose above the little boy's frightened wails. 'Don't you touch him!'

For the first time, Catherine McAdam looked puzzled. 'If you didn't want me to have him, why did you bring him to Paisley? It was meant to be – don't you see that? You were sent here to help me in my time of need.'

'Please – go away!'

Again, Catherine's reaching arms fell away. 'I must have him, and I will have him, though not today, since you've seen fit to upset him.' She turned and walked unhurriedly to the door, opening it with only the tips of her fingers as though afraid that the wooden timbers might contaminate her. Then she turned.

'My lawyer will contact you tomorrow. He will pay you an adequate sum, and you may hand the child over to him.'

18

When Catherine McAdam had gone, closing the door quietly behind her, Isla dropped into her fireside chair, still clutching Ross, murmuring reassurance. His sobs gradually died down; he was hot, and sticky with sweat and tears, but Isla, almost out of her mind with terror, couldn't bring herself to ease her grip on him.

Just when everything seemed to be working out for her, her world had begun to shatter. Losing the rent money, having to fight the rent collector off, then being robbed of the potatoes she and Drew had so carefully tended. And now this, the most frightening threat of all. She should never have come to this town. Ainslie McAdam was quite right, she should have found somewhere else for herself and the children. They would have to leave at once, go where nobody knew them and where Ainslie's terrifying mother would never find them.

Her mind raced like a mouse caught in a cage, hurling itself from side to side but unable to find a way through the bars that held it captive. She couldn't just leave Paisley, much as she wanted to. For the children's sake, she must first have somewhere to go. She thought fleetingly of asking Flora Currie for help and shelter, then dismissed the idea. Flora had been kind, but her family and the McAdams had known each other socially, and Isla herself owed Flora too much to drag her into the dreadful situation. She suddenly remembered Aunt Lally in Edinburgh. She could go there, but first she would have to find money to pay for the journey.

She and Ross both jumped as Magret came barging in from the close. 'Isla? Somethin's burnin', can ye no' smell it?' Then, after one swift look at Isla, 'God, lassie, what's happened? Ye look as if ye've seen a ghost!'

Snatching a towel from the nail by the stove, she opened the oven door, then gave a wail. 'Look at them, they're all spoiled – did ye no' smell them?' She put the tray of blackened scones on top of the cooker and flapped the towel to waft the smoke away. For the first time Isla became aware of the acrid stink of burning.

At the sight of Daisy, standing in the middle of the kitchen, her fine hair wispy round her small skull and one index finger stuck firmly into a nostril, Ross reverted to his normal self and struggled to get down. Isla resisted, but finally gave in when he began to kick and pummel at her.

'Never mind the scones.'

'Never mind? Since when did any of us have money tae throw away like that?'

Isla got to her feet stiffly, feeling as though she had aged years in the past half hour. She had to do something before Catherine McAdam changed her mind and came back for Ross. She took the towel from Magret and wet one corner under the tap, then wiped her son's sticky, protesting face.

'I have to go out. Could you fetch Barbara from school, and keep her with you until I get back?'

'But the weans is old enough to find their own way home—'

'I don't want her left to come along the street by herself,' Isla interrupted sharply, snatching her coat from the nail on the door. 'I'll be back as soon as I can – just keep an eye on her till I get home.'

Ross was getting too big for his go-chair now, and he had begun to hate it. There was no time to struggle with him, so Isla scooped him up into her arms and hurried out, regardless of her friend's baffled face. By the time she reached Moss Street and turned in at the close that bore Gilchrist Forbes' gleaming brass plate, she was staggering beneath the little boy's weight.

The receptionist, seated in her small office behind its sheltering glass window, was speaking on the telephone. She flicked a cool glance in Isla's general direction, then her eyes widened and she began to scramble from her chair as Isla, ignoring her, marched round the corner into the open waiting area outside the offices.

Sunlight poured in through the windows of Gilchrist Forbes' large office. He and his son, bending over papers on the large desk, looked up as Isla burst into the room.

'Nobody's going to take my child away from me – nobody!'

Colin's exasperated, 'For goodness' sake, not again!'

clashed with the receptionist's, 'I couldn't stop her, Mr
Forbes, she just—'

Gilchrist Forbes held up a hand for silence, looking
at the distraught young woman who had just invaded
his office, realising that she was on the verge of hysteria. 'Sit down, Mrs Moffatt. Miss Lang, could we have
some tea? And perhaps you could take the little boy into
your own office and keep him amu—'

'No!' Isla glared at him over Ross's head. 'He's staying with me!'

'Very well.' Forbes nodded at the receptionist, who
withdrew with an offended sniff, then he picked up
some blank sheets of paper and a pencil from the desk,
and held them out to Ross.

'Would you like to draw pictures, young man? Over
here, where your mother can keep an eye on you.' He
took a stool from a corner and placed it in a puddle of
sunlight. Isla hesitated, then released the little boy, who
went at once to the stool and knelt down on the carpet,
reaching for the pencil the lawyer held out to him. The
sunlight turned his downbent head into a mass of dancing flames and the sight of the nape of his neck, soft
and innocent, wrenched at Isla's heart. She couldn't
bear the thought of losing him.

'Mr Forbes, you're not going to take my son away
from me. I won't let you!'

Father and son exchanged puzzled looks. 'Why
should we want to do that?' the older man said mildly.

'Mrs McAdam . . .' Then, seeing that both men
were bewildered, Isla said, slowly and carefully, 'Mrs
McAdam came to my house this afternoon. She w-
wants . . .' The horror of the meeting swept over her

again and her voice began to waver. 'She wants Ross.'

'You mean that she offered to adopt your child?'
Colin asked.

'She just wanted him! She said that he was a
McAdam, he had Kenneth's blood in him and she could
give him things that I couldn't. She said that you'd –
you'd come for him tomorrow, with an agreement for
me to sign. She wants to b-buy . . .' Despite the warmth
of the room Isla had begun to shiver.

The door opened and Colin Forbes hurried forward
to take the tray from the receptionist. He poured tea
then put a cup into Isla's hand and said, in the gentlest
voice she had ever heard from him, 'Drink this, Mrs
Moffatt.'

The hot sweet tea began to revive her and the shivering eased. She looked up to see Ross sinking his small
white teeth into a biscuit, the crumbs glittering in the
sunlight as they sprayed towards the carpet.

'Ross, look at the mess you're making . . .' she began
automatically, but Gilchrist Forbes put a hand up to
stop her.

'Never mind the mess, m'dear, just tell us exactly
what Mrs McAdam said to you.'

Isla forced her mind back to the confrontation, speaking haltingly at first, then faster as she relived the scene.
By the time she had finished she had begun to shake
again.

'Nobody can make me give up my children. I won't
let them!'

'You've got nothing to fear, Mrs Moffatt,' Gilchrist
assured her. 'Nobody can take your children from you
without your permission.'

'I've heard of folk in George Street who've had their bairns taken from them.'

'Only if they were unable to care for the children, or if they ill treated them. Only if it was in the children's interests, surely?' He spoke gently, but to Isla's ears the words were condescending, easily voiced by a man who had never known the insecurity caused by hardship or the gnawing worry over where his next meal was to come from.

'It's not as simple as that, Mr Forbes,' she told him sharply. 'Not if you've got no money behind you and the folk with the power decide otherwise. Mrs McAdam, for instance – she's right when she says that she can give Ross more than I can, but that doesn't mean that she can love him more than I do.'

Ross, his cheeks bulging with biscuit, came over to lean against her. She put her arm about him and hugged his small body to her. The thought of him, ill or alone in a strange big house, calling in vain for her, was more than she could bear. 'She doesn't look to me like a woman who could love a wee bairn properly,' she said to the two men, the tears beginning to flow again. 'She doesn't look to me like a woman who could love anyone.'

At his father's request, Colin Forbes drove Isla back to George Street in his smart car with its smell of leather seats. The children playing in the street and the women leaning against the close-mouths, arms folded, gaped as first Ross then Isla got out.

'Are you all right?' Colin Forbes asked from the car's interior. 'Do you want me to come into the house with you?'

215

'We're fine, thank you.' He had been kind to Ross, courteous towards Isla, but the irritation was still there, every time he looked at her or spoke to her. The last thing she wanted was to spend more time in his company.

'My father will be in touch with you tomorrow,' he said, and drove off as soon as she closed the door.

Barbara sped out of the close, Greta at her heels. 'Mummy, where've you been?'

'I goed in a motor car,' Ross bragged to her, pulling back on Isla's hand to watch the car disappearing along the road as she hurried him into the close, away from prying eyes.

'Phemie,' Gilchrist Forbes asked as soon as he got home, 'did you tell Catherine McAdam where Kenneth's other – other wife lives?'

'Of course not – as if I'd do a cruel thing like that!'

'But she knows?'

His wife, setting the table for the evening meal, paused in her work. 'She told me that she'd heard about the woman, though I can't think how, since she never goes out.'

'What else did she say?'

'Nothing.' Her eyes brightened with curiosity. 'Why? Has something happened?'

'Nothing of any great importance.'

Phemie almost stamped a plump foot on the carpet. 'It has – it must have. Gilchrist, are you going to give me that nonsense about lawyers' confidences again?'

'No, my dear—'

'Because if you are, mebbe it's time I started thinking about lawyers' wives' confidences too. I don't know,' Phemie said, thumping knives and forks down on the table, 'it's one thing when you want to know something from me, and quite another when I ask you anything—'

'Dinner smells good, mother,' Colin said from the doorway.

'It'll be ready in twenty minutes. Colin, what's your father hiding from me now?'

'Hiding?' her son asked, his face expressionless.

'Men!' She glared, then shooed them out of the room. 'If you're not going to tell me what's going on, you might at least have the decency to get out from under my feet when I'm busy!'

They went willingly to the small library, where Colin said as soon as he closed the door, 'You surely don't believe what that woman told us today?'

Gilchrist was already pouring whisky into two glasses. 'Mrs Moffatt is a client of ours, Colin, and she has a name.'

'She had another name before that – but it turned out to belong to someone else.'

'That's enough,' Gilchrist said sharply, handing a glass to his son. 'I don't know why you have to be so disapproving. If an old fogey like me can accept the idea of a bigamous marriage without blinking, I don't see why a modern young man like yourself should make such a song and dance about it.'

Colin, suddenly reminded of Isla Moffatt's laughter in the dark, smelly close, her voice pointing out that Ainslie must have other reasons for ending their engagement, swallowed down a mouthful of fine malt

217

whisky. 'Being modern has nothing to do with it. She should never have come to Paisley.'

'But she did come to Paisley, and she's our client, and we must do our best by her. Whatever his faults, I believe that McAdam cared for her, and as his friend as well as his lawyer, it's my place to do the best I can for the girl. She's got nobody else.'

'Being the mother of his children doesn't give her the right to make accusations against his lawful widow.'

The older man walked to the window and looked out on the side drive where a red brick wall was covered with yellow climbing roses. After a long moment he said, 'Colin, Catherine McAdam telephoned just after you and Mrs Moffatt left the office. She told Miss Lang that she wanted me to call on her tomorrow morning at eleven o'clock.' He emptied his glass and turned to look at his son. 'To deal with an urgent and very important personal matter on her behalf.'

Colin stared for a moment, then asked, 'What are you going to do?'

Gilchrist Forbes sighed, and moved to his favourite chair, suddenly feeling very weary.

'I think that I must have a talk with Ainslie first,' he said. 'Tomorrow, at her place of work, so that Catherine knows nothing about it.'

Isla took both children into the wall-bed with her that night and lay sleeplessly staring into the darkness. It was a warm night, and the little room was stiflingly hot; the children tossed and mumbled in their sleep, faces and hair damp with sweat, throwing their arms and legs wide, digging sharp little knees and elbows into her.

Every time footsteps approached the close-mouth, or a car or cart came along the road, she sat upright, convinced that Catherine McAdam had sent someone to steal Ross away from her.

She walked to school with Barbara and Greta in the morning, then went along to Castlehead, where Flora immediately whisked her into the dolls'-house room to show her some bits and pieces she had found that might be of use for the *Little Women* house, which was already coming along well.

'She's been ferretin' in every cupboard and every drawer,' Annie said gloomily from the doorway. 'I'm at my wit's end, following her round and tidying up after her.'

'Nobody asked you to,' Flora snapped. 'I'm not in my dotage yet – I can do my own tidying.' She laid ribbons and buttons and costume jewellery and cardboard before Isla, who looked on listlessly, reacting only when Annie tried to take Ross into the kitchen.

'He's fine here, with me.' She put an arm about the little boy and drew him to her, lying to the two puzzled faces, 'He was a bit crabbit this morning. I think he might be coming down with a chill.'

Annie and Flora looked at Ross's clear eyes and happy grin, then at each other.

'Whatever you think best, dear – Annie can bring his drink of milk in here, then.' Flora signalled to the servant, who withdrew, a hurt expression on her round face. 'Is there something worrying you?' Flora ventured when the maid had gone.

'No, nothing,' Isla told her, and Flora said no more. When she took him back to George Street, Isla couldn't bear to let Ross play outside with the other children. He stormed and stamped, then bawled when she smacked him, and she gathered him up in her arms and cried along with him, rocking and kissing and soothing him until he fell asleep.

'What's amiss with ye?' Magret wanted to know when she came in and found the two of them huddled in the chair.

'I'm fine.'

'Ye've been out of sorts since ye burned those scones yesterday.' She waited, then when no explanation was forthcoming said, 'I'll make us a nice cup of tea.'

'Where's Daisy?'

'She's fallen sound asleep on the rug by the fire, bless her. She was up half the night with her teeth. She'll be fine on her own for a minute,' Magret said comfortably. Watching her as she gathered the cups together and took the muslin cover off the milk jug, Isla envied the other woman her placid assumption that Daisy, alone, was safe from harm.

Ross woke just then, and again demanded to be allowed out to play. 'Ach, let him go,' Magret advised. 'He needs the fresh air, don't ye, pet?'

'I'll go outside too. It's a nice afternoon . . .' Isla picked up one of the chairs standing by the table.

'Aye, all right, on ye go. I'll bring the tea out, and fetch Daisy.'

The afternoon was pleasantly warm and there were quite a few women enjoying the sun, some sitting on the close steps, some on chairs and stools they had brought out, others 'windae-hingin' ', leaning out of open windows, their forearms supported by cushions or blankets

220

laid on the window-sills. While they gossiped and laughed and lifted their faces to the sun and yelled at their children, Isla kept her gaze fixed on Ross.

Catherine McAdam had spoken the truth when she said that she could give the little boy much more than Isla could. Was she being unfair to him, she wondered, craning her neck round the bulk of a woman who happened to move between them, afraid to lose sight of him for a minute. Should she put her own selfish need of him aside and let him have the chance of growing up in a big house and getting a fine education? What would Kenneth have wanted for his son? She had a terrible suspicion that he would have wanted Ross to have all the things that his legal wife was offering.

'It's all right, hen, yer wean'll no' catch somethin' nasty just 'cause he's mixin' with the likes of our bairns,' the woman who had blocked her view said sharply, and Isla drew back, flushing.

'I just – Ross, come back here,' she called as he ventured a few yards further along the pavement. Magret and the other women exchanged looks, and exchanged them again when the time for the schoolchildren to be let out drew near and Isla got up and announced that she was going to fetch Barbara.

'Ye don't want tae go runnin' after yer weans all the time, hen,' someone advised. 'They'll only get spoiled.'

'I feel like the walk. Come on, Ross.'

'Ach, let him play,' Magret said comfortably, from her seat on the hollowed stone step leading to the close. 'I'll keep an eye on him.'

'No, he's to come with me. Ross, did you hear me? And stop dragging your feet like that, you'll ruin your shoes!' Isla ordered as the little boy left his friends reluctantly and went to her, his bottom lip sticking out and his toes scuffing along the pavement. She took his hand, pulling him along behind her as she hurried towards the corner of Maxwellton Street, where the West School stood.

'Yew'll ruin yewr shoes,' she heard someone mimic as she went, and there was a ripple of laughter from the women at the close-mouth. Most of their children played barefoot in the summer, and a few went barefoot through the winter too.

'Hoity-toity!' someone else said loudly. The tears that were never far from the surface now burned Isla's eyes as she walked on. It had been hard enough to win the friendship and trust of those women. If it hadn't been for the peg dolls she had made for their daughters, some of them would still be ignoring her. She was aware that her sudden possessiveness towards her children would only remind them that she was indeed an outsider, but what else, she wondered in despair, could she do? Gilchrist Forbes had been reassuring on the previous day, but his wife was a friend of Catherine McAdam's. He might be put under pressure to help Catherine rather than Isla. His son would have no difficulty in deciding between herself and Ainslie's mother, Isla thought bitterly.

By this time even the most possessive of mothers had stopped coming to fetch their children home, so she and Ross waited alone outside the school railings. Isla fidgeted, looking up and down the road every few seconds, half expecting to see Catherine McAdam, all in black, bearing down on them.

At last, a handbell clanged within the school, and a few seconds later one or two children came running out of the main door. More and more followed, until the playground was seething with them. Isla, clutching Ross with one hand and the railings with the other, strained for a glimpse of Barbara's tawny head, waving and shouting when she finally saw it.

Barbara, like Ross, came to her reluctantly, not at all pleased to see her mother waiting for her. 'What're you doing here?' she wanted to know, brows drawn down between hostile brown eyes. Greta trailed at her back, as usual.

'We thought it would be nice to walk back with you.'

Barbara gave her mother a withering look. 'Nobody's mummy comes to fetch them home! Come on, Greta,' she ordered, and ran ahead, heels flying and her curly hair, now quite long, bouncing on her shoulders. Ross, who had dragged behind Isla all the way to the school, made a futile attempt to break free of her imprisoning hand, then, unable to get away, tried to pull Isla along in an effort to catch up with his sister and Greta.

As they went, Isla turned her tired mind to Magret. It wasn't possible to keep secrets from her neighbour, she knew from experience. The safest course was to tell her something, though not necessarily everything. Isla began to put together the story of a nameless woman who had lost her son in the Glen Cinema tragedy, and after seeing Ross playing out in the street, had recognised a similarity to her own dead child and offered to raise him in the other boy's place. Isla knew that by telling that story she could enlist Magret's support in her struggle to keep Ross safe.

223

Her life, she thought wryly as Ross hauled her round the corner and into George Street, was beginning to sound like a novelette.

Gilchrist Forbes himself arrived not long after Isla got home, stepping out of his car, tipping his hat courteously to the staring women still gathered round the close-mouth.

Isla, in the middle of making the evening meal, motioned him to a chair, wiping her hands nervously on her pinny. He put his hat and cane on the table and smiled at her. 'I've come to put your mind at rest.'

She sank into a chair. 'You mean she can't take Ross away from me?'

'There was never any question of that, my dear. Mrs McAdam is – unwell. None of us realised just how unwell she was, until now. She got it into her head that you had been sent to Paisley by some higher agency, so that she could adopt your son in place of her own. I've explained to her that she cannot possibly do this.'

'But did she listen to you? She might try again—'

He held up a reassuring hand. 'I've already made arrangements for a nurse-companion to care for Mrs McAdam until such time as she recovers from her illness.'

He looked strained, Isla thought with compassion. 'Can I make you some tea, Mr Forbes?'

'It's a kind thought, but my wife expects me home. Besides . . .' he smiled down at Barbara and Ross, 'You've got your hands full. The companion I mentioned will take up her duties tomorrow, and in the meantime Ainslie will stay with her mother.' He got to his feet, saying as he reached for his hat and stick, 'She's asked me to tell you that she's extremely upset over the worry you've had.'

'Ainslie?' Isla was scarcely able to keep the disbelief from her voice.

'I can assure you, Mrs Moffatt, that she was very upset when I spoke to her this morning. Like the rest of us, she had no idea that her brother's death had had such an effect on her mother. I feel very sorry for Ainslie,' he said thoughtfully, as he left. 'She's not had an easy life lately.'

19

A few nights later, when the children were in bed and asleep, someone knocked at the door. Isla, who hadn't recovered from the fright Catherine McAdam had given her, felt her heart turn over beneath her ribs with a painful wrench.

The trousers she had been darning for Ross fell from her limp fingers to her knee, then to the floor as she pressed her body back into the chair, hoping that whoever waited outside would go away and leave her in peace.

The knock came again, more insistently. Afraid that the children would be wakened, she got up and opened the door an inch, peering through the small space, ready to slam it shut again if need be.

'Who is it?'

'Ainslie McAdam.'

'Go away,' Isla said against the crack. 'I want nothing to do with you or your family. Leave us in peace!'

'I've not come to cause trouble. I have to talk to you.'

Reluctantly, Isla opened the door, and the girl came into the room, pulling her close-fitting hat off to let her red hair fall loosely about her face.

'Are your children asleep?'

Isla nodded, watching her warily. The arrogance had gone out of Ainslie McAdam's face; as she stepped into the pool of light shed by the gas mantles above the fireplace Isla saw that her eyes were shadowed, and the skin beneath them was shaded a delicate violet, as though she too had been enduring sleepless nights.

The official year of mourning for Kenneth McAdam was over, and Isla had discarded her black armband. She would have thought that Ainslie would now be in mourning for her brother, but the girl wore a slim skirt in a deep violet shade, with a silky tailored jacket patterned with small violet and white squares. On any other redhead, violet might have been garish, but on Ainslie, it looked stylish.

The two young women eyed each other warily for a moment, then Ainslie lifted her hands away from her sides, palms out, in a helpless gesture. 'I'm sorry. I'm so sorry. I had no idea of what was in my mother's mind, none at all, until Mr Forbes told me.' Then, as Isla said nothing, 'I don't blame you for not believing me, but it's the truth. She's been in a bad way since my brother's death, but she seemed to be coming out of it. I thought that she was improving. Instead she was thinking up this – this nonsense about replacing him with your wee boy. You'll hear no more about it, I promise you.'

'How can I believe you? How can I be sure?'

'I don't blame you for mistrusting me. You've had a bad time at the hands of the McAdams, haven't you?'

'You needn't presume to speak for your father. I don't regret a moment of the time I shared with him.'

Ainslie's eyes flared with surprise – just as Kenneth's did, Isla thought, as she had thought the first time she and Ainslie set eyes on each other. Her lips tightened, and for a moment she was the Ainslie that Isla knew, arrogant and bitter. Then the look was gone. She dipped a hand into her jacket pocket, then laid a small paper-wrapped package on the table.

'This is for the children,' she said, then went past Isla towards the door, leaving the faint scent of floral perfume in her wake. At the door, she paused. 'May I call again, when things have settled down?'

'I don't see that—'

'Please,' Ainslie said. 'I need to talk to you. I need to talk about my father.'

'If you want to,' Isla said, against her own instincts.

As the click of Ainslie's smart shoes faded away along the pavement, she hoped that that might be the end of the matter. She didn't believe that the girl would come back. She herself would prefer it if Ainslie stayed away, for she had had more than enough of Kenneth's other family. They might hold her to blame for their own troubles, but they themselves had caused her more heartbreak than she wanted in one lifetime.

She picked up the small packet from the table. It smelled faintly of moth-balls and the light scent Ainslie had worn. When she pulled at the ribbon tied around it, the wrapping paper fell away to reveal two books. The first was a sturdy, brightly coloured picture book, designed for a child of Ross's age, depicting balls and kittens, kites and building bricks. The second had imaginative, well-drawn pictures and a simple story that Barbara could read for herself.

Opening it, Isla caught her breath as her eyes fell on a few words in a firm, familiar handwriting that she would have known anywhere. The few short, treasured notes Kenneth had written to her in that same hand during their brief courtship were still in her possession.

'To Ainslie Isobel McAdam,' the words said. '12th October, 1912, from her father, Kenneth Innes McAdam.'

A gift from Kenneth to his daughter. A gift that had clearly been cherished and cared for over the years, and had now been handed over as a peace offering to his other, secret daughter.

The promises made by both Ainslie and the lawyer held. Catherine McAdam didn't come back to George Street, but Isla had had such a fright that it was several weeks before she allowed herself to believe that the threat no longer existed, and Ross could safely play with his friends without her constant supervision. By then the damage had been done; although Magret remained loyal to her, the other women in the street had decided amongst themselves that Isla Moffatt thought herself better than they were, and they took to turning away when she walked down the street, or making loud asides to each other in her presence about folk who thought they were something they weren't.

'Ach, it's just the way they are,' Magret said. 'Pay no heed.'

Fortunately, the antagonism towards Isla didn't extend to the children, who continued to be accepted by their friends. The school summer holidays began and Barbara, at home all day, passed the time by organising another back-court concert.

Lena McNab, the handsome woman who lived across the close and owned the little bakery down the road, went regularly with her young husband to the Paisley Theatre in Smithhills, and took great pleasure in teaching Barbara the songs she heard at the music hall, even coming round the counter, if the shop was quiet, to dance a few steps. Barbara often came back from the bakery with another song.

'Hello, hello,' she would warble, setting down the loaf she had been sent to buy and dancing across the floor, Ross jigging up and down in her wake. 'Who's your lady friend? Who's the little girlie by your side?' Or, linking her arm with some difficulty through his, she would break into, 'Roamin' in the gloamin'.'

Unfortunately, willing though Ross was, he had none of his sister's sense of rhythm, and when he was involved, the songs usually ended with the two of them falling over because Ross had moved the wrong way, or Barbara being put off the melody by his enthusiastic, noisy off-key renderings.

'She's a natural wee music-hall turn, that lassie of yours,' Mrs McNab told Isla when she went into the bakery. 'She should go on to the halls herself one of these days.'

Isla smiled, and nodded, and wondered what Kenneth would have made of it all.

To her surprise, Ainslie came back again, and as the summer went on, her visits took on a weekly pattern. At first they talked about Paisley, Barbara and Ross, books, the auction rooms, Flora Currie's dolls' houses, circling round each other warily, keeping well away from any subject that affected them deeply.

Noticing how relaxed and animated the girl became when she talked about her work at the auction rooms, Isla suspected that life wasn't easy, had perhaps never been entirely easy, for Kenneth's elder daughter. She couldn't understand why this should be, because Kenneth had been a loving and demonstrative father to Barbara and Ross. She had often asked him teasingly what his business colleagues would say if they saw him playing with the children, or cuddling them both on his lap while he read to them.

Now that she thought of it, he had never really responded to those questions, fobbing them off with a smile, or changing the subject.

The sight of Ainslie walking down the road and into the close, smartly dressed and clearly from a different world, only added to the other women's suspicions that Isla was a 'neb in the air'. She explained her new visitor to Magret by saying that Ainslie was the daughter of the household where she worked, and then had to admit the lie to Ainslie herself.

'Just in case the two of you meet, and she says something. I sometimes feel as though I'm living two separate lives, but if the people round here knew that I owned this building they'd never accept me, and there's nowhere else for us to go just now.' She looked round the shabby room. 'It's still up for sale, but who would want it?'

'My father would be turning in his grave if he knew that his flesh and blood were living in a place like this.'

'It's not his fault.' Isla immediately went on the defensive. 'He signed the building over to me so that I'd have some income coming in – he didn't dream that we'd have to live in it.'

'He should have taken the trouble to think things through.' There was suddenly more than a hint of Ainslie's former arrogance in her voice. 'Because of him you're having to struggle along on hardly any money and tell your neighbours all sorts of untruths.'

Isla was ironing, using the table in place of an ironing board, with an old blanket folded on it to protect it from the heat. Now she set the flat-iron on its end with a thump. 'If you're going to insult your father's memory, this isn't the place to do it,' she said quietly. 'I'll not allow anyone to speak ill of him in my hearing, especially his own daughter.'

'You're beginning to sound like all the rest. Just because he was my father it doesn't mean that I have to idolise his memory. Folk should earn respect, not take it for granted.'

'Earn it? The man educated you, clothed you, fed you – and provided a nice home into the bargain. If that's not earning respect, I don't know what is!'

Ainslie's fair skin flushed crimson at the criticism. 'Are you saying that having money makes everything all right?'

'I'm saying that you should be grateful for what Kenneth did for you, and give some thought to what he must have gone through in the last weeks of his life.'

'He brought it on himself. If he hadn't been trying to support two families—' Ainslie stopped, a hand flying to her mouth, then said, 'I'm sorry, I shouldn't have said such a thing, not to you.'

Isla pushed a straggle of black hair back from her forehead. Now the truth was coming to the surface. 'Yes, you should. It's why you came here, isn't it? To try to understand your father?' The words that had gone through her mind again and again in the past thirteen months came easily to her lips. 'If only he'd told me about his worries, I'd have done all I could to help.'

'How could he tell you, of all people?'

'That's what makes it worse – thinking for five years that everything was open and honest between us, then discovering that it was all—'

'All lies?'

Isla shook her head and sat down at the table, the ironing forgotten. 'He didn't lie. He made up a story in his own mind about the way he wanted things to be, and then he tried to live it, with me.'

Ainslie, in the fireside chair, looked down at the hands clasped round her knees. 'And my mother and Innes and I were left outside, in the real life that he didn't want.'

'I didn't mean that. You were his daughter.'

'But that doesn't mean that he loved me! Oh, he liked Innes well enough, but that was because he was a boy.'

'What about the lovely books you gave the children? They were his gifts to you.'

'Where we live, everyone has nicely bound books on show. My father wanted me to have the right books, that was all.'

'You're wrong, Ainslie. Kenneth loved his children. I

mind the patience he had with Barbara, spending hours
with her on his knee, reading stories to her—'

'How nice for Barbara.' The girl jumped up and
reached blindly for her bag and her gloves. 'At least he
cared for one of his daughters—'

'Ainslie, I didn't mean – Ainslie!'

But the door had opened and closed, and Isla was
alone.

'Tell me about Kenneth McAdam.'

Flora Currie blinked at Isla, then said, 'You surely
know more about him than I did.'

They were working on the *Little Women* dolls' house,
Flora, with glue and cardboard and narrow strips of
beading, making a frame for a tiny sampler that Isla had
drawn with coloured crayons, Isla brushing pieces of
wall-paper with flour and water paste and pressing them
into place on the parlour walls.

She told Flora, briefly, about her conversation with
Ainslie on the previous day, ending with, 'I'm not asking you to gossip, or tell tales. I just think it's time I
knew more about the man I thought I was married to
for five years.'

'We all present different faces to different people, my
dear.'

'I know that – goodness knows I do it myself all the
time these days,' Isla said wryly, 'what with paying
myself rent for a building I own, and changing my
name. But for my own sake – and the children's – I
have to understand him better. For instance, *my*
Kenneth wouldn't have made money out of renting
rooms in tired old buildings to folk who have no choice

but to live there. But the Kenneth that Ainslie knew did that.'

'A lot of folk make money out of owning homes they'd not live in themselves. It's the way of the world,' Flora said evasively.

Isla, realising that the older woman heartily disliked talking to her about Kenneth, changed tack. 'Tell me about his – about Ainslie's mother, then.'

'Catherine? Her people were well off, and I mind that everyone thought it a very suitable match, though my brother Arnold – you mind I said he and Kenneth had been friends – was surprised at Catherine choosing Kenneth. He said that she'd not had much time for him before. I saw her on her wedding day, and she looked radiant. The next time I saw her was at her father-in-law's funeral, and then she looked quite ill. She wasn't long past Ainslie's birth at the time, as I remember.'

She paused to collect her thoughts, then said, 'When Catherine's parents died, I heard that she wanted to move into their big house, but Kenneth would have none of it. I don't think he could have afforded the upkeep. Catherine could – she inherited quite a lot from them – but he'd not have wanted to live on his wife's money. Come to think of it, that might have been what finished his own business, trying to show Catherine that he could make a lot of money. I always felt a bit sorry for Kenneth – I don't think he ever felt comfortable with the life he led.'

Flora Currie's words fitted in with what Isla herself had said to Ainslie about Kenneth inventing a world, and sharing it with her. Waiting for sleep to come that night, she mulled over them. He seemed to have been so many things – a husband who wasn't a husband at all, a loving father who hadn't, it seemed, shown much love towards his older children, a caring man who charged rent for sub-standard housing he had made no effort to improve.

Ross muttered, and she got up and looked into the cot. He was sound asleep, twisted in the sheet, the pillow wedged alongside him. Lifting his head and slipping the pillow beneath it, she wondered if she had ever really known Kenneth at all.

20

Mr Leckie, the toyshop owner who had spoken to Flora at the auction sale, called on her unexpectedly one day to see the half-completed *Little Women* house, and met Isla.

'You have an interesting talent, Mrs Moffatt. I wonder – would you be interested in decorating another little house for me when you've finished this one? Something simple and straightforward, that I can put on show to advertise the furniture and houses I sell.'

'Surely you could do that yourself.'

The man shook his head. 'I'm not talking about just putting furniture into a doll's house, Mrs Moffatt. Anyone can do that, but you have the ability to create a home in miniature.'

'I quite agree,' said Flora. 'Of course you must do it, Isla.'

'I'll supply the house,' the shopkeeper added as Isla hesitated. 'And the furniture, though I'd leave the choice of furnishings entirely to you, and pay for any other materials you may need.'

'But I haven't got anywhere to work on it.'

'Yes, you have,' Flora said firmly. 'You'll work here. She'll do it, Mr Leckie.'

'I can't use your home as a workplace,' Isla protested when the man had gone.

'Nonsense, I enjoy seeing you and the children, and so does Annie, though she'd rather die than admit it. And now you'll be earning some money – you can do with that, surely.'

'At least it means that I can afford to pay you for the use of your premises.'

Flora looked shocked at the very idea. 'My dear girl, it's me who should be paying you for the interest you've brought into my life. Your visits are the only thing that have kept me going, since poor Agnes passed away.'

Flora's neighbour, a woman she had known for many years, had died after a long illness, and now the house next door lay silent and empty, waiting for the next-of-kin to decide what was to be done with it.

'It reminds me of my own mortality every time I see the closed door and the curtains pulled across the windows,' Flora Currie had told Isla with a shiver not long after the funeral. 'Poor Agnes was such a lively woman before her illness, always popping in.'

Young Mr Kelly upstairs lost his job again and couldn't get another. He and his little wife began to look more and more desperate, and Mrs Leach looked more and more like a dragon.

Going into the wash-house one day, Isla hesitated as she heard the woman's voice from inside, nagging and complaining. She turned and went quietly back into the close. 'She was going on at poor Mrs Kelly about how she should never have married him,' she told Magret later.

'She's a right bitch, so she is. I'm heart-sorry for that

lassie. It's bad enough havin' yer man out of work without yer ma going on and on about it. It's not her fault, poor soul – or his.'

The Kellys fell behind with their rent, and Isla refused to let Colin Forbes, who was still collecting the rents, threaten them with eviction. 'He's doing his best to find work – where's the sense in making their lives more difficult by making threats, or putting them out?' she asked.

'People have to pay their way, Mrs Moffatt.'

'The Kellys have every intention of paying their way. They're not deliberately trying to cheat – they're not committing a crime, so why punish them?'

Colin Forbes glared. 'Mrs Moffatt, you keep asking me about repairs – when can the roof be fixed, when can the close be lit. D'you not understand that nothing can be done unless you yourself have the money to do it? And you'll not get the money while you protect tenants who don't pay!'

'In that case, wouldn't it make more sense to try to find work for Mr Kelly than to put him out of his home?' she shot back at him. 'The man's an office worker, and from what I know of him I'm quite sure very conscientious. Is there any chance of finding him a place with Forbes and Son?'

'Not at the moment. And even if there was, would it be wise to put him where he might learn who owns this building?'

She hadn't thought of that. She stuttered for a moment, confused, then rallied as she saw the cold smile on his lips. 'There are other offices. You might be able to place him elsewhere.'

'I'm a lawyer, Mrs Moffatt, not a nursemaid,' he said, and slapped the rentbook shut.

Without Gilchrist Forbes' help, Ainslie would never have been able to persuade her mother to let the nurse-companion into the house. Gilchrist, under the guise of bringing papers for Catherine to sign, talked of a respectable woman of his acquaintance, fallen on hard times through no fault of her own, searching for a position as a useful companion to some lady, and by the time he set down his empty teacup, Catherine herself had suggested that, with Ainslie busy about her own affairs, it would be pleasant for her to have someone else in the house, other than the servants.

Ann Dove, a woman of about Catherine's own age, calmly and with just the right amount of meekness, submitted to being ordered about, but Ainslie was acutely embarrassed by her mother's high-handed attitude.

'You're a nurse, not a servant,' she protested to the woman when Catherine was out of earshot.

'Your mother doesn't know that, does she? She's a very sad woman, Miss McAdam, and a lonely one – through no fault of yours,' Miss Dove added swiftly as she saw the stricken look on Ainslie's face. 'It's just part of being the sort of person she is. She needs someone to order around, and it's better that it's me and not you. And don't worry,' she added with a faint smile, 'if things get too bad, I can look after myself.'

Her presence in the house eased Ainslie's life a great deal, giving her freedom to concentrate on her work. She hadn't gone back to Isla's house since leaving it in

a rage a few weeks earlier. She wanted to, but at the
same time, she was wary at what she might find out if
she and Isla really talked to each other.

Colin called, and found her in the front garden,
weeding a flower bed. Walking up the drive, he looked
beyond her kneeling figure and saw that the curtains
were looped back from the windows. Daylight had at
last been permitted back into the house.

At the sound of footsteps on the gravel Ainslie looked
up, then scrambled to her feet, smiling. Her hair was
escaping from the green ribbon that tied it back, to curl
round her face like little flames.

'Are you here on business?'

'Strictly for pleasure, to see you.'

'Would you like to come in? Or we could sit in the
summer-house.'

He opted for the summer-house, and as they walked
round the side of the house together she dusted the soil
from her hands then took off the heavy apron she had
been wearing.

'Mother isn't pleased,' she said as she saw him glance
at her white and green dress. 'She thinks I should be in
mourning black for Innes, but I've had enough of
mourning. In any case, I don't think Innes would have
wanted us to dress in black for him.'

'How is your mother?' he asked as they stepped into
the summer-house's cool shade.

'The nurse is very good with her. I'm grateful to
your father for finding her.' She flicked a sidelong
glance at him, then asked, 'Did you know that Mother
had been drinking?'

'What?' He stared at her in disbelief.

'I knew that she was taking rather a lot of the tonic wine the doctor recommended to get her strength up, and that she had a glass of brandy sometimes. But I didn't think that . . .' She stopped, then said, 'It was Miss Dove – the nurse – who told me. Apparently the servants knew, because they were the ones who bought the bottles for her, and disposed of them. But they couldn't bring themselves to tell me, poor souls. I thought your father might have said something to you.'

Colin was appalled at the thought of Mrs McAdam, always the lady, turning to drink. 'Not a word. He probably wanted to protect your mother, but I wish I'd known, for your sake. You've been through hell over the past year or so, haven't you?'

'If it hadn't been for the auction rooms and the people there, I would probably be fighting Mother for the brandy bottle,' Ainslie agreed, with a faint laugh. She picked a leaf from her skirt and smoothed it between her fingers, staring intently down at it. 'Isla Moffatt says that my father loved her children,' she said suddenly. 'He played with them.' She began to shred the leaf, tearing tiny neat strips from it. 'It wasn't that he didn't have any love to give, Colin. He'd just chosen to give it to another wife and other children.'

'Everything comes back to Isla Moffatt, doesn't it?' Colin rose abruptly and paced to the door. After the shadows, the sun was almost like a blow against his face and arm. 'If she hadn't come to Paisley—'

'That's what I thought at first. But now,' Ainslie said, 'I'm not so sure. It hurts to learn the truth, but it's the only way forward. And that's the way I'm going from now on, Colin. Forwards.'

In the shade of the summer-house, her face swam like a water-lily within the glow of her hair. Looking down on her, Colin Forbes accepted, at last, that there was no chance now of Ainslie marrying him.

The day after Colin's visit, Ainslie went back to George Street, stepping round groups of children squatting on cracked paving stones warmed by the sun, forging her way through the huddle of women snatching what fresh air they could at the close-mouth. She stood at Isla's door, fists thrust into the pockets of the sleeveless jacket she wore, and said, 'No matter how it hurts, I want to know the truth about my father.'

Isla had been washing clothes at the sink, and her face was flushed with heat, her hair wisping across her cheeks. She stepped back, drying her hands on her crossover pinny. 'Come in,' she said.

'I wanted him to love me,' Ainslie told Isla an hour later, getting the words out at last. 'All my life I tried so hard to earn his love. That's why it hurt when I realised he'd given it freely to your daughter. Now, I'm beginning to think that my mother stood between us, for reasons of her own. She tried to stand between me and Innes, even after he died. She's always wanted to possess people, and she's always been afraid of them loving each other, because she thought that that would shut her out.'

'Poor soul. It must be terrible to be afraid all the time.'

Ainslie shot Isla a startled glance, then said, 'They should probably never have married. Mother was disappointed in my father, and perhaps he withdrew

243

because he knew it. So she turned all her ambition on Innes instead.'

Isla, wringing out the last of the small clothes she had been washing, shivered inside at the thought of the misery Ross might have suffered in Catherine's hands. 'People aren't made of Plasticine. Try to shape them against their natures, and you'll only end up misshaping them.'

Ainslie ran a hand over the back of her neck, lifting her hair to let what little air there was cool her. It had been a long afternoon and she felt bone-weary, but also as though she was on the road to recovery after a serious illness.

She and Isla had been ruthlessly honest with each other; Ainslie had heard about the human side of her father, a side she had never been privileged to see in all the twenty-one years she had known him, while Isla had discovered the darker side of his nature, the cold, reserved husband and father, the ruthless businessman.

'That's probably why he wanted another marriage, with you,' Ainslie said now. 'You knew nothing of his background or his family. You accepted him as he was, without criticism. What are you doing?' she added as Isla opened out the ungainly wooden clothes-horse and began to hang the wet clothes on it. 'It's a lovely day, they'd dry in half an hour if you put them outside.'

'You've never lived in a tenement, have you? This is Mrs Kelly's day for the washlines.'

'She might not be using all the line.'

'Even so, this is her day, not mine,' Isla said, and went on with her work.

Ainslie watched for a moment, then asked, 'D'you feel any differently towards my father now that you know more about him?'

Isla took time to consider. It had been hard to face the fact that her Kenneth had been so different, so uncaring, in his other life. But she still had her own memories of him to offset these pictures.

'He was a human being,' she said at last, 'and no human being's perfect.' She glanced up at the cracked, stained ceiling then at the warped window frame and the dripping sink, and the corners of her mouth turned down. 'I'm a fine one to talk – this place is mine now, and I haven't done any more to improve it than he did.'

'That's another responsibility he put on your shoulders – looking after this place. We're all what he made us, when you think of it,' Ainslie said thoughtfully. 'You and me, and Mother too. All McAdam's women. And there's your Barbara as well.'

'I doubt if anyone could influence Barbara,' Isla told her dryly. 'She's got a mind of her own.'

'Are you going to tell the children the truth about Father?'

'Mebbe one day, when they're grown up, if I think they can take it and understand. But not for a long time.'

As though on cue, the children arrived at that moment, hot and grimy from play, in search of food, but hanging back a little at the sight of Ainslie.

'I haven't had time to make anything yet,' Isla told them, fetching a loaf and a half-full jar of jam.

'I'm thirsty,' Barbara whined, and Ross, his eyes fixed on Ainslie, joined in.

'Make up your minds.' Isla paused, about to cut

slices from the loaf. 'I can't do both things at once.'

Ainslie got to her feet and took the breadknife from her. 'You get them something to drink,' she said. 'I'll see to the bread and jam. After that, I wouldn't mind a cup of tea. I think we've both earned one.'

In September, the *Little Women* house was finished and borne off by Mr Leckie, who brought with him another house for Isla to work on, and a box of furniture. He gave her a fair price for the finished house, and Flora insisted on Isla taking all the money.

'All I contributed was bits and pieces that were already here,' she said when Isla protested. 'The Victorian house was a gift, and I can't even remember where the other one came from. You did all the work.'

Isla, who badly needed the money, finally gave in, and they started to sift through the box of furniture from the toyshop.

'It's awful plain,' Isla said when they had finished.

'Make your own furniture, then, the way you did for the others. Mr Leckie said you could alter it if you wanted.'

'The other houses were just for show, but this one's supposed to be played with, so it needs good solid furniture. But I'd like something better than this. Something – different.' She frowned down at the sturdy little table she was holding.

'Mebbe we could find someone who's good with his hands,' Flora suggested. And suddenly Isla remembered Drew Brown, sitting on the steps in the back court, using the point of his penknife to shape a proper face for Barbara's peg doll.

She took the table back to George Street with her, and went up to his flat that evening, while the children were playing with Greta and Daisy in Magret's flat. It was raining, and too wet for them to be outside.

Isla had never gone to the upper floor before. The stone steps were hollowed in the centre, and she had to feel her way up, her outstretched hands pressed against the chill, damp walls. Drew himself opened the door, peering into the gloom. 'Mam, it's Mrs Moffatt,' he called, and his mother appeared at once, looking anxious.

'Come in,' she said, then, as Drew moved back to let Isla in, 'is there something wrong?'

'No, it's Drew I really came to see.' Isla stepped into the little flat, and instantly recognised the smell of damp. A metal bucket stood on newspapers, yellowed with age, against the outside wall near the sink, water dripping into it with a continuous, steady tinny little beat.

'You've got a bad leak there.'

'Only when it rains,' Drew said with a bleak grin, while his mother explained, 'The roof's rotten.'

'Have you not complained about it?'

Mrs Brown shrugged. 'Early on I did, but it wasnae any use. Now I just don't bother.'

'When did it start?'

'Och, three or four years ago,' the woman told her vaguely. 'We're used tae it. Ye'll have a cup of tea, Mrs Moffatt?'

'I can't stay, the children'll be looking for me soon.' Isla remembered why she had called, and held out the little table she had brought. 'Drew, could you do something with this for me? Mebbe carve the legs into a

247

better shape, full at the top here, then tapering down, with the feet curved.'

'You mean like a bandy-legged woman with nice neat ankles? I've seen that sort somewhere. Table, not woman,' he added hurriedly as his mother, shocked, said, 'Drew!'

'Could you do it?'

He studied the little table, running his thumb down over the legs. 'I think so.'

'I'll pay you for it.'

'Wait till we see if I can do it first,' the boy said, but his face was alight with interest as he studied the tiny table, and she could see that he was longing to start work.

'I think you should have another word with the factor,' she said as she left.

'I don't want to be a nuisance . . .' Mrs Brown began.

'I keep tellin' her that the man that owns this place'll be living in a grand house that doesn't leak when the rain comes,' Drew said.

The contempt in his words rang in Isla's ears as she felt her way back down the dark stairs. When the roof first started leaking, Kenneth had had the money to repair it, she thought. But there was no sense in dwelling on the faults of a man who was dead and no longer able to defend himself. She was the landlord now, and it was up to her to do what she could.

21

After careful calculation Isla divided the money Mr Leckie had given her into three lots. One was for Drew, if he managed to alter the table for her, another for herself and the children. She took the third sum with her when she went on the following Monday to collect the rent money. When she asked if she could see Mr Forbes, the receptionist shook her head.

'He's not in the office just now. Mr Colin's here, though.'

'I'd better see him, then,' Isla said without enthusiasm.

Colin Forbes stared at the coins she put on his desk. 'What's this?'

'Mrs Brown's ceiling's been leaking since I first moved here. The roof badly needs repairing.'

He frowned. 'Mrs Brown's not complained to us.'

'If she had, what would you have done?'

'I suppose we'd have had to pass the matter on to you.'

'The poor soul's scared that if she makes too much fuss she'll mebbe be put out. It's easier for her to keep emptying a bucket, and do without the use of that part of her living-room. Her son sleeps in the other room, and I've a suspicion that the rain gets in there too.'

He pushed the coins around with a forefinger. 'There's not nearly enough here to get the work done.'

'I know, but you can keep that safe for me until I can afford to give you the rest.'

'Mrs Moffatt,' he said, the familiar exasperation in his voice, 'your money would be better spent on your children.'

'I can assure you that my children are well cared for, Mr Forbes.' Isla indicated Ross, who had climbed on to a chair and was looking out of the window. 'Does he look under-nourished and neglected?'

'No,' he admitted, then, leaning forward and eyeing her, 'but you don't look as well as you might be.'

'There's nothing wrong with me!'

'A few days by the sea might do you good. You could use the money for that.'

'I'm too busy earning the rest of the money for the roof repairs.'

He looked as though he was going to go on arguing, then shrugged. 'Very well, if that's what you want, I'll see that it's put away safely, and recorded.' As she rose to go, he added, 'By the way, a friend of my father's with an office in Incle Street has an opening for a clerk. I've passed Mr Kelly's name to him.'

To Isla's delight, Drew managed to carve the plain little table into something graceful and delicate, even varnishing it before handing it over. More and more dissatisfied with the solid, unimaginative furniture Mr Leckie had given her, she asked the boy if he could make a chaise longue for one of the rooms. Together, they pored over a book he had brought from the library, then, using scraps of wood from the workshop where he was employed, Drew managed to provide just what she wanted.

Isla padded and covered the little piece of furniture, working at nights after the children were asleep. She had to work standing at the mantel on most nights, for the gas light above the mantelshelf was poor, and the work she was doing was very fine. By the time she fell into bed her legs and ankles were sore and stiff. But the chaise longue was perfect, and Flora's admiration the next day made all the work worthwhile.

Spurred on by the need to get the roof repaired before the winter came, Isla gave Drew more furniture to work on, and spent as much time as she could on the new doll's house. Her eyes felt sore and tired, and she began to suffer from headaches caused by the amount of time she spent on the detailed work of stitching tiny cushions and curtains.

'Ye'll make yersel' ill,' Annie said bluntly, leaning against the frame of the dolls'-house room door, arms folded, and Flora nodded.

'She's right, my dear, you look pale. You need to take a day off now and again. Why not take the children up to Brodie Park for some fresh air?'

'They're outside most of the time, and I get plenty of fresh air walking round here and home again,' Isla told them. Now that the little house represented much-needed money, she lay awake at nights, planning the next day's work, and hurried round to Castlehead as soon as she could in the mornings.

Magret nagged at her about not eating properly.

'It's too hot to eat,' Isla told her shortly. The early autumn was unusually warm and dry, and although the continual smell from the drains didn't seem to affect the children as badly as it affected Isla herself, she fretted in case they caught some disease from the poor sewerage. It seemed to her, sometimes, that she worried about everything. She finished the little house for Mr Leckie, and the toyshop owner, delighted with it, had promised to put more work her way. Even so, Isla fretted. Earning some money of her own, even a little, had made all the difference, and there was no jewellery left to pawn. If Mr Leckie didn't give her more work, she didn't know what she would do.

It was because her mind was full of such concerns that she didn't see the tram bearing down on her as she crossed the High Street on her way to collect the rent money one Monday morning. Alerted by a sudden jangling of bells, and shouting from the driver, frantically leaning on his brake, she finally looked up, too late.

Colin Forbes had just arrived in his office and was opening the window to let some air into the stuffy room when he glanced down in time to see the cowcatcher in front of the tram hit a young woman. Her body was tossed through the air like a discarded rag doll, and as it landed in the gutter her head glanced off the kerb.

'My God!' He ran from the office, almost knocking the receptionist over as she came through the door, a pile of envelopes in her hand.

'Telephone for the ambulance wagon,' he shouted into her startled face, and ran on, through the door and down the stairs and across the road to where a policeman was pushing his way through the gathering crowd. The officer knelt down beside the woman in the road, slipping an arm under her shoulders.

Her head lolled against his sleeve and Colin, breaking through the people who had gathered, recognised Isla Moffatt, her eyes closed and her face as white as paper, apart from a ribbon of shining crimson blood that crawled, slowly but steadily, down her face from the wound in her forehead.

'Slight concussion,' the ward sister said briskly. 'Nothing to worry about, but the doctor wants you to stay with us for a few days.' Her professional smile faded when Isla, dazed and confused, struggled to get up. 'Now don't be silly, dear.'

'My children – I have to see to my children!'

'They're fine.' The sister tucked Isla back into bed, pulling the blankets tightly over her. 'A Miss McAdam came to visit you earlier, while you were sleeping. She says you're not to worry, the children are being well looked after.'

'Better do as she says, hen, they're a bossy lot in here,' a voice said from the next bed as the sister moved away on silent feet. Isla began to turn her head, but stopped as pain washed through it. Putting a hand up to the source of the pain, she felt a padded bandage across her forehead, then sleep came, and she drifted away from the big, high-ceilinged room into nowhere.

Pictures came to her as she floated in and out of sleep – uniformed nurses crossing and re-crossing her line of vision like ships in sail, a balding man in a neat suit with a gold chain strung across his waistcoat bending over her, a woman with an elaborate feathered hat perched on her head marching past, carrying a bunch of flowers – they had come and gone before she could register them. It reminded her of her childhood, and rides on the merry-go-round's painted horses when the shows came. Up and down and round and round, clutching tightly to the pole that grew out of the back of the horse she rode, daringly freeing one hand to wave to her parents as they came into sight then fell away again.

'I must take the children to the shows,' she said aloud, and was startled when a familiar voice replied, 'That's a good idea.'

Isla's lids lifted and she looked up into Flora Currie's green eyes. 'What are you doing here?' she asked, confused and still thinking of the merry-go-round.

'I'm visiting you. You had a nasty accident crossing the road, but you're fine now, and so are the children. They're staying at my house – you'll see them in a day or so, when you're better. Annie sent some home-made scones, they're on your locker. And Ainslie will be in to visit you tomorrow.'

When she had gone, Isla slept again, wakening once or twice during the night to the sound of snoring and an occasional groan or mumbled sentence from the beds around her. A voice called a man's name plaintively further up the long ward and a nurse went past, a silent ghost in the dimly lit ward. The voice stopped, and Isla slept again, until she was wakened to face the day.

Her head still ached, but the confusion had left her, and when the doctor made his rounds she begged to be allowed home.

'You had a nasty crack on the head, and we want to

be quite sure that you're over it. Besides,' a frown crossed his face, 'you're in sore need of rest and nourishment. You've not been feeding yourself properly, have you?'

She started to protest, but he cut in with, 'It won't hurt you to be cosseted for a day or two,' and turned back to the group deferentially waiting for him at the foot of the bed. As they moved off, Isla heard him murmur something about women who allowed themselves to become rundown.

The woman in the next bed heard it too. 'It's all right for the likes of them to criticise,' she said with a sniff, then lowered her voice slightly, as the ward sister turned and looked sharply at her before hurrying after the doctor. 'They don't know what it's like, do they? What sort of mother would feed herself and leave her kids hungry?' Then, settling herself comfortably, 'But what can't be cured must be endured, eh? Make the most of it, hen – that's my advice.'

The long narrow ward, with its double row of beds and its uniformed nurses, brought back memories of Isla's training in Edinburgh. All she had wanted then was to become a nurse, perhaps rising to the post of ward sister or even matron, one day. But Kenneth McAdam had been brought into her ward from the operating theatre when she was halfway through the course, after being struck down with appendicitis during a business trip to Edinburgh. And from that moment, her life had changed.

Ainslie came in that afternoon, turning patients' and visitors' heads as she walked up the long ward. She was dressed in a blue knee-length skirt with knife pleats at the front, and a long V-necked blouse in the same colour, with a geometric pattern in gold, and a gold leather belt around her waist. Her vivid hair was tied back at the nape of her neck with a blue ribbon, and a beret dipped rakishly over one ear. She had developed new confidence, Isla thought, watching her approach the bed. Ainslie was coming to terms with herself.

She put a small basket of fruit on top of the locker. 'I'd have brought flowers, but you're not going to be here long enough to enjoy them.' Her eyes swept over Isla and she said bluntly, 'I hadn't realised that you'd got so thin.'

Isla hurriedly tucked her arms beneath the sheet. 'I'm not thin!'

'The ward sister told Miss Currie that you were under-nourished.'

'It's just this hot weather. Nobody feels like eating when it's hot. How are the children?' Isla asked anxiously. 'Have you seen them?'

'I saw them last night, and this morning too. Your neighbour told me what had happened when I called on you, and where the children were, so I went round to Castlehead. They're very well. Missing you, of course, but they know you'll be back soon. Isla, we've been talking – me and Miss Currie and Annie – and we all think that you should have a wee holiday when you come out of hospital.'

'How could I afford that?'

'Colin told me about you giving him money to have the roof repaired. You'd be better spending it on yourself.'

'But the work needs to be done. And it needs to be done before the winter comes.'

Ainslie fidgeted, then said, almost guiltily, 'Miss Currie's written to your aunt to tell her what's happened.'

'She hasn't!'

'She found the address in your house when she was getting the children's things. It's all right,' she added hurriedly, 'she just said you'd been widowed, and that you're living in Paisley now. And you'd had a wee accident, but you're fine.'

Isla stared at her in dismay. She didn't want Aunt Lally to know the truth about Kenneth, or about the struggle she had had since his death.

Ainslie and Colin Forbes took her home on the following day. Barbara, waiting on the pavement, jigging from one foot to the other in a frenzy of impatience, threw herself at Isla as soon as she got out of the car, but Ross hung back for a moment, finger in mouth, unsure of this white-faced mother with a sticking plaster on her forehead.

'We've been staying in Miss Currie's house,' Barbara said in a rush of words. 'We had a bedroom all to ourselves and a big bed, where's your bandage, Miss Currie said you'd have a bandage . . .'

'I don't need it any more. Ross?' Isla held her hand out to the little boy, just as Magret arrived at the close-mouth, her round face wreathed in smiles. Ross ducked his head and whirled round to bury himself in Magret's apron. Daisy, not to be outdone, followed suit.

'Ross!'

'Ach, they forget quick at his age,' Magret soothed. 'Come on in, hen, and sit down. I've got the kettle on. There's enough for everyb'dy,' she added, looking beyond Isla to where Ainslie and Colin stood.

'On you go, Isla. Barbara, carry your mother's case.' Ainslie handed the small cardboard case to the little girl. 'I'll come and see you this evening, when you've had time to settle in,' she said, and turned back to the car as Isla went into the close, Barbara clutching her hand and chattering like a little monkey. As she went, she was aware of the women at every window and every close-mouth up and down the street.

Ross released Magret's apron and shot across the room to climb on to his mother's lap as soon as they got into Magret's flat, while Magret herself, reaching for the condensed milk tin, confessed, 'It's just as well they couldnae stay, for there's no' enough cups. I didnae like tae say, though. Mind yer mammy's poor sore head, Ross,' she cautioned, but Isla hugged the little boy tightly.

'My head's all better. I'm all better,' she said, smiling at her children's anxious faces.

Even so, she was glad to go to bed early that night, and she felt so listless the next day that the thought of walking round to Castlehead was too much. Instead, Flora called on her, her face wrinkled with concern.

'I'll be fine tomorrow,' Isla assured her, but she wasn't. It was as though she had come up against a brick wall that refused to allow her to get on with her life. She recalled that the ward sister had warned her about this just before she left the Infirmary.

'It'll take some time before you get back to your old self, Mrs Moffatt. The accident wasn't serious, but you've worn yourself out, and you need a longer rest than you've had here.'

'I've not been doing nearly as much as most women,' Isla had argued. It was true – some of her neighbours had large families to cope with, some had sick parents or in-laws staying with them, others went out to work or took in laundry or sewing in addition to caring for their husbands and children.

'Mebbe not, but there are other ways of exhausting yourself, and continual worry's one of them. You'll have to be kind to yourself for a while,' the woman had advised.

Isla felt that the kindest thing she could do for herself was to get on with her life, but the harder she tried to spur herself on, the more difficult it became.

When a letter arrived from Edinburgh, informing her that Aunt Lally would like to see her again, and to meet the children if she cared to bring them to Edinburgh for a short visit, both Ainslie and Flora Currie urged her to accept.

'But what about Barbara's schooling?'

'She could stay with me,' Flora suggested, but Isla had got such a fright over almost losing Ross that she refused to go to Edinburgh without Barbara.

She thought that that was the end of the matter, but Ainslie went with her to the school, where the head-mistress agreed, under the circumstances, to let Barbara take two weeks off.

'She's a quick learner. If you take her school books with you, Mrs Moffatt, and undertake to see that she does some work while she's away, that would be accept-able.'

Colin Forbes called to hand back the money Isla had given him for the roof repairs, and suggest that Forbes and Son should advance the money needed to cover the most essential repairs, recovering it from the proceeds when a buyer came forward for the building.

'But it's been over a year now, and nobody's put in an offer,' Isla pointed out, adding suspiciously, 'has Ainslie put you up to this? Or Miss Currie?'

He had been pleasant to her on the day he drove her home from the hospital, but now the usual edge came into his voice and the usual irritated gleam darkened his hazel eyes. 'It's often done in business, Mrs Moffatt. You'll get more for the place if it's seen that some work's being carried out on it, and it's in our interest to try to sell at a good price because of our commission. Since you're determined to get the roof repairs done soon, my father and I feel that we should do what we can to help. But only insofar as the essential work is concerned,' he added hastily. 'It would cost more than the whole building's worth to have all the roof repairs carried out.'

'As long as Mrs Brown and her son can escape the worst of the rain when it comes,' Isla said, and couldn't help adding, 'at least you'll get a bit of peace while I'm in Edinburgh.'

He flushed. 'I don't know what you mean, Mrs Moffatt.'

That night Isla wrote to Aunt Lally to let her know that she and the children would arrive the following week.

'You're no sooner back home than you're gone again,' Magret lamented.

'That's what I think too, but so many folk are nagging at me to go to Edinburgh that I might as well give
in. Anyway, Aunt Lally seems to be eager to see the
children. Mebbe she's mellowed in her old age.'

Magret offered to lend a battered old suitcase for the
journey. 'It's only used to keep the bairns' winter jerseys
in below the bed,' she explained, 'and they'll not come
to any harm wrapped up in paper for a wee while.'

22

Barbara and Ross gaped in amazement as their great-aunt Lally Moffatt came sailing towards them in Edinburgh's Waverley Station. She had scarcely changed in the six years since Isla had last seen her. She was still tall and commanding, straight of back and large of bosom, and she still favoured startlingly bright colours and floating, wispy scarves.

On this occasion, she was dressed in a scarlet calf-length dress topped by a pale-grey overtunic splashed with embroidered roses. Crimson feathers drifted from her grey hat, and a red feather boa rustled round her throat and floated in her wake.

'Isla, my dear!' Isla was enveloped in a perfumed embrace, her face briefly smothered against the boa, then released, to be held back at arms' length and studied through narrowed blue eyes. 'Your friend was right when she wrote to say that you needed a holiday. You look like something the cat dragged in,' Lally announced in ringing tones that had once reached to the back of theatre galleries with ease. Heads turned all up and down the platform.

'And these are your little ones! Darlings, come to your auntie!' Lally stooped with an ominous creaking of stays and swept a child into each arm. When she released them, Ross sneezed.

'It's the feathers,' Barbara explained, bright-eyed. 'They got up his nose. Mine too.'

'How sweet!' her great-aunt trumpeted, and spun round, her eyes searching the platform. 'Porter!'

More heads turned. 'We only have two small cases,' Isla protested, embarrassed by the attention they were attracting. 'I can carry them.'

'Nonsense, a lady should never carry her own luggage – remember that, little girl,' Lally added to Barbara, who nodded eagerly, standing on one leg and bending the other back to catch her foot in one hand.

'I can hop. I can hop all down the platform.'

A porter was already scuttling eagerly up to them. 'Kangaroos hop, young ladies walk, head up and shoulders back,' said Lally. 'Come along!' And she set off down the platform, Barbara forging along by her side, and the porter trotting behind her.

Following, Ross's hand clutched in hers, Isla began to wonder if she had the strength to spend two weeks in Aunt Lally's company.

Lally Moffatt had lived in the same first-floor flat in a handsome tenement building ever since Isla could remember. Climbing the stairs, she recalled her aunt's claim that the flat had been bought for her by a wealthy admirer during her days in the music hall chorus, and wondered again if it was true.

The flat hadn't changed much, and the children's

mouths rounded, as well as their eyes, when they went inside. The living-room walls were covered with framed paintings, photographs, decorative plates, bows, bunches of dried flowers, fans, and programmes. Every piece of furniture held more photographs, albums, books, vases filled with more dried flowers, gloves, more decorative plates, and fancy little boxes. Even the mirror over the cluttered fireplace had its share of cards and programmes pushed into the frame. Footwear – shoes and slippers in patent leather, kid, suede, satin, velvet, buckskin, lizardskin, and snakeskin – stood in rows along the skirting board.

'Nothing's changed,' Isla said in wonder.

'I believe I've collected a few more mementoes.' Lally unpinned her hat and tossed it carelessly on to a chair already overflowing with hats, gloves, and long scarves. Her hair, which Isla remembered as daffodil yellow, was now pure white, still cut short, level with her ears. Her mouth was a bright pink cupid's bow, and her eyebrows had been plucked out and replaced by delicate arches, pencilled in. 'Now then' – she clapped her hands briskly together – 'let's have some tea!'

'Yes!' said Ross, and trotted after her as she marched off to the small kitchen. Barbara stayed where she was, still turning round slowly to take everything in.

'Look, Mummy, a piano!' She pointed to a corner of the high-ceilinged room where a small piano was almost hidden by the shawl that had been tossed over it. Barbara drew in a deep breath and let it out in a sigh, her eyes bright.

'I'm going to like staying here!' she said.

*

'I don't remember you making a fuss over me when I was small,' Isla said that night when the children had been put to bed and she and her aunt were sipping sherry on either side of the fireplace. Lally's raised eyebrows disappeared under her fringe.

'Don't tell me you're jealous of your own children!'

'Of course not, just making an observation.'

'For one thing I'm much older, and old age tends to yearn towards youth. For another, your two are really quite beautiful, whereas I remember you as a quiet, dark, sallow little girl. Such a pity you didn't take after me and your father, instead of your mother.'

'Mother was lovely.'

'She was, wasn't she, bless her,' Lally remembered, her face softening. 'But she was of Italian parentage, my dear. She still had the Mediterranean sun on her cheeks, like the bloom on black grapes. You never had that at all. You still don't.'

'We don't get a lot of sun in Paisley,' Isla said dryly.

'Your hair doesn't help – all that dark stuff round that wee pale face. You should get it bobbed.' Then, seeing Isla's involuntary glance at her own uncompromising short cut, Lally said, 'Don't worry, it'll not look like a chopped field the way mine does. You've got nice soft hair, it would lie in well round your face.'

'Mebbe so, but I've got more to do with my money than spend it on myself.'

'There's a friend of mine . . .' Lally had always had friends who could turn their hands to everything, Isla remembered. 'A dresser she was, but she could cut hair very well. She once trimmed Marie Lloyd's hair in an

emergency, and there was never a complaint. She'd do
it for nothing.'

'I'll think about it.'

'Your little ones, now – what wonderful hair! Their
father was a very handsome man, as I remember from
our two brief meetings. What happened?' Lally asked so
abruptly that Isla was disconcerted for a moment.

'He – he died. If you remember, he was older than I
was.'

'Why take up your own name again?'

'I just wanted to,' Isla said shortly.

Lally gave her a long shrewd look from beneath darkened eyelashes, then shrugged, and sipped at her sherry.
'You always were secretive – now that, you got from
your mother. D'you have plans to marry again?'

'Who would want a penniless widow with two children to support?'

'You'd be surprised.' The blue eyes studied her face.
'Whatever's happened to you, you've had to walk a
hard road. But you're still young enough to attract
men.'

'I've no wish to attract men.'

'Nonsense, there isn't a woman alive who doesn't
want to look her best,' Lally said briskly. 'You need fat-
tening up – and some stimulating company.'

'What I need is some peace and quiet.'

'Away you go, lassie,' said Lally Moffatt. 'At your
age?'

Later, in the small, crowded spare bedroom, Isla
tucked the blankets round Ross, who slept on a small
truckle bed, then turned out the gas mantle and climbed
into bed beside Barbara, who murmured sleepily and

turned over. Gradually her eyes became accustomed to the dark, and the silhouette of a macabre headless body, the tailor's dummy Lally had used in the old days to make her stage costumes on, outlined against the window.

Outside, she could dimly hear the hum of traffic passing along the main road two blocks further down, and the occasional motor car chugging its way along below the windows. With surprise, she realised that she felt homesick for the single room in George Street.

The bracing winds of Scotland's east coast seemed to blow Isla's cobwebs away. During the day she and Lally took the children to visit Edinburgh Castle and the Palace of Holyrood House, strolling down the narrow cobbled Royal Mile and along Princes Street to look in the shop windows, exploring Princes Street gardens and the warren of streets and closes in the Old Town.

Almost every night some of Lally's friends dropped in, for she loved company, and had always been famed for holding open house. Dressed in crêpe de Chine frocks with bold patterns and loose sleeves and floating sashes and scarves, a cigarette in a holder and a headdress thick with paste jewellery clamped on to her short white hair, Lally held court.

Most of her friends had been on the stage, or connected with the theatre, and almost every sentence began with 'D'you remember?' They laughed a lot and talked over each other, and spoiled the children outrageously.

Sometimes during the day Barbara and Ross went off with Lally and some of her friends, leaving Isla to enjoy some time to herself, and sometimes their great-aunt kept them amused in the house, teaching them songs and letting them dress up in the trunkfuls of stage clothes she had kept, so that Isla could wander round the streets and through the shops without worrying about them.

She never knew what would meet her when she came back from those trips. It could be a dramatic play, with the children tottering about in Lally's shoes, with dresses and jackets far too big for them falling off their shoulders and threatening to trip them up at every step. It could be a music hall turn, with Lally thumping out a song on the piano and the children strutting around the room with canes, Ross with his head tipped back so that he could see from under a top hat stuffed with newspaper, Barbara with her top hat wedged on by her hair, which had been bundled up for the occasion.

Once or twice Lally took the children to an afternoon matinee. Ross tended to fall asleep, but Barbara came back with eyes like saucers, able to recite most of the show, with some prompting from her great-aunt.

'She's got a marvellous memory, darling,' Lally enthused, 'And such style! She must have inherited it from me.'

Watching her daughter, a sailor hat tipped saucily over one eye, strutting across the living-room and bellowing out 'All the Nice Girls Love a Sailor', Isla had to agree with her. Barbara certainly hadn't inherited her outgoing personality from either of her parents.

Egged on by the children, Isla finally gave in to her aunt's insistence, and had her hair bobbed. She sat with her eyes closed, listening to the crunch of the scissors and the soft regretful sighing sound her hair made as it fell in clumps to the floor, where Barbara gathered it up. She thought, as Lally's friend worked, of how Kenneth had loved to loosen her hair at night and brush it for her, stopping now and again to bury his face in its softness, or lift it aside so that he could kiss the nape of her neck. A shiver ran through her at the memory, and the woman said at once, 'Did I hurt you?'

'No.' No sense in living in the past, Isla told herself. Lally was right, her hair would be easier to care for now, and that was all that mattered.

Even so, she was reluctant to open her eyes when the cutting was finished, despite the two women's assurances that she looked lovely. Barbara finally climbed on to her knee and said, her nose bumping Isla's, her breath tickling Isla's top lip, 'Look, Mummy, you're beautiful!'

Isla opened her eyes and found herself staring into her daughter's face. 'You're not made of glass, Barbara. I can't see through you.'

The little girl giggled, and squirmed round until she was sitting on Isla's lap. Looking into the mirror, Isla saw a neat, wide-eyed face, framed with dark wings that curved softly round on to her cheeks, staring back at her in astonishment.

'I look like a different person!'

Lally's friend, standing behind her, nodded her satisfaction, while Lally herself said, 'It's about time!'

In their second week in Edinburgh, Lally, who loved parties, held one to mark their visit, inviting all her theatrical friends. Barbara provided the entertainment all on her own, glowing at the applause that greeted each song.

Halfway through the evening, watching her children, particularly her daughter, being fussed over by all the adults, Isla knew that it was time to go back to Paisley, back to their usual life. Lally pouted when she announced the next day that it was time to start making plans for their return.

'But you've only just got here!'

'We've been here for almost two weeks, Aunt Lally, and that was the arrangement. Besides, Barbara has to get back to school.'

'Talking of Barbara,' Lally said slowly, flashing a quick look at her niece from beneath her lashes, 'she's a very talented little girl, Isla. Bertie was just saying the other day that she'd be a natural on the stage.'

'That depends on what she wants to do when she grows up.'

'But she ought to start as soon as possible. I was at elocution and dancing by the time I was her age.'

'Aunt Lally, I can't afford to pay for these things for Barbara, and even if I could, it would only set her apart from her friends. She's managed to make a place for herself in Paisley, and it wouldn't be fair to her to change things now.'

'Paisley! What chance will she have there? There are some excellent classes here in Edinburgh, and you can't deny that we have good schools – look at your own education.'

Isla put a hand up to the nape of her neck, and was astonished, as always, to touch skin instead of a heavy mass of hair. 'I've no intention of uprooting myself and the children again.'

'I'm not talking about the entire family being uprooted. Why don't you leave Barbara here with me, just for a year, until we see how things work out? I'll bear the cost of her education and her dance classes and singing classes. And for elocution too, she'll need that,' Lally went on as Isla stared at her. 'I still have some influence, you know. It could all be done on very little, and she deserves—'

'No!' The cold terror Isla had known when Catherine McAdam tried to take Ross away from her returned. The older woman looked at her in astonishment.

'My dear child, I'm not suggesting kidnap! I've no intention of coming between you and your daughter, I'm only asking you to give her one little year, to see how she does. I can guarantee that with the proper training now, she'll be a star in ten years – we'll be so proud of her—'

'No!' Isla, aware of the children in the next room, trying on Lally's clothes, fought to keep her voice calm. 'We've been through enough as it is, and all I want for Barbara is an ordinary upbringing.'

'But—'

'She's only a little girl, Aunt Lally. She has years ahead of her to make up her own mind. But not now, not yet – and don't try to persuade her,' she added swiftly as she saw her aunt's eyes narrowing. 'I'll not have it, no matter how much she pleads.'

'Do you realise what you're denying that child? She may well grow up to resent you for it.'

'That's a chance I have to take. I want her to grow up like any other child, and I know that that's what her father would have wanted, too.'

271

They eyed each other, then, 'Oh, very well,' Lally said at last, huffily. 'But I warn you, Isla, you're being most unfair!'

Barbara sulked when she was told that they were going home. 'But I like it here! Why can't we stay with Aunt Lally?'

'Because holidays don't go on forever,' Isla told her sharply, aware of her aunt's hurt looks.

The old fear of losing one of her children had been re-awakened, and she didn't feel entirely safe until the train was pulling out of Waverley Station, leaving Lally alone on the platform. Sinking back into her seat, Isla struggled to justify her decision to take Barbara back to Paisley. Lally was getting older, she couldn't possibly be expected to care for an active little girl, she told herself. Besides, she had had difficulty in getting Barbara to do her lessons every day. Barbara had objected, and Lally had supported her. If she left the child in Edinburgh for a whole year, she told herself as the train moved west-wards, the child would be quite illiterate.

But she knew that the truth was that the children were all she had in the world, all that was left of her life with Kenneth. And that, quite apart from the deep love she had for both of them, was very important to her.

'Ye'll never guess,' Magret said almost as soon as Isla got home. 'They've repaired the roof above the Browns' flat! Ye could have knocked the lot of us down with a feather when the men arrived and began to put up lad-ders.' She handed Isla a cup of her strong, sweet tinned-milk tea. 'I don't mind anyone doing any repairs on this place in all the time we've been here. Mrs Brown's fair thrilled about it.'

That evening, Drew came down to show Isla a small wardrobe that he had made. The interior was hollow, and the double doors opened. 'I minded you sayin' that you didnae like that solid wardrobe you had for the wee house, so I thought I'd see what I could do,' he explained, glowing with pride in his success and her pleasure. 'The hinges came from a box my mam had. And I've found another book in the library, and bought myself an exercise book so's I can copy the pictures down.'

'Look, it's even got a rail! Now I can make some clothes, and some cardboard hangers to put them on. You're clever, Drew!'

When she took some coins from her purse and insisted on paying for the wardrobe, Drew protested.

'Och no, you didnae ask me tae make this for you. You can just keep it.'

'I'm buying it,' she told him firmly. 'You deserve payment, and anyway, it means that I can feel free to ask you to do more, if I get another order for a house.'

'I enjoyed it,' he said as he gave in and took the money, then, 'did you hear that there's been some work done on the roof?'

'Mrs McDougall told me.'

'My mam's fair pleased,' Drew said happily. 'She cannae wait for the rain tae come, so that she can enjoy being dry.'

23

Annie beamed – a rare event – when she saw Isla on the doorstep. 'It's grand tae see ye back. She'll be fair pleased.' She nodded at the parlour door. 'She's in by.'

'Isla!' Flora Currie came forward with hands outstretched. 'My, your holiday's done you good – I've never seen you look so well. Your hair's very smart!'

Isla put a hand to her short hair. 'It was my aunt's idea, not mine. It still feels . . .' Her voice trailed away as a man got up from the chair by the window, his long body seeming to unfold in sections.

'Come and meet Philip Hannigan,' Flora said briskly. He towered over both women as she made the introductions, his teeth flashing white in a tanned face.

'My friends call me Phil. I'm very pleased to meet you.' He spoke in a soft, attractive drawl and her hand seemed to disappear into his.

'Phil comes from Canada,' Flora said proudly, as though she had made him all by herself. 'His great-aunt was my dear friend Agnes from next door. He's inherited her house.'

'You're going to settle here?'

'No, ma'am, I've got a timber business back home in

Ontario, and that's where I belong.' Philip Hannigan smiled down on his hostess. 'Miss Flora's been my guardian angel ever since I got here.'

'Och, away with you, man!' Flora flushed like a young girl. 'I just did what Agnes would have done for my kin if things had been the other way round. He's insisted on staying in that house on his own,' she explained to Isla. 'So of course I said he must have his meals with us. Ainslie McAdam's been a great help with sorting out the house – she's arranged for her employer to have a look at the furniture to see what should go for auction.'

'I'd like some of the furniture to be sold along with the house,' Phil put in. 'They sort of belong together, but Ainslie – Miss McAdam – thinks there's too much of it, and some of it should be disposed of separately.'

'Where are the children, Isla? I was looking forward to seeing them again.'

'Barbara's back at school, and Ross wanted to stay and play with Daisy. Barbara's learned a lot of new songs from Aunt Lally,' Isla said, half-ruefully. 'She's planning another back-court concert.'

'I told you that Isla's little girl was musically gifted, didn't I?' Flora asked Philip Hannigan.

The Canadian dipped his head in agreement. 'I'm looking forward to meeting both of them.'

'Isla, Mr Leckie's got a special order in for a dolls' house, from a customer who wants you to furnish it.'

'That's wonderful!'

'I said I was sure you'd want to do it, so he brought it the other day. His customer wants it for Christmas, and you can decide on the style.'

'I've heard all about your talent, Mrs Moffatt,' Phil Hannigan put in. 'It sounds to me as though you've got yourself quite a business there.'

'It's just a hobby.'

He shook his head. 'Don't you believe it. Finding out what folk want, then supplying it – that's how businesses begin.'

It would have been very easy to sit back and drown in that soft drawl, but Isla was longing to see the new house. When she excused herself Philip unwound himself from his chair, reaching the door before she did and holding it open for her.

'I look forward to meeting you again, Mrs Moffatt.'

'Isla.'

'Isla,' he agreed. 'It's a very pretty name.'

As she crossed the hall Isla glanced in the mirror and saw that she, too, was blushing. The man had that sort of effect on women, she decided, as she opened the door of the doll's-house room.

On the following Saturday, when Isla and the children arrived at Castlehead, Philip Hannigan and Ainslie were both in Flora's drawing-room, Ainslie equipped with a notebook and pencil.

'We're going to start making a list of the furniture that's going to auction. Come and have a look around,' the Canadian suggested. Isla hesitated. She had planned to spend her time at Castlehead making a mirror by glueing some tiny jet beads from an old necklace round silver paper stuck on to cardboard.

'I'm not going, because the house holds too many memories for me. But you should, Isla, you'd enjoy seeing round it,' Flora urged and she gave in.

Outside, Phil lifted the children over the hedge then swung his long legs over without any difficulty. Isla and Ainslie declined his offer of help, and took the longer route through Miss Currie's gate and along the pavement.

'He's a good-looking man, isn't he?' Ainslie murmured.

'Probably married.'

'Actually, no. Your holiday's done you good.'

'I ate far too much in Edinburgh.'

'You suit a little more weight.' Ainslie herself looked more relaxed. She wore a summer dress in pale blue, the same colour as her eyes, with an open jacket in navy to match the braiding at the dress's neck and hem.

'How is your mother?' Isla asked, formally, and a shadow passed over Ainslie's face.

'Her health has improved, but her mind . . .' She stopped, her hand on the gate leading to the neighbouring garden, then said, 'She seems to live in a world of her own making. She talks of nobody but Innes and my grandfather. She doesn't seem to be aware of my existence.'

'I'm sorry.'

For a moment Isla saw hurt in the other girl's gaze, then it was gone, hidden behind a mask of indifference as Ainslie opened the gate, then closed it behind them.

'It's that nurse I'm sorry for. Mother's become very arrogant, and she orders poor Miss Dove about all the time. Fortunately Miss Dove doesn't seem to mind, she treats Mother with just the right mixture of deference and firmness.'

'Come on, you two,' Phil called from the porch. As she went up the steps Ainslie tripped and Phil put out a hand to steady her.

'I'm all right,' she said hurriedly, pulling herself away. He raised an eyebrow.

'Do all Scottish girls hate being touched?'

She coloured. 'I don't hate it. I mean . . .'

'Only teasing. Come on in.' He stood back to let them pass, winking at Isla.

The house smelled musty, as though it hadn't been lived in for some time. The children were already on their way upstairs, Ross puffing in Barbara's wake.

'Let them go where they want,' Phil said easily when Isla called them back. 'Kids like to explore. I understand that Great-Aunt Agnes more or less lived in the drawing-room,' he went on, opening the door.

Isla, fascinated, moved about the stuffy room, edging round occasional tables, plant-pot stands, chairs and cabinets. She studied the massive sideboard, laden down with ornaments, then tipped her head back to look up at the ceiling and the cornices. The room was similar to Flora Currie's drawing-room, but not as square. There were alcoves on either side of the fireplace, and the window had more of a bay.

'It's a very graceful room, isn't it?' she said thoughtfully. 'This' – she put a hand on a small cabinet – 'suits it, and so does that corner cupboard, while this sideboard's out of place.'

'The room's big enough to take it,' Phil said.

'Yes, but the piece itself's far too big and clumsy for the lines of this room,' Isla told him, moving around, rejecting and selecting, while the other two watched.

'Try to imagine it with only a third of the furniture in it and most of the ornaments gone,' she said at last. 'Think how light and airy it would look then.'

'I quite agree,' said Colin Forbes from the doorway. She turned, and saw his eyes widen as he recognised her. 'Mrs Moffatt! I thought it was – you've done something to your hair,' he said feebly, and Ainslie laughed.

'Did you think we'd brought in an expert? I believe we have, at that. I didn't know you knew about interior design, Isla.'

'I don't, it's just that I . . .' Isla stopped on the verge of saying 'I learned a lot when Kenneth and I were furnishing our house', and changed it to, 'I like houses, and furniture.'

'I never did have any imagination,' Phil Hannigan admitted. 'I can only see what I see.'

'I understand what Isla means,' Ainslie said. 'You should shift most of this furniture out, Phil, but keep the pieces she mentioned. That'll make the house look more attractive, and easier to view as well. If the buyer doesn't want them, they can be auctioned off later.'

Forbes and Son were handling the sale of the house, and Colin, like Ainslie, had come on business, bringing notebook and pencil with him. They moved upstairs, and after taking a quick look round Isla left them there, Ainslie listing the furniture, Colin thumping walls and jumping on the floors, with the children's enthusiastic help, to test the joists. She slipped back down to the kitchen, where she washed the few dishes Phil had left in the sink. She was rinsing the dishcloth when Ainslie arrived.

'Here you are. Colin and I are going to drive Phil down to the Clyde coast this afternoon. Come with us.'

'I couldn't possibly . . .'

'The children too, they can sit on our laps, and I'm sure they'd love to see the sea,' Ainslie coaxed. Isla was shaking her head firmly when Barbara and Ross burst in, shouting, 'Mummy, we're going to the seaside!'

'Ainslie! You told them without asking me first!'

'I must have let it slip out,' Ainslie said guiltily, then brightened. 'You'll have to say yes now, won't you?'

They went to Barassie, where the car could be driven right on to a wide stretch of firm sand and the children could shed their socks and shoes and paddle in the shallow water. Ainslie went with them, while the two young men stayed by the car with Isla. They were from different worlds, she thought, looking at them. Colin Forbes, formal in a blue suit, with shirt and tie, stood staring out at the glittering water, while Phil, dressed casually in cream-coloured trousers and an open-necked checked shirt beneath a sleeveless tan pullover, sprawled bonelessly on the sand, completely at his ease.

'Look at the way the light catches their hair – they've all got the same colouring,' he marvelled, watching the three figures at the water's edge. 'They look more like Ainslie's kids than yours, Isla.'

There was an awkward silence, broken by Colin saying easily, 'Red hair's common among the Scots. By the way, Mrs Moffatt . . .'

'Is stuffiness common too? Calling Isla Mrs Moffatt,' Phil explained when Colin looked puzzled.

'Mrs Moffatt is a client.'

'So am I, but you call me Phil. What's the matter, don't you like each other?' The Canadian looked from one to the other, then grinned. 'Personally, I can't imagine anyone not liking Isla.'

If Isla hadn't been just as embarrassed as he was, she would have laughed at the mixture of expressions that chased each other across Colin Forbes' reddening face. Finally he said stiffly, 'As I was saying – Isla – I think we may have found a buyer for the tenement building.'

'Really?'

'I should be able to give you further details when you come to the office on Monday, but I need to be able to tell the prospective buyer whether the building's fully tenanted or not. Will you be moving out if you sell?'

'I don't see how I can.'

'Surely you'll be able to buy another place with the money you make from the sale?' Phil asked. His interest was so sincere that it didn't occur to Isla to feel annoyed at the question.

'I've already spent some of the money I'd get from a sale, paying for essential repairs. It would probably be wise to stay where I am, and invest the rest.'

'Why not make an offer for my great-aunt's house? It would be a great place to raise kids, with that backyard and all. And you'd have room to develop that dolls'-house business of yours.'

'I couldn't begin to afford a house like that!'

'Make me an offer,' he invited, and when she laughed, he persisted. 'Go on – I've not had any offers yet. You might as well be the first.'

'Five shillings is as much as I could afford.'

'Five shillings. There you go, Colin – the first bid's in.'

Colin Forbes grunted, and ran a finger round his constricting collar. He stooped and picked up a stick, flicking at the sand with it as he wandered down to the water's edge, where Ainslie and the children were playing.

'What's troubling Ainslie?' Phil asked when Colin was out of earshot. 'She flinched away like a startled deer when I tried to steady her back at the house. Made me feel she'd rather have been left to fall flat on her face.'

'She's – not had an easy time lately.'

'Uh-huh?' He settled his back more comfortably against the car wheel. 'I can't imagine why anyone would want to cause problems for a girl like that.'

The offer made for the tenement was lower than Isla had hoped.

'It's not a good time to be selling,' Colin Forbes explained. 'Ordinarily, we'd advise waiting in the hope of the market improving, but . . .'

'I can't afford to wait.' The repair bill for the roof was still haunting her. 'I'll have to take it.'

'And remain as a tenant?'

'I've no option. At least I can stop feeling guilty about the state of the place if I don't own it.'

'Then I'll get the papers drawn up, and let you know when they're ready for signature.'

Phil always seemed to be around when Isla went to Castlehead, and Ainslie was there often too, helping him to clear out cupboards and get the house ready for sale.

The lanky Canadian took a liking to Barbara and Ross, who both adored him, and somehow, without Isla knowing how it happened, the three of them – Phil, Ainslie and Isla, had fallen into the habit of taking the children on outings. Colin often accompanied them – so that he could be near Ainslie, Isla assumed.

To her consternation, Phil even turned up at Barbara's back-court concert with Ainslie, causing more than a ripple of excitement. The women were far more interested in him than in their children's talents, nudging each other and whispering amongst themselves. Phil, unabashed, tipped his hat and beamed at them all, then settled down to enjoy the concert, applauding each song loudly, and handing out coins afterwards to all the performers, who immediately ran off to the corner shop to buy sweeties.

'Ye've got some strange friends, Isla,' said Magret after he had gone, adding with a coy giggle, 'mind you, he's a fine-looking man, is he no'?'

'I think he's the nicest person in the whole world,' Barbara, flushed with the success of her concert, said indistinctly round a large peppermint ball.

One windy day, they all drove up to the top of the braes flanking Paisley to fly Colin's old kite.

'Phil likes your company,' Ainslie said as the two of them sat on the springy grass, watching the children jump about with excitement as the kite soared.

'He likes everyone, he's got that sort of nature. And if you're trying to matchmake you're wasting your time. I've become used to my independence, and I like it fine.'

'But think of it, Isla – life in Canada! The children would love it. Phil's got his own business, and a fine house, with beautiful countryside around it, and Lake Erie not far away.'

'He's been telling you a lot about himself, hasn't he?'

'I'm not the marrying kind,' Ainslie said at once.

'Neither am I, now.'

'Hey, look at this – it's going up to the sun!' Phil called as the two men skimmed past, Colin controlling the kite while Ross, on Phil's shoulders, reached up towards the dancing, colourful kite with one hand, and clutched Phil's thick hair with the other. Barbara raced alongside, her ribbon long since lost and her red hair streaming in the wind.

Following Isla's advice, Phil had the surplus furniture removed from his great-aunt's house and sold at auction. Left with only the smaller furniture, the house looked just as Isla had visualised it – spacious and elegant, despite the clean patches on the wallpaper where the furniture had stood for many years.

Phil, in plus-fours and a casual jacket, attended the sale, lounging at the back of the large auction room. Whenever Ainslie, who was assisting the clerk, found a moment to glance up from the lists she had to follow meticulously, he caught her eye and winked. Afterwards, he stayed behind and gave the men a hand to clear the room, carrying lots outside to pack on to carts and lorries, putting unsold goods back into storage. Then he joined them for a mug of strong tea.

'You did all right,' Charlie told him, and Phil shrugged. He was leaning against a wall, mug in hand, looking, as he always did, as though he belonged.

'It wasn't bad. To tell the truth, it goes against the grain, making money out of someone else's possessions. I prefer to know that what I've got was earned by my own efforts.'

Ainslie, eyeing the rangy Canadian, was taken by his relaxed self-confidence, his ease with his surroundings. Compared to him, the Scots seemed to be confined in invisible boxes, limited by self-imposed rules of behaviour.

'How do you get home?' he asked as they left the auction rooms together.

'By bus from the Cross.' Then she said impulsively, 'But today, I think I'd like to walk.'

'To the other side of the town? Won't your mother wonder where you've got to?'

'She won't notice,' Ainslie said, then, as they stepped out briskly together, she found herself telling him about her mother and about Innes. He was a good listener, and it seemed natural to go on to talk about her father, about giving Colin back his ring, about Isla, and her own guilt at having treated the other woman so badly when she first came to the town. She spoke freely of her need to make amends, to her half-brother and sister as well as to their mother. As she talked, the pavement seemed to skim past beneath their feet, and suddenly they were standing at her gate. She felt tired after the long walk, but it was a good, healthy tiredness, as though all the talking had cleansed and eased her.

'I wish I could invite you in for tea, Phil, but . . .'

'I understand.' He looked beyond her, to the garden and the house, then back at her face. 'This doesn't look like the right sort of place for you. It's too closed in.'

She turned to study the house where she had been born and raised. 'I feel that way too, whenever I'm in it.'

'Tell me, d'you feel bad about breaking off your engagement to Colin?'

'Yes, but I still think that it was the right thing to do.' She held her hand out. 'Thank you for being such a good listener, Phil.'

His hand was reassuring as it clasped hers. 'Any time,' he said, then released her, flipped a finger at the brim of his soft hat, and swung round, walking away with that long, unhurried step she had found easy to adopt.

For once, there was no feeling of apprehension as Ainslie went through the front door. She felt warm and at ease – and safe.

24

Isla handed the pen over, and watched as Colin Forbes scribbled his own name as witness to her signature. Over the past week or two, thrown into his company more than before, she had discovered that he could be much nicer than she had thought possible.

She had seen him glancing at Ainslie when he thought he was unobserved, and had recognised the look on his face. It was clear, in those brief, private glances, that he knew that he had lost Ainslie McAdam for ever, and was still coming to terms with the truth. Isla knew what that was like. By selling the tenement she herself had broken another of the few, delicate strands that still linked her to Kenneth.

'When the money comes through, we can discuss what you want to do with it.' His voice broke through her thoughts.

'I'm hoping that we'll be able to live on it for at least two more years. Once Ross goes to school, I'll be free to look for paid employment.'

The little boy, standing by the window where he could look down on the passing tramcars, turned at the

sound of his name and came to her. She smiled down at
him, smoothing back his hair.

'You'll not make much from the sale.'

'I've learned a lot about managing on very little
money,' she said wryly, getting to her feet. 'Most of the
folk in George Street are experts at that.'

It was ironic that just as Isla had sold the tenement,
Mrs Leach discovered that she had owned it.

The woman came storming down the street, battered
shopping bag in hand, just as Isla and Magret, on their
way back from the bakery, reached the close.

'So – what's like tae be a landlord, then?' she shouted
from several yards away. Mrs Kelly, her daughter, trotted just behind her, pale and anxious. 'You – I'm talkin'
tae ye!' A hand caught Isla's shoulder, pulling her back
as she was about to step into the close. Ross, who had
been running ahead with Daisy, came back to his
mother, his small face tight with concern.

'Let go of me!'

'Did ye know?' Mrs Leach swung round on Magret.
'Did ye know that it's her that owns this building? It's
her we pay our rents tae—'

'Ach, away wi' ye,' Magret scoffed. 'Don't be so daft.
Isla's in the same boat as the rest of us – she's tryin' tae
raise two weans on her own.'

'Mam—' Mrs Kelly plucked at her mother's sleeve.
Mrs Leach threw her off with a twitch of the arm.

'Her that's let the place fall down about our ears
while she lives on our money!'

'Ye're haverin'!' Magret was getting angry. 'Look at
the lassie. Does she look like a landlord?'

'She looks like a sly wee besom, that's what she looks like,' Mrs Leach roared back. By now there wasn't a window without a face framed in it, not a close-mouth without its group of staring women.

'I don't own anything!'

Mrs Leach sniffed. 'Not now ye don't. But ye did, didn't ye? Oh, ye thought ye were so clever, pretendin' tae be a poor wee widow. But I've found ye out – I've got yer measure now, milady. There's no' much can be kept hidden from me!'

'Tell her she's haverin', Isla,' Magret said contemptuously.

'Haverin', am I?' Mrs Leach caught her daughter's arm and pulled the distraught girl forward. 'And what about her man, was he haverin' tae, when he heard in the very office where he works that she's the one that owns this building?'

'Mam, I told ye that in confidence,' Mrs Kelly whimpered, but her mother wasn't interested.

'Tell the truth and shame the devil,' she shouted to the gathering audience. 'That's the way I was brought up.'

Magret began to waver. 'It's no' true, is it?' she asked Isla. 'It cannae be true!'

Ross, clinging to Isla's legs, started to wail, and she put a hand on his head. 'It's all right, pet.'

'See? She'll not answer ye,' Mrs Leach told Magret. 'She's scared tae answer ye!'

'But she pays her rent, the same as the rest of us.'

'Aye – and then she goes tae the factor's every week an' gets it back, along wi' our hard-earned money!' Mrs Leach's hard finger rammed into Isla's shoulder, forcing her to retreat. Her ankles collided painfully with the step, and she almost fell, but managed to stay upright, stumbling on to the step. Ross was almost hysterical now, and she scooped him up in her arms, retreating to the safety of her own room. Mrs Leach followed her along the close, her bulk shutting out the light, her voice hounding and nagging.

'We don't want the likes o' you livin' here,' she brayed, her voice rolling like thunder round the narrow close. 'The folks that live here's decent! We've no time for liars. Ye can just get out of this building – you an' yer weans!'

Even when Isla reached the safety of the room and slammed the door in the woman's face, her fist pounded on the panels and her voice kept bellowing on, magnified by the enclosed passageway.

Trembling on the other side of the door, hugging Ross to her and trying to hush him, as though afraid that his weeping would somehow give them both away, Isla heard Magret arguing, and Mrs Kelly pleading with her mother to come away. At last, Mrs Leach allowed herself to be led upstairs, after one final thump at the door. After a moment, there was another, gentle tap at the door.

'Isla?'

She put Ross down and opened the door. Magret came in, Daisy gawping at her side. 'She's bletherin'. The woman's gone clean off her head – I knew it would happen one day.'

'It's true, Magret.'

Magret's mouth opened and shut. Finally she said feebly, 'The landlord? You?'

'I did own the place, but I've sold it now. I didn't want to say anything because—'

Magret looked dazed. 'I'll have to see what he thinks about all this business,' she said, then caught Daisy by the hand as the little girl made a move towards Ross. 'I'd – I'd best be gettin' his tea ready. I'll see ye later,' and she almost ran out of the room.

Isla turned away from the door, just in time to see faces at the window, peering into the room. She managed, for Ross's sake, to swallow back her involuntary yelp of fright, then went across to pull the curtain shut. As she did so, something thumped against the glass, but didn't break it. Ross jumped at the sound and ran to her.

'It's all right, pet, it's all right,' she soothed him, but she didn't dare to venture out, or to draw back the curtain. They sat in the gloom, listening to the sound of voices outside as the news was relayed from one person to another, until Barbara came home from school, tears in her eyes, wanting to know why the women in the street had pointed at her and shouted nasty things about her mummy.

From that day, life in George Street became impossible. None of the other children were allowed to play with Ross, and Barbara, bewildered, wanted to know why the children at school had turned against her.

'Have you been bad?' she asked suspiciously.

'No, love, it's just that – this tenement belonged to your daddy, and he gave it to us when he – had to go away. But the neighbours didn't know that, and they're angry with me for not telling them.'

Barbara's eyes were like saucers. 'The whole building? Did they think he should have given it to them instead?'

Isla tried to explain, but Barbara got it into her head

that the neighbours had somehow taken the tenement away from her mother, and arrived home next day with her snub nose bloody and her blouse torn after a fight in the playground over the issue.

Isla couldn't stay in the house all the time. When she went out, people stared and pointed and made loud asides to each other about rich folk slumming, and poor folk unable to trust their neighbours. The curtains stayed closed, because every time she opened them, people stared in. The owner of the corner shop, a friendly man who had previously been willing to put Isla's purchases on the slate until the beginning of each week, refused to sell her anything until she had cleared her debts.

'But you give credit to most of the folk round here.'

'Aye, missus, because I want tae keep my customers,' the man said. 'If I serve you, most of them'll go elsewhere. I cannae afford tae let that happen.'

The other women in the shop stepped aside ostentatiously to let Isla out, muttering amongst themselves. She had no option but to go to the lawyer's office to ask Colin Forbes if she could take some money out at once.

'Is there something wrong?' His gaze moved from her to Ross, unusually silent and clinging.

'No.' She was too ashamed to tell him about what had happened. It was her problem, and she must cope with it. She was sure that if she and the children could just wait out the storm, it would die down. Once the George Street folk realised that, like them, she was struggling to support her family and worrying about where the next meal was coming from, they would surely come round.

She arrived home to find a pile of horse manure outside her door. She fetched the shovel from the back court and cleared it, then scrubbed the close out. After sluicing the water away down the street drain she came back into the close to find Magret lurking there.

'Oh, Isla, it's a rotten shame, so it is. I'd have cleaned it up for ye, but Tommy says I've no' tae talk tae ye, and the bairns cannae play together. I'm sorry . . .'

'It's all right, I can understand why he's so angry.'

Magret held back Daisy, who was trying to reach Ross. 'Why did ye keep it a secret, Isla?'

'Because I knew that if the folk round here knew the truth, they'd do just what they're doing now,' Isla told her, and went into the house.

Drew tapped on the door that night; when she was certain he was alone, she opened the door, closing it quickly behind him.

'I've finished that wee sideboard.' He handed it over and she ran her fingers over it.

'It's lovely, Drew.'

He reached into his pocket and brought out a small parcel, fragrant-smelling and still warm. 'My mam's just baked these scones. She thought you and the bairns'd like them. And here's a wee pot of raspberry jam to go with them.'

Tears of gratitude stung Isla's eyes. 'Thank you – and thank your mother for me.'

'It was you that got the roof fixed, wasn't it? If there's anythin' we can dae for ye, mam an' me, ye just have tae let us know. It's no' right, the way folks is treatin' ye,' the youth said hotly. 'It's that old Leach that's got the rest of them stirred up against ye. It'll be forgotten in a week.'

As he stepped out into the close again, she heard him say, with a boldness that she never would have believed of Drew, 'Evenin', Mrs Leach. Is there somethin' wrong wi' yer eyes? They look awful stary.'

The old woman's scandalised sniff reverberated through the close as Isla closed the door.

Drew was wrong – Isla's betrayal, as Mrs Leach and her cronies saw it, wasn't forgotten in a week. Instead, the persecution became increasingly worse, until finally one night, someone threw a stone through the window, shouting, 'See how long ye take tae repair that, land-lady! Nob'dy wants your sort here!'

The children, who had just been put to bed, screamed with fright, and Isla, working at the sink, jumped back as shards of glass flew into the washing-up water. She caught Ross up out of his cot and jumped with him into the wall-bed, where the three of them crouched together.

'Look, Mummy,' Ross said suddenly, wide-eyed, pointing at the back of her hand, which was bleeding freely. There was blood on the blanket, and on Ross's clothes.

Isla put her hand to her mouth, tasting the saltiness of her own blood. Round it she said reassuringly, 'It's just a wee cut,' to the two frightened little faces peering up at her in the wall-bed's gloom. She wound her hand-kerchief around the cut to stop the bleeding. They all stayed in the wall-bed that night, for Isla was afraid to put Ross into his cot. The children went to sleep quickly, but Isla lay awake, jumping at the slightest noise from outside, her mind conjuring up alarming pictures of people smashing the door down, robbing her, harming the children. Her hand throbbed all through the night.

Isla had been going to Flora Currie's house in Castlehead every morning as usual, and had managed to persuade Ross to say nothing about the trouble in George Street.

The day after the window was smashed was a Saturday, and after boarding the broken window up with cardboard, Isla took the children to Flora's, braving the walk along George Street, under hostile eyes. It was a relief to turn the corner into Maxwellton Street.

Barbara had been safely tucked away in her classroom during the week. Now, as they passed the West Station and made for the gate in the wall, Isla did her best to tactfully suggest to her daughter that nothing should be said about what had happened in George Street. Barbara, looking forward to being cosseted by Annie and as glad as Isla was to get away from the unfriendliness in George Street for a little while, agreed cheerfully.

Ainslie, who had become a regular caller at Castlehead, was already in the house when Isla arrived, and so was Phil. His sharp eyes fell on the bandaged hand at once. 'Been in the wars?' he asked, and before she could say a word, Barbara, completely forgetting all that she had promised, launched into a dramatic story about the broken window.

Flora tutted. 'Those children that throw stones! Do their mothers never think to teach them how dangerous it is?'

'It was a man,' Barbara chirruped. 'I heard him

shouting, "Nobody wants your sort here!"' Her clear little voice dropped to mimic the harsh taunt she had heard the day before.

'A man?' Flora asked. 'Why would a man do a thing like that?'

'It's because my daddy didn't give them the tenement,' Barbara explained, ignoring her mother's glare. 'The folk are all angry with us, and nobody'll . . .' She stopped and gave a gulp, then went on, her voice wobbling slightly, 'Nobody'll play with me and Ross—'

She stopped as Phil jumped to his feet, staggered, clutched at a chair, then limped theatrically towards the door, opening it then clutching at it for support.

'Oh, my leg – it's gone again,' he said dramatically. 'Barbara, would you and Ross go to the kitchen and ask Miss Annie if she knows what I did with my spare wooden leg?'

'You haven't got a wooden leg,' Barbara said, the threatening tears vanishing.

'Sure I have. I've got two, and this one's giving out on me. Tell Miss Annie that I think I might have left it in the biscuit tin,' he called after them as they scampered out, giggling.

'You'll drive Annie daft with your silliness,' Flora told him as he closed the door.

'Not her, she loves a bit of fun. Now . . .' Phil came back into the room, his face suddenly grim. 'What's going on, Isla?'

'It's nothing important.'

'Sounds pretty important to me.'

'She's not been herself for the past week,' Flora fretted, 'but I didn't want to pry.'

'I think you should pry,' Phil told her. 'I think it's time we all pried.'

'It's not your worry.'

'Nonsense. Anything that harms you and your bairns is my worry. Out with it.'

'Better do as the lady says,' Phil drawled. 'She can be mean when she puts her mind to it.'

'I wish Agnes could have met you, Philip. She'd have loved you! Come on, now,' Flora added with a change of tone, and Isla shrugged helplessly and started to talk.

'They can't treat you like that,' Phil exploded when she finished. 'Who do they think they are?'

'You should go to the police,' Ainslie chimed in, and Flora nodded.

'I certainly will not. They're hurt because I deceived them, and I can't say that I blame them.'

Phil's eyes were blazing with suppressed fury. 'You don't blame someone for smashing your window and terrorising your kids?'

'No – I mean yes – I mean,' Isla said helplessly, looking at her friends' tense faces. 'The trouble is that now they think I'm wealthy, when I'm not. I'm no better off than they are. It'll blow over.'

'You think so? And how many broken windows d'you think it'll take?' Phil made for the door, but Ainslie's voice stopped him in his tracks.

'Going to George Street and making a fuss won't help matters, nor will reporting it to the police. It'll only make things worse for Isla and the children. They'll have to move out.'

'I can't afford to move!'

'Colin's father owns property in Paisley. He might have a flat you could rent.'

'It'd have to be the same rent as the place I'm in now. I didn't make much money from the sale of the tenement, and part of that went to pay for the repairs. We'll have to live on the rest until Ross goes to school and I'm free to look for a job.'

'You've already got a job, doing up those dolls' houses.'

'That doesn't bring in much, Phil,' Ainslie said absently, staring into space, her neat brows drawn together in thought.

'Why don't you move in here? There's enough room.'

Isla reached out to pat Flora Currie's hand. 'It's kind of you, but I'm not going to impose two active children on you.'

'I love the bairns!'

'I know you do, but they're more lovable in small doses, believe me.'

'What are we all fretting about?' Phil said. 'There's my aunt's house, lying empty right next door.'

'I couldn't afford to pay rent on a house that size!'

'Who said anything about rent? I need to sell it and get back home. I'm not interested in renting.'

'Then it's out of the question.'

'You already made an offer for it a few weeks ago.'

'Phil, that was just a bit of fun!'

'What was it again?'

'Five shillings, and that's still as much as I could—'

'Done.' The Canadian strode over to take Isla's hand and shake it firmly. 'You've got yourself a deal, Mrs Moffatt.'

'But—'

'Don't tease the lassie, Philip,' Flora snapped, but Ainslie, her eyes bright, touched the older woman's arm.

'Wait a minute, Miss Currie, I don't believe he's teasing her at all. You mean it, don't you, Phil?'

'We shook hands on it. I've never in my life gone back on a handshake.'

'But . . .' Isla said again, feeling as though the world had been turned upside down like a snow scene in a glass ball. 'You can't sell a house for five shillings!'

'Sure I can. I can do anything I want, as long as it's not breaking the law. Listen, I've got everything I want back home – well, almost everything,' Phil added, with a swift sidelong glance at Ainslie, who coloured slightly and looked away. 'I didn't come over here to make money out of my great-aunt's death, I came to try to make up in some way for not having come over earlier, while she was still alive. I reckon that having folks like you and your redheads living in her house, and you working in it at those dolls' houses, is as good a way as any of making amends.'

'Isla, you could put a room aside for your dolls'-house work,' Ainslie said excitedly.

'Great, I've got an ally!' Phil put an arm about her shoulders. Even in her confusion, Isla noticed that Ainslie didn't break the contact as before, but stayed within his casual embrace.

'Well now, Isla,' said Flora Currie, sounding as dazed as Isla felt, 'it looks as though you've just bought yourself somewhere else to live.'

Isla had fully expected Colin Forbes and his father to show Phil Hannigan the error of his ways, and explain to him how ridiculous his scheme was. But to her surprise, both men were willing to let the five-shilling sale go through, though Colin was tight-lipped.

'Mr Hannigan has quite made up his mind that this is what he wants, and therefore it stands as a proper business arrangement,' Gilchrist Forbes said. 'For your part, it's clearly advantageous, and the papers will be drawn up as soon as possible. I understand that Mr Hannigan wants them to be signed as soon as possible, and the matter brought to a conclusion.'

'But I can't just buy a house that size for five shillings!'

'Normally, I would agree with you, but this is not a normal transaction. For five shillings, the house is yours. And from what Ainslie and Colin tell me,' the lawyer added, 'the sooner you move out of George Street and into Castlehead, the better.'

The George Street folk gathered to watch the 'flitting' in sullen silence. Both Phil and Colin were there to help carry Isla's few pieces of furniture out to the van that had been hired for the occasion, and their presence acted as a deterrent to those who might have made something of the occasion.

As the van drew away from the kerb and Phil helped Isla and the children into Colin's car, Mrs Leach, who had been standing by the close watching every move, said loudly, 'Good riddance tae bad rubbish!'

The tall Canadian immediately turned, cupping a hand behind his ear. 'I didn't quite catch that, ma'am, you've got such a quiet voice,' he said politely. 'Can you speak a little louder?'

Mrs Leach went crimson as some of the onlookers tittered, and flounced back into the close with a loud sniff. The titters strengthened into a laugh as she disappeared. The George Street folk had united against someone they saw as an outsider, but on the other hand, Mrs Leach herself wasn't popular, and many of them relished the sight of her being bested.

Phil had insisted on including the furniture still in the house in the deal, pointing out that Isla herself had said that it belonged there, and Flora donated two small beds from her attic for the children. Ross was overcome with excitement at having a real bed, instead of a cot that had become too short for him.

Isla, who was living in a daze, had thought of turning the small room beside the kitchen into her workroom, but Ainslie talked her into taking one of the two big front rooms instead.

'You may well end up with quite a lot of work, and if so, you'll need the space,' she pointed out. Isla, seeing the sense of her argument, decided that one front room should be the living-room while the other, formerly the dining-room, became a workroom. She would have no need for a separate room to eat in, the kitchen was as large as the room she and the children had lived in at George Street. She took one of the three bedrooms upstairs, and put both children into another room. It was too soon for Ross to be on his own. Once he was old enough, he could move into the smallest bedroom.

'As far as they're concerned, the most exciting place in the house is the bathroom,' she said wryly to Ainslie, who had insisted on helping her to get the workroom ready. Annie was making up beds upstairs, with the children hindering more than helping. 'I can see that I'm going to have trouble keeping Ross away from that running water.'

Ainslie, whisking a handbrush along the skirting board, sat back on her heels and looked round the room. 'This place has so much space. I never noticed until recently how dark and crowded our house is.' She hesitated, then said slowly, 'My aunt's here from the Border on a visit. She's suggested finding a small place there for Mother, so that they can see more of each other.'

'D'you think she'll agree?'

'I think she feels the same way I do – that that house has too many memories. She and her sister always got on well. I believe Mother would be the better for a move.'

'What will you do? Go with her, or stay in Paisley?'

'Mother and I both know that we can't share a house. As to staying in Paisley . . .' Ainslie hesitated again, fidgeting with the brush in her hands.

A sudden thought struck Isla, but it was so delicate that she daren't put it into words, in case she blundered. Instead she kept her voice light when she said, 'Phil's going to see what Mr Blayne has in the way of long tables and a good chest of drawers for this room. I shall miss him when he goes back to Canada.' She sneaked a glance at Ainslie. 'He's very good at knowing just how to make people happy, isn't he?'

'Yes, he is.' Ainslie looked up, her lips curved into a determined, but wavering, smile, her eyes sparkling. 'Isla . . .'

Isla decided that she wouldn't be blundering after all. 'He's asked you to go to Canada with him. He's asked you to marry him!' Then, as Ainslie nodded and burst into tears, Isla dropped to the floor beside her and hugged her. 'That's wonderful!'

Ainslie caught and held her so tightly that she felt her ribs creak.

'No it's not, it's ridiculous!' she wept into Isla's neck. 'I said – I swore – that I'd never marry. And I meant it! I scarcely know him – I might hate living with him in Canada!'

'That's not what you said when you were trying to persuade me to consider it.'

'Yes, but you're you and I'm . . .' Ainslie gave a huge sniff and sat back, scrubbing a wrist across her face just like a child. She was so like Barbara, Isla thought. Even when they cried, they both looked beautiful. 'I'm such a difficult person, Isla, such a mixture. I'd probably be a terrible wife!'

'Phil doesn't seem to think so.'

'I might not even l-like Canada!'

'You're quite right. It's all ridiculous, and you'd both be very unhappy, and Canada will probably turn out to be the most dreadful place on earth.'

'Isla!'

'Ainslie! If you love the man, marry the man!'

Ainslie burst into tears again and, this time, Isla joined her. They sat on the floor, in each other's arms, and cried their eyes out.

Ainslie McAdam and Philip Hannigan were married quietly in Oakshawhill Church on a crisp, sunny December day, just before Christmas, with Isla and Colin as their witnesses. The date of their wedding had been carefully planned to ensure that eight days later, on the anniversary of Innes's death, Catherine and Ainslie would both have left Paisley, one moving to the borders, the other on her way to Canada with her new husband.

Colin watched impassively as Ainslie, beautiful in a suit of deep green with a huge sable collar and sable at the cuffs of her jacket and round the hem of her skirt, became Phil Hannigan's wife, and even managed a cheerful smile and a kiss for the bride as they left the church. Isla, watching, felt heart-sorry for the young man.

At Catherine's insistence, a small reception was held in the house. Isla, given her own way, would have gone back to Castlehead, where Annie was looking after the children, when the ceremony was over, but Ainslie and Flora both persuaded her to see the occasion through to the end. 'The children'll be fine with Annie, and I'm going to be at the reception,' Flora said. 'We'll be company for each other.'

Even so, Isla faltered at the front door, and might not have managed to step over the lintel if Colin Forbes

hadn't taken her arm and drawn her into the long rec-
tangular hall by his side, murmuring, 'If I can go
through with the wedding, Isla, you can go through
with the reception.'

It was the first time he had spontaneously used her
given name, and Isla was so taken aback by the sound of
it on his tongue that she was inside the house and being
greeted by Flora, striking in a yellow and black dress
beneath a black coat, before she knew it.

Catherine McAdam sat in state in the drawing-room,
graciously receiving her daughter's guests. She proffered her cheek formally for Ainslie's kiss, then Phil's,
only coming to life when Colin's turn came to greet her.

'My dear boy!' She took his hands in hers, smiling
warmly up at him.

'This must be a very happy occasion for you, Mrs
McAdam.' He bent to kiss her, then drew Isla forward.
'I'd like you to meet Mrs Isla Moffatt.'

Kenneth's first, legal wife and his second, unlawful
wife looked into each other's faces, and Catherine's
gaze swept over Isla without recognition. 'How d'you
do.' She touched Isla's hand briefly, then turned back
to Colin. 'Unfortunately, my daughter's chosen a
Colonial,' she told him, her voice ringing out. 'She
never does the right thing. But at least he's wealthy.'

There was an audible, collective gasp, as everyone
within earshot swivelled towards the bridal couple, avid
to record their reaction. The colour drained from
Ainslie's face, and Isla sensed Colin tensing beside her,
ready to jump to his former fiancée's defence. Then
Philip Hannigan, an arm about Ainslie's shoulders,
drawled in a voice just as clear and carrying as

Catherine's, 'Well I'll be darned. I thought that I was
the one marrying money!'

Ainslie laughed, a peal of genuine, unselfconscious
amusement, while Catherine stared coldly at her upstart
new son-in-law and the cream of Paisley society blinked
and murmured and bridled, sensing that it had just
been mocked, and not sure what should be done about
it.

'Phil's done that girl the world of good already,'
Flora approved, arriving beside Isla. 'She's learning that
cattiness doesn't matter, even when it comes from her
own mother.'

Later, someone came and swept Flora away to meet
someone else. Isla, on her own, sipped at the glass of
champagne offered by one of the maids, looking around
the drawing-room, trying to imagine the Kenneth she
had known at home in it. It was impossible. There had
been so many Kenneth McAdams.

'Mrs – Moffatt, isn't it?' Two stylishly dressed
women bore down on her. 'The Mrs Moffatt who made
that delightful *Little Women* house?'

'Yes, that's right.'

'Dolly McNair bought it from Leckie's toyshop,' the
speaker informed her friend. 'It's really quite sweet. I
wonder if you would do one for me?'

'I'd be happy to. If you let Mr Leckie know what
you want, he'll pass the information on to me.'

'I'll do that,' the woman gushed, then, eyes sharpen-
ing, 'I understand that you bought Agnes McFall's
house in Castlehead. For five shillings, someone told
me, but of course they must have got it wrong.'

'Five shillings? Surely not,' her friend chimed in.

'My dear, I can assure you – the five-shilling mansion, people are calling it.'

'But nobody sells a house for that price – are we getting confused with your dolls' houses?'

Their eyes were bright, greedy with the desire for some lucrative gossip. Isla, taken aback by what she now realised had been a planned attack, stammered, her mouth going dry. She was looking from one face to the other, searching wildly for something to say when a hand closed on her arm and Colin Forbes said smoothly above her head, 'Pardon me, I couldn't help overhearing. Mrs Moffatt and Mr Hannigan came to a private agreement regarding the sale of his great-aunt's house, and as Mrs Moffatt's solicitor, I can assure you that everything was in order.' Then, turning his back on the two women, who had begun to quack out protests, 'Isla, my mother is anxious to meet you.'

Gilchrist Forbes stood by the window with a plump, maternal-looking woman.

'Mother,' Colin said, 'this is Isla Moffatt. I've just rescued her from that pair of nebby old crows.'

He jerked his head towards the women who had been talking to Isla, and Phemie Forbes, followed the movement, gave an outraged gasp. 'You're talking about two friends of mine. Gilchrist, speak to him!'

'Colin's too old to be spoken to, Phemie,' her husband said calmly. 'In any case, I'm more likely to agree with him than disagree. Mrs Moffatt, this is my wife.'

'Tchah!' Phemie glared at her menfolk, then turned her attention to Isla, her gaze swiftly evaluating the sage skirt and long tailored jacket with dark green trimmings that Ainslie had insisted on buying Isla for the wedding. She held out a ringed hand. 'How do you do, my dear. I hope you've settled into your new home?'

'We have. I think we're going to be very happy there.'

'I must say, though, that it's a very strange situation. Did you really only pay five—'

'Phemie!' her husband cut in hurriedly, while Colin said, 'I'd wondered where these old biddies got their information from.'

'Are you suggesting that . . .?'

'What, Mother?' Colin smiled down on the woman, who glared back at him. It was clear to Isla that there was affection between the three members of the Forbes family; it reminded her, achingly, of the bond there had always been between herself and her own parents.

'Men can be quite impossible, can't they?' Phemie turned to Isla to include her in the general conspiracy of womanhood, then her still-pretty features blurred and her eyes widened. 'I mean – that is . . .'

Suddenly, Isla knew that for all the older woman's apparent friendliness, in Phemie Forbes' eyes, she herself was outside the conspiracy, a woman apart, wife yet not wife, widow yet not widow.

It was a relief when Ainslie and Philip marked the end of the reception by leaving. They had decided to spend a few days on honeymoon before sailing to Canada. Catherine McAdam stayed in her chair, announcing that she was too tired to accompany her daughter and son-in-law to the gate. Once again, she accepted Ainslie's kiss without any show of emotion, and Phil's arm went protectively about his new wife as she turned to leave her home for the last time. She pressed her head briefly against his shoulder in recognition of his gesture, while Isla, watching, swore to herself that she would never allow anything to destroy her own small family as the McAdams had been destroyed.

As the couple made their farewells out on the driveway in a flurry of kisses and handshakes, the last of the day's sunlight struck rich copper glints from Ainslie's hair. At the gate, she left Phil's side to hug Isla.

'Write to me – long letters telling me every single thing that happens. And I'll write back, I promise. Kiss the children for me.'

She released Isla and turned to hug Colin as Phil caught Isla up in a brief embrace. 'Be happy in great-aunt Agnes's house,' he said.

As the car moved off, and Ainslie's hand fluttered from the window, the final rays of the sun sparkled on the gold wedding ring. Isla, hanging back from the press of people crowded at the gate and spilling on to the pavement, saw that Colin was beside her, his face expressionless.

'It must have been hard for you, today.'

He blinked down at her as though he had never seen her before, then his eyes cleared. Today, she saw, they were the green of deep water. 'I think she's married the right man. She's never looked at me the way she looks at him.'

The guests had started to move back towards the house. An involuntary shiver ran through Isla at the thought of going back inside.

'I think I'll just go home.'

'D'you mind if I walk with you?' Colin asked. 'I'd welcome a change of scene.'

26

'I don't expect to be long, Robert,' Phemie Forbes told her chauffeur as he opened the garden gate for her.

Walking up the flagged path between small neat lawns, each with its circular rosebed, she forced back the fluttery feeling that invaded her stomach and told herself that she was doing nothing wrong. She was merely safeguarding her son's interests; any good mother would do the same. She gave the bell-pull a smart tug, and almost at once saw movement through the stained-glass upper half of the door.

When it opened, Phemie, fully expecting a maidservant, was taken aback to see the lady of the house herself. Isla Moffatt, for her part, looked just as astonished to find Phemie on her doorstep, but quickly produced a welcoming smile.

'Mrs Forbes, what a pleasant surprise. I haven't seen you for some time. Please,' she stepped back, 'come in.'

'I've only dropped in for a moment,' Phemie said as she stepped inside and followed Isla into a room to the right of the hall, noting the young woman's blue crêpe de Chine blouse with a large bow at the throat, and the

310

navy skirt that fitted snugly over slender hips, then flared out.

'You'll have some tea, of course.' As protocol dictated in the west of Scotland, the phrase was more of a statement than a question. It was a standard joke in the west that in the Edinburgh area, where the people were reputed to be more formal, the greeting to a casual caller was, 'You'll have had your tea?'

'I only called in for a few minutes . . .'

'But I was about to have one myself, and I'd welcome the company.'

'Well, perhaps a quick cup.' Phemie allowed her hostess to relieve her of her sealskin wrap.

'I'll not be a moment,' Isla promised, and hurried out.

Taking advantage of her absence, Phemie set about a close scrutiny of the room as she drew the gloves from her plump little hands. In the five years since moving to Castlehead, Isla Moffatt had done very well for herself. It had become the fashion in Paisley and further afield to have one of her dolls' houses on show in one's home. Many of Phemie's friends had bought them, and she herself had two, both presented to her by Colin. One was based on Haworth Hall, the home of the Brontë sisters, while each room in the other house depicted a scene from *Alice in Wonderland*.

Isla's home reflected her financial success. The room Phemie stood in was furnished in modern style, with walls of pale rose, not papered, but painted, and bearing only two paintings, whereas Phemie's drawing-room walls were crowded with pictures. Long curtains in a deeper shade of rose hung at the bay windows, and the carpet was patterned in rose and pale green against a creamy background. The wooden surrounds were highly polished, and the rest of the woodwork was cream. The soft, inviting sofa and chairs were covered with a rose and pale green patterned material, with small cream and gold cushions scattered over them.

The room was fragrant with the smell of roses from a large bowl on a table by the window. Their rich colours reflected in the table's gleaming surface, and they also filled another bowl set on the hearth, in front of the empty grate. Phemie recalled noticing more flowers in a tall vase in the hall, by a telephone.

The few pieces of furniture in the room were made of polished walnut, and the overall effect was one of space, light, colour and comfort.

The door opened. Caught in the act of studying the high ceiling, which, like the walls, was painted soft rose, Phemie jerked her chin down so sharply that pain shot through the back of her neck. 'Won't you sit down?' Isla put the tray down on a small table before the fireplace as Phemie sank into one of the chairs. It was extremely comfortable, and she wondered, a trifle grimly, how often her son had sat in this very same chair.

The tea service was patterned with geometrical shapes filled in with bold colours. It looked very like a dinner set that a friend of Phemie's had recently shown to her, boasting that it was designed by Clarice Cliffe, one of the leading designers of the day.

Isla talked about her garden as they drank their tea, apparently unaware of her guest's silence. Phemie, sneaking little glances over the rim of the cup that she was now quite certain must be Clarice Cliffe, recalled how sorry she had felt for the girl at Ainslie's wedding, with her pinched, sallow face. Feeling sorry for her, she had invited Isla and her children to her home several times, and had even begun to like the little family. But gradually, as she noted the growing friendship between Colin and Isla and began to sense problems ahead, the invitations had ceased, and for the past three years the two women had only encountered each other occasionally in the town, exchanging brief greetings and moving on.

Now, five years after their first meeting at the wedding, Isla's face was nicely rounded, her skin like smooth ivory, with just a touch of dusky rose over each cheekbone. Her brown eyes, once anxious and apprehensive, sparkled with life, and her dark hair fell sleekly to her jawline, curling inwards slightly at the bottom. She looked positively pretty, Phemie thought, with a pang that gave her the courage to introduce her reason for calling.

'I understand that your little houses are doing very well, Mrs Moffatt.'

If the younger woman had noticed the deliberate condescension in 'little houses', she gave no sign of it. 'I'm continually surprised by the number of orders that keep coming in,' she confessed with a smile. 'I fully expected interest to have fallen away quite early on.'

'My son tells me that they're even selling in England, and abroad.'

Isla picked up the teapot, then put it down again when Phemie gave a decisive shake of the head. 'Ainslie took some leaflets and photographs back to Canada with her the last time she and Phil were over here, and

managed to obtain several orders for me, for both decorative and practical houses.'

'By practical, you mean houses that are to be played
with, rather than to be put on show?' When Isla nodded, Phemie forged on. 'Several of my friends have
bought your practical houses for their little grand-
daughters.' She smiled, a smile that didn't touch her
eyes. 'I'm hopeful that one day soon I'll be able to give
you a similar order.'

'Really?' Isla looked up, interested. 'Is Colin planning
to marry?'

The time had come. Phemie drew in a deep breath
and dusted an imaginary crumb from the lap of her tan
woollen skirt. 'I thought you might know more about
that than I do, Mrs Moffatt. He seems to spend a great
deal of his time in this house. I expect he confides in
you – since you're an older woman.'

The barb went home; she saw the colour in Isla
Moffatt's cheeks deepen. 'He does call in frequently,
but he's said nothing to me. And I'm quite sure that he
doesn't keep secrets from you.'

Phemie's hand again whisked across her skirt. 'The
fact is, Mrs Moffatt, my husband and I would both like
to see our son settling down, instead of gallivanting
around with this girl and that. He never used to be so –
so flighty.'

Amusement danced into her hostess's eyes, and was
suppressed. 'I never thought of Colin as being flighty,'
she observed mildly.

'Nor I, until recently. I take it he talks to you about
his thoughts, his hopes for the future?'

'From time to time, as friends do.'

Phemie pounced. 'Friends?'

Isla Moffatt regarded her for a moment, then said, 'You might as well speak your mind, Mrs Forbes, rather than dancing around your reason for calling.'

Phemie, who had been raised to believe that 'dancing around', as the younger woman put it, was the correct thing to do, blinked, then rallied. 'Very well, if you prefer it. It seems to us, Mrs Moffatt,' she stated, invoking Gilchrist's support, confident that if she had told him what was on her mind, he would have agreed with her, 'that Colin spends altogether too much time in this house. Folk are beginning to talk.'

'I'd have thought that with all the troubles in the world just now folk would have more to gossip about than friendships.'

'There's bound to be talk when one of the friends is a respectable young bachelor of good family, and the other an older woman with—'

'With a past?'

'With two growing children!' Phemie snapped. 'It's time Colin was settling down.'

Colour surged into Isla's face, and her hands, bare except for Kenneth McAdam's gold band on one finger – a ring he had had no right to put there, Phemie reminded herself – gripped the arms of her chair. 'I can assure you, Mrs Forbes, that there has been no talk of marriage between your son and myself. We've never even considered such a thing.'

'It's time Colin did consider it, and there are plenty of young women in Paisley who are eminently suitable.' Over the past five years Colin had brought some of them home – pretty girls of good family, just the right age to start bearing his children, and in many cases clearly willing to walk down the aisle of Paisley Abbey by his side. But one by one they had drifted away, married other women's sons, presented other women with grandchildren. 'You must tell him to stop calling and look elsewhere for his – friends,' Phemie said flatly, and Isla Moffatt put her cup down and got to her feet.

'Now that you've said what you came to say, Mrs Forbes, I think you should go.'

'I intend to.' Phemie began to struggle out of the chair, which showed a tendency to want to keep her within its soft depths. Eventually, she had to suffer the indignity of taking her hostess's proffered hand, and being helped to her feet.

In the hall, accepting her wrap, she said with as much dignity as she could muster, 'I hope that you'll pay heed to what I've had to say.'

'I can assure you of that,' said Isla Moffatt, opening the door.

Comfortable living had piled weight on Phemie Forbes as the years went by. As a result, her self-righteous, straight-backed march down the path to the waiting car appeared, from where Isla stood on the porch, more like the waddling of an elderly, contented bear; a bear with short legs and only a patch of gleaming fur left across the shoulders.

But Isla was in no mood to be amused by the thought. She was embarrassed, confused, and very angry, although she wouldn't for the world have let Colin's mother know that. As the car drove off with Phemie, in the back seat, resolutely staring ahead,

Barbara arrived at the gate, her schoolbag dangling from one hand, her skirt swirling round legs that seemed to be growing longer by the month. Ross was immediately behind her, and as Barbara opened the gate he tried to squeeze past. The two of them, jammed in the narrow gap, squabbled briefly before breaking free and scurrying up the garden path, both starting to talk about their day at school as soon as they saw their mother standing on the porch.

They were unmistakably Kenneth McAdam's children, Isla thought as she watched them come towards her. Although twelve-year-old Barbara's eyes were brown, like her own, her expressions were Kenneth's. She also had his enthusiasm for life, and the same swinging, easy stride that had caused the breath to catch in Isla's throat the first time she saw Ainslie walking towards her. Isla's dark hair had tempered Kenneth's red-gold head to produce, in their daughter, a rich, striking auburn.

Ross had Kenneth's blazing red hair and pale skin and light blue eyes, and he also had the more serious side of his father's nature. There were times, when he pulled at his lower lip and drew his brows down in thought, when strong memories of the man she still thought of as her husband flooded back to Isla.

'That was Colin's mother, wasn't it?' Barbara asked as she reached the porch. 'I remember seeing him with her in the town.' Her gaze was direct, just like Kenneth's. 'What did she want?'

'She was just visiting.'

'Why?' asked Ross. 'She's never visited you bef—'

'Upstairs, the two of you, and change out of your

school clothes.' Isla scooped them before her into the house. 'I've got work to do.'

'I'm too weak with hunger to climb the stairs,' announced Barbara, who possessed an excellent appetite, yet never seemed to put on any weight. Her brother was already on his way to the kitchen, where Nan, who had moved in as housekeeper when Isla's work had begun to take up most of her time, would be putting out milk and scones. The children always came home from school hungry.

'Five minutes – then upstairs and get some work done before teatime,' Isla called after them, then went into her favourite room, the dolls'-house workshop opposite the living-room.

Its cream-painted walls were lined with counters holding a variety of miniature houses, boxes of materials, small pots of paint or glue, and books on furniture and fashions. In the window recess Mabel Torrance, the seamstress who had worked full-time for Isla for the past eighteen months, sat at one of the two sewing machines. She smiled at her employer, then went back to her work. Isla sat down at the desk in one corner, where she had been planning a new house when Colin's mother had interrupted her.

She picked up her pencil, put it down, and started riffling through one of the books, staring blankly at the pages without seeing them. Instead, Phemie Forbes' visit played itself over and over again in her mind, like one of the films she occasionally took the children to see.

The whole episode had been just like a film, she thought – unreal, the sort of thing that didn't really happen. Only it had happened. She gave up all pretence of looking for something, and let the book in front of her lie where it had fallen open. After Ainslie's departure for Canada, Colin, in the double role of Isla's lawyer and Ainslie's friend, had helped Isla to settle in the Castlehead house. He had advised her on business matters as the demand for her work grew, suggesting and drawing up a contract between her and Mr Leckie, the toyshop owner.

It was Colin who had suggested having leaflets advertising her work printed and distributed to attract more clients, Colin who had taught her how to cope with the paperwork as orders started to come direct to her home. He had somehow drifted into the habit of calling in once or twice a week, occasionally taking them out in his car, even helping now and again with homework. As Ross grew from toddler to schoolboy, Colin had become, in some ways, the father-figure Ross had never known.

But nothing more than a friend. In the years following Ainslie's departure for Canada, he had plunged into the local social life and, to his mother's delight, had become one of the town's most eligible bachelors, often bringing the latest conquest to visit Isla and see the dolls' houses.

'It's more comfortable here,' he had said when she pointed out that his mother might prefer to play hostess to his friends. 'Mother would pry and simper, and probably start planning wedding outfits. Anyway, I need someone like you to tell me who should be taken to meet her, and who should be kept well away from her.'

After each introduction, he inevitably asked for Isla's

opinion of the latest girl. She enjoyed meeting them all, and became genuinely fond of one or two, but steadfastly refused to criticise any of them, insisting that he must make his own judgements. After a few weeks, or, at most, a few months, the current girl would disappear, to be replaced by someone else.

'She was too possessive,' Colin would say vaguely, sprawling at his ease in Isla's comfortable living-room. Or, 'She giggled too much,' or perhaps, 'She began to get that engagement-ring gleam in her eyes.'

'You must stop comparing them all with Ainslie,' Isla told him one day, and he stared at her, astonished.

'You think I do that?'

'Of course you do. It's not fair to them, Colin. People deserve to be judged on their own merits.'

'Mmmm,' Colin said, and gradually, fewer girlfriends had been brought to Castlehead for Isla's inspection. She hadn't even realised that, until now.

'People are bound to talk – a respectable young bachelor of good family – an older woman . . .' Phrases the older woman had used came back to her as she stared down at the open book, taking on new meaning, turning an easy, happy friendship into something suspect and distasteful.

'I'll see you tomorrow morning, Mrs Moffatt.' Isla came back to the present with a jerk. Mabel was covering the sewing machine, which meant that it was five o'clock.

'Yes, Mabel, thanks.' She rubbed a hand over her eyes, then panic flared through her as she heard a man's voice in the hall, talking to Mabel. Colin sometimes looked in on his way home from the office.

Isla stood up, almost knocking the book to the ground. She couldn't face him now – she needed time to think things through—

But when the door opened it was Drew Brown who came in, pulling his jacket on over his overalls. 'That's me away home. I've varnished the table, it'll be dry by tomorrow.' He looked down at the open book and gave a low whistle. 'That'll take some work. Still, I reckon I could manage it.'

Isla, glancing down, saw that the book had fallen open at the picture of an elaborate three-seated chair in green velvet.

'I've not decided, Drew, so don't worry your head about it yet.' She closed the book. 'You go off and enjoy your evening at the theatre with Mary.'

'I will. G'night, then.' He went off, whistling cheerfully.

Only days after Isla had left George Street, Drew had come shyly to Castlehead to offer to go on making furniture for her.

'I'd not want to get you into trouble with your neighbours, Drew.'

'Ach, what happened was just a storm in a teacup. My mam and me both think it's only right for me tae go on helping ye, seeing as it was you that got our roof fixed,' he had said, standing in the hall, twisting his cap round and round in his hands. 'Anyway, I like making the wee furniture.'

For three years he had worked for Isla in the evenings and weekends. As the orders began to flow in she had become increasingly dependent on the young man's talents, and when he was dismissed from the joinery shop after finishing his apprenticeship, Colin had suggested that she employ Drew herself.

He had scribbled figures on paper, convincing her that she could afford to pay Drew, suggesting that the carriage-house, still packed with its former owner's rubbish, could be pressed into service.

Between them, Drew and Colin had turned the carriage-house into a decent workshop, and Drew had settled in happily. Now, two years later, he had become an essential part of Isla's life, thanks to Colin.

Isla bit her lip realising that, unbidden, Colin had managed to steal back into her thoughts. He would have to go, not just from her mind, but from her life. It would be hard to turn her back on him, for although she knew a lot of people now – neighbours, clients, acquaintances – her only close friends were Colin, Ainslie, far away in Canada with her husband and twin sons, and Flora Currie, who had become frighteningly frail during the past year. But if, as his mother had said, folk were gossiping, a break had to be made. Since Kenneth's death, Isla had developed a dislike, almost a fear, of being talked about.

She heard the children leaping down the staircase on their way to the kitchen for tea, and was grateful beyond measure for their existence, their casual conviction that life would never change. As long as Ross and Barbara were in her world, she would never be alone, or lonely.

Cheered by that thought, Isla squared her shoulders and went out to meet her children in the hall.

27

With relief, Isla remembered during tea that that evening Colin, who had joined the Territorial Army as Britain uneasily watched the steady growth of strength and power in Germany, would be attending the weekly meeting in their headquarters, and wouldn't come to Low Road.

Too restless to sit and read after the evening meal, she went into the garden with the intention of tiring herself out with some brisk weeding. Ross was playing with several other boys in a garden further along the road, and as she worked, Isla could hear their voices on the soft evening air, while the beautiful, sad strains of 'Ol' Man River', floated from the open window of Barbara's room. A steady stream of girls, like a line of ants, had begun to converge on the house immediately after tea, trotting up the stairs to Barbara's room to rehearse yet another of her concerts.

Aunt Lally had died in 1934, leaving everything she had to Barbara and Ross. Isla had put the proceeds of the sale of the flat and the furniture, together with the little money her aunt had left, into trust for the children, but Barbara had insisted on keeping all Lally's scrapbooks and sheet music. A cupboard had had to be bought specially to house it all in her room. She used the music for her concerts, which had already raised considerable sums of money for various charities.

After her sudden, enforced move to Low Road, Isla had decided – largely on Colin's and Flora's advice – to keep Barbara at the West School, rather than unsettle the child by moving her elsewhere. Once they were away from George Street, the animosity Barbara had begun to experience in the school playground had ebbed away, and in no time at all she was bringing her former friends from the street home to play at the end of each school day.

Greta and, once she began to go to school, Daisy, were among the group. Only weeks after the 'flitting', Isla had encountered Magret in a shop, and her former neighbour had greeted her as though nothing had happened.

'Ach, life's too short tae bear a grudge,' she had declared, her face wreathed in smiles. 'It's only sourfaces like that Mrs Leach that never forget. Mrs Leach, and elephants, eh?'

Since then, Magret had called in at Low Road now and again, refusing to sit anywhere but in the kitchen, where she and Isla and, eventually, Nan, enjoyed many a cosy gossip over a cup of tea. With Daisy at school, Magret had gone back to work in the mills, only five minutes' walk from Low Road. She was saving hard in the hope of moving to a better house. There was a good chance, being overcrowded, that the McDougalls would get a house in the new scheme at Ferguslie Park, but Magret wanted to stay near the mills and near her friends and neighbours. She had her eye on a rented flat further along George Street, on the other side of Maxwellton Street.

In June, Barbara's stint at the West School had come to an end, and now, in early September, she and Greta had just started attending Camphill Secondary School. Most of the Low Road children were attending the John Neilston Institution or the Grammar School, both fee-paying, but Barbara insisted on staying with her former classmates, and Isla, who would have found it difficult to pay school fees as well as wages for Drew and Mabel, had been content to go along with her daughter's wishes.

All Barbara asked of her friends was that they were willing to take part in her back-court concerts, now back-garden concerts. As a result, the children who marched up the path most evenings and weekends were a mixture from the Paisley schools, and at each of Barbara's concerts, held in the garden in fine weather and the living-room in bad weather, mothers from comfortable homes and cramped tenements gossiped and laughed and applauded side by side.

Isla straightened up, rubbing at her back. It was almost dark now, and the house-lights looked inviting. There was just a touch of autumn in the air, the slightest hint of approaching winter. As she gathered up her trowel and fork and locked them in the little shed, then walked down the path towards the house, the turmoil Phemie Forbes had caused began to fade away.

'I don't know, Drew,' Isla said the next day, studying the sketches Drew had made of the three-seater chair he had seen in the furniture book the day before. 'It looks very complicated to me.'

Glancing up at Drew, she could tell by the gleam in his eyes that he had already made up his mind. Drew loved a challenge.

'Not when you think of it piece by piece. It'd look bonny in that fancy house you're doing for – oh hullo, Mr Forbes.'

Isla, taken off guard, spun round to see Colin leaning against the frame of the open carriage-house door, grinning at her. 'What are you doing here at this time of day?' she asked sharply, and his eyebrows rose.

'I'm running the old man home for some lunch because his own car's having some work done on it. I thought I'd look in and ask if you and the kids want to go to the Regal tonight.'

'John Gilbert,' Drew said enthusiastically. 'I've seen it, it's good.'

'No, I don't think so.'

'It's Friday – no school tomorrow.'

'We're already going out.'

'Where?'

'Just out.' She bustled Colin out of the workshop, blinking in the sunshine. 'Look, I'm really busy, and your father's waiting . . .'

'Is there something up?'

'Of course not.'

'Then come to the cinema. The kids'll enjoy it—'

'I told you, I'm busy, we're going out.' She had managed to get him as far as the gate, but as she moved to open it, Colin put his hand on the top rail, preventing her.

'There *is* something wrong.'

'It's nothing – just . . .' she wavered, then said in a

rush of words, 'you spend too much time with us, Colin.'

This time his eyebrows soared. 'I enjoy your company, and Barbara's, and Ross's.'

'But we've all got our own lives to lead. We can't be in each other's pockets all the time.' She glanced up at him, and saw the smile die out of his eyes.

'In other words, I've outstayed my welcome.'

'Colin, I'm very grateful for all you've done for me – for us – but—'

'But you'd prefer not to be – pestered.'

'I didn't say . . . .' Isla began, then, realising that he had offered her a way out of her dilemma, and she must take it, she said lamely, 'well, yes.'

'You should have said something.'

'I just have,' she said to a spot just beyond his right shoulder.

'So you have.' His voice was cold now. She risked a swift glance at him, and saw that he was looking at her just as he had at their very first meeting. Then, she hadn't understood why. Now, she did.

'Colin, I really am very grateful for—'

'Good day, Isla,' he said, and turned away, striding out of the garden and along the road towards the gate that led to the main road and his car and his father and his real life.

It was over, just like that. She had expected an argument, perhaps even a quarrel, but now she realised that that wasn't Colin's way. He had his pride, and if he felt that he wasn't wanted, that was that. It had happened swiftly and easily, and as she turned back to the carriage-house and Drew, she told herself that she should be glad of that, at least.

Before she reached the carriage-house, the sun had gone in behind a cloud.

A week dragged by. The invigorating tingle that had been in the air as summer's dying blended with winter's approach vanished, washed away by drizzling, constant rain. Barbara and Ross came home from school each day soaked to the skin, and squabbled a lot because Ross hated to be indoors all the time. Drew was depressed because the little Victorian loveseat had proved to be too difficult for him after all, and a very particular customer made a fuss over a dolls' house that wasn't ready on the agreed date. It seemed to Isla that everything was going wrong, and the low cloud and persistent rain made her feel tired and despondent.

The previous winter had laid both Flora and Annie low with 'flu; Flora had battled her way through it, but despite all that Isla and the doctor could do, Annie had developed pneumonia and died.

Isla had found another housekeeper, kindly and efficient, but although the woman did everything she could to make Flora comfortable and content, it wasn't the same, and a lot of Flora's old fire and drive had evaporated.

'It's the fighting I miss,' she confided in Isla when she paid her usual daily visit. 'Whenever I snap at Betty her lip trembles and she almost turns cartwheels trying to please me. Annie knew how to give as good as she got.' Her green eyes, still lovely although the sparkle had gone from them, were wistful. 'You know you're still alive when you're having a good quarrel.'

Then she leaned forward in her chair and fixed her

gaze on Isla. 'You've heard my grouse against life, now tell me yours.'

'I don't have any, other than being tired of this wet weather.'

'Something's been troubling you for the past week, lassie, and it's not the rain. Anyone living in this part of the world should be used to that. Come on now, what is it?'

'It's nothing.'

'Fiddlesticks! But if you won't say, you won't. Go ahead and treat me like a stranger, see if I care,' Flora said with an echo of the little girl she had once been.

'You do so care,' Isla mimicked the childish note in the old woman's voice, and Flora grinned at her.

'Of course I do, you daft lassie. Is that not what friends are for?'

'I'm just being silly. Colin's mother called on me last week and she's got some daft notion in her head that I'm getting in the way of him finding himself a suitable wife. It upset me a bit.'

Flora snorted. 'Phemie Forbes was always kind-hearted, I'll give her that, but as thick as a plank, even as a young woman. You're surely not going to take any heed of what she says?'

'Flora, she said that folk have started to talk. I don't want to be the subject of gossip, I've had my share of that.'

'Gossip should always be ignored, even if it's telling the truth,' Flora said blithely. 'Have you talked to Colin about this?'

'I've spoken to him, but I couldn't bring myself to tell him what his mother had said. I just said that I didn't want him to come to the house so often.'

'That's a fine thing to say to a man whose got his pride. So he's not been back since?'

'No.'

'I'm not surprised. So that's why you've been going about with a face like a wet washing. You're missing him.'

'I'm not – but I enjoy his company, and the children like him. They've been asking about him, and I don't know what to tell them. I didn't mean that he shouldn't come at all, just that he shouldn't come so often.' Under the steady green gaze, Isla floundered, then said feebly, 'Mebbe I didn't make myself clear.'

'And mebbe you don't even know what you want yourself,' Flora said dryly.

'I just want to live my life in peace, without folk talking about me.' Isla got to her feet and roamed about Flora's drawing-room restlessly. 'Oh, I wish his mother had never come near me!'

'Poor Phemie.'

'Why? She's got what she wanted. She must be really pleased with herself.'

'For the moment, mebbe. But she'd have been well advised to tend to her own business and let Colin tend to his. He's old enough. Sometimes,' said Flora, 'if you throw a stone in the wrong place, it comes bouncing back and hits you. Phemie should have thought about that before opening her mouth.'

Mercifully, the rain stopped on the following day and the weather brightened. Over the next two days the sun, together with a fresh, drying wind, made it possible for the once-a-week gardener Isla employed to

330

gather up the fallen leaves and old vegetation and burn them at the bottom of the garden. The bonfire smouldered all afternoon, scenting the air with its smoke, and after the children had gone to bed Isla went out to make sure that it had died down.

Dawdling back up towards the house, she stopped halfway to sink down on to the swing that Colin had put up for the children years earlier, resting her heels on the grass and letting the swing drift to and fro, trying to slough off the lethargy that was still troubling her.

She was just beginning to feel the tension easing from her body when a voice from the darkness said, 'Isla Moffatt, just what the hell are you playing at?'

Her startled reaction sent the swing spinning, and she might have hit her shoulder against the wooden supports if Colin hadn't caught at the ropes and steadied her. Still holding them, standing so close that she could smell the familiar, comforting smell of soap and tobacco from him, he said again, 'What are you playing at?'

'What are you talking about?'

'Don't pretend. Did Ross not tell you I met him this afternoon?'

'No.' Trapped by his body, she had to crane her head back painfully to look up at him.

'He stopped to watch me playing cricket on his way home from school. I went over to talk to him and he happened to mention that my mother had called on you last week — the day before you decided that you didn't want me hanging around any more.'

His head was a dark mass, surrounded, from her viewpoint, by stars. 'I did not say—'

331

He gave the ropes a little shake, and the swing jiggled. Their knees were pressed together, and she could feel the warmth of his legs against hers. 'That's what it sounded like. I thought . . .' he stopped, then said, 'I thought you must have met someone, some man.'

'It was nothing to do with another man! You've been very good to us, Colin, but you've got your own life to live, and your own friends and interests—'

'And my own right to choose my friends?'

'Yes, but . . .'

'Thank you for that concession, at least.' At last he released the ropes and took a turn away from her, towards the edge of the lawn.

'Poor Mother,' Colin said out of the darkness as Isla got up from the swing, rubbing at the back of her neck, 'she never could understand that actions must have consequences.'

A breeze rustled the bushes and Isla shivered. 'I'm going indoors. D'you want some tea?' she asked automatically.

'I want you to hear me out first. You listened to my mother, so it's only fair that you listen to me.' Colin took her place on the swing. 'It wasn't until Ross told me about Mother's visit that I realised how wise she had been.'

'Wise?'

He edged the swing seat back until he was almost upright, supported by his feet on the ground. 'Very wise. She'd sensed something that I hadn't, fully. That I'm in love with you.'

'You – what?' Isla couldn't have been more astonished if the stars had suddenly swooped down to turn the garden into a circus ring.

'Think about it, Isla. Would I have kept coming here all those years if I didn't love you?'

'That's nonsense,' she said briskly, sounding, to her own ears, just like Flora. 'You think of me as a – an older sister. Why else would you bring all your girlfriends to this house and ask for my opinion about them?'

'Exactly. I put that very question to myself, and the answer was so obvious that I can't think why neither of us saw it before. You once accused me of looking for another Ainslie, remember?'

'Yes,' Isla said cautiously.

'Yet none of the girls I brought here were redheads, were they? They were all dark, like you. I suppose,' Colin mused, 'that I must have been making comparisons, and each time I found the others lacking, and stopped seeing them. The only woman I kept on seeing was you, Isla Moffatt, because the only woman I wanted to see was you – and my clever little mother was the first to see it.'

'Have you been drinking?'

'Not a drop. Oh, I thought about it, after you sent me away and I thought that perhaps you'd found someone else. But I didn't get around to it, thank God. Nor did I realise why I felt so miserable until I met up with young Ross. Talk about babes and sucklings,' said Colin with sudden jubilation. 'I'm going to take that lad out on Saturday and buy him a Knickerbocker Glory, whether you approve or not.'

'You have been drinking! And I'm going indoors n—'

Colin lifted both feet and the swing, released, soared through the air. As it reached the end of its curve, he let the ropes go and landed lightly in front of Isla, who was turning towards the house. Before she had time to utter more than a faint squeak, she had been spun round and into his arms.

Her first thought was that it was all wrong to be kissed by a man who was almost like a brother. Her second thought, arriving almost immediately on the heels of the first, was how wonderful it was to be kissed passionately after all those years of abstinence, and to want to dissolve in the kiss and return it fourfold.

'It's all wrong,' she said shakily when he finally released her.

'No it isn't, it's all very right,' Colin whispered, and kissed her again.

'You're younger than I am,' she protested a few minutes later.

'Only by a couple of years. And before you think of any more objections, let me say that I like your children, and I'd enjoy being their stepfather. Think about young Ross, surrounded by women,' he urged, his mouth moving against her ear, sending ripples of desire through her awakening body. 'It's your duty to bring a man into his life, and I'm recommending myself for the position. Officially, on Forbes and Son headed office notepaper, if you insist.'

'Your father—'

'Who cares?' Colin kissed her again, and again she melted into his arms, her mouth softening and opening beneath his. The past week's depression had vanished, to be replaced by joy that seemed to bubble up from the depths of her body to fill her with golden fire.

'Your mother,' she protested weakly, 'will be dreadfully upset.'

'I'll buy her a Knickerbocker Glory too,' Colin promised. 'If it wasn't for her, heaven knows how long it would have taken us to realise how much we needed each other.'

'You can't be serious,' Phemie Forbes whimpered the next morning, a piece of toast falling from her fingers.

Colin beamed at her. 'I've never been more serious in my life, Mother.'

'But – an older woman, with two children! A woman who's—'

'Who's what? Who's struggled against incredible odds to raise her family with no help from anyone? A woman who's built up a business and earned respect from the community?'

'She's tricked you into this!'

'I'm thirty-two years old, Mother. If I was as easily led as you seem to think, I'd have been married to some scheming minx years ago. As for being tricked, it took me some time to talk Isla into accepting me.'

'Gilchrist,' Phemie appealed frantically, 'make him come to his senses before it's too late!'

'You've already done that yourself, Mother,' Colin told her, then, as she stared blankly, 'because of your visit, she sent me packing, and that was when I realised how much I wanted to be with her. I'll never be able to thank you enough for that.'

'Gilchrist!' Phemie almost screamed through the lacy handkerchief clutched to her mouth. 'I demand that you speak to your son!'

'My dear, Colin's old enough to make his own decisions,' Gilchrist Forbes pointed out, then, as the door slammed behind his wife, he laid down his fork and sighed. 'God knows if she'll ever get over this.'

'She'll have to. I meant what I said, Father, I won't give Isla up.'

The older man's brow was furrowed. 'Colin, you'll be taking on all the responsibilities of a ready-made family. Are you quite sure that Isla Moffatt means that much to you?'

'I've no doubt of it. I'd like you both to be happy for me, but if needs be, I can do without your approval. I'm going to marry Isla, as soon as possible.'

Gilchrist pushed back his chair, eyeing his half-eaten breakfast with regret. 'In that case,' he said, 'the sooner I can bring Phemie round to the idea, the better.'

28

Isla opened her eyes to darkness and the soft murmuring of the River Clyde breaking against the shore across the road from the Helensburgh hotel where she and Colin had spent their three-day honeymoon. In a few hours they would be on their way back to Paisley, back to Low Road and the children and their new life together.

Although their bodies weren't touching in the large bed she could feel his warmth lapping against her just as the broad river outside lapped the shore. Isla smiled drowsily and wriggled across the mattress until she could feel his body against hers. In spite of the chill November weather they had had three wonderful days, walking and driving together, talking, laughing, getting to know each other in an entirely new way. And there had been three wonderful nights, too, rediscovering the joy of lying in a man's arms, of loving and being desirable and loved, a luxury that she had thought would never be hers again.

They had been married quietly in the vestry of Oakshaw West Church, the church Colin's parents worshipped in, with Barbara and Ross present, and Mabel and a friend of Colin's standing as witnesses. They would have liked Ainslie and Phil to be their witnesses, but the Hannigans' twin sons had just started school, and Ainslie was reluctant to leave them with Phil's sister at such a time.

The reception had been held at Low Road. Phemie Forbes, who had no option but to accept the marriage once she realised that her son wasn't going to change his mind, had wanted to hold the reception in her home, but Colin refused.

'Miss Currie isn't strong enough to go to Stanley Drive, and we both want her to be there, so it has to be in Low Road,' he said firmly, and Phemie had no option but to give in, and be a guest at the home of her new daughter-in-law.

'You look very – pretty, my dear,' she said graciously, eyeing the pale blue wool and angora dress that Barbara had helped Isla to choose. Barbara had insisted on the hat to go with it – a slouched felt decorated with a jaunty curve of dark blue feathers. Isla had settled it at an angle on her dark head with foreboding, but when she saw the look in Colin's eyes when she stepped from the hired car at the church, she knew that Barbara had been right.

Phemie presented a powdered cheek, and Isla dutifully kissed it, knowing that Colin's mother would never fully accept her as a member of the Forbes family.

Flora, on the other hand, had regained all her former animation for the wedding reception, her cheeks flushed and her green eyes sparkling. 'I knew you two were right for each other,' she said smugly, surveying the couple before her. Colin, laughing, put an arm about his wife's shoulders.

'I wish you'd told me, then, instead of letting me waste all those years blundering about in the dark.'

'Och, I knew you'd find out for yourself eventually. Best to let things work out naturally. Anyway, you've got the rest of your lives together.'

Isla, recalling the words in the dark hotel room, smiled drowsily and brushed her lips against her husband's warm, naked shoulder. He wakened at once, turning over to scoop her into his arms. His face, already scratchy with the night's growth, snuggled against her neck.

'What time is it?'

'Go to sleep,' she whispered. 'It's not morning yet.'

'Good.' His hands slid over the silky nightdress she wore, rousing her body to an instant response. As they met and merged in the bed's warm nest, Isla felt that nothing could ever hurt her again.

In the summer of 1938, Catherine McAdam took a bad stroke and Ainslie, summoned to Scotland, arrived too late to see her mother. After the funeral she and Phil, together with their twin sons, came to Paisley.

'If I'm honest, the only emotion I have is pity,' Ainslie told Isla during one of their long talks together. 'She wouldn't let me love her, but she couldn't stop me from feeling sorry for her. She didn't really have much of a life, did she?'

'By her own choice. She could have got some pleasure out of seeing Mike and Jamie.' Isla had been appalled to hear that when Ainslie offered to bring her sons on a visit while they were still small, Catherine had refused. Ainslie had never made the offer again.

Now, she shrugged. Over the past seven years, she had absorbed much of Phil's easy-going nature. She was more relaxed than Isla had ever seen her, happy in her marriage, and delighted with her active sons. 'That was just Mother. I never could understand her, any more than she could understand me.' She stretched luxuriously. 'Isn't the house lovely and quiet?'

'For once,' Isla agreed. Phil had taken all four children down to the seaside for the day, and Colin was at work. The two women were in the kitchen, Ainslie sitting at the table, Isla icing a cake for the twins, who were to celebrate their sixth birthday in Scotland.

'What affected me most, after the funeral, was realising that I'm the only one left. There we were, the four of us, Mother and Father and me and poor little Innes – I thought that we were there for ever, and now there's only me.'

'And Phil, and Jamie, and Mike,' Isla reminded her. The boys were clearly Phil's sons, wiry and cheerful, but they both had their mother's blue eyes, and Jamie, the younger and slightly smaller twin, had red glints in his thick brown hair.

'And Barbara, and Ross,' Ainslie said. 'I'm their half-sister, remember?' She hesitated, then said carefully, 'They don't know about their father yet, do they?'

'Only that he died when they were both very small. They get on so well with Colin, and I don't want to throw any stones into the pond.'

'But isn't it time they knew the truth? Barbara at least is old enough to understand. She'll be fourteen soon.'

Isla put the icing knife down and wiped her sticky

fingers on a towel. 'I want to be sure that it's the right time – and I want to tell them myself, in my own way.'

Ainslie gave her a long look, then had the sense to change the subject. 'You and Colin are perfect together. I've never seen a couple who looked so right together. You're like—'

'A set of book-ends?'

'What I'm trying to say is that you fit each other. Colin wouldn't have been nearly as happy if he'd married me. I can be prickly at times, but Phil copes so well when I'm being difficult. He knows when to steer clear, and when to tell me to shut up and calm down.'

'He's wonderful. I just wish he would let us pay the proper price for this place.' After their marriage, Colin had tried to persuade Phil to take the market price for Isla's house, but the Canadian refused point-blank.

'We made a deal, and we shook hands on it. If I went back on it now I'd never live it down,' he drawled.

'But when you made the deal Isla was on her own, with very little money. Things have changed now. We can afford to pay the proper price.'

'No way,' Phil said flatly, then added, a gleam in his eye, ' 'Sides, at the time I got a real kick out of telling the folks at home that I'd sold a house for a few dollars. I don't want to ruin my reputation.'

'He's got no intention of taking a penny more for the house,' Ainslie said now. 'As far as Phil's concerned, the deal was fair. Do people still call it the five-shilling mansion?'

'Some, sometimes. It used to bother me, but not any more.'

'Good.' Again, Ainslie stretched her arms catlike over

341

her head, then gave a lazy laugh. 'If anyone had told me
eight years ago that I'd move to Canada and settle happily into marriage, I'd have called them a liar. Isn't life
strange?'

'Mmmm. But it's good, too.'

Ainslie used a finger to scoop up some icing that had
fallen from the knife.

'Very good,' she said indistinctly, but enthusiastically, round the fingertip in her mouth.

The Hannigans tried to persuade Isla and Colin to
return to Canada with them for a visit, but Gilchrist
Forbes had retired shortly after his son's marriage, and
it was difficult for Colin to leave the business just then.
Instead it was agreed that the family would spend the
following summer in Canada.

But while Isla was enjoying the happiest phase of
her life for many years, clouds had begun to gather
over Europe. German soldiers had marched into
Czechoslovakia; Jews in Germany were being system-
atically terrorised and stripped of all rights, and by the
summer of 1939 it looked as though war was becoming inevitable. The Territorial Army was being
strengthened, and as well as finding the task of running the office without his father's presence
demanding, Colin found himself spending more time
than ever before at Army headquarters as 1939 pro-
gressed. Isla, too, was flooded with orders from
clients, and before the school holidays arrived it
became clear to them both that the planned Canadian
holiday would have to be cancelled.

Barbara and Ross, who had been looking forward to

the trip, were heart-broken at the news. 'You promised!' Ross said accusingly, a tremor in his voice.

'I know, but that was before we realised how busy we were going to be,' Isla tried to explain, while Colin chimed in with, 'We'll go next year.'

'That's what you said last year,' Barbara pointed out, tossing her long red hair back over her shoulders.

It was pleated into pigtails for school, and combed out when she came home. Colin reached for a handful and tugged it gently.

'We'll go to North Berwick for two weeks instead. You like it there, don't you?'

'Not as much as we'd like Canada,' she told him sharply, twitching away and jerking her hair free.

'You promised!' Ross said again, his voice breaking and the gathering tears spilling over, despite all his attempts to hold them back. He scrambled to his feet and ran out of the room, banging the door.

Colin put out a restraining hand as Isla began to get to her feet. 'Leave it, love. Let him have a good bawl without being fussed over.'

'Why can't we go on our own?' Barbara persisted. 'I'm old enough to look after the two of us.'

Isla's temper began to rise. She was as disappointed as the children about their cancelled plans. Like them, she had been looking forward to seeing another country, and visiting Ainslie's home. 'For goodness' sake, Barbara, don't be so silly,' she snapped. 'We couldn't possibly do that!'

Barbara scowled, her lower lip pushing itself forward. 'I think it's very unfair!' she said hotly, and flung herself out of the room.

Listening to the sound of her daughter bounding up the stairs, Isla sighed. 'At times like this, you must regret marrying me.'

Colin reached out and raised her hand from the arm of her chair, squeezing it hard. 'Not me. They're disappointed, and who can blame them? But they'll get over it.'

But the children refused to get over it. They moped to school in the mornings and moped back again in the afternoons, long-faced and sulky. They squabbled with each other almost all the time, and refused to become interested in any plans Isla and Colin tried to make for the summer.

Isla had already written to Ainslie to explain the situation, and her reply arrived while both children were still sunk in gloom. 'We're really disappointed about your change of plans, particularly the twins. Phil and I have talked it over, and we think that you should let Barbara and Ross come for the summer anyway. You needn't worry about them travelling alone, it would give me a marvellous excuse to come to Scotland, to bring them back with me. You and Colin could surely take a little while off at the end of August to come over and take them home. It would be better than nothing. Please say yes.'

Luckily, Barbara and Ross were at school when the letter arrived. Isla kept it in her pocket, out of sight, and showed it to Colin that night when the children were in bed.

'I think we should agree,' he said when he had read it.

Isla gaped at him. 'Of course we can't agree! For one

thing, we can't have Ainslie coming all the way here just to fetch them, and for another, it would mean them being far away from us for at least six weeks.'

'I'd rather be apart for six weeks and know they're happy than have them sulking around all summer because we ruined their holiday,' Colin said reasonably. 'It's Ainslie's own idea to come for them, so we're not imposing on her. It sounds as though she'd like the chance to make the trip, and it would be good for them – and for us – to spend a little time apart. You know they'd be safe as houses with her and Phil, and they'd have a wonderful time.'

'But what if the war comes while they're away?'

'I don't think it'll happen all that quickly. We'll have time to fetch them back. I think I should be free by the end of August – it only means asking their schools to let them start the autumn term two weeks later than usual. They'll probably agree to it under the circumstances.'

'But they've never been away from me before,' Isla argued in growing panic. Colin put the letter aside and came to kneel by her chair, his hand warm against her cheek.

'Darling, I know how much they mean to you, and I've not forgotten that time Ainslie's mother tried to take Ross away from you, but that was a long time ago. Barbara's going to be fifteen in August, and Ross is eleven. You can't tie them to your apron-strings for ever.'

'I don't!' she said at once, vehemently. Then, as he said nothing, 'Do I?'

'Not exactly, but you do have a tendency to worry over them like a mother hen.' Colin's voice was light, but with a serious undertone. 'It's understandable, but at the same time, it's not good for them to be over-protected, Isla.'

'I'm going to bed.' She got up quickly, the movement knocking his hand away from her face. Alone in their bedroom, brushing her hair, she stared into her own eyes in the dressing-table mirror. Colin's words had hurt, but they had to be faced.

For years, between the time of Kenneth's death and her marriage to Colin, the children had been her sole responsibility, all that she had. Every meal they ate, each day they survived, had been the result of her efforts. She could still recall, as though it had happened only the day before, the terror of almost losing Ross to Catherine McAdam, and the lesser, but still frightening, threat of losing Barbara to Aunt Lally. But as Colin had pointed out, these fears belonged to the past, to a time of deep insecurity and uncertainty. The children were growing up now, Colin was part of their lives, and Ainslie was nothing like her mother. There was no threat as far as she and Phil were concerned.

The brush slowed, and stopped. When Colin came into the room some time later Isla was still at the dressing-table, gazing into her own reflected eyes. She jumped slightly at the light touch of his hands on her shoulders, looking up to meet his gaze in the glass.

'You're right, I do tend to fret about them too much,' she said slowly, reaching her fingers up to cover his. 'It's time to start letting go.'

The cloud that had been hanging over the household lifted as soon as Barbara and Ross were told that they

346

could spend summer in Canada after all. They immediately began to shower Isla with assurances of their
very best behaviour during the visit to Ainslie and
Phil.

'If they keep their vows, you'll find yourself playing
hostess to a pair of saints,' Isla said wryly to Ainslie
when she arrived in Scotland a few days before Barbara
and Ross were due to finish school.

'I hope not, I couldn't take the strain. Try to come
over before the end of August,' Ainslie coaxed. 'If you
wait until then you'll have very little time with us, and
I've been so looking forward to introducing you to all
our friends.'

'We'll try. But Colin's really busy, and for some
strange reason everyone wants to buy dolls' houses –
I've never had so many orders all at once.'

'Mebbe they're trying to hold on to the good things
of life while they can.'

'You sense it too?'

Ainslie was curled up in an armchair in Isla's living-
room, her feet tucked beneath her. She was still lithe,
though motherhood and maturity had softened and
rounded her body. Her curly red hair had been cut
short, framing a tanned face with freckles sprinkled like
a drift of gold dust across nose and cheekbones. The
twins were also freckled, but much more heavily. 'With
more freckle than face,' Barbara had teased them the
previous summer.

'It's hard to ignore the atmosphere in this country at
the moment. People don't actually come out and talk
about the possibility of a war, but I can see it in their
eyes, hear it in their voices.' She gave a sudden,

involuntary shiver. 'We talk about it in Canada, too, but the threat of it seems to feel closer here. Britain's such a small country, and everything's more concentrated in a place that's surrounded by water.' She shivered again, then, said briskly, 'Listen to me – all gloom and doom. It probably won't come to anything, and the children'll have a wonderful time with us, I promise.'

Upstairs, a door opened and shut loudly several times. Voices clamoured shrilly above the noise of feet thundering down the stairs and across the hall. The front door opened, then closed, and the voices rocketed past the window, fading as the group of boys, led by eleven-year-old Ross, ran round the house to the back garden.

'Are you quite sure you want to take on the responsibility of my two?' Isla asked as the noise died away. 'Ross never seems to tire, and Barbara can be quite an insufferable little madam at times.'

'It'll be fine, don't worry. There's lots of space at home to run wild in, and Phil's great with kids. He knows when to put his foot down without stamping on anyone. As for Barbara – I'll enjoy getting to know my kid sister,' Ainslie said.

She and the children sailed from Greenock a week later. Ross, who hadn't quite shaken off the little-boy look, and was chubbily cherubic in grey shorts and a grey jacket over shirt and tie, couldn't wait to start the great adventure that lay before him. He gave Isla then Colin a strangling hug, then raced up the gangplank of the steamer waiting to take the passengers out to the Tail of the Bank, where the liner lay. One sock, Isla noticed as she watched him go, was already coming down, and his ginger hair had broken free of the cold-water combing she had given it not much more than an hour earlier.

Barbara, already a stranger in her first grown-up costume, hugged her mother, then Colin, more sedately, but with warmth.

'I'll write every week – I'll tell you everything that happens,' she promised.

'And I'll make sure she does – that they both do,' Ainslie said. 'Don't fret. And take good care of yourself, and each other.' She hugged them both, then said in a choked voice, 'Come on, Barbara, let's go and get it over with. I hate goodbyes. They make me cry, and I hate crying even more than I hate goodbyes!'

As the two of them went towards the gangplank, Barbara's flared skirt swung round slim, sleekly stockinged legs and the sun sparked red lights from her hair, peeping out from beneath the green beret set stylishly to one side. Isla had never felt so desolate in her life. She clung to Colin's arm, convinced that if she didn't restrain herself she would run up the gangplank and snatch her children back.

'They change so quickly,' she said tearfully as she and Colin drove home after watching the liner move regally down-river towards the open sea, tugs fussing round her. 'They'll be entirely different by the time we see them again!'

'It won't be all that long. We'll be joining them in a matter of weeks,' Colin reassured her. 'In the meantime, just think about the fun we're going to have, with some time to ourselves for a change. It'll be like being newly-weds. We'll start tonight – I'll take you out for dinner in a restaurant, somewhere special, with candles on the table.'

That summer seemed to pass more swiftly than any other. In August, Barbara celebrated her fifteenth birthday in Canada, and Ainslie and Phil gave her a big party. Judging by the letters they wrote every week, both children were having a wonderful time.

But the news from Europe grew more ominous, with the Germans poised to march into Poland. Towards the end of August it became clear that Colin wouldn't be able to get away from the office after all, and Isla would have to go to Canada on her own. But when she tried to book a passage, she discovered that all the shipping lines were busy because of a flood of bookings from Canadians returning home, and parents sending their children away from Britain to the safety of another country.

Reluctantly, because she had never flown before, she tried the airlines, only to find that they were in the same situation.

'If it comes to it, you could go on a one-way ticket,' Colin suggested. 'I'd rather have the three of you safe in Canada if we do go to war.'

'I don't like the idea of leaving you here on your own for goodness knows how long,' she said, then tried to make light of the situation. 'Your mother would probably start introducing you to eligible young women as soon as my back was turned.'

'Oh, I think she's realised by now that I'm a very married man.'

'I'm not so sure,' Isla said dryly. Since the wedding,

she and Phemie Forbes had only met each other when they had to, and on those few occasions there was still a coolness in the air. It was clear that Phemie could not get over her disappointment at her son's choice of wife.

'Isla, I may not be here for long.'

'But you're thirty-four, Colin. They'll be calling up younger men, surely.'

'I'm not exactly Methuselah,' he protested, then, his smile fading, 'I'm in the Territorials, love. I've been trained, and if they want me, I'm willing to go.'

'What about the business?'

'My father's going to come out of retirement, so that he can take over when the time comes. We've already discussed it and I think he's quite excited at the thought of being in the office again. So you see, you might be left here alone. At least in Canada you'd be with the children.'

'If it comes to war, the children will be fine with Ainslie. And if you do go away, I'd want to be here for you when you have leave. Anyway, there's Flora to consider − I'd not leave her now, after all she's done for me.'

Ainslie phoned, her voice crackly and distant, coming and going as though the telephone cable was being swung to and fro on waves, to say that she had investigated the possibility of bringing Barbara and Ross back to Scotland herself, only to find, as Isla had, that liners and aeroplanes alike were fully booked. Ross and Barbara both spoke to their mother, sounding excited at the prospect of staying on in Canada for longer than planned. Ainslie had taken the first step towards enrolling them in local schools, just in case, and Ross was looking forward to that.

'It won't be like being in school at home, because of them sounding different because they're Canadians,' he explained.

Barbara at least had the tact to say, just before the call ended, 'We miss you both, Mum, but everything's fine here, and it won't be for long, will it?'

'Not long,' Isla agreed, praying that she was telling the truth.

Colin, struck to the heart by the look on her face as she put down the phone, redoubled his efforts to get her to Canada, and almost managed to get her a berth on the liner *Athenia*. But even as Isla was packing for the trip the booking fell through, and the liner sailed without her.

Two days later, the German army marched into Poland, and Britain declared war.

'There's still the chance of getting the children back,' Isla said hopefully as Colin switched off the wireless, Neville Chamberlain's war announcement still ringing in their ears. 'Surely nothing will happen for a little while. I'll keep trying.'

On the following evening Colin came into the kitchen where Isla and Nan were getting the evening meal ready, his face like stone.

'Look . . .' He held his newspaper out and Isla took it, sinking into a chair as she read the headlines. The *Athenia*, packed with passengers, had been torpedoed on the previous day, only hours after Britain had declared war on Germany. More than a hundred people had died, including children on their way to safety in Canada.

'That's that,' Colin said flatly. 'You stay here, and Barbara and Ross stay with Ainslie, until this business is over.'

Later, in the privacy of their bedroom, he said wretchedly, 'Isla, I'm so sorry. I should never have talked you into letting them go. If it hadn't been for me, they'd be here, with us. I should have known better!'

'You weren't to know that things were going to happen so quickly. And you were right – it was time they learned to spend time away from me.' She summoned up a smile. 'We're more fortunate than some of those poor souls that are having to send their children away from the cities without knowing who they're going to. Barbara and Ross will be fine with Ainslie and Phil – they'll look on the whole thing as an adventure.'

But behind the smile was the icy realisation that the die was cast, and her children thousands of miles away from her, perhaps for years. There was no chance, now, of getting them back until the matter was resolved. Isla kept on smiling reassuringly into Colin's worried, guilty face, but inside, she felt as though her heart was breaking.

Paisley, like every other town in Britain, seethed with preparations for war. Policemen were to be seen on the streets with gasmasks hanging at their sides and tin helmets slung over their shoulders, and Isla stood in long queues to obtain heavy black curtaining for the windows, and sticky netting which she and Nan and Colin, with Drew's help, put over every window to prevent shards of glass flying into the rooms in the event of the windows being smashed during air-raids. As there was no basement to shelter in if a raid came, she bought a large solid table from Charlie Blayne's auction room and had it placed against the back wall of the living-room.

'It's hideous,' Colin said flatly when he saw it.

'But it's solid. If there's a raid, Nan and I can pull the couch across in front of it and even if the whole window comes in we'll be safe.'

'And if the house collapses about your ears?'

She banged on the table with her knuckles. 'It won't, but even if it does, Nan and I and Flora, if we can get her under it, will be quite safe beneath that table until we're dug out.'

'For God's sake, woman, don't say things like that!' Colin pulled her into his arms and held her tightly. She clung to him, knowing, though she would never admit it to him, that the thought of his going away from her, possibly being badly hurt or killed, was far more frightening than the fear of anything happening to her. For the time being, at least, she had lost her children; she couldn't bear the thought of losing Colin, too.

First Aid posts were set up, one of them in the West School, and Drew came back from registering for the services and proposed to his girlfriend, who accepted him.

'We're not going to get married before I go,' he explained to Isla, shyly but proudly. 'But when I'm away from Paisley it'll be good to know that she's mine. It'll give me something to stay alive for.'

'I hope you both have a very long and happy life together.' On an impulse Isla reached up and kissed Drew, who went crimson and escaped to his workshop as soon as he was released. He was twenty-five now, but, to her, he was still the shy teenager who had helped her to dig the potato patch in George Street. Isla watched him hurry from the room, and hoped that the war might be over soon, before too many young lads like Drew were dragged into it.

A blackout was imposed at once, and by the end of the year a number of local people were among the first victims of the war, some of them knocked down in the darkened night streets by cars and buses and tramcars, others killed or injured by tumbles down narrow stone stairs in unlit tenement buildings. Gas masks were issued and after trying hers on, Isla hurriedly tore herself free of the constricting straps, dragging in gulps of air.

'I'd rather take my chances with the gas!'

'You'll wear that mask if you're told to, for as long as you must,' Colin told her grimly.

'But I couldn't breathe!'

He caught her by the shoulders and shook her. 'Listen, Isla, I've been through a gas tank in training, and believe me, you're much better off with the mask. So wear it!'

Magret, too, hated the gas masks. 'It doesn't seem to bother the lassies,' she said mournfully on a visit to Isla's kitchen. 'They go off every day with their masks over their shoulders in wee cardboard boxes, and not a care in the world, and there's me worried sick, wondering what would be worst – me choking in that nasty smelly thing, or them coming home to find me gassed on the floor,'

'I'll be wearing mine,' Nan said firmly. 'I'm all for

staying alive.' Nan had already volunteered for duty in one of the town's first-aid posts, and was an avid collector of silver paper and waste paper and cardboard for the war effort.

Shy little Mrs Kelly, Mrs Leach's daughter, had given birth to a son almost a year earlier, and to George Street's astonishment, Mrs Leach, the dragon who had been the bane of the street children's lives for many years, had become a doting grandmother. When 'baby helmets', the small compartments intended to hold the entire child and protect it against gas attacks, were made available, Magret's account of helping to fit little Boyd Kelly into his helmet had Isla and Nan in tears of laughter.

'Honest tae God, ye'd need at least a week's warnin' tae get that wean ready,' Magret insisted, elbows on the kitchen table. 'As fast as we got an arm in, a leg popped out. It was like trying tae fit a chicken back intae its egg three days later. What with the wee soul roaring his head off, and Mrs Leach giving orders, the place was in an uproar. Finally she pushes the lot of us out of the road and says she'll dae it herself – you know what she's like, Isla, aye has tae be in charge. Then she lifts the bairn up and starts tellin' him that Gran wants him tae be a good boy and let her tuck him intae the contraption.' She beamed at her listeners. 'That was when his nappy fell off and he peed all down the front of her good blouse.'

Despite all the haste of the war preparations, a strange lethargy fell on the town as 1939 gave way to 1940. Men who had registered for call-up continued to work, and for a while life went on as before. Orders still came in for dolls' houses, and in the little spare time he had, Colin, following exhortations to dig for victory, helped the elderly gardener who came once a week to dig up most of the back lawn and plant vegetables for future consumption. It was like waiting for the starter's gun to start the race, Isla thought, and being unable to move until it was fired.

Canada, too, had declared war on Germany, but to his chagrin, Phil was unable to sign up because of a knee injury he had sustained shortly after the twins' birth, when he had been caught in the path of some timber that had broken loose in his yard.

'He's needed here in any case, because the yard's important to war work,' Ainslie wrote. 'Several of his friends are going, and I've given them all your address in case they ever find themselves in Scotland. Barbara and Ross have settled in very well at school. Barbara's keeping her piano lessons going, as well as studying dancing. She wanted to take singing lessons, too, but Phil and I thought that that might be too much for her to cope with on top of everything else. A music teacher I know heard her sing, and says that she has a natural talent that shouldn't be suppressed, so thankfully Barbara's given up on that idea.'

For their part, Ross and Barbara's letters were filled with enthusiasm and excitement.

'It's all a big adventure to them,' Isla told Magret bleakly. 'They're having a wonderful time.'

'Bairns is like men and pet dogs, hen,' her friend said knowledgeably. 'As long as there's someone around tae keep their bellies filled and give them a fireside tae sit by and a roof over their heads, they're happy enough.

357

But that doesnae mean they're no' missing ye. They will be, but they'll no' want tae say too much about that, because they know that it'd worry ye. Everything'll turn out fine, you'll see.'

Busy though Colin was with the garden and further training with the Territorials, and with organising the office so that his father could run it in his absence, Isla sensed a growing restlessness about him.

'You can't wait to go, can you?' she asked one evening as they stumbled home arm in arm through the pitch-black night, with only a pencil-thin line of light from a hooded torch to guide them. At Colin's suggestion, they had been to the Regal Cinema to see the Ritz Brothers in *The Three Musketeers*, but even during the film, with people laughing all around them, she had been aware of his tension.

'In one way I don't want to go at all, but in another – well, I've got this daft notion that if I can just get away and do something, the whole rotten business might be over and done with and we can all get on with our lives. I hate all this waiting!'

Isla, who had put her name down with the Nursing Reserve and was waiting to hear from them, understood how he felt. But they had no option but to wait.

Greta reached her fifteenth birthday and went to work in a shop in the High Street. Not long after that, Magret achieved her greatest ambition when she and her family moved into a two-bedroomed flat in a more modern tenement further along George Street. There was a tiny scullery, only large enough for one person at a time, and a bathroom.

With three of the family working, Magret achieved another long-term ambition, and got Tommy's auntie's clock out of the pawnshop. It sat on her new mantelshelf in pride of place – a huge and hideous black marble creation like a Greek temple, complete with a roof and pillars. Magret was in her element.

Isla and Colin celebrated Christmas quietly with Nan and Flora Currie, and early in 1940 the dolls'-house business was put into mothballs when Drew was called up and Mabel went into the Women's Auxiliary Air Force.

In April, Hitler's army invaded Denmark and Norway. Colin was summoned to Aldershot for further orders and Isla started nursing in the Craw Road Sanatorium, about ten minutes' walk away from Low Road.

Suddenly, the starter had fired his pistol, and the grim race to win the war was on.

29

All the sanatorium patients who were well enough to be sent home had gone by the time Isla started work there, and the remainder were put into two small wards. The other wards dealt with a mixture of patients, so that the Royal Alexandra Infirmary, Paisley's largest hospital, could be freed for incoming wounded, or people injured in the air-raids that were already hitting southern England.

As a partially trained nurse, Isla was given the more mundane tasks, fetching and carrying, emptying bed-pans, helping to clean the wards and serve meals and bathe patients. But despite that, and despite an aching back and feet that were so sore at the end of a shift that they could scarcely carry her home, she enjoyed being back in a hospital routine. For one thing, it kept her occupied, easing the helpless frustration of missing Colin and the children and worrying about them continuously.

Colin was sent to France, and had scarcely landed there when the German tanks broke through and the British Expeditionary Forces found themselves outnum-bered and in retreat. He came home only a month after leaving for Aldershot, with one arm in a sling after being hit by flying shrapnel at Dunkirk, embarrassed at being wounded before he had had a chance to do any fighting, and bitter with memories of the nightmare on the French beaches, where men under fire from the enemy clawed their way desperately through the shallows, trying to scramble aboard the mongrel flotilla of ships and boats that had come to snatch them to safety. Two short weeks later he returned to his regiment, fit for action again.

Letters arrived regularly from Ainslie, Barbara and Ross. Ainslie sent photographs, and parcels of tinned meat and fruit that were gratefully received, for rationing was already biting deep into civilian life. Isla shared the food with Flora Currie, and with Magret and, through Magret, the residents of the old tenement. Although she no longer lived there, Magret still took a keen interest in the place. She had even persuaded young Mrs Kelly, whose husband had been called up, to secure a job in the mills, and now the two of them worked beside each other.

Only Mrs Leach, who looked after her grandson while his mother was at work, declined to take anything from Isla. She did her best to make her daughter follow suit, but Mrs Kelly, with a growing son to feed, defied her mother and accepted her share of the tins gratefully, as did the others.

'Is that no' what life's all about?' Magret asked. 'War or no war, if we don't help each other we deserve all we get. Never mind that Mrs Leach, there's no understanding her at all, but the lassie's really nice, when ye get her away from the old woman. She must take after her da, rest his soul.'

Phemie Forbes threw herself into war work with enthusiasm. She joined the Women's Voluntary Service, and in her spare time she knitted for the troops. She was hardly ever to be seen these days without knitting needles in her hands and a half-finished garment in khaki wool on her lap. Isla, who for Colin's sake made a point of calling on Phemie at least once every week, sitting on the edge of a chair in the Forbeses' drawing-room and making small talk to the background of clicking needles, often thought that her mother-in-law looked like a fly perched in the middle of a khaki web.

Gilchrist, guiltily revelling in the luxury of having the reins of the business in his own hands again, referred to his wife's continual industry as knitting for victory, or stitching up the war. He and Isla got on well together and he often called in on her on his way back from the office, sitting in the living-room with his feet sprawled over the carpet, just as his son had once done.

Colin, in England for the remainder of 1940, was able to come home on leave fairly regularly, but at the end of the year his regiment was sent overseas and Isla was forced to settle down to a life bereft of husband and children. Throughout 1940, radio broadcasts had conveyed reports of the horror of the interminable raids on London and Coventry and Liverpool; once 1941 arrived, Paisley's sirens started sounding more frequently, and Isla and Nan, both busy with their war work, saw little of each other.

Clydebank, a shipbuilding town not far from Paisley, was almost destroyed by a devastating two-night air raid in March. Isla was on duty both nights, and as most of the patients were kept awake by the unnerving wail of the sirens, the sound of wave after wave of German planes rumbling through the sky, and the distant thump of anti-aircraft guns, all the staff on duty had a hard time of it. Hurrying from one building to the other on the first night of the raid, Isla saw the searchlights weaving back and forth across the sky. A faint rosy glow on the horizon, almost like the early promise of a beautiful sunrise, marked Clydebank's agony by fire.

Some of the 'Bankers' who had been bombed and burned out of their homes came to Paisley, and a family of four, a dazed young mother and her three children, spent a few weeks in Isla's home. It was like the old days, when Barbara and Ross were home. Both Isla and Nan revelled in the luxury of having children around, and Nan, the most efficient person that Isla had ever known, worked wonders when it came to finding enough food to keep ever-hungry little stomachs content. They were both sorry when the family moved on, to stay with relatives in Stranraer.

Early in May it was the turn of Greenock, another Clydeside town famed for its large shipyards. It, too, was bombarded for two nights, and again, the enemy bombers flew over Paisley, but this time they didn't pass by harmlessly. On the first night, an incendiary bomb landed not far from Low Road, on the railway embankment close to Ferguslie Mills.

On the following night, Isla, who was off duty, was wakened by the mournful wail of the sirens. Nan was on duty that night, and Isla was alone. She dressed hurriedly and ran through the dark to Flora's house, blundering into bushes, fumbling impatiently with the stiff catch on Flora's gate.

Betty, the housekeeper, opened the door to Isla. 'Thank goodness you're here, Mrs Forbes. She refuses to let me help her to get dressed. She'll not leave her bed!'

'I'll see to her.' Isla hurried across the hall to the little room that had once housed Flora's dolls' houses. Not long before the war began, they had been moved upstairs so that the ground-floor room could be turned into a bedroom for the old lady, who was finding it increasingly difficult to cope with stairs. Colin had supervised the installation of a small ground-floor bathroom adjacent to the kitchen.

In spite of all Isla's pleading and coaxing and threatening, Flora refused to leave the comfort of her bed. 'After all those years, I see no sense in trying to prolong my life by making it a misery,' she announced. 'Squatting beneath a table isn't dignified. I decided the last time you got me to do that that I'd never do it again. I'm fine where I am.'

She could scarcely be heard over the noise of the planes passing overhead. The sky must be thick with them, Isla thought, glancing fearfully up at the ceiling. It was hard to credit that so many could crowd into such a small patch of sky. The mind-picture of big heavy machines colliding with each other and falling on the houses beneath came to her, and refused to leave. 'Flora, you might get hurt if you stay here. You're right beside the window. It's far safer in the living-room.'

'If my end's coming, it'll come no matter whether I'm cowering on the carpet or lying comfortably in my bed.'

'What about Betty? And me? If you insist on staying here, we'll have to stay with you.'

'No you don't.' All that could be seen of Flora were bright eyes, grass-green in the lamplight, peering over the edge of the quilt gripped in her two hands. Her voice was muffled, but determined. 'I don't want your deaths on my conscience, but I'm not stirring one step. I'm too old to be bothered by all this palaver!'

'Flora Currie, if you don't let us help you up right now, we'll just have to drag you out of your bed and carry you into the living-room.'

There was no reply. Isla and Betty looked helplessly at each other, knowing that they couldn't leave her, or risk a heart attack by forcing her into safety.

Isla thought wistfully of the big solid table in the living-room next door, then said slowly, 'There's that old folding screen we found in the attic and put in the drawing-room.'

After a struggle, the two women managed to fit the large, ungainly screen between the window and the bed, then settled down in the dim light of a torch to wait the raid out. Flora dozed, and was still asleep when there was a great blast of sound from somewhere and their empty teacups, placed on the bedside table, jangled together with the vibration. The entire house shook, and Isla threw herself across the bed to protect the old woman against breaking glass. Betty screamed, then went scrambling after the torch, which had rolled from the bedside table to the floor, as Flora, waking with a start, hit out with her fists at the sudden weight across her.

'In the name of God, lassie, I thought I'd been attacked,' she said reproachfully when the torch was found and order restored.

'I was trying to keep you from getting killed.'

Flora tutted. 'It's you that needs saving, not me. Didn't I say that if my time's come, it's come? There's a man and two bonny children that'll be wanting to see you safe and well when this nonsense is over.'

'D'you think it landed in Low Road?' Betty whispered when Flora had drifted back into sleep.

'It wasn't that close. Maybe the mills – or George Street.' The day before, the railway embankment close to the mills had been set alight by incendiary bombs. Some thought that the mills had been the real target.

'Whatever it was, it was close,' Betty said. 'And it was big.' They stared at each other, wondering what the dawn would bring.

They finally slept, huddled in armchairs by the bed, sleeping right through the All Clear and waking to blessed silence, broken only by the birds' dawn chorus.

Leaving Betty to snatch an hour's sleep in her own bed, Isla went back home. It was early yet to expect Nan home; if the night's explosion had meant death and injury to some poor souls, she might be later than usual, kept busy at her first-aid post.

Isla went to bed, but couldn't sleep. Finally she got up again, dressed, and made breakfast, expecting to hear Nan's key in the lock at any moment.

She was drinking her second cup of tea when Mr Smith from further up the road came to the door, wearing his official ARP tin helmet and armband. He looked as though he hadn't slept for a week.

'Mrs Forbes, I'm afraid I've got bad news,' he began. 'Colin—'

'No, no, it's got nothing to do with your husband,'

he said hurriedly, then, 'that explosion last night – a landmine scored a direct hit on the first-aid post at Woodside . . .'

The church at the foot of New Street had been set aside as a temporary mortuary. Isla walked to it down George Street, her feet crunching on broken glass, and waited in line to go in to identify Nan. War meant queuing for everything, she thought drearily. Buying food, buying clothes, identifying the dead. She caught snatches of talk from the others waiting with her. The landmine had been clearly seen, drifting down through the searchlights, swinging from its parachute. If the wind had only carried it a hundred yards further on, it would have landed on the cemetery where Kenneth and his son lay. Almost immediately after the landmine had hit the first-aid post, killing doctors, nurses, ambulance drivers, and helpers like Nan, another bomb had landed on the east wing of the West School, used as an auxiliary fire station, killing several firefighters. Again, the general belief was that the mills, so close to both explosions that most of their windows had been blown in, had been the target.

When her turn came, and the corner of the blanket was lifted aside, she looked down at Nan, eyes closed, mouth slack, her greying brown hair, always in such a neat roll, untidy and darkly clotted at one side. 'Yes, that's Nan – Mrs Agnes Urquhart,' she corrected herself.

'Is she from Paisley?'

'Her sisters live in Stirling. She's been widowed for years. I'll write to her family,' Isla said. Her guide nodded and dropped the blanket.

367

'Ninety-two killed in all,' he said as he escorted her from the church, 'and every last one of 'em decent folk doing their duty. When's this terrible business going to stop?'

Isla left the building, passing the people who still waited outside, to claim their own dead, and walked home, heedless now of the broken glass under her feet. At that moment, she was glad that Barbara and Ross were safe in Canada, where the bombs couldn't reach them.

The house seemed very empty when she let herself in. Once there had been Colin and Drew and Mabel and the children – and Nan, who had, in her own way, been the very heart of the house. Now there was only Isla. She paused at the foot of the stairs, the newel post solid beneath her hand, and looked up towards the landing, remembering all the times she had stood there in the past, calling to the children to make less noise.

For a moment she knew blind, suffocating panic, wondering how she was going to be able to keep going on her own, then, quite unexpectedly, the tears came. She clung to the polished post, letting all the grief come out, crying noisily like a child, because now there was nobody there to be disturbed by her misery. When the tears finally ebbed then stopped, she went into the kitchen – Nan's kitchen – and sluiced her face with cold water, then made herself a cup of tea before going to tell Flora about Nan.

At the end of the year, the Japanese bombed Pearl Harbor, and America came into the war. And the terrible business continued.

*

'Here, let me give you a hand.'

Isla, who had assumed that she was alone in the garden, jumped and almost sliced off the toe of her wellington boot when she heard the voice. For a moment she thought that the easy drawl was Phil's, then as she spun round she saw a stranger advancing towards her from the corner of the house.

'Sorry, did I startle you?' He took the spade from her and eyed the rows of green shoots. 'They're too small to be dug up.'

'I know, but I wanted to give my neighbour some new potatoes.'

'Okay.' Effortlessly, he buried the spade to its shaft in the earth. Isla stepped aside and left him to it. She had no idea who he was, but she was glad of the chance to straighten her aching back.

The man bent to the spade, then heaved it up with a soft grunt. The potato shaw keeled over and small pale potatoes gleamed through the crumbling earth. He put the spade aside and knelt to run his hands through the soil, gathering the frugal harvest.

'There aren't many.'

'There's enough.' Isla held out her basket and he put the potatoes into it, then dusted his hands together as he stood up.

'Are you Isla? Isla Forbes? Phil and Ainslie told me to look you up if I was in the area.'

'You're Canadian?'

A grin split his thin face. 'Most folks can tell that the minute I open my mouth,' he said, then thrust his hand out. 'Gregg Marshall.'

A sudden April shower began to fall, and Isla, who

hadn't slept well earlier in the day despite being exhausted by her busy night on duty, smothered a yawn and collected her wits. 'I was just going to make myself a cup of tea. Would you like one?'

'That'd be fine, if it's not too much trouble.'

She led him into the house through the back door and put the basket of potatoes down on the dresser, then began to ease her first wellington off.

'Sit down.' He knelt before her, taking her muddy foot in his hands, levering the tight boot off skilfully. 'There we are – now the other one.'

'That one's always hard to get off.'

'I've never yet met the boot that could get the better of me. Tod, my eldest, has the darnedest knack of getting his socks wedged down inside his boots, so I learned at a hard school.'

Sitting on a wooden chair, clinging to the seat to avoid being pulled off by the final tug on the boot, Isla looked down on a mass of curly light brown hair. The boot came off and he tipped his head back to smile triumphantly at her before setting it to one side with its companion, then washing his hands at the sink. Isla, padding barefoot across the kitchen in search of her slippers, was uncomfortably aware that she didn't look her best in one of Colin's jerseys and an old skirt. She hadn't been expecting anyone to call.

'D'you mind if I get these potatoes ready for Flora?' She eyed the clock. 'We'll be eating in an hour, because she likes to get to bed early and I'm going on duty.'

'Not at all. Can I help?'

When she declined the offer, he peeled off his leather jacket then sat down at the table. 'I'm stationed down at

Prestwick Aerodrome, and Ainslie said that if I found myself in Scotland I had to call and say hello from the Hannigans, and from Barbara and Ross.'

Isla, washing the tiny potatoes, turned from the sink, heedless of the water dripping from her hands. 'You know the children? How are they? Are they happy?'

'I know them well. We live pretty close to Phil and Ainslie. You've got a couple of nice kids, Mrs Forbes – and they're doing fine, believe me. Barbara has a wonderful voice. She sang in a concert for the troops just before we left for Europe. She's doing a lot of singing, helping to raise money for the war effort as well as singing for the troops.'

'She's always loved music.'

As she put the potatoes on to cook and made the tea Isla told Gregg Marshall about the back-court concerts Barbara used to run, and he listened with genuine interest, then said, 'You know she's been on radio a few times?'

'Oh yes, she wrote to tell me all about it.'

'Pat – my wife – envies you, you know. She always wanted a girl, just like your Barbara, but after three boys she's given up hope. Maybe when this is all over . . .' He paused, lost for a moment in his own thoughts, then said, 'You must miss them a lot.'

'I do. I miss them dreadfully,' Isla said, fussing over the potatoes in order to hide the tears that had gathered in her eyes.

Luckily, she had managed to make some buns the day before. She put them out on a plate, together with a precious pot of raspberry jam Nan had made a year earlier from Flora's raspberry bushes, and watched with carefully hidden concern as Gregg Marshall spooned precious sugar into his cup. She herself had learned, like most civilians, to get used to drinking tea without sugar.

'Ainslie told me your husband's in the Army.'

'The artillery. He's with the Fifty-first Highland Division now, in Egypt as far as I know.'

'I thought most of the Fifty-first were captured in France?'

'They were, after Dunkirk. They were cut off, trying to get to the beaches. But the regiment's been rebuilt with men seconded from other regiments. That's how Colin came to be with them.'

Gregg put the sugar bowl down and started stirring his tea, then stopped suddenly. 'Oh heck!' He looked across the table at Isla, his eyes, very clear blue, concerned. 'I've just realised – is this all the sugar you're allowed?'

'It's all right, I don't use much.'

His thin, rugged face flushed. 'I should have thought – we're not used to this rationing you folks have to deal with. I'll bring you some from the base.'

'You don't need to do that, I can manage very well.'

'You live alone?'

'Our housekeeper, Nan, used to share the house with me, but she was killed last year by a landmine.'

'I'm sorry.'

'So am I.' Isla felt the tears threatening again, and blinked hard. 'I still miss her very much.'

'You must get very lonely, with your husband and kids away.'

'Not really. Most of the time, I'm working at the sanatorium, or with my neighbour. Life's so frantic at times that on the few occasions I'm on my own here, I've learned to quite enjoy the solitude.'

'Pat would hate it. She could never stand her own company, not that she gets the chance now, with three boys to raise on her own.' Gregg reached for his jacket and brought a handful of photographs out of an inner pocket, proudly showing off his pretty blonde wife and his three sandy-haired sons. To Isla's delight, Ross was in a few of the photographs, squinting into the camera as he always did, and seventeen-year-old Barbara was in one, long-legged and mature in trousers and a blouse, perched on a wall, laughing into the camera, her mane of curly hair blowing about her face.

Isla studied the children she hadn't been able to touch for almost three years, hungry for every detail. Ross, who had lost the last trace of infant plumpness, was only a week away from another birthday. She had posted a long letter to him, and a book inscribed on the flyleaf, 'To Ross on his fourteenth birthday, with much love from Mum and Dad. April 1942.'

When she relinquished the photographs to Gregg he separated those with Ross and Barbara in them and gave them back. 'They're for you.'

'But your own boys are in them, and Ainslie's been very good about sending letters and photographs. I'm filling my third album now.'

'Keep them anyway, I've got plenty of snapshots of the boys.' He looked at his watch. 'I'd better be going.'

'Come next door and meet my neighbour first. She doesn't get out now and she loves company. Stay and have a meal with us,' Isla urged.

'If you're sure—'

'I'm quite sure. It won't be much, but we'd both be glad of the company.'

The rain had stopped when they left the house, but enough had fallen to give the earth a fresh, cool smell. As they walked out of her gate, then along the pavement for a few yards and in at Flora's gate, Isla tried to work out how to stretch the meal to cover another person. She had made some vegetable soup, and had handed her meat ration over to Betty so that she could make a stew for the three of them. They often pooled their resources.

Flora, looking almost like a faded photograph of the woman Isla had first met outside the West School, was in her usual chair in the front room, a blanket that Isla, Barbara and Nan had knitted for her tucked over her knees. Her white hair covered her skull in soft wisps and her face was gaunt, but her green eyes were still able to sparkle up at the tall airman when Isla introduced him.

'It's just like having Phil here again. So you're at Prestwick? A pilot?'

'Nothing as grand, ma'am. I'm ground crew – a mechanic to trade.'

'You'll have some whisky,' Flora stated. 'The bottle's in the sideboard, Isla, and the glasses. No need to worry, young man, we'll not send you back to the aero-drome drunk. There's not that much whisky left, so you'll only get enough to make you thirst for more.'

Gregg took the tiny glass from Isla and looked at its spoonful of amber whisky. 'I see what you mean, Miss Currie.'

'It's the thought that counts – and I can assure you

that the thought's worth half a tumblerful of Scotland's finest malt,' Flora told him. His laughter followed Isla out of the room as she went in search of Betty to tell her that there would be a guest for dinner.

'But, Mrs Forbes, there's scarce enough to feed us, let alone a man!'

'We'll manage. We'll have to – I thought it would be good for Flora to have some new company for a change, and anyway, it was good of the man to come and visit.' Isla lifted pot lids and peered inside. 'We can use small plates for the soup, and with Flora eating the wee new potatoes, there'll be enough of the others to go round. If I'd known he was coming I could mebbe have got a rabbit,' she fretted, studying the stew that would be hard put to it to stretch to four helpings. 'D'you have any corned beef left?'

'Just a slice, but I was keeping it for Miss Currie's lunch tomorrow.'

'I can let you have some of mine for her lunch,' Isla said rashly. 'Break the slice up and mix it into the stew, and beat a slice of bread in as well, to make it look more. Add some water to the gravy, too. I brought the rest of the buns, so we can fill up with them afterwards, with a cup of tea. He's heavy on the sugar, but we'll get by.'

Even though she and Betty served the meal on the smallest plates they could find, it didn't amount to much. Gregg Marshall made no comment, but Isla noticed that he took only one spoonful of sugar with his tea.

'She's a wonderful old lady,' he said when the two of them left Flora's home.

'She enjoyed your company. You must visit us again.'

'I surely will – and I'll bring you some sugar.'

'There's no need for that.'

'I feel bad about taking your supply. Can I give you a lift to your hospital?' he asked as they stepped on to the pavement. Isla eyed the motor-cycle propped on its stand outside her gate, and explained that the sanatorium was just a step away, and she would walk there. When the machine had roared off up the road, bringing one or two neighbours to their windows, she went into the house to get ready for work.

Flora was in bed, her eyes still bright, when Isla looked in, as she always did on her way to and from the sanatorium.

'It was nice to see a new face, wasn't it? He was just like Phil – these Canadians seem to get such enjoyment out of life. Not like the dour Scots at all. I hope some of that rubs off on your bairns, Isla. It'd be good for them.'

30

Gregg came back often, roaring up to the gate on his motor-cycle, bringing delicacies such as sugar or a small packet of butter, and occasionally some delicious crunchy doughnuts from the canteen. These gifts, like Ainslie's food parcels, were shared with Flora and Magret and the people in the tenement in George Street. Tommy McDougall had been called up now, and was stationed in England.

Isla's gardener had had to give up work because of ill-health, and she hadn't bothered to find anyone else. Gregg willingly helped her in the garden when he called, or sat for hours in the kitchen talking about his home and his family, frequently introducing Barbara and Ross into his reminiscing until Isla felt as though she had been present with her children at the sledging parties in the winter, the picnics, the visits between the Hannigan and Marshall houses to view new kittens or puppies. These word-pictures of her children in Canada made the temporary separation more bearable for her, and went a long way to easing the pain of being without them. Gregg also spent a lot of time with Flora, who

377

had developed a new interest in life since his unexpected arrival.

'You've done her so much good,' Isla told him gratefully. 'She needs company, and I can't spend as much time as I'd like with her these days.'

The Canadian tipped the kitchen chair back and stretched his legs across the linoleum floor. 'I'm the one who's getting all the favours. You and Miss Currie have been like family to me, and it's great to be able to visit a real home.'

Isla looked around the kitchen, which had grown noticeably shabbier since Nan's death. 'I'd scarcely call this place a real home nowadays. The house used to be full of people coming and going, and now I almost live in this room. I hate to see the place so – alone.'

'You're like my Pat – wherever she happens to be is home to me. I get that same feeling when I'm around you.' Gregg smiled at her, then asked, almost shyly, 'Could I have a look at those dolls' houses I kept hearing about from Ainslie and Phil and the kids?'

Isla rarely visited the dolls'-house room now. Walking into it with Gregg, she felt for a moment as though time had looped back. As far as this room was concerned, the war had never happened, her family hadn't been scattered far and wide, and Nan was still alive, bustling round the kitchen pouring out milk and putting fresh-baked scones on a plate, ready for the children's return from school.

Gregg, unaware of the memories she was experiencing, was moving carefully round the tables, fascinated by the little houses and the miniature furniture. 'I wish more than ever now that I had a daughter. It would have been great to give her something like this.' He stopped in front of one with a murmur of delight. 'Hey, this is just like the place my grandparents used to have!'

'It's supposed to be from *Anne of Green Gables*. I'm hoping to complete it one day, but at the moment my furniture maker's in the Navy.'

'He certainly loved his work,' Gregg marvelled, his fingers gently caressing a tiny rocking chair in pale gold wood. 'Listen, would you make me a house just like this, to give to Pat?'

'Of course, but you'll have to wait until after the war. Even if I had the time, I can't get the materials just now. Anyway, I couldn't do it without Drew to make the furniture.'

Gregg was still admiring the little chair. 'I can't get over how perfect this is. I can almost see my grandma sitting in it!' He held the miniature piece gently, lovingly, just as Drew would, Isla thought, and on an impulse she took him out to see the workshop.

Despite being locked up, the place still smelled of fresh wood and paint and glue and textiles. 'Your carpenter certainly cares about his trade. These tools have been well looked after.' Gregg turned his head and smiled at her, and suddenly she was looking at Drew, hearing her long-ago voice saying, 'How are things coming along?' and his voice replying, 'Fine. I'll have time to finish this before I go home for my tea, and it'll be dry in the morning, ready for the handles to be put on.'

Drew was thin, whereas Gregg was as lean and strong as a whip. Drew had serious grey eyes, Gregg's were blue and full of a love of life. Both had light brown hair, but Gregg's was fairer, and curly, whereas Drew's was straight and often flopped over his eyes. The two men were unlike each other in many ways, yet their shared love of fine craftsmanship, and the way Gregg had just turned and smiled absently at her, reminded her so strongly of Drew that to her horror, she burst into tears.

At once he was beside her. 'Isla? What is it? Did I say the wrong thing?'

She shook her head and tried to explain, then gave up and rested her head on his shoulder, letting the tears have their own way. Gregg said nothing more, just stood and held her while she sobbed out her grief over Nan's violent and unnecessary death, her longing to see Barbara and Ross again, her fears for Colin's safety, her exhaustion and loneliness, and her continuous, strength-sapping fear.

When at last the weeping had slowed to sniffs and hiccups, he mopped her face dry with his handkerchief, then locked the workshop door and led her into the house, where he sat her down at the kitchen table and made some tea.

'I shouldn't have asked to see your workplace. It brought back too many hurtful memories.'

'It wasn't that – I'm just being daft.'

'You're not daft,' Gregg told her, the Scottish word sounding so different on his lips. 'You're worn out with work and worry and not getting enough to eat.'

Isla flopped in her chair like a rag doll, completely drained, shaken by an occasional involuntary shudder. When he put the cup into her hands she sipped at it, then wrinkled her nose.

'It's t-terrible!'

'I'm not used to making tea,' Gregg said matter-of-factly, taking a seat at the other side of the table. Eyes closed, he inhaled the steam rising from his cup, then sipped. 'It tastes fine to me.'

'It's too strong, and too sweet, and . . .' She sipped again, then it was her turn to sniff at the brew. 'You've put something in it.'

He dipped into the pocket of his leather jacket, hanging from the back of his chair, and held up a small silver flask. 'A few drops of brandy, that's all.'

'No wonder it tastes terrible!'

'Don't look a gift horse in the mouth, that's what my grandma used to say. Drink it up, it'll do you good.'

Although she grimaced at every mouthful, she had to admit that she did feel better when she had drained the cup. She got up to put it in the sink, then gave a gasp of horror as her gaze fell on the small mirror hanging nearby. Her face was stained, her eyes and mouth swollen with weeping. 'I look awful!'

'Everyone looks awful when they've been crying as hard as you were. Splash cold water on your face.'

She did, and looked marginally better, though her eyelids were still puffy. Gregg rinsed the cups and set them on the draining board while she was still peering into the mirror and making small sounds of horror. 'Take a couple of aspirin and go to bed with a hot-water bottle. You'll feel fine after a sleep.'

'But I said I'd call in on Flora this afternoon. She'll know at once that I've been crying, and it'll upset her.'

Gregg dried his hands and reached for his jacket, moving about the kitchen comfortably, as though in his own home. 'I'll go. I'll tell her you've got a headache and you've had to go to bed.'

'Gregg,' she said as he opened the back door. 'I've never in my life made such a fool of myself. You've been very kind.'

'What are friends for? Listen, Isla, nobody can be strong for ever, not even you. Don't be so hard on yourself – you needed a good bawl, and today just happened to be the day for it,' he said, and went out, closing the door.

In July, Colin came home on leave. Isla had been living for that day, but as he stepped off the train at the West Station and came towards her, his nutbrown face almost split in two by his grin, she suddenly felt ridiculously shy. He was like a stranger, bronzed and more muscular than when he had first been called up, his teeth astonishingly large and white against his tan. Then she was swept up into his arms and despite the rough khaki uniform and the bronzed skin, she knew that he was still the man she had married.

She had worked hard in preparation for his return, putting in extra hours at the sanatorium in order to win some time off, cleaning the house from top to bottom with Betty's help, saving her coupons and the extras Gregg had brought so that she could feed him well.

He paused for a moment in the hall. 'The house hasn't changed a bit. I've dreamed of the smell of that furniture polish you always use.'

'Is that all you thought about while you were thousands of miles away? Furniture polish?'

He caught at her hand as she started to move towards

the kitchen, spinning her round and into his arms. 'Oh, I've thought of other things as well,' he murmured against her mouth, then scooped her into his arms.

'Colin, your parents are coming round in a little while!'

'And we'll be the perfect host and hostess when they arrive,' said Colin, marching up the stairs as though his wife weighed nothing at all. 'First, there's a little matter I've been dreaming about since the last time I was with you.'

'I've missed you,' he whispered later as they lay together in bed. 'Looking up at all those beautiful stars in the sky at night, and wishing that you were there to see them with me.'

Isla trailed her fingers down the side of his face and he caught at her hand and nibbled on her fingertips, then stretched and yawned. 'I suppose we'd better get ready to entertain our guests.'

She lay for a moment, watching him dress. His body had been tanned all over by a sun much more fierce than the sun that shone over Scotland.

'D'you think we'll ever get back to the way we were?'

He grinned down at her, his fingers moving nimbly down the front of his shirt, popping buttons into buttonholes with practised speed. 'Back together as a family? Of course we will, there's no doubt about it.' The grin faded. 'Though we're all going to miss Nan such a lot.'

'Yes, we are.'

'I felt even worse about persuading you to let Ross and Barbara go away when I heard about Nan,' Colin said sombrely. 'Now you're all alone and I can't do a damned thing about it. I often wish I could turn the clock back.'

'I'm managing – and they're fine where they are.

Mebbe it was for the best after all. At least I don't have
to worry about a bomb mebbe falling on them at school.
It's helped to hear so much about them from Gregg
Marshall.'

'When am I going to meet him?'

'At the weekend. He offered to stay away and let us
have time to ourselves while you were home, but I said
you'd want to meet him. You'll like him, Colin, he's a
very nice man.'

'I'm sure I will.' Then, stooping to kiss her nose, he
added, 'But if you don't stop lying there, Mrs Forbes,
looking so desirable and so tempting, I'll not be in a fit
state to meet him, let alone my parents in about ten
minutes.'

As Isla had expected, Gregg and Colin got on well
together, and the Canadian paid several visits before
Colin had to report back. When the time came, Isla
found it hard to let him go, to step back and watch the
train carry him away, knowing that his regiment was
being sent to North Africa, where the fighting had been
fierce and the Eighth Army forced back almost to
Alexandria by Rommel's troops.

She missed him even more this time. The big bed was
an island of loneliness, and she often lay awake, despite
being exhausted by her work at the hospital, yearning for
Colin. She knew, from the talk she heard from the rest of
the staff at the sanatorium, that she wasn't the only
woman to have such feelings. One or two of the nurses
confessed, sometimes defiantly, sometimes tearfully, that
they had found comfort with some other man.

For her part, there were times, particularly in the

first weeks after Colin's leave, when Isla found herself glancing at Gregg as they worked together in the garden, or sat on opposite sides of the kitchen table. She found herself wondering what it would be like to be held in his arms, caressed by those large, well-shaped, sure hands. She thrust the thoughts away as soon as they arrived, embarrassed and angry with herself. Once or twice she considered asking him not to come back, but he got such pleasure out of the visits that she couldn't bring herself to be so cruel.

Drew came home, no longer a gawky lad but a man in his naval uniform with the cap tilted jauntily over his eyes. He came to tell Isla that his sweetheart Mary had agreed that on his next leave they would marry.

'Our mums are going tae save their coupons, and their clothes coupons too, tae give us a smashing wedding,' he said happily, 'I can't wait to see my Mary as a bride. She's a lovely dresser – makes all her own now. She even knows how to paint her legs to look as if she's wearing stockings – the seam down the back and all!'

In the workshop, he ran his hands lovingly, just as Gregg had done, over the tools awaiting his return. 'It'll be good to get back to work again.'

'I'm not going to lose you to the Navy after the war?' Isla asked, and he looked round and grinned – again, just as Gregg had done.

'Not a chance. I'm enjoying the life, but I'm looking forward to coming home, too, and settling down. I've been sketching furniture in my spare time. I've got all sorts of plans – just you wait and see.'

For her part, Isla was afraid to look too far ahead. All her thoughts these days were with Colin, in North

Africa. His letters home made no mention of the life and death struggle for supremacy that they both knew couldn't be far away now. Instead, he wrote about everyday life in the desert.

'I suppose the flies were here before we were, but you'd think they'd be willing to have discussions with us about what should be theirs and what should be ours. They're even more obstinate than Rommel, and insist on being my food tasters, often getting eaten themselves if they don't get out of the way in time – and if I don't spot them in time. As to the sand, I wonder if eating and drinking sand with everything means that my teeth will benefit? They're constantly being scoured with the stuff. You'll be heading into winter now. It's cooler here, thank goodness, but still hot compared to home. I wish I was an artist, and able to capture the sunsets on paper and send them to you, my darling. They're beautiful, but they'd be even more beautiful if we could only be watching them together. Perhaps one day, when this war's over, I'll take you to Africa and show you those sunsets.'

The inevitable battle came in October, a fight that, once started, had to be fought to the bitter end. Even after the news came through that the Eighth Army had succeeded, at El Alamein, in forcing the enemy back and winning a massive victory, Isla couldn't rest until Colin's letter arrived, telling her that he had come through without injury. Then, and only then, she allowed herself to weep with relief.

Early in December, while Gregg and Isla were playing cards with Flora in her drawing-room, Gregg asked Isla to go with him to the Christmas dance at Prestwick Aerodrome.

'It'll be fun,' he coaxed when Isla refused. 'It's time you had some fun in your life, and you'd be doing me a big favour.'

'I'm not a dancer.'

'That doesn't matter, it's just a case of moving with the music.'

'On you go, Isla,' Flora urged. 'Everyone needs time off, and if you're not at the sanatorium you're dancing attendance on me. It's time you enjoyed yourself. It's Christmas!'

Isla finally gave in and agreed, then wished she hadn't when she surveyed her wardrobe in search of something to wear. The two evening dresses she possessed were rejected as being too formal, and all she could find was a pale pink silk blouse, and a dark blue evening skirt. They still fitted, but a glance in the mirror showed that they looked dated and uninteresting.

Magret called in at least once every week after her shift at the mills, since there was no longer any need to have 'his' dinner ready on time each evening, so Isla put on the blouse and skirt and paraded round the bedroom for her friend's benefit.

'I see what you mean,' Magret said. 'They've no' got much life tae them, have they?'

Isla lifted a handful of skirt, then released it. It fell limply against her thigh. 'I haven't time to make anything, and I'm not going to waste coupons on something I'll probably never wear again. Besides, I told Drew that I'd save some clothing coupons to help towards his wedding. I'll have to tell Gregg that I've changed my mind.' Peering in the mirror again, this time at her face, she added, 'Anyway, I'm thirty-nine, not nineteen. Far too old to go gallivanting off to dances.'

'Ach, ye're only as old as ye feel.'

'All right – forty-nine.'

'If that's the truth, it's probably time ye had a good night out. I tell ye what, I'll bring our Greta over tonight tae have a look at them. She's awful clever at making things over.'

'She'll have to be a miracle worker to make anything of this outfit.'

'Don't give up hope yet, hen,' Magret advised, and later that evening, she arrived on the doorstep with Greta.

Isla hadn't seen the girl since Barbara had gone to Canada, though she frequently heard from Magret about Greta's job in a draper's shop, and about her boyfriend, who was on important war work in the India Tyre factory at nearby Inchinnan. To her astonishment, the thin, plain little girl who had always been in Barbara's shadow had blossomed into a self-possessed young woman, casually smart in a red woollen jersey that showed off her full breasts and slim waist to advantage, worn over a snug-fitting tweed skirt. Greta's hair, once nondescript brown, had a chestnut glow to it, and was swept up to form a halo round her skilfully made-up face.

'How's Barbara?' she asked.

'She's fine – she's singing with a band now.' Isla produced some photographs that had just arrived from Canada, and Magret went through them, exclaiming over each one.

'My, wee Ross's nearly a man now, isn't he? Oh, Greta, look, isn't Barbara just beautiful?' She handed her daughter a photograph that Isla had looked at again and again, unable to believe that the lovely young woman standing at the microphone in a tight-bodiced, long-skirted dress with a sweetheart neck and short puffed sleeves, her long hair curling on her shoulders, could be the schoolgirl who had gone off with Ainslie.

'I like the frock,' Greta said. Later, in the bedroom, she eyed the pink blouse and navy skirt critically. 'I see what ye mean.'

'I haven't got anything else.'

'Mind if I have a look?' Greta riffled through the wardrobe and drew out a summer dress in navy, with large white spots, navy buttons down the bodice, and a cluster of artificial navy and white flowers pinned to the collar.

'The buttons are pretty, I could use them, and mebbe the flowers, but it'd mean spoiling yer dress. The skirt hangs well, though, ye could still use it, with a new waistband.'

'I doubt if I'd be wearing that dress again anyway. Do what you want with it – keep the skirt for yourself, if you can use it.'

'Oh, great!' For the first time, Greta looked animated. 'That Peter Pan collar on the blouse'll have tae go. All right if I change it about a bit?'

She took the clothes home with her, and returned them the day before the dance. When Isla put on the blouse and skirt she was stunned by the difference. The blouse now had a plain round neck, enlivened by a row of navy blue flowers from the bunch on the dress, alternating with pink flowers that Greta had made from the discarded collar. The plain pink buttons down the front of the blouse had been replaced by decorative navy buttons from the dress, and the starched skirt and underskirt swirled and rustled as Isla moved around the bedroom.

'Ye look bonny, Isla,' Magret marvelled, adding with justified pride, 'I told ye our Greta was clever with a needle, didn't I? Have ye noticed her skirt?'

Greta gave a twirl. She wore the same red jersey as before, but tonight her skirt, snug-fitting over the hips then full to the hem, was navy with white spots.

'Nothin' tae it, I just made up a waistband from the bodice,' she said casually. 'Sit down and I'll cut yer hair.'

She was as good with scissors as she was with a needle. Isla's dark hair was neatly trimmed, then washed. Then, using a poker heated in the kitchen range, Greta curled the ends under.

'Ye're gettin' a bit grey at the temples,' she said matter-of-factly. 'Wearing yer hair like this'll help tae hide that.'

She tore up some newspaper into strips and used it to put Isla's hair into curlers before she left.

'It'll be uncomfortable in bed tonight, but it'll be worth it.' Then, delving in the large shoulder-bag she had brought to produce bottles and boxes, 'Now I'll show ye how tae do yer face.'

31

Greta was right – the newspaper curlers meant that Isla spent an uncomfortable night, but on the following evening, when she went over to show Flora her outfit, she had to admit that her suffering had been worthwhile. Her hair had brushed out into a soft bell about her face, and the blouse and skirt looked as though they had been made for each other.

For once Gregg had left his beloved motor-cycle in Prestwick and borrowed a car. When he arrived at Flora's, as arranged, to collect her, he stopped in the drawing-room doorway, staring. It was the first time Isla had seen him in uniform; they gaped at each other for a long moment, then caught each other's eyes and laughed.

'Stand side by side, and let me take a look at you,' the old woman commanded, nodding her satisfaction when, self-consciously, they obeyed. 'Very nice indeed. You make a smart couple. Now mind and give her a really good evening, she deserves it,' she commanded Gregg as he helped Isla into her everyday navy serge coat.

'I surely will, ma'am,' he promised solemnly.

In peace-time, Isla and Colin had often taken the children for summer holidays to Troon, close by to Prestwick. It was a pleasant part of the Clyde Firth, with great stretches of sand, and shallow water just right for paddling. She hadn't been back there since the war began, but had heard that the sandy beaches were covered with rolls of barbed wire to defend the Clydeside towns against invasion, and most of the hotels and gift shops and tearooms and ice-cream kiosks were closed and shuttered.

They drove down in the dark, so Isla had no chance to see the changes for herself. The dance was held in the canteen, which Gregg called the PX. It was a long wooden hut, with paper chains looped over the ceiling and walls, and a Christmas tree on either side of the stage where the band sat. They stepped through the dark entrance into a dazzle of light and a clamour of music and voices, and for a moment Isla hesitated. Gregg put an arm about her and steered her confidently round the edge of the dance floor, crowded with men in uniform and women, some uniformed, others in their best dresses, to a table where they were clearly expected. Chairs were hauled out for them, and Isla was introduced to more people than she could possibly remember.

'Now before she sits down, I'm taking her off to give her a few words of advice on how to handle you lot. Get her a drink, Gregg, we'll be back in a minute.' A young woman with blond hair swept up into a mass of curls at the top of her head took Isla by the hand and led her to the ladies powder room, where she leaned against a wash hand basin and took out a cigarette packet, lighting one for herself when Isla shook her head.

'I'm Doris, you're staying at my house tonight.' She blew a smoke-ring and studied Isla with bright blue eyes. 'I know they're a bit much when you're not used to them, but they're all nice lads. Far from home, and desperate to have as good a Christmas as they can, bless 'em.'

'You've been here before?' Isla combed her hair, then studied herself in the mirror.

'Here . . .' Doris took the comb from her and deftly flicked a stray wisp of hair into place. 'I work here, so I know them all. Gregg's one of the nicest. He's talked about you a lot – I'm glad you agreed to come to the dance, he didn't think you would.'

'Neither did I. I'm not used to socialising any more, it terrifies me.'

'There's no need, none of us bite. He really wanted to give you a good night out, in return for all the kindness you've shown him.'

'He's done more than enough, bringing us things, and helping in the garden.'

'But you've provided a home he can feel comfortable in, and that means a lot to all those lads out there. He's a real family man, is Gregg. It's a shame, what this war's done to his sort. Ready to go out and face them now?' Doris paused at the door and winked reassuringly. 'Just give yourself time to get used to us all, and make up your mind to have a good time.'

She was right. As Isla began to concentrate on the people around her, her nervousness faded. It returned when Gregg drew her on to the dance-floor, but he was a good dancer, and in his blue-uniformed arms she learned how to relax and follow the music. During the

evening she danced with several of the men, but discovered that she was most comfortable with Gregg.
They danced well together, moving in easy unison, and
it came as quite a shock when the band struck up 'Auld
Lang Syne' and she was whisked on to the floor to
squeeze into a great circle, arms crossed, one hand in
Gregg's, the other in the grip of Doris's partner, a nav-
igator called Mike, to mark the end of the evening.

Gregg and Mike drove the two women to Doris's
house in Prestwick, but didn't come in, because Doris's
parents were asleep, and her father, a baker, had to get
up early the next morning to start work in the bakehouse.

Declining Doris's whispered offer of a cup of tea, Isla
followed the girl upstairs on tiptoe, carrying the small
case she had brought with her. There were two beds in
Doris's room, one of them the property of her sister,
who was in the WAAC.

'I hope it didn't spoil your evening, having to come
back here with me,' Isla said into the darkness when the
two of them were in bed.

'No goodnight kiss from Mike, you mean?' Doris
chuckled softly. 'Don't worry about that, we're just
mates. My boyfriend's in a German PoW camp.'

'I'm sorry.'

'So am I.' For the first time Doris's voice was bleak,
devoid of laughter. Then she said firmly, 'But he'll be
home soon, you wait and see. Winnie says we've
reached the beginning of the end, and I think he's right.
G'night.'

Gregg drove Isla home on the following morning and
they had lunch with Flora, who was waiting to hear all

about the dance. Gregg, who had to go on duty that evening and would remain on duty over Christmas, presented Flora and Betty with their Christmas presents, a soft woolly bed-jacket for Flora, two pairs of stockings for Betty, and enthused over the hand-knitted scarf and the bottle of whisky he received in return.

'I'll savour this drop by drop,' he said, eyeing the whisky, but Flora snorted.

'Nonsense, man – half a tumblerful at a time, and don't forget to drink a toast to me.'

'Miss Currie, I'll be doing that for the rest of my life, believe me,' Gregg said sincerely. Later, in Isla's kitchen, he took a wrapped packet out of his pocket. For her, too, there were stockings, as well as a small box containing a butterfly brooch. She gave him a tie-pin, with matching cufflinks.

'Thank you for a lovely evening,' she said as he reluctantly got up to go.

'It's me who should be thanking you. You looked beautiful.' Then, as she began to move past him to open the door, he stopped her with a hand on her arm, and bent to kiss her, his mouth warm and hard on hers. In a reflex action, Isla's arms went round him, and his own embrace tightened. Suddenly overwhelmed by the need to be close to someone after all the months of abstinence, she clung to him, and he responded. When they finally stood back from each other, she saw her own hunger, her own need, mirrored in his rugged, normally laughing face.

As they stared at each other, their faces only inches apart, thoughts spun giddily through Isla's head. She wanted him to go away and never come back. She wanted him to kiss her again, to stay with her. She wanted to be able to turn the clock back, only five minutes, to the time before the kiss and the turmoil it had caused.

Finally, 'I have to go,' Gregg said, his voice husky, unsure of itself. 'Have a happy Christmas.'

'You too,' she said, and stood looking at the door long after he had gone through it.

'The man's a fool!' Flora glared at the wireless, where the Radio Doctor's fatherly voice was giving Boxing-Day advice on how to deal with the discomforts of overeating on Christmas Day. 'Overeating indeed – it seems to me that a fragment of chicken and a spoonful of potatoes followed by mashed parsnips with banana flavouring's not that far away from bread and water. How can anyone overeat on the rations we get? Switch him off, Isla, for goodness' sake!'

Isla obeyed, and silence fell on the room. Flora seemed to be dozing, as she often did these days, and Isla was startled when the old woman said abruptly, 'I've a feeling I did you a wrong when I persuaded you to go to that dance.'

'What?'

'Isla, we've known each other long enough to be honest. You've not been the same since you went to Prestwick.'

'There was nothing wrong with Prestwick, the folk there were very nice. I just miss the children, and Colin. Christmas is a bad time to be apart from your family,' Isla said shortly, burying her nose in the magazine she had been pretending to read.

She had been in a panic all through Christmas Day.
Gregg's kiss had altered their relationship for ever. The
memory of his mouth on hers, his arms about her, had
haunted her ever since. Everything had changed, and
suddenly he was no longer the friendly, likeable
Canadian she had grown to depend on. He was a man,
a very attractive man, who had succeeded in stirring up
emotions that had lain dormant since Colin's last leave.

'It's more than just Christmas,' Flora said. 'I'd no
worries about coaxing you to go to the dance with
Gregg, for he could never be anything but a gentleman.
But now I've a suspicion that that very thing might be
the trouble.'

'Are you sure you didn't overeat? You're talking a lot
of nonsense.'

'Am I? You're two decent people, and you've both
been away too long from those you love. I should have
thought of that, instead of just telling myself how nice
it would be for the two of you to have a break from all
this war business.' Flora's fingers twisted restlessly at
the blanket about her knees.

'Flora, you've got nothing to reproach yourself about.
Nothing happened!'

'No? There was a glow about the two of you when he
brought you back the next day. I thought it was just the
pleasure of the dance, but you've been ill at ease ever
since, lassie, worried about something.'

'Who wouldn't be worried with her man . . .' Isla's
voice wavered and she got up and made a business of
stacking the used tea things so that Flora couldn't see
her face. 'Her man away fighting?' she finished, gaining
control over herself.

'One man away fighting, another nearer at hand, and both of them good caring souls,' Flora said from behind her. 'I nearly married once, you know.'

'You?'

Flora nodded. 'The marriage was all but settled, then a friend of my family's who'd been away from Paisley for years came back, and suddenly everything was changed. I swithered from one to the other, and I swithered too long. They both lost patience and looked elsewhere.' Flora gave a soft chuckle. 'It's as well for them that they did, for if they'd had the patience to wait, they'd be waiting still. To this day, I don't know myself which I wanted the most. But one thing I do know to my cost, Isla – it's possible for a woman to love two men.'

'In all the years I've known you, you've never said a word about this before,' Isla said suspiciously.

Flora's eyes, normally heavy-lidded now, flashed emerald fire at her. 'That's because I've never had need to,' she said.

Letters arrived early in January from North Africa, where Colin expected to remain for some time, and from Canada. Barbara, who at eighteen had left school and was singing with the band every week, wrote excitedly about their regular slot on radio. Ross, still at school, working for Phil at weekends and holidays, wrote about the timber-yard. Colin wrote about the flies and the sand and the other men. Isla had little to tell them in her replies, other than that she had been moved from nightshift to dayshift. Her days off were always the same, filled up with gardening, queuing outside food shops, visits next door, the petty annoyances of rationing and queues and having to do without, and the endless longing for peace and a return to normality.

She had dreaded meeting Gregg again, but when he roared up on his motor-cycle a few days after Christmas he was his usual relaxed self, and his visits continued as usual, though Isla noticed that, like her, he tended to avoid any physical contact with her, no matter how small or how innocent. By mutual, unspoken consent, they spent most of his time in Paisley with Flora.

Returning on a pleasant April afternoon from a dutiful visit to Colin's mother to find Gregg's motor-cycle on its rest at the front gate and Gregg himself working in the back garden, his jacket slung over the clothesline, Isla stood for a moment at the corner of the house, unnoticed, watching him. She knew that his father had been a farmer, and that Gregg had expected to follow in his footsteps. But a growing interest in machinery had led him to leave the farm in his late teens and set up his own business, supplying farm machinery. He still had a deep love of the land and enjoyed working it, no matter how small the scale. He was digging now to an easy rhythm, his lean body bending and swinging, his arms tensing then relaxing as he worked. As Isla watched him, she knew that Flora was right – it was possible to love two men, to want to be with one as much as the other.

He looked up just then, and the broad grin that was never far away spread over his face when he saw her.

'Hi there – I got an unexpected afternoon off, so I thought I'd get some work done on this ground before the weeds take over.'

'You shouldn't have bothered.'

'Why do the Scotch always say that?' Gregg asked.

'Scots. Scotch is the drink.'

'We learn something every day. You look very nice.'

Isla looked down at the suit she was wearing, a misty blue-grey check that Colin particularly liked. 'I always try to look smart when I visit Colin's mother. She expects it of me. I'll get changed.'

Later, working alongside him, sharing his countryman's pleasure in the good dark soil that slid from their spades, she felt soothed by his companionable silence. One day, she might have to face up to her feelings for him. But not yet.

They walked round to Flora's for tea, then returned to finish the digging, completing the task just as dusk brought out the clouds of tiny midges that made life outside unbearable. Then they drank cocoa in the kitchen and listened to the news broadcast on the radio, then to *ITMA*, which Gregg loved. He was roaring with laughter at something Tommy Handley had said when the back door burst open and Betty erupted into the room, heedless of the need to prevent the lamplight from spilling out of the door.

'Thank God you're still here, Mr Marshall.' Her face was as white as paper. 'It's Miss Currie, I think she's fallen in the bathroom and I can't get the door open—'

Gregg was on his way out of the kitchen before she had finished. The two women caught up with him just as he put his shoulder to the locked bathroom door. It flew open to reveal a small slight figure huddled on the floor.

'Let me by!' Isla pushed past the Canadian. Flora

400

was unconscious but still breathing. Her pulse was erratic and the area round her mouth had gone blue.

'Betty, telephone for the doctor.' Isla deftly drew Flora's nightdress and dressing-gown, which had rumpled up in her fall, down over her skinny legs, then Gregg carried the old woman across the hall and laid her gently on the bed.

'He's coming right away,' Betty said. 'He should be here in ten minutes.'

Isla, her fingers on Flora's pulse, laid her friend's hand down very gently on the bed, then tucked the blanket round Flora as though to protect her from the chill that was already on its way and would not be denied. 'There's no hurry,' she said.

32

Flora's family had been Baptists, and had worshipped at the Coats' Memorial Church, the church with the great sweep of stairs that Isla vaguely remembered passing on her way to visit Kenneth McAdam's grave, the first time she came to Paisley. That day seemed to belong to another life entirely, she thought, as she climbed the stairs to attend the funeral service, Gregg by her side.

The church's interior was beautiful and spacious, but even so it was quite well filled with people who had come to pay their respects to the last member of a family well respected and remembered in the town. Isla spotted Charlie Blayne, the auctioneer, among them and later, after Flora had been laid to rest in the imposing family plot not far from Kenneth's grave, she introduced him to Gregg.

The auctioneer's hair, a mixture of brown and grey when Ainslie had worked for him, was now a mass of tight silvery curls. He beamed at Gregg and shook his hand enthusiastically, then introduced his wife, a small neat woman almost hidden by his big sturdy body.

'How's Ainslie?'

'Very well, and busy looking after my two as well as her own boys. The twins'll be eleven next month.'

Charlie shook his head in wonder. 'Time flies when ye measure it against youngsters growing up. Give the lassie my regards the next time ye write, and tell her we still miss her at the auction-rooms. She could've done very well as an auctioneer if she hadnae lost her head and run off to Canada.'

'I think it was her heart she lost, Mr Blayne,' said Gregg, amused.

'Call me Charlie, son, everyone does. Aye, well, I suppose we all let our hearts away with too much.' Charlie put an arm about his wife and hugged her. 'Eh, Lizzie?'

'Aye, we all have a daft streak in us,' she said dryly, then to Isla and Gregg, giving Charlie a dig with her elbow, 'this is mine, and the older he gets the dafter he gets.'

Once again Gregg had borrowed a car from someone at the aerodrome. As it moved down the cemetery drive Isla asked him to stop for a moment. 'I'll not be long,' she said as she got out.

It was only a short walk along a side path to where Kenneth and his son lay. Catherine, at her own wish, had been buried in Dumfries. Isla stood for a moment, wishing that she had thought to bring flowers, even a single blossom, from those heaped round Flora's grave.

'Someone special?' Gregg asked as she went back to the car and settled herself beside him.

'Someone very special.'

The nieces whom Flora had never been able to give dolls' houses to were at the funeral, and so were the nephews. Because none of them belonged to Paisley, Isla had offered to hold the reception at her own house where, by dint of a lot of careful planning, and help from Betty and from Gregg, who brought provisions from the PX at Prestwick, she managed to provide everyone with food and drink.

Nobody stayed long, for many of the mourners had come from outside Paisley, and were anxious to get home before dark because of the blackout.

'We're grateful to you for all your help,' one of the nieces said as she was leaving. 'We'll be back next week to clear the house out and see Mr Forbes about selling it.'

Betty, who was going back to her family in Bishopton, a nearby village, was the last to leave. 'I'll never forget Miss Currie,' she said at the door, tears in her eyes, then she left, and Isla went back to the living-room, where Gregg was gathering up cups and plates.

'I'll help to clear things up,' he offered. 'I don't have to be back at the airbase for a few hours yet.'

After washing the dishes, they put the living-room to rights and Gregg got out the carpet sweeper while Isla made tea. It was growing dark, and he made sure that the blackout curtains were all in place before joining her in the kitchen. 'She had a very happy time, that last day,' he said gently, after a long silence. 'We all did, remember?'

Isla nodded, remembering how Flora had had them both laughing, Gregg until the tears ran down his cheeks, with some story of friends of her parents. 'I'm not being malicious, you understand,' she had said, her green eyes gleaming. 'Just a wee touch wicked – but that makes for a better story, doesn't it?'

'It's good to spend your last hours in life with friends,' Isla said now, summoning a smile.

'Are you sure you'll be all right on your own tonight? You look worn out. I can phone the base and tell them I can't get back until morning.'

'Of course I'll be all right,' she said at once, and knew by the way the colour rose in his face that her voice had been too sharp.

'I didn't mean . . .'

'I know. I'm sorry. I'll be fine.'

'Take some whisky before you go to bed, it'll help. Here . . .' he started to reach into his jacket pocket for his flask, but Isla stopped him with an upraised hand.

'Not brandy in my tea again, thank you, I remember the taste from last time. I've got some whisky, I'll make myself a hot toddy before I go to bed.'

'Okay.' Silence fell between them, companionable at first, almost like the old days, then gradually taking on a meaning of its own. It couldn't be allowed to continue, Isla thought, and jumped up to switch on the radio. A man's voice came through, talking about architecture in Italy. She twirled the dial in search of some music, or a comedy programme, but tonight every station she could find had people talking. All except one, but it was playing gloomy funereal music that she knew would reduce her to tears on such a day. She wished that she had thought of sitting in the living-room, where there was a gramophone.

Instead of sitting down at the table again she picked up her cup and drained it, then took it over to the sink.

'I'm so tired that I don't think I'll need that whisky,' she said over her shoulder.

Gregg brought his own cup to the sink. 'In that case, I'll clear out and leave you in peace.'

Isla took the cup from his hand, almost dropping it in her eagerness not to let their fingers touch, and started washing it vigorously, listening to the sounds he made as he picked up his jacket and put it on.

'I'm going to miss Flora a lot,' he said, his voice sombre. 'You've both been family to me since I came over here. She was like a favourite aunt, and you . . .' He stopped, then said slowly, 'Isla, we have things to talk about.'

'Not tonight.' She swung round from the sink, and pulled the tea-towel from its hook so roughly that the material caught and tore.

'You know what I mean, don't you?' Gregg asked. 'We've been scared to look at each other ever since the dance.'

'I don't know what you're—'

'For God's sake, Isla,' he suddenly burst out. 'Don't start behaving like a flirty teenager! That's not you at all. We're grown-up people, old enough to face up to what's happening.'

'We're married people too, with growing children, and responsibilities.'

'I know that.' He sounded so defeated that she wanted to go to him and hold him and comfort him. Instead, she folded the towel with great care, hung it over the back of a chair, and sat down at the table, so weary that she could no longer stay on her feet.

'I know,' Gregg said again, quietly, letting his lean

body fold down into the opposite chair, resting his curled fists on the scrubbed wooden table. 'I love Pat – but now I love you too.' The fists tightened. 'I never thought there could be room in my life for another woman, but there is. A great empty hole I knew nothing about, just waiting to be filled to the brim by you.'

'I wish I'd never gone to that dance!'

'I wish I hadn't asked you. I wouldn't have, if I'd had any idea of the harm it was going to do. But there's no use in wishing the past away. One kiss,' he said in wonder. 'One little friendly Christmas kiss between friends. That's all it was supposed to be. But I've not been able to get you out of my mind since, not for a minute.'

'It would have been better if you hadn't come back.'

'I know, but I couldn't have stayed away. Isla . . .'

He looked up from his hands, catching her gaze before she could turn away. His look seemed to light up the kitchen, his love was like a soft blanket, waiting to enfold and cherish her. She wanted to draw its warmth around her and stay in its folds for the rest of her life. But she couldn't, she mustn't.

He read her thoughts, and tried to lighten the tension between them. 'Of course, there was another reason why I couldn't stay away. I knew that the vegetable bed needed digging.' For a moment, as they laughed together, the clock was turned back and everything was all right again. Then, watching the laughter fade from Gregg's eyes, seeing the bleak despair that replaced it, Isla knew that, like her, he knew what must be done.

'There's no future for us, is there?' It was a statement, not a question.

'No future at all, Gregg. My Colin, your Pat – they don't deserve to be hurt.'

'I don't want to hurt you either.'

'At least I'll know why, and I'll know it's for the best.'

Gregg suddenly lifted his fists then slammed them down hard on to the table. 'God damn it, how can it be so wrong to love somebody and want to be with them? I could wring Adolf Hitler's damned neck! If it wasn't for him, I'd never have come to Scotland, or met you . . .'

'If you want to wring his neck, you'll have to stand in a very long line,' Isla said wryly, and he gave a grunt of laughter that was almost a sob. The sound of it hurt her unbearably.

'Right. Anyway, I guess I'd prefer knowing you and losing you to not knowing you at all.' He put his hands flat on the table and studied them. 'We seem to have talked ourselves into a decision.'

'Yes, we have.'

He got up, reached for his cap, then turned, his eyes pleading. 'Isla, can I stay here tonight? Just one time, once to remember for the rest of my life?'

It would have been so easy to say yes. Nobody need ever know, nobody would be hurt. But against all her own instincts, Isla shook her head. 'I think you should go now, Gregg. And I don't think you should come back.' It struck her that this was the second time she had sent a man away. The last occasion had had a happy ending, but that couldn't, wouldn't happen again.

Gregg gave a long defeated sigh, then got to his feet. Isla stared down at the table, praying that he wouldn't touch her, knowing that one touch from a finger-tip would be enough to destroy the wall she had managed to build round herself.

'You know something? I'm glad I took you to the dance,' Gregg said. 'At least I got to hold you in my arms, even though there were about a hundred other people round us.'

The door opened, then closed swiftly, to keep the light from spilling out. Isla got up and fumbled her way through the dark hall and into the living-room to the window, bumping into furniture as she went. She drew the blackout aside, but it was so dark outside that she could see nothing. She stood clutching the folds of material, hoping that he would change his mind and come back, but at the same time praying that he would just go away and get it over with.

Outside, a car engine hiccuped, then roared into life. The sound dwindled away into the distance, and faded to nothing.

The days trailed by, each just like the one that had gone before it. Gregg stayed away, and didn't make any attempt to get in touch with her, and with the house next door lying empty, Isla felt completely alone. Several times she found herself hurrying down the path on her way to visit Flora, and had to turn and trail back to the house. The only bright moments in her life came when she received letters from Colin and the children and Ainslie. She carried their letters and photographs around with her, reading and re-reading the written words until she could have recited every single one of them in her sleep, running the tips of her fingers hungrily over the photographs. Her longing for the children, assuaged a little by Gregg's descriptions of them, came back as strong as ever, to torment her.

Flora's relatives returned to clear everything out of the house, and a 'For Sale' sign went up in the garden.

'Heaven knows why,' Gilchrist Forbes said when Isla paid her weekly visit to him and his wife. 'It's not a through road, so there's no passing traffic to see the sign. But it's what they wanted, and the client is always right.'

Isla fell heir to Flora's dolls' houses, because nobody else wanted them. 'I don't know what she collected them for,' one of the nieces said when she made the offer. 'They just gather dust. I understand that you like that sort of thing, Mrs Forbes, so perhaps you'd care to take them. I seem to remember that there was a very nice Victorian house – you don't happen to know what happened to it, do you?'

'It was refurbished and auctioned to raise money for the families of the children killed in the Glen Cinema disaster.'

'Oh yes, I remember hearing about that,' the woman said vaguely. 'What on earth made her think of selling the little house, though? It must have been worth quite a bit – why couldn't she have just donated a pound or so to the fund and be done with it?'

The houses, together with a few boxes containing a jumble of furniture and dolls, had to be stacked on the upstairs landing, because Isla couldn't get them up into the loft by herself, and Gregg was no longer around to do it for her. One of them, Isla noticed, looked quite like the house next door. She took it into her bedroom so that she could study it, and decided that once the war was over, she would furnish it and turn it into a copy of Flora's house, just for herself.

The thought cheered her and gave her something to do in her spare time, sketching the rooms in Flora's home from memory, and sorting through the boxes of odds and ends in search of pieces she might be able to use for the task.

In May, the Allied forces, Colin among them, took Tunis, and it began to look as though the war was beginning to swing, slowly, in the Allies' favour.

Drew came home on leave, and as soon as Isla opened the door and saw him standing in the porch she knew that there was something wrong. He was wearing civilian clothes this time, and all his jauntiness had vanished. He followed her through to the kitchen, but declined her offer of a cup of tea.

'Mary's married,' he said bluntly.

'Married? Oh, Drew, I'm so sorry!'

'Not half as sorry as I am,' Drew said between clenched teeth. 'She met up with some damned Geordie soldier in the NAAFI and off she went. She'd only known him a matter of weeks, her mum said. I knew she should never have gone to work in that NAAFI, I said so at the time. But she wanted to do her bit.' He drooped over the kitchen table, the picture of misery. 'She did that, all right. Sent me one of those "Dear John" letters.'

'Mary's not the only girl in the world. You'll find somebody else, somebody more worthy of you.'

He wasn't impressed. 'That's what my mum says, but I don't want anyone else, I just want my Mary.

411

She'll be sorry, you know. I reckon she married the uniform, not the bloke. He'll look a lot different in civvies, doing a nine to five job and moaning because his tea's not ready.'

In an attempt to take his mind off Mary, Isla asked him to store the dolls' houses in the attic for her. He agreed in a lackadaisical way, but had brightened up a little by the time the job was done, even going out to his workshop to give some of his tools a good cleaning. Standing by the door, watching him at work, Isla was able to pretend for a little while that the war had never happened, that Nan was bustling around the kitchen and Colin was in his office and the children were due home from school at any minute, fighting to be first through the gate.

When Drew had finished they went back into the house, where he downed a mugful of cocoa and ate a jam sandwich as they made plans for future dolls' houses once he was back on civvy street.

Drew liked the idea of the Flora Currie house. 'She was a nice old soul, Miss Currie. I was sorry when Mum told me she'd gone.'

On the doorstep on his way out, he stopped to say, 'Mum and me are going to have a slap-up meal before I go back, with the coupons she was keeping for the wedding. And I've given her some money and told her to go out and put the clothing coupons she was keeping towards a fur coat for herself. They'd have been wasted on that Mary anyway.' And he went off with the slightly rolling step common to all seamen, leaving Isla to struggle with the mental picture of little Mrs Brown, thin and stooped, creeping along George Street in a fur coat.

Colin had survived the desert, and the taking of Sicily, and his letters had grown confident and cheerful, certain of victory now that the list of Allied victories was steadily increasing. In Canada, Barbara had gone on tour with the band, to Isla's consternation, though Ainslie's letters were reassuring.

'Phil and I felt that it would be wrong to insist on her staying here instead of going. She'll be nineteen in two months' time, Isla, she's not a child any more. The band leader's wife is travelling with them, a sensible soul who can be trusted to keep an eye on Barbara. Anyway, you've got a level-headed daughter, and I'm sure she's well able to make her own decisions.'

It seemed to Isla, who still tended to think of Barbara and Ross as she had last seen them, that she was caught in a time warp. Even with the photographic proof before her, she found it hard to think of Barbara as a young woman and Ross, now fifteen, as a youth on the brink of manhood.

Gilchrist Forbes sold Flora's house in September to a couple with a young family. A lot was done to it before they moved in, and the quiet road, which had once known the roar of Gregg's motor-cycle, now echoed to the sound of hammering and sawing, and workmen calling to each other.

Another letter came from Ainslie, a thick envelope. Isla knew, just by looking at it, that it carried bad news. She had recently received Ross's usual fortnightly letter, but nothing from Barbara, who had fallen into the habit of sending cards from wherever she and the band were playing, and photographs of herself and the grinning musicians. There were usually some fans in the photographs too, young men, and the occasional young woman, autograph book in hand.

She carried the envelope into the kitchen and laid it on the table. If Flora had been alive, she would have gone next door to open it, but Flora wasn't there any more, Colin was far away in Sicily, and Isla was on her own. After five minutes, during which her imagination ran riot, she opened the envelope.

Ainslie's writing, normally neat, sprawled across the pages, launching into the story she had to tell without wasting time on chat about the weather. Because the Canadian government had become somewhat edgy about the number of British children evacuated to their country and left there for much longer than had first been anticipated, they had recently been checking on all the British people temporarily resident in their country. Ainslie had explained that Barbara and Ross were not technically evacuees, but her half-sister and half-brother, visiting her on an extended stay.

This had been accepted without comment, but unfortunately, now that Barbara required a work permit in order to travel with the band, she had had to deal with some paperwork on her own, and had seen, in black and white, the details about her relationship with Ainslie.

'She managed to get time off, and came here in quite a state,' Ainslie wrote. 'I explained that you had thought it best to leave things alone until you were able to tell her in person, but I'm afraid she was in no mood to accept that. She's very hurt, Isla – she wouldn't discuss it with me, just went storming back to Ottawa. She's since written to Ross, but not to me. Ross, by the way, is quite pleased to find that he's related, through me, to Phil and the boys, and not in the least bothered. I suppose Barbara's just more emotional than he is.'

Isla groaned softly as she reached the end of the letter. She should have told Barbara the truth earlier, but by the time the girl reached the age when she might have started asking questions about her real father, she was in Canada and involved in a new life.

She waited and worried for a few weeks, hoping that her daughter would write, reluctant to burden Colin with her problems when he was so far away and engaged in the day to day business of just staying alive. But there was no word from Barbara. Ross wrote, bubbling over with the joy of discovering that he had a whole set of relatives. 'I think it's great,' his untidy scrawl said. 'It makes me feel as if I'm really part of the Hannigan family. I expect Ainslie's told you that Barbara's not so happy about things, Mum. I can't think why, because she really likes Ainslie. I suppose it's something to do with being female. Don't worry, she'll come round to it.'

But Barbara didn't come round to it. Eventually, deciding that she could wait no longer for a letter from the girl, Isla steeled herself to sit down at Colin's desk on one of her days off, and start writing a long letter to Barbara.

The only way, she thought, chewing the end of the pen, was to tell the whole story, from the first day she had set eyes on Kenneth McAdam in the men's surgical ward of the Edinburgh hospital where she was a probationer. She wrote steadily for several hours, keeping nothing back, forcing herself to go once again

through all the pain of Kenneth's death, and the discovery of his other marriage and the first, terrible,
meeting with Ainslie. It was even harder than she had
expected it to be, but Barbara already felt as though she
was being deceived, and now she needed, and deserved,
every bit of the truth.

She stopped to eat and to rest her hand and wrist,
which were stiff and painful, then drove herself back to
the desk. 'I meant to tell you and Ross when you were
old enough to understand, but by the time you both
reached that stage, you were in Canada. Your real father
loved you very much, Barbara, and so do I. Colin thinks
of you as his own daughter. I know it must be hard for
you to discover that your father and I were never legally
married, but surely you must see that the important
thing is that you're part of a family, and nothing will
ever change that.'

It was late when she finished, signing and sealing the
letter without reading it over, partly because she was
afraid that she might then lose the courage to post it,
partly because having just relived years of her life on
paper, she couldn't bear to go over it all again. She had
even taken Kenneth's final letter, the letter Gilchrist
Forbes had given her when he came to tell her of
Kenneth's death, from the tiny drawer below her jewel
box, and copied it out word for word.

She slept badly that night, and went out to post the
letter as soon as the post-office opened, before walking
to the sanatorium.

It was a difficult day. For some unknown reason, the
patients were all irritable, and two of the nurses on her
shift were ill and off work. A group of officials chose

that day of all days to inspect the place, and the matron took her nervousness out on her staff. Worn out though she was, Isla welcomed the hard work, because at least it kept her from fretting about Barbara, and reliving the submerged memories that had been released by the letter, and thrown up to the surface of her mind.

She stayed on duty for a few hours longer than necessary to help the night staff, also short-handed, to settle the patients down, then walked slowly home through a dark night lit, now and again, by the moon glancing through scudding clouds. She was halfway down the hill when she saw a sudden tiny flare of light appear then disappear as someone at the foot of the hill pulled on a cigarette. Isla stopped, listening, but there was no sound of footsteps either approaching or walking away from her, and no voices. She stared into the night until her eyes were aching, and eventually glimpsed another tiny glow, just where the first had been. Someone was standing near the wooden door she had to go through to reach Low Road.

Isla fumbled for the torch she always carried in her bag. She hadn't used it on the walk because the batteries were low, and she knew the way from sanatorium to Low Road so well that she could have walked it blindfold. She switched the torch on, but the light was so weak and wavery that it was no use to her at all.

She bit her lip. The moon had been hidden for the past few minutes, and she was in total darkness. She was on her own, faced with the prospect of trudging back to the hospital, or going on. Home was nearer. It had been raining when she left the house that morning, and she was carrying her folded umbrella. She gripped it firmly and walked on, the tap of her heels on the roadway loud in the silence.

She had almost reached the door when she heard the sound of movement, the heel of a shoe scraping on the pavement as someone turned. Just then the moon slid out from the clouds and shone on the man turning towards her. It was Gregg Marshall.

'Isla,' he said, 'I couldn't stay away.'

Gregg lit a fire in the living-room and they talked half the night, sitting on the rug before the fireplace. He had applied for a transfer to an air base in England, and it had come through. He was leaving in a few days' time.

'When it came to it I couldn't just leave without seeing you, just one last time,' he said, and Isla, happy for the first time since Flora's death, unable to believe that he was really there, really with her, reached out and allowed her fingers the luxury of touching his face. He put his own hand on hers, turning her hand so that his mouth could brush over her palm. 'How've you been?' His eyes travelled over her face. 'You look worn out, Isla. What's wrong?'

She told him about Barbara, the words spilling out. It was such a relief to be able to talk about it. He listened in silence, and when she had talked herself out, he took his handkerchief and dabbed gently at her face, drying tears that she hadn't even noticed.

'Isla, Barbara's a very nice girl who's growing up to be a very nice, very beautiful, very sensible woman. I've got no doubt of that. You're going to have to give her time, honey – as much of it as she needs. She'll come to terms with everything, and while you're waiting, just keep on writing to her. She's been hurt, but she needs to know that this doesn't make any difference to the way you love her. What does Colin have to say about it?'

'I haven't told him. He's got enough to worry about.'

Gregg's eyebrows rose. 'Honey, he's the only father Barbara's ever known, and she's his daughter now. Don't try to cut him out of what's happening; if you do he'll resent it when he finally finds out.'

Isla looped her hands about her knees, staring into the fire. 'Oh, Gregg, I've made a terrible mess of things!'

He shifted so that he could put an arm about her. It was good to be able to lean back against a man's shoulder again. 'You haven't made a mess of anything, you've just been trying to save other people from grief. You've been so used to coping on your own all the years you were raising your kids that you've forgotten how to let others help.' He squeezed her shoulder. 'You need to loosen up, lady. Nobody can take the cares of the world on their shoulders, not even Isla Forbes.'

'Oh, Gregg, I'm so glad you came to Paisley tonight.'

She felt a laugh rumble through his body. 'I aim to please, ma'am.'

They sat together in silence for a long time, looking into the fire. Then Isla stirred, turned, and found his mouth waiting for hers.

Loving Gregg in the firelight, being loved by him, was inevitable and natural and, in its own way, right. At the beginning they were hungry for each other, hungry for contact, demanding and taking, almost devouring each other. Then, with the first urgent need satisfied, their lips and hands and bodies gentled into true loving and giving and receiving in mutual pleasure, both anxious, in this first and last time together, to give as much happiness to the other as possible. They spoke to each other with their bodies, their mouths, their hands. Questions were asked and answered, pledges made, assurances given, without a word being spoken aloud.

The years seemed to drop from them, and they loved like teenagers, rather than the parents of growing children. Isla felt no self-consciousness at all over exposing her aging body to his gaze and his touch, nor was there any guilt. Colin had always been an enthusiastic lover, though considerate; Gregg brought a form of poetry to his lovemaking, worshipping and celebrating their union with every part of himself, finally flowing into her and around her, enclosing her, merging the two of them into one being.

She sensed, as she responded with a fluidity that she had never known before, that this was not the way he and his wife made love, just as it was nothing like the way she and Colin coupled. This was unique, belonging only to the two of them, and only for this one magical night. It was a primitive celebration of their meeting at a time when their great need of each other surpassed everything that had been in their lives before, or would come again.

At last, they slept in each other's arms, lying on cushions, wrapped snugly together in the large woollen shawl that was normally draped along the back of the couch. Isla wakened to find Gregg kneeling by her side, his lips moving slowly, gently, across her breasts. The fire had gone out, and because of the blackout, the room was dark, but she could hear birdsong outside.

'It's five o'clock, honey,' he said against her shoulder. 'I'll have to go.'

She wrapped her arms about him, drawing him close. 'Not yet . . .'

'Not quite yet,' Gregg agreed, his body responding to the movement of her limbs. This time the magic of the night before had gone, and they made love comfortably, completely, like a man and a woman who were dear friends, as well as sharing a mutual physical attraction. But his leaving couldn't be put off for ever; they dressed swiftly in lamplight, then walked to the door, their arms around each other. It was almost daylight outside, the air fresh after the previous day's rain.

'Are you sure you won't have something to eat before you go?'

'If I stay any longer, I'll never leave.' He kissed the tip of her nose, and said, 'I'll wheel the bike to the end of the road, otherwise the neighbours'll start talking about you.'

They looked at each other, a long look that they both knew would have to last the rest of their lives. 'I won't write,' Gregg said. 'I mean, I will, often, but I won't send any of the letters. Best to end it here and now.'

'When the war's over, we might go to Canada to visit Ainslie.'

'If you do, I'll stay away. I don't think I could bear to see you and not be able to touch you.' He kissed her, his mouth hard on hers. 'Take care,' he said, then she was alone, straining for one last glimpse of him through the bushes as he kicked the bike off its stand and wheeled it along the road.

When he had gone, Isla bathed in the few inches of tepid water allowed by the war regulations, dressed, and had breakfast before going into the living-room to open the blackout and restore the spilled cushions and shawl to their rightful places. She cleaned the ashes from the fireplace, washed the mugs and plates they had used, then set off for the sanatorium.

Although she had had very little sleep she strode briskly up the hill and along the road, ignoring the heavy rain-filled clouds that had begun to gather overhead. She felt fit and well, refreshed and renewed by Gregg's loving. Catching sight of her reflection in the glass panel of the sanatorium door as she was about to go in, she made a face at herself, then smiled.

She was forty years old, but she felt as young as Barbara. She would never cease to be grateful to the big Canadian for blessing her life, reminding her what it felt like to be young again, and happy. A mere fifteen hours earlier she had felt old and tired and depressed. Now, stepping into the sanatorium, she felt strong and optimistic. Although she had no knowledge of what lay ahead, she was sure that everything was going to be all right.

At last, in September, Barbara sent a letter. It was brief and somewhat cool, but at least it was a letter.

'I feel as though after all these years of being me, I'm not me at all,' she wrote. 'I'm a different person altogether. You should have told me, or Ainslie should have told me, instead of leaving me to find out the way

I did. I still don't know right now how I feel about it all, but I guess I should thank you for finally telling me everything.'

Although she wanted to reply at once, Isla restrained herself for a week, then wrote a chatty and affectionate letter, making no further reference to Kenneth other than to assure her daughter that she understood how Barbara felt, and would leave her to sort out her own feelings in her own time.

Christmas came and went, bringing with it bitter-sweet memories of the dance at Prestwick aerodrome the year before, and Christmas Day with Flora. This year Isla worked during Christmas Day and visited Colin's parents in the evening. On Boxing Day she went to Magret's to admire Greta's new engagement ring and meet her fiancé, a plump, fair-haired, shy young man content to sit in a corner and watch his beloved with adoring brown spaniel eyes. He and Greta didn't plan to marry for a year, at least. They had already put their names down for a Corporation house in one of the housing schemes built before the war.

'We don't mind which,' Greta told Isla. 'Whitehaugh, or Lochfield, or Ferguslie Park. The houses are all very nice.'

The Gillespies, the couple who had bought Flora's house, had moved in just before Christmas. They had two young children, a boy and a girl, and Isla welcomed the sound of the children's voices as they played in the garden. Early in January Janice Gillespie appeared at the dividing hedge as Isla walked up the path to her own door and invited her in for a cup of tea that afternoon.

Isla hesitated. 'I've got rather a lot to do,' she lied, reluctant to go back into a house which held so many memories.

The young woman looked disappointed. 'Just for a little while,' she begged. 'I wanted to ask you about something.'

So Isla agreed, then discovered when she nerved herself to step over the door lintel that it wasn't so difficult after all, because the house had changed out of all recognition. All Flora's dark wallpaper had been stripped off and replaced by pale distemper, 'stippled' with clusters of colour applied by dipping a sponge in paint then dabbing it over the walls. The furniture was modern and lightweight, and the couch and chairs in the living-room were covered with dark brown material, heaped with small cushions in vivid colours and patterns.

Janice Gillespie, pouring tea from an elegant, pale green fluted china pot into matching cups, suited her surroundings. She, too, was smart and modern, with short, well-cut dark hair, and red fingernails. She wore a dark green linen dress beneath a short-sleeved yellow coatee. Isla had heard that Mrs Gillespie came from a wealthy family, and her husband held down an important job at the munitions factory in Bishopton.

'Won't you have a biscuit? You'll probably think this is very impertinent of me, Mrs Forbes,' the young woman said a little nervously, putting the plate down. 'But I understand that you run a very successful business, furnishing dolls' houses.'

'I did, before the war. I'm nursing at the Craw Road sanatorium now, but I intend to start the business up again when I can.'

'Oh, I see.' Janice Gillespie looked disappointed. 'My daughter Angela's going to be six years old next month, and my sister's offered us the dolls' house her own daughter used to play with. But it's all very shabby now, and I'd hoped to persuade you to furnish it for her.'

'I do have some furniture, but it's rather ordinary,' Isla said hesitantly. 'I usually use specially made pieces, but my craftsman's in the Navy.'

Hope came into her neighbour's face. 'We wouldn't want anything too elaborate at this stage. Angela's too young to appreciate it, so we thought – just an ordinary little house that she can enjoy—'

'Ask your husband to bring it round tonight, when she's in bed,' Isla told her impulsively, 'and I'll do my best.'

Clearly, there was a genuine mother beneath Mrs Gillespie's sophistication. She beamed her delight. 'That's so kind of you!'

Later, showing her visitor out, she said, 'I understand that you knew the previous owner well. It must be strange to see how much we've changed the house.'

'I'm glad you did.' Isla looked round the hall and said, 'I think it rather likes the changes.'

'Really? We loved the place the moment we set eyes on it. It has a good feeling about it. I hope the children haven't disturbed you, playing in the garden. They're thrilled to be able to get out – we were in digs before, and there was nowhere for them to go. We had to spend most of the day in the park.'

'I enjoy hearing them – it brings back memories. My own children are in Canada for the duration of the war.'

'How dreadful for you, being apart from them!'

'They're not really children any more, almost grown up. But yes, I miss them very much, so it's good to hear your youngsters. And I think,' Isla said warmly, 'that the previous owner would be pleased if she knew that there was a family in the house again.'

Walking home, taking the old familiar route down one path, along the pavement, and up the other path, Isla was glad that she had thought of doing a copy of Flora's house eventually. Although the real house had changed out of all recognition, she would have her replica full of memories.

Mr Gillespie brought the dolls' house round that evening. When he had gone Isla eyed it thoughtfully. It had four rooms and an entrance hall and a flight of stairs to the upper floor, and once it had had a cheerful red roof, now scratched and faded. She ferreted in the cupboard in the workroom, unearthed some small pots of paint, brushes, items and furniture and scraps of material, and got to work.

The little house kept her happily occupied in her spare time over the next four weeks, and when she handed it back to the delighted Gillespies, fresh and colourful and furnished, she began work straightaway on what she now thought of as the Flora house, doing what she could and leaving the more difficult tasks until the day when Drew would be back in his workshop.

Another letter arrived from Barbara, still cool, but a little longer than the last letter, with some news of the band tour. Ainslie wrote to say that Barbara had asked her for photographs of Kenneth, which had been sent to her.

427

In March, Colin came home on leave, and insisted on taking Isla to Largs for a holiday by the Clyde. He booked a comfortable room in a comfortable hotel, and they spent most of their days braving the weather, walking along the front, wrapped up in their warmest clothes. Colin looked, on those outings, as though he was about to set out on an expedition to the North Pole. Largs, an attractive and very popular holiday town, was noted for its stiff sea breezes and Colin, used now to a much warmer climate, felt the cold intensely.

Isla had wondered, nervously, in the time between hearing that he was coming home and his actual arrival, if Gregg would come between them, if Colin might somehow taste the Canadian on her skin, read about him in her eyes, sense him in her touch. But once she was with him, held in his arms, she knew that there had been nothing to fear. Like Flora, she had learned that it was possible to love two men deeply. What had happened between herself and Gregg had come about because they had had a great need of each other at a certain stage in their lives. It had been written into their stars at birth, and it had also been written that, physically, their union would be brief. In every other way, it was real, and lasting, and guiltless.

Gregg would always be with her, locked away in a deep, secret compartment that nobody else would ever know about. But Colin was her husband, her love, her future, her life. He had asked, casually, about Gregg, and Isla had told him, just as casually, that the Canadian was in England.

'I dreamed of wet streets at night,' he said as they leaned on the rail on their first day in Largs, watching the waves race each other down the Firth of Clyde and the small boats at anchor rocking and tugging on their cables like horses trying to break free, 'with lamplight shining on puddles, and of the way falling rain dimples water, and sometimes I dreamed about snowball fights and zooming down a hill on a sledge. We must take the children sledging the first winter we have together.'

'They'll probably feel that they're too old for that sort of thing by then. Anyway, they've had lots of snow in Canada. Ours might be a comedown.'

'I don't care what they think – we're all going sledging in the first peacetime snow, and that's that,' Colin said stubbornly, then shivered and pulled the brim of his soft hat down as another gust of wind came chasing along the front towards them. 'I can't say I missed the gales, though.'

'We should have stayed at home.'

'No we shouldn't. You badly needed a holiday, and I wanted us to spend some time alone together. If we'd stayed in Paisley my mother would have been knocking at the door every day.'

'She's missed you, too.'

'I know, and I promise that I'll make a fuss of her when we get back, but you come first,' he told her. 'I want you to get the sea air into your lungs. Breathe deeply, or you'll end up as a patient in that sanatorium of yours.'

'I'm perfectly well!'

Colin put an arm about her and held her close, bending to nuzzle his cold face against hers. 'I don't know how you've been able to stand it. At least we're well fed, and we get the feeling that we're getting things done,

429

bringing an end to this damned war. It's you and the other folks left at home who've had to bear the brunt of it – not knowing half the time just what's going on, coping with rationing, worrying about air-raids and about whether I'm all right and not seeing your kids for years.' His other arm wrapped itself about her and he kissed her. 'I'll make it all up to you one day, darling,' he whispered when he lifted his mouth from hers. 'I promise!'

'Colin, people are looking at us!'

'Let them,' he said, and kissed her again.

Later, in bed, he started to laugh. 'No wonder people were staring at us this afternoon. I'm as brown as a berry and you're white as a ghost.' He caught her hand and raised their bare arms in the air, pressed together. 'The two of us must look like a half-eaten chocolate cream when we're out together.' Then, as their hands, still linked, fell back on to the bed he added, 'Isla, I'm not going back to Sicily. I've to report to a unit down south.'

Relief swept over her. 'You're staying in Britain?'

'For a while, anyway. There's something special on the way, and they're reorganising things so that the older men can relieve the youngsters to prepare for it.' He turned his head on the pillow and kissed her shoulder. 'In military terms I'm a has-been. God, the very thought makes me feel old.'

Isla raised herself on one elbow and looked down at his tanned face, familiar, yet not familiar. There were lines there that she had never seen before, some caused by laughter, some by squinting into a fiercer sun than she had ever known. But most of the lines were grim and hard, engraved deeply into his skin by sights and sounds and experiences he would probably not talk about for many years.

'You're not old. You'll never be old,' she said fiercely, and he reached up to pull her close.

'If this war's taught me anything, Isla, it's how much I love you and treasure you.'

The week in Largs was like a honeymoon. They spent every minute together, talking, walking, loving, rediscovering each other.

Following Gregg's advice, she had told Colin about Barbara. Now that they were together, they were able to talk about it in depth. Colin, like Gregg, believed that the girl should be left to her own devices. 'I don't think you'll lose her, darling. You did the right thing, telling her the whole truth once she'd found out about it.'

'If I could just talk to her face to face, answer all her questions, I'd feel better. Oh, Colin, it's been so long since I last saw them both!'

'I know, love, but I don't think it's going to be much longer now.' He gave her a sidelong glance, then said, 'Has it occurred to you that they might want to settle in Canada? They've both enjoyed their stay, and Barbara seems to have established a career there.'

She looked at him in dismay. 'They wouldn't do that, surely?'

'They might. If they do, it's not the end of the world. We could settle there ourselves if it came to it.'

'But what about the business?'

Colin gave a short, grim laugh. 'After what we've all been through in the past five years, the business doesn't seem to be all that important any more. Not nearly as important as being with you and Barbara and Ross, and being happy. If it comes to it, I'm game.'

Isla thought of Gregg, of living in his country, perhaps meeting him, seeing him with his wife and his sons. He had said that he couldn't bear a meeting under such circumstances, and she knew that she felt the same way.

'They'll want to come home, I know it,' she said obstinately, and Colin shrugged.

'No sense in crossing our bridges. I just thought I'd mention it.'

34

In June, Allied forces stormed the beaches at Normandy, the 'something special' that Colin had spoken of in Largs, and began to drive the Germans back. British losses were comparatively light, but that meant little to Isla, because Drew Brown was among them. Her letter to Colin was smudged with tears that had refused to stop trickling for days.

'I went at once to see Mrs Brown, but the place was filled with neighbours, so there wasn't much left for me to do. The poor woman was just sitting there, huddled in her chair, lost and bewildered by what's happened. Drew was all she had. The only thing she said while I was there was that perhaps it was for the best that he hadn't got married after all. I'm not so sure. At least if he had, she would have had a daughter-in-law to share her grief. Now, she's got nobody.'

She stopped writing in order to dab at her eyes with a handkerchief that was already damp, then, seeing that some tears had splashed on to the paper, she tried to blot them and only succeeded in smudging the ink. She contemplated starting the letter over again, but it was almost time to set out for the sanatorium, and she wanted to post it on her way there. She sniffed hard, gave her eyes another swipe with the handkerchief, and went on.

'Magret has done a lot for Mrs Brown since the news arrived, and Mrs Leach was a tower of strength while I was there, so gentle with Mrs Brown that I could scarcely believe it. She's older now, of course, which might have mellowed her. And poor Mr Kelly's death in Italy might have had something to do with it. Magret says that since then, Mrs Kelly has become much stronger, and won't allow her mother to bully her any more. Her little boy is a beautiful child – completely spoiled by his grandmother, who looks after him outside school hours when his mother's at work. Would you believe it, Colin, Mrs Brown even managed to rouse herself when I was saying goodbye, and thank me again for getting her roof mended all those years ago.'

Although the war was swinging in the Allies' favour now, the Germans were fighting back viciously. At the end of June, flying bombs started ravaging London.

'It must be like being attacked by a swarm of bees, only a million times worse,' Magret said, shaking her head and showering Isla's kitchen with the white fluff that always clung to the mill workers' clothes and hair. 'Bees don't stop buzzing then start exploding. These poor souls down south, they've had the worst of it!'

The Allies marched into Paris, then on to Belgium, while rockets being fired from Germany and Holland added to the misery of the flying bombs for the London civilians, and set Isla fretting afresh about Colin. She had thought he was safe in England, but now he was involved with anti-aircraft guns and, she knew from his letters, rarely able to enjoy a trouble-free night.

Unable to do a thing to help him, she concentrated her spare time on doing as much work on the Flora dolls' house as she could. That helped her a little, though every now and again dark depression swept over her as she recalled that once the war was over, Drew wouldn't be there, after all, to create miniature replicas of Flora's massive, dark furniture.

Eventually she set it aside and, buying a plain little house from Mr Leckie, who was still running his toyshop, she turned to copying the room she and Barbara and Ross had inhabited in George Street.

'I didnae know that there were this many folk in Paisley,' Magret bawled into Isla's ear. The two of them stood on the bridge spanning the River Cart at Paisley Cross, at the exact spot, Isla suddenly realised, where she had stood looking down at the river on her first visit to the town.

Only this time she wasn't alone; it was VE-Day, and every inch of the Cross and the gardens on the river-bank was crammed with people singing, dancing if they could find the space, hugging and kissing each other, celebrating the end of the war.

A group of soldiers to one side were bellowing out a Welsh song, on the other, a bunch of girls and service-men, arms linked, were jigging up and down, singing, 'Pack up Your Troubles In Your Old Kitbag'. Cars and buses caught in the crowd shrilled their horns in cele-bration, people leaning from the windows of the surrounding buildings waved Union Jacks and cheered, and all the statues in the gardens, even Queen Victoria's, were being used as footholds and handholds for folk trying to get above the crowd.

A burly man in naval uniform, a beer bottle in his hand, set up in competition with other singers with 'Roll Out The Barrel!' in a powerful voice that was soon joined by others, including the Welshmen and the girls and their escorts. Magret roared the tune out lustily, beating time in the air with clenched fists, then broke off and grabbed at Isla's hand. 'I'm dyin' for a cup of tea. C'mon, we'll find the lassies and go home.'

Half an hour later they had only travelled a few yards, to the other side of St Mirren Brae, and there was no sign of Greta or Daisy.

'Hell mend them,' their mother said cheerfully. 'We'll just go on home and let them come back when they're good and ready.'

Together the two women battled down St Mirren Brae, Magret stopping to hug every man she met, with an extra warm hug for anyone in uniform. 'Take yer chances where ye find them, that's what I say,' she said cheerfully after a particularly enthusiastic encounter with a good-looking naval rating. 'There's none of them'll bother tae pass the time of day wi' a middle-aged biddy like me once we get used tae the idea of peace again.'

The crowds were thinning by the time they had reached the end of George Street and begun to walk up its length towards Magret's new home. They stopped at the old tenement to visit Mrs Brown, and Magret tried to persuade her to go with them, but she shook her head and said with an apologetic smile, 'I'd just as soon stay here on my own today.'

'All right, hen – but ye know where I live,' Magret patted her hand. 'Ye'll be welcome there any time ye feel like it. Any time at all, mind.'

They covered the rest of the distance in subdued silence, both thinking of Drew, and young Mr Kelly, and finally arrived at the flat to find that Greta and Daisy were already there, holding an impromptu party with Greta's fiancé and Daisy's boyfriend and several other people, the gramophone the girls had bought between them thumping out a Glen Miller tune.

Magret's usual high spirits returned at the prospect of a party. Towing Isla behind her, kissing and hugging to left and to right, she fought her way through the crowd to the tiny scullery, which she called a kitchenette. 'Won't be long before your two are back, Isla,' she shouted above the noise as she set the kettle on the gas stove. Then, with a swift glance at her friend's face, 'Are ye still frettin' about Barbara?' Isla had told her about Barbara's discovery, but had withheld Kenneth's name. Although there were no longer any McAdams living in Paisley, she couldn't bring herself to betray him. For once, Magret hadn't pried.

'I can't help fretting.'

'Ach, she'll get over it. She'll have tae. And when all's said and done' – Magret, heedless of rationing on this special day, spooned sugar generously into both their cups – 'you're her mammy. It'll be fine, just wait and see.'

In July the blackout curtains were pulled down and the street lights went on again. Isla packed the hated gas mask into a cupboard and out of sight, relieved beyond measure that she had never had to find out whether or not she would have used it in a gas attack, and prepared, nervously, for the return of her son and daughter from Canada. To her relief, Barbara had decided to fly back with Ross, and Ainslie was coming with them.

'I'm more than ready for a reunion,' she wrote. 'Phil, bless him, will stay here with the boys. He reckons that on this occasion, we should be on our own. I can't wait to see you again. Prepare for a shock when you see Ross, he's so like the McAdams, though I would say that he has your temperament, thank goodness. Every time I look at him I'm reminded of poor little Innes.'

Isla, who was still at the sanatorium, and would go on working there until the local Hospital Board got everything sorted out and their nursing staff up to its required level, arranged to take time off on the day they were due to arrive. It had been agreed that they would come to Paisley from Prestwick Aerodrome by train, then get a taxi to Castlehead, where Isla would be waiting. As the expected time for their arrival came near, she was so nervous that she couldn't sit down, but had to pace the ground floor, going restlessly from room to room until she was certain she must have worn a track in the carpets. When at last she heard the taxi stopping at the gate, she rushed to the door, then paused at the top of the porch steps, terrified. It had been so long, and so many things had happened since she had last seen her children.

Ainslie was first out of the vehicle. Sophisticated though she looked in a tailored navy skirt and fur jacket, her red hair still fiery beneath a smart navy and white hat, she nevertheless gave a Red Indian whoop of excitement as she spotted Isla. She fumbled with the gate, then ran up the path as Isla ran down the porch steps. They met halfway along the path, thumping straight into each other's arms.

'I thought today would never come! You look—' Ainslie held Isla back for a moment. 'My God, you look as though you've been through the mill,' she said with brutal honesty, then gathered Isla close for another swift, hard hug before turning towards the two young people coming in at the gate.

'Come on, you two – let your ma see what a disaster I've made of your upbringing.'

Ross came forward first, grinning, and Isla saw with a catch of breath what Ainslie had meant. It was almost like seeing Kenneth again, though Ross's eyes were a darker blue and his face rounder. He caught her up in a bear hug that almost squeezed the breath from her. At sixteen, he was a good head taller than Isla herself.

'You've grown!'

'No, you've got smaller.' His eyes were bright, his voice deep, with just the trace of a drawl to it.

Then it was Barbara's turn. In spite of the photographs, Isla had been unable to think of Barbara other than as the leggy schoolgirl she had last seen going up the gangplank of the steamer at Greenock. Now she was confronted by an elegant young woman in a tan and cream checked costume, her lovely face carefully but lightly made up, her shoulder-length hair a glowing mass against the cream hat perched like a halo on the back of her head. For a moment mother and daughter eyed each other warily, then Isla opened her arms and

Barbara came into them, briefly, dropping a light kiss on Isla's cheek before freeing herself.

'Hello, Mother.'

'It looks so small!' Ross broke the awkward moment, staring up at the house. 'I remembered it as a big house.'

'Your mother's right, you daft lump – it's you that's grown,' Ainslie told him. 'Didn't I keep saying that you were eating too much?'

The taxi-driver, still waiting by the gate with a pile of luggage, cleared his throat loudly, drawing their attention to his patient presence. There was a flurry of activity, paying the man, getting the luggage into the hall, then they were all indoors, the door shut, grinning self-consciously at each other. All except Barbara, Isla noticed, avoiding eye-contact, looking around as she drew her gloves off.

'Same room?' Ross asked, and when his mother nodded he scooped up two cases and ran up the stairs, calling back, 'I'll fetch the others in a minute.'

'Ainslie, I've had to put a bed for you in Barbara's room.'

'Oh, no,' Ainslie said in mock horror. 'The indignity of it, having to share a room at my age with my kid sister!' ·

Barbara grinned at her, and for the first time, Isla caught a glimpse of the daughter she had known. 'First there gets the best bed,' she said, and ran lightly upstairs after her brother.

'She hates me,' Isla said in a panic.

'No, she doesn't.' Ainslie put an arm round her and gave her a swift hug.

'But she's so formal with me, and so relaxed with you.'

'She hasn't seen you for years, and anyway, she's inherited the McAdam pride, that's for sure. You'll have to give her time, Isla. Come and make me some tea, I've been dreaming about a cup of tea all through the flight.'

As they sat at the kitchen table waiting for the kettle to boil, they could hear Ross running up and down the stairs collecting the luggage, the thump of footsteps above, Barbara and Ross calling to each other, the slam of doors.

'This house has been so quiet, for so long,' she said in awe. 'And suddenly it's come alive again.'

'Everything'll soon be back to normal.'

'It'll never be the same again, but if we're lucky, we can start all over again.'

'Any word of Colin coming home?'

'Next month, he hopes.'

'You'll be pleased about that.'

'So will his father – he's worn himself out looking after the office. This time, he's looking forward to retiring.'

'Gregg Marshall arrived back just before we left, much to Pat's relief. She's missed him terribly. They've always been a very close family. It was good of you to give him hospitality while he was based in Scotland.'

'He's a very nice person.'

'That's exactly what he said about you,' Ainslie said. 'You'll be looking forward to getting back to your dolls' houses.'

'Mr Leckie's had some enquiries already. And Mabel's written – she'll be demobbed soon, and she wants to come back to work for me. I'll have to find another furniture maker.' She swallowed, then said, 'There'll never be anyone like Drew, though.'

'I know.' Ainslie reached over and touched her shoulder. The kettle began to whistle and Isla got up and poured some boiling water into the teapot, then emptied it out and reached for the tea-caddy.

'I was thinking of asking Mrs Brown if she'd like to be our housekeeper.'

Ainslie went unerringly to the right cupboard to fetch cups and saucers. 'Drew's mother? D'you think she'll want the job?'

'I think she might. It'd be good for her to be part of a family. If we are still a family,' Isla added, a tremor in her voice, as she set the empty kettle down.

'Of course you are. It's funny how things that happened years ago keep affecting our lives, isn't it?' Ainslie sat down again, putting her elbows on the table and leaning her chin in cupped hands. 'It's been over sixteen years since my father died, and yet when Barbara started asking about him, and the two of us spent hours going over the photographs I'd found for her, I could almost see the change coming over her. She matured, Isla. She's found qualities in herself that she'd never noticed before. Even though he died when she was little, Father shaped her, just as he shaped us. Remember when we talked it all over years ago, and I said that we were McAdam's women?'

Ross, yelling to his sister to hurry up, came thundering down the stairs and into the kitchen, a camera in his hand. He stopped suddenly, then said, 'I almost expected to see Nan here.'

'So do I, every time I come in,' Isla told him.

'It must have been awful for you.'

'It was – but now you're back home, and everything's going to be all right.'

Ross blinked rapidly, swallowed, then opened the back door. 'Outside, everyone,' he said briskly. 'I want to take some pictures.'

'But I want my tea,' Ainslie wailed.

'Later. I'm preserving this moment for posterity.' Ross tossed the words over his shoulder as he plunged into the garden.

Ainslie, groaning, got to her feet. 'We gave him that for his last birthday, and right now I wish we'd never thought of it. He's camera mad, I warn you. Come on, we might as well fetch Barbara and get it over with.'

They found Barbara in the workroom, standing over the dolls' house that Isla was working on. She turned as they went in, wonder in her eyes. 'This looks just like our old room in George Street!'

'You remember it?'

'Of course I do. That was where I learned to play peevers.' For the first time, Barbara gave her mother a genuine smile, and Isla, heartened, went to stand by her.

'I wanted to keep my hand in, and I thought it would be an easy one to do.'

Barbara reached into the little house and withdrew a matchbox tray, painted creamy yellow to resemble an orange box. Gently, she drew back the scrap of cloth hung on a thread across the opening. 'You've even put the little dishes on the shelves. Can I have it when it's finished?'

'Of course you can.'

Barbara gently replaced the little makeshift cupboard

in the dolls' house, then her index finger, tipped with pink nail polish, touched each of the dolls in turn. 'A mother doll, a girl doll, a boy doll. I insisted on having a daddy doll, didn't I?'

'Yes. You were quite right,' Isla said. 'There should have been one. I'll make one.'

'No, don't.' The silky fall of Barbara's red hair hid her downbent face. After a moment she straightened. 'We seemed to manage well enough without one,' she said matter-of-factly, and swung out of the room.

'She's thawing,' Ainslie whispered as they followed her through the kitchen and into the back garden, where Ross was standing by the edge of the vegetable patch, staring round in amazement.

'The swing's gone. Where's my swing?' he asked in his man's voice.

'You're old enough to make your own now,' Barbara said, and he made a face at her.

'I might just do that. Now, over against the garden wall, the three of you, with Mum in the middle.'

They grouped themselves, and he studied them through the viewfinder, then flapped a hand at them. 'Closer together.'

Barbara's scent, fresh and flowery, wafted towards Isla as they obeyed, arms about each other.

'That's good. Hold it,' Ross instructed.

'McAdam's women,' Ainslie murmured, just as the camera shutter clicked, freezing the three of them, Isla, Ainslie, and Barbara, entwined in an embrace for all time.

Pebbles On The Beach

1

'Lachlan!'

Trace horses dragging a loaded cart up Mearns Street from the docks to the nearby sugar refinery clattered by just as Elspeth shouted her cousin's name across the width of the playground, ironbound wheels and hooves rumbling and sparking over the cobblestones.

The figure leaning against a tenement wall opposite the school gates, studying a newspaper, didn't move. Frustrated, Elspeth put two fingers to her lips in the way Thomas and Lachlan had taught her years before, and blew a piercing whistle that cut through the chill autumn air.

This time Lachlan looked up at once, his young face splitting into a huge grin as he saw her at the bottom of the school steps. He wasn't the only one to look in her direction; all through the playground and in the street beyond the railings heads turned. Women gossiping to each other from the tenement windows opposite the school, most of them with their arms comfortably folded on cushions or blankets protecting them from the stone sills, gaped and craned to see where the noise had come from.

'Elspeth Bremner! Kindly remember that you're a young lady and not a steam whistle down at the shipyards!' snapped the teacher who had just emerged on to the steps, and Elspeth whirled guiltily, the movement whipping her skirt against her long thin legs.

'Yes, Miss Scott, sorry, Miss Scott. It's just th-that—' She was stammering in her excitement at seeing Lachlan right there in Greenock, when she had thought him to be in some army barracks in England, '—that's our Lachlan over there. He m-must have come home on leave and I didn't know about it—'

The woman's face softened. 'In that case, run along – but don't you ever let out that dreadful noise in my hearing again.'

'Yes, Miss Scott, thank you, Miss Scott.' Elspeth set off at a run across the playground, weaving around the loitering groups. Her schoolbooks, held together by an old belt, were clutched to her chest, and the thick brown plait that hung down her back bounced against her spine with every step.

The headlong rush didn't stop until she was through the gate and across the street, letting the bundle of books fall unheeded on the pavement, running straight into Lachlan's open arms, being swung up into the air and round in a circle.

'I didn't know you were coming home!' she said breathlessly as he put her down.

'Neither did I till yesterday. God, Ellie, ye've put on weight! Ye were just a wee scliff of a thing when I last saw ye.'

'I'm older now.' She prodded him in the stomach. 'You've got fatter yourself.'

'Och, that's the stodge they feed us in the army,' Lachlan McDonald said, then glanced over Elspeth's shoulder. 'Hello, Molly.'

'Hello.' Molly McKibbin's round face was strangely blotchy. She looked, Elspeth thought, surprised, as though she was coming down with something. 'You dropped your books, Elspeth.'

'I didn't drop them, I threw them down.'

'Without looking? They could have landed in some old man's spit,' Molly said self-righteously, turning the bundle over and examining it carefully.

'They're fine.' Elspeth knew that her voice was too sharp,

2

but with good reason. It was true that she and Molly always walked home from school together, but surely today, with Lachlan arriving so unexpectedly, Molly should have had the tact to leave the two of them on their own. Elspeth reached for the books, but Lachlan stretched a long arm out beyond hers, and got to the shabby strap first.

'I'll carry them. I'll take yours as well, if you like,' he added, and Molly promptly handed over her own armful of books, simpering foolishly.

'You've both shot up while I've been away,' he teased, and Molly's simper became a silly little giggle. Best friend or not, Elspeth could have slapped her.

'What's that on your face?' she asked instead.

Molly's hand flew up. 'Where?'

'Your cheeks are all blotchy – and your neck, too. Big red blotches all over. Have a look at yourself in that shop window there.'

'Stop teasin' the lassie,' Lachlan told her, amused. 'It's nothin', Molly, just a wee bit red – from the wind, mebbe. It's cold enough. Come on, I've only got till tomorrow and I don't want to spend my leave standin' here.'

Behind their wire-framed spectacles, Molly's eyes shot a look of pure venom at Elspeth, who gave a bland smile in return.

'Where's your uniform?' Elspeth slipped her hand possessively into Lachlan's free arm as they turned towards home, leaving Molly to trail behind them.

'Ach, I couldnae wait to get out of it and intae my own clothes. It's scratchy, and it doesnae fit me properly. They never do.' Then, squeezing her arm against his side, 'Happy birthday, Ellie.'

'You remembered?'

'Of course I remembered, that's why I'm here. I said to the Sergeant-Major, "Listen, sir," I said. "Our Ellie'll be thirteen years old next Thursday, so I'd be much obliged if ye could see yer way tae stoppin' the war for a couple of days so's I can go home and taste a bit of that dumpling my mum'll be making for her.'''

'You did not!' Molly gasped from Elspeth's other side.

'Of course he didn't, don't be daft!'

'But I would have, if he hadnae come up with the idea himself before I even got a chance tae speak tae him.'

'I wish it was longer than just till tomorrow!'

'Aye, well, I've not quite managed tae see the Kaiser off yet, so they need me tae go back and finish the job properly. Then I'll be home for good. Here – try my jacket pocket.'

Elspeth slipped her hand into the nearest pocket, as she had often done on cold days in the past, before the war. The familiar warmth of his body against her fingers, the confident swing of his hip, brought back comforting memories. She had missed Thomas, the first of the two brothers to go off to war, but Lachlan had always been a special favourite. When he was called up, only weeks after his seventeenth birthday, she had cried herself to sleep for several nights after he left.

Her fingers encountered a tiny glass bottle; she drew it out and gave a gasp of delight.

'It's toilet water! Oh, Lachlan—!'

He flushed. 'Well, ye're growin' up now, aren't ye? I thought that'd please ye more than sweeties.'

Molly pushed in between them, so close that she tramped on Elspeth's heel. 'It's bonny,' she agreed, her voice hushed with awe as she peered at the pretty little bottle with a delicate spray of lavender pictured on the label. She reached out an avaricious hand, but Elspeth pulled her own hand back and opened the bottle to allow the light fragrance of lavender to tickle at her nose. She flipped the bottle deftly over then upright again, then dabbed her wet fingertip below each ear.

'Can you smell it, Lachlan?'

He sniffed, his nose cold against her earlobe. 'Aye, but I'd as soon smell dumplin'. Come on, I'm hungry!'

Ignoring the silent plea in Molly's eyes, Elspeth refastened the bottle and put it into her pocket. Tomorrow after school she would let Molly have a dab of lavender, but not today. This was her birthday, her special day, and she wanted to keep its joys to herself for a little while, at least.

The three of them reached the top of the slight hill leading up from the school, and Elspeth stopped, as she usually did, to drink in the view. So did Lachlan; she had known he would, in spite of his claim to be hungry. Like her, he loved any view of the River Clyde.

The rest of Mearns Street ran down the hill that Greenock was built on. From where they stood, the tenements on either side, dropping away below them, framed the width of the River Clyde and the soft green hills on the far side. At the bottom of the street could be seen a clutter of cranes in one of the shipyards fringing the river all along the Greenock shore.

Today, both the September sky and the river below it were grey, but that didn't bother Elspeth, nor, she knew, would it concern Lachlan. The Clyde fascinated them both in all its moods, at all times of the year.

'It's grand tae taste this air again, and see the hills,' Lachlan said after a moment. 'They don't have a lot of hills in England.'

He drew in a deep lungful of air and Molly, standing demurely on his other side, did the same. 'Wee bizzum!' Elspeth thought resentfully, for normally Molly fussed and fretted impatiently when Elspeth stopped at this point every day. Peering round Lachlan, she glared at her friend, who smiled sweetly back at her.

She got her revenge a few short minutes later, when they reached the corner of Roxburgh Street. 'See you tomorrow then, Molly.'

'Eh?'

'This is where you turn off for your own house,' Elspeth said slowly and clearly, as though talking to a small child, taking

Molly's books from Lachlan and handing them back to their owner. 'Unless you've moved and not thought to tell me?'

Embarrassment spread the blotches over poor Molly's face until they joined together to create a full blush. 'Oh. I didn't realise we were here already.'

'I'll see you tomorrow morning, then.'

As the two of them crossed Roxburgh Street, leaving the other girl behind, Elspeth took Lachlan's arm again, hugging it tightly against her side. He wasn't going to be home for long and she wanted to make the most of this short, precious moment together. In the evening the neighbours would crowd into the small flat to greet the returned warrior and hear about his experiences, which meant that there would be little enough private time to spare.

Lachlan's mother, she knew, would feel the same way. Flora McDonald, fair though she was in most things, had always favoured her sons more than her daughters.

'What's the army like, Lachlan?'

'Ach, it's OK.'

'Have you done any fighting yet?'

'We've just been trainin' so far,' he said vaguely. 'How's school?'

'It's OK,' she mimicked, and he gave her a friendly punch on the shoulder.

'Don't you be so cheeky tae one of His Majesty's brave soldiers! Just a year to go, eh?'

Elspeth hesitated, then decided to let him be the first to hear her news. 'Miss Scott said this morning that she thinks I should stay on for another year.'

'Oh? So we've got a clever-clogs in the family, have we?'

'It's not just me – Mattie's done well too, in spite of having to be off so much.' Mattie, Lachlan's sister, was in the class above Elspeth's. She suffered from asthma and was at home that day, recovering from an attack. Mattie should have left school the previous June, but her parents had agreed to let her stay on for an extra year, to make up for the time she had missed.

'Right enough, ye write a grand letter. Half the lads in the unit look forward tae your letters arrivin'.'

'You don't show them to anyone else, do you?' Elspeth asked, alarmed.

'Why not? Reading them makes me feel as if I'm back home again, and they're funny, too. The other lads enjoy them. But ye'd not want tae stay on at the school, would ye?' asked Lachlan, who had been desperate to leave school as soon as possible and join his father in one of the shipyards.

'I think I would. I like school, and Miss Scott says I could get a better job if I stayed on longer. She says that mebbe I could learn to be a teacher myself.'

'God, imagine havin' a teacher in the family! Have ye told Mam?' It would never occur to Lachlan to mention his father first. Henry McDonald was an easy-going man, happy to leave the family decisions and the family budget in his wife's capable hands.

'I've not told anyone yet, except you. D'you think Auntie would agree?'

Although Flora McDonald and her husband were the only parents Elspeth had ever known, Flora had always insisted on her calling them Auntie and Uncle.

'I don't know, Ellie. Mebbe she will. The war'll be well over by then, surely, and that means that Thomas and me'll be back home, so that'd help with the money. Mind you, I've still got my apprenticeship tae finish.'

'I thought that with Rachel earning a wage now, and Mattie out of school by then—'

Elspeth's voice trailed away. Flora and Henry McDonald had been good to her as it was, taking her in when her mother, Flora's dearest friend, died giving birth to her. But they had their own family to worry about, and they might not be prepared to support her for longer than they had to.

7

They were at the spot where Regent Street cut across Mearns Street now, the corner where their tenement building stood. 'I've got something else for you,' Lachlan said as they stepped into the spotless close with its tiled walls and scrubbed stone floor, edged all the way from the pavement to the top landing with white pipeclay. 'I came across it on the train and thought ye'd like it.'

'Something you found? A kitten?' Elspeth asked doubtfully, following him up the first flight of stairs. Flora refused to allow any pets in her house, not so much as a canary, on the grounds that it might aggravate Mattie's asthma. A kitten would only cause trouble.

'Wait and see.'

The tenement consisted of a ground floor with three floors above. There were six sets of stairs to climb before the flat was reached, and three half-landings where the stairs took a bend. Each half-landing was lit by a window set with a mosaic of coloured glass. Elspeth loved these windows, for on sunny days the colours spilled over the stone stairs in a fallen rainbow.

The kitchen, which also served the family as living room and dining room, was cosy and welcoming as usual, warmed by a small coal fire as well as the heat from the gas stove. Today, the whole flat was rich with the smell of the dumpling Flora always made to celebrate a family birthday. Rachel, her oldest, was setting the table, assisted by Mattie, still pale and drawn from her bout of asthma. Rachel worked as a laundrywoman and seamstress in a large estate a little further along the coast, and as luck would have it, she had that afternoon off.

Flora McDonald was in her usual place by the stove, but it was the young man busy at the sink by the window, dressed only in a pair of khaki trousers, who caught Elspeth's eye as soon as she stepped into the room.

'Thomas!' She threw herself at him, regardless of the water spraying from his face and hands as he swung round from the sink.

'Steady on, Ellie,' he spluttered, at the same time returning her hug enthusiastically, while Flora, her face flushed with heat, her hair detaching itself strand by strand from the loose bun at the back of her head, snatched up a towel and began dabbing at the two of them.

'For goodness' sake, lassie, ye'll soak the place with yer carrying on!'

'Lachlan, why didn't you tell me?'

'I wanted tae surprise ye. She thought I'd brought her a kitten, Tom.'

'It's as well ye didnae, for it'd have gone straight out again,' his mother told him. 'Take this towel, Thomas, and let me get back tae my stove.'

'Mebbe ye'd've preferred a kitten, Ellie.' Thomas towelled himself vigorously.

'I'd rather have you two home any day of the week!'

'That reminds me—' He hung the towel up by the sink and fumbled at the khaki tunic hanging over the back of a chair, finally withdrawing a small cardboard box, slightly squashed. 'Happy birthday, Ellie.'

Inside the box, pinned to a small square of card, was an oval brooch made of polished pebbles. The centre and largest stone was dark and glossy, while those set around it were red and green, pale blue and the soft pearly grey of the sky and the River Clyde on a still, mild autumn day.

'As soon as I saw it, I was minded of the times we've collected pebbles along the beach,' Thomas explained as Elspeth stared in silence at the brooch. Then diffidently, 'D'ye like it?'

She found her voice, though it was only a whisper at first. 'Oh, Thomas, it's beautiful!'

'It is that,' Rachel agreed as she and Mattie came to look. Then she sniffed at the air. 'What's that smell? It's like – flowers.'

'Don't be daft,' Lachlan said swiftly as Elspeth, suddenly remembering the toilet water, cast a guilty look at Flora, who didn't approve of lip colours, perfume, powder or scented soap. 'How could ye have flowers at the top of a tenement?'

He glared at his sister, who grasped the message in his brown eyes and sniffed again, loudly. 'It's gone now – my nose must've gone funny for a minute.'

'Pin it on for me, Thomas.'

He did as he was bid, his fingers damp and cool against Elspeth's chin. 'There. It looks nice.'

She reached a hand up to caress the little brooch. It was the first piece of jewellery she had ever owned. And Lachlan's gift was the first scent she had ever had, apart from the illicit bottles of rose-water she and Mattie sometimes made from crushed rose petals in the washhouse during the summer.

Looking from Thomas to Lachlan, she loved the two of them with all her heart, for today, her thirteenth birthday, they had combined to remind her that from that day on, she was grown-up.

'So neither of ye knew that the other was comin' home on leave?' Henry McDonald pushed his empty plate away an hour later and leaned back in his chair, stretching strong, sinewy arms above his head. After a thorough wash in the sink to remove the grime of the shipyard, he smelled of carbolic soap, and his greying curly hair, still damp, stood up in a spiky halo round his broad moustached face. His two sons and two daughters had all inherited his curls instead of their mother's straight hair.

'Not a bit of it. The first I knew was when Lachlan here got out of the next carriage when we reached Glasgow.'

'Does a twenty-four-hour leave not mean they're going to send you abroad?' Rachel wondered aloud. Her brothers exchanged brief looks, and for a moment a chill seemed to threaten the room's warmth before Lachlan said casually, 'Mebbe it does, and mebbe it doesnae. They never tell us much about their plans.'

'That's what happened when they let Bob Cochran home for twenty-four hours,' Rachel persisted.

'How's Bob doin' these days?' Thomas wanted to know.

'Fine, the last letter I got.'

'It must be serious if ye're writin' tae each other,' Lachlan said.

'She sleeps with his letters under her pillow,' Elspeth said.

11

Unlike the house servants on the estate, Rachel didn't live in. The three girls shared one tiny bedroom, Rachel with a cot of her own, the two younger girls squeezed into a bed little larger than a single, but not as broad as a double bed.

'Does she now?'

Rachel's pretty round face went pink. 'I do not! Don't listen to her, Thomas, Ellie's just a wee liar,' she flared, but Mattie came to Elspeth's rescue.

'You do so. And you keep his photograph under the mattress'

'Here, here – no fightin' when we're all together at last,' Flora ordered. 'Clear the plates, Elspeth.' She waited until fresh plates, spoons and a large jug of custard were on the table before carefully bringing the rich, round, steaming birthday dumpling to the table. Amid a murmur of anticipation, she picked up a long sharp knife and cut into it, releasing a further gout of steam and the mouth-watering aroma of currants and raisins and treacle.

A second cut parted the first generous soft slice from the dumpling, and as it was skilfully flipped on to a plate Elspeth's heart quickened as she noticed the gleam of white paper against the moist brown interior. It was the custom, on special occasions like birthdays and Christmas and Hogmanay, to wrap silver threepenny bits in paper and bake them in the dumpling.

Normally the first slice would have gone to Elspeth, since it was her special day, but instead Flora laid the plate before Thomas, her first-born and favourite.

He immediately handed it across the table. 'Here ye are, Ellie – it's your birthday after all.'

With the tip of a spoon she dug into the slice, withdrew the tiny bundle, and opened it, the paper hot against her finger tips, to disclose a shining silver threepenny piece.

'Lucky you,' Mattie said. 'Think of the sweeties you can buy with that.'

'Or a nice bit of ribbon,' Rachel suggested.

'Far better tae put it away – the time might well come when ye'll be glad of it,' Flora put in, but Elspeth shook her head to all the suggestions.

'Uncle Henry, could you drill a wee hole in it for me, so that I can hang it on a bit of wool round my neck?'

'If ye want, hen,' her uncle agreed amiably, ignoring his wife's scandalised tutting.

'Ye're never goin' tae spoil a good thrup'ny piece by turnin' it intae a necklace, lassie!'

'It won't be spoiled. I'm going to keep it always, to remind me of today, with all of us together again.'

'Ye'll forget all about that the minute ye go intae the corner shop and see those jars of raspberry balls and liquorice straps,' Thomas told her.

'I won't.' She looked round the table at the only family she knew, and contentment surged through her. At that moment, life was perfect, she thought – then happened to meet Flora's eye.

In the older woman's glance she saw, not for the first time, a distant expression that made her feel that she was being singled out, set aside from the others round the table. Elspeth had seen that look several times during the past thirteen years; when she was a small child, it had set her off into inexplicable bouts of frightened tears which Flora, all at once her usual motherly self again, had soothed away. Now there were never tears, just a numbing, bewildering sense of being different, a chill reminder that she didn't really belong to the only family she had ever known.

'The army cooks can't cook as well as you do, Mum,' Thomas said just then, and Lachlan, his mouth full of warm, spicy dumpling, mumbled enthusiastic agreement.

Flora smiled, and the moment of uncertainty was gone as though it had never existed.

Elspeth could think of no reason for her aunt's flashes of hidden resentment. But she knew, from experience, that they would come again; always, like today, when she least expected them.

'It's not fair!'

'It's perfectly fair – and don't use that tone of voice tae me, lady,' Flora snapped, hanging Mattie's school blouse on the clothes horse to air and lifting the next garment from the pile waiting to be ironed. 'Ye've already had an extra year at the school tae set ye up for the future.'

'Mattie's had two extra years!'

'Mattie's already missed out on a lot because of her bad chest, and she's just as clever as you. Ye're not the only one with brains in this house, remember that. When she came this afternoon tae speak tae me about it all, Miss Scott could dae no more than agree with me. We cannae afford tae keep two of ye – d'ye not think Mattie deserves her chance just as much as you dae?'

'Y-yes, but—'

'There ye are, then.' Flora thumped the iron down on its end. 'We can just about manage with one of ye stayin' on, but not both. Anyway, fluff an' dust bothers Mattie's lungs, and it'd be more difficult tae find work for her than for you. So – it's only right that she's the one who gets tae stay on at the school.'

Tears crowded behind Elspeth's eyes, and she had to blink hard to hold them back. She had dreamed of becoming a teacher, had let herself believe during that extra year of schooling that it was going to happen. The sudden shock of hearing that her dream had crumbled to dust was more than she could bear. She made one last appeal. 'Uncle Henry—?'

'Now don't go encouragin' the lassie, Henry,' Flora warned at once. 'Ye know as well as I dae that one of them'll have tae go out tae work.'

Henry McDonald shifted uncomfortably in his chair, lowering the newspaper he had been holding before his face. 'I'm sorry, lass, yer auntie's right. We cannae afford tae keep the

14

two of ye on at the school, with the lads both still away.'

'I know,' Elspeth said wretchedly, 'I know.'

'My heart's broken for the lassie,' Henry said when she had gone out of the room. 'Did ye see the way the light just went out of her eyes there?'

His wife smoothed the iron over his work shirt. 'She's too quick at wantin' her own way, that one. And she's old enough tae know that we all have tae deal with disappointment from time tae time.'

'I know, but—' He bit the words off, but it was too late. The iron was banged down so hard that the sturdy table shook, and Flora whirled to confront him, hands fisted on her hips.

'But what, Henry McDonald?'

He rattled the newspaper noisily, trying to find the right words. 'Sometimes I feel you're a wee bit too hard on that lassie, Flora.'

'Too hard on her? You're sayin' that tae me, who took her in when her own grandmother would have nothin' tae do with her? Me that raised her when I'd more than enough tae do carin' for my own bairns? Don't haver, man,' Flora said witheringly. 'I'm hard on them all – I have tae be. We've not got the money tae spoil any one of them, as ye well know.'

'Aye, but – it's just that sometimes I feel ye're harder on Ellie than the others, and I cannae think why, when I mind how you and her mother were closer than sisters—' His voice died away as he looked up and saw the rage in his wife's eyes and the colour rising in her face.

'Sometimes ye've got a nasty tongue on you, Henry, and a nasty mind, accusin' yer own wife like that!'

'I didnae mean anything by it,' he protested. Henry McDonald was a strong man, afraid of nothing. All the men who worked with him in Lithgow's shipyard respected him and thought highly of him. They would have been amazed if they had seen the way he seemed to shrink into his chair before his wife's anger. 'I just thought—'

'Aye, well, thinking's no' bringin' more silver intae the house, is it? If I was as soft as you are, we'd all of us be in the poors' hospital by now,' Flora said scathingly, and returned to her work, attacking the shirt with the heavy, hot iron as though Henry was inside it.

Prudently, he went back to his paper. Flora was a good wife, but he knew from experience that he'd do best to hold his tongue, rather than bring even more scalding anger down on his head.

In the privacy of the small bedroom, Elspeth sat on the edge of the bed she shared with Mattie and revelled in the luxury of a good cry for a full five minutes. Her shoulders shuddered as she gasped and sniffled and wept for the future she had wanted so much, and had lost for ever. She would have enjoyed a good loud, babyish bawl, but instead she wept quietly, determined not to let her aunt and uncle hear her grief. Fat tears poured down her face and dripped off her chin, some trickling between her lips to lie salty on her tongue.

Lachlan's comment on her thirteenth birthday kept coming back to her: 'The war'll be well over by then, surely, and that means that Thomas and me'll be back home, so that'd help with the money.'

But almost a year later the war was still going on, and Lachlan and Thomas, both over in France now, hadn't been home since her birthday. Although their mother never spoke to anyone, not even Henry, of any fears she may have harboured for them, more silver glittered through her fair hair than ever before, and her mouth had tightened.

At last the tears began to ease off and Elspeth's wet face started itching unpleasantly. She scrubbed her hands over it, smearing tears over her cheeks, then got up and washed them away, dipping a face cloth into the chipped bowl of cold water that stood on the tallboy, then drying her face on the well-worn towel drooping from a nail in the wall.

She was just in time; as she put the towel down the door to the flat opened and Mattie, who had been packed off on an errand, passed the bedroom door on her way to the kitchen.

Elspeth peered into the foggy mirror that stood on a rickety table at the window, and saw that her eyes were pink-edged. Dropping to her knees by Rachel's bed, she pulled out the cardboard box that held the older girl's good shoes, lifting them out then scooping up the sheet of cardboard below. This was where Rachel kept her secret hoard of powder, lipstick and perfume, bought out of the few pennies the girl was allocated from her weekly pay packet, and well hidden from her mother.

Elspeth opened the little box of powder with fingers that shook in their haste, and dabbed the puff round her eyes. She put it back exactly where she found it, then replaced the cardboard and the shoes before pushing the box well out of sight beneath the bed.

Referring to the mirror again, she saw to her horror that now clumps of powder stuck to her lashes, which were still damp, and that the skin round her eyes was thick with the stuff. Hurriedly, she smoothed the surplus powder away with the tips of her fingers, then used her handkerchief to wipe up the grains that had fallen on the table. Mattie came in just as she finished.

'What're you doing?'

'Nothing. Just thinking.'

Mattie's nose wrinkled. 'What's that smell?'

'What smell? '

'It's—' Mattie sniffed again. 'You've not been at Rachel's perfume, have you?'

'Of course not!'

'You know what she's like if she thinks we've touched her stuff.'

'I told you – I've not touched it!'

Mattie hesitated, then sat down on the bed she and Elspeth

shared, linking her fingers tightly on her lap. 'Mam says that Miss Scott came to visit her today.'

'I know. She told me.'

'Imagine, a teacher coming to the house to talk about you and me, and in the holidays too.' There was awe in Mattie's voice, and Elspeth fully understood why. Teachers belonged in school, not in houses; it had never occurred to either of them that teachers had any other kind of existence. For all the two girls knew, Miss Scott might well be hung up in the classroom cupboard out of school hours, waiting patiently with the boxes of chalk and shelves of books for the next school day to begin.

'Did Mam tell you what's been decided?'

'Yes.' They were both silent, then Elspeth went on, her voice sharp with accusation, 'I didn't know you wanted to be a teacher.'

'I didn't, till Mam said that Miss Scott said that I was clever enough. With me being off school so much, I never thought—' Mattie's voice trailed away, and her fingers writhed in her lap, getting into such a tangle that Elspeth began to wonder if the girl's hands could ever be separated again. 'Ellie, it's not fair that you have to be the one to leave.'

'Yes it is.' Hard though it was to say the words, Elspeth recognised that Aunt Flora had right on her side. Mattie was just as clever as she was, and the girl had been off so often during the past ten years that if the days at home were added up she must have missed at least a year's education. And Mattie was Aunt Flora's own daughter, while Elspeth wasn't.

'I feel terrible about it, Elspeth.'

'Aunt Flora's right, they can't pay for us both. I'll enjoy going out to work,' she lied. 'I'll try for a job in an office. Mebbe I'll learn how to typewrite, and do book-keeping.'

The thought of it cheered her up a little. She had always thought that working in an office would be interesting. She might even turn out to be good at it.

Mattie smiled at her gratefully. 'I'll tell you all about

everything I learn. I'll show you all the books I have to read, so that you'll know all about how to teach.'

'And I'll tell you all about my office work.' For a moment, Elspeth felt better about everything. Peering into the mirror again, she was relieved to see that the puffiness had begun to fade from around her clear blue eyes.

Then, as her aunt called the two of them through to help her with the evening meal, realisation hit her. The summer holidays would be over in another five days, and two weeks after that she would be fourteen, a birthday that marked the end of her schooldays.

Panic swept over her, and as she followed Mattie into the kitchen she felt as though she was falling, and there was nothing to hold on to.

Flora McDonald, a trained seamstress, had dressed her family almost entirely by her own efforts, using a large heavy sewing machine that was her pride and joy. She had even made most of the clothes her husband and sons wore, and had taught the three girls to sew as soon as they were old enough to be trusted with needle and scissors.

The skills Rachel had learned from her mother had led to a position with one of the wealthy families living on the hill above the town, and Elspeth, too, had shown talent. In her constant eagerness to please her aunt and justify the day Flora had taken her in, she had worked hard and learned well, and by the time she was in her teens she was making most of her own clothes. To her dismay, her own diligence turned out to be her undoing, for as the school summer holidays drew to a close, Flora announced that she had arranged an interview for Elspeth with the sewing-room supervisor at Brodie's, the town's largest department store.

Her plea to be allowed to seek work in an office had been turned down flat.

'Office work indeed! What next? Yer poor mother and me

were seamstresses, and that's what you'll be too. Brodie's is the best store in the town – ye're very lucky, gettin' an interview there. When ye've got a man and bairns of yer own tae clothe ye'll be glad of the trainin' Brodie's'll give ye,' Flora said, and would hear no more about offices.

Elspeth, who had never been inside Brodie's in her life, gazed around, fascinated, as she followed her aunt through the entrance and found herself in a world she had never known existed. Despite the hardships of the war, the counters scattered throughout the ground-floor area seemed to her to be well stocked with rolls of ribbon and lace, buttons, hooks and eyes, and banked rainbows of sewing thread in little display boxes.

'Don't dawdle, Elspeth.' Flora tossed the words over her shoulder as she hurried towards the stairs. 'We're expected, and I'll not have them thinkin' ye're a poor timekeeper.'

Up a flight of stairs they sped, to another open area, this time set out with men's and children's clothing. The third floor held women's clothes; Elspeth caught a glimpse of gloves on one counter, petticoats on another, as Flora stopped to ask directions, then the two of them went through a door and into a narrow dark corridor, quite unlike the spacious areas they had just left.

'First door on the right,' Flora muttered, fidgeting along the corridor and pausing before a door that almost vibrated with a humming sound from the other side of the panels. It sounded to Elspeth as though a lot of sewing machines were being operated within the room.

'This'll be it,' Flora muttered, tapping tentatively with her knuckles. They waited for several long minutes, but there was no answer.

'They'll not hear you for the noise,' Elspeth ventured. 'You'll just have to go in.'

'Ye don't just walk intae strange rooms – ye wait tae be told!' Flora snapped, and they waited in vain for another few minutes before, clearly remembering the passing of time, she gave an anguished little whimper and steeled herself to open the door and reveal a large, stuffy room. An enormous table holding an impressive number of sewing machines, all in use, took up most of the space. A few of the machinists flicked a brief glance at the newcomers, then returned to their work. One of them, a pretty, red-haired girl, smiled and winked at Elspeth. A tall, cold-eyed woman examining the output of one of the machines finally noticed them, and straightened up.

'Yes?'

'We've got an appointment with Miss Buchanan – about a job.' Flora, unusually nervous, stumbled over the words.

The woman surveyed them both for a moment as though amazed that two such ordinary people should dare to approach her, then said shortly, 'This way.'

They followed her in single file along the edge of the room to a doorway that led into a tiny office, with only enough room for a cluttered desk and two chairs. 'Miss Buchanan is with a client at the moment,' the woman told them. 'I'll inform her of your arrival when she's free. What name shall I say?'

'Flora Mc— I mean, Elspeth Bremner,' Flora almost whispered. Elspeth had never known her aunt to be so cowed; the woman's nervousness started to affect her, and her knees began to shake. As soon as they were alone Flora pounced on her, brushing imaginary fluff from her best woollen coat, setting her beret straight, whirling her round to tweak at the thick dark brown plait hanging down her back.

'Stand straight, for any favour! Speak out when Miss Buchanan asks ye anythin', but don't talk unless ye're invited tae. And don't fidget!'

The inspection over, Flora sat herself down on the small plain chair at their side of the desk, drumming her fingers on her knee, while Elspeth pulled her shoulders back and stared at a crack on the wall behind the desk, wishing that she hadn't turned out to be so good with a needle.

The drumming of the sewing machines on the other side of the wall reminded her of the little she had been able to glimpse of the sewing room as she and Flora were whisked through it. The only windows she had noticed were small, and ran along the upper wall area on one side of the room, so that the girls working at the machines couldn't see out. Her heart sank, and she wanted to run from the room and from the building. Only the thought of what Aunt Flora would say and do to her kept her in her seat.

They waited in silence for a further ten minutes, both jumping when the door finally opened and Miss Buchanan arrived, small and elderly, slightly stooped and with a permanent frown tucked between eyes magnified by her spectacles.

'Mrs – er—' She fluttered a hand towards Flora in greeting, then withdrew it and edged in behind her desk, leaving Flora with her own hand outstretched. 'And – um,' she added, settling herself into her chair.

'It's about the interview,' Flora said too loudly, her cheeks pink with embarrassment as she sank back into her own seat and folded her hands together. 'You said you'd see Ellie – Elspeth – about a post.' She was speaking, Elspeth thought, surprised, as though her mouth was full of wee pebbles that slowed and restricted her speech.

'Oh yes, I did agree to consider her for employment in our workshop.' Miss Buchanan's small hands sifted through a pile of papers on the desk before emerging with a sheet of notepaper bearing Flora's careful handwriting. 'What age is she?'

'Almost fourteen,' Flora offered as Elspeth opened her mouth to reply. 'Fourteen in September. She'll be leaving school then.'

'And you want to be a seamstress?' Miss Buchanan's artificially large eyes studied Elspeth, who opened her mouth to reply, and was forestalled.

'She's very good with her needle. I taught her myself. Her mother and me were both seamstresses in Glasgow,' Flora contributed, rummaging in the depths of her worn shopping bag and bringing out a piece of snowy linen, carefully folded. She opened it to reveal two pieces of embroidery. 'These are the lassie's own work.'

Miss Buchanan opened a drawer and took out a pair of thin gloves. Slipping them on she studied the material, holding it close to her eyes to examine the fine stitching. Laying it down again, she took off her spectacles, which dangled from her neck by a ribbon. Immediately, her eyes became small and insignificant. She studied the work again, this time holding it almost at arm's-length, then, sounding surprised, she commented, 'This is quite good.'

'Oh yes.' Flora's nervousness had vanished for the moment; her voice was clear and firm and smug, for all the world, Elspeth thought, resentful at not being allowed to say a word on her own behalf, as though she had done the work herself.

'As you probably know, we now have a large ready-to-wear department, and most of our seamstresses' work involves making alterations in our ready-to-wear stock for our customers,' Miss Buchanan told Flora, as though Elspeth was invisible. 'We do a certain amount of dressmaking for our special clients, but that work, of course, is only undertaken by our most talented seamstresses. Few girls attain that standard.'

'I'm sure Elspeth'd be able to reach it, in time,' Flora snapped back, and Miss Buchanan's brows rose.

'As to that, Mrs – only time will tell.' For the first time, she looked at Elspeth studying her carefully. 'Would you like to work here?'

'I'd prefer to work in an—'

'She would.' Flora said swiftly.

'I believe that she might fit in here quite well. We'll give her a three-month trial, Mrs – er—'

Ten minutes later it had been arranged between the two women that Elspeth should start work the week after her birthday. 'What d'ye think ye were doin'?' Flora hissed in her normal, unpebbled voice as soon as they were back among the shoppers again. 'For a minute there I thought the woman was goin' tae say ye were too cheeky for the job.'

'I only wanted to ask if there was any work in the offices.'

'There isn't. It's not everyone that gets tae work at Brodie's, for they're very particular. Ye're lucky ye've been accepted as a seamstress, so let's have no more nonsense about offices. Yer mother'd be pleased,' she added as an afterthought as they descended the stairs.

'I might as well not have bothered going to the interview myself,' Elspeth wrote to Thomas that evening. 'It was a bit like being sold at a cattle market. Maybe I should be grateful that Miss Buchanan didn't insist on opening my mouth and having a look at my teeth, the way they do with horses.'

3

Elspeth's final day at school was one of the worst she had ever known. Usually, the 'leavers' lolled about on their last day, doing nothing, eyed enviously by those still bound to the classroom. But Elspeth worked hard, savouring every moment.

'This is the last time I'll walk into school – the last time I'll hang my coat up on this peg – the last time I'll sit in this seat—' The litany kept ringing through her mind, each 'last' clanging like a bell summoning mourners to a funeral.

When the real bell rang to mark the end of the day, she lingered at her desk, making a business of emptying it, until there were no more corners left to study in search of an errant eraser or a missing pencil.

'Come on,' Mattie said impatiently from the doorway.

'I'm coming.' Elspeth closed the desk – 'this is the last time I'll close this desk' – and followed her cousin from the room, her hands hanging uselessly by her sides. There were no books to carry, for they had all been handed in for some other pupil to take home and study in future.

Miss Scott stopped her in the hallway. 'Good luck, my dear. I'm sorry you weren't able to stay on any longer.'

'Yes, Miss Scott, thank you, Miss Scott,' Elspeth mumbled to the teacher's sturdy shoes, unable to meet the sympathy that she knew would be in the woman's eyes.

'Come back and see us. We'd like to know how you're getting on,' Miss Scott said, then, mercifully, she let them go, and for the last time, Elspeth walked out of the school door, down the steps, across the playground. Molly, a few months older, had left joyfully at the beginning of the summer holidays, and was working in a bakery in West Blackhall Street.

'I wish it could have been you staying on instead of me,' Mattie said by her side.

'No you don't, you want to stay as much as I do.'

'You're right. I suppose I meant that I wish we could both have stayed.'

'No, Aunt Flora's right – you've not been at school as often as me because of your chest.'

'That doesn't help to make me feel any better about it.'

'Nor me,' Elspeth thought as she walked out of the school gates for the last time.

Working in the sewing room at Brodie's wasn't as bad as Elspeth had feared. For one thing, she was allowed to pin up the long brown plait that had been a temptation all through her schooldays to boys who pulled it in the classroom and sometimes in the street. She hinted at getting it cut, but Flora wouldn't hear of it.

'Ye've got lovely hair, just like yer mother's, rest her soul. It'd be sacrilege tae cut it off. One day ye'll thank me for no' lettin' ye dae it!'

There was also the pleasure of taking a wage packet home every Friday. True, it had to be handed over to Flora unopened, just like Uncle Henry's and Rachel's wages, but at least she was earning her keep, instead of being an added burden. The fourpence handed back for her own use each week was a fortune compared with the twopence spending money she had received before.

The small, high windows in the workroom couldn't provide enough ventilation for the number of women and girls there, so the place was airless, and noisy with the continual whirring of the machines, but once the strangeness of everything and her shyness among people she didn't know wore off, Elspeth found that she was good at the work, and took pleasure in getting the occasional word of grudging praise from Miss Arnold, well known for her high standards and sharp tongue.

'If they'd left the men at home and just sent her tae fight the Jerries instead,' muttered Lena Stewart, who worked on the machine opposite Elspeth's, 'she'd've cut the legs from the lot of them with one sentence and saved us a lot of bother.'

Elspeth was surprised into a giggle, quickly disguised as a cough as Miss Arnold's cold eyes swept in her direction. Nobody was allowed to talk during working hours, but she discovered on her first day that there was always a certain amount of conversation going on, sometimes in whispers and murmurs hidden by the continual sound of the machines, sometimes by means of signals, or silent mouthing and lip-reading.

'Everyone needs tae talk,' said Lena, the redhead who had winked at her on the day of her interview. 'It's not natural tae expect women tae keep their mouths shut for hours.'

She was very pretty, with the type of looks that would have caused Flora MacDonald to tut disapprovingly. Her curly red hair continually escaped from the ribbons that were supposed to hold it back from her face, and she was well rounded, her creamy skin dusted with freckles. Her brown eyes sparkled, and even without artificial colouring her mouth was full and red.

Lena, Elspeth had quickly discovered, was a rebel, dressing in bright clothes despite Miss Buchanan's insistence on muted colours for her staff, and talking when she was expected to be quiet. She only kept her job because she was an excellent seamstress.

'Are ye stayin' in for yer dinner?' she asked when Elspeth's first morning's work ended and she was following the other girls out of the room – not through the door leading from the store, but through another, smaller door at the back of the room which led to narrow wooden stairs.

27

'I'm going home. I only live in Mearns Street.'

'Ye should bring a piece and eat with the rest of us.' As they reached the bottom of the stairs, Lena gestured towards an open door in front of them. Peeping in, Elspeth saw a large room with benches set at long tables. Men and women were settling down at the tables, unwrapping packets of sandwiches.

'The nobs have a place of their own upstairs,' Lena explained. 'Counter staff and floorwalkers and the like. This is for folk like us and the packers and carters. There's hot water and milk and mugs, and ye bring yer own tea and sugar in wee screws of paper.'

Elspeth, hurrying home through a drizzle of rain, liked the idea of sharing her midday break with Lena and the other girls, but when she suggested it to Flora, her aunt was horrified.

'Eating down in the basement with the carters and all? Ye don't know what ye might catch! Ye're better off with a good hot dinner here.'

'But I don't have much time – it would surely be better for me to eat something at the store instead of running home and running back and mebbe being late.'

Flora put a bowl of soup before her. 'I ate my dinner with Mattie. I can see tae it that ye're not late back.'

'That's another thing – I get out later than Mattie, and that means you've got two dinners to see to. If I stayed at work there'd only be hers.' A fresh shower, hurling itself against the window, gave Elspeth further ammunition. 'And winter's coming in, Auntie Flora. I might catch cold running to Mearns Street then back, and if I did I'd have to stay home, for Miss Buchanan and Miss Arnold would never let me cough and sneeze over the customers' clothes.'

'Aye, well, there is that,' Flora said slowly. 'But I hope I'd not be expected tae make up pieces for yer dinner – I've got enough tae see tae in the mornings as it is.'

'I'll do my own. I'll get up earlier.'

To her joy, Flora gave in, and Elspeth spent her midday

breaks in the canteen, drinking scalding-hot tea out of a tin mug that would have sent her aunt running for the disinfectant if she had known of it, and eating her sandwiches at a wooden table. At last, she began to feel like one of the crowd.

It was during those midday breaks that she discovered that Lena was a singer. Every time a music-hall company came to Greenock Lena was in the audience, treating her fellow workers the following dinner-time to an impromptu concert of every song in the programme. She had a good memory, and only needed to hear a song once to recall tune and lyrics.

Her voice was lovely, strong and confident when the song required it, or so sweet and pure that even the gruff carters could be seen to buff a tear away with the back of a hand when she sang a ballad or lullaby.

'It's what I like doin' best,' she confided to Elspeth. 'I sing in our local pub on a Saturday night, and at gatherin's.' Then, her eyes glowing, 'One day I'm goin' tae sing on a proper stage, like the Hippodrome or the King's Theatre. D'ye go there?'

Her eyes widened when Elspeth admitted that she had never been inside a theatre. 'But they're so bonny, with crimson velvet curtains tied back with gold ropes, and pillars right up tae the ceilings, and folk on the stage with beautiful clothes. There's lovely scenery on the stage too – come tae the Hippodrome with me on Saturday night.'

'I can't. My Aunt Flora doesn't like theatres.'

'I'm no askin' yer Aunt Flora,' Lena pointed out. 'I'm askin' you.'

'But I'd have to ask her, and she'd say no.'

'Don't tell her, then. Say ye're goin' out with a friend – it wouldnae be a lie.'

'She'd find out anyway,' Elspeth said, but finally agreed, after much coaxing, to ask her aunt's permission.

Flora's reaction was just as she had predicted. 'The theatre? Indeed you'll go tae no such place, milady.'

'But it's with one of the girls at the store.'

'I don't know what her mother's thinking of, lettin' her watch folk cavorting about on a stage.'

'Her mother's dead. She lives with her father.'

'There ye are, then – there's no woman in the house tae guide her. No wonder the poor lassie's goin' wrong. That'll no' happen tae you – ye're just out of the school and still a bairn.'

The unfairness of it stung Elspeth. 'How can I still be a bairn when I'm old enough to earn my own keep?'

Her aunt's head snapped up, eyes blazing. 'I'll tell ye how – while ye behave like a bairn ye'll be treated like one. The very idea,' she clucked like an agitated hen, 'answerin' me back after all me and yer Uncle Henry've done for ye!'

'I didn't ask you to take me in!'

Flora's patience snapped. 'Ye cheeky besom, ye!' she railed. 'Times like this I think we should have left ye tae yer Grandma Bremner. She'd've packed ye off tae the orphanage, and I don't see *them* lettin' ye stay on at the school for another year!'

No matter how hard Elspeth worked at holding her tongue and keeping the peace, Flora managed time and time again to overturn her attempts to be a dutiful foster daughter. The argument raged on, ending, as sometimes happened, with Flora ordering her out of her sight, and Elspeth running off to Granjan's tiny kitchen, tears of frustrated anger running down her cheeks.

'I never mean to upset her, but I keep doing it!' she sobbed, and Janet Docherty, Flora's mother, hauled herself out of her chair and crossed the faded rag rug to pat her bowed head.

'Yer Auntie Flora's awful hard tae please at times. It's just her nature, she doesnae mean tae sound as hard as she does.'

'I know, but I don't make things any better when I answer back. Why can't I stop myself?' Tears dripped from Elspeth's chin and made damp circles on her woollen skirt. She was huddled into a chair with her knees drawn up to her chin and her arms wrapped around them.

'If it was that easy for folk tae hold their tongues, there wouldnae have been any wars,' Janet pointed out, then, as the sobbing eased to a sniffing, hiccuping stop, 'Feelin' better now? Here—' A clean dishtowel was thrust into Elspeth's hands. 'Dry yer face, pet, an' I'll put the griddle on. Pancakes and a cup of hot tea'll make the world look better.'

Janet Docherty never threw anything away if she could get some use out of it. Greaseproof papers that had wrapped squares of butter were neatly folded and stored in a drawer once the butter was finished; now she produced one and ran it over the large black iron griddle to grease it. A paper spill from a vase on the mantelshelf was lit at the fire and used to light a ring on her small gas cooker, then she lifted the griddle by its hooped handle on to the ring to heat.

'You're awful good to me, Granjan,' Elspeth said gratefully, scrubbing at her eyes with the dishcloth.

'Ye're a good, obedient lassie and we all need a bit of comfortin' now and again.' Janet took a bowl down from a shelf and collected flour and an egg and milk.

'If I was good I wouldn't anger Aunt Flora so much.'

'Ach, Flora gets het up too quickly. She always did, even as a wean,' said Flora's mother cheerfully, measuring flour into the basin. 'Wash yer face at the jawbox now, and fill the kettle for me.'

After obediently splashing her face with cold water at the tiny sink set below the window, Elspeth dried it before filling the kettle, while Janet whipped the contents of the mixing bowl into a creamy, pale golden liquid. Scooping a spoonful up, she dropped it on to the heated griddle, which started to sizzle. The soft dough spread to just the right size, then halted, bubbles forming on its surface, as Janet dotted the large griddle with more spoonfuls. Then she started flipping them over deftly with a fish slice, disclosing the golden-brown cooked side of each.

Nobody could make pancakes as swiftly or as well as

31

Granjan, Elspeth thought contentedly, setting the table and opening the window to fetch a pat of butter from the larder, a small wooden box with a mesh door to let air in, fastened to the windowsill to keep any meat and milk and butter stored inside it fresh and cool. Her stomach gave an unladylike rumble as she turned back into the room and smelled the delicious aroma of fresh-made pancakes.

Although her own children had been raised to call Janet Gran, Flora had tried hard to make little Elspeth address her mother as Auntie Janet. 'She's got a gran of her own, it wouldnae be right tae let her call you gran too,' she had said when Janet protested.

'Ach, away wi' ye – there's nothin' wrong with her havin' two grans, like most bairns. Yours'd have two if Henry's mother was still livin', God rest her.'

'It's not right,' Flora had insisted stubbornly. Elspeth, only just over a year old and confused by this sign, the first she received, that she wasn't one of Flora's children, had found her own compromise and began calling Janet Granjan, to the old woman's secret delight. Flora, frustrated in the face of the child's determination, had given in and let the name remain.

Now, while they ate, Elspeth told Granjan about Lena. 'She's a good seamstress, but she's awful casual about her work.' She bit into a pancake, and Janet clucked, shaking her head.

'I hope she's not leadin' ye intae bad ways, lassie.'

'Oh no, I'm doing well. Miss Arnold set me to sewing some lace on a petticoat yesterday, and it's not everyone that's given work like that. She says I've got a deft touch. It's lovely material, Granjan – so soft and silky. Wearing it must be like wearing a sunbeam.' She stopped to wipe melted butter from her chin, then giggled. 'Imagine walking round all day wearing a sunbeam under your clothes.'

'Ye're awful like yer mother,' Janet said without thinking. 'She could jump from sorrow tae laughter in the blink of an eye too. Not that she was often sad, even when things were goin' against her. Maisie always saw the good side of life – and of folk.'

'Am I really like her?' Elspeth was greedy for all that she could glean about her mother.

'I've told ye often enough. Ye've got her hair, and her bonny face.'

'But not her eyes.'

'Did Flora say that?' Janet asked, taken by surprise.

'She's like Grandmother – neither of them ever tells me about my mother. I wouldn't know anything about her if it wasn't for you, but you never say I've got her eyes, Granjan.'

'Ye're gettin' altogether too sharp for yer own good, young lady. Watch out ye don't cut yerself.'

Elspeth nibbled at her pancake, then said, 'I've got his eyes, haven't I?'

'Whose?'

'My father's.'

Janet poured a second cup of strong tea for herself. 'I never saw him, so I cannae tell,' she said shortly, her discomfort so obvious that Elspeth, much as she longed to ask more questions, changed the subject.

'Thomas thinks I should take evening lessons in typewriting and shorthand.'

Janet set the teapot down with a thump and stared at her. 'What on earth for?'

'Because I want to work in an office, only Aunt Flora won't let me. Thomas said in his last letter that there's no reason why I shouldn't try to learn office skills, so that I could mebbe use them one day.'

'Don't you let him unsettle you, pet.' Janet Docherty's voice was uneasy. 'Ye're a seamstress, and that's an end of it.'

'He's not unsettling me, he's just saying that one day I might decide to do something else. He's learned to drive in the army, did you know that? He says he didn't realise how

33

interesting engines were. He might be thinking of a change himself one day.'

'Thomas is doin' very well as a gardener. And anyway, who's tae pay for those evening lessons he's got ye talkin' about? Not Master Thomas, I'll be bound.'

'I'd pay for them myself. I'm saving up already, for I like the idea,' Elspeth said eagerly. 'I'll mebbe learn book-keeping as well, if I can afford it.'

'Now don't go rushin' intae anythin',' Janet warned. 'Here – have another pancake.'

'I wish Grandmother was more like you,' Elspeth said, doing as she was bid.

'Tuts, lassie, it'd be a dull world if we were all alike.'

'But I should be closer to Grandmother than I am. After all, she's my real mother's mother. D'you think she'd really have sent me to the poors' hospital if Aunt Flora hadn't taken me in?'

Janet, about to sip her tea, spluttered into the cup and almost choked. Elspeth hurried out of her chair and round the table to pat her on the back. 'Sit down, sit down, I'm fine,' Janet gasped when the coughing fit was over. 'God save us, child, what gave ye an idea like that?'

'Aunt Flora says that's what Grandmother would have done. That's why I was crying so hard when I got here.' Elspeth, who had gone back to her pancake, put it down again, her appetite fading as she remembered the anger in her aunt's face, the pain of the words she had hurled.

'What a thing tae say tae a bairn!'

'I'm not a bairn any more, Granjan, I'm a working woman, old enough to know the truth.'

'And how can Flora have any notion of what Celia Bremner would've done?'

'She didn't take me in when my mother died. Surely that shows that she didn't want me,' Elspeth said round a lump in her throat that wasn't for her, but for the helpless baby she had once been.

'Only because Flora wouldnae hear of anyone but herself takin' ye in. Wasn't she yer poor ma's best friend? Does that not show ye how much she wanted ye?'

'Yes, but – Grandmother doesn't have any photographs of my mother in her house, nor anything that belonged to her. I don't think she'd have taken me if Aunt Flora hadn't wanted me.'

'Now ye're just haverin',' Janet said sharply. 'And we'll have no more of it. Eat up that pancake, and stop fiddling with it. It's time ye were getting back home.'

4

A large red hand suddenly imposed itself between Elspeth's eyes and the table, whipping her exercise book away before she could do more than give a squeak of surprise at the interruption. She had been so involved in writing the letter that she hadn't noticed anyone approaching.

'What's this ye're scribblin' at – a letter tae yer sweetheart?' The ginger-haired messenger boy danced round to the opposite side of the table, waving the book.

'Give it back – please.'

'In a minute. Let's see, now. "Dear – er – dear L-lachlan,"' he read aloud, struggling over the words like a small child learning to read. 'Who's Lachlan, yer fancy man?'

'My brother.' Elspeth stood up and reached for the book, her face burning with embarrassment as a few people sitting at the long table looked on, laughing. 'Give it back.'

The boy pursed his lips. 'If this Lachlan's yer brother, what's yer sweetheart's name, then?'

'I don't have a sweetheart.' Elspeth, unused to being the centre of attention, felt humiliating tears stabbing at her eyelids, and wished that she could just crawl under the table and hide.

'A bonny lassie wi' no young man of her own? Tell ye what, I'll give it back if ye'll promise tae come tae the pictures with me tonight,' the lad suggested, smirking.

'Just give it back.'

'Aw, come on – a wee visit tae the—' he began, then it was his turn to yelp with shock as a hand skelped lightly across his ear, while at the same time its partner whipped the book away from him.

'Stop yer nonsense, Johnny Crawford, and leave the lassie alone,' Lena Stewart ordered, handing the exercise book back to Elspeth.

'What d'ye think ye're doin', you? That was sore!'

'Ach, away ye go, I scarce touched ye. Ye'll get a lot worse than that from the Boche if ye're ever old enough tae go and bother them,' Lena teased. 'Away and play with yer pals, and stop pretending tae be a man when ye're nothin' but a wee laddie.'

The boy's face went scarlet as an elderly carter shouted from further down the table, 'Ye're right there, Lena hen – he's that young he's still walkin' all bandy-legged!'

'Bitch!'

'Here, here – another word out of ye and I'll learn ye what a proper slap feels like,' Lena told him sharply, and he subsided, slinking away, crimson to the tips of his ears. 'Don't let the likes of him bother ye, he's just tryin' it on. He's fancied ye ever since ye started workin' here.'

'Lena!'

'Have ye never noticed the wee glances and the wee smiles? Ach, there's no harm in him, but ye could do better for yerself. Why not come tae the dancin' tomorrow night?' Lena coaxed, not for the first time. 'There'll be plenty of men there, and there's somethin' about a uniform and a foreign accent that can set a lassie's heart racin'.'

The deep-water area off Greenock, known as the Tail o' the Bank because it marked the end of a vast mudbank, was always busy with warships these days, and the townsfolk had become used to sharing their streets with foreign seamen in unfamiliar uniforms, speaking different tongues. The local people held concerts and dances for these young men so far from home, and in turn they provided plenty of company for local girls with sweethearts in the services. Lena and most of the others who worked in the sewing room attended the dances.

'You know Aunt Flora won't let me.'

'Why not?'

'She says I'm too young.'

'Ye're old enough tae earn a wage,' Lena pointed

'That doesn't make any difference to her. I don't really want to go to dances anyway.'

She was grateful when Lena shrugged and accepted her decision without any further attempt to get her to change her mind. She had no wish to cause further trouble with Auntie Flora by sneaking out behind her back. One way or another she was certain to be found out, and then there would be another row. In any case, she was intent on saving every penny she could so that she could pay for evening classes.

Although she spent very little on herself, the tiny hoard of coins kept in an old tobacco tin in her bedroom never seemed to grow. She had borrowed a book on book-keeping from the lending library and worked on it in her spare time, but it was difficult, on her own, to grasp the finer points of crediting and debiting and cross-referencing.

Once, sent along to the accounts office to deliver a note from Miss Buchanan, she had looked enviously at the confident young woman sitting at a desk before a large, solid typewriter, tapping briskly on the keys. She longed to try her hand at typewriting.

Reaching the bottom of the page, she awoke from her day-dream to find that her pencil had written, 'Yesterday when I was typewriting to Mattie' instead of 'talking to Mattie'. Vexed, she began to tear the sheet out neatly.

'What's wrong?' Lena wanted to know.

'I wrote the wrong word.'

'Scribble it out, then. I've tae dae that all the time when I'm writin' tae George.' Lena's young man was in the navy.

38

'I don't like pages with mistakes scribbled out, it looks untidy. I'll do it over again at home.' A glance at the large clock on the wall showed that it was almost time for the loud bell that summoned the sewing girls and the carters and cleaners and packers and messenger boys back to work. The counter and office staff ate their sandwiches upstairs, in a room next to the offices.

'Ye're awful fussy,' chimed in one of the other seamstresses, leaning on Elspeth's shoulder so that she could have an upside-down look at the unwanted page. 'Ye should see the letters I write tae my young man – they're that untidy, he sometimes says he cannae make out what I'm sayin' tae him.' She hesitated, then asked diffidently, 'Would ye mebbe write tae him for me, Ellie? It'd please him tae see a tidy letter for once.'

'I couldn't do that.' Elspeth was shocked at the idea. 'It wouldn't be your letter then, and that's what he'll want more than anything.'

'What he wants is tae be able tae read what I'm tellin' him. He says that when ye're in a shell hole with all that mud, and the bullets flying around, ye don't want tae have tae keep peerin' at a piece of paper, tryin' tae make out what it's sayin'. Anyway, I'd tell ye what tae write. I just want it put down nice. Ye could do it in the dinner hour tomorrow,' the girl added eagerly.

'I don't know—'

'If she writes a letter for anyb'dy, Cora Simpson, she'll write one for me,' Lena broke in jealously. 'She's my friend more than yours, and I don't like writin' either. I only do it because George is desperate for letters.'

'I'd pay ye, Ellie,' Cora said at once. 'I'd give ye a penny tae dae it for me.'

Lena knocked the girl's arm off Elspeth's shoulder. 'And I'd pay her tuppence, so there!'

'I haven't said I'll do it yet,' Elspeth protested as the two girls glared at each other. She couldn't believe that anyone would be silly enough to pay to have something done when they were perfectly able to do it themselves.

'If ye do, it'll be for me, because I'm yer friend.'

'But I asked first!'

As they wrangled, Elspeth put aside the absurdity of writing other people's letters, and started to consider the benefits. If she wrote the two letters, she would be able to add thruppence to the money she was putting by to pay for her evening classes.

'I'll do them both,' she announced, 'for a penny halfpenny each. One tomorrow and one the day after – you can toss a coin to pick which one I write first.'

And to her astonishment, both girls agreed.

Cora won the toss. It was strange, writing someone else's letter at their dictation. At first, Elspeth, who had done well in grammar at school, found herself wanting to make corrections, much to Cora's indignation.

'Listen, it's my letter tae my lad,' she snapped. 'Just write what yer told – and I'll have an extra page of that book when ye're finished, so's I can write my own wee private bit tae him. He'll just have tae put up with my own scribbling for that bit.'

Once Elspeth settled to writing down the dictation, the way her class had been taught in school, the work came easily, and two days later the tobacco tin in her drawer at home was richer by three pennies. To her astonishment, once the others who ate their midday meal in the basement room caught on to what she was doing, a few more girls asked her to write letters for sweethearts and fathers and brothers away at the war. Then one of the carters asked if she would write to his daughter, married and living in Stirling.

'Her mother was the one that always wrote tae her, once a week without fail.' He took off his cap and scratched his bald head. 'Since the wife died our Betty expects me tae keep up with the letters, but I was never a letter-writer, and it comes awful hard.'

'She just wants to know what's been happening to you and the neighbours, now that she's not here to find out for herself,' Elspeth suggested, and he nodded.

'I know that, lass, and that's the sort of things I talk about all day tae my horse. It's easy with the horse, but when it comes tae puttin' it all down on paper for our Betty I'm tongue-tied. Ye'd be daein' me a right favour if ye'd see tae it for me.'

Then an elderly cleaner timidly asked her to write a letter to the factor about rainwater pouring in through her kitchen window.

'When I'm in front of them, all they see's an auld woman no worth botherin' about, but a letter in a nice hand's different. It's more—' She searched for a word, and beamed when Elspeth suggested, 'More businesslike?'

'That's it, hen – ye've the right way with the words. Will ye dae it for me?'

'Tell me what you want to say.' Elspeth drew the exercise book towards her. 'I'll write it down, then I'll do a proper letter tonight and give it to you tomorrow.'

When word that the factor's men had repaired the window went round the store, Elspeth was inundated with requests. She spent her evenings writing letters, and once or twice had to call on Mattie for assistance in return for helping her cousin with her homework.

'Imagine people paying to have letters written for them, when they could manage for themselves,' she wrote to Lachlan and Thomas. 'I'm getting to know as much about this town as the journalists who write in the *Greenock Telegraph*. Only they know about the important things, while I know about varicose veins and who's had a baby and how someone's Uncle William's come down with the bronchitis again. It's just as well that I can keep secrets.'

'It'll bring you out of your shell, and high time too,' Lachlan wrote back, while Thomas's letter said, 'You're discovering that everyone has some talent that's needed by others, Ellie. It's called supply and demand, and if you're wondering how I know such high-flown things, it's because I've learned a lot myself, mixing with so many different folk. That side of the war's interesting, but I'd give anything to be back home, waking in the morning and knowing that I'm going to be working in the Bruces' nice garden without having to duck every time a Boche shell comes screaming past. They don't have gardens here, only mud.'

'It's a lot of nonsense,' Flora announced when she discovered what was going on. 'Folk should see tae their own letter-writin'.'

'You rely on Ellie to do most of the writing to Thomas and Lachlan,' Mattie pointed out, and earned a cuff on the ear for her disrespect.

'That's different, milady, and well ye know it. I've got more than enough tae see tae as it is. I'd certainly not go askin' a stranger tae write letters for me. And I'm not so sure that it's right for ye tae take money for doin' it, Elspeth.'

'They want to pay their way,' Elspeth explained hurriedly, anxious in case her aunt put a stop to the letter-writing and the money she was earning towards night school. 'I don't ask to be paid.'

'Ye should be proud of the lass, Flora.' Henry's voice came from behind his newspaper. 'She works all hours at that writin' she's daein', and she surely deserves tae be paid for it.'

Flora frowned and muttered, but to Elspeth's relief she raised no further objections. Sometimes, but only sometimes, Flora McDonald listened when her husband spoke.

By January 1918 Elspeth had saved up enough money to start evening classes twice a week in typewriting, shorthand and

42

book-keeping at Greenock Higher Grade School.

On the other three evenings and at weekends she was kept busy coping with the demand for letters, which grew until she had to rise half an hour earlier in the mornings to fit them all in.

Typing and shorthand and book-keeping satisfied her love of order and neatness, and from the start she enjoyed evening classes, getting even more pleasure out of them than she had done from day school.

She quickly realised, too, that office work brought far more satisfaction than machining a neat hem on a skirt, or even stitching the pretty petticoat Miss Arnold entrusted to her one day with the comment, 'You're one of our more careful seamstresses, Elspeth. I can trust you not to make a mess of this.' Sewing had always been part of her life, but office skills brought a fresh challenge, one that she took on with enthusiasm.

Shorthand, a written language that could never be spoken, fascinated her. She took great pleasure in her newfound ability to cover a page with its crisp, swift hooks and strokes and curls, then translate the symbols back into real words. In book-keeping, she loved to see lists of figures growing on the pages of her cash-book, each amount neatly ranged beneath the figure above, each corresponding with a figure on another column, another page.

She particularly enjoyed sitting at a typewriter, tapping on the keys and watching the letters forming on the paper that moved regally upwards, line by line, from the carriage. Sometimes the teacher tapped out the alphabet on the blackboard with a cane, and the whole class was supposed to hit the correct keys to the rhythm she was setting. When the exercise worked, the sound of the keys all crashing together to the beat of the cane was music to Elspeth's ears, and it set her teeth on edge when slower girls missed the beat and threw the rhythm out.

Most of all, she treasured the knowledge that her precious evening classes were being paid for by money she herself had earned. She was doing what she had always wanted to do, and she hadn't had to turn to anyone else for help.

She envied those classmates who had already gained entrance into offices, and had been sent to night school by their employers.

'One day,' she told Mattie, her only confidante apart from her letters to Thomas and Lachlan, 'I'm going to work in an office. If you're determined enough, you can do anything.'

5

When Elspeth first started her evening classes, she didn't say a word about them to Grandmother Bremner, in case they turned out to be a mistake and she had to accept failure and give up. But by May they were going so well that she felt free to talk about them on her monthly visit to the old lady. Grandmother, she felt sure, would be pleased to hear that she had even managed to pay for them herself, and was beholden to nobody.

Celia Bremner lived near Bogstone railway station in Port Glasgow, a shipbuilding town adjacent to Greenock. The tenants in the row of tenements in which she lived were envied by others, because the railway line, which the tenement faced, had been built above the shore road to Greenock. The line was flanked on one side by a sheer drop of at least thirty feet to the shore road, and on the other side by Grandmother's street, which ran parallel to the line, but a little above it. This meant that the tenement windows had an excellent view of the Clyde, looking right over the railway line and even over the shipyards beyond to the open stretch of water and the soft green hills on the opposite shore.

The Bremners were, as Grandmother often told Elspeth, of good stock. Looking at Celia Bremner, erect as a soldier on parade, pride stamped into the hard lines of her face, Elspeth had no reason to doubt her words. During her regular visits to the house, which had started after Celia Bremner was widowed, the old woman always sat in an upright, heavily carved chair, her lower arms laid along the wooden armrests, her hands, twisted with rheumatism, curving precisely over the polished knobs at the ends. She and the chair fitted each other so well that as a child Elspeth had wondered if the chair had been specially made to her grandmother's measurements, and had supposed that somewhere in the house stood a series of identical chairs, starting with a small one made for her grandmother when she was a child, then ranging in size to the imposing adult chair standing now by the fireplace.

Grandfather Bremner, who had, as far as Elspeth knew, never set eyes on her, had been paymaster in one of the sugar refineries; a man, according to his widow, who had been looked up to by his staff and highly regarded by his employers.

Elspeth's secret hope was that if she did well enough at night school, her grandmother might be willing to put in a good word for her at the office where her grandfather had once worked.

She began by talking about the letters she was writing for other people, and was interrupted before she could get to the part about the night school classes.

'I trust you're not asked to write anything vulgar or sensational in those letters?'

'Oh no, Grandmother. Just news of what's happening in the town and with the soldiers' families.'

'In that case I believe your grandfather would have approved,' Celia Bremner said in her dry, flat voice. 'We should all use our God-given talents, and your ability to write comes from him. He himself wrote excellent letters.' Her glance travelled briefly to the mantelpiece, where a photograph of herself and her late husband stood in an elaborate carved wooden frame.

Every item of furniture in Celia Bremner's three-roomed house was carved. Wherever the eye landed it was met by a profusion of balls and claws, bunches of grapes, climbing vines, and formal flowers, all in a state of suspended animation, as though some wicked witch had cast a spell over them and stopped the flowers just at the point of opening, the leaves when they were about to toss in the wind, the grapes at the moment before they were plucked.

Even the photograph of Grandmother and Grandfather Bremner looked as though it had been frozen in time, Elspeth thought, following the old lady's gaze. He, richly moustached but balding, his eyes staring coldly through the glass, sat in a chair – surely a photographer's chair, since it was plain, with no sign of any carvings – his wife on her feet, slightly behind him, one hand firmly planted on his shoulder as if to show that he was hers and nobody else's, her sculpted hair glimpsed beneath a feathered hat.

Studying the photograph, Elspeth found it hard to imagine her grandparents in any other, less formal pose, sitting eating their dinners, for instance, or sleeping in the large carved bed in the bedroom. It was certainly impossible to imagine them talking, laughing, moving freely.

She wondered what it must have been like for her mother to grow up with these two people. From what Granjan said, Maisie Bremner had been a happy young girl, full of fun. Perhaps, thought Elspeth, feeling an itch on her calf and unable to scratch it in front of Grandmother Bremner, that was why there were no photographs of Maisie on the mantelpiece. Even a pictured image of her might hint at too much movement, too much liveliness, in this immaculate flat where the only thing allowed to move was the pendulum of the grandmother clock in the corner of the living room. Even that was strictly regulated to make sure that it didn't recklessly drop or add a second.

Deciding that a respectable interval of time had been given over to contemplation of her grandparents' portrait, she moved tentatively towards the core of her news. 'I enjoy writing letters. I'd like to work in an office one day – like Grandfather.'

47

To her surprise, her grandmother's nostrils flared and her already stiff back stiffened further. Her large-knuckled hands gripped at the armrests.

'Offices are not suitable workplaces for respectable women!'

'But a lot of women work in offices now, Grandmother.'

'That's between them and their consciences,' the old woman rapped out, eyes flashing. 'If this letter-writing is going to lead to such foolishness on your part, Elspeth, I trust that your Aunt Flora has the sense to put a stop to it at once. You're fortunate in having found a good position as a seamstress with a reputable firm, and with diligence, you may do very well for yourself there. I'll not have any more talk of office work from a granddaughter of mine, d'you hear me?'

Elspeth was completely taken aback. She had no idea what she had done to deserve this outburst, but instinct told her that retreat was the safest option. 'Yes, Grandmother.' The itch was worse now, nagging and niggling, demanding to be scratched. She shifted slightly in her chair in an attempt to relieve it.

'Don't twitch, child, it's unladylike. I expect it means that you want your tea,' Celia said reprovingly. 'Very well, you may go to the kitchen and fetch the tray.'

Elspeth, disturbed by her grandmother's sudden change of mood, was only too happy to leave the room. Clearly, there was no question of talking about her night classes now. She felt sure that if the old woman knew about them, she would put a stop to them.

Despite her rheumatism, Grandmother Bremner kept her kitchen, like the rest of the house, spotless, with never a thing out of place. The kitchen was actually a scullery, a walk-in cupboard barely large enough for the gas cooker, sink, and closet it held. The kettle, sitting over what Granjan called 'a wee peep of gas', was ready, pluming subdued little puffs of steam into the air.

With some difficulty, for the scullery was so small that

there wasn't room for even one person to bend down when the door was closed, Elspeth indulged in the luxury of clawing at her calf until the itch was subdued, tears of relief coming to her eyes. She was sure that another minute of sitting in the living room while the itch grew to monstrous proportions would have set her screaming.

The itch finally gone, she warmed the teapot then emptied it into the sink before, mindful of her grandmother's wishes, measuring a precise half-spoonful of tea into the pot from the elaborately painted caddy with its picture of Queen Victoria. After pouring boiling water into the pot she refilled the kettle from the kitchen tap.

A tray had already been set with cups and saucers, plates, milk jug and sugar bowl. Elspeth added the teapot, covered it with the knitted cosy Grandmother always used, and took four biscuits from the biscuit barrel on the shelf, laying them neatly on the blue leaf-shaped plate already on the tray. Back in the living room she put the tray down on the small table between their two chairs and poured tea, first putting in the correct amounts of milk and sugar.

They had their tea in silence, because Grandmother didn't believe in talking while taking refreshments. Sipping at the pale liquid, which she found tasteless compared to the sturdy, strong brew she was used to at home, Elspeth wished that she was back there, practising her shorthand and book-keeping, and perhaps writing two letters that she had promised for Monday morning.

She wished, too, and with all her heart, that Grandmother Bremner was more like Granjan. The two women were like chalk and cheese. Both had given birth to one child, a daughter, and both were widowed, but that was as far as any resemblance went. Granjan was small and plump and cosy, with twinkling grey eyes and a ready sense of humour, while Grandmother was tall and bony, with a long unsmiling face and cold blue eyes. Both wore their hair in a bun, but there

again, they were quite unlike each other. Granjan's hair was
grey, and always making attempts to escape from captivity;
Grandmother's was pure white and drawn back tightly,
enhancing the skull-like look of her face. Grandmother spoke
very properly, articulating each word clearly, while Granjan
chattered on in the local dialect, saying 'tae' and 'ye' instead of
'to' and 'you' and scarcely bothering with word endings like
'th' and 'ing'.

On leaving school, Granjan had worked in Boag's factory,
where the bags from the many sugar refineries in Greenock
were washed and prepared for re-use, while Grandmother had
obtained a position as lady's maid in one of the big houses in
Largs, a residential town further along the coast, where many
of the wealthy manufacturers from Glasgow had built seaside
homes.

Both women had given up work when they got married,
Granjan to a labourer at Caird's shipyard, Grandmother to an
ambitious wages clerk in one of Greenock's sugar refineries.

Granjan, forced to become the breadwinner within two
years of her marriage, when her husband, still in his twenties,
was crippled in an accident at the yard, had taken work wherever she could find it, as a cleaner and washerwoman.
Widowed in her mid-thirties, she still paid her way by washing for women who could afford to pay someone else to see to
their laundry.

Grandmother's husband had achieved the position of paymaster before his death, leaving his widow with enough money
to continue living in the comfortable flat they had shared, and
to cover her frugal lifestyle. It was once she was on her own
that Celia Bremner had acknowledged the existence of her
dead daughter's illegitimate child, insisting on monthly visits.
Flora had taken Elspeth to Port Glasgow in the early days,
leaving her at the door and waiting for her in the street an
hour later. As soon as Elspeth was old enough, she started
making the visits on her own, although as far as she could tell,

her grandmother didn't derive any more pleasure from their meetings than she herself did.

When they had finished tea Elspeth removed the tray and carefully washed and dried the fragile fluted cups, then put them away in the cupboard. As always, her grandmother took advantage of her absence to visit the lavatory.

Unlike most residents in the three towns – Port Glasgow, Greenock and Gourock – strung together along the banks of the Clyde, Grandmother was fortunate enough to have an indoor lavatory. While this was a blessing to be envied, Elspeth was aware that as far as Grandmother was concerned it was more of a curse if anyone else happened to be in the flat, as it meant that they could hear the cistern flushing.

She had learned early in her visits to remain quietly in the scullery until the noisy rush of water had ceased and the old woman had had enough time to settle herself carefully back in her chair, as though she hadn't moved from it at all. Celia Bremner hated to let anyone know that she did anything as common as using a lavatory.

Elspeth often wondered how her grandmother would have managed in the Mearns Street tenement, where all the tenants on one landing shared the privy on the half-landing below, and the folk on the ground floor had their privy in the back yard. She was sure that Grandmother Bremner would rather have burst than admit that she was prey to the same physical actions as other human beings.

Waiting in the scullery until it was time to return to the living room, Elspeth recalled her own sense of shock on hearing from Molly McKibbin, one of a large family, about how men and women made babies. It had been then, and still was, very difficult to think of Auntie Flora and Uncle Henry indulging in such goings-on in the large kitchen wall-bed they shared, but quite impossible to fathom out how the couple in the photograph on Grandmother's mantelpiece could ever have conceived her mother.

Even now that she was older and had had Molly's scarlet-faced, giggling whispers confirmed by some of the girls in the sewing room, she couldn't believe it of her grandmother. Surely a woman who hated to have it known that she had to answer calls of nature like everyone else would never have permitted herself to get involved in that way with a man!

'I hope you've not chipped any of my china.' Celia's cold, creaky voice brought her back to the present just when her thoughts were threatening to get completely out of control.

'No, Grandmother.' She returned to the living room, hoping that her expression carried no hint of the impure thoughts she had been having. 'I was just dusting the biscuit barrel.'

'And how is everything in the sewing room?' Celia Bremner asked when they were facing each other across the fireplace again.

'Very well, thank you, Grandmother. Miss Arnold allowed me to hand-stitch a hem on a petticoat last Thursday, and she was pleased with it when I'd finished.' In her enthusiasm at the memory of Miss Arnold's grudging praise, Elspeth hitched herself slightly forward in her chair. 'It was beautiful material, lovely to touch—'

'Sit up, girl, you're slouching. I'm glad to hear that you're giving satisfaction. You get your sewing ability from me, of course – when I attended Miss Hope Childes, I was well known for my delicate stitching,' Celia said firmly, giving no credit at all to the hours of hard work Flora McDonald had put into teaching Elspeth and her own two daughters how to sew.

'Miss Arnold says that she might let me do some more work for clients who have their clothes made for them.'

Her grandmother inclined her head. 'You could do well for yourself, then.'

The clock in the corner gently chimed the half-hour, and Elspeth sighed inwardly. Thirty more minutes must pass before she was free to make her excuses and go.

'Thomas wrote to me last week,' she volunteered. 'He's in Belgium now. Lachlan's still in France, and we don't hear so much from him just now. I hope he's all right. Thomas says things are just as bad as ever before.' She looked down at her hands, and tried hard not to let her voice shake as she went on, 'I'm so worried about the two of them. I couldn't bear it if they didn't come back home.'

'They're doing their duty by their king and country,' Celia Bremner said implacably. 'You must fix your mind on that, and accept whatever the Lord may choose to send.'

Elspeth was startled by the sudden jolt of anger that ran through her. She longed to ask why anyone should accept without protest a war that was killing hundreds and thousands of ordinary young men like Thomas and Lachlan, but she didn't dare. Instead, she folded her lips together to contain her fury, and waited for the clock to chime four times and release her.

When it finally, grudgingly, did so, she held back until she had rounded the street corner and was well out of sight before starting to run, rejoicing in her freedom and the pleasure of stretching her limbs after having to sit so still in the claustro-phobic room she had just left.

6

Spring made little impact on the cobbles and slabs of Greenock's streets and back yards, though flowers and trees and bushes could be seen stirring with life in the town's parks and in the wealthier townsfolk's gardens and the countryside beyond. Most of the residents, though, marked the arrival of the spring season by the soft green shading on the hills at the other side of the Clyde.

In the battlegrounds of France and Belgium there was even less indication of the release from a long, cold, wet winter. Elspeth gathered from Thomas's letters that the rain had eased somewhat, and smoke from the guns drifted across blue skies, but the mud was still there. In one letter he wrote about spending a night in the ruins of a big house, similar to the house his employers, the Bruce family, had in Gourock, describing graphically the glassless windows, the odd scrap of wallpaper still clinging here and there to what remained of a wall, a door hanging askew on one twisted hinge.

'It was hard to believe that it had once been a cosy home where a family had lived,' he wrote. 'I wonder where they are now, and what's become of them? We thought we were in clover when we arrived, because almost one entire room was left standing, complete with a fireplace and a bonny ceiling, with carving all round. We gathered up wood and lit a fire, only to discover that the chimney had fallen in, so we were driven out of the place by clouds of smoke. We were so pleased at being able to sit at a real fire in a real fireplace that we hung on for as long as we could, until we were all wheezing and coughing, the tears running down our faces.

'I managed to find time to go out into the grounds before we left. It reminded me a lot of the Bruces', for this place had a kitchen garden and a rose garden and once it had had some bonny box hedging and statues on the terracing, all broken and destroyed now. All the glass was gone in their greenhouses, of course, but I did find a pot with a hyacinth blossoming in it, a lovely deep blue flower. I cleared the broken glass from it and moved it to a sheltered spot. Maybe after the fighting is over and the folk come back to rebuild their house, the hyacinth will still be there, waiting for them. It was good to think that all this destruction can't entirely kill Nature off.'

As Elspeth had told her grandmother, Lachlan's letters to her and to his parents had become sporadic. When he did write, his letters were short, and tended to be filled with memories of the past: 'Do you remember that day we all walked over the hills to Loch Thom and had a picnic?' or, 'I was thinking this morning about the time Thomas and me went to Gourock and hired a boat and rowed out into the river so far that we thought we weren't going to get back before the hire time was up.'

She knew from what the other girls in the sewing room said that men on active duty often clung to thoughts of home. One of the carters who had fought in the Boer War in South Africa told her that it was important to soldiers to know that everything was the same at home, just waiting for them to return and slip back into the place they had left.

'Not that anything's ever the same,' he said, scratching his bristly chin, 'for the man himself's bound tae be changed by the things he's seen an' heard an' done. But even so, he needs tae believe that his real life's still waitin' for him back home. That's what keeps him goin'.'

*

55

In the summer, as the tide of battle slowly began to turn in the Allies' favour at last, a War Office telegram arrived at the McDonalds' flat. Lachlan had been wounded, and was in hospital in France.

To Elspeth, who had become increasingly superstitious about both Thomas and Lachlan, and had taken to lying awake night after night, fretting over them, the news was welcome. The war had dragged on far longer than anyone had at first believed possible, and by now almost every family she knew had lost a young man in the fighting, or had had word of wounds received in battle.

So far this hadn't happened to the McDonalds, and she had got it into her head that Thomas and Lachlan had escaped harm for too long while men were injured and killed all around them. Some form of blood sacrifice, she had begun to believe during those long dark sleepless nights, might have to be made before they could be truly safe.

Now she saw Lachlan's wound as just such a sacrifice, an omen that both he and Thomas would survive and return home safely when the war was finally over. She was even relieved for Lachlan's sake, happy to know that for a little while, at least, he was distanced from the fighting and able to rest in safety and without fear.

But when she tried to express these thoughts to Flora, who had almost fainted away at the sight of the War Office envelope, her outraged aunt was in no mood to listen.

'All I know is that my poor laddie's lyin' hurt and in pain in some foreign hospital, with none of his own there tae see tae him,' she snapped. 'I see nothing tae be happy about – and neither would you, if ye'd the sense God gave ye!'

Once again, Elspeth thought in despair, biting her tongue to prevent herself from trying to explain and thus annoying Flora even further, she had caused trouble without meaning to. Would she never learn to keep her opinions to herself?

She was already feeling low that summer. The evening

classes had ended, and wouldn't begin again until September, and as Mattie's school was also closed there was no homework to study with her.

More orders for letters were coming in, and her savings for the next evening-school session were growing, but she missed working on the typewriter, and found a sewing machine a poor substitute. She begged a large sheet of cardboard from a local shopkeeper, and carefully, working from memory, drew out on it a typewriter keyboard. Working on it helped to keep her fingers supple, but at the same time she missed the crisp tapping of a real typewriter's keys.

August brought some excitement to the sewing room. Catherine Bruce, the elder daughter of the family for whom Thomas worked in peacetime, was engaged to a young captain in the Scottish Rifles, and when he was sent home to recuperate from wounds, the couple decided to marry before he went back on duty. The bride's mother, Mrs Lorrimer Bruce, was insistent on a proper church wedding complete with bridesmaids. There was also to be a full trousseau for her daughter's honeymoon, brief though it must be, as the groom was to rejoin his unit by mid-September.

Because the war and the lack of time made it difficult for the trousseau to be made in Glasgow, as would have happened in peacetime, Brodie's store was pressed into service. The sewing room suddenly became a whirl of activity, with all the seamstresses enlisted to help meet the deadline. Even the 'plain' sewing women, who normally only dealt with alterations to ready-made clothes, were given something to do for the wedding.

Miss Buchanan rushed about like a dandelion ball caught up in a whirlwind, her arms filled with sketches and patterns and materials, and Miss Arnold, two bright spots of colour high on her normally pale cheekbones, seemed to be everywhere at once, instructing, checking, criticising, while at the same time soothing her near-hysterical superior.

'This is a great honour for the department,' she told the staff at least once every day. 'We must show Mrs Bruce that we can do as well as any big Glasgow store.'

'The gentry won't even let a war deprive them of their bit of show,' Lena said with a sniff as they all stitched and cut and trimmed.

'What's wrong with a nice dress and jacket?' one of the other women wanted to know. 'That's what my sister wore when she married her sweetheart a few months ago. It's the marryin' that counts, not the show.'

'When ye're a nob, it's the show that counts more than the marryin',' Lena retorted disparagingly. 'What I'd like tae know is, where did they get all this lovely material? It's hard tae find stuff like that nowadays.'

'I heard that a lot of it comes from Mrs Bruce herself,' one of the other girls ventured. 'She put it by before the war began, just in case it was needed for somethin' like this.'

'God! The rest of us makin' do with what we can find, and the likes of the Bruces even hidin' away good cloth!' For a moment Elspeth thought that Lena was going to explode. Her face went red and her hair seemed to give off flashes of light. She opened her mouth to speak, then bent over her work, almost choking with suppressed anger, as the door opened and Miss Arnold swept back in to urge her staff to further efforts.

Elspeth didn't object at all to the hustle and bustle, because the hard work gave her something to do and took her mind off the loss of the evening classes. She enjoyed handling the beautiful materials chosen for the trousseau, and loved the sight of all the colours spilling across the worktables, brightening the drab room.

Once, when she was sent to the fitting rooms with a lawn petticoat she had just finished, a beautiful garment trimmed with pink ribbons and lace, she caught a glimpse of the two Bruce sisters.

Catherine Bruce, the bride-to-be, was a pretty young woman with soft dark hair framing a round face. She was standing before a full-length mirror, garbed in a crimson silk underdress beneath a sequined net overdress in the same colour. Two of the seamstresses were on their knees beside her, working on the hem, while Miss Arnold watched critically, her back to Elspeth, who hesitated at the door, unwilling to interrupt.

She had never seen a more beautiful dress, but the wearer's brows were drawn together above dark-lashed green eyes, her full small mouth turned down at the corners in a sulky pout.

'I still don't like the neckline. It doesn't look right.'

'I think it very flattering, Miss Bruce.' Elspeth had never heard Miss Arnold speak in that soft, soothing voice before. 'Just your style.'

'That's very well, but you're not the one who has to wear it, are you?' the girl snapped without taking her eyes off her own reflection. Elspeth saw Miss Arnold's back stiffen, but when the woman replied it was in the same quiet, reasonable voice.

'If we change the neckline, we change the entire style of the dress, madam.'

'For goodness' sake, Kate, stop fussing. It's lovely, and you know it,' a new voice cut in, and for the first time Elspeth, spellbound up to now by the beauty of the dress, noticed the girl sitting in the corner. Clearly this was Catherine Bruce's sister, for there was a strong family resemblance; but while the bride was pretty, the other girl was breathtakingly beautiful. Her hair was hidden beneath a turban striped in two shades of green, the darker shade an exact match for her wide, clear eyes, and a dark green feather swept up from it. Her silk suit, also in dark green with a lighter shade picking out the lapels, cuffs, and facing, was cut in a severe military style, and her small, narrow feet wore soft green kid button boots. Her face was less rounded than her sister's, almost angular, with a small yet soft mouth.

'It's all right for you, Aileen, all you need is one

59

EVELYN HOOD

bridesmaid's dress. I wish Mother had come with me,'
Catherine Bruce fretted, turning back to the mirror.

'So do I,' her sister agreed, then the lovely green eyes discovered Elspeth. 'Someone's waiting to speak to you, Miss
Arnold,' she said, and the supervisor turned.

'What do you want, Elspeth?'

'You asked for this, Miss Arnold.'

'Yes, I did. Run along now,' Miss Arnold said briefly, taking the petticoat and turning back at once to her client.

The bridesmaids' dresses, Elspeth knew, were to be in pale
yellow muslin, cut straight across from shoulder to shoulder
and trimmed with silver and yellow roses. Aileen Bruce would
look beautiful in hers, she thought, hurrying back to her
work.

As the wedding date approached, Miss Buchanan, clearly
convinced that the clothes would never be ready in time,
worked herself into a frenzy.

'If she's not careful, one of these days she'll go whizzin' out
the door and bump intae hersel' coming back,' Lena remarked
during a midday break in the basement. 'Either that, or she'll
run right up her own arse by accident. We used tae have a dog
that was forever chasin' its own tail – it never did catch it, but
she's in danger of catchin' hers.'

'I wish she'd just keep out of the way and stop telling us to
leave what we're doing and go on to something else,' Elspeth
complained. She was working on another petticoat, one with a
lot of tucking in the bodice that required careful and time-
consuming work, and twice that morning Miss Buchanan had
tried to make her stop what she was doing and turn to another
garment.

If it hadn't been for Miss Arnold's cool efficiency, Miss
Buchanan would have got the entire sewing room into such a
tizzy that work on the wedding clothes could well have
descended into chaos. She took to following Miss Buchanan
around, calmly and quietly countermanding her superior's

60

conflicting orders and ensuring that one garment was finished before work started on the next.

'It's Miss Bruce that's the real problem.' Lily, one of the women who had been in the fitting room the day Elspeth took the petticoat in, leaned across the table. 'Talk about fussy – she doesnae like any of the things she ordered. Keeps wanting them all tae be changed, and she should know better than anyb'dy how little time we've got left. She's spoiled rotten, that one, thinks money's all that matters. Thank goodness her man comes from Perth – the folk up there are welcome tae her.'

'Remember that she's tae stay with her mother till the war's over,' someone else cautioned. 'We'll not get rid of her until her husband's back home for good, so let's hope nothing happens tae him.'

'I can see the day he'll wish something had,' Lily sniffed. 'Courtin' 's one thing, marryin' 's another. I should know – it wasn't until my man went off to the fighting that I realised what a pain in the neck he is. Once Miss Catherine's new husband's got her all the time he might wish he'd never proposed.'

'The sister seems to be quite nice,' Elspeth offered, and Lily shrugged.

'She's decent enough. Mind you, she's been away at some posh boarding school, so she's mebbe learned a few manners there. Once she's been under her ma's wing for a year or two she might be just as bad,' she said, then, coaxingly, 'Elspeth, ye wouldnae have the time tae write me a wee letter tae the factor, would ye? He's tryin' tae tell me I'm still owing my share of those roof repairs, and I know I'm not. But I cannae seem tae put the words down the right way.'

Preparing the trousseau in time for the wedding date began to resemble being in a locked room with the walls slowly moving in to crush the life out of its occupants. As the wedding day approached, the seamstresses worked almost every evening until quite late. Miss Buchanan tottered continually on the verge of apoplexy, while Miss Arnold's controlled serenity was magnificent to see.

It was just as well that there were no evening classes, for Elspeth would have had to miss them. She had been put almost entirely on to fine work that couldn't be done on a machine, and her fingers were red and stiff, the skin rough from plying a needle, her back aching with tension after long hours bent over the worktable. At home, she had to work into the night and get up early in the morning to keep up with her letter-writing as well, but she was determined not to let it fall behind, for it had turned out to be a lucrative sideline.

Between the letters and overtime in the sewing room, her savings had grown considerably and she now had enough to ensure another year at night school, even though she had given a percentage of her overtime earnings to Flora.

To her surprise, her aunt was reluctant to take it. 'Ye've been workin' hard, lassie, with never a word of complaint. Ye deserve tae keep it,' she said, but Elspeth insisted, constantly aware of the debt she owed Flora and Henry McDonald, and anxious to do what she could to repay them.

Secretly, she dreamed of buying them a nice house one day, and furnishing it throughout, to show them how grateful she was for all they had done for her, and to make up for all those occasions when she had inadvertently annoyed Aunt Flora.

One evening when the seamstresses were working late on the last part of the wedding trousseau, a list of the clothes completed went missing, together with two essential patterns. Everyone stopped work and the sewing room was searched, but it was nowhere to be found. Miss Buchanan had had to go home at dinner-time with a severe headache, and as it was her habit to scoop up every piece of paper she could find during her dashes into the sewing room to interrupt and harangue her long-suffering workers, Miss Arnold searched her tiny cubby-hole, but came back empty-handed.

Elspeth and Lena, who had both just finished the work they had been doing, were despatched to the main office, where a copy of the list was kept in case of emergencies, while the overseer continued to hunt for the patterns.

'Mr James Brodie's still on the premises, so he'll be in his room, off the accounts office. He'll know where the list is. Remember to speak clearly, don't gabble, and don't stare at the floor when he speaks to you. I don't want him to think that we employ mindless idiots in the sewing room. And remember that the staff call Mr James "sir",' Miss Arnold cautioned, and the girls, their minds seething with instructions, obediently scurried off up the narrow stairs to the top floor, where the main office and accounts department were housed.

'Why send two of us?' Elspeth wondered as they went.

'So that we can keep each other out of mischief.' Lena was bounding ahead. 'It's great tae get out for a few minutes, isn't it?'

There was no reply when they tapped at the door of the main office. After waiting for a moment or two, Lena nudged Elspeth in. The room was empty, and so, they realised after tapping at the inner door, was the small office belonging to Mr James Brodie, manager of the store, and son of the owner, who had retired.

'Now what do we do?'

'Wait here. There's no sense in goin' back empty-handed,' Lena advised. 'The lights are on and the door's not been locked, so he can't be far away. He'll have gone tae the privy.' She stood in the middle of the main office, turning slowly, taking everything in. 'It's awful tidy, isn't it?'

'That's because they don't have patterns and cloth everywhere.' The office's neatness delighted Elspeth. The high desk along one wall was swept clear of books and papers, pens were laid in the grooves provided and the inkwells were free of stains. All the drawers and cupboard doors were closed, and neat rows of files filled the shelves that lined another wall.

'It's brighter here during the day than it is in the sewing room.' Lena indicated the skylights let into the ceiling. 'I wish we'd some daylight, I hate workin' under the electric light all the time.'

Elspeth didn't hear her. Her eye had fallen on the small table in the corner, with the unmistakable shape of a typewriter filling out its protective dust cover. Envy and longing flooded her mind and her fingers started to itch. She edged over to the table to run her fingertips over the cover, then, after a quick look at the door leading to the corridor, she whipped it off to reveal the typewriter itself.

'Here – what're ye doin'?'

'Just looking.' Her eyes devoured the machine greedily; it was high and shining and solid, the round keys, each with its letter or number clearly stamped on it, as mouthwatering to her as a glossy heap of liquorice allsorts would have been to a hungry child staring in through a sweetshop window.

Her fingers yearned to touch those keys, her ears longed to hear them at work. Several sheets of paper lay by the machine, white and untouched as a fresh snowfall, waiting for letters to be tapped briskly across their pristine surfaces. It was almost too much to bear, being so near a typewriter again and not being able to touch it.

'Mr James can't be at the privy,' she said without taking her eyes from the machine. 'He'd have been back by now.'

'My dad can spend hours in our privy,' Lena said from behind her. 'He suffers terrible from constipation, and when he manages tae go it takes a while. The neighbours have tae pee intae buckets when that happens. Here, what're ye doin' now?' she added in alarm as Elspeth drew out the chair tucked in beneath the desk.

'Just looking.' Elspeth sat down and let her fingers rest on the keys. A shiver of pure pleasure ran through her, and she knew that she couldn't leave things at that. She had to try the typewriter, to find out whether, during the summer, she had lost her recently learned skills.

'Keep an eye on the corridor,' she said, reaching for a sheet of paper and rolling it into the machine.

'Elspeth Bremner! You'll get us both the sack!' Although she could be a rebel in the sewing room, Lena was intimidated by the office, a room she had never been in before.

'I'll not be a minute. Just watch the corridor and tell me if you hear him coming.'

Beneath her fingers the keys leapt into life. 'The cat sat on the mat,' she typed, then ran the carriage back to start a new line. 'The quick brown fox jumped over the lazy dog' was followed by a swift, sure alphabet, every stroke true and clear like a run of notes on a piano.

'That's clever! Where did ye learn tae dae that?' Lena asked in wonder, coming to lean over the desk.

'I've been going to evening classes.' Elspeth hadn't told any of her workmates about her studies for fear of being laughed at, but now, with her ability clear for all to see, she didn't mind talking about it. She ran off another alphabet, her wrists at just the right angle, her fingers skimming over the keys, her eyes fixed on the paper and not the keyboard. Her teacher would have been proud of her, she thought, tossing the carriage back with a flick of the wrist to begin a new line.

She was so taken up with the joy of touching a typewriter again that she didn't even register the fact that Lena, who was supposed to be keeping watch, was in fact standing beside her, equally entranced. Neither of them heard the footsteps in the corridor, or the door opening behind them. When someone suddenly stepped into their line of vision and a male voice, as crisp and sharp as the tap of the keys on the paper, asked, 'Just what do you think you're doing?' the two girls jumped and squealed.

7

James Brodie's long, handsome face was grim, his brows drawn into a frown as he surveyed the two young women trembling before him. 'Well?'

Lena, gasping like a landed fish, her hand pressed tightly to her heart, was for once lost for words. Elspeth, suddenly aware of the enormity of her actions, stood up slowly.

'I – we – Miss Arnold sent us for a copy of Miss Bruce's wedding list, Mr – s-sir.' The words stuck in her throat, on her tongue, behind her front teeth, and it was difficult to get them out. Mindful of Miss Arnold's orders, she lifted her chin when all she really wanted to do was to hide her face against the linoleum on the floor.

The eyes surveying her were frosty, and so was his voice when he said, 'Did she ask you to fetch the list, or to type it out?'

'You werenae here, sir.' Lena finally found her voice, and her wits. 'We were waitin' for ye.'

'You were doing more than waiting.'

Elspeth swallowed hard. 'I – I was just trying out the type-writer – sir.'

'But you're a seamstress, not a typist.'

'She goes tae the night school,' Lena said eagerly. 'She knows how tae work it.'

'Then she'll know how to leave it as she found it, won't she?

And while you're doing that, I'll find this list you're supposed to be fetching.'

Silently, cheeks burning and mouth trembling, Elspeth rolled the sullied sheet of paper from the machine and laid it down on the desk before lining the carriage up properly. In a futile attempt to erase her crime, she used her clean handkerchief to wipe the surface of the keys before replacing the dust cover. By the time she had finished, Mr James had returned from his own small office. He handed the list to Lena.

'Take that to Miss Arnold, and tell her—' He stopped, looking from one flushed face to the other, then said ominously, 'Never mind, I'll tell her myself. I'll have that, young woman, it's my property.'

Elspeth had picked up the used sheet with some idea of removing all traces of the sacrilege she had just committed. Scarlet with mortification, she laid it in the outstretched hand.

'Now you can go back to where you belong,' the manager said dismissively, and the two of them crept out and along the corridor, running down the stairs as though the devil was at their heels, not stopping until they were back on the level where the sewing rooms were situated.

'Sweet Jesus, I near died when I saw him standing there,' Lena gasped, clutching at the banisters with her free hand.

'You were supposed to keep watch for him!' Elspeth blazed at her, fighting back tears of humiliation. It had been the worst moment of her whole life.

'I wouldnae have heard him even if I'd been at the door. It's unnatural for a grown man tae be so light on his feet. Anyway, it's all your fault for touchin' the thing in the first place. I wasnae doing anything wrong – it was you,' Lena said virtuously.

'D'you think he'll tell Miss Arnold?'

'He's sure tae. Did ye see the look on his face? He was ready for throwing us out of the place there and then.'

'What'll we do?' Elspeth wailed. 'What'll Aunt Flora say if I'm turned off?'

Her distress cooled the older girl's anger. 'Ye'll get another position, surely.'

'But it was her that got me this one! She'll say I've let her down again – I'm always doing it! Oh, why couldn't I have kept my hands to myself?' Elspeth wrung the offending hands, in such a state that Lena put an arm about her.

'Don't fret, hen, it'll all work out somehow. Come on, we'll have tae get back tae Miss Arnold, she'll be in a state about this precious list of hers. Don't say anything tae her, what she doesnae know won't hurt her – and no doubt she'll hear about it soon enough. There's one thing,' she added consolingly as they went along the corridor, 'at least yer typewritin' was nice and neat. He cannae accuse ye of doin' it badly.'

Fortunately, Miss Arnold, who had found the missing patterns just before they returned, was less harassed by the time they arrived back in the sewing room. She took the list from Lena, then looked from one to the other. 'You took a long time.'

'Mr James was in the – wasnae there,' Lena said smoothly. 'We had tae wait for him tae came back.'

The supervisor peered more closely at them. 'You're both looking flushed. What have you been up to?'

Elspeth, in the grip of her own private terror, stared dumbly back at her, but Lena was ready with another glib answer. 'We ran down the stairs, 'cos we knew you'd be waiting.'

'Well, you've wasted enough time away from your work. Elspeth, I want that skirt I left by your machine hemmed, and Lena, you can stitch the ribbons on to that camisole,' the supervisor ordered, and bustled off to the cutting room.

Elspeth sank thankfully into her chair and picked up the skirt. It was just as well that she had to machine instead of sew by hand, for she was shaking so much that she couldn't have threaded a needle. As it was, it took all her concentration to guide the material through the machine in a straight line.

*

Normally, when she got home from working overtime, she was as hungry as a horse, but that night she couldn't touch her supper.

'I hope ye're not sickening for something,' Flora fretted. 'I've got enough on my mind worryin' about our Lachlan without you falling ill as well.'

'I'm fine.'

'You don't look it,' Rachel said, eyeing her.

'I've got a sore head. It's all that sewing. I'll go to my bed early.'

'I'll be glad when this wedding's by.' Flora removed her untouched plate and covered it with a clean cloth. 'I'll put this in the oven, mebbe yer uncle'll be glad of it when he gets back from his meetin'.'

Elspeth lay sleepless, racked by guilt and wishing that she had never gone near the typewriter. When Mattie came to bed, tiptoeing about in the dark, trying not to waken her, she pretended she was asleep. A little later, Rachel came in with a candle and was about to light the gas mantle when Mattie hissed. 'Leave it, you'll wake Elspeth.'

Rachel sighed gustily, but did as she was told, though she would have been better to light the mantle, as she kept falling over things in the candle's weak light, yelping and muttering and loudly hissing, 'Shush yourself!' each time Mattie tried to quiet her.

At last she settled down, and soon both she and Mattie were breathing slowly and evenly, with the occasional fluttering snore. Elspeth lay awake, listening to the movements of her aunt and uncle, and the sounds of the tenement – the faint gurgle of water in the pipes, the clump of heavy footsteps on the stairs, the wailing of a child startled awake by a nightmare. She heard Mr McAllister from the flat below returning late from the pub, raising his voice in song then shouting at his wife and being shouted at in return.

Gradually, all the noises eased off as the tenement settled

down for the night. Then there was only the occasional plaintive toot from one of the many ships out on the river, or the melodious sound of a church clock striking the hours and half-hours.

Elspeth was still awake, feverishly going over and over those few moments of temptation in the office, wishing that she had pushed her hands into her pockets, or even cut them off, rather than allow them to touch that typewriter. One hand sought the little silver threepenny bit she had found in her birthday dumpling more than a year earlier, clutching it tightly. True to his word, Uncle Henry had drilled a hole in it for her, and she had worn it round her neck ever since, day and night. One of the first things she had bought with her earnings had been a fine chain to replace the piece of wool it had hung from. It had helped her in moments of stress, but tonight, not even the feel of it biting into her palm could comfort her.

The thought of having to tell her aunt that she had been turned away from the good, respectable job that had been found for her set her moving restlessly in the bed. Mattie, sound asleep, gave a moan of protest as an elbow jabbed into her back, and Elspeth made herself lie still, picturing the look on Flora's face when she heard the dreadful news.

The next two days, busy as they were, dragged by. Every time Miss Arnold or Miss Buchanan came into the sewing room Elspeth cringed, her heart thumping so hard that it was like a drum beating in her ears. She scarcely ate a thing, and it was all she could do to concentrate on her work, and on the letters she wrote during the midday meal break.

Lena, on the other hand, behaved as though nothing had happened, talking when she was supposed to be concentrating on her work, chattering like a budgie during their breaks, laughing and joking with the carters and the errand boys.

'Ach, he'll have forgotten all about it,' she said airily when

Elspeth wondered aloud when retribution was going to fall on them both. 'If he'd meant tae tell on us he'd have done it right away. Besides, we didnae steal anythin', or break anythin', did we?'

'I touched the typewriter, and spoiled a sheet of paper.'

'With the money he has, he can afford tae lose a hundred sheets of paper. And it'll teach you tae keep your hands tae yourself in future, miss. Now stop worryin' about it,' Lena ordered. 'Ye're like a wee ghost. Ye'll make yerself ill if ye don't watch out.'

Flora already thought that Elspeth was sickening for something, and had made her take a spoonful of her favourite cure-all, brimstone and treacle. For once, Elspeth had swallowed it down without protest, for she knew that she wouldn't feel better until she had received some form of punishment for what she had done, and if Mr James Brodie had indeed decided to let them off this time, the nasty-tasting medicine would do instead.

When nothing had been said after three days, she allowed herself to relax, trying to push the shameful episode to the back of her mind so that she could concentrate on the last frantic whirl of getting the trousseau finished.

To everyone's surprise, they managed it. Mrs Bruce and her daughter gave their grudging approval to the garments that had been made in a very short time, Miss Buchanan stopped behaving like a whirling dervish and Miss Arnold permitted herself a slight smile as she congratulated the seamstresses on their hard work.

There was even a small bonus payment made to each of the women. Elspeth used hers to buy a little brooch for Aunt Flora, some tobacco for Uncle Henry, ribbons for Rachel, and a new pen for Mattie.

'Ye should have spent it on yerself, lassie,' Flora said, surprisingly, when the gifts were handed out. 'Ye've worked hard and almost made yerself ill intae the bargain.'

But Elspeth, still suffering from guilt over what she had done in Mr James Brodie's office, had no desire to spend a penny of the money on herself, or even to put it into her savings. As she saw it, she was buying back a clear conscience by spending her bonus on others. She bought a small poke of raspberry balls for Granjan, who doted on them, and since she couldn't think of a gift for Grandmother, she went out into the countryside on her way to visit the old lady and picked a bunch of flowers.

Celia Bremner's eyebrows shot up at the sight of the pale pink wild roses and red campion. 'What's this?'

'I thought you'd like them, Grandmother. The fields are looking pretty just now, and I wanted you to see what's growing there.'

'Unexpected gifts,' said Grandmother shrewdly, 'are usually the sign of a guilty conscience. Have you been up to something, child?'

Elspeth's mouth dropped open, and she felt the beginnings of a blush warm her face. 'No, Grandmother.'

'I hope not. Very well, you may put them in the small glass vase you'll find at the back of the middle shelf above the sink. And bring a tray cloth with you, to put under the vase. Flowers drop petals and make a mess. It'll be easier to gather it all up if it falls on the cloth.'

Filling the vase and drying it carefully before arranging the flowers in it, Elspeth wished that she hadn't bothered picking them. She was sure that under Grandmother's baleful stare the poor things would wilt and die earlier than they might have in anyone else's house. She wondered if this was the way her grandmother had treated her mother, and if so, how Maisie had managed to be as bright and happy as Granjan said she was. Elspeth was sure that if she herself had had to grow up in Grandmother's house she would have wilted away very quickly.

Carrying the vase carefully back into the living room, a

72

clean tray cloth draped over one arm, she was grateful to Aunt Flora for having taken her in, instead of leaving her to her grandmother's tender mercies.

On the day of the Bruce wedding, the last Saturday in August, Mattie, Lena, Elspeth and Rachel walked to Gourock to see the bridal party emerge from the church. It was a beautiful day – 'It wouldnae dare tae be anythin' else, for the Bruces,' Lena said scornfully – and the bride's white satin dress, embroidered with silver threads, shimmered in the sunshine as she and her groom emerged from the church's cool darkness and paused on the top step.

An awed murmur rose from the women clustered round the gate. Many of them were pale and thin, grey-faced from over-work and worry and lack of nourishment. In the main, the clothes they wore were shabby, and most of them carried small children and had toddlers whining impatiently round their skirts. Marriage had done little for them, and yet, Elspeth thought, taking a moment to note the way their tired, dull eyes brightened and softened at the sight of the newly married couple, they still loved to see a wedding, and still clung to the hope that for someone else it would turn out to be the roman-tic, happy-ever-after story they had dreamed of for themselves as young girls.

'Would you look at that dress,' Rachel sighed, eyeing the panels of embroidered lace draping into points at each side of the mid-calf-length skirt.

'And the veil,' Mattie marvelled, as a light breeze caught the fragile lace, causing it to drift round the bride's head. 'Isn't it bonny? Was it made at Brodie's too?'

'I heard it was her mother's,' Lena informed her. 'Italian lace. It must've cost a fortune just on its own.'

As the rest of the wedding party came out to join the bride and groom, the women at the gate crowded closer, peering through the bars at the beautiful clothes, the smart hats, the

73

jewellery sparkling at the women's throats and ears and wrists and fingers.

The precious stones were no doubt real and very beautiful, but Elspeth, putting her hand up to caress the pebble brooch Thomas had given her, wouldn't have exchanged it for all the diamonds and rubies and pearls and sapphires adorning the Bruce women and their guests. The minister, moving here and there among the guests in his sober black robes, looked like a crow socialising with a flock of peacocks.

The five bridesmaids were as pretty as a bunch of daffodils as they grouped together in their yellow muslin gowns. Wide-brimmed straw hats in the same shade as the dresses were tied under their chins with long pale gold ribbons.

As one of them stepped aside from the rest to talk to a tall young man in naval uniform, she took her hat off to reveal the pale gold rose nestling against the crown. She turned to smile at the women clustering round the gate, and Elspeth recognised her as Aileen Bruce, the girl she had seen in the fitting room. Her hair, black as ebony, was cut short and clung to her small, neat skull.

Lena's eyes were on the naval officer. 'Ooh, he's a bit of all right! Lucky her, with him for a sweetheart!'

One of the women standing beside them let out a cackle of amusement. 'That's not her sweetheart, that's Ian, her brother. I should know, 'cos I used to work in Mrs Bruce's kitchens before I got married.'

'Which of them's *his* sweetheart, then?' Lena wanted to know, and the woman shrugged.

'Don't ask me. When I worked there he was only a lad at school, but even so, every girl who came tae the house made eyes at him.'

'I'm not surprised.' Lena clutched at the railings, almost forcing her body through them in her attempt to watch Ian Bruce as he moved with his sister through the throng on the gravel sweep before the church. 'He's lovely!'

'I wouldnae mind a few hours alone with him,' one of the other women said, and there was a squeal of laughter when Lena wriggled her shoulders and retorted, 'You're slow – I'd only need a few minutes!'

Hooves clattered on the road behind them as the carriages that had been waiting a short distance away came up to form a line at the gates. The elderly horses that drew them – all the young, fit horses had been commandeered for the war effort – had been groomed until their coats shone, and flowers had been pleated into their manes and tails. Ushers crunched down the gravel drive to open the gates, and the onlookers fell back to form a guard of honour on the pavement as the wedding party prepared to leave for the reception at the Bruces' large house.

Elspeth raised herself on tiptoe and craned her neck to take in everything she could. Seen close to, the wedding dress and veil were the loveliest, most fragile things she had ever seen. A thousand points of light blazed from the small tiara on the bride's dark head, and the cloudy veil was so fine that it surely must have been spun by angels from happy dreams, she thought, lifted into a rare and unexpected transport of poetic fantasy by the colour and excitement of the occasion.

The bridegroom, a thin-faced young man smart in the uniform of an army captain, walked with a very slight limp, a relic from the wound which had sent him home from France for a few months and made this summer wedding possible. The limp and the uniform added to the romance of the occasion, and a faint sigh of sympathy rippled across the onlookers as he handed his bride into their carriage. Its seats were covered with white satin, and flowers were scattered here and there among the rich snowy folds.

Aileen Bruce dipped a slim hand into her brother's pocket and brought out a small paper bag. Hurrying after the newly-wed couple, she sprayed a fountain of rice over them just as they were getting into their carriage. The women crowding the pavement on both sides of the open gates squealed and laughed as stinging pellets of rice fell among them, and Aileen laughed back at them before gathering up her skirt and springing nimbly into the second carriage, followed by the other bridesmaids.

Mr and Mrs Bruce, he in top hat and tails, she in powderblue silk with a cluster of deep blue feathers pinned to the brim of her hat, were ushered into their carriage by their son, who then stepped up to sit beside them, looking neither to right nor to left. Viewed from close quarters, he was the handsomest man Elspeth had ever seen, even on the cinema screen. Lena clutched at her wrist as he passed by, her nails digging into the skin, and hissed dramatically, 'I'd die for a man like that, so I would!'

After the guests had swept away in their carriages, a small group of men and women who had followed the others out of the church and had hung back during the general movement to the carriages, came down the drive, accompanied by the minister. The four women were in nursing uniforms, and some of the men also wore uniform – the dark blue of the navy, or army khaki, with two in the lighter blue of the air force. Others were in civilian clothing. Some wore slings, some had crutches, one was missing an arm, his empty sleeve neatly pinned up.

One or two members of the small group bore no outward sign of wounds, but like many of the women on the pavement, they were gaunt and stamped with the marks of suffering. One young man, who had a tearing, rasping cough that sounded as though he was shredding his lungs, pressed a large handkerchief to his mouth every time an attack started, as though ashamed to be associated with such a harsh sound.

The onlookers fell silent, knowing that these were some of the men living at the Bruces' big house, part of which had been turned into a convalescent home for wounded military. Some of the women on the pavement reached out to touch a shoulder or a hand, or called, 'Good luck tae ye, laddies,' or

'Bless ye,' as, with the help of the nurses, the men boarded a wagon that had halted at the church gate.

When the wagon had departed and the church gates were closed the girls strolled silently back to Greenock, each caught up in her own thoughts. Glancing at them, reading their expressions, Elspeth was certain that Rachel was thinking longingly of the bride's clothes, and Lena of the bride's brother. Mattie looked as though she was musing over the pleasure of being involved, even briefly and from the sidelines, in something out of the ordinary.

Elspeth herself, as they walked home, started composing her next letter to Thomas, who, as he worked for the Bruce family and hoped to continue working for them when he was finally free of his war duties, would surely want to know all about the wedding. She was also thinking of the convalescent men she had just seen, and about Lachlan.

8

Although at first it was understood that Lachlan's arm wound was not serious, he was still in a French hospital at the end of August. His letters, dictated to one of the nurses there, were very brief, merely informing his worried parents that he was recovering and being well looked after. There were no letters for Elspeth, nor did she expect any under the circumstances.

She herself wrote to him every week, as usual, making her own letters as cheerful and amusing as she could, avoiding any reference to his wound, or to the likelihood of him being sent back to his battalion when he was fit again.

Flora continued to fret about her younger son. 'If it's takin' so long for him tae get better, how can it only be a mild wound?' she repeatedly asked her family, who knew no more than she herself did. 'It must be worse than they're lettin' on. It's gone gangrenous, that's what's happened. He'll have tae have it cut off, and what'll become of him then? How can he work in the shipyards with only one arm, tell me that? Or mebbe they'll not cut it off in time, and he'll die, out there in that hospital where he doesnae know anyone, and they don't even talk the same language as he does—'

'Come on now, lass,' Henry would interrupt at this point, his voice rough with his own worry. 'If he was as bad as that they'd tell us. Anyway, there'll be army nurses and doctors there, as British as he is. Who d'ye think writes his letters for him? A Frenchie nurse couldnae do that, now, could she? He'll be fine, you wait and see.'

Thomas, still in Belgium, did his best to find someone who knew about his brother's battalion and could tell him what might be happening to Lachlan, but with no luck. There was nothing to do but wait and worry and hope.

By the end of September the tide of war had firmly turned in the Allies' favour. The Germans were being swept back all along the Western Front, yielding yard by yard at first, then mile by mile. This meant that Thomas, in Belgium, was now in the thick of it all, and between fretting about him at war and Lachlan in hospital, Flora, weakened by worry, fell victim to the Spanish 'flu that swept across Europe, killing hundreds of people already battered by years of deprivation and suffering because of the war.

In Flora's case, it was so bad that she had to be taken into the Greenock and District Combination Hospital. Without her, the small flat immediately began to resemble a yacht at sea, suddenly deprived of sails and keel and tossing helplessly on the waves. The three girls did their best to keep things going, but without Flora at her usual place in the kitchen, there was a frightening sense of uncertainty about the place.

Nobody was allowed to visit the ward where Flora lay with other 'flu victims, in case the visitors themselves caught the infection. The nurses and doctors, it was said, were going down like flies themselves.

Henry, a strong and confident man in the shipyard, collapsed like a deflated ball, and spent all his time at home sitting gazing into the fire, scarcely hearing a word that was said to him, his pipe, usually puffing tobacco smoke into the air, empty and clenched between his teeth.

'It's like looking at a whipped dog,' Mattie said nervously one evening as the three girls sat in their tiny bedroom. They had taken to spending most of their time there, because they felt like interlopers, sitting in the kitchen with Henry and his silent grief.

'He's hurting, and he doesn't know what to do about it. If he could just see her it might help him.'

'It wouldnae do her any good, though, would it?' Rachel said. 'It'd only make her feel worse, that long face of his hanging over her bed. She'd be certain that she wasn't going to survive.'

When Granjan moved in and took over her daughter's responsibilities, things became a little easier. No matter how worried she herself might have felt about Flora, she didn't show it in the slightest. Instead, she bustled round the kitchen, cooking delicious meals, chattering cheerfully, bullying Henry out of his trance and on to his feet.

She found all sorts of odd jobs for him to do, fastening down a corner of linoleum in the hall that had been threatening for months to trip up unwary feet, tightening drawer handles, whitewashing the kitchen ceiling.

'Now's yer chance tae get things done,' she would say, almost forcing a brush or a hammer or a screwdriver into his hand, nagging him to his feet when all he wanted to do was sit and stare into the fire. 'Think how pleased Flora'll be when she comes home tae find everythin' done. Ye know how much she hates a mess – best see tae it all while she's tucked up in her hospital bed, not knowin' a thing about it.'

She made him paint the woodwork throughout the small flat and re-paper the kitchen, searching Greenock and Port Glasgow herself for paint and paper, scarce commodities. With the help of the three girls she herself scrubbed the rugs and polished the linoleum and washed the curtains and cleaned the windows.

'We've got tae get it all done before Flora comes home,' she kept saying, and gradually, in the face of her persistence, Henry and the girls began to think of the time when Flora was well again, instead of wondering if that day would ever come.

At night, Elspeth lay in bed long after Mattie and Rachel

had drifted off to sleep, praying for Flora's recovery, suffering agonies of guilt over the number of times she had upset and annoyed the older woman, wishing that she could have been a model foster daughter, worthy of all that had been done for her, and that she herself had been struck down instead of Flora.

She even promised herself that she would never again upset Flora, if only she could recover and come home. Knowing all too well from bitter experience how easy it was to do or say the wrong thing without even knowing that in Flora's eyes it was wrong, she was uncomfortably aware that she would probably not be able to keep those promises.

It was so difficult, she thought, to live by other people's standards.

When she woke up one morning with a sore throat and aching joints, she was convinced that her prayers had been answered, and that she had been given the chance to bear Flora's illness in her place. But it turned out to be ordinary influenza, and after a few days of Granjan's nursing, she was up and about again, though pale and shaky.

By that time, Flora was on the mend, and had been moved into an open ward. Elspeth had to stay behind when the others visited her, in case, in her own enfeebled state, she re-infected herself or her aunt. Mattie and Rachel were awed by their mother's fragility.

'I've never seen her like that before, all pale and thin and just lying there, with her hair down in two plaits,' said Mattie.

'I have,' Rachel told her. 'When you were born.'

Henry, who stayed on by his wife's side when the others left, looked more like his old self when he got back. 'She gave me dog's abuse when I told her we'd been paintin' and paperin' the place. Said I should've waited until she was home tae see what I was up tae. That's your fault,' he accused his mother-in-law.

'Indeed it is not, it's yours for waggin' yer silly tongue,' she

81

snapped back, a gleam in her eyes. 'She's quite right when she says ye should've known better – better than tae go tellin' her!'

'Ach, she got it out of me. I was never good at keepin' anythin' from Flora.'

'That's the best way for a married man tae be,' his mother-in-law told him drily. ''Specially if it includes his wages. It saves a lot of quarrelling.'

'It didnae save me from a tellin'-off. The whole ward was listenin', tae. I didnae know where tae put my face.'

'That shows she's getting better.' Janet, who only reached halfway up Henry's waistcoat but matched him in width, craned up towards his chin, sniffing loudly. 'I didnae know they sold beer in the hospital.'

He reddened and retreated to his usual armchair, picking up his pipe and reaching for his tobacco pouch.

'Ach, I met some o' the lads on my way home and went for a wee drink with them.'

'That's another thing ye don't want tae go tellin' Flora when ye visit her tomorrow night,' Janet said, grinning at the girls, who beamed back. After almost two weeks of sucking at an empty bowl, the man of the house was filling his pipe again. Flora McDonald was going to recover, and all was well with her household.

A few days later Elspeth returned to the sewing room, which was almost empty because many of the women, including Miss Buchanan, were off with 'flu.

'But not Miss Arnold,' Lena said sadly after getting a lecture from the overseer for chattering when she should have been working. 'There's not an influenza germ that'd dare tae touch her.'

'I notice you didn't get it,' Elspeth pointed out, and her friend grinned.

'The devil looks after his own. Any word about your Lachlan?'

'He's been moved to a hospital in England.'

Lena's brows rose. 'What for?'

'I don't know. The letter just said that he'd been moved, and they'd let us know when he was coming home.'

'That means he's finished with the fightin'. My dad says it'll all be over soon, so they'll surely not send him back now.'

'I suppose not.' Elspeth knew that she should be happy for Lachlan, safe in Britain and away from the front line. Wasn't this what she had wanted for him? But as she settled some material beneath the sewing machine, she wondered, as they were all wondering at home, why Lachlan was still in hospital, and why they hadn't been told more about his condition.

Flora, who firmly refused to go to a convalescent home, returned to her family, pale, thin, still weak, but determined to take up her usual everyday life as quickly as possible. She inspected the decorating that had been done during her absence, and grudgingly admitted that it 'wasn't too bad'.

'It was mebbe as well tae get it seen tae, with our Lachlan comin' home soon,' she decided, sinking into a fireside chair. 'Mattie, put the kettle on, I've been parched for a decent cup of tea these last few weeks. I cannae be doin' with being ill. It's all a nonsense.'

A nonsense that had claimed victims throughout the town, including two in their tenement, an elderly woman who lived alone on the ground floor, and a three-month-old baby, the first child of a couple on the second floor, conceived during her father's last leave from the Royal Navy.

Flora had fully recovered her strength by the time the war finally came to an end in November. That evening, Greenock held one big street party, and Elspeth, Rachel and Mattie wandered round the packed town, enjoying a sense of freedom that they had never known before. Hundreds of thousands of men and women on both sides had lost their lives during the struggle, and proper mourning for them would come later, but for that evening, all people wanted was a chance to mark the end of the conflict.

From the shipyards and from the vessels moored at the Tail o' the Bank came the clamour of sirens, and in the town itself everyone who could play a fiddle or an accordion or even a penny whistle had brought it along. Cars and buses and tramcars, nudging their way slowly and patiently along the streets, tooted their horns or clanged their bells, while those hanging out of the windows had plenty of time to shake hands with the people all around before passing on their way.

Groups of women and children and old men leaned on every tenement windowsill, calling down to the crowds below. Folk were hugging and kissing total strangers, talking and laughing with them like old friends, drinking and dancing together. Here and there, couples had opted out of the crush and could be seen closely entwined in shop doorways and close-mouths, oblivious to everyone else.

They met Lena and some of the other girls from the sewing room, arm in arm with a group of foreign seamen, most of the men clutching bottles of beer. When they were introduced, Lena's escort, a young giant of a man with a thatch of black curly hair, insisted on kissing all three of them. His mouth was wet and rubbery, and tasted of drink, and it was a relief when he and Lena moved on and Rachel, Mattie and Elspeth were able to scrub at their mouths with handkerchiefs.

'I don't know how Lena can enjoy kissing the likes of him.' Mattie's face was wrinkled with distaste. 'It was terrible! I think he tried to put his tongue in my mouth, too.'

'He did not!' Elspeth was scandalised at the very thought.

'Either that, or he'd three lips. If that's what kissing's like, I'm not going to bother getting myself a boyfriend.'

'Bob doesn't kiss like that at all,' Rachel put in quickly. 'It must be because that man's foreign.'

'Oh, so Bob's kissed you, then?' Mattie winked at Elspeth as her sister blushed deeply. Until now, Rachel had refused to admit that she and Bob were anything but good friends.

'If you must know, he kissed me goodbye the last time he was home on leave. And he's asked me to marry him.'

'Rachel!' The two younger girls stopped and eyed her with a new respect.

Rachel preened and simpered, enjoying her moment in the limelight. 'I haven't said I will, so don't you go telling Mam when there's nothing at all to tell.'

'But you'll say yes, won't you? When he comes home from the army?' Elspeth thought it was all very romantic.

'I might – and I might not, so not a word,' Rachel cautioned, and they both crossed their hearts, then Elspeth, looking beyond Rachel, said in astonishment, 'Granjan! What are you doing here?'

'Celebratin' the end o' the fightin', same as you.' Janet Docherty was bright-eyed and flushed with excitement. One arm was closely linked to her neighbour, Mrs Begg, and from the elbow of the other dangled the shiny black leather handbag only brought out on special occasions. It was bulging, as usual, because Janet made a point of taking everything of importance with her when she went out, just in case she got knocked down and taken to hospital, and needed her personal papers. 'Bein' old doesnae mean we cannae have a celebration, does it, Teenie?'

'I'm just glad I lived tae see the day,' Mrs Begg confirmed, dipping her head up and down energetically. With her small sharp eyes and her long thin nose, the gesture made her look like a bird drinking from a puddle. 'Though we'll no' be out too long. The town's too crowded for my liking.'

'Ach away wi' ye, it's just grand tae see all the folk so happy,' Janet chided her. 'How's Flora? Are Henry and her not out in the streets too?'

'My dad went to have a drink with his mates, but Mam's at home,' Rachel explained. 'She says she's happy just sitting on

85

her own, thinking about Thomas and Lachlan coming home soon.'

'Aye, right enough, it's grand tae think that we'll get them back again,' Janet agreed. 'Come on now, Teenie, we'd best be off and let the lassies enjoy themselves,' and the two elderly women forged on through the crowds.

A group of people were dancing in Cathcart Square; for a while the girls stood and watched, then they too were pulled into the dance. Elspeth's partner was a burly man in civilian clothes, probably a shipworker who, like Uncle Henry, had been excused military service because he was needed in the yards. As they revolved under a streetlamp, she saw that beneath a bushy moustache his grinning mouth revealed tobacco-stained teeth. His hands were hot and damp as they clasped hers, spinning her round and round until her feet were almost lifted from the cobbles.

'Don't worry, hen, I'll no' let ye fall,' he bellowed, seeing the panic in her face. It was a relief when the music ended and she was able to stop, one arm looped about a lamp standard because the square was still whirling about her head.

'Here – this'll steady ye,' the man said, pushing an opened bottle under her nose.

'No – no thank you.' She tried to pull back, but the bottle followed, nuzzling insistently against her mouth.

'Go on, a wee drop'll no' hurt ye.'

'I don't want it.'

'Let's have another dance, then,' he wheedled as the accordionist started up again. He tried to draw her back on to the cobbles, a hand about her waist, but she clung to the lamppost, shaking her head.

'It's time I was getting home.'

'On a night like this? The war doesnae end every day, hen. We'll dance the night away an' have somethin' tae tell our grandweans, eh?'

'I have to go,' Elspeth insisted, breaking free, backing away from his clutching hands. There were so many people about that it was easy to plunge back into the crowd, away from him. That same crush, however, made it impossible for her to find Mattie and Rachel. She worked her way round the square in search of them, then, deciding that the task was impossible, she began to struggle out of the square, along Hamilton Street. There was no fun in being out on her own; she might as well make for Mearns Street and home.

It had been possible to walk along the crowded streets when there were three of them linked together, forging a path through the crush. Alone, Elspeth found, it was a different matter. She kept getting forced back by the sheer numbers moving towards Cathcart Square, drawn by the jaunty music. It seemed to be a matter, as Flora McDonald tended to say on a busy day, of one step forward and two steps back all the time.

Once, when a drunken French sailor unexpectedly scooped her up and whirled her round above the heads of the passers-by, she thought that she glimpsed Rachel on the other side of the road.

''Ello, pretty mademoiselle,' the young man yelled above the general noise as he set her down again. He attempted a gallant bow, but his feet betrayed him, sending him stumbling sideways. His friends, roaring with laughter, caught him before he landed among a sea of feet, and carried him off with them, while Elspeth, beginning to lose her nerve now that she was on her own, launched herself off the edge of the pavement and across the road.

9

When she got to the opposite pavement Rachel was nowhere to be seen. Elspeth struggled on in the direction of home, then realised after a few stumbling steps that she had turned round without being aware of it and was heading back to Cathcart Square. She started to retrace her steps, only to run into the man who had danced with her earlier.

'There ye are, hen, I've been lookin' for ye. Come on, just a wee dance—'

He got a firm grip on her wrist this time, and started towing her back in the direction of the accordion music, pushing his way through the crowds. Elspeth pulled back, but couldn't break his grip. A gap cleared to one side of her, and she wrenched herself towards it in the hope that her change of direction would catch him by surprise, only to find that she had made a mistake. Her sudden sideways lunge had taken them to the inside of the pavement, and instead of pulling her onwards, he now crowded her against the wall of a tenement building.

'D'ye no' want tae dance?'

'I want to go home!'

'A wee kiss first, eh? A wee kiss tae celebrate a great day—'

'No!' She tried to wriggle away, but she was pinned between his large body and the wall. He clamped his arms round her, at the same time shuffling along sideways like the crabs she had sometimes seen on the shore when she played there as a child. Elspeth couldn't understand what he was doing until the wall suddenly dipped away from behind her and she staggered back a step or two before coming up against another solid obstruction. He had eased her into the doorway of a shop, out of the way of the people flocking past.

Elspeth, panicking, kicked out at him and tried to push him away. He laughed at her, crowding her more closely against the shop door.

'I like a lassie wi' spirit,' he said, then kissed her hard, pushing her lips against her teeth, forcing her head back until it was jammed against the door. It was as though he was trying to force his own face right through hers. She was sure that he was going to succeed, and the bones of her face were going to give way. Mattie had been right about Lena's boyfriend kissing her with his tongue as well as his mouth. This man was doing the same, and disgust and revulsion almost choked her.

One of his hands managed to insert itself between their bodies, crawling like a spider over her until it reached her breast, where it fastened hungrily. A year earlier, he would have had nothing to clutch, but since the summer her body had fleshed out, maturing at what seemed to Elspeth to be an incredible and embarrassing speed. Before then her measurements had been more or less the same from shoulder to thigh, but now her waist had slimmed down, while her breasts and hips had rounded out.

She tried to scream, but he was pinioning her mouth with his own, and it was difficult enough to breathe, let alone shout. Even if she had been able to make any sound it was unlikely that anybody would have heeded; there was so much noise in the street that even a loud yell could have gone unnoticed.

He was pushing himself against her now in short, rhythmic thrusts, while one knee tried to intrude between her legs.

The separate, onlooking part of her mind suddenly fled, unable to tolerate what was happening, and sheer terror gripped Elspeth. She couldn't breathe, she was at the mercy of this man she had never met or seen before. She was going to die, her mind screamed at her. She was going to die, either of suffocation or from what he was about to do to her.

Her understanding of the sexual act had always been sketchy, made up as it was by only half-believed information from her schoolfriend Molly, giggling comments overheard in the sewing room, and magazines and novelettes she and Mattie had smuggled into their bedroom. The foster-sisters had mulled over what they knew of the subject frequently, and between them had tended towards the romantic side, with the men always honourable and respectful towards their women-folk.

Now, as the stranger's knee managed to prise her legs apart and his hand tightened painfully on her left breast, Elspeth knew that she and Mattie had been wrong in their assumptions. Love wasn't as essential as they had thought – there was a physical relationship too, one that had nothing to do with tenderness or respect, but everything to do with hurting and perhaps even killing.

The noise that had been beating in her ears since she had ventured on to the streets began to fade, the glow of the gas streetlights to dim. She closed her eyes tightly to shut out the face pressing against hers, and flashing lights seared the inside of her lids.

The man lurched back slightly, releasing her mouth and breast, moving his hand downwards. She felt his knuckles pushing painfully into her stomach as he apparently fumbled with his belt. Sucking air into her starving lungs, Elspeth made one last bid for freedom, lurching towards the pavement with its continual flow of passers-by. He reached out a long arm and wrapped it about her, hauling her back against the door, moving his body so that it formed a blockade between her and the people only a matter of a yard away in the street.

'Hold still, ye stupid bi—' he started to say, then suddenly grunted, lurching hard against her so that the air she had managed to drag into her lungs was forced out again by the weight of his body.

'Ye dirty midden, ye,' a familiar voice yelled. 'I'll teach ye tae put yer mucky hands on my grandwean, Johnny Lafferty!'

The man pulled back, spinning to face the street. 'Ow!' she heard him yelp as a well-aimed blow from Janet Docherty's best handbag landed on his nose. He tried to retreat sideways along the shopfront, hands thrown up before his face to protect it from the blows raining on him. 'For God's sake, missus!'

'Keep God out o' it, foul-tongued blasphemer that ye are!' Janet was smaller than he was, but she managed to keep aiming blows at his face by bouncing like a rubber ball with each swing of the bag. Mrs Begg, bleating, 'Oh dear, lassie, oh dear!' put her arms about Elspeth, who was sagging at the knees.

Despite the noise in the street, Janet's outraged yells and the howls of the man now cowering against the shop front attracted attention. A small crowd gathered to watch and laugh, their backs forming a wall around which the rest of the revellers flowed.

'The dirty bastard was tryin' tae attack my grandwean,' Janet informed them between blows. 'And her only a wee bit of a lassie!'

'I didnae ken she was yer grandwean,' the man wailed, then, appealing to the onlookers, 'I didnae ken!'

'Mebbe no', but ye must've kent she was someone's grandwean, ye filthy pig, ye! An' you a grown man wi' a wife, God help her, an' six weans of yer ain!' said Janet, and aimed another blow at him. Because he had lowered his arms in order to appeal to the crowd, her best handbag landed fairly on his nose, and he yelped like a beaten dog.

The onlookers were all on Janet's side. 'That's right, missus, you show him,' a man shouted, while others jeered at the drunk, and a woman screeched, 'I ken him tae – a worthless piece o' scum that's nae use tae his wife except for fatherin' more and more bairns on the poor sowl!'

'Mercy me,' said Mrs Begg in distress, doing her best to cover Elspeth's ears.

'Here's a polisman, missus,' someone called out. 'Hand the rascal over tae him.'

Janet stood back, the first white-hot rush of anger spent. 'Ach, let him run tae his hole, stinkin' rat that he is,' she said with sudden dignity, and the crowd, respecting her right to decide, stood back to let the man go, then melted away as the policeman approached.

'Are ye all right, pet?' Janet asked anxiously, gathering Elspeth from Mrs Begg's arms, then, as Elspeth nodded, beyond speech for the moment, 'Here, Teenie, you take her on that side and I'll take her on this, and we'll get her out of here.'

'Are ye taking her home tae her mammy?' Mrs Begg asked above Elspeth's bowed head as the three of them struggled along towards Nicolson Street.

'Have ye lost the wits God gave ye, woman? Can ye see our Flora's face if we take the bairn back lookin' like this? We'll take her tae my house and get her tidied up first.'

Back in Granjan's cosy little flat in Nicolson Street, Mrs Begg made tea while Janet washed Elspeth's face and hands and combed her hair, talking soothingly as she worked.

'Thank goodness I caught a sight of ye when ye were tryin' tae get away from that drunken lout. No sense frettin' over what didnae happen, is there? Ye've got a split lip on ye, hen.' She dabbed gently at Elspeth's mouth. 'But that's easy explained tae yer Auntie Flora – ye'll no' be the only one in Greenock tonight tae walk intae a lamppost in all that crush.'

'I've got a wee bit of whisky in my kitchen cupboard. Will I fetch it and we can put some in her tea tae help her get over the shock?' suggested Mrs Begg, who lived across the landing.

'And take her back tae Flora smellin' of drink? For goodness' sake, Teenie! She'll be fine, won't ye, pet? All she needs is a good strong cup of tea with plenty of sugar in it.'

She was right. By the time the cup was half empty Elspeth was feeling more like herself, though Granjan was still seething.

'That Johnny Lafferty's always been a midden, so he has.'

'He was drunk, he didn't know what he was doing.' Now that the nightmare was over Elspeth felt a shred of pity for the man who had so quickly turned into a whining child under her grandmother's relentless attack.

'The man's never sober. That poor wife of his has a lot tae put up with!'

'Where d'you know him from, Granjan?'

'From here. He lives up above.' Janet Docherty glared up at the ceiling. 'I should push the handle of my broom clean through right now an' hope it'd come out right where he's standing. I'd do it too, if it wasnae that I feel so sorry for Liza. She's got no chance of a decent life with him, and most of her bairns'll probably grow up tae be like their wastrel of a faither, then she'll have even more heartbreak.'

She shook her head in sorrow, then went on briskly, with a change of tone 'Now – finish yer tea, and Teenie and me'll see ye back home. Flora'll be frettin' about ye, specially if Rachel and Mattie are home already. Mind, now, all ye need tae tell her is that ye met up with some friends, then got pushed intae a lamppost by accident in the crush. And put that man out of yer mind, hen. There's plenty of fools like him in the world, but with any luck ye'll never meet up with another of them. If ye do, and yer as close tae him as ye were tae Johnny, take my advice and bring yer knee up like this – see? It fair takes their mind off any further ill-doin'.'

'Janet!' Mrs Begg screeched as Granjan demonstrated by lifting one plump knee up sharply, almost overbalancing.

'Ach, stop yer scrakin', Teenie Begg. Lassies should know these things. That's what saved me more than once in my own young days. Come on, then, pet, time you were home. And I'd be grateful,' Janet added as she helped Elspeth on with her coat, 'if ye'd no' let on tae yer Auntie Flora that I used the word "bastard" in front of ye. It was all said in the heat of the moment, hen.'

Elspeth had always thought that once the war was over, everything would get back to normal, but instead, life went on as usual for several months. There was still a shortage of food and clothing, and most of the men were still away from home. Women still did men's work in the factories and shipyards, and on the buses and trams as clippies and drivers.

Round about Christmas time the foreign ships began to depart from the river and the first of the Greenock men returned home. Among them was Bob Cochran, Rachel's sweetheart. Rachel went about with a permanent smile on her face, but Bob, never a chatterbox, had become even more morose during his time away. When he did speak it was usually to complain about the way the soldiers had been treated by officers who knew nothing, but thought they were superior just because they had been brought up in posh houses and went to posh schools.

His other complaint was about conditions in the shipyard where he had taken up his former job.

'What did we fight for, tell me that?' he would demand, sitting opposite Henry in the McDonalds' kitchen, his booted feet sprawled across the rag rug. 'What did we risk our lives for, and live in muddy water up to our knees for? Tae build a better world, they told us.' A contemptuous jerk of his close-cropped head towards the hall door indicated that 'they', the officers and shipyard owners and others of their ilk, existed somewhere outside the tenement. 'But what's better about it, tell me that? I'm no' paid any more than I was before I went

94

away. I'm no' treated any better. A land fit for heroes? That's not what I'd call it!'

'He's an awful moaner, isn't he?' Mattie said in disgust when she and Elspeth had escaped to the bedroom, Elspeth to write letters, Mattie to do her homework. 'I don't remember him making such a fuss about everything before. He was quite nice then.'

'He's got a right to be angry, I suppose.' Elspeth was curled up at the head of the bed, trying to get as close as she could to the gas mantle, which didn't give out much light. Mattie was sitting on Rachel's bed, beneath the other mantle. 'He must've had a hard time of it, and then he comes home to find that things are no better than they were before.'

'I'd think more of him if he made the best of it,' Mattie said flatly. 'I don't know what Rachel still sees in him. He looks so – hard, doesn't he? Mebbe he'll look better when his hair grows back.'

They collapsed in giggles, remembering Bob's first visit to the flat after leaving the army. Before going off to war, he had had a fine head of light brown hair, thick and soft, but to Rachel's dismay he had come home for good with his hair cropped even more ruthlessly than army regulations demanded, so close to his scalp that the skin shone through. The shaven head, accentuated by his thick, short neck and powerful shoulders, gave him a menacing look.

'Och, Bob, why did you let them cut your nice hair so short?' Rachel had asked, running her hand over the stubble. Then she pulled her fingers back sharply as her beloved said, 'Nits.'

'Nits?' Rachel almost screamed the word, wiping her hand hurriedly on her skirt, while Henry stopped in the act of knocking out his pipe, and Flora gasped. Head lice were common in the Greenock tenements, but Flora had worked hard to keep her own children's heads clean, combing their hair with a special close-toothed comb every day, washing their heads with strong-smelling coal-tar soap that they all hated. To the McDonald household, nits meant dirt and squalor.

'We was alive with the wee bu—' Bob shot a look at Flora and suddenly remembered where he was, '—blighters in the trenches. If we hadnae had our heads shaved we'd've been too busy clawin' at ourselves tae shoot back at the Jerries.' Then, as Rachel moaned softly, 'Ach, don't make such a fuss. I've been well scrubbed wi' disinfectant since then. They're all gone – and the body lice tae. What else can ye expect?' he went on as Rachel retreated from the arm of his chair, shuddering. 'We was crowded together for weeks on end in these trenches, never findin' the time tae change our clothes, let alone clean them.'

A sneer brushed across his mouth as he surveyed the horror in the faces around him. 'Ye know a pal's really a pal when ye've shared nits an' fleas with him,' he said, then the sneer changed to a hoot of derisive laughter.

'D'you think Thomas and Lachlan'll have their hair all cut off too?' Mattie said when the girls' giggles had died down. Without being aware of her actions she ran a pencil through her own brown curls, using it to scratch at the scalp beneath.

'How should I know?'

'You write to them both.'

'Nits aren't the sort of thing you ask about in letters. I see that Aunt Flora's bought in some extra-strong soap, and another bottle of Jeyes fluid,' Elspeth said, then she and Mattie shuddered in unison.

10

Thomas arrived home in the middle of February, a week after his twenty-third birthday. His brown hair had been cut short, but not nearly as short as Bob's. It clung round his scalp in curls, and his boyish body had filled out, not with fat, but with muscle. There was a new awareness in his eyes, too, but apart from that he was the Thomas they all knew well, still cheerful, happy to be back, with none of Bob's bitter resentment at the war that had torn him from home and family.

'It wasnae a picnic, and I'd not want tae go through it again,' he said as he enjoyed his first home-cooked meal, 'but a lot more had it worse than me, losing their lives or bits of their bodies, or their homes and everything they had in life. And I'm talking about civilians too, not just soldiers. Those poor souls in France and Belgium that saw their towns and villages turned into battlefields – it'll take them a long time tae get back to a normal life.'

He waited until the meal was over, and the neighbours who had crowded into the flat to welcome him back had eventually returned to their own homes, before telling his family that he had visited Lachlan on his way home.

Flora was overjoyed. 'How is he? How's his arm?'

'It's fine, Mam, all mended, and only a wee scar to show where the bullet went in. Lucky for him it didnae do any permanent damage. His arm'll mebbe never be as strong as it used tae be, but there won't be much difference.'

'Than why isn't he home? He'll do far better here than in any hospital where there's nobody of his own blood tae comfort him. I would've gone tae visit the laddie, but what with the influenza and yer dad needin' me here tae see tae his meals for him when he comes in from—'

'Mam, will ye just wheesht a minute and listen tae me?' Thomas asked quietly, but with a gravity in his voice that brought all their heads swivelling round in his direction.

'There's more tae it than they said, isn't there?' Flora's clenched fist went up to her mouth. Above it, her eyes were anguished. 'I knew they werenae tellin' us the truth of it!'

'Flora—' Henry reached across from his own chair to put a large hand on his wife's knee. 'Just dae as the laddie asks, and give him the chance tae tell us what's amiss wi' Lachlan.'

Thomas looked from one face to the other. 'He's fine, in his body,' he said at last, carefully. 'But in his head—'

'He was wounded in the head as well?' Rachel asked sharply, while Flora whimpered into her fist, her free hand finding and clutching Henry's fingers.

'Just in the arm, and I've already said that that's fine. It's inside his head I'm talking about. He'd a hard time of it in France, with all the noise and the business of seeing laddies he knew and fought beside being injured or killed. It's all been too much for him.'

'Shell shock.' Elspeth didn't know she had spoken until they all looked at her.

'That's what the hospital folk said. It's somethin' that can happen tae a soldier.'

'How did you know what it was called, Elspeth?' Henry asked.

'One of the girls I write letters for, her lad's cousin had it. He'd to come home early from the war. He's getting better now,' Elspeth added swiftly to her aunt.

'I don't understand.' Mattie's thin face was puzzled. 'How can he be shell-shocked if a shell didn't hit him?'

'It's the noise,' Thomas explained. 'The noise all the time of those big shells screamin' past day and night, sometimes for days on end without any stop tae it. Ye've no idea of the noise unless ye've lived through it.' He paused for a moment, then said, 'It's a wee bit like standin' in a very big railway station, with trains runnin' through every platform, one after another, never stopping, never givin' yer ears a rest, even when they're dingin' wi' the noise and ye'd give anythin' ye had tae get a bit of peace and quiet, only nothing'll make it stop.'

He paused, looked at his family's perplexed faces, and shrugged. 'I don't have the words tae explain it any better. It's like something in a nightmare. The place where Lachlan was based was very bad for the shellin'. If he hadnae been shot in the arm, I don't know what would've happened tae him. He'd mebbe have gone mad, poor soul.'

'By the sound of it, he has.'

The words were no sooner out of Rachel's mouth than Thomas rounded on her, jumping up from his chair to grab her shoulders. 'Our Lachlan's not mad,' he said vehemently into his sister's startled face. 'And don't ever let me hear ye say that about him again!'

'Here—' Henry cut in sharply, getting to his feet. 'No need for that!'

As they all stared at Thomas in astonishment, his hands fell away from his sister's shoulders, and he stepped back, his Adam's apple lurching visibly in his throat as he gave another gulping swallow.

'I'm sorry, Rachel. I – I didnae—'

'You frighted me!' Rachel's pretty face was red with shock and embarrassment.

'I'm sorry,' Thomas said again. 'It's just that – Lachlan's not mad, and I'll not hear anyone sayin' it. Nobody.'

Henry took his son by the arm, drawing him to his own armchair. 'Sit down here, lad, by the fire, and tell us more about what's ailin' him.'

Thomas resisted the hand on his arm, moving back to the table, where he sat down. 'You sit in yer own chair, Da, I'm fine here.'

'What's wrong with Lachlan?' Flora had scarcely noticed the interruption.

'He's a wee bit confused, Mam. He's spent so much time under fire that he can't grasp the fact that it's all over and he's safe. He jumps at the slightest noise. He – he cries a lot,' Thomas said, and Mattie and Elspeth stared at each other. Men didn't cry. Crying was for bairns and small children. They couldn't imagine Lachlan, who found a laugh in everything that happened to him, even the bad things, in tears.

'He'll get better, though?' Mattie's voice was very small, and Thomas reached across the table to give her hand a reassuring squeeze.

'Of course he'll get better, given time. The nurses and doctors are working with him. They're very kind tae him, you need have nae fear about that. He's well looked after.'

'Not as well as he would be in his own home. I want him back here,' Flora said firmly.

'When he's a bit better I'll—'

'Never mind when he's a bit better, I want him home now. He's my son, and I want tae look after him myself!'

'Mam—' Thomas began, but she ignored him.

'Are ye tryin' tae tell me they won't let him out? Is it a hospital or a prison he's in – tell me that?'

'It's a hospital, and of course they'll let him out, but should we not give them a wee while longer with him?'

'We've been without the two of ye for near enough four years, and we want ye both back here, where ye belong!' Flora insisted.

She was adamant, refusing to settle for anything less than a firm promise that Thomas would write to the hospital the next day, and travel back down to England within the week to bring Lachlan home. At last, worn out from a long day of

100

travelling and talking, he gave her that promise, and the family all went to bed.

In the narrow lobby Elspeth asked fearfully, 'Thomas, is Lachlan going to be all right?'

'Of course he will, but it might take longer than Mam thinks.' There was no gas lighting in the boys' tiny room, and in the glow of the candle he carried, Thomas's face was drawn with tiredness, his eyes deep black pits. 'We'll all have tae be very understandin' with him.'

'We will be. Get a good night's sleep, you look as if you need it.'

He smiled slightly. 'I've learned tae sleep in all sorts of places at all sorts of times. Don't you worry about me, I'll be snoring as soon as my head touches that pillow.'

On the following day Flora made Thomas write to the English hospital. He posted the letter on his way to Gourock to see Mr Bruce, his former employer, about getting his old job back.

All that day in the sewing room Elspeth fretted about him. The men working in factories and shipyards had been assured of their own jobs back when the fighting was over, which meant that Lachlan would be able to return to the shipyard. But Thomas, employed by one man instead of a company, couldn't be so sure of returning to his old employment. He might have to seek work elsewhere, in a job market in turmoil, with returning servicemen expecting to be reinstated at once, to the resentment of some of the women who had kept the shipyards and factories and shops going by taking over men's work. They had worked on the buses and trams, even carrying sacks of coal on their backs, and had enjoyed being independent at last, and earning decent wages.

Now many of them were rebelling against a return to their kitchen sinks and dependency once again on their menfolk. Many women whose men either didn't return or were too badly wounded to work were terrified of losing the wages they had become accustomed to, and ending up with their children in the poors' hospital.

As Miss Buchanan refused to allow what she called 'unnecessary adornments' among her workforce, Elspeth couldn't wear Thomas's little pebble brooch at work. She kept the silver threepenny bit hidden beneath her blouse, and several times that day she felt for its outline, wishing on it for Thomas.

When she got home that evening he was in the kitchen, peeling potatoes for his mother and grinning from ear to ear.

'He's not only willin' tae have me back, he's goin' tae buy himself a motorcar, and I'll have the job of looking after it and driving him and his family around as well as helping in the gardens,' he announced proudly. 'It's a good thing I learned tae drive in the army.'

'Here, give that knife tae Elspeth, now she's home, and let her see tae the potatoes,' Flora fussed, but Thomas shook his head.

'Elspeth's been workin' hard all day while I've been enjoying myself, getting to know Greenock again. I can see tae them.'

'It's not seemly, a grown man doing a woman's work!'

'Mam, in the army we'd tae turn our hands tae everything. If I'd a pound for every potato I've peeled in the past four years I'd not need to work ever again. Imagine,' he exulted, wielding the knife so vigorously that peelings flew all over the kitchen and Flora, always a thrifty housewife, was driven to the point of apoplexy, 'me, drivin' a fine car and gettin' paid for it!'

Two days later a letter arrived from the English hospital, advising against taking Lachlan away so soon. Flora's mouth tightened as she read it. 'He's been in hospitals quite long enough. It's time he was with his own folk.'

'Mam, the doctor's working with Lachlan just now, and if we give him a wee while longer—'

But Flora would have none of it. 'Write back, Thomas, and

tell them ye're on yer way there and they've tae let our Lachlan go.'

Thomas's eyes met Elspeth's, and his shoulders lifted in a faint shrug. 'Aye, Mam, if that's what ye want.'

As he didn't have to start working for Mr Bruce until the following Monday, he left for England early the next day, taking with him money that Flora had somehow managed to scrape together to pay for the train fares. That day and all during the next, as her sons travelled homewards, Flora worked on their room, hauling the narrow beds out from the walls, scrubbing the floor, polishing the small window and washing down the woodwork. She even managed to whitewash the ceiling and put some cream paint on the walls.

They were due home on Saturday, which meant that all the members of the family would be free to greet them. When Elspeth got back from the department store, breathless and red in the face from running all the way, Mattie was pacing the pavement outside the close, so wrapped up against the chill February air that only her red nose could be seen peeping from the scarves wound round her head. Elspeth could hear the breath whistling in the other girl's lungs.

'What are you doing out on a cold day like this?'

Mattie coughed wheezily into a mittened hand. 'Mam's been beating every cushion in the house, and my chest got so bad with the dust I had to get out of the place.'

'But she knows you can't take the dust! She shouldn't be beating cushions while you're home.'

'She can't see past Lachlan just now. She's so desperate to get things nice for him that everything else's gone clean out of her head. Go on up and see if the place is clear.'

Elspeth could smell the dust in the air as soon as she walked into the flat. Flora, down on her knees, giving the shining brass tongs and poker and hearthbrush an unnecessary final polish, looked as though she hadn't stopped working all morning.

'There ye are, at last. Put the kettle on, will ye? My throat's dry. Did ye see our Mattie on yer way home? I was wantin' her tae give me a hand, but she's been out half the morning.'

'She's outside in the cold wind, because the dust from the cushions brought her asthma on again.'

For a moment, Flora had the grace to look slightly ashamed, then she rallied. 'I couldnae have the place lookin' like a midden when Lachlan's coming home after all these years!'

'Aunt Flora, this house is never a midden, it's as clean and as neat as a palace.' Elspeth lit the gas ring under the kettle, then took a cup and saucer out of the cupboard.

'Ye can cut some bread and bring out the cheese, and we'll have somethin' tae keep us going.' Flora glanced at the clock and sucked her breath in. 'Would ye look at the time! Yer uncle and Rachel'll be home any minute. Fetch Mattie up and she can give ye a hand gettin' things ready for them.'

'She can't come up yet, Aunt Flora. I can still smell the dust in the air, it'll only make her chest worse.'

'Of course it won't – she's growin' out of the asthma, she's not as bad as all that,' Flora snapped. She had always gone out of her way to help Mattie during her bouts of asthma, sitting up at nights with the girl without a word of complaint, boiling kettles to create steam and making bread poultices to ease her daughter's chest. Now, guilt at having made Mattie ill in her eagerness to get everything ready for Lachlan brought a sharp note into her voice. 'Go down and fetch her.'

'She'll only start wheezing again as soon as she comes in. You'll need to wait until the dust—'

'That's enough, miss!' Flora McDonald snapped, her cheeks, already flushed with activity, flaring with added colour. 'Do as I say!'

Arguing would only have added fuel to her anger and precipitated yet another row between them, so Elspeth held her tongue and did as she was told. On the first landing she stopped and unbuttoned her coat so that she could fumble in her skirt pocket. She brought out some coins she had been paid that morning for writing two letters, balancing them thoughtfully on her outspread palm. They had been intended for the old tobacco tin used for saving money to pay for her evening classes, but today Mattie's need was greater than her own.

With a small, regretful sigh she slipped the coins into her coat pocket and continued on down the stairs.

Mattie was still pacing, her nose redder than before. 'Can I go up?' she asked eagerly when Elspeth appeared.

'The dust's still in the air. Aunt Flora says we're to buy three meat pies and have our dinner at Granjan's,' Elspeth lied, drawing the coins from her pocket. 'She gave me the money for them.'

Mattie's eyes brightened. 'I'm starving,' she admitted. 'And freezing.'

'Come on, then.' Elspeth linked arms with her and the two of them set off, walking as quickly as Mattie's breathing would allow. Aunt Flora was going to be awful angry, Elspeth thought as they went. The trouble she would get into when they returned would be well deserved for deceiving both her aunt and her cousin. But on the other hand, she couldn't have let Mattie go back up into the dusty air of the flat, or hang about any longer on the windy pavement.

11

For once, the angels were on her side. When she and Mattie, the latter breathing more easily now, returned to Mearns Street later that afternoon, Granjan was with them.

'Ye don't think I'm goin' tae let our Lachlan come back home from the war without his granny there tae greet him,' she had insisted, and Elspeth was happy to agree, knowing that Flora wouldn't make a fuss about her deception in front of Granjan.

The place was spick and span and dust-free, and Bob Cochran was waiting in the kitchen with the rest of the family, dressed, as they all were, in his Sunday best. He got up to let Granjan have his seat by the fire.

'Where have you two been?' Flora wanted to know.

'At Gran's,' Mattie answered cheerfully. 'We bought meat pies and had our dinner with her.'

'It was a kind thought, Flora hen,' Janet Docherty chimed in. 'The three of us had a good gossip, and all the dust's cleared out of the lassie's lungs now.'

Flora's eyes narrowed as they met Elspeth's. She opened her mouth to speak, but just then Mattie, at the window, shrieked, 'I see them – I see them!'

'Where?' There was a rush to the small window, and Mattie narrowly escaped being knocked into the sink by the crush of bodies at her back.

'There, look, coming up the hill.'

'It's them all right.' Bob's height gave him the advantage of being able to see over everyone else's heads. 'That's Thomas, carrying the suitcase, and the other—' He paused, then said, his voice puzzled, 'The other's surely Lachlan.'

'Now sit down, the lot of ye, and I'll go tae the door on my lone.' Flora's voice, trembling with anticipation, rang out over the excited chatter. 'Mind that the laddie's no' been well, and don't all rush at him at the one time.'

As the others did as they were bid, almost falling over each other in their haste to take their places, Elspeth craned across the small sink to look down at the street. She saw Thomas walking slowly towards the tenement building, a suitcase in one hand, the other holding the arm of the man who walked by his side, head bent, huddled into his coat.

Often in the past she had waited at this same window, watching for Lachlan returning from the shipyard. Despite the hard day's work he had just finished, he always ran up the hill effortlessly, craning to look up at the kitchen window, waving to her with both arms sawing through the air above his head. It had become a ritual for the two of them.

But if Lachlan was indeed Thomas's companion today, he was walking like a feeble old man. Some of the joy of seeing him again began to seep away, to be replaced by anxiety, and an eerie sense of dread.

It seemed a long time, long enough for them to exchange puzzled glances before they heard Flora opening the door and saying tremulously, 'Oh, Lachlan!'

When she finally came into the kitchen tears were trickling unashamedly down her face, and her smile was almost a grimace. 'Here he is, at last!' she announced, then, turning back to the door, 'Come on in, son. Everything'll be all right now ye're home.'

Lachlan came in hesitantly, stopping in the doorway as he took in the crowd waiting for him in the small kitchen. For a moment Elspeth thought that he was going to turn and go out again, then she heard Thomas say, low-voiced, 'Go on, you're doing fine,' and Lachlan McDonald, home from the war at last, stepped into the kitchen.

The greetings died in their throats. His head was down, his eyes fixed on the floor or on his hat, which was clutched between hands that turned it round and round unceasingly. His light brown hair was much longer than Thomas's, and untidy, as Lachlan's soft fine hair had always been, but the shine had gone from it and it hung lank and lifeless.

'Well, well.' Henry McDonald, swallowing back his shock at first sight of his younger son, got to his feet and moved to clap the young man's shoulder. Normally his large, strong hand landed on backs and shoulders heartily, but this time it paused for a fraction of a second in mid-air as Lachlan flinched, then landed gently, more of a caress than a clap. 'Welcome home, son,' Henry said, his voice gruff. 'Come on in and sit down – here, sit in my chair, near the fire.'

'He'd be best at the table, Da,' Thomas said swiftly, managing to reach round his brother's painfully thin figure to pull a chair out for him. He eased Lachlan out of his coat and into the chair, talking cheerfully all the time, his eyes, moving from one person to the next, carrying clear warning that Lachlan must be treated gently.

They all understood. One by one, they offered a few words, a touch of the hand. As Lachlan's pale, drawn face bobbed up at each of them through a ragged fringe of hair, his lips curved in a forced smile and he spoke their names – 'Mattie . . . Rachel . . . Elspeth . . . Gran' – in a slow, puzzled way, as though surprised to see them there. After each naming he ducked his head down again, pushing his chin against his chest as if he was afraid of drawing too much attention to himself.

Thomas stood behind and slightly to one side of him, his hand on Lachlan's stooped shoulder; now and again a quiver ran through Lachlan, and each time that happened Elspeth saw his brother's hold on his shoulder tighten very slightly in reassurance.

When they settled themselves round the table to eat, Thomas, beside Lachlan, talked cheerfully and continuously, though he himself looked exhausted, his face grey and his eyes heavy with strain. Every now and again he sprinkled his chatter with, 'Isn't that so, Lachlan?' or, 'Didn't we, Lachlan?' And each time Lachlan gave a quick, shy nod, and a muttered 'Aye.'

'We thought we'd never get here, didn't we, Lachlan? The train was busy, and it crawled all the way. I think myself it was an English train, with no liking for coming over the border, for it seemed tae get even slower after that. We were luckier than some, though, weren't we, Lachlan, for we found seats beside each other, and the hospital had given us a packet of sandwiches, so we didnae starve.'

It was painful to watch Lachlan's terror and the efforts he made to keep it under control. It was as though he was with hostile strangers, Elspeth thought, rather than his own bloodkin, the people he had grown up with. She wanted desperately to put her arms around him and hold him close, safe from the world. But she sensed that even a touch of her hand might send him into a panic.

Watching the way he pushed the food around his plate, it was clear to her that he should have stayed in the hospital until he was more able to face the world. She looked round the table, seeing the tears in Mattie's and Rachel's and Granjan's eyes, the stunned horror on Henry's face, and, even worse, the mingled incredulity and distaste on Bob Cochran's coarsely handsome features, and experienced a rush of anger at Flora for having insisted on dragging her son home with no thought to how he might feel about it.

Flora herself was clearly determined to make the most of the situation. Like Thomas, she talked cheerfully, pretending that everything was all right, even laughing now and again, a harsh, forced laugh that made Lachlan jump.

'D'ye not want yer nice mince?' she asked him, as though he was a child, when every other plate had been emptied and Lachlan's reduced to an unappetising congealing mush of meat, gravy and mashed potatoes. 'I made it specially for ye. It was always your favourite – mind how much ye liked it?'

'I think he got enough to eat on the train, Mam.' Thomas picked up the cold plate and handed it to her. 'They gave us a lot of sandwiches, didn't they, Lachlan?'

It was the same with the dumpling and custard. Scarcely a spoonful went into Lachlan's mouth, although Granjan and Elspeth, in an attempt to draw attention away from him, started up a conversation about nothing in particular, glaring at the others until they took the hint and joined in.

A few minutes later, glancing back at Lachlan, Elspeth was horrified to see a large tear drop from his lowered face into the yellow and brown soup he had made of his pudding. It was followed by another, then another.

'Thomas—' she began, just as Lachlan's shoulders began to shake and a muffled whimper escaped from his throat.

'I think it's time we went tae our beds,' said Thomas swiftly, getting to his feet. 'It's been a long day, and I'm tired out. You must be too, eh, Lachlan? Come on, old son,' he added gently, and his brother allowed himself to be eased to his feet and turned towards the door.

'I'll help ye,' Flora and Henry said at the same time, but Thomas shook his head.

'We'll be fine. We'll see ye in the mornin', eh?'

When the door had closed behind them, the people left at the table stared at each other blankly. Mattie began to weep, and Elspeth felt the tears she herself refused to shed forming a solid ball of grief in her throat.

'Mattie, stop behavin' like a daft wean!' Flora's voice was over-loud. 'We're all home together at last, and there's nothin' tae cry about! Ye'll take a cup of tea now, Mam?'

110

But Granjan excused herself, saying that it was time she was off home. Bob immediately offered to walk back to Nicolson Street with her, and Rachel said that she'd go too. Elspeth got the impression that Bob couldn't wait to get away from the flat.

Once the three of them had gone, Flora sent Mattie and Elspeth off to bed, announcing that she would wash the dishes herself. Although it was still early they went without argument.

'That's not our Lachlan at all,' Mattie burst out as soon as they were alone in the bedroom. 'What's happened to him?'

'I don't know.' Elspeth spoke with difficulty round the great lump of tears in her throat. 'But whatever it was, it must have been terrible.'

'Bringin' him home was a nightmare,' Thomas admitted to his family the following morning. Lachlan was still asleep, and the rest of them had gathered in the kitchen. 'It was hard for him tae be outside the hospital, with crowds of folk in the streets and the railway station, and in the train. Times I'd tae coax him every step of the way, and once when a train whistle blew he threw himself under a bench and I'd the devil's own job getting him tae come out again. We nearly missed our train over the head of it.'

His lips twisted in the ghost of a grin. 'I've never seen our Lachlan move as fast as that in my life. It gave one or two other folk a shock, too. The rest of the time he was clutching my arm so tight it felt as though it had been caught in a vice.' He rolled up his shirtsleeve to reveal the bruises made by Lachlan's fingers on his muscular, hairy arm.

He himself still showed some of the previous day's exhaustion, having had his sleep interrupted each time Lachlan awoke and cried out in terror at finding himself in unfamiliar surroundings.

'But he doesnae need tae be scared of anything now,' Flora fretted. 'He's home, in that room he's slept in ever since he was old enough tae spend a night away from my side.'

111

'I know, Mam, but Lachlan's not the laddie he used tae be,' Thomas tried to explain patiently. 'The things that happened tae him in the war have changed him. He's coming tae folk and things he used tae know like a stranger, seein' them for the first time. We must give him time tae get used tae being home again. The Sister at the hospital told me he took time tae settle in there, and the same'll have tae happen here.'

'But you haven't changed, Thomas, and Bob didn't change.' Rachel's pretty face was twisted with the effort of trying to understand. 'Why should Lachlan?'

'I've seen it happen tae more than one poor soul. Mebbe it's because they're more sensitive than the rest of us, mebbe it's because they were in the worst of the fighting, or mebbe a mixture of the two. There's no discredit tae them, for at times we all saw things that no human being should have tae see.' Thomas paused, his warm brown eyes darkening with bleak memories. Then he blinked, shrugging himself back to the present.

'It was easier for me, for we were moving on, over the French border and through Belgium, fightin' as we went. We'd a job tae do and we were able tae get on with it. But there was a time when Lachlan's unit was pinned down under fire for days on end, then more time spent advancing a wee bit, then being driven back again, then tryin' tae advance again. And they suffered heavy losses.'

'What can we do for him?' Flora wanted to know.

'Just – accept him, Mam. Don't try tae push him intae gettin' better. The doctor I saw says it's best just tae treat him gently. Let him know he's not on his lone, and leave him tae work things out in his own time.'

'I don't know how long the shipyard'll keep his job open for him,' Henry said doubtfully.

There was a note of suppressed irritation in Thomas's voice when he answered. 'Then he'll have tae find a new job when he's able, Da.'

'Will he ever get back to himself?' Mattie asked.

'Of course he will, given time.'

Elspeth, glancing at Thomas, saw the flicker of doubt that crossed his face as he spoke, and a shiver ran through her.

As Thomas had said, the Lachlan who had come back to them after the army finished with him wasn't the Lachlan they had known. It was as though some stranger had put on Lachlan's body as he might have shrugged on his jacket. It didn't quite fit, it didn't look right, and yet in some eerie way it was still undeniably Lachlan.

It was hard for them, but hardest of all for Lachlan. He spent most of his time huddled in Flora's armchair by the fire, or in his tiny bedroom, occasionally with a newspaper in his lap, though he rarely read it. He jumped at sudden noises or movements, and responded timidly and haltingly when spoken to, searching for the right words, his voice often tailing away in mid-sentence. At night, in the grip of nightmares, his screams frequently woke the entire household, and the neighbours too.

Used to working in the constant din and clatter of machinery in the shipyard, Henry McDonald tended as a result to speak loudly at all times, and to move about noisily at home. After startling Lachlan into a fit of hysteria when he barged noisily into the kitchen on his return from work on the day after the boy's arrival home, he had to work hard at learning to change his ways.

That first day alone in the house with Lachlan was bad for Flora. He panicked when he saw her getting ready to go to the shops, and was equally panic-stricken when she suggested that if he didn't want to be left alone, he could go with her. Finally she had to take her coat off, and stay at home. As it was her custom to shop each day, there was nothing in the house for that night's dinner. When Mattie arrived home from school she was sent back out again to buy pieces of fried fish for the evening meal, and Flora suffered the humiliation of seeing her family eat their first shop-cooked meal.

After that, Janet Docherty came every morning to sit with her grandson while Flora went to the shops. The old woman's placid nature was good for Lachlan; when she was there he relaxed more than he could with his mother, who watched him anxiously all the time, trying to anticipate his every need.

'Ye don't need tae treat the laddie as if he's made of fine china, Flora,' Janet tried to explain to her daughter. 'He'll no' break. It's just as if he's had a blow tae the head—'

'It's nothin' like that at all, Mam!' Flora swatted the words aside impatiently. 'It wasnae his head that got hurt, it was his arm – and what I'm sayin' is, how can a bullet in anyone's arm make them go the way our Lachlan's gone? Tell me that.'

'I didnae say he'd been hit on the head,' Janet said patiently. 'I'm just sayin' it's like a blow tae the head, and – wheesht for a minute, will ye, and let me explain,' she added as Flora opened her mouth to protest. 'If ye get a hard knock on the skull, ye feel all dazed and out of place for a minute, don't ye? Mind that time ye fell off the wash-house roof that ye'd no right tae be on in the first place, and ye felt dizzy for a whole day after it? That's the way poor Lachlan's feeling right now, with all that's been happenin' tae him.'

'But he's not just been like that for a day, has he? It's been months, from what we've heard, and there's no betterment.'

'Aye, well, as far as he's concerned, the fallin' off the wash-house roof business must've happened tae him time after time, day after day, and nob'dy knew, so it just kept gettin' worse and worse. The longer it went on and the worse it got, the longer it'll take him tae get over it,' Janet ended triumphantly. 'D'ye see?'

Flora sniffed. 'There's a queer difference between fallin' from a wash-house roof and bein' in a war,' she said, and Janet, realising that she wasn't going to best her daughter, held her peace and went back to her knitting.

Elspeth, who had come home for her midday meal, as she now did two or three times a week to see how Lachlan was, had been listening to the exchange, but for once she had the sense to keep out of it and avoid bringing Flora's wrath down on her head. But she was impressed by the old woman's grasp of the situation.

'How did you manage to work out all that about the wash-house roof, Granjan?' she wanted to know as the two of them went out of the close together, Janet heading back to her own home and Elspeth bound for the sewing room.

'Ach, there's nothin' tae it, hen. Christ did that sort of thing all the time in the New Testament tae explain things tae the folk, and if it's good enough for Him it's good enough for me,' Janet said breezily, adding, 'Mind you, I don't know if He'd've managed with his wee stories so well if a lot of the folk listenin' tae Him had been like our Flora.'

It was difficult to explain to friends and neighbours just what had happened to Lachlan. Normally when a soldier returned from the war, everyone in the tenement where his family lived, and sometimes everyone in the entire street, flocked to welcome him back and hear about his experiences. Lachlan had always been popular with young and old alike, and quite a few people were offended when asked not to come to the house on his return.

'Their experience of men getting hurt in the war's kept to bullet wounds or sword slashes, or coughing their lungs up from the gas,' Thomas explained to Elspeth. 'They can understand amputation and death, but not someone being hurt in the head without anything actually smashing through his skull.'

'You said there were a lot of soldiers hurt like Lachlan.'

'Aye, but some of them are still in hospitals, where Lachlan should still be, and there were some poor devils couldn't take it any more and took their own lives, while others' – Thomas stopped short, then went on cautiously, watching her from the corner of his eye – 'others were killed for it.'

'What d'you mean?'

'Shot as cowards, or as deserters.' Thomas's voice was so matter-of-fact that for a moment she couldn't take in what he was telling her. When she did, she gaped at him in horror.

'Killed by their own side, you mean?' There was something about the unexpected sight of blood and flesh normally kept

116

tidily where it should be, beneath intact skin, that made the onlookers' stomachs twist and knot in sudden revulsion. Elspeth had experienced it at school more than once, when a child tripped and cut its head open, or someone tore an arm on one of the spiked railings that surrounded the playground. She felt it now.

'That couldn't happen!'

'I've seen it, Ellie.' The bleak, dark look was in his eyes again. 'There was one in our own unit, a decent enough laddie, just seventeen years old. We could all see that it was gettin' tae him, but the officers wouldnae listen when some of us tried tae tell them. The way they saw things, a soldier had tae be brave all the time, else he was lettin' his king and country down. I sometimes wondered how the King himself would've managed if he'd been there instead of safe at home. Anyway, one day this poor lad couldnae take any more. We were goin' intae battle, and he threw his rifle away and started crying like a bairn. Crying for his mam, he was, with his eyes squeezed shut and his mouth open and the tears and the snot runnin' down his face.'

'What happened?'

'They arrested him, and held a court martial as soon as they could. Then they found a bit of wall that was still standing and they stood him up against it with a blindfold round his eyes, and they shot him. He wasnae the only one it happened tae, but he was the only one I knew as a comrade.'

Elspeth felt sick. 'Did his parents know?'

Thomas's shoulders had hunched as he relived the experience. Now they straightened, and he went on polishing his shoes for work the next day. They got muddy, working in the Bruce gardens, but Thomas liked to start the day with clean shoes, and he always scraped off all the mud and polished them every evening.

'They were told he died in the line of duty. At least they never knew the truth of it, and there's not one man in the unit that'd tell them different if he was tae meet up with them. So now ye know why our Lachlan's one of the lucky ones, in spite of what he's goin' through just now. That's why I'll do anything I must tae get him better. I'm not lettin' the army destroy my brother the way they destroyed that laddie and all the others, pushing them intae a hell they couldnae handle, then punishing them for allowin' it tae get tae them.'

It was difficult for Elspeth to explain about Lachlan to the girls at work. They all knew that her foster brothers had come back safely from the war, but nobody could understand why, with his arm wound fully healed, Lachlan showed no signs of returning to the shipyard.

Lena, who had an eye for the opposite sex and had tried on several occasions to coax Elspeth to agree to a visit to the local Hippodrome in a foursome – the two of them, Thomas, and Lachlan – couldn't understand it at all. 'If he's got the right number of arms and legs and he's not even lost his sight like some poor buggers have, why's he ill?' she wanted to know. 'What else can be wrong with him?'

'It's his head—' Elspeth began, then, realising that they would all think she was talking about a head wound, she amended it to, 'I mean, inside his head.'

'Ye mean he's a daftie?' one of the girls suggested, and Elspeth rounded on her.

'I do not! Our Lachlan's a clever lad – everyone knows that!'

'Aye – clever enough tae pretend that there's somethin' wrong with him when there's nothin' at all,' Betty Jardine sneered. 'If you ask me, he's just swinging the lead.' Betty's brother and one of her cousins and the young man she had been walking out with had all been killed during the war. She and her family had suffered badly, and because of this she was treated more gently than usual by the rest of the girls, though she was sharp-tongued and carping by nature, and before her tragic losses she had been thoroughly disliked.

'He's not! How dare you say such a thing about our Lachlan!' Elspeth was furious, and close to tears with frustration.

'What else is there tae say?' Betty shot back, and there was a murmur of agreement round the large table. Elspeth stopped her sewing machine and half rose from her seat, sheer rage closing her mind to everything but the need to punish Betty for the terrible things she was saying about gentle, suffering Lachlan. Just then Miss Arnold walked in, her presence putting a stop to what might have become a nasty confrontation, and the girl sitting next to Elspeth grabbed her skirt and hauled her back down to her chair.

'Just as well,' Lena said during the midday break. 'That Betty's got sharp fingernails on her, hen. Ye might've got the worst of it – and lost yer job, too.'

'I'll not have her saying such things about our Lachlan,' Elspeth muttered sullenly, but she was secretly relieved that the overseer had arrived when she did.

She had only once in her life been involved in a fight, and that had been a shoving and hair-pulling playground clash with another six-year-old who had tried to steal her new pencil-case. Even now the memory of it made her face burn with shame. She vividly recalled the humiliation of being made to stand in front of the entire class afterwards, the shocked outrage in her teacher's voice as she said, 'Elspeth Bremner, I never thought I'd see you behaving like a guttersnipe!' The final word, spoken with the utmost contempt, had hurt her far more than the two strokes of the belt the teacher had then delivered on her small, wincing palm.

A month after she started work, two of the women from the packing department had come to blows in the basement room during the midday break, kicking and clawing, dragging at each other's hair, screeching like harlots, and eventually rolling on the ground, with a crowd gathered round them, yelling encouragement. Elspeth had stayed well back, the sound of the fight stirring unpleasant memories of her own single lapse.

119

Both women, eventually separated by a floorwalker drawn to the scene by the noise, had been dismissed on the spot. The very thought that the same thing could have happened to her if Miss Arnold hadn't come in when she did made her cringe, and resolve to say nothing in future about her home life, or Lachlan.

He had been damaged as cruelly as any man blinded or crippled in the war. The real tragedy of it was that in Lachlan's case, nobody could see the wounds.

Although it was only April, the sun was warm on Thomas McDonald's back as he raked and smoothed the gravel of the long curving driveway leading to Overton, the Bruces' house. Occasionally he stopped to stretch and ease stiffened muscles, leaning on the long-handled rake and taking a moment to look about him.

One side of the drive was bordered by a wall of rhododendrons a good twelve feet high. In a month's time they would be studded with crimson and pink and white flowers, each as large as a dinner plate. Where Thomas stood, almost at the top of the drive and near the point where the gravel opened out into a great forecourt in front of the graceful grey-stone mansion, the opposite side of the drive was a smooth grassy bank topped by a row of peony bushes. They had already started blooming, each individual blossom made up of hundreds of tight-packed velvety crimson petals. Beyond, in flowerbeds dotted over the smooth green lawns, the last of the daffodils and tulips could still be seen, and in the woods edging the estate, where he had been working the day before, he had seen stretches of bluebells beneath the trees. Thomas loved this place, and had clung to the memory of it during the war. To him, the gardens of Overton represented peace and serenity and an assurance that while they were there, nothing totally evil could happen.

Returning to his work, he thought of Lachlan, sitting at

home day after day, and longed to bring him to this place with its wide sweeps of smooth green lawn, the walled kitchen and rose gardens, and the lily pond. Surely in gardens like these, with grassed paths leading between flowering bushes to secret little glades, each holding a surprise – a sundial, a huge stone urn filled with flowers, a statue, a graceful gazebo to rest in – his brother's troubled mind would mend.

Thomas believed in the healing power of the open sky and the sight and smell and touch of growing things. He had tried to persuade Lachlan to walk with him to the open land behind Greenock, where they had once played as boys, but Lachlan had lost his nerve once he got to the street, and bolted back to the flat.

It would help if Lachlan could be transported most of the way in the handsome dark blue car now standing in a former carriage-house at the rear of the Bruce house. But Mr Bruce wasn't the kind of man to permit his car to be used for the benefit of his chauffeur-cum-gardener's brother.

Thomas's mouth was dry; he looked up at the sun, and estimated that soon it would be time to go round to the kitchen for a cool glass of lemonade, unless Ina brought one out to him before then.

Ina, one of the Bruces' housemaids, had shown her interest in him from his first day back after the war. She was a pretty girl, with large blue eyes and fair curly hair, and Thomas had been happy to start walking out with her.

Hooves crunched along the drive from the double gate and Thomas moved to the verge and kept working. To his surprise the horse stopped instead of passing by.

'Hello. I thought you were the chauffeur now.'

Startled, he looked up at the girl sitting straight-backed in the saddle.

'I'm a gardener as well, Miss Aileen, when the motorcar's not needed.' The smart grey chauffeur's uniform, complete with gloves and peaked cap, was kept in a small room off the kitchen, so that he could change into it when the car was required.

'Isn't gardening a comedown after driving the car?'

'Not for me, I like working in the garden just as much as I like driving.'

'D'you like horses too?'

Thomas glanced at the handsome chestnut she rode. 'Yes, miss.'

'In that case,' Aileen Bruce said hopefully, 'would you mind very much taking Cavalier round to the stables for me? I should do it myself, but I've stayed out too long and we have guests arriving soon. I must go and change or my mother'll be furious.'

'Of course, miss.' Thomas laid the rake down carefully on the grass verge and went to the handsome chestnut cob, taking the reins in one hand and running the other down the animal's soft nose. The girl slipped from the saddle with ease to stand beside him, her own hand caressing the horse's neck. The other took off her brown leather peaked cap to reveal sleek black hair cut close to her neat skull.

'He's beautiful, isn't he?' She spoke easily, as though Thomas was a friend rather than one of her father's employees. 'I should stay with him until he's been unsaddled and rubbed down and settled into his stall – it's a poor rider who doesn't look after her mount, you know – but I daren't upset Mother. Give my abject apologies to Alfred, and tell him I promise it'll never ever happen again.'

'Yes, miss.' Thomas glanced down at the girl, a good head smaller than he was, and suddenly the world shifted abruptly on its axis. He had often seen her in the gardens, a pigtailed schoolgirl, but while he was away she had become a beautiful woman, and this was the first time he had ever been so close to her. He stared, unable to help himself, at her perfect face, the vivid green, thick-lashed eyes looking up into his.

She blinked, then glanced away from him and back at the

horse. 'Thanks,' she said, then, as though she could no more help it than he could, she looked into Thomas's eyes again.

They might have stood there forever, if a voice hadn't called her name. Wrenching his eyes from her, looking over her head, Thomas saw his employer's wife standing at the top of the steps.

'I'd better go – thanks again,' Aileen Bruce said, and set off at a run across the great sweep of gravel to the house. The scarlet jersey she wore with fawn riding breeches made an exotic splash of colour against the grey walls, and a shaft of sunlight on her black hair made it gleam like a blackbird's wing as she followed her mother into the house.

Thomas watched until she had disappeared, then ran his free hand through his own hair, which had grown longer since he came home from the army, and had fallen into its usual casual waves. He clicked his tongue at the horse and gave its warm silky neck a final caress before leading it round the side of the house, towards the stables.

'We'll never manage it!'

'We will, Aunt Flora.' Elspeth put another pin into the paper pattern, and slid the muslin cloth carefully along the table so that she could reach the next stretch of pattern.

'We'll have to manage, for I'm not letting Annie Cochran outdo me.' Rachel emphasised her words by stabbing at the air with a large pair of scissors.

'I don't know why ye didnae just insist on waitin' till the end of the year, like we agreed,' her mother lamented, pushing back a strand of hair that had come loose from the bun at the back of her head.

'Because I want to get married, and it's a long time till the end of the year.'

'Aye, well, ye'll find that marriage lasts a long time too,' Flora muttered. Her face was red and shiny, for it was a lovely day outside, and the kitchen was hot. They had tried opening the window, only to close it again because the refreshing breeze had riffled the cream-coloured muslin Rachel had chosen for her wedding dress, making it impossible for them to cut it out.

Rachel paid no heed to her mother. 'Anyway, it means that we'll have a nice wedding breakfast in a hotel, instead of all crowding in here.'

'Da's not pleased about that – there's no drink sold in the Anderson Waverley Temperance Hotel,' Mattie put in from the window, where she was perched on the draining board, stitching a broad brown ribbon round a straw hat.

'It'll not do him any harm tae drink lemonade for once,' Flora told her, adding, 'If we ever get there.'

Bits of ribbon and material lay all over the kitchen. It was as bad, Elspeth thought, pinning another section of pattern and material together, as the time the sewing room at Brodie's were all trying to get Catherine Bruce's wedding trousseau ready.

Ever since Bob Cochran had come home from the war he and Rachel had been saving and planning for their wedding on New Year's Eve, the traditional date for Scottish marriages since it enabled the happy couple to start both a new year and a new life together. But at the end of April Bob's parents had suggested that since his sister Annie was marrying in May, there should be a double wedding, followed by a joint reception in the back hall of the Anderson Waverley Temperance Hotel in West Blackhall Street. The booking was made possible because Archie Cochran, Bob's father, was a leading member of the local temperance movement.

With very little time in which to prepare for the wedding, life in the McDonald household had become chaotic. By some miracle, Bob had managed to find a two-roomed flat to rent down by the river, and he and a band of helpers, including Thomas and Henry, were working there at that moment in an effort to make the place habitable in time.

'Where's the light brown thread?' Flora asked, and they all stopped what they were doing to hunt for the elusive bobbin.

When it was finally located under a pile of ribbons, she dislodged Mattie from the draining board so that she could get enough light to see as she threaded her needle.

'I'm tellin' ye,' she said again, her eyes crossing as she tried to fix them on the thread wavering close to the needle's eye, 'we'll never manage it.'

'We will so, Mam.' Now that she was almost a married woman, Rachel felt bold enough to defy her mother. 'We will.'

They did. And, thought Elspeth as she stood in the hotel's back hall watching Rachel dance past on Bob's arm, her pretty face glowing with happiness and excitement beneath the bell-shaped brim of her straw hat, it had been worth it. It was a lovely wedding, marred only by Lachlan's absence. Thomas had volunteered to stay at home with him, but Flora wouldn't hear of it.

'Ina'll be expecting you to take her, and Mam's already said she'll keep Lachlan company, so that's that decided.'

'Of course, we all know why the Cochrans were so eager,' Elspeth heard Flora murmur now as the other happy couple whirled past on the small dance floor. 'They had tae get their Annie married off quickly. Would ye look at the size of her?'

'Ach, Annie was always a plump lassie,' Henry said placatingly. Seeing him glance at the glass of lemonade in his hand before taking a tentative sip, Elspeth nudged Mattie's elbow and both girls stifled giggles. Clearly, Henry McDonald was missing his usual glass of beer, and wishing that his daughter's new in-laws weren't in the temperance movement.

'Don't talk nonsense, Henry – Annie Cochran was solid all over before, not just in front.' Flora tugged at her new gloves. 'She's either gone too far too soon with that young man of hers, or the fat's slipped.'

She brushed a piece of thread from the skirt of the dark green suit she had bought just before the war. It was a bit tight for her now, and as it was a heavy winter suit she was hot, but she couldn't bring herself to take the long jacket off, for she was tormented by the suspicion that the skirt fastenings, unable to hold her in place any longer, might give way, treating the wedding guests to a glimpse of her petticoated hip bulging through the gap.

'It'll mebbe be our Thomas's turn next, him and Ina,' she added, spotting her elder son's fair head among the dancers. 'If they get married, mebbe Mr Bruce'll give them a nice house on the estate.'

13

'Which of you,' Miss Arnold asked from the door of the sewing room, her voice so cold that the words might have been carved from ice, 'is the girl who apparently had the audacity to touch the typewriting machine in the accounts office?'

Elspeth felt as though someone had hit her hard and unexpectedly in the stomach with a rolling pin. The material she was holding dropped from her fingers; her mouth dried and her face flamed as a shockwave ran through her entire body.

Lena, too, was stunned into blushing confusion by the question, coming as it did so long after the crime had been committed. Before she could prevent herself she turned and looked at Elspeth, but even if she had been able to hide her reaction, it would have made no difference, since the culprit's guilt was so obvious that every eye in the room, including Miss Arnold's, was on her.

'I—' Elspeth started to speak, but no sound came out. She cleared her throat and tried again. 'It was me, Miss Arnold.'

'And when was this?'

'When we were working late on Miss Bruce's wedding clothes. You sent me to the office—'

'I sent— I did no such thing!'

'Yes you did.' Elspeth was too caught up in the need to explain to realise that she was not only contradicting Miss Arnold, but implicating her. 'It was when we were busy with

127

Miss Bruce's trousseau, and you sent me to ask Mr James for a list.'

The woman's face crimsoned. 'For a list – not to make free of the office and touch things!'

'She didnae dae any harm.' Lena rushed to defend her friend. 'You sent me as well, Miss Arnold, and I saw what happened. She just touched the machine, then Mr James came in and—'

'That's enough! Get on with your work. As for you, Elspeth Bremner, you're to go at once to Mr James's office!'

Elspeth's knees were so weak that she could scarcely walk along the corridor. She swallowed convulsively several times, blinking hard to clear her sight, which had misted over. How could Mr James do this to her? How could he be so cruel, waiting for months before deciding to punish her for her lapse?

Then a far more frightening question crowded into her head, obliterating her anguish over James Brodie's betrayal. What was Aunt Flora going to say?

By the time she reached the accounts office she had made up her mind that when the ordeal to come was over she would walk out of the department store with her head high – then run away somewhere, anywhere. She couldn't face Flora and tell her that she had been dismissed for bad conduct, with no reference to show to a future employer.

In the accounts office the typewriting machine, the cause of Elspeth's shameful downfall, sat smugly on its table in the corner, shrouded by its dust cover. A young man and an older woman were sitting on tall stools at the high sloping desk running along the opposite wall, each writing in large ledgers.

The woman twisted her head over her shoulder. 'Yes?'

'I'm—' Elspeth swallowed hard, then tried again. 'I'm to see Mr James. I was sent from the sewing room.'

The young man looked up, his gaze sweeping her from top to toe.

'Oh, yes,' the woman said, and to Elspeth, the words had an

ominous sound. Everyone, it seemed, knew about her crime. 'He's expecting you.' She nodded at the closed door leading to the inner office. 'Knock on the door first, and wait till he tells you to go in.'

Wiping her palms nervously down the sides of her serviceable blue skirt, Elspeth approached the door, knocked tentatively, waited for a moment, then knocked again.

'It's all right, he only bites on Wednesdays,' the young man said. She turned, surprised, to be met by a wide grin.

'You've got enough to do without poking your nose in where it isn't wanted, Graham Adams!' the woman snapped, just as a voice shouted, 'Come in!' from the office.

Elspeth, faced with the choice of confronting James Brodie again or showing abject cowardice and running away, grappled with the door handle and almost plunged forward into the lion's den without giving herself further time to think.

'Yes?' The man who had caught her tampering with the office typewriter looked up from his crowded desk.

'You wanted to see me, Mr James? Elspeth Bremner,' she added as he stared blankly at her.

'And what did I want to see you ab—?' he began, then recognition came into his eyes. 'You're the one I found typewriting that night.'

'Yes, sir.'

'Your friend said you went to night school?'

'Yes, sir. I've been studying for eighteen months. Typewriting and shorthand, and book-keeping,' she added, since he seemed to be expecting her to go into detail.

'And what does a seamstress want with book-keeping and all the rest of it?'

'I – I want to work in an office one day,' she said, then shied back nervously as he got up and surged round the desk towards her, dislodging a pile of papers as he went. He and Elspeth both caught at it as it prepared to launch itself into space, then Mr Brodie took a sheet from the top.

129

'This'll do.' He opened the office door. 'Follow me, Elspeth Bremner.'

She did, and together they surveyed the covered typewriting machine, until Mr James said impatiently, 'Well? It's a good machine but it hasn't learned to uncover itself yet, so take the cover off, sit down and put some paper into it. Now,' he went on when she had done as she was told, 'make it type something.'

'What, sir?'

'Anything – I just want to see if you know what you're doing.'

'The cat sat on the nat,' Elspeth typed, then, professional pride overcoming fear, she pushed the carriage back and corrected her mistake. 'The cat sat on the mat,' the second line said, with confidence. As her fingers recognised the familiar, pleasant sensation of keys yielding beneath them, the third line appeared. 'Peter Piper picked a peck of pickled peppers.'

'Now try copying that.' The paper he had brought with him was thumped down beside the typewriter. Elspeth picked it up and looked at it, appalled. It was a long handwritten list of materials, complete with measurements and prices which would, she knew, have to be laid out in neatly spaced columns.

'What's the matter?' James Brodie asked from above her head. 'Do they only teach you quotations and nursery rhymes at the night school?'

'No, sir, but – I'll need môre paper.'

'Then take that one out, and put another one in,' he said, exasperated.

'Excuse me, Mr James, I think the lassie would do better on her own, without anyone standing over her,' the woman at the desk suggested.

'Hmmpphh. Very well, Elspeth Bremner, bring the copy to me when you've finished it – and I'll expect to see it before the sun sets and the moon comes up,' the manager said, and stamped back into his small office, shutting the door noisily behind him.

When a fresh sheet had been rolled into the machine, Elspeth, grateful that she had reached tabulating in her studies, set up the machine, and began to type.

Ten minutes later she laid the typed sheet on James Brodie's desk, with the original list beside it. He picked them both up, comparing them line by line, while she waited, hands linked. In spite of her confusion and bewilderment, she had enjoyed typing again, and the need for concentration had soothed her.

'Very good,' he said at last. 'Go back to the sewing room now, and tell Miss Arnold that I'd be grateful if she would allow you to begin tomorrow morning at half past eight sharp.'

'Begin?'

'Begin,' he repeated, then, eyebrows raised, 'Did she not tell you?'

'Tell me what – Mr James,' she added hurriedly.

He laid the papers down. 'What d'you think you're here for?'

'To be dismissed, because I typed on the typewriter that time.'

'Well, well,' James Brodie said thoughtfully. 'Isn't that a bit of malice?' Then, just as Elspeth opened her mouth to assure him that she had intended no malice at all, but had only wanted to try the typewriter, he returned to the business in hand. 'The fact of the matter is, Miss Bremner, my typist has fallen ill and I need someone to take her place until she comes back. I recalled being told that you were taking lessons, and so I asked Miss Arnold to send you along. You may go now – and remember, half past eight, and not a minute later. There's a lot to be done.'

She ran all the way home from work that afternoon, bursting into the flat to announce that she was to leave the sewing room and work in the department store office and be a real typewriter, for a little while, at least. Mattie and Rachel were delighted for her, and when he came home, Thomas picked her up and swung her about the room.

'Good for you, Ellie!'

Uncle Henry joked about Elspeth running her own office next, and Auntie Flora said that Elspeth had done well – then launched into a lecture about the need for her to mind her manners and do as she was told and not make a nuisance of herself in the accounts office.

'She's not going tae make a nuisance of herself, Mam.' Thomas was brushing his shoes, and preparing to meet Ina on her evening off. 'They need our Ellie's talents – she'll do well for herself, just wait and see.' Even Lachlan smiled and hugged her and said how pleased he was. Then, putting the tip of a finger against the little silver threepenny piece at her throat, 'It's brought you luck right enough.'

'It has,' she agreed, and wished that she could find some way of bringing a little luck to Lachlan, who sorely needed it.

It wasn't until that night that she remembered Mr James's comment about malice, and told Mattie.

'I thought he meant me, touching the typewriter when I shouldn't have, but now I'm thinking it was Miss Arnold he was talking about, not telling me why he wanted to see me.'

'Jealous old cat,' Mattie said absently, peering at a textbook. The single cot had been taken out of their room when Rachel married, giving them a bit more space. Mattie was studying, sitting on her haunches at the end of the double bed, while Elspeth herself, leaning against a pillow propped against the bedhead, was writing letters, using her drawn-up knees as a desk.

'It's all water under the bridge now. No harm was done, after all.' Elspeth put the writing pad aside and eased herself on to her knees, her face alight. 'The important thing – the wonderful thing – is that I'm going to get to work in an office!'

'Until the real girl comes back, just,' Mattie cautioned.

'Even so, I'm going to be able to type all day long.'

'And this time,' Mattie cast her work aside too and bounced

up on her own knees, taking Elspeth's hands in hers, 'you're going to get paid for it!'

It had been cloudy all day, threatening rain, but not following the threat through until early afternoon, when Thomas, giving a final trim to the box hedging round some herbaceous borders, felt the first drops on the back of his neck. He ignored them, and worked on, but within minutes the rain was falling hard and fast, soaking him, and there was no sense in continuing.

The nearest shelter was a small hexagonal summerhouse in the nearby rose garden; Thomas pulled up the collar of his thick working shirt, and ran, skidding slightly on the wet paving stones between the rose beds. He cleared the three steps up to the summerhouse in one stride, threw open the double doors with their diamond-shaped panes of coloured glass set into the top sections, and catapulted into the little building.

Something already inhabiting the space within moved and gave a shriek of fright. Before he could stop himself, Thomas, too, gave out a sharp, startled cry, then felt like a complete fool as he saw Aileen Bruce crouched against the opposite wall, green eyes wide, one hand pressed to her mouth and the other to her heart, a handful of rosebuds scattered on the floor round her feet.

For a moment he stared at her dumbly, unable to believe that she was really there. Ever since the day he had spoken to her in the drive, Thomas had been unable to get the girl out of his mind. He saw her occasionally, on the tennis court, or out riding, or sitting a short distance behind him as he drove her and her parents. He had developed a strange sixth sense where she was concerned – when she was nearby he knew it, even before he actually saw her.

Once, when she was gathering flowers for the house, he had cut off a spray of lilac that was difficult for her to reach. He would never forget the light, sweet touch of her hand against his as she took the spray, the wide smile as she thanked him.

'Thomas! I thought – you came barging in like—' She gave a nervous giggle. 'I feel such a fool.'

'So do I.' In his dreams over the past months he had rescued her several times from runaway horses, or saved her from drowning. In reality, he thought grimly, sick with humiliation, he had gone crashing into the summerhouse and scared the life out of her. Desperate to get out of the confined space and go somewhere where he could slam his fist, or at least his stupid head, against the good solid trunk of a tree, he muttered an apology and turned to the door, just as the shower settled in and rain started drumming hard on the wooden roof just above their heads.

'Wait – you'll get soaked out there. There's room for us both.' She moved forward to stop him, then gave an exclamation and bent to pick up a rosebud. 'Oh, the poor thing, I've stepped on it.'

'Let me, miss, some of those thorns are wicked.'

'They can draw your blood just as easily as mine,' she objected as he knelt to gather the roses.

'I'm used to thorns.' He picked the flowers up and laid them carefully in the trug she held out to him.

'You must think I'm empty-headed, screaming and giggling like that,' she said, sitting down on the bench and settling the trug by her side.

He wanted to tell her that he thought she was the most beautiful, most wonderful woman he had ever met. Instead, he cleared his throat and said, 'Not at all, Miss Aileen. I've seen plenty of men during the war yelling because they thought a shell was going to get them, then laughing like idiots with the relief when it didn't. I've done it myself.'

'You were in the war? So was my brother. He enjoyed it.'

No doubt he had, Thomas thought grimly. Ian Bruce, an arrogant, handsome young man with never a glance or a word for the servants, was employed by a firm of lawyers in Glasgow, and lived in the city, driving to Gourock most weekends in his own smart two-seater car. When he was at home during the summer there were tennis parties, either on the Bruce court, which was kept in immaculate condition for them, or at friends' courts.

Ian Bruce, Thomas thought, would have been an officer. True, some of the officers had suffered just as much as their men, but others – and he had a feeling that Bruce was one of them – had never really had to face the realities. Aloud, he said bluntly, 'There's not much pleasure in killing and being killed.'

'Tell me about your war.'

He could have told her about the mud and the misery and the naked fear. He could have talked about the helpless certainty at times that the war would never ever stop, that he and those with him would spend the rest of their lives struggling with the enemy for a few hundred square yards of ground that for some unknown reason mattered tremendously to both sides.

He could have told her about the times when all he had wanted was to feel the impact of that final, fatal bullet, and get it all over and done with; about what it was like to see close friends screaming and dying.

Instead, his words underlined by the rain hammering on the roof, he told her about Lachlan, and what the war had done to him.

She listened without interruption, her green eyes luminous in the summerhouse's dim light. 'That's – terrible,' she said, when he had finished. 'That poor young man. My brother made it all sound like a bit of a lark. I'd no idea what it was really like.'

Thomas came back to earth with a jolt, cursing himself all over again for his stupidity. Her brother had probably tried to protect her from the truth, and he had come lumbering along and told her things she should never have heard.

'It was a bit of a lark, quite a lot of the time,' he lied. 'I expect your brother made a better job of it than I did.'

'I expect,' said Aileen Bruce shrewdly, 'that his war was easier than yours. What's going to become of your brother? Will he get better?'

'I don't know,' Thomas said honestly. 'I keep telling the rest of them that he'll be fine, but it's been so long now that I'm not sure. The nightmares have almost gone, but he's not got any of his confidence back.'

'Would a doctor not be able to help?'

'No!' He spoke so fiercely that she jumped. 'He's had his fill of doctors and nursing. I should have insisted on him staying in that hospital for a while longer instead of bringing him home because my mother wanted it. They might have made a difference then. But it's too late now tae think of ifs and buts. If we were tae send him back tae hospital now it would only make him think we'd given up, or that we don't want him. Besides, it'd more likely be the asylum now than the hospital, and I'm not having our Lachlan put intae that place.'

He stared down at his hands. 'Mam – my mother – she's beginning tae treat him as if he was a bairn again, and that's not good for him. The other day I caught her running a brush through his hair. Next thing we know she'll be dusting him, as if he was part of the furn—'

He halted, realising that something was missing, and glanced up at the roof. 'The rain's stopped.'

They made for the door at the same time, reaching out for the latch simultaneously, so that his hand landed on hers.

'I think, miss—' he started, just as she began, 'Perhaps we should—' Then they both stopped, laughing. She was so close that he could smell her skin, fresh and flowery, like a summer's day. He began to remove his hand from hers, but just then Aileen turned her own hand round so that their fingers became entwined. The trug fell to the floor for the second time, and her other hand came up to touch his face lightly, then moved over his shoulder to the nape of his neck, while his arm reached around her waist, drawing her closer.

Ina kissed boldly, her mouth open and her tongue teasing his, but Aileen Bruce's kiss was chaste and innocent, and all the sweeter for that.

It was a short kiss, but long enough for Thomas's entire life to change for ever. When they separated and he looked down into her face, he saw her eyes filled with the things he himself wanted to say. He bent towards her again, then a voice calling some distance away broke the embrace and sent them springing away from each other.

'I'm – I'm sorry, Miss Aileen, I had no right—'

The hand that had cupped the nape of his neck touched his mouth, stopping the words. 'I wanted you to kiss me,' she said, then, with sudden urgency, 'You must go. I'll find you tomorrow.'

Blessed by the rain, the garden smelled fresh and faintly perfumed, like her skin. Thomas, dazed by what had just happened, and by the strength of his own reaction, blundered out of the summerhouse and through the bushes, heedless of the light sting of branches against his face, and the soaking he got from them.

He reached the place where he had been working just in time; as he retrieved the shears from under the bush where he had stored them, Aileen and her brother met at the other side of the tall beech hedge a few yards away from him.

'I've been looking for you everywhere,' Ian Bruce said irritably. 'Where have you been?'

'Picking roses. I took shelter in the summerhouse.' Her voice, Thomas thought, stirring to the memory of her mouth beneath his, was like little bells chiming.

He bent his head over his work just as the two of them turned the corner and came towards him.

'If you wanted flowers,' Ian Bruce said shortly, ignoring the figure kneeling at the side of the path, 'you should have asked one of the gardeners to get them for you. That's what they're there for.'

'I'm quite capable of doing things for myself,' she retorted, then they were past, and Thomas looked up as they went through an archway of green and out of sight, Ian Bruce carrying the basket of rosebuds, his free arm about his sister's shoulders.

The thought came to him that while Ina fitted snugly in his arms, Aileen Bruce belonged in them. He knew what his grandmother would have said if she had known what had happened in the summerhouse: 'It'll all end in tears!'

Maybe so, but he had never been happier in his entire life than he was at that moment.

14

The typewriter clacked nonstop, turning out a continuous flow of lists, letters, and memorandums to the many departments housed within Brodie's store. As the days flew past, Elspeth's confidence grew and her initial shyness eased off. James Brodie was a fair employer, a man who put in a decent day's work and expected the same of his staff. He didn't hover over them all the time as Miss Arnold and Miss Buchanan did in the sewing room, nor, if he was in a bad mood, did he vent it on them. Wilma Morgan, the older woman, was a sharp-eyed clerkess who ruled over the accounts office, but was friendly enough as long as she was given the respect she considered due to one who had worked there for ten years. Graham Adams, still serving his apprenticeship as a clerk, was a cheerful nineteen-year-old with ambition.

'If I play my cards right, I'll be the boss in here, in time,' he bragged to Elspeth when Wilma and Mr Brodie were out of the office.

She pressed the tabulating key, and the large heavy carriage sped on its way, then crashed to a standstill at the correct place. 'D'you think so?'

'The way I see it, once the old man dies and Mr James inherits the store, he won't want to be stuck here day in and day out. He's got no choice just now, for his dad expects him to do as he did. He never missed a day at his desk himself, until the bronchitis got worse and he had to stay at home.

Imagine owning a place like this and sitting behind a desk like one of the staff!'

He had swung round on his high stool and was leaning back against the sloping desk, his elbows hooked nonchalantly on the ridge that prevented the heavy ledgers from sliding off. 'Once Mr James owns the place, I reckon he'll want to have more time for yachting. He's got his own boat at Gourock – takes it out every Saturday afternoon, and does some racing in it, too. He'll want a second-in-command here, and that'll be me.'

He jabbed at his own chest confidently with a thumb. 'So keep in with me, Elspeth, and you could do well for yourself.'

'I'm not going to be here for long. The typist'll be back one of these days, then I'll have to go back to the sewing room.'

'I can still do you some good there, for Mr James's manager would be in charge of all the departments.'

Elspeth rolled a sheet of paper out of the typewriter and put a fresh sheet in. 'I won't be here by then. I don't want to spend the rest of my life as a seamstress. I want to work in an office.'

'I could arrange that for you, when I'm in charge.' He paused; although she was concentrating on her work, he knew that he was running his eyes over her, a habit of his that she disliked intensely. 'Have you got a sweetheart?'

'My aunt says I'm too young.'

'What age are you, then?'

Lena would have come up with a pert return, or slapped his face for his cheek. Elspeth merely answered the question. 'I'm fifteen.'

'A bit young, but still, I'm not particular,' Graham said magnanimously. 'I'll take you out tonight, if you like.'

'I'm visiting my grandmother tonight.'

'Tomorrow.'

'I'm helping my Aunt Flora to do the weekend cleaning.'

'When, then?'

He was smirking confidently, appearing to think that Elspeth would be flattered by his attentions. Instead, she merely found his persistence irritating. What with the excitement over her temporary move to the office, worry about Lachlan, and her letter-writing she had enough to think about.

'I don't know.'

Graham's eyes hardened and his mouth turned down at the corners. 'I'll not wait around for ever.'

'I'd not expect you to,' she retorted, just as Wilma's heavy tread could be heard in the corridor outside. Graham spun round to the desk, snatching up his pen.

'Damn!' he muttered, and Elspeth glanced up to see a large blot of ink, dislodged from the pen as he grabbed it, spread itself over the page he had just completed.

Then Wilma was in the room, wailing over the mess he had made, and suddenly Graham, reaching for a sheet of blotting paper, protesting that it had been an accident, seemed a far cry from being Mr James Brodie's manager, and lord of all he surveyed.

Although Elspeth, as an office employee, could have eaten her midday sandwiches in the upstairs canteen, she continued, despite Wilma's obvious disapproval, to join Lena and the others in the big basement room. For one thing, she knew that soon she would have to return to the sewing room, and she had no wish to annoy the women there by appearing 'snobby', and for another, her letter-writing was still in demand, and she depended on the money she earned from it for her night-school classes.

She had thought that once the war was over her talent for writing letters would no longer be of use, but she was wrong. As well as the usual formal letters voicing complaints or asking advice, girls who wanted to keep in touch with soldiers and sailors who had been in the town during the war sought her assistance, and once the returning brothers and cousins heard of her skills they, too, contacted her, eager to keep in touch with young women they had met elsewhere, but unable to put together the things they wanted to say.

Elspeth, who had long since passed the stage of being embarrassed at requests to write about love and longing, and had in fact become famed for her ability to write love letters, sat patiently, exercise book in one hand and pencil in the other, while her clients blushed and stammered and said, 'Ach, just tell him I love him, and I cannae wait tae cuddle him again,' or, 'Can ye put down somethin' nice about her bonny face in the moonlight, and how I'll never forget that night when we – tae hang wi' it, just say that night, she'll know what I mean.'

The pennies and halfpennies filled her tobacco tin to capacity, and were exchanged for sixpences, then shillings, then half-crowns. Only Thomas knew how much she had saved, and he advised her to keep her own business to herself.

'But it seems underhand, not letting Aunt Flora know.'

'There's nothing wrong with it. You pay your wages into the house the same as the rest of us, and anything extra's yer – your own business,' said Thomas, who had been working hard on improving his speech since donning a chauffeur's uniform. 'You might need something some time, and be glad of the money.'

He urged her to open a bank account, and after she had approached the bank door three times then turned away again, unable to walk into such a place on her own, he went with her, handsome and reassuring in his smart grey chauffeur's uniform.

As they stepped back on to the street, the bankbook clutched in Elspeth's hand, Thomas said, 'I'm fetching Mrs Bruce in ten minutes. There's time to give you a lift back to Brodie's.'

Sitting in the deep, comfortable seat beside him, gliding through the streets with the mingled smell of leather and Mr Bruce's cigars tantalising her nose, was like glimpsing heaven. She had just begun to imagine herself a titled lady, dressed in the best Brodie's had to offer, on her way to take tea with the Provost's wife, when Thomas broke the spell. 'I'm worried about our Lachlan. He's not gettin' any better, is he?'

'He still needs time,' Elspeth offered, but without much

conviction, for she knew what he meant. Lachlan, who had always had some artistic skill, had taken to drawing, first on the margin of newspapers with a stub of pencil he had found, then in a blank exercise book Mattie had given him, together with a better pencil.

At first the family had looked on his new hobby as a step forward in his recovery, but all the drawings turned out to be of men in battle, some yelling defiance at the enemy as they charged, bayonets fixed on their rifles, others screaming in agony as they writhed on the ground. They were appalled by the pictures, drawn with such ferocity that the pencil dug deep into the paper.

'Mebbe we're treatin' him the wrong way,' Thomas fretted. Glancing sideways at him, Elspeth saw that his face was bleak with worry. 'Mam treats him as though he's a bairn again, and he's content to let it happen. Mebbe he needs to be pushed into doin' more for himself, instead of havin' things done for him.' He turned the wheel, easing the big car round a corner. 'He's only just gone into his twenty-first year – his whole life's still in front of him. Times I lie awake at night worryin' that he'll spend it just the way he is now.'

'But if we try to push him, could it not make him worse?'

'Mebbe, but being kind to him isn't making him any better, is it?' Thomas said in despair as they reached the corner of the street where the department store stood. 'I'd best let you out here, so's nobody in the store sees you.'

Standing on the kerb, watching Thomas drive off, Elspeth decided that one day she would like to have her own car and her own chauffeur. Patting the pocket that held her new bankbook, she felt that by opening a bank account, she had just taken the first step to future affluence.

'I will not have it!'

Elspeth, who had just stepped into the flat, halted as she heard the words booming from the kitchen.

She recognised the voice – one she had never expected to hear in Mearns Street.

'There's nothin' wrong with the lassie workin' in an office,' Flora rapped back. 'What d'ye think she'll do, Mrs Bremner – help herself tae one of the clerks?'

Elspeth opened the door on a gasp of outrage from her grandmother to see Flora McDonald and Celia Bremner facing each other across the kitchen table. Flora was red in the face, and two bright red blotches stood out on Celia's sallow cheekbones.

'You're a bad besom, Flora Docherty,' Celia hissed, using Flora's own name, as was the custom among local women. 'I never liked our Maisie going about with you – it's no wonder she went wrong!'

'It wasnae me that did for Maisie, and well you know it,' Flora almost shrieked. 'If anythin' harmed that poor lassie, it was growin' up with all the bitterness and vindictiveness in that house of yours. Oh, she told me about it – she had tae tell someone!'

Celia gave a strangled cry, her hands forming themselves into claws. For a moment Elspeth, still transfixed in the doorway, thought that her grandmother was going to throw the table aside and launch herself on Flora, then another voice broke in, high and desperate.

'Stop it!'

She hadn't even realised that Lachlan was in the room until he cried out, for he wasn't in his usual chair by the fire. Instead, he huddled in the corner between the sink and the wall that held the curtained bed-recess, his thin body pressed against the wall as though trying to force its way through the plaster and bricks. His face was ashen, and his body shaking so much that water splashed over the edge of the cup he clutched tightly in both hands.

'Stop it,' he said again through clenched teeth, his voice thin and raw. 'Stop it, stop it, stop—'

'It's all right, Lachlan, all right.' Elspeth erupted into the room, pushing past her grandmother, and squatted down beside him, talking soothingly, trying to take the cup from him. As his fingers began to relax, a ship's siren suddenly blared out from the river below. It was too much for him. He gave a short, high, animal-like scream and his body jerked at the sudden noise. Cold water slopped over Elspeth's hands, soaking through her gloves, and Lachlan's fingers spasmed, tightening round the cup until she feared that it might break.

Then Thomas was pushing her aside, raising his brother to his feet, coaxing him away from the wall and out of the room, talking in the low, soothing voice he always used for Lachlan.

Celia Bremner watched him go, her face frozen in a grimace of astonishment and distaste. 'What in the world's wrong with the laddie?' she wanted to know when the two young men had gone from the room.

'I told you, Grandmother, it's what happened to him in the war. He can't help it.'

'He should be in the infirmary – or the asylum.'

'You hold yer tongue!' Flora almost spat the words at the old woman. 'There's nothin' wrong with my laddie that a wee bit of peace and quiet cannae cure. Ye've said yer say, Mrs Bremner – now ye can get out of my house.'

'Elspeth, you will come with me. This is no place for any granddaughter of mine.'

Elspeth felt as though the ground had been pulled from beneath her feet. Panic caught her heart and squeezed it painfully as she backed away from her grandmother, groping with one hand for the sturdiness of the wall at her back. Her fingers caught instead at the bed-curtains, gathering a handful of the material.

'I don't want to,' she heard herself saying.

'It's not a question of what you want. I'll not have my own flesh and blood living in this house.'

'Ye never wanted Ellie before, so why should ye have her now?' Flora wanted to know. 'I'll not let you waste her life the way ye wasted poor Maisie's.'

'You have the nerve to say that to me, when your own son's no better than—'

'Mam!' Thomas's voice was like the crack of a whip. He moved quickly from the door to intercept his mother, who was on her way towards Celia Bremner. 'Sit down, Mam, I'll deal with this.' His mother's body stiffened, like that of a small child unwilling to be put in a seat, but Thomas's youthful strength won, and Flora had no option but to sit down. Then he turned to Celia. 'Mrs Bremner, I think you should go home now.'

She eyed him warily, moving back a step. 'Elspeth—'

'Elspeth's staying here for the moment. If she wants to live with you, she'll make her own way.'

'She'll do as her grandmother tells her!'

Thomas's face was like stone, though his voice was still low and reasonable. 'Elspeth's old enough tae earn her keep, and she's old enough tae make up her own mind. Not one person in this house'll try tae influence her, one way or another. You have my word on that. Now – I'll walk with you down tae the tram stop, and see you on your way.'

Celia summoned up the last of her strength. 'Elspeth, I'll expect you in Port Glasgow!' With one last, scathing look at Flora, she made for the door, but by that time her fingers were trembling so hard that they fumbled helplessly with the handle.

Thomas reached round her to open the door. 'I'll not be long,' he told the others as he followed Celia out. 'Ellie, look after Lachlan.'

As the outer door closed, Flora slumped in her chair. She, too, was shaking, her face grey and old. 'Elspeth, see tae Lachlan.'

'Aunt Flora, why is my grand—'

'Do as yer told!' Flora snapped, summoning such a steely edge to her voice that Elspeth fled at once from the room.

Lachlan was sitting on his bed; when she sat down beside him, her arm against his, she could feel him trembling.

'It's all right, Lachie, it was just my grandmother in a temper.'

'I don't like folk shouting,' he whispered through white lips.

'I know. I don't either.'

'She was shouting about you, Ellie. What've ye done tae make her so angry?'

'I've not done anything. She's just awful strict, like a teacher.'

'She told Mam that ye've tae go and stay with her.'

Elspeth felt a shiver run through her at the thought of living in the cheerless house she could scarcely bear to sit in for even two hours.

'I'm not going.'

'Good.' Lachlan took her hand in his. He was like a child, Elspeth thought sadly, remembering how she had always looked up to him in her own childhood, always longed to be as grown-up as he was.

She started talking about times they'd had as children, and about her work, and gradually he relaxed. She heard Thomas return eventually, going directly to the kitchen. Then Mattie and her father came in and the small flat grew fragrant with the smell of the midday meal. And still she talked, until, at last, Thomas appeared in the doorway.

'It's dinner-time.'

Lachlan went off cheerfully enough, while Elspeth lingered to ask, 'How's Grandmother?'

'I went all the way back with her, to be on the safe side. She was in an awful state, poor old soul.' A faint smile touched the corners of his mouth. 'She wouldn't talk to me. I had to sit at the back of the tram and pay my own fare. I think she was glad enough to have someone keeping an eye on her, but she'd have died before she'd admit it. Don't say anything to the rest of them,' he added as they went through the hall. 'Mam won't want them to know what happened.'

15

Flora refused to discuss Celia Bremner's visit, and Elspeth was left puzzling about what she had overheard, and trying to make sense of it. Finally, she ventured to speak to Granjan about it.

'It's no business of yours or mine, pet.'

'But it is my business,' Elspeth said, exasperated. 'The quarrel was about me. I thought Grandmother would be pleased about me wanting to work in an office like my grandfather. But when I mentioned it she was so sharp that I didn't even dare to tell her I was going to night school. What have I done wrong?'

'Nothing at all,' Janet Docherty hastened to assure her. 'It wasnae you who did wrong.'

'Who did, then?'

Janet sighed. 'I suppose ye should know – but not a word tae anyone. If Flora knew I'd told ye she'd be ragin'.'

'Not a word, I promise.'

'It was yer grandfather.' Granjan spoke as though every word was being dragged out of her. 'It seems there was this woman worked in the same office as him, and he – liked her.'

Elspeth gaped at her. 'He fell in love with another woman while he was married to Grandmother?'

'It happens tae folk sometimes – but not often,' Granjan added hurriedly. 'Marriage is marriage, and nothin' should come between man and wife. But I'll admit that Celia Bremner was never what ye'd call a warm, lovin' sort of woman.'

'Did she find out about it?'

'If she didnae know before he went off, she must have known then,' Janet said drily. It was almost too much for Elspeth to take in.

'You mean he ran away – with this woman?' Her voice rose to a squeal, and Janet winced.

'For any favour keep yer voice down – the neighbours'll hear.'

'But Grandmother said he died.'

'So he did, as far as she was concerned.' Janet bent stiffly to pick a piece of fluff from the carpet. 'Marriage is important tae a woman, Ellie. There's a certain respect in havin' a ring on yer finger an' bein' called Missus. There's as much respect for a widow, but little for a deserted wife.'

'Folk must have known, surely.'

'Of course they did. The whole place buzzed with it, and I felt that sorry for Celia – not that she was a woman who'd let anyone sympathise with her. The gossip soon died down, the way gossip does. As tae her sayin' he died – he might well have by now, for all folk know. An' give the man his due, he saw tae it that she wasnae left destitute.'

Elspeth sat silent, trying to understand the new picture Granjan had painted of Celia Bremner. She was such a proud woman, and she must have suffered greatly over her husband's desertion.

'Was it just after that that she started wanting to see me?'

'I believe it was, hen.'

'She wants me to go and live with her,' Elspeth said, and shivered. 'But I can't. I'm sorry for what happened to her, but it doesn't make her a different person.'

'We all have our own lives, and nobody else can live them for us. You do whatever's best for you,' Janet told her. 'But whatever you do, mind what I said – not a word about this tae a soul!'

*

As the day for her usual monthly visit to Port Glasgow drew near, Elspeth was in a quandary. She had decided, after the quarrel, never to visit her grandmother again, and the decision had been a relief, for she hated the duty visits. But Granjan's story had made her feel guilty about turning her back on her maternal grandmother, who had already lost her husband and her daughter – or, rather, driven them both away from her.

She was still unsure when the day came, and was taken aback when Flora said after the midday meal, 'Is it not time ye were gettin' ready tae go tae yer grandmother's?'

'You want me to go, after what happened between the two of you?'

Flora glared. 'That has nothin' tae dae with you doin' yer duty by her. She's yer own flesh and blood.'

'I'll come with you, Ellie,' Mattie volunteered as Elspeth hesitated, and her mother rounded on her.

'Ye'll do no such thing, lady. Elspeth's old enough tae tend tae her own business.'

Apprehension settled in a solid lump behind Elspeth's ribs as she prepared for the visit. By the time she reached her grandmother's door it had become a hard, jagged boulder. She banged the polished brass doorknocker the way she had been taught, loud enough to be heard, but not loud enough to annoy Grandmother, then stepped back, hands folded protectively across the part of her stomach where the boulder lay.

After a moment she heard movement behind the door, then it opened to reveal Celia Bremner, as erect and as awesome as ever.

'It's you,' she said, as she always did. Then, moving back, 'You'd best come in.'

The visit went along its usual lines, with not a thing said about Celia's visit to Mearns Street. In the kitchen, the teatray was set out as usual, as though there had been no question of Elspeth staying away.

After tea, instead of waiting in the kitchen until

Grandmother emerged from the lavatory, Elspeth tiptoed into the living room to study the photograph more closely. Surely that balding, respectable man behind the protective glass couldn't possibly have had a sweetheart, she thought, but a more intensive study showed that in actual fact he was quite a good-looking man.

Noting afresh the possessive hold his wife had on his shoulder, Elspeth began to understand why he had felt the need to escape. Then the cistern was flushed, and she fled, mouse-like, back to the kitchen, reaching it just in time.

Flora sank into a chair by the table and fanned herself with one hand. 'That washhouse was like a furnace today,' she said, then, as she always did when she returned to the house, 'Put the kettle on, Elspeth, I could do with a cup of tea.'

Thomas, studying a book at the table, put a detaining hand on Elspeth's wrist as she moved past him to the cooker. 'Lachlan,' he said blandly, 'put the kettle on, will you?'

Lachlan, who had been idly gazing into space, stared. So did his mother.

'What?'

'Elspeth's been helping you with the washing, Mam. She's just as tired as you are, and I'm tryin' to read this book about car engines. Lachlan's not doing anything.'

'But Lachlan's—'

'—as able as any of us to make a cup of tea,' Thomas said evenly. 'It's time he was doing something round the house.'

Flora went red. 'Don't talk nonsense. Elspeth, do as you're told.'

Thomas's fingers tightened. 'Sit down, Elspeth, and let Lachlan see to it.' His brown eyes flashed a clear message at her, and she sank into a chair, her heart thumping, and her palms clammy.

'I'll make it myself,' Flora said icily, but Thomas's free hand caught at her sleeve as she started to rise.

151

'He can manage, Mam. He's a man, not a bairn.'

'He's not well!'

'And he'll not get well if you keep fussing over him. It's gone on long enough. You heard me, Lachlan,' Thomas told his brother, his voice suddenly hard. 'Get up and put the kettle on.'

Lachlan, who had been looking wide-eyed back and forth between his mother and brother during their argument, did as he was told. Seeing his hands shake as he filled the kettle, Elspeth longed to get up and do it for him, but didn't dare.

'Now put the cups on the table,' Thomas said, his voice crisp and hard. An officer's voice, Elspeth suddenly realised. The voice of authority, one that Lachlan had been trained in the army to obey automatically.

Step by step, keeping one hand on his mother's wrist, Thomas talked his brother through the ritual of making tea. Uncertainly, moving like an old man, Lachlan did as he was told, while Flora sat motionless, her mouth so tight that it could scarcely be seen, her eyes like icy pebbles.

When the time came for Lachlan to pour boiling water from the kettle to the large shabby tin teapot, his hands were trembling so much that Elspeth was convinced that he was going to scald himself. She half rose from the chair, then as Thomas said her name very quietly, forced herself to sit down again.

After Lachlan had placed a cup in front of each of them, he began to take his own tea back to his chair, where he took all his meals, a towel tucked into the neck of his shirt by Flora. Thomas's voice halted him. 'Sit at the table with us, Lachlan.'

The young man hesitated and half turned, his eyes pleading. 'Here, beside me,' Thomas said implacably, drawing out a chair, and Lachlan obeyed.

It was more like a funeral than four people enjoying a cup of tea. Thomas talked about car engines, while Flora stared at the table, making no attempt to drink her tea, and Lachlan, after trying to lift his cup two-handed and being forced to put it down again because his trembling hands threatened to splash hot liquid all over the table, gave up the attempt.

Elspeth, glancing over at him, saw that he was weeping silently. She put her own cup down, determined this time to do something about his misery, but just then he got to his feet and left the room, scrubbing one sleeved arm over his face in a heartbreakingly childish gesture.

'Are ye satisfied now?' Flora hissed at her first-born as soon as Lachlan had gone. 'D'ye not think the poor laddie's got enough trouble without you bullyin' him? Wait till yer father—'

'Sometimes, Mam, we have to be cruel to be kind.' Thomas got up with an abrupt movement and went to the door.

'Where d'ye think ye're goin'?'

'To Lachlan.'

'Leave him – ye've done him enough harm!'

'It's me he needs. Sit down, Mam, and drink your tea.'

'I don't want it!'

'When we behaved like that, you called it cutting off our noses to spite our faces,' Thomas said, and left the room. Flora scraped her chair back from the table, poured her tea down the sink, and began to scrub the potatoes for the evening meal, the water flying in all directions a testimony to her inner fury.

The next morning Thomas, who had until then been helping Lachlan to dress and undress, got his brother up half an hour earlier than usual, and stood over him while Lachlan laboriously dressed himself.

Flora tutted when he appeared in the kitchen with his shirt buttons in the wrong buttonholes. 'Lachlan, will ye look at yerself, laddie! Come here till I sort ye out.'

Lachlan started to move obediently towards her, but Thomas, coming into the room at his back, stopped him.

'Leave him be, Mam. Look, Lachie—' He hooked a finger into the loop of shirt on Lachlan's thin chest caused by an

153

unused buttonhole. 'You've missed one. You'll have to undo them all and start again. From the top now, and work your way down.'

From then on, the battle for Lachlan was under way. Flora's fingers itched every time she saw her son with his braces twisted or his shoelaces untied, but Thomas continued to push his brother into looking after himself, and saw to it that Elspeth and Mattie and his father did the same.

At first, Lachlan's struggles were painful to see. Often he was in tears of helpless frustration, but gradually, the tears gave way to bouts of anger, mainly directed against Thomas, who shouted back at him, goading him on.

'He never used to lose his temper,' Elspeth said nervously after Lachlan had stormed off to bed following a particularly bad flare-up.

'It's time he learned, then.'

'Thomas, are you sure you're doing the right thing, treating him this way?'

'It's that, or seeing him turn into a helpless invalid.' Thomas pushed his thick fair hair from his face, but, as usual, it fell back across his brow as soon as it was released. 'And what'll happen to him then, Ellie? Who's going to care for him when Mam's gone? D'ye want to see him put into the asylum or the poors' hospital, or left to walk the streets because he can't fend for himself? I know I'm hurting him, but it's like thawing out someone who's been frozen. It's sore, but if he isnae thawed out he'll die. That's what's happening to Lachie.' He caught at her wrist, shook it slightly. 'And you've got to help me, for none of the rest will.'

Picking up Lachlan's discarded sketch book he leafed through the pages, then gave a short laugh. 'Take a look at that.'

The battle scenes concentrated now on one soldier. In every sketch he was injured and suffering, and in every sketch he bore a clear likeness to Thomas.

'The man's got talent,' Thomas commented drily.

He didn't let up for a moment, and as the days and weeks went by, Lachlan began to show unmistakable signs of improvement. Tormented by his brother's jibes about grown men who let their mammies look after them, he began to shrug his mother's hands away when she tried, in Thomas's absence, to do something for him.

Looking at the expression on the older woman's face each time that happened, Elspeth sympathised with her, for she was only trying to do what she saw as the best for Lachlan. She herself felt ashamed of the times she had answered Aunt Flora back and been difficult, and tried to be kinder and more understanding.

Unfortunately, Flora, wounded to the core by what she saw as Lachlan's rejection, interpreted Elspeth's overtures as pity. She became even more irritable with the girl than before, and gradually, Elspeth's good intentions flew out of the window, the two of them reverting back to the uneasy relationship they had known for years.

Flora's bitterness over Thomas and Lachlan was eased when Rachel plucked up the courage to tell her that she was expecting a child.

'There's just one thing,' the girl went on nervously. 'It's due in January.'

Flora, as used to mental mathematics as any housewife forced, week after week, to make the money available go as far as possible, did a swift calculation in her head, then glared at her daughter. 'A seven-month bairn?'

'Eight months, Mam.'

'Don't quibble with me, lady, it's still too early. Some of the neighbours might be daft, but they're no' fools. No wonder ye were so keen tae take up the Cochrans' offer of a double weddin'!'

'What with Bob coming back safe from the war, and all . . .' Rachel's words faded under her mother's look, then she made one more try, 'At least we're not as bad as Annie Cochran and her man – their bairn's born already.'

'Just because she just made it tae the kirk in time, it doesnae excuse what you did. After the way I've tried to bring you up well,' Flora foamed, 'here ye are, giving yer father and me a showin' up before the whole street.'

'It happens to other folk,' Rachel protested tremulously.

'But it's never happened to us. If this is a lassie ye're carryin', wait and see how you feel if she comes tae you with the same tale. Ye'll not be so pleased about it then.'

Tears were shimmering in Rachel's eyes now. 'Don't be like that about it, Mam, Bob's bad enough without you starting on me.'

'What d'ye mean? Is he not pleased about the bairn?'

Rachel sniffed. 'He doesnae want a family so soon. He says I should have been more careful.'

'He what?' Flora's maternal instinct flared up. 'The cheeky monkey! It takes two tae make a bairn, just you tell him that from me! And when it comes, it'll be a lot bonnier than that wee red-faced greetin' thing his sister Annie's got. All my bairns were bonny.'

'Does that mean you're not angry with me, Mam?'

Flora had gone too far to draw back now. 'Aye, well, what's done's done,' she conceded, 'and it'll be nice tae have a grand—' She broke off as the door opened and Thomas walked in.

'Thomas?' She glanced at the clock. 'What are ye doin' here at this time of the day?'

He was in his chauffeur's uniform, the peaked cap tucked beneath one arm. 'Ma – Mother, I've brought Miss Bruce to visit you,' he said awkwardly, just as Aileen Bruce, in a beige silk dress under a long deep green linen jacket, came into the kitchen at his back.

Her smile, as she advanced on Flora, a slim hand extended, was radiant. 'Mrs McDonald – I've been looking forward to meeting you.'

Flustered, Flora and Rachel scrambled to their feet.

'Where's Lachlan?' Thomas asked as Aileen's soft, cool hand met Flora's rough and reddened fingers.

'In his room. Thomas—' Flora said as he went into the hall, then belatedly remembered her manners. 'This is my eldest, Rachel. Ye'll have a wee cup of tea, Miss Bruce?'

Aileen beamed at Rachel, who smiled shyly in return, one hand trying to tidy her hair unobtrusively. 'It's very kind of you, but we're hoping to take your other son for a drive.'

'Our Lachlan?' Flora signalled to Rachel to scoop up the cups sitting on the floor by the two fireside chairs.

'I thought he might enjoy a run to Loch Thom. It's lovely up there.'

'Ye'll take a seat, at least.'

'Thank you.' Aileen Bruce sank gracefully into a chair by the table and, apparently unaware of the tension in the room, chattered easily until Thomas returned with Lachlan, who, much to his mother's relief, had put on a jacket and tie and brushed his hair. His brown eyes were wary, and he was rubbing his hands nervously down the sides of his trousers.

'Here we are.' There was a forced cheerfulness in Thomas's voice. 'Miss Bruce, this is my brother Lachlan.'

Aileen's wide smile broke over Lachlan, making him blink. 'How do you do? I'm sorry you've not been well. Thomas tells me you're feeling better, though.'

'H-how d'ye do?' He shook her hand as though it was made of porcelain.

'I hope you'll come out with us for a wee run.'

'Of course he will,' Thomas said heartily. 'We'd best be on our way – we'll not be long, Mother.'

16

Lachlan was still out when the rest of the family arrived home, and the flat was spotless, for Flora had spent the rest of the afternoon, with Rachel's help, cleaning every inch of it. But there was no evening meal waiting for them.

'I'm not havin' that Bruce lassie findin' us sittin' eatin',' Flora said firmly. 'She'll not catch me unawares twice. Ye'll have tae wait until she's been and gone before ye eat. Henry, away tae the wee room and change intae yer best clothes. I've left them out for ye.'

'Put on my good clothes on a weekday? The lassie's flesh and blood the same as the rest of us,' Henry protested, his stomach rumbling. 'She knows that we eat, there's no shame in her seein' us doin' it.'

'That's not what I think – and for goodness' sake do somethin' about that noise,' Flora snapped as his empty stomach protested again. 'D'ye want tae shame me entirely?'

Hurt and hungry, he took himself off to the pub, announcing that he would buy a pie to keep body and soul together. Flora, her mouth a thin, tight line, started to clean the spotless sink.

'D'ye think she will come back?' Mattie asked hopefully. 'I wish I'd been home earlier to see her!'

Flora, plying a washcloth energetically, sniffed. 'There was nothin' tae see, just a wealthy lassie who'd no business to be here.'

'It was nice of her to think of taking Lachlan out,' Mattie protested. 'Most posh folk are too neb-in-the-air tae come near a tenement.'

'Not Miss Aileen,' Elspeth said. She, too, was disappointed at missing the girl's visit, but at least she could claim to have seen her at close quarters before. 'She was in the fitting room at Brodie's once, when she and her sister were having clothes made for the wedding. I thought then she would be nice to know. D'you not mind, Mattie, when we went to see her sister comin' out of the church after she got married? Miss Aileen was the chief bridesmaid.'

'Oh, yes – a bonny girl, she was, with black hair and a lovely smile.'

'There's more tae folk than a nice smile and clothes that cost enough tae feed a workman's family for a week,' Flora interrupted. 'Dust that skirtin' board if ye've nothin' else tae dae, Mattie. And Elspeth, take a dry mop over the hall linoleum.'

To the girls' disappointment, Lachlan came home alone shortly afterwards, glowing with fresh air and exercise. Aileen and Thomas had taken him over the hills to Loch Thom, the town's reservoir.

'It was grand tae see the grass and the water again, and hear the birds,' he said with an enthusiasm Elspeth hadn't seen since his last war leave. 'We'd a right good walk round the water's edge, the three of us. She's kind, that Miss Aileen. Mam, Thomas says tae tell ye he'll get somethin' tae eat at the big house. He'd tae take Miss Aileen home, then tonight he's drivin' her mother and father.' His eyes swept the empty, polished table. 'Have I missed my dinner?'

Flora's dread of another visit from Aileen Bruce turned to insult because the girl hadn't returned to see the result of all her polishing and scrubbing. 'There's cold meat, and I'll fry up some cold boiled potatoes,' she said shortly. 'That'll have tae dae ye for once.'

*

Thomas didn't come home till late, tiptoeing into the dark, silent hall. When his duties as a chauffeur kept him at work in the evenings, he always went straight to bed without disturbing the sleeping household, but tonight the kitchen door opened to reveal his mother's silhouette.

'In here.'

The kitchen was dimly lit by one gas mantle, and Henry's snores wafted from behind the curtains closing off the wall-bed. Flora had changed into her long-sleeved, throat-to-ankle nightdress, with a large shawl over it. Her grey hair, released from the bun she put it up in every morning, hung down over her shoulders, giving her a vulnerable look. But there was nothing vulnerable about her voice.

'Well?' Thomas asked when they were confronting each other.

'You know fine!' his mother told him, low-voiced, mindful of her sleeping husband. 'Bringin' that lassie intae my kitchen without warning and giving me a right showin'-up!'

Thomas had changed out of his chauffeur's uniform and back into his own clothes. 'Mam, the kitchen was spotless. It always is – there was no need for you to be ashamed of it.'

'But she's used tae a lot better than this, isn't she?' Flora glanced round the small room where the entire family ate and washed and spent their spare time. Ever since Aileen Bruce had stepped into it, she had been looking at it through different eyes, seeing what she imagined Aileen had seen – a crowded little room with handmade rag rugs laid on linoleum that was kept spotlessly clean, but was also faded from all those scrubbings, and cracked in places.

'That doesnae mean that there's anything wrong with the place. She's a nice lassie, Mam, she didnae come here to look down on us.'

'Why did she come, then?'

'To take Lachlan out, and to meet you. She's heard all about you and the rest of the family from me.'

160

Flora pulled the shawl more tightly about her body. 'Since when does a gardener talk about himself and his family tae his employer's daughter?'

He flushed angrily, his patience almost spent. 'I'm a chauffeur as well as a gardener—'

'Fancy names don't change folk.'

'—and sometimes I've to drive Miss Aileen places,' Thomas forged on, refusing to let the jibe get to him. 'She's interested in folk – where's the harm in that?'

'There's plenty harm when a man workin' for a lassie's father looks at her the way you did today.'

His flush deepened. 'What d'you mean by that?'

Flora put her hands flat on the table, grunting a little at the pain in her stiff wrists, and looked hard at her elder son, the first-born who had always meant more to her than any of the others.

'Ye know fine what I mean. Stop yer nonsense now, Thomas, before ye make a fool of yerself.'

Their eyes met and locked, then Thomas turned and walked out of the room.

Lachlan, worn out by excitement and unaccustomed exercise, was sound asleep, and didn't stir as Thomas undressed and slipped into bed. Tired though he was himself, he lay awake in the darkness.

'Your mother doesn't like me,' Aileen had said as they drove back to Gourock after dropping Lachlan in Mearns Street. She had moved into the front seat, close enough for him to smell the scent she always wore.

'Of course she does! Who could dislike you? Lachlan thinks you're an angel come down from heaven,' he told her, grinning. They had reached a quiet stretch of road, and he drew the car in to the side and stopped. 'You'll have to get into the back now. You can't let your parents see you sitting beside the chauffeur.'

161

She put a hand on his arm, preventing him from getting out. 'And what do you think about me?'

'You know what I think,' Thomas said hoarsely, and as though it was the most natural thing to do in the world, she came into his arms, her mouth hungry for his. He kissed her, quickly and softly at first, then hard, with passion. She responded just as passionately, and he crushed her even closer, heat racing through his body.

Ever since that first kiss in the summerhouse they had been meeting when and where they could. At first the excitement of their secret trysts had been enough, but over the past few weeks their feelings had deepened.

Now, as they drew apart, he said, 'I can't bear the thought of you going away for a whole month.'

'Neither can I, but they wouldn't dream of letting me stay behind.' She reached up and traced his eyebrows with the tip of one finger. 'We'll write to each other, every day.'

'Where can we send the letters?' Thomas asked in despair. 'There's nobody we can trust. You'll meet someone, and fall in love and forget about me – and mebbe that'd be for the best.'

'No!' It was a soft, urgent cry, followed by a rain of butterfly-light kisses on his chin and mouth.

'That's what's going to happen sooner or later, Aileen. I don't see your parents letting you marry their chauffeur.'

'There must be some way!'

Thomas doubted it. He had known from the start that nothing could come of their feelings for each other.

'We have to go,' he said reluctantly, opening the car door. 'They'll be wondering where you are.'

After tucking her tenderly into the cool recesses of the back seat, he resumed his place behind the wheel, taking a moment to glance at the river, lazy and mirror-like beneath the blue, sunny sky. Downriver, the surface was gashed by a passing ship on its way up the Clyde to deliver its load in Glasgow, passing a trim, brightly painted passenger steamer taking day trippers round the islands scattered thickly at the mouth of the river. The disturbed water at the wake of both vessels broke into white ruffles that spread slowly, in long rolling waves. Eventually, those waves would break on the banks.

On the far side, dolls'-house-sized dwellings could be seen, the hills rising behind them soft and green and peaceful.

'I love you, Thomas,' Aileen said softly from the rear of the car as he eased it back on to the road. He smiled at her in the mirror.

'I love you too,' he said.

Now, remembering their stolen moments, Thomas tossed restlessly in the dark of the night, wishing with all his heart that he could have turned the wheel just then and taken the car safely over the surface of the river and on to the far shore, then up into the rich, placid green hills beyond, driving forever with Aileen, never to be found by anyone.

In August, Theresa McCabe, James Brodie's typist, was well enough to return to the office, and Elspeth was sent back to the sewing room.

She was apprehensive about her reception, worried in case the other seamstresses would accuse her of being 'posh', or having airs and graces after spending time as an office worker, but thanks to her decision to continue spending her midday breaks with them, and her friendship with Lena, there was no trouble from the others.

The only person who caused her grief was Miss Arnold. 'I hope this won't be beneath your dignity,' she would say scathingly when giving Elspeth work to do, or, 'You'll be sure to let me know if you think this will ruin your hands, won't you? We never know when Mr James might need your invaluable assistance again.'

'Pay no attention,' Lena advised. 'She's jealous because she cannae do anythin' but sew, and she's not all that good at it. Well, she's not,' she protested as the girls huddled round the table greeted this sacrilege with gasps. 'When does she ever do any sewin' herself?'

'She worked on Miss Bruce's trousseau last year,' one of them volunteered.

'Only plain sewin', though. She got where she is by makin' up tae Miss Buchanan. I'll grant ye she's quite good at organisin', but when it comes tae plyin' a needle or usin' a machine we're all better than her. Mebbe we have tae put up with her behaviour, but we don't have tae be frightened by it.'

'Miss Buchanan'll be getting retired in a few years,' someone pointed out. 'Then Miss Arnold'll get her job. You should try tae get Miss Arnold's place when the time comes, Lena.'

'Me? I'll be long away by then. I'll be on the halls, see if I'm not,' Lena said haughtily.

Following her friend's advice, Elspeth swallowed hard when Miss Arnold's tongue lashed at her, and trapped her own tongue between her teeth to hold back the retorts that so swiftly came to mind. Gradually, as the weeks went by, the woman grew tired of baiting her, and life settled back to normal.

Unable to believe what her casual passing glance had revealed, Elspeth spun round, almost bumping into a fat elderly man, and hurried back to the small shop window.

It badly needed cleaning, and the space beyond it was crowded with the richly varied collection to be found in any pawn shop, but the typewriter in the middle of the clutter stood out like a precious stone in a box of costume jewellery, large and black and solid, its great carriage scarcely demeaned by the bracelets and necklaces that had been looped around it.

She put down the bag containing the exercise book she used to list details of letters to be written, and cupped her hands against the glass to cut out the sun's reflection. Peer as she might, she couldn't see a price ticket.

She straightened up and turned to the shop door, then had

to lean against the window instead as her legs suddenly went weak. For a moment she doubted if she had the strength to take the few steps needed to reach the door, but as she stood there, quivering with excitement, the bell jangled as a woman went in. The thought that she might be enquiring about the typewriter, might even buy it, gave Elspeth the energy she needed, and she followed the woman in so closely that she narrowly avoided being hit in the face as the door swung back.

She trembled in the background, relaxing slightly when the woman produced a vase from her shopping bag and began to haggle with the thin, stooped man behind the counter. The two of them argued comfortably for some time while Elspeth shifted from foot to foot and tried to choke back a sneeze as dust tickled at the back of her nose.

At last, client and pawnbroker reached agreement. Money was handed over and the woman hurried out, while the pawnbroker gathered up the vase and carried it off into the back shop, tossing, 'I'll no' keep ye a minute, lass,' over his shoulder.

After a moment, the bell above the street door jangled and a young man came in, brushing past her to duck round the edge of the counter.

'Can I help you?'

'Th-that typewriter in the window – is it for sale?'

'The Underwood? Yes, it is, the man who pawned it didn't come back for it.' He pulled a ledger from beneath the counter and flipped through it. 'Nine shillings.'

Elspeth did a swift sum in her head. 'I could manage three shillings and sixpence just now, and pay the rest up, if that would be all right.'

'Is it for yourself?'

'Yes. I can type,' Elspeth said quickly in her own defence. 'I'm attending night school, but it's not on just now.'

'Have a look at it, while I ask my uncle.' He cleared a space on the narrow counter, then, after a tussle, managed to heave the typewriter out of the window. As he went into the back

shop, Elspeth caressed the typewriter keys gently, dizzy with
the thought of owning such a machine.

The young man returned and thrust a sheet of paper at her.
'You'll want to try it out,' he said, and watched with interest
as she rolled the paper into the carriage, lined it up, and
dashed off the first thing that came into her head. Rolling the
paper out of the machine, she studied the result.

'The t's not working.'

He came round to her side of the counter to look over her
shoulder. '"Wee sleekit cow'ring tim'rous beastie",' he trans-
lated, with some difficulty. 'You're a Burns fan?'

'It's a good poem for practising.'

He tested the keys, then announced, 'That one's sticking. I
can oil it for you, and dust it.' Then, straightening up as the
older man came through from the back shop, 'What d'you think,
Uncle George? Can the young lady buy it in instalments?'

'Well—' The pawnbroker scratched at his chin, the rasping
of fingernails against beard-stubble loud in the small claustro-
phobic space.

'It's been sitting in the back shop for long enough,' his
nephew urged. 'Not many folk in this town are desperate to
buy a typewriter.'

The pawnbroker glared. 'It's a valuable machine.'

'I'd not expect to take it away until the money's all paid up,'
Elspeth put in hurriedly.

'And when'll that be?'

'I'll put something towards it every week, and it'll be paid
up by the end of the year – earlier, if I can manage it.'

With almost two-thirds of the asking price still to be found,
it was a reckless commitment, but she couldn't afford to ask
for longer. She might lose the typewriter altogether, and when
would another chance come along? She would make every saving she could, and add in the little she got back from Auntie
Flora each week.

'How can I be sure ye'll no' lose interest and stop payin'?

This is a valuable piece of machinery, ye know.'

'If I do stop you can keep what I've paid so far.'

She remembered another barrier to her ownership, and drew a deep breath. 'I've not got the three and sixpence on me, but I'll bring it in tomorrow.' Her whole body was tense with urgency; she felt her mouth trembling, and put a hand up to hide this sign of weakness.

'Come on, Uncle George, it's a fair offer,' the young man urged, and his uncle, after deliberating, nodded creakily, as though the decision he had just come to hurt physically as well as emotionally.

'As long as I get the first payment tomorrow. If I don't, or if ye miss a week, the machine goes right back into the window, mind. Kenneth, I'll hold you responsible.'

Elspeth almost wept with relief. 'I don't know how to thank you!' she said when the pawnbroker had shuffled back through the curtained doorway at the side of the counter.

'For a start, you could give me your handkerchief.'

'My – what?'

He grinned down at her. He had a nice face, round and cheerful. His hair was dark, and his brown eyes crinkled at the corners when he smiled. 'The typewriter needs cleaning – you've smeared dust all over your face.'

'Oh!' Luckily her handkerchief was still spotless and unused. She gave it to him and he wiped her chin and cheek carefully before returning it to her.

'That's better. I'll put it away in the back shop for you, and get it into working order. I'll need your name and address for our books.'

'I'll type it for you,' Elspeth said proudly. 'But you'll have to fill in the t's yourself.'

'Miss Elspeth Bremner,' he read aloud when she had finished, then, holding out his hand, 'Kenneth Monteith.'

'How do you do?' She felt colour rising to her cheeks as they shook hands.

'Are you planning to use the typewriter to start up in business for yourself?'

'Oh no, I'm a seamstress – but I'm going to work in an office one day,' she explained as he raised his eyebrows. 'I write letters for folk, sometimes business letters, so a typewriter of my own would be useful.'

He was about to say something else, but his uncle called on him from behind the curtain. 'Well,' he came round the counter to open the street door for her, 'I'll see you tomorrow, when you make your first payment. Good afternoon, Miss Bremner.'

Her feet skimmed the pavement as she went home. She couldn't believe that at last she was going to have her very own typewriter! She could write letters on it, and maybe papers for Mattie. She was on the threshold of a new life, and the possibilities ahead were endless.

17

There was very little left in her bank account once she'd taken out the deposit for the typewriter, but that couldn't be helped, she thought, hurrying to the pawn shop with the money. She peered in the window as she passed, but the typewriter had gone.

To her relief, Kenneth was behind the counter. 'It's all right, it's in the back shop,' he reassured her as soon as she went in. 'I started working on it today.'

After checking the money and entering the amount into a ledger, he wrote the date and amount on a small card and handed it over. 'This'll help you to keep the payments in order. I've put the full amount at the top,' he explained, then, diffidently, 'I was wondering – there's a good film on at the Central Picture House this week, and I don't like going on my own. Would you care to come with me?'

Elspeth, aware of a sudden warmth in her face, could have wept. Kenneth Monteith would soon begin to think that she was a red-faced clown at this rate. But this was the first time a young man had ever invited her out, apart from the Brodie's messenger boy, and Graham in the office. She hadn't taken either of them seriously, but Kenneth was different. He had been very helpful about the typewriter.

'Yes,' she heard herself say, though she was sure that she hadn't definitely made her mind up. He grinned, showing strong white teeth.

'Tomorrow night? I'll call for you at half past six.'

'I'll meet you outside the Central at quarter to seven,' she said hastily, explaining to Mattie later, in the privacy of their room, that she wasn't at all sure what Aunt Flora would have to say about a gentleman caller.

'She might not let me go at all. It's safer to let her think I'm going out with Lena and the others.' She had been permitted to attend the cinema once or twice with girls from work.

Mattie wrinkled her nose. 'I couldn't be bothered walking out with a young man just now – not when I'm getting ready to go to college.'

'We're not going to start keeping company, it's only a visit to the pictures.' There were times, Elspeth thought, when Mattie had a bit of an opinion about herself. She had left school now, and soon she would leave for Glasgow to start her teacher-training course. In the meantime she had found work during the summer months as a sales assistant in a Gourock dress shop. Since starting the job, a distinct loftiness had crept into her manner.

'He's taking me to the Central Picture House,' Elspeth told her importantly. The Central in West Blackhall Street was one of Greenock's newest and most impressive cinemas.

'D'you like him? I'd need to like someone an awful lot to let them take me to the pictures.'

'He's nice enough, but I'm only going because he's been so kind about the typewriter. Anyway,' Elspeth added honestly, 'I fancy seeing the inside of the Central.'

Fortunately, Kenneth was already waiting outside the picture house when she arrived, so she didn't have to stand around in the open, where one of the girls from the sewing room might have spotted her. To her embarrassment, he insisted on paying for both seats, and buying her a small box of liquorice allsorts.

'You're saving for that typewriter, remember?' he said as they stopped to admire the large fireplace in the foyer, a special feature of the Central.

'I know, but you'll not earn much in that wee shop.'

'I'm fine, don't worry about me. I don't work for Uncle George all the time, just in the holidays,' he said casually as they headed towards the auditorium. 'I'm going back to Glasgow in October to start my second year at the university. I'm hoping to be a doctor.'

They were going up some stairs, and Elspeth tripped over her feet and almost fell flat on her face. Wait till Mattie heard about that, she thought gleefully when she had recovered. And Aunt Flora. To think that she, Elspeth from the sewing room, was going out with a university student – and a future doctor!

She had scarcely recovered from that shock when they entered the auditorium. For a moment, she stood still, looking around. It was magnificent, with its chandeliers and decorative ceiling and plush tip-up seats and uniformed attendants. They took their seats just in time, and as the film flickered on to the screen, Elspeth, glancing round the dark auditorium, saw that some of the young men had their arms about their girls' shoulders.

She sat primly upright, wondering what she should do if Kenneth put his arm about her. He had bought her ticket, and given her sweets, so it would surely be rude to push him away. On the other hand, she wasn't certain that she wanted to be hugged. Fortunately, she didn't have to make the decision, for Kenneth was too engrossed in the film to make any overtures.

Glancing sideways at him, she decided that she liked his profile. His nose was straight and not too long, and he had quite a nice-shaped chin. She offered him a sweet, but he was so engrossed in the cowboys and Indians racing across the screen that he didn't notice, and finally she had to tap him on the elbow, making him jump.

'Liquorice allsort?'

'Oh – thanks.' He fumbled in the box, found a sweet, and turned back to the screen.

Elspeth relaxed into the soft plush seat and began to concentrate on the film herself. She became so involved in it that towards the end, when a fearsome Red Indian warrior, tomahawk in hand, suddenly hurtled down from a tree and on to the hero's back, she yelped and jumped. To her horror, the sweets still left in the box she held shot out of it and all over the floor, rattling against the seats in front. A few heads turned, and there was a low ripple of amusement.

'Oh!' She tried to duck down so that she could scoop up some of the sweets, which were rolling around the carpeted floor, but Kenneth's hand came out of nowhere to stop her.

'Just leave them.' He didn't take his hand away again; it felt warm and comfortable and not in the least threatening. Under its touch, she relaxed again, and they sat companionably together for the rest of the film. When it ended with the heroine running into the hero's arms and resting her trusting head on his manly shoulder, it felt quite nice to be holding – or being held by – a man's hand. Elspeth felt a sisterly bond between herself and the heroine, who now had THE END running across the face lifted for the hero's kiss.

But when the lights went up again she was brought back to the present with a bump. 'Oh, look—' She stared in dismay at the sweets dotted about their feet, then squeezed down into the narrow space between the rows of seats and started gathering them up.

'Don't bother,' Kenneth said above her head. 'We can't eat them now.'

'I can't leave the place looking like this!'

'They've got folk who come in and clean it.'

'But they'll think I'm an awful slitter, leaving such a mess!'

'They won't know who did it.' He drew her to her feet. 'Mind you, we'd better get out quickly, before they come in and catch us at the scene of the crime.'

Her face was burning. 'You're laughing at me!'

'Mebbe just a wee bit. But I like your sense of what's right.' He glanced beyond her, and added, 'We'd better go, there's folk wanting out.'

172

Turning, she saw that there were indeed some people waiting patiently for her to get out of their way. Scarlet now with embarrassment, she snatched up her coat and moved on, feeling a liquorice allsort squash beneath her foot as she went.

'It was a terrible waste of good sweeties, after you spending your money on them,' she lamented as they stepped out on to the street.

'We'd eaten most of them anyway.' He took her arm and steered her round two drunken men who were staggering along the middle of the pavement. Again, he maintained the contact.

It was dusk when they reached Mearns Street. Elspeth wondered if he expected to be invited up to the flat, but he stopped at the close-mouth, touching her pebble brooch lightly with the tip of a finger. 'I like your brooch.'

'It was a birthday present from my brother Thomas, during the war. We used to collect pebbles together by the river, and he bought this to remind me about that.'

'I like the river. Mebbe we could take a walk down there some night?' Kenneth looked down the hill to where the Clyde could be glimpsed between tenements. The lamplighter came into sight, using his long pole to open the gas lamps. Just a touch of the pole against the wicks within turned them into soft golden globes of light.

'This is a lovely time of the evening,' Kenneth said quietly, looking down at her. 'Your eyes are like very deep, dark pools in this light.'

'Are they?' Nobody had ever talked to her like that before; she hoped that he couldn't see the colour warming her face.

'In daylight, they're so blue. You've got beautiful eyes,' he said, then, 'Before the lamplighter gets this far—'

With an unexpected movement he whisked her up the step and into the dim close. A hand beneath her chin tipped her face to his and he kissed her, his lips first brushing hers, then claiming them, just like the couple on the cinema screen.

'Goodnight, Elspeth,' he said a few moments later. 'Mebbe

we could go out for a walk tomorrow evening?'

'I'll look into the shop on my way home,' she promised, then she was alone, breathless with happiness at the realisation that in spite of the liquorice allsorts, he wanted to see her again. She leaned against the close wall, her mouth soft and a great sense of wellbeing flooding through her, and smiled dreamily at the opposite wall until the lamplighter suddenly invaded the close.

'Aye, lassie,' he said heartily, brushing past her on his way to the lamp at the foot of the stairs. 'A grand night for it, eh?'

'For what?' she asked, still dazed.

Soft gas light filled the close. The lighter, an elderly man, turned and winked at her.

'For bein' alive,' he said, and went on his way, while Elspeth fled upstairs, her mouth still tasting Kenneth's lips, her nostrils filled with the fresh soapy smell of him.

Kenneth was returning soon to Glasgow, but he and Elspeth made the most of the time that was left, seeing each other every day. Because he couldn't afford the cinema or the theatre often, they walked along by the river, or over the hills at the back of the town, sometimes talking, sometimes silently enjoying being together.

Like Elspeth, Kenneth was ambitious. He didn't find her yearning to work in an office at all strange, and with him, she felt that she could be herself, saying whatever she wanted without being laughed at, or accused of trying to get above herself.

He took her to his home in Gourock for tea, and his parents made her welcome. She plucked up the courage to invite him to Mearns Street, where, to her delight, he fitted in well. They all liked him, even Flora, once she had recovered from the shock of realising that Elspeth was walking out with a young man who was clever enough to become a doctor.

He and Granjan took to each other at once, and even

Grandmother approved. 'A civil young man,' she told Elspeth in the kitchen when she took Kenneth with her on her monthly visit. Then, delivering the highest accolade, 'Your grandfather would have been pleased.'

The best part of it was that Kenneth understood about Lachlan. He knew about shell shock, and admired the way Thomas was working to rebuild his brother's confidence.

'It'll take time,' he told Elspeth, 'just as it would if he had broken his leg badly. The hard thing is that in Lachlan's case the damage doesn't show, so folk don't know how to deal with it.'

Lachlan continued to improve. The drawings of Thomas being hurt and killed were a thing of the past; now he sketched the views from the windows, covering page after page with drawings of cranes and ships in construction, and the water and hills beyond. The nightmares that had plagued him, and the entire family, night after night were easing. He nerved himself to go out more, especially down to the shore, where he could sit for hours on end looking at the water.

'The river's not afraid of anything,' he explained to Elspeth. 'It just goes its own way, and it takes its own time, and it always gets where it wants to be. The river knows what's best for it.'

A week before Kenneth was due to leave, he and Elspeth went on an afternoon picnic with Mattie, Thomas and Lachlan. Because the shore at Greenock was lined with ship-yards, they took a short bus ride along the coastline to Largs, a handsome residential town popular with holiday-makers. It was the first time Lachlan had been in a bus since the war; sitting behind him, Elspeth saw his thin shoulders tense with the effort of keeping his nerves under control as the vehicle rattled along. Kenneth, beside her, leaned forward.

'Look at the water, Lachlan,' she heard him say. 'Just keep watching it and we'll soon be there.'

Lachlan's fair head immediately craned to the right, and the tension eased from his back. When they descended at Largs Pier, his eyes were bright with triumph at having broken through another barrier.

They found a sheltered pebble beach beyond the town, with rocks scattered here and there, useful as seats or back-rests. The long, low green shape of the Greater Cumbrae, one of the Clyde islands, lay across the water. Its small town, Millport, was also popular with holiday-makers and day-trippers, and passenger steamers were to be seen regularly plying between the island and Largs.

They paddled in the cold clear water, then ate the sandwiches and ginger beer they had brought with them. Afterwards, Mattie wandered off along the beach in search of shells and Lachlan perched on a rock, his eyes on the river. Thomas tossed pebbles into the water while Kenneth propped his back comfortably against a rock and opened a book he had brought with him.

Elspeth waded into the river again, braving the agony of walking without shoes over the pebbles, gasping as the water enfolded her feet in its cold grip. Her long brown plait swung over her shoulder, the golden hairs glinting in the sunlight. She found a half-submerged rock and leaned against it, watching her bare toes shimmering beneath the surface, then looking up as a passenger steamer passed quite close, tiny arms waving from the crowded rails. A gust of wind almost dislodged her straw hat; she pinned it down with one hand and waved back with the other, then as a slightly larger wavelet broke against her calves, she kilted her skirt higher and made her way back to the beach.

'I've been thinking,' Kenneth said lazily, watching her drying her feet, which were as scarlet as lobsters from the water. 'Why should that typewriter be sitting in the back shop, when you could be using it?'

'But I've not finished paying for it yet.' She handed back the clean handkerchief he had loaned her. Thomas flipped a round, flat pebble into the water and it bounced twice before disappearing beneath the surface.

'I know, but I've got work to do for the beginning of the university year. You could type it out for me if you had the machine – I'd pay you for it.'

'I couldn't take your money!'

'Of course you can,' Thomas said shortly. 'The very best money is the money you can get out of other folk's pockets and into your own. Or so I'm told.'

Kenneth looked puzzled, and Thomas grinned back at him, cold-eyed.

'What I mean is, Kenneth, we all need money, don't we?'

'That's what life's about.'

'I thought your life was going to be about making sick folk well,' Thomas said at once, and Kenneth flushed.

'It is, but I'll have to get paid for it. How else can I live?'

'There's your answer, Ellie.' Thomas sent another pebble into the air with a flick of the thumb. This time it bounced four times, and was quite far out before it sank. 'Folk need money to live, and you've as much right to live as anyone.'

'You earn a wage yourself,' Kenneth's voice was defensive, and Thomas laughed.

'Aye, but I'm only paid enough to enable me to exist.' He started to prise a large stone out of the ground. 'While the man that employs me lives very comfortably because he has a lot more money than me.'

The stone came free, and he held it up, gesturing around the beach with his other hand. 'Suppose this big stone's that man, and the rock our Lachie's sitting on's a man with even more wealth. But when you look all around, what d'ye see?'

His free hand dropped, to indicate the beach around them. 'Wee pebbles, all over the place. These pebbles are us, and all the folk like us. They're necessary, because without them there's no beach, but most folk don't realise that. Most folk

177

think the pebbles don't matter, 'cos there's so many of them, and they're only wee.'

He scooped a handful of pebbles up and tossed them towards the water. They hit the surface with a series of soft plops. Then he hurled the stone viciously after them. It crashed into the river noisily, throwing up spray.

'Pebbles don't make enough noise tae be noticed, but the big stones do, because they're important – important enough to throw their weight around,' said Thomas, then scrambled to his feet, rubbing moisture from his hands.

'So take the lad's money, Ellie. Take all the money you can get. The more you earn, the bigger the pebble you'll be – and the more folk'll take notice of you, and see you as a person,' he said, then strode off along the beach, leaving them to gape after his retreating back.

'What's bothering him?' Kenneth asked, his voice subdued.

'I don't know. He's been like this for weeks. It's not like Thomas at all,' Elspeth fretted.

Kenneth shrugged. 'Whatever it is, it's not our worry. What I was saying is, I've been working in the pawn shop to earn money to help me through university. And it would help me if you'd type some of the papers for me.'

'What would your uncle say?'

'I've spoken to him about it, and he agrees. He's a businessman – he realises that if I pay you to do work for me, you can pay him what you owe on the typewriter sooner than you expected. And that suits him.'

Kenneth brought the typewriter to Mearns Street the next evening, trundling it through the streets on a handcart, then carrying it up the stairs to arrive, red-faced and breathless, at the McDonalds' door.

They all crowded into the small bedroom to watch as the typewriter was settled carefully on to a sturdy little table that he had brought from the pawn shop.

'A present from the management,' he explained casually.

Elspeth, shaking with excitement, settled herself on the side of the bed, because there was no room for a chair, and sent her fingers flying deftly across the keys. Listening to their admiring exclamations as she explained the workings of the machine, she glowed. Perhaps she wasn't going to be a teacher, like Mattie, or a doctor, like Kenneth, but this was something that she, and nobody else in the room, could do. She felt important, and gifted.

Kenneth, hunkered down on his heels by the table, his elbows on its edge, caught her eye, and gave her a warm, conspiratorial smile. She beamed back at him, remembering that she owed it all to him. If he hadn't coaxed his uncle to trust her, she might not have got the typewriter, her most precious possession.

Flora had wanted her younger daughter to continue living at home while studying at teacher-training college, travelling by train to Glasgow each morning and returning in the evenings.

But Mattie, suddenly ready to spread her wings, had argued that this was quite impossible; as well as being costly, it would give her little time to study.

To her relief her mother finally gave in. The headmistress of the school Mattie and Elspeth had attended was consulted, letters – typed by Elspeth – were sent out and replies received, and Flora and Mattie spent a nerve-racking day in the city, inspecting a recommended hostel for young women. When they arrived home, Flora flustered and Mattie giddy with excitement, it had all been arranged.

On Mattie's final evening at home, neighbours and friends flocked to the flat to wish the fledgling teacher well. Even Bob, who didn't often visit now, came with Rachel, who wore the dress that had been made for her wedding. It would soon have to be put aside, Elspeth thought, noticing how the skirt, which had hung so neatly back in May, was now tight over the girl's swelling pregnancy.

'Have you noticed the bold Bob?' Thomas murmured to her during the evening. 'That's never ginger he's drinking.'

'Of course it is. Bob's temperance.'

'I'm not so sure.'

It was true that Bob had changed. He was restless, and louder than usual, and she noticed that he had developed a habit of passing a hand over his lips, as though they were parched, although he had a glass in his hand every time Elspeth saw him.

She didn't have time to wonder at Thomas's words, because just then Kenneth, who was also leaving for Glasgow the following day, sought her out.

'It's too crowded in here, I'm going out for a breath of fresh air. Come with me.'

'You'll look out for Mattie, won't you?' she asked as they went through the close to the back yard. 'She'll mebbe feel lost in such a big city on her own.'

'I'm going to be busy, but I'll do what I can. Elspeth, Uncle

George was wondering if you'd look in at the shop tomorrow to have a word with him. I've told him that you might be willing to look after his books.'

'Me?'

'You've been taking book-keeping at night school, haven't you? It'd be good for you get some practice at it.' He put an arm about her. 'You're shivering. Here—' He drew her to where the wash house used by all the women in the tenement bulked against the tenement wall. The door was never locked; the interior smelled of bleach and soda, soap and wet clothes, but at least they were out of the chill night wind.

Kenneth was a silhouette against the small window, his breath warm on her cheek. 'I've done what I can with his books during the summer, but he needs someone to see to things properly. And he'll pay you fairly, I've seen to that too. Will you do it?'

'I'll have a word with him about it.'

'Good,' he said, then he kissed her, and suddenly she felt quite tearful at the thought of being without him. She clung to him in the soap-smelling gloom. 'I'm going to miss you!'

'I'll be home for the New Year.'

'But that's months away yet!'

Kenneth kissed her again, and she returned the kiss with passion, running her fingers through his hair and over the nape of his neck. She knew that he liked that.

'Oh – Elspeth!' he whispered, nuzzling at her neck then her shoulder, his mouth hot through the barricade of her woollen jumper.

Whether it was because of the darkness, or the small space they were enclosed in together, or because his kisses were more passionate than usual, she couldn't tell; she only knew that her stomach was churning, her knees so weak that she was grateful for the support of the big brick boiler against her back. She had heard from Lena and the other girls in the sewing room about love and passion, and had seen it on the cinema screen, but nothing had prepared her for such a sense of elation. She wanted to blend right into Kenneth, to be part of him and for him to be part of her . . .

For a long moment it was wonderful, then the sudden waft of cold air against her stomach when he began to unfasten her blouse brought her back to earth. His hands were sliding over her bare shoulders, his fingers slipping under her bodice to touch her breasts, his body shuddering against her. A strange, pleasant thrill was running through her own body, but at the same time a tingle of doubt flared in her mind.

'Kenneth—'

He didn't hear her, and she had to struggle inelegantly to push his hands down to the comparative respectability of her skirt waistband.

'What is it?' He sounded strange, as if he had just wakened from a sound sleep. 'Oh, Elspeth, please!'

Please, her aroused body begged along with him, but her brain, which had started to function again, said otherwise. Mind and body, longing and common sense – it was like being in a whirlpool. She wanted whatever was happening between herself and Kenneth to go on, but at the same time she knew that it was wrong.

'We'd better not,' she said, squirming away from him, pulling the edges of her blouse together, pushing buttons through buttonholes with nervous haste.

'But I'm going away – can we not just love each other a wee bit so that we've got something to remember?'

'Not like this.' Now that the heat was slowly draining from her, she knew that this wasn't the way she had imagined it would be. Not in the wash house, with the smell of soda and harsh yellow soap.

'Come on, Elspeth—' As he reached for her, light from the small window glinted off the whites of his eyes, and she suddenly realised that in the dark, he could be anybody. For all she knew, Kenneth might have been spirited away somehow, and his place taken by someone – or something – else. Memories flooded back of the man who had dragged her into the shop doorway during the street celebrations at the end of the war.

'Leave me be!' Spurred on by her over-strong imagination, she squirmed away from him, pushing at him frantically, then ran to the door. Her sense of direction had gone, and she panicked when her outstretched hands came up against the brick wall instead of the rough wooden door. She fumbled to her right, found planks beneath her fingers, and burst out of the wash house into the chill darkness.

'Elspeth!' Kenneth caught at her arm and turned her round. And there he was, clearly seen in the light spilling through a ground-floor window; Kenneth, her Kenneth, with his hair tousled and his round face perplexed.

She fell against him, half laughing. 'Kenneth, it's you!'

'Of course it's me, who else could it be? What's wrong with you?'

She sucked in a deep breath, smoothing his jacket with her hands. 'I'm sorry, Kenneth, I just – I had to get out into the fresh air.'

He said nothing, but moved back slightly, so that her hands dropped away from him.

'I have to go, I told my parents I'd not be late home.'

'Kenneth, don't be angry with me—' she began, then jumped away from him, startled, as Thomas spoke from the darkness of the close.

'Elspeth, it's time you were back in the house.'

'I'm just going.' Kenneth brushed past him without another glance at Elspeth.

'What was going on?' Thomas asked as Kenneth's footsteps disappeared along the close.

'Nothing was going on! What did you have to go creeping about like that for?'

'I saw you from the landing window, bursting out of the washhouse. What were the two of you up to?'

183

'Doing the washing, what d'you think?' She flung the words at him, pushing past him to reach the stairs. He had ruined everything. Because of him, Kenneth had gone, without giving her a chance to explain. She was so angry that she could have hit him.

He caught up with her on the first landing, stopping her and spinning her towards him with his hands on her shoulders. 'Ellie, you're still only a bairn.'

'I'm old enough to look out for myself!'

'You're not. No harm to Kenneth, he's a decent lad, but he's older than you, and he knows more about the world. Don't try to grow up too soon, Ellie,' he said, 'There are bad things as well as good things in it, and once you've taken the final step you can't change your mind and go back to being a bairn.'

'Leave me be!' She pulled free and ran up the stairs, away from him.

In bed later, Mattie clung to her, her tears on Elspeth's neck just where Kenneth's mouth had been, and just as hot. 'What if I don't like it, Ellie? What if I'm a dunce after all, and nobody wants to be my friend, and I'm all alone?'

'You'll be fine. You're clever, and of course folk'll like you. If you get too homesick, we're only a train ride away. You'll be fine,' Elspeth said again. 'Anyway, what about me, left here while you and Kenneth are in Glasgow? I'm going to be lonely without you.'

'But you've got Mam and Dad and Lachlan and Thomas.' Mattie sniffed. 'I'll not have anyone I know!'

By the time Mattie was soothed into sleep, Elspeth was wide awake, her mind filled with the scene in the washhouse. In the safety of her bed, her body tormented by the memory of Kenneth's touch, she wished that she hadn't pushed him away. She moaned softly as she recollected how his fingertips had brushed against her breasts. Would he forgive her for the way she had treated him?

Then she imagined herself having to tell Aunt Flora that a

bairn was on the way. The very thought of such a scene cooled and calmed her burning, restless body. Maybe she had done the right thing after all. Maybe one day she would be glad that she had done the right thing, hard though it had been.

With that thought held firmly in her mind, she fell asleep at last.

George Monteith was standing behind the counter when Elspeth went into the pawn shop after work the following evening. His presence more than anything else brought it home to her that Kenneth was far away in Glasgow now, and for a moment she knew a great sense of loss.

The pawnbroker invited her upstairs to his kitchen, a room furnished with a fireplace, gas cooker, table, chairs and sideboard, but with shelves holding a wide variety of items, all sporting pawn tickets, lining the walls. He laid the books before her on the kitchen table, together with an old tin biscuit box adorned on the lid with a splotched and faded picture of a basketful of kittens, and crammed with pawn tickets and scraps of paper. Each time the bell jangled in the shop below he scurried off, leaving her to find her way through the maze of paperwork.

Elspeth was appalled at the size of the task she had been asked to take on. George Monteith's idea of financial dealings was to scribble all his transactions down on scraps of paper and toss them into the biscuit box. His ledger was shamefully bare and neglected, with nothing balancing.

At first, she was inclined to make some excuse and get out of the place as quickly as she could, but on the other hand, the challenge interested her, and she had some idea in her head that by helping his uncle, she could make up for her childish behaviour towards Kenneth the night before. By the time she returned home, she and the pawnbroker had come to an agreement.

Flora was horrified when she heard that Elspeth was to do

Mr Monteith's books. 'I don't care if he is Kenneth's uncle, he's still a pawnbroker,' she said in outrage, 'and I'll not have you standing behind the counter of that pawn shop. As tae what your grandmother'd have to say if she heard – I've no wish tae have her round here again, makin' more accusations against me!'

'Aunt Flora, it's not going to be like that at all. I'll call in at the shop every Friday evening to collect the books, then bring them back here and work on them over the weekend. I'll hand them back in on Monday morning on my way to work. There's no shame in it,' Elspeth coaxed, horrified at the prospect of having to admit to Mr Monteith that her aunt had forbidden her to do his books. That was no way for a book-keeper to behave!

'Well, ye can give it a try,' Flora said at last, grudgingly. 'But if anyone talks about seein' you goin' intae a pawn shop, it stops at once, d'ye hear me? I've no wish to have folks thinkin' we're havin' tae pawn things in order tae eat.'

From then on, Elspeth was so busy with the task of organising Mr Monteith's books at the weekends and letter-writing in the evenings that she had very little time to miss Kenneth.

She wrote to him, apologising for her behaviour on his last evening at home. His reply was somewhat cool, but she kept writing, and gradually his own letters, never very frequent or very long, took on more warmth, and she felt that she had been forgiven.

Thanks to her work for Mr Monteith, the typewriter was fully paid for by October, and each morning when she woke and saw it sitting by the bed, she glowed with the pride of full ownership. Her bank account, sorely depleted by the money she had had to pay for the typewriter, began to flourish once more.

By the time Mr and Mrs Bruce and their daughter returned from their holiday in the south of France, Thomas, who had tormented himself during their absence with thoughts of

Aileen laughing and talking and dancing with other men, had resigned himself to the fact that he had lost her.

When she came home, he told himself during sleepless nights, he would learn that she had been promised to some handsome, confident, wealthy man. After all, that was what her parents wanted and expected. That was what she had been born to, and the sooner he accepted the truth the better. At least, he tried to tell himself, he had known more happiness with her than he had ever dreamed of. He would always have that to remember. But such thoughts were cold comfort. Aileen was the woman he wanted, and there could never be anyone else.

Ian Bruce, who had returned to Scotland before his parents and sister because of business commitments, went with Thomas to collect them from the station, travelling in state in the back of the car because it wouldn't have occurred to him to sit beside the chauffeur.

When the train came in, Thomas went directly to the guard's van to collect the luggage. By the time he emerged from the station with a porter and began packing the cases into the trunk the family were seated.

After making arrangements to have the rest of the luggage brought to the house in a hired cab, together with the valet and lady's maid who had accompanied their master and mistress on holiday, he took his place behind the wheel and drove from the station, his ears straining to catch Aileen's voice. Every laugh, every word she spoke, squeezed at his heart. Opening the car door at the house, he stared stiffly ahead like a sentry on duty, then glanced at her, startled, as she paused and said, 'Hello, Thomas.'

'Welcome home, Miss Aileen.' He tore his eyes away from her almost at once, afraid of staring, almost choking with anger as he heard her brother say clearly as he accompanied her up the steps to the front door, 'If you must chat with a servant, Aileen, at least use his surname.'

Although he had glanced at her only briefly, the image of her, cool and slender in a lemon jacket and skirt that emphasised her perfect golden tan burned in his mind's eye for the rest of that day and all through the night. He woke up the next morning with it strong and clear in his brain.

She came into the garage that morning when he was polishing the car, touching his shoulder lightly and making him jump.

'Miss Aileen—' One glance over her shoulder showed that she was alone, and he added, low-voiced, 'You're not supposed to be in here—'

She was dressed for riding, in a green shirt that emphasised the colour of her eyes. 'I had to see you.' The words sent a jolt of astonished joy through his entire body. 'I've missed you so much, Thomas. I wrote every night, then tore up the letters because I had no way of sending them to you.'

He swallowed hard, scarcely able to believe her. He had worked so hard at convincing himself that her feelings for him would have died by now. 'I – I thought you'd have found someone else.'

'How could you think that?' Her eyes caressed his face. 'How could you doubt me?'

'I – you must have met so many men while you were away.'

'I did, but I wasn't interested in them. I don't want anyone else, surely you know that by now? Oh, Thomas—'

She reached up to touch his cheek, her fingers sending the blood racing round in his veins. He wanted to pull her into his arms and hold her and never let her go; instead, he put his own hand up to cover hers, trapping it against his face for a few joyous seconds before lifting it away.

'You must go. What if someone comes in?'

'Where are you going to be later?'

'I'm taking your father to Glasgow. We'll not be back till late afternoon.'

'Tonight, then.'

'There's a dinner party tonight.'

'After dinner. I'll pretend to have a headache and meet you in the summerhouse.'

Someone walked past the slightly open garage door. 'You must go,' Thomas said again, in a panic.

'Nine o'clock,' she whispered, and left, not bothering to peer out first to see if the coast was clear, but leaving confidently, as befitted someone who had legitimate reasons for going into her own father's garage.

A few minutes later, Thomas, weak with relief at the knowledge that she still cared, heard her horse's hooves clattering on the cobbles outside. Hungering for another sight of her, he left the car and moved to the door to see her go by, straight-backed as ever, her small hands confident on the reins. He watched until she had ridden round the corner of the house and out of sight, then, about to turn back into the garage's gloom, he saw Ina standing by the kitchen door opposite, a basket of washing on its way to the drying green balanced on one hip.

He had put a stop to his meetings with Ina after he first kissed Aileen in the summerhouse, suddenly unable to bear the housemaid's kisses and caresses. It hadn't been easy, for since Rachel's wedding the girl had become very possessive, constantly urging him to agree to marriage, and Thomas couldn't explain to her why he no longer wanted to walk out with her. Finally, he had precipitated a quarrel over nothing, and told her that they were finished. Ina had taken it badly, and hadn't spoken to him since.

Now, she gave him a long, bold, cold look, then her eyes narrowed and she swung away with a toss of the head.

Thomas returned to his work, his joy over the meeting with Aileen suddenly tempered with apprehension. There had been something about Ina's calculating, knowing look that chilled him to the bone.

19

Although Elspeth missed Mattie, having the bedroom to herself meant that she could type without disturbing anyone. Lachlan took to coming in to watch her at work and to marvel at her skill. He was still quiet and withdrawn, but much more independent than he had been since coming home from the army. His father had hoped to get him back to his old job, but the continual noise in the shipyards still panicked him.

When, in the middle of September, Elspeth heard that there was a vacancy for someone in the packing office at Brodie's, she suggested it to Lachlan.

'It's not much, just packing up things that customers have ordered, ready for the carters. But it'd be a start. What d'you think?'

Lachlan, sitting on her bed, plucked nervously at the corner of the quilt, thinking for a while.

'I cannae go on like this all my life, can I?'

'It would be good for you to get out and about again. There's not many in the packing room, and I'd be near to hand. We could go to work together, and walk home together too.'

He looked up at her, fear in his eyes, but determination in the set of his mouth.

'I'll try.'

As luck would have it, Miss Arnold was off with toothache the next day, and Miss Buchanan busy with a client, so Elspeth was able to slip out of the sewing room and go to the office, where Theresa McCabe rattled efficiently at the type-writer and Wilma and Graham worked at the big desk.

Wilma raised her brows when Elspeth asked if Mr James was free. 'What d'you want to see him about?'

'I'll tell him that.'

Wilma gave an offended sniff, but got down from her stool and tapped on the office door, closing it behind her when Mr James called to her to go in. She returned in a few minutes and said sulkily, 'He'll see you.'

James Brodie's greeting was more welcoming. He shook Elspeth's hand, and waved her to a chair before asking, 'What can I do for you?'

She told him about Lachlan's shell shock and how he couldn't return to the shipyard because of the noise and the bustle of the place. Then, twisting her fingers nervously in her lap, she ventured, 'I've heard there's a position free in the packing department. I think he could do that.'

'Do you? And what does he think?'

'He'd like to try for it. He needs to do something, Mr James, before it's too late,' she added, trying hard not to beg.

He pursed his lips for a moment, then to her great relief he said, 'Bring him with you tomorrow morning and I'll have a word with him.'

She fretted half the night in case Lachlan's nerve failed him at the last moment, but the following morning, pale and tense, dressed in his best, he walked with her into the store. She took him to the office but then had to go to the sewing room. It wasn't until after work, when she got home, that she found out that he had been given a month's trial.

After all they had been through with Lachlan, it was as if he had gained a place at Glasgow University. Flora and Henry could scarcely conceal their elation, and Thomas, who had finally emerged from the moodiness that had dogged him for a full month and reverted to his usual cheerful self, slapped his brother on the back and insisted on taking him out for a drink.

When they returned, he tapped on Elspeth's door.

'You did well.'

She twisted round from the typewriter to look up at him. 'D'you think he'll be all right?'

'I don't know – it's up to him now. But at least you've got him this far,' he said, then let her get back to her typing.

As well as the letters she was commissioned to write, Mattie and Kenneth were correspondents now, just as Thomas and Lachlan had been during the war. Mattie's letters were long and enthusiastic; she was settling in well at college and in the hostel, making friends and enjoying her studies. Kenneth's letters were usually brief reports on the subjects he had studied that week.

To his family's relief, Lachlan settled into the packing department quite well. At first, going to work was a daily trial, but having made the initial effort, he refused to let himself give in and stay at home.

'If I give up now, I'll not go back,' he told Elspeth tersely one morning when he looked so strained that she tried to persuade him to stay at home. As the days grew into weeks she saw the tension easing from his mouth and eyes, and knew that he had broken through yet another barrier.

Night classes had started again, and thanks to her own typewriter and her work with Mr Monteith's books, her typing and book-keeping abilities had improved. She was even allowed, in the typewriting class, to take over the beginners now and then while the harassed teacher dealt with the more advanced pupils.

'You're good at helping them to understand,' the woman commented one evening. 'Have you thought of teaching typewriting yourself, once you get your diploma?'

'Oh, no.' Elspeth was taken aback by the very idea, but the teacher was serious. 'I think you should. You have the right approach.'

Elspeth almost danced her way home that night. She was still set on working in an office, but if nothing came of that, there was now teaching to consider. Gradually, her ambitions were coming closer to being realised.

In October, a few weeks after Elspeth's sixteenth birthday, Thomas came home, grim-faced, and told his parents that he had lost his job.

'You can't have!' Flora's lips were suddenly ashen, and one hand clutched at her chest. Because her own father had been unable to support his wife and child due to poor health, Flora, who had had a harsh childhood despite all her mother's efforts to be the breadwinner, had grown up with a terror of unemployment. 'What did ye do wrong?'

'I did nothing wrong. There was a difference of opinion between me and Mr Ian. He's an arrogant bastard, that one,' Thomas added bitterly.

'What d'ye mean, a difference of opinion? What was it about?'

'Nothing that concerns you, Mam.'

Flora gave an animal-like whimper. 'For God's sake, man, ye lose yer job and say it's none of our concern? D'ye know how many men are bein' turned off these days?' Her voice began to rise. 'D'ye know how hard it is tae find work?'

'I'll manage.' Thomas, Elspeth saw with concern, looked grey and ill. 'I'll find another place.'

'How d'ye expect tae find another position just like that when ye werenae able tae stay in the one ye already had?' Flora almost shouted at him. 'Are ye goin' tae get a good reference from Mr Bruce?'

Thomas looked away from her searching glance. He was her favourite, and there was little he could hide from her.

'Well – are ye?'

'No.'

'No – and how can ye, if ye quarrelled with his son! Can ye no' keep yer tongue quiet when ye're around yer betters, ye daft fool?'

Thomas was stung into rounding on her. 'A man like Ian Bruce isn't my better!'

'Is he no'? Whatever sort of man he is, he's got money, and what d'you have, tell me that? Not even a job!'

'Don't get yerself all upset, Flora.' Henry put a hand on her arm. 'The laddie's got a good head on his shoulders, he'll find somethin' else.'

'Ye think so?' Flora shrugged his hand from her arm and whirled back to Thomas.

'It's her fault, isn't it? That lassie ye brought home with ye – Bruce's daughter?'

His eyes blazed at her. 'Leave it, Mam – I'm going out.' He turned to the door, but before he could open it Flora was on him, clutching at his jacket, hauling him round to face her. 'Don't you walk away from me! It was her, wasn't it?'

'Who?' Henry asked, bemused.

'That Bruce girl – that lassie he brought here tae my house!' She flailed at Thomas with her fists, forcing him to duck and wrap his arms about his head in self-protection.

Elspeth and Lachlan and Henry watched open-mouthed, too stunned by the suddenness of the attack to intervene. They had never seen Flora in such a state before; her face was crimson, her eyes wild, her hair escaping from its pins. Her voice was a harridan's shriek, the words pouring from it as she belaboured her son.

'Dirty, filthy midden that ye are, runnin' after yer master's daughter,' she screeched. 'An' she's no better, flauntin' herself before decent folk! I saw the way ye looked at her that day! I told ye, didn't I? I told ye she'd bring harm on ye!'

'That's enough, Mam!' Thomas had been forced back against the door; now he straightened up, suffering the blows, grappling with her until he managed to catch her wrists. His own face was distorted with rage. 'I'll not have ye foul-mouthin' her!'

Henry, coming to his senses, caught his wife round the waist

194

and dragged her away from Thomas. 'For God's sake, woman, d'ye want the neighbours tae call the polis? Leave the laddie be!'

'Look at the guilt in his face. Ask him if I'm no' right,' Flora panted. 'It was her that cost him his place – let him try tae deny it!'

'I'm not denying it,' Thomas said steadily. 'I love her – and she loves me.'

'Oh aye – it's love that made her stand by and let ye lose yer place, is it?'

'She knows nothing yet about what's happened,' Thomas flared back at his mother. 'She's away for a few days. It was Ina – she found out and told Mr Ian, and he went to his father.'

'Godsake's, man,' Henry groaned. 'Have ye no sense at all? You and Mr Bruce's daughter – how could ye think there was any future in that?'

'I knew there was no future to it, Da, but I cannae help my feelin's—'

'Can ye no'?' Flora stormed. 'Look at the shame yer precious feelin's've brought on us, ye—' Henry's grip on her had relaxed, and all at once she lunged forward, one arm lifting above her head, then swinging down to deliver a hefty open-handed slap across Thomas's cheek. The sharp crack of it rang through the room, then Flora, her rage spent, slumped back against her husband, sobbing, while Thomas put a hand to his reddening cheek. He stared in disbelief at his mother, then turned to the door.

'Come back here, Thomas, and let's get this business sorted out,' his father said.

'I'll come back when I get work, and not before. I'll not be a burden on anyone.' Thomas flung the words over his shoulder, just before the door closed behind him. A moment later, the outer door slammed.

Flora's knees gave way and she would have slid to the floor if Henry hadn't caught her and bundled her into a chair. 'What's goin' tae become of him now?' she whimpered, raising a face that was wet with tears, and aflame with angry red blotches now, as though she herself had been hit repeatedly.

'He'll survive, the way we all have tae.' Henry's voice was old and bleak. 'Ellie, ye'd best make yer auntie a cup of tea.'

Turning in a daze to do as she was told, she saw Lachlan standing in one corner, stooped over as though in pain. Elspeth's heart seemed to drop down through her ribs; this was the way Lachlan had been just after the war, before Thomas started dragging him out of his trauma.

Henry had noticed him too. 'Come on, son, sit over here,' he said, his voice gentle as he eased his son to a chair. 'It's nothin' tae get upset about.'

'How could Thomas do it?' Flora wailed as Elspeth made tea. 'Upsettin' his own brother, too, with never a thought of what he's been through already.'

Elspeth's blood boiled along with the kettle on the stove. If anyone had upset Lachlan it was Flora herself, with her venomous attack on Thomas. She bit the accusation back with an effort, saying instead, as she put a mug of strong, sweet tea into the older woman's icy hands, 'It's over now, Aunt Flora. Don't upset yourself.'

Flora glared up at her, looking like a witch with her untidy hair and narrowed eyes and blotched face. 'What d'ye mean, it's over? There's our Thomas out of work and the whole town'll be tattling tomorrow about what he's been up to with his employer's daughter—'

'He's not been up to anything,' Elspeth was stung into protesting. 'He said he loved her, but that doesn't mean that they've – they've—' She bit her lip, remembering that although she had been earning a wage for two years now, in Flora's eyes she was too young to know anything about what could happen between men and women.

'Love?' Flora gave a contemptuous laugh. 'Ordinary folk like us were never meant tae fall in love! Yer poor mother found that out the hard way – and it was me that was left tae raise the result. I'm not havin' my Thomas goin' along that road!'

'Flora, that's enough,' Henry barked from where he stood over Lachlan.

Despite the warmth of the room, a chill descended over Elspeth, as if someone had just dropped a flexible sheet of ice on her from above. Without a word, she poured out tea for Henry and Lachlan.

Thomas didn't come home that night. Flora, distraught, sent Henry out to look for him, and he came back at midnight to report that Thomas was staying with his grandmother.

'He says he'll come back when he's got a job, and not before.'

'Now look what's become of us.' Worry and exhaustion had taken their toll on Flora, dimming her anger to a feeble spark. 'That lassie's cursed this house!'

'For pity's sake, Flora,' her husband said wearily, 'She's done nothing of the sort. Now let's get tae our beds – we've got work tae see tae in the mornin'.'

On the following evening Elspeth and Lachlan hurried along to Granjan's little flat as soon as they could get away without rousing Flora's suspicions.

'Thomas isnae in,' the old woman said as soon as she opened the door. 'Come on in, the two of ye.'

'How is he?' Lachlan asked anxiously as they followed her into the kitchen.

'In a right state when he arrived here. He'd a good drink in him, and he's still in a right takin'. He cannae see past that Bruce lassie.'

Elspeth looked round the little room. 'Where did he sleep?' There was only the wall-bed, where Granjan slept.

'On the floor, wrapped in a quilt an' with a cushion under his head. He'll sleep there again tonight, for he's determined not tae go back home without a wage packet. Flora's in a terrible takin'.'

197

'She's been here?'

'Oh aye, most of the day. She's torn between wantin' Thomas home an' wantin' him dead. Ach, she doesnae mean it, though. She dotes on that laddie – on all her bairns,' she added hurriedly, a hand on Lachlan's fair head. 'The trouble with Flora is that she's never learned how tae love folk. She punishes them instead.' Janet Docherty sighed. 'I don't know how that came about, for she had plenty love herself as a bairn. Never be scared tae tell someone if ye love them, Elspeth, even if they let on they don't want tae know. It's the greatest compliment ye can give tae another human bein'.' Then, as the outer door opened, 'Mind what ye say, he's feelin' as tender as if he's been run over by the horse as well as the cart.'

Thomas, pale and drawn, stopped in the doorway when he saw the two of them. 'What are you doing here?'

'We came to see how you are.'

'I'm fine.'

'There's a pot of soup waitin' for ye.' Granjan bustled to the cooker. 'I got a nice bit of flank mutton tae taste it, so there's a good mutton stew as well.'

'I don't want anything to eat.'

'Of course ye do. Ye cannae seek work on an empty stomach.'

'Plenty have to,' Thomas said shortly.

'Aye, poor souls, but I've no intention of lettin' my own grandwean do that – not while I'm alive. Ye'll have a drop of soup too?' she asked Elspeth and Lachlan, who both hesitated. They had already eaten, but the broth smelled good.

'Come on,' Janet coaxed. 'Lachie can do with a bit more fat on his bones, and I'm sure you could manage a wee taste, Elspeth.'

As they squeezed round her little table, Elspeth marvelled at the difference between mother and daughter. Flora was always jumpy and on edge, while Janet was so serene. It would be better for Thomas, she thought, to spend time with his

grandmother while his unseen wounds healed. When Lachlan
tried to persuade his brother to return home with them, she
said firmly, 'I think Thomas is fine here, for the time being.'

He smiled gratefully at her. 'I'll come back when I've got
another job, Lachie.'

'When'll that be?'

'Soon, I can promise you that.'

When they rose to go, Granjan announced that she would
go with them to visit Flora. As she and Lachlan set out along
the road, Thomas detained Elspeth at the close-mouth.

'I've made a terrible mess of it all, Ellie,' he said wretchedly.
'I should never have let it come tae this!'

Elspeth thought of Aileen Bruce as she had seen her in the
fitting room at Brodie's and at her sister's wedding. 'She's very
bonny.'

'Aye,' Thomas said huskily. 'Why did Ina have to show
such malice? Ian Bruce was fair pleased to find out something
against me. He was there, in his father's study when I was sent
for – I could see the gloating in his eyes.'

'Are you sure it was Ina?'

'She saw us talking once, not long ago. She must have been
watching ever since, following one or the other of us. I should
have ended it long since, but I kept wanting just one more
meeting. Mam's right, I was a fool!'

'Will you try to see her again?'

'No. The damage is done, best leave it at that and not make
things worse.' He rubbed his hand hard over his face. 'You'd
best go.'

Hurrying along the darkening road after the two figures, one
dumpy, the other tall, ahead of her, Elspeth wished that she
could have stayed with Thomas. He was strong for others, but
vulnerable in his own grief. She wanted to comfort him, but
knew at the same time that the comfort he really needed could
never be his.

20

It wasn't an easy time to find work. Men were being laid off everywhere, and there was always a crowd waiting down at the docks in the hope of finding even a few hours' paid employment.

Thomas went out every morning and came back every evening, worn out from trudging round the streets. His ability to drive and his skill with engines stood him in good stead; a week after being turned away by Mr Bruce he found work in a small garage run by Forbes Cameron, a man with a deep interest in motorcars and enough money to set up his own business.

Even though he was bringing a pay packet home again, things weren't the same between Thomas and his mother. In the past, he had been the only member of the family able to tease Flora without giving offence; she usually wrangled with him amiably, or, if she could think of nothing to say, reached up and boxed his ears. Now, mother and son were civil to each other, but too much had happened for forgiveness on either side, and the special bond between them had vanished.

Nor could Elspeth forget what Flora had said to her that night. She had always known that she wasn't really part of the McDonald family, but it had never been made so cruelly clear before. She wished that she could find some way of striking out on her own instead of being beholden to the McDonalds.

Early in November, Brodie's typist had to take time off work because of illness in the family, and to her delight, Elspeth was asked back into the office. This time she took over the task confidently, impressing Mr Brodie with her ability to rattle away on the typewriter instead of pecking nervously at the keys.

She was more confident, too, in the way she handled Graham Adams when he started pestering her to go out with him.

'I've got a young man,' she told him loftily. His face dropped, and dropped even further when he discovered that Kenneth was studying to be a doctor. He made one more feeble try: 'If he's away in Glasgow studying, there's no harm in you finding someone to keep you company in the meantime.'

Elspeth whisked a sheet of paper out of the typewriter and rolled another in. 'I couldn't do that. He's very jealous,' she lied, and he said no more.

Rain rattled against the windows as the hands of the clock on the kitchen mantel shelf reached nine o'clock. Flora, who had been throwing surreptitious glances at the clock for the past half-hour, put her darning down. 'Where's that laddie got tae?'

'He'll be working on an engine, Aunt Flora,' Elspeth said, though she herself was becoming concerned over Thomas's absence.

Flora got up and opened the oven, letting the smell of overheated food into the room. 'He'll be more able tae heel his boots with this than eat it, the time it's been waitin' for him!'

Thomas's new job meant erratic hours. He had thrown himself into it feverishly, often working past his official stopping time.

Flora's complaints about the number of times she had to reheat his evening meal only met with a cool gaze and an indifferent, 'I'm not bothered whether the food's burned or cold, Mam – I'm not even bothered whether you make it or not,' that frustrated and frightened her.

'He's never as late as this,' she said now, picking up the sock she was darning, then tossing it down and giving her husband a firm dig in the ribs. He woke with a start from his comfortable doze.

'Henry, that laddie's never back yet – away tae the garage tae see if he's still there.'

Henry McDonald stretched and yawned. 'He'll have stopped in at a pub tae have a drink with some of his pals.'

'Not without comin' home first tae change out of his workin' dungarees. Our Thomas'd never stand in a pub covered with oil and filth. Not like some I could name,' she added with a sniff and a meaningful look at her husband.

'I'll go,' Lachlan offered, just as the knocker rattled.

Elspeth reached the door first, to find a policeman standing on the mat.

'Is yer daddy in, hen?'

The door across the landing had opened a crack; respectable tenements were never visited by the police, and there would probably be an ear pressed to every door the man had passed on his way up.

'Come in,' she started to say, but Flora was already pushing past her to scoop the officer in and shut the door against eavesdroppers. Henry, alerted by hearing a strange voice, appeared at the kitchen door, his shirt open to show his semmit, his braces looped at his waist.

'What's amiss?'

The constable drew his helmet off and tucked it under his arm as he made his way along the short, narrow hall into the kitchen. 'Mr McDonald? I've got some bad news for ye,' he said ponderously. 'It's yer lad, Thomas. We found him an hour since, in a back court. Someone's given him a right beatin'.'

Flora sagged heavily against her husband, just as she had done on the night she and Thomas had had their bitter quarrel. 'Is he – will he—'

'He's been taken tae the Infirmary, missus,' the man told her. 'They'll be able tae tell ye more when ye get there.'

'I'm going too,' Elspeth and Lachlan both said as soon as the policeman had left, but Flora shook her head.

'We cannae all rush there – they'll no' let a crowd of us in.

Better for you two tae stay here and we'll go on our own.'

They had two long hours of waiting before Flora and Henry returned with the news that Thomas was going to be all right.

'There's no bones broken, but he'll be kept in for a few days, just so's they can keep an eye on him. He's in a terrible state, the poor laddie.' Flora's face was streaked with tears, her eyes red.

'Someone gave him a right hidin',' Henry confirmed.

Elspeth opened her mouth to speak, but the words wouldn't come out. It was Lachlan who said, 'But who'd do that to our Thomas? Was it money they were after?'

'And him in his dungarees and covered with oil? Even in the gaslight anyone could see that he'd no' have money on him,' Flora snapped. 'The polis think he was mebbe mistaken for someone else.' Then, wringing her hands, 'What a thing tae happen – a polisman at our door! What'll the neighbours think?'

When Elspeth went to the Infirmary the following evening she didn't recognise any of the men in the beds at each side of the long ward. It was only when he called her name that she found Thomas.

Tears came to her eyes as she reached the bed where he was propped against pillows, with one arm strapped against his chest. His face was a mass of bruises, and both eyes were half shut. 'Oh, Thomas!'

'Now don't start greetin', Ellie,' he said with difficulty through swollen lips. 'Mam's done enough for the whole town. She cried so hard they almost had to change the bed when she left last night, and she was at it again this afternoon.'

Elspeth blinked rapidly to hold the tears back. 'Your face looks like the map of Europe that used to hang on our class-room wall.'

Thomas started to laugh, then winced and stopped abruptly. 'You should see my ribs – they're a world map; but it's not as bad as it looks. My arm's strapped because they put the shoulder out of place.'

She took his left hand in hers. 'There was more than one man?'

There had been two men at least, one stepping out of a close right in front of Thomas, another moving swiftly up behind him. After beating him unconscious they had apparently dragged him through a nearby close and into a neglected back court.

'I'm just lucky someone happened to come into the court and find me, else I'd have lain all night,' he finished.

Elspeth's palms stung; looking down she realised that she had doubled her hands into such tight fists as she listened that her nails were digging into the tender skin, leaving angry red crescents. 'Who would do such a thing?'

Thomas, exhausted with telling the story, slumped back against the supporting pillows. 'Ian Bruce might have the answer to that. I've seen him passing the garage a few times. I think he wanted me to know he was keeping an eye on me.'

'But you've not seen his sister since you lost your job.'

He began to shrug, then stopped as pain flickered across his face. 'He must think I'm still a threat to the family. He'd not find it hard to get men to do his work for him.'

'Did you tell the police?'

'Can you see them accusing Ian Bruce of having an ex-employee beaten?' Thomas asked drily. 'There's no sense in telling them anything.'

'If his sister knew—'

'Leave, it, Ellie. How's Lachlan?'

'He wanted to come with me, but as soon as we walked in the hospital door he started shaking. He'd to turn and go out again – he was awful vexed about it.'

'Tell him I'd not want him to force himself. I'll be home in a day or two. And don't you fret yourself, Ellie, I probably deserved what I got, playing with fire the way I did.'

'Nobody deserves to look like that.'

The words rang in her mind for the rest of the night, and

were still with her in the morning as she walked to work. Just because the Bruce family had money, it didn't give them the right to hurt folk.

The typewriter rattled ferociously that morning as she fumed over the injustice of what had happened to Thomas. Aileen Bruce was surely as responsible as he was for the love that had grown between them, and to Elspeth's mind, Aileen should know just what her brother had done in her name.

She thought of going to the Bruce estate and confronting the girl, but common sense prevailed. If she went to the door and asked to see Aileen she would almost certainly be refused admittance. If the girl's brother happened to be there, she might even put herself into danger. Anyone who could pay people to do what had been done to Thomas would think nothing of hurting a woman. A letter would have a better chance of reaching Aileen.

She had never before done her own work during office hours, but this was an emergency, she told herself, putting a blank sheet of paper into the typewriter. It didn't take long to do, for her fingers flew over the keys, and it was finished and in an envelope without anyone noticing. During the midday break she used some of her precious letter-writing money to bribe one of the messenger boys to deliver it during his rounds.

That evening, Flora came back from the Infirmary in a towering rage that spilled out in a flow of words as soon as the outer door closed behind her. Elspeth and Lachlan heard her squawking in the hall even before the door flew open and she stormed in, with Henry at her back, trying to placate her.

'The lassie was just visitin', Flora.'

'Visitin', d'ye call it? Well, I call it humiliatin'!'

'Miss Bruce came tae the hospital tae see our Thomas,' Henry explained to Lachlan and Elspeth as his wife paused to draw breath.

She wrenched the long pin from her hat. 'She'd no right! Walkin' intae the ward with a bunch of flowers that must have

cost a month's wages! Everyone in the place stopped talkin'.'
She whipped her hat off and stabbed the pin back into it
fiercely for safekeeping. 'It was the silence and the look on our
Thomas's face that made me turn round. And there she was,
marchin' right past us as if we werenae there, lettin' the flowers fall over the bed and on tae the floor, and takin' his hand for
all the world tae see—'

'She was cryin', poor wee lass,' Henry put in.

Flora glared at him. 'I was near cryin' myself. I've never seen
such an exhibition! If one of my lassies ever behaved like that in
public she'd feel the back of my hand, I can tell ye.' The
witch-like, venomous look that Elspeth had seen on the night
Thomas lost his job blotched the woman's face again. 'I didnae
know where tae look—' All at once, she started to weep.

'Come on, hen,' Henry soothed, easing his wife into her
chair. 'Best leave her,' he said over her head to the other two.
'It's Thomas bein' hurt an' all.'

It was more than that, Elspeth thought as she and Lachlan
crept from the room. It was the realisation that Thomas was lost
to her, now and for ever.

When Thomas came home a few days later, his face still bruised
and swollen, Flora's wrath had not abated.

As a result, mother and son had another quarrel, even more
vicious than the last, and again it ended with Thomas leaving
home. His employer, who already thought highly of his abilities
as a mechanic, let him sleep on a cot in the garage office. Ian
Bruce found out, too late, that far from keeping Thomas away
from his sister, his actions had forced Aileen to choose between
Thomas and her own family. She chose Thomas, braving her
family's wrath, accepting without flinching her father's refusal
to help her in any way.

She ignored Thomas's protests too, and when he found a
two-roomed flat to rent, she insisted on selling her personal
jewellery in order to buy furniture for their new home.

Flora, just as proud and determined as Mr Bruce, also refused to forgive them, mainly because the story had gone through the town like wildfire and the gossips had had a wonderful time discussing it all.

'She's a snob in her own way, is our Flora,' Janet Docherty told Elspeth. Janet herself had infuriated her daughter by taking a liking to Aileen and refusing to turn her back on the young couple.

When they married at the end of November, only Elspeth and Lachlan and Janet were present. Watching Thomas and his bride standing before the minister in the empty, echoing church, Elspeth thought of Catherine Bruce's fine wedding at the end of the war. Aileen could have had a wedding day like that, with no expense spared, but the happiness on her lovely face as she turned to leave the church, her hand tucked under her husband's elbow, showed that in her own eyes she had made the right choice. Despite the fading yellow and blue and purple bruises still discolouring his face, Thomas, too, was glowing with joy.

It was very hard for Aileen, used as she was to servants seeing to her every need, to settle to such a different life, but she was determined to make her marriage work, turning to her husband's grandmother for help in learning the basic skills of running her new, tiny home.

'It's no' the lassie's fault that she's been brought up tae money and servants,' Janet said. 'As long as her and Thomas make each other happy, what does it matter where they were born and raised? Mind yer hair, pet, it's too bonny tae burn.'

The two of them were in Janet's little kitchen a week after the wedding. Elspeth, making toast at the fire, obediently pushed her long plait back over one shoulder. She always put it up for work, but let it hang free at other times. She had been considering having her hair cut short, but Flora still refused to allow it. Turning the slice of bread on the long toasting fork and thrusting it back towards the glowing coals, she said, 'They say in the sewing room that Mrs Bruce has taken to her bed with the shock of what's happened.'

'Ach, that's just a ploy rich women use tae hide away from folk till the fuss dies down. I daresay poor Flora'd enjoy doin' the same, but she'll just have tae thole it till the gossips get tired. It's a strange world, right enough – the rich don't like tae see their bairns marryin' the poor, and a lot of ordinary folk like Flora don't like tae see the poor marryin' the rich.'

Janet put the teapot on the table and covered it with the woollen cosy Elspeth had crocheted at school, then came to sit by the fire, turning up the hem of her skirt so that her plump legs, richly decorated with varicose veins, could bask in the heat. 'Folk have short memories where scandal's concerned. Another week and they'll have found somethin' else tae whisper about.'

She was right, as usual. With no more fuel to keep it going, the gossip about Thomas McDonald and his new bride died down as the year drew to its close. When Mattie returned home for Christmas and New Year she had blossomed and matured, put on some much-needed weight and gained an air of confidence that startled her family. Contrary to Flora's conviction that her younger daughter would die of asthma within weeks of arriving in smoky, industrial Glasgow, the childhood ailment didn't bother Mattie as often now.

Warned by Elspeth's letters, she said nothing about Thomas and Aileen. Neither did Flora, and the others knew better than to mention Thomas's name. But as soon as she and Elspeth were in their bedroom on Mattie's first night home, propped, as usual, at either end of the bed, she asked, 'What's happening with Thomas? There's a new pinched look about Mam – I didn't dare say his name.'

'They're both fine, and very happy. You must go and see them.'

'I'll go tomorrow. Will they not be coming to see the new year in with the rest of us?'

208

'I don't think Aunt Flora'll allow it,' Elspeth said, and Mattie's eyes clouded.

'But it's Ne'erday! Everybody's with their own folk at Ne'erday, to start the new year off!'

'She's set her face against accepting Aileen.'

'I never thought she'd turn away from Thomas,' Mattie said wonderingly, then, 'Well, you and me and Lachlan'll just have to go and see them after the bells, for I'm not going to leave my own brother without his family at a time like that, whatever she says. She'll be busy with all the neighbours then anyway.'

'Tell me about Glasgow, and college.'

Mattie's eyes brightened. 'It's grand, Ellie! Teaching's the right thing for me – the only thing. I was born to it.' She adjusted her pillow, which had started sliding down. 'Kenneth's been kind, he kept an eye on me at the beginning, and I see him now and again, but I'd have managed anyway. He said to let you know he's coming home tomorrow. Studying's not as hard as I thought it would be, and I can't wait to get into the class-rooms.'

She talked for a while about her life in Glasgow, and Elspeth drank it all in, wishing that she, too, could have had the opportunity to go to the city.

Mattie's yawns became more and more frequent, and finally she stretched her arms, then slipped beneath the blankets. 'I'm getting sleepy – I'll tell you more tomorrow. Lachlan's looking much better – that work you found for him's doing him good.'

'It's not much, but it's a start. He's been helping out with painting some of the departments, too, and Mr Brodie's talking about giving him more responsibility.'

'All we need now,' Mattie said drowsily, 'is for Mam to stop being so silly about Thomas and Aileen, and everything'll be all right.'

Kenneth was waiting outside the department store when Elspeth left work the following evening. She wanted to run to him, but hesitated, recalling their last meeting, and its sudden end when Thomas came across the two of them in the back court.

He, too, looked awkward; he held out his hand, and Elspeth shook it, aware that Graham Adams and Lena and some of the other girls from the sewing room were nearby. Lachlan, who usually walked home with her, had prudently disappeared.

To her relief, Kenneth drew her hand through his arm as they walked away. 'You've done a grand job with Uncle George's books. He's fair delighted.'

'It was good practice for me.'

He laughed. 'A challenge, more like. Anyone who can get *his* affairs into order must be clever.'

Pride and pleasure warmed her, and she relaxed a little.

That evening he took her to the cinema, and kissed her on the way home.

'I've been thinking, while I was away, about that last time – in the wash house,' he said awkwardly. It was as well that it was dark in the corner where they stood, for Elspeth felt her face burn at the memory. 'It was wrong of me, to try to—'

'I shouldn't have made such a fuss.'

'I shouldn't have—' He stopped, then said, 'I forgot that you're still very young. It'll not happen again.'

'Never?' She tried to get a teasing note into her voice in an effort to lighten the situation. She had missed him, and now she wasn't entirely sure whether she was relieved or disappointed at his words.

'Well – not till you're older, and I'm further on with my studies,' he said firmly, then put an arm about her and turned her towards the lighted street. 'Come on, it's too cold to be standing here. D'you think your Aunt Flora would be willing to offer me a cup of tea?'

Despite her family's arguments and pleas Flora obstinately refused to invite Thomas and Aileen to Mearns Street for New Year, so after midnight on Hogmanay, Lachlan and Mattie and Elspeth and Janet left the house shortly after the church bells and the ships' sirens out on the river had noisily welcomed 1920.

'I don't like leaving Mam on her own at New Year,' Lachlan said as they gained the street at last, having been stopped all the way down the stairs by neighbours wishing them a happy new year. As, traditionally, first-footers couldn't go into anyone's home empty-handed, he was armed with a bottle of whisky.

'It's her own choice,' said Mattie, who was carrying a lump of coal, denoting good wishes to the house they were going to enter, and wrapped in newspaper to save marking her hands or her coat. Elspeth's gift was a black bun – a rich fruit cake – that she had baked herself. When Thomas and Aileen came to the door their callers were arguing over who should go into the house first.

'It has to be you, Ellie,' Mattie was saying as the door opened. 'Your hair's not all that dark, but it's darker than ours.'

Thomas, his face split by a huge grin, put one arm about Aileen and reached his free hand out to draw them into the house. 'I've got my own luck-bringer,' he said, 'and nobody here's got hair as dark as hers, so come in, the lot of you. And welcome!'

•

To mark the new year, Lena had persuaded Elspeth to accompany her and her latest young man to the music hall at the Hippodrome Theatre.

'D'you not want to go on your own with Drew?' Elspeth had asked doubtfully when the outing was first proposed.

'I do not,' Lena said bluntly. George, the naval sweetheart Lena had been writing to when Elspeth first met her, had vanished from the scene almost as soon as the war was over, and since then Lena had changed escorts several times. 'I'm tired of lookin' at Drew, but he's too thick tae take a hint. That's why I want you tae come too, so's I'm not stuck with him all evening. I can scarce get tae the privy in our back court without him trailin' along at my back. Bring yer sweetheart, and Mattie and that nice shy brother of yours that works in the packin' room. He's got bonny eyes.'

'Bonny eyes or not, he's too quiet for you.'

Lena winked. 'I can be quiet and shy when I want tae be. Go on and ask him. Ye neednae fret, I'll not affront ye.'

Mattie agreed enthusiastically, and to Elspeth's surprise, both Kenneth and Lachlan accepted the invitation. When Thomas and Aileen heard what was afoot they announced that they wanted to go too, so there were eight of them in the third row that night, much to Drew's annoyance.

Lachlan, who insisted on sitting at the end of the row in case it all got too much for him and he had to leave hurriedly, glanced frequently and nervously round at the crowded auditorium and up at the boxes flanking the stage. Once or twice Elspeth, sitting next to him, thought that he was going to lose his nerve and make a bolt for the exit, but he stayed where he was, and when the lights went down and the crimson plush curtains swept open to reveal the three lines of chorus girls ready to sweep into 'Put on your Ta-ta, Little Girlie', she felt him relaxing in his seat.

It was an enjoyable evening. The comedians were exceptionally funny, the dancers and acrobats exceptionally lithe, the soprano and baritone of an exceptionally fine quality. The problem came towards the end of the evening, when it was announced that Miss Dolly Burnett, the popular soloist, had had to cancel her appearance because of illness, and someone else was taking over her spot in the programme. An ageing lady in a flouncy pink shepherdess costume then appeared onstage, and the orchestra struck up.

Almost as soon as the substitute raised her wavering voice in song the audience became restless. Murmurs rippled from all directions, and to her horror Elspeth heard Lena say clearly from further along the row, 'That reminds me, Drew, I forgot tae put the cat out before I left home.'

The applause at the end of the first song was sparse, and when the poor woman launched into a second melody, trying to achieve notes that her voice couldn't possibly reach, catcalls and jeers began to be heard from the gallery. The noise grew until the orchestra wavered into nervous silence, and the singer, crimson with mortification and anger, was forced to stop. The Master of Ceremonies rushed on to the stage to appeal for order.

'Ladies and gentlemen, this lady has very kindly agreed to step in at short notice. The least you can do is to give her a hearing.'

'We have,' Lena bawled back at him, bouncing to her feet and ignoring Drew's attempts to pull her back into her seat. 'Now the least she could do's tae stop givin' us an earache!'

The audience applauded, and Elspeth cringed back against her seat as the Master of Ceremonies glared down at the row where they sat.

'If you can do better, miss,' he said crushingly, 'you're welcome to try.'

Lena needed no further invitation. 'Right,' she yelled back, 'I will!' and jumping to her feet she started to push her way along the row towards the aisle.

The man's jaw dropped. 'This is a music hall, not a street

party. Please return to your seat, miss!' He danced at the edge of the stage, his arms making distracted, shooing motions.

'Away with ye, man,' someone bellowed back from right behind Elspeth and Lachlan, making them both jump. 'Ye asked if the lassie could dae better – let her have a try at it!'

The call was taken up across the auditorium and in the gallery as Lena continued to forge towards the aisle. When she reached it, she stopped and turned, taking Lachlan's face in her hands and smacking a hearty kiss on his astonished mouth.

'Wish me luck,' Elspeth heard her say beneath the audience's applause, then she was on her way up the steps to the stage. Glancing down the row, Elspeth could see Drew, red-faced with rage, leaning forward to glare at Lachlan, who was too dazed to notice.

Seemingly undaunted by the lights and egged on by the crowd's noisy encouragement, Lena marched to the centre of the stage. As she knelt to have a brief discussion with the orchestra conductor, the Master of Ceremonies hustled the bewildered shepherdess into the wings, shrugging and murmuring in her ear.

'I expect he's telling her that they might as well let Lena make a fool of herself,' Kenneth said, applauding vigorously with the rest of the audience as the conductor had a quick conference with his musicians, and Lena straightened up to face the auditorium, whipping off her felt hat and loosening the ribbon that kept her long red hair under control.

As it fell in curls over her shoulders the spotlights caught it, turning it into a burst of brilliant colour that distracted attention away from her plain dark coat and heavy practical shoes. Then the music started, the applause died down, and Lena began to sing.

She had chosen a song that began with a serious verse; as the introduction was played she stood alone in the centre of the large stage, head up and face solemn, her hands meekly before her, one holding her hat, the other her ribbon. Her voice was clear and sweet, reaching the high notes without effort. At the end of the verse, she held the final note for several beats, then paused, her eyes sweeping boldly over the waiting audience, before suddenly swinging into a saucy chorus, deepening her voice as she slapped the plain felt hat back on her head, this time at a cheeky angle, and began to dance along the front of the stage.

'My darling daddy never ever puts sugar in his tea,' she sang, then, winking at her listeners, ''cos my sugar daddy says his only sugar's me—'

As cheers and whistles broke out around her, Elspeth stared, dumbfounded, at this new Lena, who was behaving as if going on to a stage was a common occurrence. It was as though she had been born to it.

The applause at the end of the song was tumultuous, and when Lena made to leave the stage, the audience roared for more. This time she sang, 'Poor Butterfly', standing straight and still, her hands clasped before her; her voice, sweet and pure, bringing a lump to Elspeth's throat. She wasn't the only one to be moved – the noisy audience had fallen into attentive silence as soon as the first notes rose from Lena's throat, and now there were a few sniffs from somewhere behind Elspeth, and the occasional gruff clearing of a throat. She glanced at Lachlan, and saw that he was totally absorbed in the lone figure on the stage, his lips parted and his eyes shining.

The applause was again deafening when the last wistful notes faded away, with some members of the audience on their feet. Lena beamed at them, knelt to whisper to the conductor, then announced with a cheeky grin, 'One more song and that's all ye're gettin'!' For the final song, she completely changed her style again, swinging into a pert rendering of 'I Can't Find My Way Home'.

When the song ended, she blew kisses to every part of the theatre, then to the orchestra, before picking up her hat and hair ribbon and walking demurely to the steps. The Master of

Ceremonies appeared as she got there, and they spoke briefly before she continued back down to her seat.

'Thanks for the luck,' Elspeth heard her say to Lachlan, putting a hand on his arm as he stumbled to his feet to let her brush past him.

As the party made their way to the exit after the show they were halted time and again by people crowding round to speak to Lena. She shrugged off their praise modestly, but her pretty face glowed.

'I've always wanted tae dae that,' she said when they finally grouped together on the pavement.

'You were wonderful!' Mattie's voice was awed. 'I could never do what you did tonight.'

'Och, it's easy. Ye don't pay any heed tae the audience, ye just think about the songs and enjoy singin' them.'

'An' make a right exhibition of yerself,' Drew said sourly, glaring at Lachlan, who hadn't said a word but couldn't take his eyes off Lena. 'Come on, it's time we were gettin' home.'

'I've tae go round tae the stage door first. That man wants a word with me.'

'Aye, an' I can imagine what it is,' Drew snarled. 'I'm goin' tae no stage door. I've had enough of a showin'-up tonight as it is!'

'I never said you were goin' with me,' Lena snapped back at him. 'I can manage fine on my own.'

He stared at her wordlessly, then turned on his heel and stamped away. Watching him go, Lena shrugged.

'Good riddance tae bad rubbish.'

'D'you want us to go with you?' Thomas offered as she turned away.

'No, I'll be fine.' She tossed the words over her shoulder as she headed for the side street where the stage door was located.

On Monday morning, she arrived at Brodie's department store to give in her notice. That night she went onstage again at the Hippodrome, and a week later, when the company finished its Greenock booking, Lena left town with them, telling

Elspeth before she went that both Miss Buchanan and Miss Arnold had prophesied a terrible future for her.

'They seem tae think I'll either end up as a white slave or starvin' in a garret,' she said, amused. 'I told them that anythin's better than dyin' of boredom in a sewin' room.'

'It's like a fairy story,' Elspeth marvelled, and Lena shrugged.

'It's just a matter of doin' what ye want tae do. Mind that when yer own time comes. Anyway – it was your Lachlan that gave me the good luck.'

She winked, just as she had winked on the Hippodrome stage. 'He might be quiet, but he's a lovely laddie,' she added, then she was gone.

As Lena's sudden decision to go on the stage meant that the sewing room was short-handed, Miss Buchanan demanded Elspeth's return from the office.

'As it happens, I'm expecting Miss McCabe back next week,' James Brodie said when he broke the news to Elspeth, 'so you would have been returning to the sewing room then in any case. But Miss Buchanan tells me there's a fairly large order in, so she can't wait.'

'I could do some work for you in the evenings, if I can take it home with me,' Elspeth offered, astonished by her own audacity. 'I've got my own typewriter there.'

His brows shot up. 'Your own typewriter? How did that come about?' She felt colour rise to her face as she explained, finishing with, 'It's old, but it's in good order.'

'But you shouldn't have to work in the evenings as well, my dear.'

'I don't mind. I don't go out much anyway,' she told him truthfully. Kenneth and Mattie had returned to Glasgow, and time was hanging on her hands.

He agreed, and each evening after that she went along to the office to collect the evening's work before going home. She was able to fit it in because the demand for her letter-writing skills had finally begun to ease off, though there were still several requests each week.

The work she had to do for Mr Brodie was easy compared to making sense of Mr Monteith's erratic book-keeping on crumpled scraps of paper. That task had seemed at first sight to be quite impossible, but Elspeth, determined not to let it defeat her, had worked hard, thankful, as the little bits of paper spread over the typing table, then the bed, and finally the floor, that she now had the room to herself and there was nobody there to complain.

Mr Monteith's writing was deplorable, his methods haphazard, but as time went by she had begun to read and decipher the scribbles more easily, and to grasp his strange logic. Gradually, the muddle had been transferred from torn-off scraps of papers and used envelopes into the large ledger. She had bought a smaller book and tethered it to the counter, persuading Mr Monteith to enter each transaction in it, rather than using bits of paper. He grumbled at first, but finally gave in.

It had occurred to Elspeth that most local folk took their most precious possessions into Mr Monteith's shop on a Monday morning, redeemed them on Friday, and pawned them again on the following Monday. Once James Brodie's typist had returned to work and Elspeth had more time in the evenings, she drew up a list of the items going through the pawnbroker's hands each week. When it was completed to her satisfaction she started listing the unclaimed or longer-term items stored in the back shop and the flat above, sneezing as the dust tickled her nose.

The listing meant that she spent far more time in the pawn shop than Aunt Flora would have allowed, had she known about it, but fortunately Flora was too wrapped up in her new grandchild to notice what Elspeth was up to.

Rachel's little girl, named Mary, after Mary Pickford the film star, was born less than two weeks after New Year. Once she was back on her feet, Rachel seemed to spend almost as much time in her old home as she had before she was married. Flora had no objection, for it meant that she could spend hours with her little granddaughter on her lap, cuddling her and crooning to her.

'Who's gran's best wee dumplin'?' she would say with a gentleness that amazed her family. 'Who loves her old granny?' Watching her joy in the baby, Elspeth saw another side to the woman she always thought of as sharp-tongued and difficult to please. Clearly, Aunt Flora loved babies, and it was easy to see, now, why she had taken her friend's orphaned child in with no thought to the cost of another mouth to feed.

'Mr James sent for me.' It was strange, Elspeth thought, to be visiting the office she had come to think of as her own workplace. Her eyes strayed to the typewriter, now under Theresa McCabe's control.

'I'll tell him you're here.' Wilma squirmed down from her high stool, saying as she went to the inner office, 'This is the lassie that did the typing while you were off, Theresa.'

'Oh aye?' The typist looked Elspeth up and down, then sniffed, clearly finding her wanting. It was a relief when Wilma reappeared, holding the office door open for Elspeth then closing it behind her.

To her astonishment, James Brodie reached over the desk and shook her hand. 'I wanted to thank you for the work you did in the office, and at home. And' – he held out an envelope – 'to give you this.'

Puzzled, she opened it, and her eyes widened as she saw that it held two crisp one-pound notes.

'But – I'm not due any wages till the end of the week.'

'That's from me, to express my appreciation.'

'Mr James, I can't take money I've not earned.'

'Of course you've earned it,' he said firmly, ignoring her outstretched hand. 'You'll have to learn to value your own skills – that's what business is all about.'

She didn't dare show the money to Aunt Flora, who had always warned the three girls about taking gifts from men. According to her, that was the swiftest way to hell. Surely, Elspeth thought as she left the office, Mr Brodie wasn't that sort of man. But Aunt Flora might not agree.

On the following day, she put the money into the bank.

At the end of January, a postcard arrived from Lena, addressed to Lachlan and bearing a view of Glasgow's George Square. According to the few words scrawled on the other side, Lena was appearing onstage in one of the city's theatres. Flushed with excitement, for he never received any post, Lachlan read it again and again, studying the photograph until Flora told him tartly that he'd wear it away with his eyes.

'I don't know what that lassie's thinkin' of anyway, sendin' cards tae a respectable house,' she added sourly. 'I don't like a son of mine gettin' messages from a woman who flaunts hersel' on the stage in front of goodness knows who.'

'There's nothin' wrong with goin' on the stage,' Lachlan retorted sharply, reducing his mother to open-mouthed astonishment. It was unheard of, even before the war, for him to answer her back.

When another card arrived a month later, this time from Aberdeen, he seized it and bore it off to his bedroom, refusing to discuss it with anyone, though he reported proudly to Elspeth later, 'She says she's doin' fine, and she's askin' after you. They're off to Dundee soon; she says she'll send me a card from there.'

But there were no more cards. As the weeks passed and Lachlan's eager anticipation turned to disappointment, Elspeth became furious with Lena for letting him down. There was nothing she herself could do about it, though, other than deciding that if Lena ever returned to Greenock she would have a few things to say to her.

22

Thomas, wearing trousers and a vest, opened the door to Elspeth.

'I've just arrived home,' he explained hurriedly, 'Aileen's cut herself, and I'm washing the dirt from the garage off my hands so that I can see to her.'

In the kitchen, fragrant with the smell of simmering broth mingled with an undercurrent of stew from the oven, Aileen was sitting on a chair by the stove, one hand nursing the other, a clumsy bandage wrapped about one of her fingers.

'I'll see to it,' Elspeth offered, but Thomas, already back at the tiny sink, shook his head.

'I can manage.'

Aileen smiled apologetically. 'It's just a wee cut where the knife slipped when I was peeling potatoes. I'm so clumsy – it's nothing to fret over.'

'You never know with cuts,' her husband insisted, reaching for the towel while Elspeth picked up the knife that Aileen had dropped and got on with the work of peeling the potatoes, noticing that the girl had cut the peel thick, taking a fair portion of the potato with it. Flora McDonald would have been mortified if she or any of the girls she had raised had indulged in such wastefulness.

Elspeth liked spending time in the little flat, and called in often. Although Thomas and Aileen couldn't afford much in the way of furniture, their love and joy in each other

221

permeated their home, turning it into a warm, welcoming place. Aileen, determined to be as good a wife as she could, worked hard at learning how to look after her new home; the small room was neat and bright and welcoming, the table set, the fireplace swept, the fire well tended.

The only untidiness was unavoidable – Thomas's oily working dungarees, which were lying on a sheet of newspaper in the corner. He himself washed them every Saturday, Elspeth knew, refusing to allow Aileen to take on the heavy, daunting task.

'How's Lachlan doing?' he asked as he tossed the towel down and knelt before his wife, carefully unwrapping the bandage.

'He's working late at the store this evening, helping with some painting.' Elspeth noticed that although Aileen had filled a pot with water in readiness for the potatoes, she hadn't yet put it on to the stove to heat, thus slowing down the cooking process.

'I want to do everything right for Thomas. He's given up so much for me,' Aileen had told Elspeth once, ignoring the fact that she herself had given up even more. She hated to let Thomas see the mistakes she made, although he never found fault.

Now, Elspeth signalled silently to Aileen with the pot before putting it on the stove, and the girl, understanding, gave an imperceptible nod, her green eyes flashing her gratitude. Just then Thomas's fair head dipped swiftly to let his lips brush the tiny cut on Aileen's work-roughened hand. Elspeth looked away quickly, feeling that it was wrong to spy on such special moments between man and wife.

Aileen was showing signs of strain, she thought as she began to cut the potatoes into quarters. A little worried frown was settling in between her brows, and there was an air of tension about her. It couldn't be easy for someone from her background to have to deal with the daily grind of trying to make a small wage stretch as far as possible.

'You'll stay for your dinner?' Aileen invited when the bandage was firmly in place and Thomas had freed her to join Elspeth at the stove.

'I'm expected at home. I just looked in to see how you were.'

'We're both fine,' Thomas said cheerfully, replacing the towel he had been using on its nail beside the window. He hesitated, sniffing the air, then pulled back a corner of the window curtain. Elspeth heard an intake of breath from Aileen as he turned, holding out a small bowl containing a deep blue hyacinth. Its delicate, haunting fragrance began to spread over the room.

'Aileen, pet, I told you we cannae afford to spend money on—'

'I didn't buy it,' Aileen interrupted, fingers twisting nervously at her apron. 'It was a gift. Ian brought it.'

Thomas's jaw dropped and his brown eyes widened. 'Your brother was here?'

'Just for a minute, to see how I was. He brought the wee plant.'

'From the greenhouses,' Thomas said, then swallowed hard. 'To remind you of everything you've turned your back on.'

'It isn't like that at all.' She stepped forward and put her hands over his, so that they were both cradling the bowl. 'He came because he just wanted to see me.'

'And he saw you in this tiny room that's all I can give you.' His shoulders slumped, and his voice was bleak with humiliation. 'Did he ask you to go back home with him?'

'I am home! He's my brother, Thomas, you're surely not going to forbid me to see him now and then, are you?'

'I'd never forbid you to do anything, you surely know that.' Then, with a visible effort, he forced a smile. 'I'm not complaining, lass, of course your brother'll want to see you. It was just – a surprise, that's all.'

'I wish Ian Bruce hadnae come back into our lives,' he told

223

Elspeth, low-voiced, as he accompanied her to the close-mouth a few minutes later. 'I'd never deny her, but I don't trust the man.'

'He can't come between you and Aileen,' she tried to reassure him. 'You're man and wife, and she'd not turn her back on you now.'

'I know, but—' Thomas sighed, then said, 'The man's a troublemaker.'

Ian Bruce visited his sister regularly from then on, though never when Thomas was home. Elspeth herself found him lounging in his sister's flat when she called one day. She slowed as she saw the smart sports car outside the close, circled enviously by a group of wide-eyed children giggling at their reflections in the gleaming scarlet paintwork. On the nearby street corner loitered the inevitable group of men unable to find regular work. They stared enviously at the handsome automobile that had cost more than a year's wages and muttered amongst themselves, hawking into the gutter.

Elspeth hesitated. She would have turned and hurried away, but she had promised to buy some meat for Aileen on her way home from work, and she had no option but to deliver it.

The girl looked worried when she came to the door, then smiled when she saw Elspeth waiting in the close. 'Come in and meet my brother,' she said, and Elspeth, who had intended to hand the parcel over then leave, was drawn into the kitchen.

She had only glimpsed Ian Bruce, in full uniform at his elder sister's wedding, and had thought then that he was the most handsome man she had ever set eyes on. Close to, out of uniform and in an open-necked white shirt, dark blazer and white trousers, he was like a Greek god. As he rose to his feet and took her hand in his cool, firm grip, his closeness set her pulse fluttering. He knew it – she could tell by the lazy amusement in the green eyes gazing down on her.

'You'll have some tea, Elspeth?' Aileen asked.

She recalled the reason for her visit, and withdrew her fingers hurriedly from Ian's. 'I can't stop, I'm just handing this in.'

Aileen unfolded the parcel and studied the piece of flank mutton, her brow wrinkled. 'How did you say I should cook it?'

'Wash it, then put it into the soup, to get the flavour,' Elspeth gabbled, aware of Ian Bruce's presence only inches away. 'Then take it out before you serve the soup, and put it on two plates with boiled potatoes and some carrots. That way you'll get full use from it.'

Aileen's hand flew to her mouth. 'The soup! I was doing the vegetables when Ian arrived.'

They lay in a small pile on a chopping board, onions and carrots, turnip and potatoes and a halved leek.

'There's still time. I'll see to the meat while you finish the vegetables.'

'How delightfully domesticated,' Ian Bruce drawled, as the two of them set to work.

'Oh, I've learned a lot,' Aileen told him proudly. When the vegetables were in the pot she dried her hands and reached for her purse. 'I'll pay for the meat now, Elspeth, before I forget.'

Glancing at the young man, Elspeth saw his mouth tighten as he watched his sister scrabbling in the small purse, then counting coppers carefully out on to the table. As Elspeth scooped them up and straightened, his gaze moved away, travelling round the room that was so unlike the grand house he and his sister were used to. His lip curled, and suddenly despising him for his dislike of the home Thomas had provided for Aileen, Elspeth stuffed the money into her pocket.

'I must go. Don't bother to see me out,' she added as Aileen moved towards the door.

'I'm sure your friend can manage to find her own way,' Ian agreed, detaining his sister with a hand on her arm. 'Sit down and have a rest. I hate to see you working like a skivvy.'

Outside again, Elspeth almost ran along the street, wondering how she could have been charmed, even for a moment, by the man who had had Thomas beaten unconscious as punishment for loving his sister. She, too, wished that Ian Bruce hadn't come back into Aileen's life.

But Aileen welcomed his visits. 'We were always close, and I've missed him more than I've missed my parents,' she confided to Elspeth the next time she called.

'After what he did to Thomas?' Elspeth's voice was sharper than she intended, and Aileen flushed.

'He knows he did wrong, and he's sorry about it. He even went to the garage to apologise, but Thomas wouldn't speak to him. But mebbe one of these days' – her face brightened – 'I'll get the two of them together. And Ian's trying to persuade my parents to change their minds. One day everything'll be all right.'

'I can't see your parents being happy about the sort of life you lead now.' Elspeth hated to throw cold water on the girl's hopes, but she felt that Aileen was expecting too much.

'They might, and so might Thomas's mother, now that—' Aileen stopped, a hand flying up to her mouth, and said guiltily from between spread fingers, 'Thomas wanted to tell you when we were all together. I'm going to have a child.'

'Oh, Aileen!' Elspeth hugged her. 'I'm pleased for you – for both of you.'

'So are we, and now I've spoiled it for Thomas. You'll not let on, will you?'

'I won't,' Elspeth promised, and managed to be convincingly surprised and delighted when she heard the news officially a week later. Thomas was almost bursting with happiness and pride.

'I'm going to work every hour I can to get somewhere better than this before the bairn comes,' he said exultantly, and when Aileen protested, 'There's nothing wrong with it, we'll manage fine,' he shook his head, hugging her tightly to him. 'I want to do more than manage.'

'And all I want is for our families to be happy for us, and for that to happen soon.' As she rested her head against her husband's chest, Aileen's lovely face was determined.

Outside, it was May; great clumps of golden broom splashed across the hills above the town and the sun's rays sparkled on the river beyond the dockyards, turning the water into a vast treasure chest filled with diamonds. But inside the Infirmary the long ward looked drab and dreary. Here and there, where the sunlight managed to squeeze through the tall, narrow windows, small pools of light dappled a locker top or a sheet.

Celia Bremner lay very still, as she had since being admitted, her bony hands folded on the stiff coverlet, her grey head scarcely denting the snowy pillow. Her eyes were closed and her mouth slightly open, the breath rattling unevenly in and out of her lungs. She hadn't fully recovered consciousness since being brought into the Infirmary after a neglected cold turned to pneumonia. Occasionally she moved, or muttered something unintelligible; once or twice she had opened her eyes and gazed vacantly around before lapsing back into her coma.

During the ten days her grandmother had been in the Infirmary, Elspeth had visited every evening and on Saturday and Sunday afternoons as well. Flora had accompanied her on one occasion, but this was the ward she had lain in during her influenza attack, and the memory of it made her fidget restlessly, anxious to get back home. Lachlan still had a morbid fear of hospitals, but both Thomas and Aileen had gone with her once or twice; as had Mattie and Kenneth during brief visits home at Easter, but preoccupied as they were with the thought of approaching exams they had both been poor company.

Granjan, who had declared from the first that visiting the

sick was no task for a young lassie to tackle on her own, was Elspeth's favourite companion, sitting patiently and calmly by the bed, occasionally reaching out to pat Celia's hand.

'Poor soul,' she murmured now from the opposite side of the bed, 'She'd hate tae know she's been brought tae this.'

A bell tolled in the corridor beyond the ward, and all down its length visitors began to get up and file out. Elspeth, with one last look at the grey, stern face on the pillow, rose and followed Granjan, guilty at the feeling of relief that always came over her as she stepped through the ward doors.

'Best go afore me, for I'm slow on stairs,' the old woman advised the people just behind her on the landing, adding carefully as the two of them waited for the flow of visitors to ease to a trickle, 'Have ye given any thought, pet, about yer grandma mebbe not gettin' better?'

'I know she's very poorly,' Elspeth said doubtfully. She couldn't imagine a world without Grandmother, couldn't imagine the still figure they had just left allowing herself to die.

'She is, poor woman. Best tae be prepared, just in case.' The stairs were clearing now, and Granjan gripped the rail firmly, taking the steps one at a time. When they reached the foyer she headed towards a nearby bench, as she always did. 'I'll just sit here for a wee minute tae catch my breath.'

Someone called Elspeth's name and she turned to see a girl who had attended the typewriting and shorthand classes with her.

'Peggy, what are you doing here?'

'Visiting my dad, he's had a bad turn again.' The girl looked tired and tense, and Elspeth recalled that she kept house for her father, who had a weak heart. 'He'll be all right, they say. Home again next week. What about you?'

'My grandmother's got pneumonia. How are you? Are you working?'

Peggy, who had been one of the star pupils in the typing

class, shrugged. 'Just in the early mornings, in a bakery. It's the only way I can bring in some money and see to Da as well. He can't be left on his own all day, so there's no hope of working in an office. They all want someone who can be there all the time.'

'I did some typing in Brodie's accounts office, but I'm back in the sewing room again.'

Peggy sighed. 'It's a terrible waste of all that learning we did, isn't it? I keep tellin' myself that mebbe one day I'll get to use a typewriter again, if my fingers are still up to it by then . . .'

Walking home with Granjan, Elspeth felt guilty about the typewriter sitting in her bedroom. At least she had her own machine, and some work to do on it, unlike poor Peggy.

Celia Bremner died a few days later, without regaining consciousness, and was buried in the same lair as her daughter. Flora, Henry, Granjan and Lachlan attended the funeral, and so did Thomas and Aileen. When she heard about the coming baby, Flora had finally given in and admitted her elder son and his wife into the family circle, though she was still somewhat stiff and formal with them both. Life was too short to bear grudges, Elspeth thought as she watched her grandmother's coffin being lowered into the ground.

As the undertaker's men withdrew the cords and stepped back, she suddenly felt completely alone. Cold and grim though she had always been, Grandmother had at least been of her own flesh and blood. For all Elspeth knew, her father and grandfather had both died long ago. She shivered, wishing that Kenneth could have been beside her. He, at least, was hers in some measure. She tried to console herself, as the minister's voice droned out the final words of the service, with the thought that he would be home for the summer in only two months' time.

23

A few days later she turned the key in the door and stepped nervously into Grandmother's flat, Rachel crowding in behind her.

'It's lovely!' the older girl breathed, staring at the carpeted floor and the large walnut coat-stand with its carved panels and decorative mirror. Celia Bremner's everyday coat and hat still hung on their usual hooks, and a long umbrella, neatly furled, waited in the stand for a hand that would never again lift it.

The flat was filled with her grandmother's presence, and she wouldn't have been at all surprised if the old lady had suddenly appeared at the parlour door. Crossing the hall and reaching out to open it, she was glad that she had thought of asking Rachel to help her to start clearing the place.

'I'm afraid that there is very little money involved,' the lawyer had said, sitting at his paper-littered desk and peering at Elspeth over the top of his half-moon spectacles. 'Your grandmother had a little money of her own, and used it frugally, but there's not much left. The proceeds of the sale of the furnishings will go to you, Miss Bremner, as sole surviving relative – that is, after my legal fees have been settled.'

'Sole survivor? Are you certain of that?'

'Of course,' the man said abruptly, and Elspeth swallowed hard, the nails of one hand digging into the palm. It had to be said. Everything had to be above board.

She swallowed again, then said, her voice little more than a whisper, 'My grandfather—'

The lawyer's bushy eyebrows shot up. 'You know of your grandparents' – er – situation?'

'I had heard something—'

He looked at her as though she had just shouted his own innermost secrets to the whole town, then said stiffly, 'Your grandfather died several years ago, Miss Bremner. As the family lawyer, I can assure you that you are indeed your grandmother's sole surviving relative.' Then he had changed the subject, and she didn't dare ask him for further details.

Elspeth had put the emptying of the flat off for as long as possible, but now time was running out and it had to be done so that the factor could rent the place to new tenants. Granjan would have helped, but stairs made her breathless, and Flora had made it clear that she had no wish to become involved.

'Never mind that nonsense about no' speakin' ill of the dead – I didnae like the woman and she didnae like me, so I want nothin' tae dae with her possessions,' she had said bluntly. 'I cannae abide that house anyway, it was always cold and unforgivin'.'

Rachel, on the other hand, seized the chance eagerly when asked to help, confessing that she loved seeing other folks' homes. Flora had agreed to take wee Mary off her daughter's hands for a few hours, and had borne the baby off to visit Granjan.

Although Elspeth had called at the house once a month for years, she had only seen the hall and kitchen and bathroom and parlour, and had never set foot in her grandmother's bedroom, with its vast wardrobe and double bed and marble-topped washstand complete with floral ewer and basin, or in the smaller bedroom that had once belonged to her mother. While Rachel exclaimed over the large sideboard and the slippery buttoned-leather *chaise-longue* in the parlour, Elspeth tiptoed into the smaller room, holding her breath, hoping desperately that she would come across something that had belonged to her mother.

But to her disappointment the small bed had been stripped bare and the single wardrobe was empty and smelled strongly of mothballs. The plain yellow ewer and basin on the wash-stand were bone dry, and the tallboy drawers only held spare blankets which also reeked of mothballs. Every trace of her mother had been swept away. It was as if she had never existed.

'I wish I'd a room like this for wee Mary,' Rachel said wistfully from the doorway, then, briskly unfastening her jacket, 'Well, we'd best get on with it.'

The grandmother clock in the living room chimed the half-hour just as she spoke, underlining the shortage of time available, and Elspeth reluctantly stripped her own jacket and hat off and donned the apron she had brought with her.

They worked hard all morning, opening drawers and cup-boards, clearing shelves, sorting some forty years of Celia Bremner's life into various piles. The flat had been rented, and Elspeth was pleased about that, for she herself could never have lived in it. But once piles of clothes and sheets and towels and boxes filled with old-fashioned underwear and clothes and shawls and gloves and ornaments and cutlery and dishes and pots and pans began to litter the floor space, blur-ring the edges of the flat's former identity, she changed her mind. If it had been left to her, she could have given it to Thomas as a fitting home for his wife and coming baby.

The clock chimed again, and she closed the bottom drawer she had been emptying and went through to the kitchen, where Rachel was clearing out cupboards.

'We'll have a wee cup of—' she began, then stopped, staring. 'Rachel, where did you get that?'

Rachel, stretching up to a high cupboard, looked blankly at her over one shoulder. 'What?'

'That bruise on your arm.'

Rachel immediately dropped her arms and stepped away from the cupboard, tugging one sleeve down. 'I don't know what you're talking about.'

'Yes you do.' Elspeth caught at the other girl's wrist, and after a brief struggle managed to push the sleeve up to reveal a nasty yellowing bruise on Rachel's upper arm. 'There.'

'Och, that? I banged my arm against the close wall.' Rachel put her free hand nervously to her throat, and Elspeth's eyes followed the movement.

'Did you bang your chest against it too?' Before Rachel could move, Elspeth drew the neck of her blouse aside to reveal another bruise marring the creamy skin.

'I just – I—' Rachel pulled back. 'It's nothing.'

'Rachel—'

'I deserved it,' Rachel said defensively, then, sudden tears filling her eyes. 'Let it be, Ellie!'

'I'll do nothing of the sort. Does Aunt Flora know about this – and Uncle Henry?'

Rachel flew into a panic at mention of her father's name. 'Don't tell him, Ellie, for God's sake! He'll go for Bob, then Bob'll go for me and—'

Elspeth picked up the kettle. 'Sit down, I'm going to make some tea.'

'But there's still a lot of work to do!'

'Never mind the work, just sit down. We'll have some tea, and then,' she added over her shoulder as she wrenched at the tap and began to fill the kettle, 'I want to know what's going on – all of it, Rachel.'

Half an hour later, when Grandmother's teapot, which for the first time in its existence had been filled to the brim with strong dark tea instead of the pale liquid it had normally held, had been emptied, the whole sorry story of Bob Cochran's brutality had been spilled out.

'He doesnae mean it,' Rachel said for the fourth or fifth

time, her face puffy and wet with the tears she had shed. 'It's the drink – he's not used to it.'

'But Bob's teetotal.'

'He used to be.' Rachel took a moment to blow her nose and dab at her eyes. 'It was the war – it changed Bob just as much as it changed Lachie, only nobody knew it at the time because there was nothing to see. He worries about things – whether he's goin' to be turned away from his work, and what'd become of us if he was. He even worries in case there's ever another war and he has to go away again. And then he has to have a drink to stop the worrying, then another. And when he comes home wee Mary's crying bothers him, though she can't help it, poor lamb, and one thing leads to another.'

'What about his parents? Do they know he's drinking?'

Rachel's body quivered. 'They found out. Now they'll have nothing to do with him, or me. They won't even look at my poor wee M-mary . . .' The tears began to flow again.

'You have to tell Uncle Henry, Rachel. He'd not let this happen to you if he knew.'

'I daren't, because of what he'd do to Bob. And Mam says—'

'You've told Aunt Flora?' Elspeth asked, astonished. 'She knows about this?'

'I had to tell someone.' Rachel had worked her way through both her own handkerchief and Elspeth's. As more tears streamed down her face Elspeth delved into a drawer and found a tray cloth.

'Here, take this.'

'I can't,' Rachel protested, trying to push it away. 'It's far too bonny – look at the nice stitching!'

'Go on – Grandmother'll never know the difference now. What were you saying about Aunt Flora?'

Rachel mopped at her face. 'She says I have to deal with it myself.'

'What?'

Rachel sprang to her mother's defence. 'She's had enough to worry about with Lachlan, then Thomas and Aileen. And she's right – Bob's my husband, and I married him for better or worse. It's up to me to stop him from drinking and h-hitting me.'

'How?'

'Well—' The tears welled again, and Rachel refolded the tray cloth to find a dry spot. 'If I was a better wife to him, he'd not hit me.'

'Did she say that?' Elspeth asked, outraged, then, as Rachel nodded, 'That's terrible!'

Rachel reached across the table and clutched at her hand. 'Promise me you'll say nothing to anybody!'

'But Rachel—'

'Promise!' the girl insisted, and Elspeth chewed her lower lip for a moment, then said reluctantly, 'If that's what you want.'

'It is.' Rachel gave her nose a final blow, and got up to splash cold water on her face. 'It's helped, just talking about it – now, let's get on with the work.'

It took two weeks to clear the house, working at weekends and in the evenings. Every time Elspeth thought she had finished at last, she discovered another drawer stuffed with half-finished knitting or sewing or boxes of buttons.

When it was done, she gave all the bed linen and napery to Rachel, urging her to sell what she didn't want, and spend the money on herself and Mary.

'Don't let Bob take it for drink.'

'I can't stop him,' Rachel said listlessly. She had lost all her confidence, Elspeth realised, and wondered why she and the rest of the family hadn't noticed the change in the girl before. 'If he sees me buyin' stuff we can't afford on his wages he'll want to know where the money's coming from.'

'Then put it aside, to use when you need it.'

'He'll only find it,' Rachel said, and in the end Elspeth sold the linen and napery herself to the owner of a small second-hand shop, and banked the money for Rachel.

Granjan and Aileen also benefited from the flat clearance, but Flora refused to accept anything. Celia Bremner's clothes, together with the small household items left, were collected by a charity happy to get them, and Elspeth called in an auction-eer to take the furniture and carpets off her hands.

Taking a final look round on the day the furniture was to be removed, she discovered that a small drawer tucked away in her grandmother's large mothball-smelling wardrobe refused to shut flush with its framework. After struggling with it for a few moments, she pulled it clear and knelt to feel in the space behind it. The blockage had been caused by a few letters with-out envelopes, tied together with a piece of string.

Replacing the drawer, which now slid smoothly into place, she sat back on her heels and loosened the string, which had been tied in a neat bow. The pages, released, fell across her lap like dead leaves, and she gasped as the word 'Whore!' seemed to fly up at her from among them. It was scrawled across one of the sheets in a large, angular hand, written so viciously that here and there the pen had broken through the paper. It was repeated on every sheet, almost obliterating the cramped cop-perplate writing beneath.

The doorknocker crashed on to its brass plate in a way that would have set Grandmother's eyes flashing. Elspeth jumped, then hurriedly gathered the pages up and thrust them into her pocket as she went to let the auctioneer's men in.

Their loud voices and the tramp of their feet across wood and linoleum banished the last trace of Celia Bremner from the house she had lived in for so long. When they had gone, taking the furniture with them and leaving only its imprint on the papered walls, the flat was large and echoing, a place that Elspeth had never been in before.

She closed the door behind the last man and took the letters out of her pocket, moving into the parlour to hold a sheet up to the light from the window, squinting at it until she managed to make out the words, 'My dearest Robert.'

Her eyes flew automatically to the mantel shelf where her grandparents' photograph had stood. Now it was packed into a box under her bed in Mearns Street, together with the few pieces of jewellery she had come across. It was only then that she realised that there had been no trace of her grandfather in the flat either, apart from the photograph. Celia Bremner had wiped both daughter and husband from her life. Everything apart from a few letters written to her grandfather, Elspeth discovered as she strained to decipher the faded writing on the pages in her hand, and even they had been defaced until it was almost impossible to make much out.

As she grew accustomed to the writing, she realised that she was looking at love letters, signed with the name 'Ann'.

Time was passing; she pushed the letters into her pocket and got on with the task of sweeping the floors and making sure that everything was clean and neat for the new tenants.

Leaving the flat for the last time, she walked to the factor's office in Port Glasgow to hand the key in, then squandered a few pennies on a tram ride back to Greenock, too tired for once to walk home.

There was nobody in the flat when she got back. Flora would no doubt be at Rachel's, Lachlan often visited Thomas and Aileen on a Saturday afternoon, and Henry would be at the bowling green with his cronies. In the kitchen, she pulled the letters from her pocket, recalling the story Granjan had revealed about Robert Bremner leaving his wife, eloping with a colleague. At the time Elspeth had struggled to put the tale out of her mind, fearful that Grandmother's sharp eyes might bore right into her skull and discover what she knew. She had succeeded so well that she had almost forgotten it, until reminded by the letters.

Somehow, her grandmother had got hold of them, and had kept them hidden away, perhaps taking them out to read now and then, tormenting herself, stoking the flames of bitterness, nursing her hatred and keeping it alive. Even when the man was dead – and surely the lawyer must have informed her that she was then, truly, widowed – she had kept the letters, refusing to let the matter end.

This, Elspeth thought with horror, was the woman whose blood ran in her own veins. She vowed there and then that she herself would never, ever bear a grudge, or allow bitterness to warp her life as it had warped Celia Bremner's. She lost all desire to decipher the letters further; even lying in her hand they seemed to radiate a pain that she couldn't bear.

Instead, she crumpled them into the empty grate, then took the big box of matches that always stood on the mantel shelf and struck one. Afterwards, she crushed the ashes into powder which she swept up and took down to the midden in the back court, watching with relief the last grains fall from the shovel.

Now the letters were where they belonged, out of harm's way at last.

24

As Elspeth went back upstairs, she paused on the final landing where the colours from the stained-glass window lay like a spilled rainbow on the stone floor. The letters Celia had kept hidden all those years had suddenly become linked in her mind with the present; a thought occurred to her that surely couldn't be right. And yet . . .

She ran up the last flight of stairs, anxious to make the most of the little time she had left to herself in the empty flat. In the kitchen, she drew aside the curtains hiding the wall-bed and went down on her knees to scrabble in the space beneath the bed. Flora McDonald kept a large biscuit box there, right at the back, a box that nobody, including Henry, was permitted to touch.

Elspeth's groping fingers found it, and she drew it out into the open, prising the lid up and riffling hurriedly through Flora's most precious possessions – her marriage certificate, her children's birth certificates, letters written by Thomas and Lachlan during the war. She had reached the bottom of the box and begun to think, with relief, that she had been mistaken, when her fingers touched a slim bundle.

For the second time that afternoon, Elspeth drew a well-kept secret from its hiding place. This one, like the letters in Celia Bremner's flat, was tied with string; she had no need to unfasten it, for one glance showed that it held half a dozen postcards, bearing pictures of various Scottish towns and addressed to Lachlan.

Flora was the first of the family to return home, arriving just after Elspeth had returned the box to its proper place and closed the curtains. She retained the small package of postcards, and as soon as her aunt came in she silently laid them on the table.

Flora's eyes almost bulged as they took in the postcards, and her mouth worked silently for a few moments before she managed to speak.

'Where did ye get these?'

Elspeth swallowed hard. She had done a terrible thing, but surely right was on her side. 'I went looking for them and I found them. They belong to Lachlan, Aunt Flora, not to you.'

Again, Flora McDonald's mouth worked for a second or two before she said, 'I'll not have any son of mine gettin' involved with a woman that earns her livin' on the stage!'

'There's no harm in the postcards – you saw how pleased he was to get the first two.'

'Oh, I saw all right – why d'ye think I held the others back? He's had enough hurt, without her givin' him more.'

'Hiding the cards didn't save him any pain – he was hurt at the thought that Lena had forgotten about him.' Elspeth pushed the postcards across the table. 'Give them back, Aunt Flora. Tell him they must have been held up somewhere and they all arrived today.'

'I should've put them in the fire when they first came!'

'If you burn them now I'll tell him about them.'

'So this is what it's come tae? After all I've done for ye, this is the thanks I get?' Flora pulled her hat off and thrust the hatpin through it savagely, then attacked her jacket, wrenching buttons from buttonholes. 'Have I not had tae suffer enough shame over Thomas as it is? I'm not lettin' our Lachie go the same way. This is a respectable family!'

Exasperation flared beyond caution. 'It'll not be a family for much longer if all you worry about is what the neighbours think. Thomas and Aileen are happy together – surely that's all that matters!'

'She's not the right woman for our Thomas.'

'You thought Bob Cochran was the right man for Rachel, and look what's happened to her.'

'There's nothing wrong with Rachel's marriage,' Flora flared.

'I've seen Rachel's bruises, Aunt Flora, and heard about Bob's drinking and the way he treats her. She's told me that you know all about it, yet you've done nothing to help her.'

'Mind yer own business!' Flora McDonald slammed both hands down hard on the table. Seeing the rage in the woman's face, Elspeth thought she had gone too far. She took a step back, clutching at a chair for support.

'Ye've been nothin' but a troublemaker since ye left the school,' Flora hissed into the space between them. 'Sidin' with Thomas when he came between me and Lachlan, sendin' that girl tae the Infirmary when Thomas was hurt – oh, I knew your hand was in it somewhere, madam, for ye cannae keep out of other folk's business, can ye?'

She hauled open a drawer in the dresser, and fumbled through it, then extracted an opened letter and tossed it on to the table.

'Here's another thing ye can poke yer neb intae. This came yesterday, and I was tryin' tae find the right time tae tell ye about it, but ye might as well read it for yerself,' she said coldly. 'Go on – read it!'

Slowly, Elspeth drew the letter from its envelope. It was from Mattie, and ran along the lines of the letters Elspeth herself received from the girl, telling about her progress at a school she was teaching in as part of her training. Puzzled, Elspeth looked up at her aunt, who stood watching her closely. Her face was hard and unforgiving.

'Try the next page,' she ordered.

At first, Elspeth's eyes ran along the close-packed lines without taking in the words, then she blinked, focused, and started again.

'There's something you should know, Mam,' Mattie had written. 'I need to tell someone before I come home for the summer, because I don't know what to do about it. Kenneth and I—'

Elspeth read to the end, a paralysing chill descending on her and numbing her body until she had no physical sense of her feet on the floor or her fingers holding the letter. Just as she finished, the outer door opened and Henry's tuneless whistle was heard in the hall. Flora scooped up the postcards with one hand, reaching the other across the table to pluck the letter from Elspeth's unresisting fingers.

'One word from you about Rachel,' she hissed, 'and you're out on the pavement – d'ye understand?'

Then Henry was in the room, filling it with noise and movement as usual, quite unaware of the tension between his wife and their foster child.

It was easy enough for Elspeth to slip out of the kitchen and out of the flat without arousing comment. She sped down the stairs; once outside she started to walk quickly, not thinking of where she was going.

Sickened by the ugly scene in the kitchen, she wished that she had never thought of looking for Lachlan's postcards. Then, remembering the sudden radiance in his face after Lena had kissed him at the theatre, and when he received the first postcard, she knew that he had been cruelly wronged, and deserved her help. Lena's fondness for him was probably too fragile to last, but Lachlan was entitled to know that at least she had cared enough to keep in contact, and hadn't forgotten him so soon.

But she had had to pay a bitter price for defending him. 'Kenneth and I—' The words sang mockingly in her head as she walked. Kenneth and Mattie. Kenneth being kind to Mattie at Elspeth's request, helping her to settle into her new life in Glasgow.

Their meetings must have continued, first of all by chance, then by arrangement and choice. Kenneth and Mattie, falling in love, planning to marry when he had gained his degree, and at a loss as to how to break the news to poor Elspeth.

'Could you tell her for me, Mam?' Mattie had written. 'Do it as gently as you can. I don't know how I'll face her. Kenneth's working in Glasgow for most of the summer, so he'll not be home for long. I won't either, I'm coming back early to be with him.'

Aunt Flora had certainly found a way of breaking the news, and at the same time had found a way of punishing her foster daughter for having dared to interfere in family business.

Elspeth wondered if Kenneth had tried to go further than kisses and cuddles with Mattie. If so, how had Mattie responded? She was older than Elspeth, and probably more worldly-wise since moving to Glasgow. Instead of panicking as she, Elspeth, had done in the wash house that night, Mattie might have given Kenneth what he wanted, and given it gladly.

Turning a corner, Elspeth was astonished to see the garage where Thomas worked only yards along the street. She looked round, down over the rooftops to the sun-blessed river below. Without noticing, she had climbed almost to the inland edge of the town.

Thomas was working on a car in the yard. Alerted by her footsteps on the cobbles, he looked up. 'Ellie?' At once, his expression changed. 'Has something happened to Aileen?'

'No, of course not. Why should it?'

'You looked so serious.' He reached for a rag and wiped his oily fingers, then glanced at her again. 'If it's not Aileen, what is it?'

'Nothing, I was just passing.'

243

'Nobody just passes along this street.' Thomas came round the bulk of the car he was working on. 'What's wrong?'

The concern in his voice was her undoing. She felt her face melt as though it was made of candle grease, and Thomas's figure, as he came towards her, shimmered as tears filled her eyes and began to spill over.

'Come on, I'll make us a cup of tea.' He put a firm hand beneath her elbow.

'Your work—' she protested as he began to lead her over the cobbles towards a door.

'I can take a few minutes off, and Mr Cameron's not here this afternoon, so you don't need to worry about him.'

He urged her through the door and she stopped in her tracks, staring round at the small, filthy kitchen.

'This is terrible!'

'It serves its purpose,' Thomas said blithely, pulling a chair forward and filling the kettle at a squeaky old tap. 'We only use the place for making tea now and again.' Then, as she continued to stare round in horror, 'Never mind the state of the place – sit down and tell me what's bothering you.'

At his reminder, her misery came flooding back. She collapsed into the chair, not caring about her skirt, and poured out the story of Kenneth and Mattie while salty tears trickled, one after another, down her cheeks.

'Well, well – Mattie and Kenneth.' Thomas pushed a mug of tea into her hand. 'Drink that down, now.'

She did as he was told. The tea was very sweet and very hot. The first tentative sip burned its way down into her stomach, and the second set up a glow that began to thaw out the numbed feeling. She looked gratefully at Thomas, who was propped against the sink, cradling his own mug in both hands. Dirty and oily though it was, his face was kind and concerned and his sympathy was so obvious that she felt that if she had reached out a hand she could have touched it.

'How do you really feel about it?' he asked, taking her by

surprise. She opened her mouth to reply, then sipped at her tea instead, giving herself time to think about the question.

Kenneth had never said much in his letters, and he had certainly not made any declarations of love. The letters had eased off over the past month or so, but she had been too busy visiting Grandmother in hospital then clearing out her house, to notice. She had assumed that in the summer, when he came back from the university, everything would go on as before.

'I want him to be mine, not Mattie's,' she said at last, slowly. Then, tipping her head back to look up at Thomas, 'But mebbe I only want him because now he's Mattie's.'

'D'you want to spend the rest of your life with him?' Thomas probed, and smiled when she replied, irritably, 'I don't know – I'm too young to think of the rest of my life.'

'You're right there – you're still far too young to tie yourself down. And no matter what age you are when the right one comes along, you know about it when it happens. Take my word for it – and let Mattie have Kenneth, if she wants him so badly.'

'I'd not want to keep him against his will – but it hurts,' she admitted candidly, 'knowing that he prefers someone else to me.'

A smile pulled at the corners of his mouth, and was quickly subdued. 'I know, Ellie. It's happened to me too, and it always hurts. But that's the way life is sometimes.' Then a frown puckered his brow. 'But I don't understand why Mam let you read the letter without giving you any warning. She didnae need to be so cruel.'

Again, Elspeth opened her mouth then closed it. She had promised Rachel that she would say nothing about Bob's ill-treatment, and if she was to tell Thomas about Lachlan's postcards being kept from him, it would probably do the new and fragile relationship that he and his mother had started to build no good at all.

'What is it?' He was watching her closely. 'You're gasping

like a baggy minnow that's just been scooped out of a pond.'

She got up and eased him aside so that she could rinse out the empty mug. 'I was cheeky to Aunt Flora, so she gave me the letter to punish me.'

'You must have been awful cheeky to deserve what you got.'

'I was,' she said shortly, and he had the sense to leave it at that.

As they left the kitchen, Elspeth to return to Mearns Street, Thomas to get back to his work, she put her arms about him and hugged him closely. He smelled of cars and oil and, faintly, of the soap Aileen kept by her kitchen sink.

'Here—' he protested, surprised and embarrassed.

'I don't know what I'd do without you, Thomas.'

'Ach, away ye go and let me get on with my work,' he said gruffly. Even so, he returned the hug for a moment before opening the door and shooing her out into the yard.

Going back down the hill, she felt warmed and healed by that moment of contact with another person. The coming baby was very fortunate to have such loving parents as Thomas and Aileen, she thought, then pushed the thought away hurriedly because it reminded her of her own situation, orphaned and, as far as she knew, without kith or kin.

When she got back to the flat Elspeth went straight to her own room and peered into the small mirror on the wall. The tea, the talk with Thomas, and the walk home had cleared all traces of tears, though her mouth had a downward twist. She forced a smile at her reflection, pulling a comb through her hair at the same time, and vowed to herself that she would never let Flora McDonald know how much Mattie's letter had hurt her.

When Lachlan tapped at the door a few minutes later she was ready to face him, her hair neat and her smile pinned firmly in place.

'Look!' He was almost incoherent with pleasure. 'Postcards

from Lena, lots of them from all over.' He began to spread them across the bed, reciting, 'Dundee, Inverness, Fort William, Perth, Paisley, Ayr. They must have been stuck somewhere, then they all arrived together. You can read them,' he offered magnanimously.

Although she felt that she had had more than her share that day of reading other people's letters, Elspeth did as she was bid. Lena's spelling left much to be desired, but her enthusiasm spilled across the small space allowed for messages. She seemed to be having a wonderful time, and pleasing audiences everywhere the troupe went. Each card, Elspeth noted, ended with a casual, 'Love, Lena.'

'They're lovely, but Lachlan, Lena's always been a bit' – she searched for the right phrase, but could only think of – 'generous towards folk. She treats everyone the same way.'

'You're worried in case I believe it when she sends her love,' he said in a surprisingly matter-of-fact voice, gathering the cards into a neat stack. 'I don't, but it's great tae have a friend. For a wee while there I was so shy and scared that I was like a wean again. I thought I'd never feel comfortable with anyone outside this house. Now I feel differently, and Lena's helped.' He gave her a slightly embarrassed smile. 'When the cards stopped I was a bit hurt because it was so sudden, but I got over that. If they stop again, it won't bother me.'

Flora was unusually quiet that evening. Throughout the evening meal, she slid sidelong glances at Elspeth, who was deliberately cheerful and carefree. It was, she thought later when she had escaped to her room, a performance that would surely have won her a place in the troupe that Lena worked with.

25

By unspoken agreement, a truce was decided between Elspeth and Flora, with neither making any further reference to the ugly quarrel they had had. But as far as Elspeth was concerned, the harm had been done, and the animosity she had sensed in her foster mother, even in babyhood, had been brought into the open. Nothing, she thought, absently fingering the little pebble brooch pinned to her blouse, would ever be the same again.

Mattie and Kenneth both wrote to her, their letters arriving on the following Saturday morning. They lay unopened in her pocket until the afternoon; she finally opened them on the beach where she and Kenneth had often picnicked with the others, and where she was free to settle her back against a rock and read with only the seagulls for company.

Both were short and apologetic, both spoke of fighting against their growing feelings for each other, and losing. They both expressed a hope that Elspeth would be able to understand, and to forgive.

She stared out across the water, seeing the two of them in her mind's eye, writing their letters together, comparing words and phrases. The waves washing almost to her feet echoed their sighs of relief when they finally signed their names, folded the single sheets of paper, and sealed them into envelopes. She pictured them walking together to a postbox, slipping the letters into its waiting mouth, then hurrying away, fingers entwined, thankful that the difficult task was over, and free, now that they had confessed, to enjoy their love.

She wanted to cry, but there were no tears left. Instead, she tore the letters up, tossing the shreds of paper to the breeze, which then committed them to the water. She had had enough of letters that had been kept and agonised over – the past was past, and only the future mattered.

As the time for Mattie's return from Glasgow drew near, Elspeth sought for ways and means of keeping herself too busy to think about the summer she had once looked forward to. Mr Monteith, well pleased with the work she had done for him, had told her several weeks earlier about a friend of his, a second-hand furniture dealer in Port Glasgow, who could do with some help with his paperwork. Elspeth put on her best hat and coat and paid a visit to the man, coming home with an armful of books to work on.

Lachlan offered to take Elspeth to the pictures on the day of Mattie's arrival, and was surprised when she refused.

'But Kenneth'll be coming as well, for his tea, and Mam'll probably make a fuss of them both. You'll not want to be there when that's going on.'

'I have to be there. I have to face the two of them sometime, Lachie, and it might as well be now.' Even to her own ears she sounded very cool and grown-up, although her stomach was full of butterflies.

He scowled. 'I think our Mattie's got a cheek, parading him in front of you.'

'She's got every right to bring her fiancé to her own home.'

'Are you telling me that you don't mind?'

Elspeth had never lied to Lachlan or Thomas, and wasn't going to start now. 'I minded a lot when I first heard, but I've got used to the idea now. I'd not have wanted Kenneth to stay with me against his will. And I'm going to be here when Mattie brings him home.'

'Oh, all right – but if you feel that you want to get out of the place, tip me the wink and I'll think of something.'

When the moment came, it was hard for her to see the happiness in Mattie and Kenneth's faces and to hear Flora making such a fuss of the two of them. But Elspeth had worked hard to prepare for the ordeal, and she managed to deal with it calmly, congratulating them both and admiring the engagement ring Kenneth had given Mattie. That made it official, she thought, gazing down at the small diamond. There was no chance now of Kenneth changing his mind and asking her to take him back.

Lachlan hovered around Elspeth protectively all afternoon, giving Kenneth a curt nod when he arrived, then eyeing him coldly across the table during the meal. Henry, too, tended to sympathise with her, but Kenneth and Mattie both looked so guilty each time they caught Elspeth's eye that she found herself making a point of being nice to them both.

As the rest of the family were there as well – Granjan and Thomas and Aileen, Rachel and wee Mary – things were easier for Elspeth. The kitchen was so crowded that it was easy for her to avoid the happy couple after greeting them.

Flora, glowing with pleasure and triumph at the good marriage her younger daughter was making, found herself eclipsed somewhat when Thomas announced at the table that his employer, Forbes Cameron, had decided to buy a partnership in a larger garage in Gourock.

'He's going to spend most of his time there, and I'm to run the Greenock garage for him,' he said proudly. 'I've not been there long, but he's pleased with my work and says he couldn't find a better man for the job. I'm to get in another mechanic to work under me. And it means more money, so' – he put an arm round Aileen, sitting by his side – 'we'll be able to afford a better flat before the bairn arrives.'

As the two girls were going to bed that night, Mattie tried to explain, as she had in her letter, that she and Kenneth hadn't intended to fall in love. Elspeth, who couldn't face the prospect of another discussion about the matter, broke in almost at once.

'Mattie, Kenneth and me were just friends, nothing more. I don't mind about what's happened.' She wasn't sure whether that was a lie or not. She was still hurt, but at the same time she was aware of a faint sense of freedom. 'He cares more for you than he ever did for me, and there's nothing else to be said about it.'

Mattie's eyes, which had been sliding away from Elspeth ever since she arrived, brightened. 'You're awful generous, Ellie.'

'I'm just being sensible,' Elspeth told her briskly, then, longing to change the subject, 'It's good news about Thomas, isn't it?'

Celia Bremner's furniture was sold not long after Mattie and Kenneth returned to Glasgow, raising more money than Elspeth had expected. She would have liked to spend it on the others, but realised that in view of the tension between herself and Flora, that would not be wise. Instead, she bought small gifts for Granjan and Rachel and wee Mary, and a pretty scarf in different shades of green to match Aileen's eyes.

'I'm so glad to see you!' the girl welcomed her when she called with the gift. 'Thomas is working late again, and I'm tired of my own company.'

The note of complaint in her voice, unusual for Aileen, put Elspeth on the defensive. 'He's trying to make a success of running the garage on his own, so that he can earn enough to give you and the bairn a good life.'

'I know, but—' Aileen hesitated, then said slowly, 'Has he told you that Ian's offered to give us a loan until things get better?'

'Your brother? Thomas would never agree to that!'

'Thomas,' his wife said shortly, 'has more pride than he can afford. I don't see why we shouldn't accept – Ian's my brother, after all, and he only wants to help. It would make such a difference to us, yet Thomas refused to even discuss it.'

'Can you blame him, after what happened?'

Aileen flushed. 'That was ages ago, and Ian's done everything he can since then to make up for it. It's Thomas who's being difficult now. You'd think he'd want what's best for both of us. For a start, we could move out of this place and into something with more room.' She threw her hands out to indicate the small kitchen that she had so lovingly painted and furnished less than a year ago, then said with sudden hope, 'Would you speak to him, Elspeth? He thinks highly of you, and he'd listen to you. You could explain to him that Ian only wants to help us.'

'But I couldn't interfere in Thomas's life,' Elspeth said wretchedly, then, as Aileen opened her mouth to argue, she held out the small package. 'Grandmother's furniture's been sold, so I brought you a wee gift to celebrate.'

To her relief, Aileen brightened at once, exclaiming with delight over the scarf then tying it round her neck and admiring herself in the small wall mirror.

Thomas arrived just then, his eyes suddenly wary as he stepped into the room and saw the pretty green scarf about his wife's throat.

'Is this another of your brother's wee presents? Aileen, I've told you—'

'Elspeth gave it to me. I suppose that's acceptable, since she's a member of your family, not mine?' There was a sharpness in Aileen's voice that Elspeth had never heard before, and she wished that she had left before Thomas's arrival.

He flushed scarlet beneath the streaks of dirt and oil from the garage. 'I'm sorry, Ellie, I didn't realise,' he said, then as he looked again at his wife, the wariness fled and he smiled. 'The colour matches your eyes. You look lovely.' He moved to hug her, but she backed away.

'Don't get oil all over it. I wish you'd wash at the garage, Thomas, and not walk through the streets looking like that.'

'I told you, if I take the time to heat water on the gas ring, a customer's sure to arrive while I'm doing it, then I'm trapped for another half-hour.' He poured hot water from the kettle on the range into a basin and snapped open the metal fastenings holding the shoulder straps of his dirty dungarees. 'It's best to just lock up and go while the place is empty. As for walking home like this, a wee bit of dirt's a badge of honour. There's plenty of poor souls in this town that'd give anything they had for the chance to get their hands dirty from work.'

He stepped out of the overalls and tossed them on to the newspaper waiting in the corner for them, then reached for the harsh yellow soap by the sink and began to wash.

'I'd best go and let you have your meal in peace,' Elspeth said, but Thomas, dousing his face, spluttered through a veil of water, 'Wait a bit, Ellie, I want to ask you about something.'

'What did you buy for yourself?' Aileen wanted to know.

'A new pair of gloves.' Now that the angry flush had left the other girl's cheeks, Elspeth saw that there were shadows beneath her slightly slanted eyes, and the corners of her mouth were drawn down. The baby was showing now and increasing weight had robbed Aileen of her usual grace; as she picked up a jug and went to rinse Thomas's hair she put her feet down heavily, moving with the sway-backed walk of pregnancy.

Her blouse and skirt strained tightly over her rounded belly, so that the hem at the front of the skirt was dragged up, giving the garment an uneven look.

Elspeth felt a stab of pity for the girl. If she had married her own class, she would have been pampered throughout this pregnancy, not allowed to lift even a finger. She would have worn clothes specially made for the occasion, cut skilfully to conceal her swelling figure. Instead, she was denied the luxury that was hers by birthright, forced to cope as best she could. It was little wonder that she was tired and irritable.

'How would you like me to make you a new dress?' she offered impulsively. 'Something loose and more comfortable.'

Aileen handed Thomas a towel and he buried his head and face in it. 'Could you?' Her eyes lit up, the weariness and stress vanishing. For a moment she was pretty and carefree again, then her eyes clouded. 'How much would the material cost?'

'Whatever it is, we'll find the money,' Thomas put in quickly from the folds of the towel. 'It's well past time you had a new dress.'

'Don't worry about the cost – we get remnants for nothing at work, and there's a lovely piece of silky material lying in the sewing room just now, a nice bluey-green that would suit you.'

It wasn't true. Miss Arnold didn't allow the girls in the sewing room to take even the smallest scraps that were left over from their work. As Lena used to say, the overseer wouldn't have given her nail-clippings away free. But Elspeth had been admiring the piece of blue-green material on the remnants counter at Brodie's that very day. It wouldn't cost much, and she could use some of Grandmother's money.

'I'll bring the material in tomorrow, on my way home from work,' she promised. 'We can decide on the style once you've had a look at it.'

Aileen nodded eagerly, her face radiant, as Thomas turned from the sink, running his fingers through his wet hair. 'I'm looking for a favour from you as well, Ellie.' He looked embarrassed. 'With me being in charge of the garage now, it means that I've to balance the books and send out the accounts. I've never in my life had to see to that side of things – I just handed my pay packet to Mam and she handed back my spending money. It was much the same in the army. And Aileen here has no more idea of working with money than I have, though' – he shot a proud look at his wife – 'I've never seen anyone make a few coppers go further than she can.'

Aileen coloured, and said quickly, 'I'm learning, but I can't deal with ledgers and payments and all that sort of thing. I'm still finding out about the cost of vegetables and washing soap.'

'So I thought mebbe you could show me how to do the books,' Thomas went on. 'I'll try to learn from you so that I can take them over myself soon.'

He was running a comb through his hair now; it clung to his skull, combining with his newly scrubbed face to take years off his age. He and Aileen, Elspeth thought as she looked from one to the other, both looked too young to shoulder all the responsibilities and worries that crowded in on them. At that moment, she felt older than either of them, though she was several years their junior.

'Of course I will. Can you bring them home with you tomorrow? I'll have a look at them after I've measured Aileen for the dress.'

Studying the ledgers and cash-books spread before her, Elspeth could see that although Forbes Cameron had known what he was about, Thomas didn't. His financial dealings since taking over the garage reminded her of Mr Monteith's book-keeping.

'I've not got the time to do it all properly as well as getting on with my own work,' he explained anxiously, watching as she riffled through the notes he had made. By his side, Aileen caressed the dress material Elspeth had bought that morning from the remnants counter.

'To tell the truth, it would take too long to sit down and teach you how to keep your own books, but I could see to them for you if you want, and teach you what I can when you've got the time. I could type out your bills properly while I'm at it.'

His eyes lit up. 'That would be grand! How much will you want for it?'

She thought fast, guessing that any money he paid her would have to come from his own wages.

'You've got an office at the garage, haven't you?'

'It's not much – a room with a desk and a gas ring and a paraffin heater.'

'Could I move my typewriter in and work there? I think Aunt Flora's getting tired of the noise the typewriter makes,' she hurried on as Thomas raised his eyebrows. 'If I could use your office I'd do your books in place of paying rent – unless you think Mr Cameron would object.'

'He'll not bother his head about it. But it's not a very cosy room, Ellie.'

'That'll make me work faster, so that I can get away to somewhere more comfortable.'

'In that case, you've got a deal.' Thomas took her hand and shook it vigorously. 'I'll collect the typewriter from Mearns Street tomorrow.'

The garage workshop had at one time been the stable and carriage-house of a sturdy Georgian family home on the hill above Greenock. As the town expanded the garden had disappeared beneath cobbled streets and small factories, but the house still remained, its brickwork badly in need of repointing, its high, wide windows either boarded up or so dirty that it was impossible to see through them, its once-handsome front door dingy and permanently sealed.

The only usable entrance to the old building was the kitchen door, which opened from a cobbled yard where horses had once been led out to be yoked to carriages. The upper floor and the attic had been closed off, and only the front two ground rooms were in use, one as a storeroom, the other an office of sorts.

Thomas was right, Elspeth discovered at first sight of the room. It was the most cheerless place she had ever seen. Large and high-ceilinged, it had once been a drawing room, but now the timbered floor was scuffed and scored, faded paper hung dismally from the walls, and the mouldings on the ceiling could scarcely be seen in the dim light from a filthy window. The enormous fireplace lurked against one wall like the mouth of a dark and dismal cave, and the furniture consisted of a few chairs, a paraffin stove, a large sideboard piled with books and papers, a sagging *chaise-longue* that looked as though it had crept into the house to die, and a dusty table where Thomas set down her typewriter. The bulky machine, which had dominated her little bedroom, suddenly seemed small and quite forlorn in the middle of the long table.

'I told you it was cheerless,' Thomas said from behind her as she gazed round. 'Are you sure you want to work here?'

'I'm quite sure. At least I can make as much noise as I like without disturbing anyone,' she added wryly as a loud crash came from the direction of the yard.

'I'd better go and see what Joe's up to,' Thomas said hurriedly, and left.

Now that she was alone, Elspeth took time to study the place more closely, noting the dust that lay everywhere, and the grime on the windows, cutting down considerably on the amount of light in the room. At least something could be done about that. Tiptoeing across the hall, a square, gloomy place with a curved stairway leading up into total darkness, she found that the room at the other side was filled with bits of machinery. She hurriedly closed the door after one brief glance and returned to the office, wiping her dusty hands on her handkerchief.

'I hope you're not going to start fussing,' Thomas said anxiously when he returned to find her rubbing hard at the table with a rag she had located. 'It's only an office, mind.'

'I know, but nobody could work in there the way it is. All that dust'll ruin the typewriter. Don't worry, I'm not going to expect you or Joe to start painting and papering.'

Rachel willingly agreed to help, and the two of them spent the following weekend scrubbing and sweeping and climbing precariously on to chairs in order to knock down spiders' webs with mops lashed to broom handles. They wrapped themselves in huge aprons and swathed their heads in scarves to protect their hair against the dust. Baby Mary slumbered in her perambulator in a safe corner of the yard.

'It's been a bonny house,' Rachel said breathlessly, balancing on the windowsill and rubbing hard at the glass. 'Imagine living in a place like this, with nice furniture, and flowers outside the windows instead of just the street and folk passing by.'

'And a servant to come and turn the pages of your book for you,' Elspeth agreed from the sideboard, where she was sorting through the books, shaking each one vigorously to clear the dust from it. She was enjoying Rachel's company. They had never really known each other before, for Mattie was nearer Elspeth's age and Rachel had always been the older sister, contemptuous of the two younger girls. Now, Elspeth discovered that Rachel was a good companion, with a sense of fun she had never demonstrated before.

As the other girl stretched up to the top of the window, Elspeth noticed a few bruises on her arms. Clearly, Bob was still ill-treating his wife. But she had the wit to say nothing, taking her frustration and anger out instead on a fragment of wallpaper dangling above the sideboard, wrenching it savagely from the wall. It came away with a satisfactory ripping sound, showering her with grit.

'Ellie, what're you doing?'

'It might as well be off as hanging there.' Elspeth stepped back to look at her handiwork, refastening the scarf round her head. 'If we brush over the plaster it'll look better than the way it was.'

'Let me.' Rachel deftly stepped from the sill to a chair, then caught at another drooping piece of wallpaper and tore it free. 'It feels good, doesn't it?' she said with enthusiasm. When she laughed, Elspeth noticed, she looked years younger.

Half an hour later, when Thomas glanced in to see how they were getting on, there was a small pile of paper in the middle of the floor.

'You don't mind, do you?' Elspeth asked, noting Rachel swiftly tugging her sleeves down to ensure that the finger-shaped blue marks on her arms were hidden. 'The walls looked worse with the paper than they do without it.'

He shrugged, and handed over two mugs of strong tea. 'As long as you get my books into order I don't care what you do.'

Their throats were clogged with dust, so they went out into the yard to drink their tea, Rachel going at once to the perambulator to look at her daughter. Six-month-old Mary, oblivious to the noise from the workshop, was sound asleep on her back, one arm thrown above her head, long dark lashes brushing her plump cheeks.

Joe, the man Thomas had hired when he took over the running of the garage, came over to admire the baby. He was a cheerful man in his forties, a marine engineer who had lost his job as a seaman after an accident damaged one leg. Although he could no longer shin up and down the narrow metal ladders of an engine room he was well able to cope with garage work, and enjoyed dealing with cars and motor bicycles instead of ships' engines.

He touched the baby's half-open hand very gently with the tip of one finger, taking care not to dirty her white skin. 'That's a right bonny wee lassie ye've got there, hen.'

Rachel smiled shyly, then said when the man had gone back to work, 'I wish she'd been a laddie.'

'Why?'

'Women don't have much of a time – not women like us, anyway.'

'Are things still bad?' Elspeth ventured, and the older girl shrugged.

'They're no worse, and I suppose I ought to be grateful for that. Never marry for love, Ellie, it doesnae buy food or pay the rent, and it only makes folks bitter in the end.' She bent to draw the blanket gently round her slumbering daughter. 'I'm going to try to teach her that when she's older.' Then, straightening, she said suddenly, bleakly, 'I'm expecting again, Ellie, but don't say a word to anyone till I tell Mam. She'll want to be the first to know.'

'What does Bob say?'

'It's not something I'm in a hurry to tell him. I'll have to pick my time.'

'He'll be pleased, surely.' And surely, Elspeth thought, he'd be kinder to Rachel when she was carrying his child.

Rachel's mouth twisted wryly. 'I was daft enough to think he'd be pleased when I fell with Mary, but that's when the trouble started. To him a bairn's just another mouth to feed and one less drink. That's why I'm hoping this'll be a wee laddie – he might take that a bit better.'

'Why don't you do sewing for folk to make more money, since Bob's drinking most of his wages?'

'I couldn't,' Rachel said at once, startled.

'Yes you could. You earned your living by sewing before you married, and you're good at it. Look at the bonny wee clothes you've made for Mary. There must be neighbours who can't sew – you could offer to help them.'

'They'd not be able to pay me.'

'Money's not the only way to pay for things. They could look after Mary for an hour and let you get some time to yourself, or mebbe give you a few scones, or – there are lots of ways folk can help each other,' Elspeth pointed out. 'If any of your neighbours does cleaning for someone with money, she could mebbe mention your name, then you might get work from people who can afford to pay.'

'I'll think about it. We'd best get back to work.'

'You should have told me about the bairn,' Elspeth said as they rinsed their mugs in the kitchen. 'I'd not have let you climb up on the windowsill or the chairs.'

Rachel threw her a sidelong look from the corner of her eye. 'Why else did you think I was so keen to do it?' she asked, and went back to work.

With the layers of dust removed and daylight filtering in through the cleaned windows, the office, while still shabby and neglected, was at least usable. Elspeth started working there the following weekend, relishing the space she now had.

In her bedroom, papers had been strewn over the bed and

the floor, but here the table was large enough to accommodate them all. It was satisfying, too, to hear the crisp tapping of the typewriter keys and the crash of the returning carriage echo in the large room, knowing that Flora wasn't going to bang on the door to tell her to stop the noise.

It didn't take her long to put the garage books into order. She did Mr Monteith's work there too, as well as Mr Leslie's, the shopkeeper who had heard of her skills from Mr Monteith. Normally, she would only have been able to work in the office on a Saturday morning, but Thomas, in his eagerness to do his best for Aileen and their coming child, often worked into the evenings from Monday to Saturday, and always spent part of every Sunday at the garage, making it possible for Elspeth to put in longer hours than she had expected.

He was driving himself too hard, but her attempts to tell him that were brushed aside.

'It's only rich folk who deal with stocks and shares that make money without getting off their backsides,' he said contemptuously. 'And I'd not want to earn my bread that way, by the sweat of other men's foreheads. If I don't make this place a success Mr Cameron'll close it down, then where'll we be – me and Aileen and the bairn?'

'And where'll Aileen and the baby be if you make yourself ill?'

'Stop girnin' at me, Ellie,' he said, irritated. 'I've got enough on my mind as it is.'

She held her tongue after that, though she continued to worry about him, and about Aileen. She was busy in her spare time making the new dress she had promised Aileen, and she had met Ian Bruce more than once at the flat. Aileen was always animated when her brother was there, and it was clear that he adored her. Surely, Elspeth told herself, it was only natural for Aileen to want to keep in touch with the only member of her family who, at the moment, would have anything to do with her. But at the same time she had the uncomfortable feeling that Ian Bruce was encouraging Aileen's growing dissatisfaction with her surroundings.

Once, rounding the corner on her way to visit, she was in time to see Ian Bruce handing his sister into his car. It was a cool, breezy day and the green scarf Elspeth had given Aileen was tied around her head. Her thickening figure was enveloped in a warm fur coat that Elspeth had never seen before – presumably a garment brought from the wardrobe she had had to leave behind when she walked out of her parents' mansion to marry Thomas.

Neither of them noticed Elspeth; as the red car roared past her, she saw that all Aileen's attention was fixed on her brother.

'I love Thomas, and I'd not want to be away from him,' she said to Elspeth a few days later. The new dress was almost completed, and Elspeth was kneeling at her feet, pinning up the hem. 'But I'm so tired of having to do without and count the pennies. If he'd just let Ian help us, things would be much easier, and we'd have more time together. Ian's sure that once the baby's born Mother and Father will come round. And there's no reason why Father shouldn't buy Thomas a garage of his own.'

'Thomas would never allow that, Aileen,' Elspeth said carefully, and the skirt twitched in her hand as the other girl shrugged.

'He could, if he'd give up this stubborn pride of his.'

When the dress had been taken off, Aileen opened a drawer and showed her a lovely pair of gloves, soft and beautifully made. 'Ian gave them to me, to wear at the baby's christening.' Her eyes shone as she stroked the material with work-reddened hands. 'Don't tell Thomas – I'm going to hide them away until the time comes.'

She had asked Elspeth to buy some mince on her way to the flat; when she opened her purse to pay for it, Elspeth saw that there was more money in it than usual. Remembering Thomas's boast about his wife's ability to make a pound note go a long way, she wondered if Ian Bruce was giving his sister money.

There was nobody she could talk to about her suspicions, not even Granjan, in case she inadvertently let a word slip out in Flora's hearing. So Elspeth held her tongue and tried to assure herself that once the baby arrived Aileen would revert back to her former self.

The garage books gave an impressive picture of Thomas's ability to run the place. Once she managed to sort out the paperwork she found that business was brisk, although she already knew that from the number of people who called in at the garage every day, and from the telephone calls.

Before her arrival, Thomas had dealt with the telephone, which stood in the kitchen. Now it was Elspeth's job to answer it when she was in the office. At first, unused to the machine, she had been nervous.

'Ellie, I've got enough to do without running in here every time the telephone rings. It's only a machine,' Thomas told her impatiently. 'Machines are made for folk's convenience – no need to be afraid of them!'

Stung by his words, she had made herself master the instrument, and within a week had become used to it, though she was thrown into alarm when one of the callers barked, 'Tell McDonald to come to the phone,' as soon as she answered.

There was so much authority in the voice that she obeyed, and had reached the kitchen door before realising that nobody had the right to order her around like that. She returned to the machine.

'Please.'

'What?'

'C-courtesy costs nothing,' she said, then tried to force the nervous quiver from her voice. 'You could have said please.'

There was an exasperated sigh, then the man at the other end of the line asked, 'Will that bring McDonald to the phone any faster?'

'It will.'

'In that case – please.'

'If you'll just hold on, I'll go and get him,' Elspeth said primly, and went to call Thomas from the workshop.

He came into the office a few minutes later. 'What did you say to that man?'

Elspeth finished the entry she was making before looking up. 'The man on the phone? He was impertinent, so I made him say please, that's all.'

'Ah. I don't think anyone's ever made him say that before.'

'I wasn't impertinent back to him. If he says I was, he's lying.'

'He didn't,' Thomas said, and turned to go.

'Who is he?'

'Forbes Cameron, the owner of this place,' Thomas said, and returned to his work.

Forbes Cameron strolled into the office the following weekend to introduce himself.

'And to apologise for my boorishness on the telephone,' he added, and Elspeth flushed.

'I didn't realise it was you.'

'That shouldn't make any difference. You were quite right, I behaved badly. My only excuse is that I'm so used to working among men that I've lost my manners. I'm sure my mother would wholeheartedly agree with you that it was time someone pulled me up about it.'

He was a stocky, broad-shouldered man, a few years older than Thomas. Dark hair that looked as though it had been brushed that morning, but had then found a way of breaking free, topped a square, tanned face. His eyes were grey, and his mouth wide above a determined chin. She knew from what Thomas had said that Forbes Cameron had been born into money and had travelled extensively. He was a racing-car driver and yachtsman.

265

He glanced around the room, then back at her. 'I never realised what good lines this room has before.'

'It just needed cleaning.'

'It needs more than that.' He looked at the wall behind her, covered here and there by wallpaper, but mainly showing the bare plaster. 'It needs re-papering, for a start.'

'It's not worth papering an office.'

'Painting, then. What colour would you like?'

'There's no need to—'

'Blue? Yellow? Purple? Tell me what you think.'

Elspeth studied the walls. 'If I was doing it, I'd choose a soft shade, mebbe a parchment colour, mebbe a bit lighter than that.'

He strode over to where her coat hung on a nail. 'Come into the town with me and choose something. We'll get a decent coat-stand while we're at it.'

'But I'm in the middle of some work.'

'Give yourself an hour off to choose paint.'

'The room's fine as it is.'

'It's my room, and I say it needs painting. So—' She was scooped from her seat and being helped into her coat before she knew what was happening. Ten minutes later the two of them were choosing paint.

'What about the doors and skirting boards and window frames?' Forbes Cameron asked when she had opted for a pale fawn shade.

'It's too beautiful to be covered, even though it's all marked.'

'Varnish, then, with some treatment first,' he decided briskly. 'Now come and have a cup of tea, and tell me about yourself.'

'This is ridiculous,' she protested as they sipped tea in a small tearoom.

'Not at all; you deserve a proper office, especially after you've done such excellent work on our books.'

266

'You've seen them?'

'I call in every week to keep an eye on things. McDonald tells me you've refused to take any money for the work.'

'Thomas has enough to do with his wages. He lets me keep my typewriter in the office, and do work for other people there in return for what I do for the garage.'

'Nevertheless, it's me who should be paying you, not McDonald. I've been very lax about that. We'll arrange proper payment on the way back, and I'll see that the room's painted during the week, so that it's all ready for you by next Saturday.'

But by the following Saturday a freshly painted office was the last thing on Elspeth's mind. Three days after she met Forbes Cameron, Ian Bruce's handsome red car spun out of control on the hill road to the Loch Thom reservoir, smashing into a stone wall.

Ian and his passenger, his sister Aileen, both died immediately.

A clerk from Mr Bruce's lawyer's firm called at Mearns Street, where Thomas was staying with his parents, to inform him of the arrangements Aileen's father had made for the double funeral.

The family, at their evening meal, sat in awkward silence as the man, his bowler hat tucked beneath one arm, talked to Thomas. When he had finished he left, politely refusing Flora's flustered offer of a wee cup of tea.

'Ye'd've thought they'd've had the decency tae call at a better time – and to consult ye,' she raged when the man had gone. 'They've not even invited ye tae the house, and you their son-in-law!'

'Leave it, Mam,' Thomas told her brusquely. He had scarcely spoken since hearing the news.

'But she was your wife, an' carryin' your bairn—'

'The lassie I was married to's gone, and so's the bairn that never was. No point in quarrelin' over what's left. Anyway, she was a Bruce more than a McDonald.' He got up from the table, pushing his chair back noisily, and left the kitchen. A moment later the outer door shut.

'Now where's he goin'?' Flora wailed.

'Probably back to the garage, Mam,' Lachlan said.

'But he's already put in his day's work, and scarcely touched his food. If he's goin' tae insist on workin' every hour of the day an' night he'll have tae eat tae keep his strength up!'

'Leave it be, Flora, the laddie needs tae go through this in his own way,' Henry said with a rarely heard ring of authority in his voice. 'Don't fuss him.'

She glared, then went over to the sink, leaving her own plate half-full, and began to crash dishes about. 'I don't know – ye'd think he'd talk tae us about it, or even cry if it takes him that way. But this is no' like our Thomas at all.'

'He'll be all right,' Elspeth tried to assure her, though she too was worried about the way Thomas had completely withdrawn from everything and everyone since his wife's death.

'Come and eat yer own food,' Henry added.

'I don't want it.'

'Sit down and eat, woman!' He all but shouted the words. Elspeth and Lachlan glanced at each other, then dipped their heads over their own plates. Although there was nothing wrong with the food, it was as interesting as cardboard to Elspeth, and she was sure that Lachlan felt the same way. They were both making a show of minding their own business in order to avoid the confrontation that seemed inevitable. Henry McDonald, Lachlan had once told Elspeth, could be a feared dictator at work, but he had always been content to let his wife rule the house, until now.

The confrontation didn't come. Flora flounced away from the sink and sat down, picking up her fork and knife.

'It's as if he doesnae care,' she muttered to the cooling, congealing mince and potatoes and carrots.

'Of course he cares – can ye no' see it in his eyes? He cares so much that he cannae speak for the pain of it.'

'Then why doesnae he let his own folk comfort him?' Flora asked, a tremor in her voice, 'When I think of that bonny wee thing, no more than a child hersel' – and how could he say she wasnae a McDonald, when they were wed in front of a minister and her own family's had nothin' tae dae with her since? It's us should be buryin' her, not them!'

'Flora—' Henry said quietly, with real steel in his voice this time. To Elspeth's relief the woman subsided.

Thomas hadn't set foot in the flat he shared with Aileen since hearing about the accident. He had moved into his parents' house at once, unable to return to his home, sending his father to collect clothes for him. He had insisted on working at the garage as usual, and when he was at Mearns Street he sat alone in the tiny room he once more shared with Lachlan, or in the kitchen making a pretence of reading the newspaper. He had aged overnight, and his brown eyes, normally lively and bright, were dull pebbles set in bony hollows.

Neighbours calling to express their sympathies were met with a set, withdrawn expression, and he usually left the kitchen or even the flat when outsiders called, letting his mother do the talking for him.

As a result of this, Elspeth knew, the neighbours were muttering to each other that he was too stuck-up for his own good and no longer interested in his own folk after marrying one of the gentry. She wanted to shout at them that it wasn't true, that Thomas should be left in peace to grieve in his own way, but she couldn't. That would only have incensed Aunt Flora, and made matters worse.

The funeral service was held in the grand church Catherine Bruce had been married in not long before the end of the war. Aileen's flower-bedecked coffin lay beside that of her brother, almost exactly where she must have stood on that long-past wedding day in her pretty yellow bridesmaid's dress.

As Thomas led his family in, an usher scurried up to tell him in a discreet murmur that there was a place for him in 'the family pew'.

'I wasn't welcome in their company when she was alive, and I see no reason to sit with them now,' Thomas said in a low, clear voice and ushered his family into a row halfway up the church while the man retreated, red-faced.

Flora wanted to sit by her bereaved son, but he had paid no heed, and as church was no place for an argument, she had to submit to his wishes, following Janet Docherty to the end of the empty row while the others huddled nervously in the aisle, anxious to be seated as quickly as possible and out of the view of the rest of the congregation.

Thomas chose the seat by the aisle for himself, looking straight ahead and seemingly oblivious to the stares and murmurs as the mourners coming down the aisle recognised him as Aileen's husband. He seated Lachlan beside him, then came Elspeth and Mattie, who had arrived that morning from Glasgow to attend the funeral. Rachel, who was having an uncomfortable pregnancy and looked pale and drawn in her borrowed black coat and a hat that didn't suit her, sat between Mattie and Bob.

As they waited for the service to begin, Flora fretted about Thomas's refusal to sit at the front of the church. 'They'll think he's snubbin' them,' Elspeth heard her say in an agitated whisper, loud enough to set heads in her vicinity turning.

'It doesnae matter any more what they think, does it?' Henry retorted gruffly, and Elspeth could positively hear Flora's withering glare as she subsided.

Many of the people pouring into the church were young, presumably Ian's friends – and former friends of Aileen's, thought Elspeth, though not one of them had visited her after her marriage. Forbes Cameron paused by Thomas, who got to his feet and shook hands with his employer and with the elderly couple by his side before the trio moved on to take their places elsewhere in the church.

The sombre organ music and the heavy scent of the massed funeral flowers had given Elspeth the beginnings of a headache by the time Mr Bruce and his daughter and son-in-law arrived, Catherine's face hidden by heavy veiling. She was the Bruces' only surviving child, Elspeth realised as the three of them walked down the long aisle, and she pitied these people who in their arrogance and insensitivity had turned their backs on Aileen in the final year of her life. For all their money and all their pride, the Bruces were still parents, and this must be a terrible day for them.

As soon as the family was seated the minister began to speak at length about the tragedy of two premature deaths. He talked about Aileen without once making reference to her marriage, her husband or her unborn child. Slipping a glance at Thomas, Elspeth saw that his profile could have been carved out of stone. Not a muscle twitched, not an eyelid flickered, even when the service finally ended and his wife's coffin was carried out, so near to him as it went by that he could have reached out and touched it. Mr Bruce and his daughter and son-in-law, walking behind the coffins, passed Thomas without a glance.

As she rose to make her way out of the church Elspeth saw some of their neighbours from Mearns Street sitting at the back, together with others who were probably Bruce servants.

Outside, the sun was shining, oblivious to the fact that today of all days the sky should have been overcast and weeping cold rain. As the McDonalds hesitated on the gravel drive, clustered in a knot for mutual comfort, Forbes Cameron brought over the elderly couple he had escorted into church, introducing them as his parents. They, at least, were friendly, and Elspeth, who had noticed with concern that Flora had begun to look pinched and shrunken and was clinging to Henry's arm for support, was relieved to see the woman expand a little under Mrs Cameron's kindly warmth. Just like a little Japanese flower, she thought, remembering her childhood, when she had loved to watch tiny dried-up flakes of apparently colourless paper blossom into bright flowers when dropped into a cup of water.

The usher who had spoken to Thomas in the church arrived by his elbow again to inform him that there was a place for him in one of the leading cars.

'Thank Mr Bruce,' Forbes Cameron told him blandly, 'and explain that Mr McDonald and his family are travelling with us.' Then he swept them off to where three handsome black limousines, each with a uniformed chauffeur, waited in the long line of cars.

In the cemetery, Thomas took hold of Elspeth's arm as she stepped out of the car. 'Stay with me,' he said; startled, for it was the first thing he had said to her since hearing of Aileen's death, she allowed herself to be drawn along with him through the crowd of mourners to where the two coffins waited beside the open graves.

In death, as in life, the Bruce family believed in their right to own land. An elaborate wrought-iron fence defended the considerable area set aside solely for their dead; each well-tended grave was watched over by a handsome headstone, and in the middle of the lair a marble memorial soared above the heads of the gathered mourners, the names of all those buried within the fence inscribed on its four smooth sides.

'Hold your head high, Ellie,' Thomas murmured as they took their places on the opposite side of the graves from Mr Bruce and his daughter. She did as she was bid, raising her head, topped by a wide-brimmed, high-crowned black straw hat, on the long stem of her neck, proud to be standing by Thomas, who, although his black suit hadn't cost a fraction of the money that most of the mourners had clearly paid for their funeral clothes, seemed to her to be the most elegantly dressed man there. Aileen, she thought with tears aching in her throat, would have been proud of him.

Arm against arm, they stood motionless during the shortened version of the church service, separating only when Thomas stepped forward to take hold of one of the cords to help lower his young wife and their unborn child into their final resting place.

Ian Bruce had been buried first, his father and brother-in-law throwing handfuls of earth in on top of his coffin. As the undertaker's men took over the cords, smoothly lowering Aileen to the bottom of the grave, Thomas stooped and gathered a firm fistful of soil from the pile nearby, then held his arm out over the void, opening his fingers to let the earth patter down in a final salute to his wife.

It was hard not to gape when the funeral party went into the Bruce house. Although she had known that the place would be sumptuous, Elspeth was unprepared for the massive hallway they passed through after entering the house.

'It's almost big enough to hold our entire tenement,' Mattie murmured at her side as they stepped through the front door, staring at the huge staircase rising to the next floor. The fireplace in the vast drawing room was as broad as one of the kitchen walls at Mearns Street. Looking around at the paintings, the furniture, the wide, high windows opening on to a terrace where flower-filled stone urns stood, Elspeth felt her heart break for Aileen.

No wonder the girl had been suffocated in the tiny flat that was all Thomas could provide. No wonder she had been so pleased to make contact with her brother, and so eager to urge Thomas to take advantage of an offer that would have given them a larger home.

Mrs Bruce, her face grey and old against her black dress, her eyes filled with a sorrow that would never leave her, put in a brief appearance once the mourners were gathered. Supported by a uniformed nurse, she spoke to a few people, but neither she nor her husband or daughter came near Thomas. If it hadn't been for the kindness of Forbes Cameron and his parents, the McDonalds would have been completely isolated.

The Camerons fussed over Flora in particular, making certain that she had enough to eat, seeing to it that her cup was refilled, although Elspeth could tell by the flickering of Flora's lashes as she sipped carefully at the fragile china cup that the weak tea it held wasn't to her liking.

Standing close to her mother as though for protection, Rachel kept an anxious eye on Bob, who had eagerly accepted a glass of whisky and drunk it swiftly. Flora hadn't noticed, but Henry did, frowning in puzzled disbelief. Now Bob's eyes thirstily watched the silver trays of glasses being carried round the room by immaculately uniformed maids. His face was flushed, and he continually plucked with one finger at the collar of his shirt, or tugged his jacket down. Like Rachel, he must have borrowed his funeral clothes from a more affluent neighbour, for they were too tight for him. When one of the trays moved in his direction his fingers trembled and the tip of his tongue flicked across his lower lip, but somehow Henry, clearly realising that his son-in-law had broken the teetotal pledge made as a child, managed to step between Bob and the crystal glasses half filled with amber liquid.

Watching Bob's suffering, Rachel's misery, Flora's discomfort and Thomas's stoic indifference to his surroundings, Elspeth longed to sweep them all away from the magnificent house which had been the cause of so much heartache. None of them deserved to be treated like this. It was a relief when Forbes Cameron suggested leaving.

'We've been here for an acceptable length of time, and I see that some other people are preparing to go. My mother's tired, and I'm sure that you are too, Mrs Docherty.'

Janet was the only member of the group to have been at her ease, taking in her surroundings and the fine clothes of the women in the room with swift, birdlike glances that carried not a sign of envy. 'I'm f—' she began, then, with a look at her daughter, who was beginning to wilt again, she amended it to, 'I'm fair exhausted, tae tell ye the truth. Would ye mind if we went home, Flora?'

Mrs Bruce had long since retreated from the room. They made their farewells to Mr Bruce, who held each hand limply for a second and made murmuring noises, gazing past their heads, then Cameron saw them into the limousines, which were magically waiting before the door when they went out on to the steps.

Elspeth rode with Rachel and Bob, who were taken straight

home because Rachel was worried about wee Mary, being cared for by a neighbour. She arrived back at Mearns Street in time to see the garage owner assist Flora on to the pavement, under the interested stare of half the street, and bow over her hand before she summoned up the last of her strength and swept regally into the close.

'Such a nice man,' she said when they had gained the kitchen, stripping her hat and gloves off. 'A real gentleman. Elspeth, for pity's sake put that kettle on, I'm parched for a decent cup of tea. That was nothin' but coloured water they were pourin' out of they silver teapots.'

'They're a right gutless lot,' Henry grunted, sinking into a chair and easing his shoes off. 'I'd like tae see them try tae manage a decent day's work in the yards – it'd kill them off before they got properly started. Here – what was Bob Cochran doin', drinkin' whisky?'

'He wasn't,' Flora said at once.

'I'm no' daft, woman, I know whisky when I see it. He'd have had more if I hadnae worked it so that we both got lemonade the second time.' He wrinkled his face up. 'It meant I'd tae do without more whisky mysel', and it was the best I've ever tasted, tae.'

'The lemonade was made from real lemons,' Elspeth said in an attempt to make peace.

'Lemonade?' Henry snorted. 'The only decent drink in this country's the one made with grain and good Scottish water, and I'd tae miss out on my share because of that eejit our Rachel married.' Mention of Bob reminded him of his earlier question. 'And what happened tae the pledge he signed?' he demanded to know.

'Where's our Thomas?' Flora jumped up from her chair and her husband waved a carefully polished black shoe at her.

'Will ye stop jumpin' about like a flea on a dog?'

'He didn't come upstairs,' Lachlan reported. 'He said he wanted a bit of a walk.'

'There ye are, then, he's fine.' Henry relaxed into his chair, wriggling and stretching his stockinged toes. 'An' there's Elspeth made yer precious tea for ye. Now for pity's sake will ye put yer backside down on that chair and drink the stuff?'

Flora, having achieved her main aim and taken his mind off Bob, did as she was told, for once.

'Never bother with me, lassie,' Janet Docherty said that evening, poking the coals in her grate into a blaze. 'I've been tae more funerals than you've had hot dinners, and though this was one of the hardest tae thole, I'm old enough tae accept whatever the good Lord chooses tae throw at us. It's Thomas that's needin' a friend tonight, poor soul.'

'He doesn't want anyone.' Elspeth had gone round to Janet's flat to keep the old woman company.

'Aye he does, it's just that he hasnae realised it. His mother's nae comfort, for she fusses too much, and we all know she never wanted that marriage in the first place. With all the goodwill in the world, Flora'll no' be able tae stop hersel' from remindin' him time and again that she's been proved right after all. But you're different, lassie. It was you he chose tae stand by him at her grave. Seek him out, Elspeth. Don't push intae his grief, but let him know ye're there if he needs someone.'

When Elspeth knocked on the door of the flat Thomas had lived in with Aileen, there was an empty, desolate echo to the sound. Convinced that he wasn't sitting inside, refusing to answer, she went back out to the pavement, thinking hard. It wouldn't be his way to seek solace in the noisy, smoky atmosphere of the town's pubs, and if he had gone walking in the country above the town or along by the river, there was no hope of locating him. There was only one place she could try before conceding defeat.

To her disappointment, the garage and workshops were dark and silent. Without hope, she threaded her way round the hulking shadows of vehicles parked in the yard, sliding her feet cautiously along the cobbles at each step, wary of banging her shins or ankles on the pieces of machinery that usually littered the place.

The back door to the house was unlocked, creaking open eerily to reveal a pitch-black cave beyond. Elspeth hesitated. There was a box of matches on the gas stove only a few steps to her left, and candles on the shelf above, but the thought of reaching out into the dark, fumbling for the shape of the cooker and perhaps encountering something else – a hand, a face – was unnerving. Forcing her imagination under control, she proceeded as best she could without seeking light that might attract attention from a policeman passing by on his patrol, and cause further bother.

Gritting her teeth, she inched forward, her outstretched fingers identifying the back of a wooden chair, the corner of a cupboard. Her eyes had become accustomed to the darkness now, and by the time she reached the door leading to the hall she could just make out the outline of the kitchen furniture in the very faint grey light from the window behind her.

The hall was a deep black well. She stood still for a while until her eyes again became accustomed to her surroundings, breathing in the smell of damp and dust and metal and oil that permeated the house. There was a new, sharper smell too, which she puzzled over briefly before identifying it as the smell of paint from the newly decorated office. When her straining eyes finally found the fan-shaped wedge of grey that was the window above the sealed front door, she began the perilous journey across the hall towards the office, lifting each foot elaborately high, then putting it down gently, quietly, on the wooden floor she couldn't see.

She was halfway across, by her own reckoning, when she heard sudden movement from above. She had been trying hard not to think about the staircase to her right, leading up into unknown territory, but now she spun round to face it, her heart leaping into her mouth.

'Thomas?' Her voice, squeaky and trembling, startled her, and she clapped a hand to her mouth. There was no reply, and she didn't dare call again. She wanted desperately to run back through the kitchen and out into the comparative safety of the yard, but she knew that if she panicked now she would lose all sense of direction, with little chance of finding the back door quickly, so she made herself stand still, breathing deeply to calm her racing heart, refusing to accept the sudden picture that had flown into her mind of Thomas on the upper floor, swinging from some hook in the ceiling.

Mice, she told herself – the noise would just be mice, making free of the abandoned rooms. She had seen their droppings on the ground floor, and some of the paperwork piled on the old desk when she first came to the office had been nibbled by tiny teeth. There were rats, too, about the yard.

She was no stranger to rats and mice and cockroaches, for the working class and the poor always shared their lives with such creatures. She had little fear of them, apart from a dislike of their way of appearing suddenly, without warning, and on the whole she accepted their right to exist. But now, alone in the dark, she felt that their presence was menacing. This was their time of day, their territory rather than hers.

All had fallen quiet upstairs, and she told herself firmly that now she had come this far it was better to continue rather than to retreat.

At last she gained the office door and opened it, wrapped in the smell of fresh paint as she stepped inside. Mercifully, the moon was shining on the front of the building, and there was more light in here, enough for her to make out the comforting shape of the desk she worked at, and the smaller hump that was her covered typewriter. She started towards them, then spun round, giving a muffled yelp, as Thomas said from behind her, 'Who is it?'

'Oh – Thomas!' He was sitting on the sagging old couch that stood against the wall opposite her desk. In her relief she wanted to rush into his arms, but managed to hold herself back.

'I came looking for you.' Her voice was still weak and shaky. 'We were worried – nobody knew where you'd gone.'

'You surely knew I'd be all right – or did you think I was going to kill myself?'

'Of course not,' she lied.

He moved, and the *chaise-longue* creaked. 'I'd not do that,' his disembodied voice said. 'It'd be too easy. I just needed to be on my own, to think about things.'

She waited, letting the silence between them gather, then at last he said, 'I was going to ask you. Ellie – would you see to the house for me? I can't bring myself to go into it, and I'd not want to ask any of the others.'

'Of course I will. What d'you want me to do with—'

'Get rid of it all,' he interrupted harshly. 'Everything. I don't want anything from it. The rent's paid up for another two weeks, that should give you enough time. Here's the key.'

She could see well enough now to cross the room quite easily. His hand was cool and dry, the metal key warm as it passed from his fingers to hers. She slipped it into her pocket and retreated to the desk, sensing his need to be on his own.

After another long silence he spoke again, bleakly. 'I did a terrible thing, marrying Aileen. If it hadn't been for me she'd be alive today, probably wed to some man who could have given her everything she deserved.'

'Don't be daft, Thomas McDonald!' The words rushed hotly to her lips. 'Aileen came to you of her own free will, and she didn't regret one minute of it.'

'Ellie, you saw that house today – the servants, the comfort of it all. Who'd willingly walk away from that?'

'It was when I saw the house that I knew how much she must have loved you, to give it up for you. And I understood why,' Elspeth said passionately. 'There wasn't an ounce of warmth in that place, while your wee house was brimming over with love and happiness. As for the folk I saw today – they didn't deserve someone like Aileen. There was no – no joy in them.'

'Would you expect them to be joyful on a day like this?' he asked sarcastically.

'You know fine what I mean. They were all wrapped up in themselves. What sort of folk would turn their backs on a lovely lassie like your Aileen just because she insisted on going her own way?'

'Mam did.'

She swatted the words impatiently into the dark shadows of the room. 'Aunt Flora's always like that when she's defied. Anyway, she'd come round to accepting your marriage. Don't be hard on her, Thomas – she's suffering torments over the way she treated the two of you when you first married. I doubt if Mr and Mrs Bruce feel as bad as she does.'

There was a pause before he spoke again. 'Mr Bruce's lawyer offered me money. I got the letter yesterday. One thousand pounds, he'll pay me, if I'll sign a bit of paper promising I'll make no claim on the Bruce family.'

Elspeth almost choked with outrage. 'That's insulting!'

'It's the only way they know. They think that even people can be bought, especially people like us.'

'Pebbles on the beach.'

'What?'

'That's what you said, one day when we were all on the beach at Largs. You said that ordinary folk are like pebbles, too many and too small to be noticed.'

'I don't mind saying it, but it's true. I went to the office and told the man that I'd not take a penny from the likes of the Bruces, not even if I was starving in the gutter. The only way to get respect from folk like that is to show them that you're

282

as good as they are. That's what I'm going to do, Ellie. I'm going to work even harder for Aileen than I did when she was here. I'm going to show the Bruces and the whole town that given time I could have provided her with everything she wanted.' His voice was low and level, but intense. 'I'll make my own thousand, then another thousand, and another. I'll make them admit that they were wrong about me, even if I have to ram bundles of notes down their throats to do it!'

Elspeth shivered though the room wasn't cold. She felt as though someone had just walked over her grave.

'Don't become bitter, Thomas.'

'Of course I'm bitter! Can you blame me? If I hadnae been so opposed to her seeing her brother she wouldnae have gone off with him in his car. We'd had words about it just the day before.'

She thought of the day she herself had seen Aileen drive away in Ian Bruce's car. There had probably been other times that neither she nor Thomas knew about.

'But she must have been in her brother's car hundreds of times before she met you. The accident could have happened at any time.'

'You're talking nonsense.'

'I know,' she said wretchedly, confused by her own clumsy attempts to reason with him. 'It's hard to find the right words. I'd do better if I was putting them down in a letter.'

He laughed, an unexpected barking sound. 'Mebbe you should write to me, then,' he said, his voice suddenly weary, 'Come to me, Ellie.'

When she did as she was told he drew her down on to the couch, putting an arm about her and holding her close. 'Are you cold?'

'No, it's warm enough.'

'You don't need to find the words.' His breath was warm against her ear. 'Just wheesht for a wee while, and let me listen to them for myself.'

283

Timidly, she put her own arms around him. He was so tense that it was like wrapping her arms round the trunk of a tree. They sat in silence for a long time, long enough for his body to relax gradually, until he was leaning quite heavily against her. She wondered if he had fallen asleep. The couch was lumpy and uncomfortable, thrusting small hard fists into the softness of her buttocks, but she didn't want to move in case she disturbed him. Instead she stayed still, inhaling the clean soapy smell from his hair, listening to his breathing, feeling the slow steady thump of his heart echoing against her own ribs. The street outside was silent, for this was an industrial area and not many people had occasion to pass through it at night. Once, she heard a scampering above her head, but with Thomas close beside her there was no need, now, to be afraid.

Finally, when she was almost asleep herself, he stirred and straightened and sat upright. 'You'd best go home, Ellie. Mam'll be wondering where you are.'

Her arms were stiff and numbed. She moved her fingers surreptitiously. 'Come back with me.'

He was still so close that disturbed air brushed her cheek when he shook his head.

'I'm staying here tonight.'

'But—'

'I'll be fine. Come on, now.' He rose and pulled her up from the couch. The life was just beginning to come back to her hands, and they felt as though they were clad in thick woollen gloves. Thomas led the way, sure-footed, through the hall and kitchen with Elspeth clinging as best she could to the back of his jacket. In the street he said, 'Tell Mam I'm fine, and I'll look in on her tomorrow. You'll manage home all right?'

'Yes.'

His hands cupped her shoulders, his lips touched her cheek. 'Thanks, Ellie,' he said 'You're a grand sister.' Then, turning her about to face the empty street, he gave her a little shove. 'Go on, now.'

Pins and needles danced all the way up and down her arms. She welcomed the sensation, because it promised eventual normality, something that had been lacking in her life ever since Aileen's death.

At the corner she stopped and looked back. Thomas's hand was a tiny pale movement against the darkness of the building behind him as he waved.

She waved back, and set off for Mearns Street.

29

Elspeth walked in through the main entrance of Brodie's department store and across the carpeted floor to the elegant lift provided for those paying customers who declined to use the staircases. Patrick, the lift operator, gaped as she stepped in and said, 'The top floor, please.'

'Lassie, what're ye doin'?'

'I'm going to see Mr James.'

Patrick peered out, glancing furtively from right to left. 'But ye cannae use the lift. It's for the gentry!'

'I can do as I please. Will you get on with it, or do I have to see to the buttons myself?'

Alarm flared into his eyes. 'Don't you touch they buttons, Elspeth Bremner! This is my lift and I'll be the one tae—' He broke off as two well-dressed women stepped into the silk-lined lift, and asked, with a noticeable change of accent, 'Which floor, moddom?'

'The third,' the older woman ordered curtly.

'The top,' Elspeth said just as curtly, adding after a pause, 'Please.'

The woman glared, and settled her fox-fur more comfortably on her shoulders, while Patrick, shrugging helplessly, slid the door shut and set the lift in motion.

'Are ye sure?' he asked plaintively as the two women stepped out at the third floor, leaving behind them the powerful scent of expensive perfume too lavishly applied, and an undertone of perspiration. It was May, and too hot for fox-furs.

'I'm sure.'

'It's mair than yer job's worth, lassie, usin' the customers' lift.'

'I'm not bothered.' She had been awake half the night, fretting over the news she had heard that evening, and by morning she had decided on a course of action. It was too late, now, to change her mind. She had already used the main entrance, and the lift. She might as well go the whole way.

It had been over a year since she had worked in the accounts office, but little had changed. Wilma and Graham still laboured over huge ledgers at the sloping desk, and Theresa McCabe typed busily in her corner, though the brisk clatter of keys slowed and stopped at Elspeth's entrance.

'I want to talk to Mr James,' she told Wilma.

'He didn't ask to see you.'

'I know that. It's me that wants to see him.'

The typewriter keys stopped altogether. Graham gaped and Wilma bristled. 'He's dealing with this morning's post. Try again in an hour.'

'I must see him now. It's very important.' The anger that had been burning in Elspeth for the past fifteen hours or so gave her voice a crisp edge. Wilma hesitated, then slipped down from the high stool.

'I'll see what he says.'

'You're looking well, Elspeth.' Graham's eyes travelled slowly down her body.

'Am I?' She had decided not to wear her usual working skirt and blouse today; instead, she had on her best blouse, striped in different shades of brown, and a fawn pleated skirt beneath a smart brown jacket she had made herself. The pebble brooch was pinned to the jacket's lapel, and beneath the blouse's high collar her lucky silver threepenny piece nestled against the hollow of her throat.

The typewriter keys rattled again as James Brodie himself opened his office door and ushered Wilma out.

'Miss Bremner – come in. Take a seat,' he invited, closing the door behind her.

She shook her head. 'I'll only be a minute. I believe you've taken on a new typist?'

'That's right, Theresa's leaving to get married. I was surprised you didn't apply for the job yourself,' he went on, taking the wind out of her sails. She stared, then rallied.

'I would have, if I'd known. I only heard about it last night, when I met a girl I knew from my typing class and she said she'd applied and been unsuccessful.'

It was Brodie's turn to be taken aback. 'But you were the first person I thought of when Theresa said she was going. Miss Arnold told me that you'd decided to stay on in the sewing room.'

Elspeth's knees suddenly went weak, and she sank into the chair she had just declined. 'She told you that?'

They stared at each other for a moment, then James Brodie said slowly, 'It seems that you've been deceived. I'm very sorry, my dear. I would have been happy to give you the position, but unfortunately it has already been filled.'

'Elspeth Bremner, d'you know what time it is?' Miss Arnold squawked as soon as Elspeth went into the sewing room. 'And just what d'you think you're wearing? You know that you girls aren't allowed to—'

'I'm late because I've just been along to see Mr James about the typist's position, Miss Arnold.'

The woman flushed, then rallied. 'Without asking me to arrange an appointment for you? You'd no right to burst in on Mr James like that!'

'And you'd no right to tell him that I wanted to stay in the sewing room instead of applying for the typist's job without consulting me first.'

There was a concerted gasp from the listening women round the large table, and the usual muted roar of sewing machines in operation faltered, then died.

Miss Arnold's face was almost purple. 'Miss Buchanan and I discussed the matter fully and agreed that you're of more value to Brodie's in this department. You're a good seamstress, and a lot of work's gone into training you. In a few years you could mebbe even become supervisor.'

'I won't be here in a few years, Miss Arnold, or even a few minutes,' Elspeth told her, and turned towards the door.

'Stop,' the woman shrieked. 'I'll not have such insubordination!' Then, as Elspeth put a hand on the handle, 'If you persist in this nonsense, Elspeth Bremner, you needn't think you'll get a reference from Miss Buchanan!'

'I won't require one. I'm going to set up in business for myself,' Elspeth said, and walked out of the sewing room for the last time, closing the door on a babble of excited voices.

Flora McDonald was beside herself with rage when she heard the news. 'After all the trouble I went to tae get ye that position! How could ye dae it? Ye'll never get work as a seamstress in the town again once word of this gets out. What have I done tae deserve this?'

The cold anger that had seized Elspeth when she first heard of the position she had lost through deceit still held her in its grip.

'It was you that wanted me to be a seamstress, Aunt Flora, not me. I'm seventeen now, old enough to make up my own mind. I've been thinking about it all, and I'm going to set up my own business, doing typing and book-keeping for folk like Mr Monteith who can't afford to employ someone all the time.'

'Are ye wandered in yer head, lassie? How could the likes of you manage that? Ye're too young, for a start!'

'I don't think I am.'

'And where would ye go? Not in my bedroom, I'll tell ye that!'

'I think I already know of somewhere,' said Elspeth, refusing to let anything her aunt said affect her. She had burned her boats, and now the only way to go was forward.

At Christmas Forbes Cameron, stammering like a schoolboy, had invited Elspeth to dinner at the large house where he still lived with his parents. Surprised, but somewhat flattered, she had accepted, and had enjoyed herself. Mr and Mrs Cameron were kindly people, as she had discovered at Aileen's funeral, and Forbes himself was an entertaining and considerate companion. They had been meeting each other ever since, a relationship that had almost caused a quarrel between her and Thomas.

'I've nothing against the man – he pays my wages – but he's a good ten years older than you are,' he said baldly.

'Does that mean that he's not to be trusted?'

'No, but—'

'Mebbe it's me you don't trust?'

'Don't be daft,' Thomas said, exasperated.

'I'm not a child, so don't treat me like one.'

'I know you're not, but even so, you'd be better with someone more your own age.'

'Like Kenneth?' she asked sarcastically.

'Oh – go your own way, you'll do that anyway. There's no reasoning with you, Elspeth Bremner,' he snapped, and stormed out of the garage office.

As it happened, she and Forbes were going to the theatre in Largs the day she left Brodie's for good, then having supper in a small restaurant.

Prudently, she waited until the meal was almost over before putting her plan to him.

'The old house? My dear girl, it's in a terrible state – you couldn't set up this business of yours in a place like that.'

'It's neglected, but the building's still sturdy. At least let me have a look at it. Please, Forbes – I've got to find some way of earning my living quickly, and this is my chance to do what I've always wanted.'

'Have you really thought about this idea of yours, Elspeth? You're young to start up in business, and it's not that easy.'

'Why does everyone keep going on about my age? Seventeen isn't all that young, and there are times when I feel much older than that. I know of two girls from the typing and book-keeping class who'd probably be glad to come in with me. Neither of them has been able to find work in an office.'

'Do they have money to invest in the idea?'

'No, but they've got office skills, and that's what I need. Peggy has a sick father who can't be left on his own for too long at a time, and Kirsty's got a baby to care for. I could offer them working hours to suit their domestic responsibilities, and there must be a lot of small businessmen like Mr Monteith who could do with typists and book-keepers but can't afford to employ somebody. With two more typists, I could go out to look for new clients. I'll need to buy another two typewriters and some office furniture, but I got my own machine in a pawn shop – I might find others there. And there are good second-hand furniture shops.'

'What about financial support while all this is happening?'

'I've still got the money from the sale of my grandmother's furniture, and I've been saving what I've made working for Mr Monteith and Mr Leslie.'

'And if this venture of yours fails?'

'Then I'll have to admit defeat and look for other employ-ment for myself. I know enough about keeping accounts by now to put an end to it before I run myself into trouble. But it will work – I know it will.' She leaned across the table in her urgency to convey the strength of her feelings for this new venture. 'I want this too much to let it fail.'

'You're taking on an awful lot, Elspeth,' said Forbes

Cameron, who had always relied on his parents' financial support in any venture he attempted.

'I'm not afraid of hard work. Please, Forbes?'

'You look so beautiful when you're enthused about something that it's very difficult to deny you anything,' he said wryly. 'I suppose there's no harm in having a proper look at the place.'

'Oh, thank you! I'll go tomorrow morning – I'm trying to keep out of Aunt Flora's way anyway, in case she starts on about finding another job for me.' she said happily.

It wasn't until she was getting ready for bed that night that she recalled his exact words. At the time she had been too intent on persuading him to let her explore the old house to pay much attention. Now, she peered wide-eyed into the mirror in an attempt to find out why he had described her as beautiful.

The ends of her long brown hair, freed from its plait and fresh from a good brushing, caught the gaslight as it swung about her face. Her blue eyes were clear, but quite ordinary, and her nose and mouth weren't too large or too small. She smiled at her own reflection, and decided that, again, her smile was ordinary.

'You're certainly not beautiful, miss,' she told her mirrored self. 'But you'll do. You'll have to – you're all I've got.'

True to his vow, Thomas had devoted himself to making the garage a success after his young wife's death. Under his single-minded supervision, it had already gained a reputation for excellent service and fair dealings.

Business had done so well that Joe, Thomas's assistant, had been promoted to the position of foreman, and two more mechanics taken on to enable Thomas to concentrate on the sales side. At his suggestion, Forbes had agreed to move into the area of car sales, and to this end the workshops had been expanded and improved and the original garage frontage removed to add a forecourt. During the work, Forbes had had the outside of the old house refurbished and painted.

Car engines were still dear to Thomas's heart, and when Elspeth arrived at the garage on the following morning she found him in his dungarees, working on an engine. She waited, trying to curb her impatience, until he was free, then explained her new plan to him.

His first reaction was a scowl. 'Is this going to mean a bunch of women traipsing through my yard and getting in the way?'

'The front door could be opened up for our use.'

Thomas grunted, then wiped his hands on a rag. 'I suppose you wound Cameron round your little finger?'

'I just asked him if I could have a good look at the house, and he agreed.'

'It's his house,' Thomas said, and called to one of the mechanics to take over.

'The keys to the upper rooms are here somewhere,' he said vaguely, rummaging in a kitchen drawer while Elspeth hovered, trying not to fidget. She had been waiting for so long to realise her dream, and now it was so close that every second's delay was unbearable.

She looked around the kitchen in an attempt to take her mind off her own impatience. She had managed to improve it, scraping years of grease from the gas stove, replacing the cracked linoleum with a remnant piece, clearing and cleaning the cupboards. Now that the garage covered car sales as well, the other downstairs room had been cleared and painted and turned into a proper office where Thomas, in a smart suit, could deal with possible buyers.

He had changed a lot since Aileen's death. Long, bitter months of grief had aged him, but not altogether unkindly. Though his first youth had gone he had taken on a new maturity that suited his lean features. The laughter in his eyes had given way to solemnity, and his body, used now to long hours of hard work and little rest, had a whip-like strength.

In recent months Elspeth had noticed sudden interest flickering into the gaze of more than one woman accompanying a husband or sweetheart to the garage to buy a new car from Thomas McDonald. A few of them had even found ways of making opening advances, but Thomas, steadfastly following his vow to show the Bruces that he was as good as they were, paid them no heed. He had moved his possessions into the old office in the garage house, refusing to give in to his mother and move back to Mearns Street permanently.

'Mam would expect everything to go back to the way it was before,' he told Elspeth. 'She can't understand that life can never go back, only forwards. I couldn't abide her fussing, anyway.'

Because she understood what he meant, and never fussed over him, Elspeth was one of the few people Thomas trusted now, and the affection that had been between them since she was a baby had strengthened.

'Here they are.' He waved a bunch of keys at her, then made for the inner door. 'Let's get this nonsense over with, then I can get back to my work.'

Elspeth kept close behind him as he led the way upstairs to a large, dark landing and unlocked the first of the three doors.

'Hold on.' He paused at the threshold and stamped hard on the floor. There was a scuttling, rustling sound, then silence.

'Mice – mebbe rats.' He crossed the room to wrench at the wooden shutters nailed across the windows.

'I'll get a cat – or a dog, if necessary,' she told him lightly, though she paused on the threshold for a moment before venturing in.

'What about the cockroaches?'

'Jeyes fluid and a scrubbing brush.'

Thomas grunted something, and pulled once more at the shutters, which gave way, dust and grit showering to the floor like a hail storm. The room was revealed, large and handsome and empty.

'It's just like the downstairs rooms. Once the windows are cleaned and the walls painted—'

'And the spider's webs cleared away,' Thomas put in, moving to the other window.

'—and some furniture installed,' she went on, ignoring the interruption, 'it'll make a fine office.'

The second room held the sagging remains of a metal bedstead and the third door, situated above the kitchen, led to a bathroom complete with a huge, stained claw-footed bath.

'Oh, look at this!' Elspeth, brought up in a house with a privy on the landing, was delighted. She tried to turn one of the taps in the cracked hand-basin, but it was too tight for her. After a brief struggle Thomas managed to loosen it, and a trickle of rusty water emerged. Elspeth pulled experimentally at the chain hanging above the privy, and it came away in her hand.

'It'd need a lot of work.' Thomas's voice was heavy with disapproval.

'But it would be worth it.'

'Ellie, you're daft!'

Standing in the ruins of the bathroom, dust streaking her face, cobwebs in her hair, the rusty cistern chain dangling from her fingers, she laughed. 'Mebbe I am, but it'll all work out – just you wait and see.'

It was the busiest summer Elspeth had ever known. Kenneth and Mattie came back to Greenock for the summer holidays, which meant that Kenneth spent a lot of time in the Mearns Street flat. Seeing the two of them together didn't trouble Elspeth a bit. She was too involved in her own life to mourn any further over what might have been.

When she wasn't at the garage, working on books for the clients she already had or chivvying the workmen upstairs, she was tramping the streets, calling in at every small business she could find – not only in Greenock, but in the neighbouring towns of Gourock and Port Glasgow. By the time the building was ready for scrubbing brush and broom she had invested some of her savings in two more second-hand typewriters and found a dozen employers, enough to get her new business off to a start.

When the time came to prepare the upper floor before furnishing it, Peggy and Kirsty, her future employees, arrived to help with the cleaning. So did Rachel, who had given birth to a second daughter, Pearl, in February. This time Elspeth insisted on paying her for the hours she put in.

'But I'm already making something from my sewing,' Rachel protested.

'That's got nothing to do with what you're doing for me.'

'It's thanks to you, for it was your idea in the first place, and you're looking after it for me.' They had agreed that the safest thing was for Rachel to admit to Bob that she was earning a certain amount – most of which he took from her to spend on drink – while she handed over the rest to Elspeth, who banked it along with the money from the sale of Celia Bremner's napery and bed linen.

'I'm still going to pay you for the work you do here. I just wish you could use a typewriter, for I could have taken you on in the office,' Elspeth said, struck to the heart by the older girl's wan, tired face.

'Even if I could type, it wouldnae work, not with the bairns still so wee,' Rachel said wistfully. 'It'd be nice to have something different to do with my life, though.' Then, squaring her shoulders and taking up a broom, she added, 'But Mam's right – I've made my bed and I must lie in it.'

The two of them were alone in the big room that was going to be the office. Kirsty and Peggy were scrubbing out the smaller room, and Mary was playing in the hallway with Sandra, Kirsty's little girl. Pearl, the baby, had been fed, and settled down in a blanket-filled box in a corner.

'It depends who's lying beside you,' Elspeth said, though

she wished she could say much more, and to Thomas and his
father. Bob was still violent towards his wife, and Flora still
refused to acknowledge what was happening, let alone tell
Henry.

'Ellie! Don't be coarse! And mind your tongue in front of
the weans,' Rachel added as Mary and Sandra scampered
through the room.

'I'm just saying what I think.'

Forbes Cameron followed Elspeth's progress with keen interest.

'Let me start you off with a loan,' he suggested one day,
finding her at the downstairs desk frowning over columns of
figures and chewing the end of her pencil.

'I wouldn't dream of it. This is my idea, and I'll not risk
anyone else's money.'

'Does that mean that you think there's a danger of failure?'

'Of course not.'

'Make it an investment, then. Call me a shareholder and
start paying me dividends at the end of your first year.' Then,
when she still hesitated, he suggested, 'If you don't like that
idea, I could offer a reduced rent for the first year instead,' and
went on to name a very low sum.

She squinted at him suspiciously. 'What benefit would you
get out of that?' In her opinion, the suggestion smacked of
charity.

'The pleasure of helping you to get started, for one. And for
another,' he went on hurriedly as she opened her mouth to
refuse, 'I'd insist on a more realistic rent after that, to make up
what I lost in the first year. And I'd want the chance to get
first refusal if or when you decided to sell shares to raise more
money.'

'But you've already put a lot into getting the house put to
rights. You shouldn't be thinking of spending even more on
me.'

'But I've already made an investment of my own. If your business should fail, you'd get nothing back, while I'd still have the house, in better condition than ever before. I could recoup all my outlay by renting the upper floor to someone else.'

Elspeth studied the page before her. Her savings had dwindled quite frighteningly, and soon there would be wages for Peggy and Kirsty to take into consideration. She couldn't afford to be too proud.

'I accept,' she said at last, and he beamed.

By the time she celebrated her eighteenth birthday the upper floor was ready. Three sturdy desks, made for her by Peggy's brother, a carpenter, had been set up in the larger of the two upper rooms to hold the typewriters. Two cupboards bought from a second-hand shop were ranged along one wall, and a polished brass sign – Forbes' birthday gift to Elspeth – engraved with the words 'Bremner Office Agency, First Floor' had been fastened by the front door, which was now in use again.

Forbes held a party to celebrate the opening, inviting a number of guests, including all Elspeth's clients. His parents were there, as were the McDonalds – Lachlan and Henry bursting with pride at Elspeth's achievement, Flora torn between possessive pride and embarrassment. She had been shocked at first by Elspeth's 'walking out', as she put it, with Forbes, agreeing with Thomas that the garage-owner was too old for her, but he had soon charmed her doubts away.

'You know what she's hoping for, don't you?' Lachlan said now, nodding at his mother, deep in conversation with Mrs Cameron. 'You wed to a wealthy man and Mattie wed to a doctor. That'd give the folk in Mearns Street somethin' tae talk about.'

She laughed, and shook her head. 'If that's true, she'll have a long wait on my part. I'll be too busy with my business to think of marriage for a good long while.'

Lachlan himself was doing well in the maintenance department at Brodie's store, and still corresponding with Lena. It was his hope that soon she would appear onstage in Greenock.

'Come on, Elspeth, time to declare the agency open.' Forbes called from the hall, and the crowd of guests parted to let her through. Dazed with the sudden realisation that she had achieved her ambition, she walked between them to the foot of the stairs.

The scissors crunched through the ribbon, it fluttered away on both sides, and the dream she had held close to her heart for the past four years had come true.

30

In January, almost exactly two years after leaving Greenock, Lena Stewart returned to appear for a week in the King's Theatre.

Lachlan was beside himself with excitement when he received the news. At the family's traditional New Year's Day dinner his happiness helped to mask the fact that the annual meal, once a landmark in the McDonald calendar, was quieter than usual. Janet was there, but Thomas had refused to join them, and Mattie was spending the day with Kenneth's parents, much to her mother's disappointment. Rachel had brought her daughters to Mearns Street, but Bob wasn't with her, to Henry's surprise. Flora and Rachel had both had a difficult time fobbing off his questions. Between that, and Lachlan's constant talk about Lena's return, Flora was noticeably irritable before they even sat down at the table.

'Ye'll mebbe get a surprise,' she informed her son crustily. 'She'll have got too high-and-mighty for the likes of you. Ye'll not likely see hide nor hair of her off the stage.'

'You're wrong there, Mam,' he told her breezily, helping himself to another slice of bread and winking at wee Mary, who doted on him. 'I'll see quite a lot of Lena, for she's arranged for me to work as a stage hand in the theatre during her week there.'

Soup spoons clattered against Flora's best china bowls all

round the table, and he smirked as everyone stared at him, enjoying the sensation he had caused.

'She's what? Well, ye can forget that, for no son of mine—' Flora began, but he interrupted her.

'It's already arranged, Mam, and I've said I'm doin' it. I've been to see the stage manager at the theatre and it's all agreed.' Lachlan dunked his bread in his soup, something Flora abhorred, and took a mouthful.

'And not a word tae us about it?'

'Leave it, Flora,' Henry advised quietly. 'Lachie's a man now, old enough tae join a circus as the elephant trainer if he chooses. Now – take yer soup before it gets cold. You too, Rachel.'

Rachel had been staring down at her bowl, the spoon drooping from her hand. She jumped, and began eating again, while her father watched her, his brows knotted with concern.

'Are ye ailin', hen?'

'Of course she's not ailin',' Flora snapped.

'She looks awful pale,' Henry said, and Janet nodded.

'I think so too.'

'And so would you look pale if ye'd two weans under yer feet day and night. I'd as soon do a day's labourin' in the shipyards as look after weans.'

'Will ye give the lassie the chance tae answer for hersel'?' Henry asked in a rare burst of impatience, then, as Flora's mouth clamped into an offended line, and she got up and collected in the plates that had been emptied, 'Ye're no sickenin' for somethin', pet, are ye?'

Rachel shot a sidelong look at her mother, then said, 'I'm fine, Da. It's this weather, I've never liked the winter.'

'It's not the winter, you've been looking poorly for a while now.' Elspeth was unable to keep silent any longer.

Despite the fact that not everybody had finished the first course, Flora banged a huge bowl of potatoes down so hard on the table that the cutlery jumped and jangled, and Mary, sitting on a pile of cushions to enable her small face to peep over the table, and tied into her chair for safety, burst into tears. Her sister, on Rachel's lap, immediately followed suit.

'Now look what ye've done!' Flora accused her husband, while in the ensuing rush to comfort the children Rachel whispered to Elspeth, 'Leave it be, for pity's sake!'

By the time the little girls had been calmed, Henry, waiting impatiently for the main course, was too hungry to remember what had caused all the fuss.

Forbes had tried to persuade Elspeth to spend the day at his parents' home, to meet some friends of theirs.

'My mother will be disappointed if you don't. You know how much she enjoys your company.'

'I can't let Aunt Flora and Uncle Henry down, not when Mattie and Thomas are both staying away.'

'But it's not as if they're really your family, is it? Not your own flesh and blood,' he added as she stared at him, puzzled.

'For goodness' sake, Forbes, they're the only family I've ever known!' On occasion, she thought with irritation, Forbes was capable of displaying a grating insensitivity towards others. 'If it comes to that, you and your parents aren't my family either.'

'Mebbe that'll change by next New Year,' he murmured, drawing her into his arms, his mouth seeking and finding hers. The anger ebbed as she closed her eyes and let her body blend with his, parting her lips against the moist warmth of his mouth.

She was very fond of Forbes, she thought, returning kiss for kiss. He had done so much for her, and had become a dear friend as well as a pleasant companion. He had never tried to force himself on her as Kenneth had, so long ago in the wash house, but his kisses and caresses were exciting and desirable, and Elspeth felt that one day quite soon she would want more from him than this chaste loving.

She hadn't as yet decided what she would do when that day

came, but the thought of it warmed her. She was a woman now, no longer a naive girl.

Although she wasn't the star of the music hall her company staged in Greenock, it was Lena that most of the folk in the audiences came to see. When the Master of Ceremonies introduced her as Greenock's own songbird, the storm of applause made the chandeliers high above the auditorium tremble and tinkle.

Elspeth gripped Forbes' arm as the curtains parted and Lena stepped forward, hands outstretched to receive the adulation of her public. The gasp that greeted her appearance could be heard even above the applause. She wore a sea-green gown, cut low in front to reveal her smooth white throat and the shaded hollow between her full breasts. Skilful draping along the top of the bodice enhanced the swell of her bosom, while below the tiny waist the skirt hugged her hips and thighs, then swirled into deep frills. The sleeves were long and tight, and hundreds of sequins caught the light with every movement she made, so that her entire body shimmered. Her red hair was caught up in an intricate pile of curls, with a large bejewelled Spanish comb thrust into them at the back.

Graciously, she acknowledged the applause from every corner of the theatre, then waited, still and erect, until it had ebbed away completely before giving the orchestra conductor a nod.

She had come a long way since her first impromptu appearance on the stage two years before. The voice that filled the theatre was stronger now, clearer and more confident. As before, she slid from one mood to another without effort, singing a ballad then swooping to the wings to collect a cloak and umbrella before launching into a comedy number that was greeted with howls of approval. Then came a slow, sad song that brought a catch to her listeners' throats.

'Didn't I tell you she was good?' Elspeth asked Forbes,

clapping until her hands stung as Lena finally left the stage, blowing expansive kisses to her ecstatic audience.

'You did, and you're right. She'll go a long way,' he predicted.

When she and Lachlan finally arrived in the hotel where they had arranged to meet for supper, Lena walked the length of the dining room like royalty, halted at almost every table by people who had been at the theatre earlier and wanted to congratulate her. She had changed into a narrow, ankle-length deep brown velvet dress, sleeveless, with a silvery silk-chiffon cape floating from beaded shoulder straps. Her hair was still up, and her only ornament was a beaded sash around her hips. Lachlan, in an evening suit, followed closely behind her, glowing as he basked in her success.

Arriving at last at the table Forbes had booked for the four of them, Lena shook his hand, hugged Elspeth, then collapsed into a chair. 'My feet are killing me!'

Forbes was enchanted by her, but it was Lachlan who absorbed all Elspeth's attention at first. 'Lachie, where did you get those clothes?'

He grinned self-consciously, and put a hand up to the bow tie at the collar of his dazzlingly white shirt. 'D'ye like it? Lena made me borrow it from the wardrobe department.'

'I like it very much.' The formal clothes had transformed him from the Lachie she knew into a stylish young man. 'You look so handsome!'

'He is handsome,' Lena said. 'You've just been too used to looking on him as a brother.' She flicked a teasing sidelong glance at Lachlan, and he beamed back at her, comfortable in her presence. 'I saw him as he really is the first time I clapped eyes on him in that big room at Brodie's store where we all ate our dinners. He was a poor wee thin creature then, in an overall that was far too big for him, but I knew what he'd look like in different clothes – and I was right.' Then she leaned across the table, her eyes brimming over with laughter. 'D'ye mind those days, Ellie?'

Clearly, although the sewing room rebel had become a sophisticated and elegant artiste, Lena's zest for life hadn't changed. She entertained them all throughout the meal with her memories of the sewing room, followed by a string of stories about her life in the theatre, each one more outrageous than the last. Diners at the other tables glanced across enviously at the four young people rocking with laughter, so obviously enjoying their evening out. Finally Lena announced that she had said more than enough, and demanded to know all Elspeth's news.

'I knew you were wasted in that dreary wee sewing room,' she said when she had heard something of the new business. 'You wrote such lovely letters. Wait and see – we're both going to become very famous and earn lots of money.' Then, with a wicked gleam in her eyes, 'And we'll have our clothes made at Brodie's, and criticise every stitch, and drive Miss Buchanan and Miss Arnold mad.'

'Miss Arnold's in charge now. Miss Buchanan retired a month or so ago.'

'Then we'll invite ourselves to Miss Buchanan's for tea as well, and criticise her taste in crockery,' said Lena.

She called in at the office two days later, all work coming to an abrupt halt when she swept into the room in a loose-fitting calf-length black woollen coat with a wide collar and deep cuffs at the wrists. Her red hair was tucked under a small black hat with a wide brim turned up all round and trimmed with jet beads. A large white satin bow was pinned at one side.

'I admire you,' she said as the two of them stood in the smaller of the two upper rooms where, Elspeth had explained, she hoped eventually to install more typewriters. 'You've done so much in such a short time.'

'Not as much as you, travelling all over the place and appearing in front of hundreds of people.'

Lena shrugged, smoothing her black gloves. 'The life's not as romantic as it looks. There are a lot of nasty little boarding

houses I'd not put a cat into, and a lot of audiences more interested in throwing insults than flowers. Anyway, I was lucky –
I got the chance to climb up on to a stage and sing. My voice
did the rest. Now you – you've changed your life right here in
your home town, and that's far more difficult. I can be anyone
I like when I'm far away from the folk who knew me before.'

'Your father must be pleased to see you home for a wee
while.'

Lena threw her head back and laughed. 'Him? I'm not so
sure. D'you mind old Miss Lambert that lived upstairs from
us? The retired schoolteacher? It seems that she took to "keeping an eye on poor Mr Stewart when his daughter upped and
left him"' – she imitated an elderly woman's dry, genteel
voice to perfection – 'and now she's got her feet tucked very
comfortably under his table. If you ask me, they'll be wed by
the time I come back again.'

'At their age?'

'Love doesn't worry about birthdays,' Lena said blithely.
'She's not my choice as a stepmother, but if she's his as a wife,
good luck to the two of them.' Then, her lovely turquoise eyes
fixed on Elspeth, she said thoughtfully. 'Talking of marriage,
Forbes seems a nice man.'

'He's helped me to set up the agency, and he's a good
friend, but I'm not looking for marriage.'

'He is. I could tell by the way he looked at you. No need to
put that face on, Ellie Bremner, you could do worse than
marry money. I nearly fell over when he ordered champagne
the other night!'

'I'd as soon earn my own fortune.'

'Then mebbe you should make that clear to Forbes before
it's too late,' Lena advised, moving to the window to look
down on the windswept cobbled street below. 'It's a grey old
town this, isn't it? But I'm still fond of it.'

As Elspeth escorted her down to the door Lena said casually, 'Lachlan's working well in the theatre, you'd think he'd

done it for years. The rest of the crew like him. He's fairly come on since I went away.'

'Your cards and letters helped.' Elspeth thought of Flora, hiding the cards, then decided to say nothing of that to her friend. 'It was kind of you.'

'Away with you – I've never been kind in my life. I did it because I like Lachlan. I always have and I always will,' Lena said, and left, her feet seeming to skim over the cobbles.

The local people, proud to know that one of their own had become a public performer, flocked to see Lena and the company played to packed houses throughout the week. Each night after the show there were crowds waiting at the stage door to speak to her, and by mid-week her photograph was on the billboards at each side of the theatre entrance.

'Dolly Costello's not pleased,' she reported gleefully to the girls in the agency. 'She's had star billing since before I was born – so mebbe it's time she got used to the idea of moving over for someone younger.'

'It must be hard for her, though,' Elspeth said, and Lena retorted, 'It's life. One day the same thing'll happen to me.'

She called in almost every day, perching on a stool in the corner, enthralling Peggy and Kirsty with her stories about theatrical life. Delighted though she was to see Lena again, Elspeth was secretly glad to know that she was only in town for a week. If it had been longer, she thought ruefully, reminding the other two yet again that there was work to be done, she might go out of business.

Despite the fact that Lena arranged free tickets for all the family, Flora steadfastly refused to attend the music hall. 'I've never approved of women flaunting themselves on a stage, and I never will,' she said coldly when Lachlan tried to coax her.

He reddened with suppressed anger. 'Lena doesn't flaunt herself. She's got a beautiful voice and folk love to hear it. Where's the harm in that?' he argued, but got nowhere.

Thomas refused as well, but civilly, and to Lena's face when she met him in the garage.

'I'm pleased for you, lassie, but I'm not ready yet for enjoyment.'

For once, Lena's pretty face was solemn. 'I can understand that, but would your Aileen want you to shut yourself away from the rest of the world and work yourself to death?' she asked bluntly.

Thomas didn't take offence. 'I've asked myself that, and the answer's no, she wouldn't. Nor would I have wanted her to mourn for ever if it had been me killed instead of her. But something inside me says I'm not ready to face things yet. Mebbe I will be, the next time you perform in Greenock.'

'I hope so,' she agreed, then put a hand on his arm. 'Don't punish yourself forever over something that wasn't your doing, Thomas.'

As they walked out on to the street, she said to Elspeth, 'When you see a decent man like your Thomas with all the life taken out of him, then look at some of the folk walking around that the world could do without, you wonder what God's thinking of at times.'

Janet Docherty and her neighbour, Mrs Begg, spent an enjoyable night at the theatre, and even Bob and Rachel took advantage of Lena's generosity. Elspeth looked after the little girls for them that evening. She was rarely in Rachel's home, and now that she had the time and the freedom to study her surroundings properly, she was struck by the dreariness of the place.

Everything was spotlessly clean, but the linoleum and the fireside rug were badly worn and the furniture cheap and uncomfortable. Mary and Pearl tended to be shy, though at the garage they usually blossomed in the warmth of Joe's kindness. But here, in their own home, both little girls seemed very withdrawn. Given the bleak atmosphere of the small flat, Elspeth could understand why.

Rachel and Bob didn't come home until about an hour after the show ended. When they did arrive Bob smelled of drink and Rachel's eyes were anxious despite the pretty flush that the chill night air had brought to her cheeks.

'I'm sorry we're late,' she burst out as soon as they arrived. 'We met some folks and got talking.'

'I'm in no hurry,' Elspeth assured her, although she had been nodding over the book in her lap for the past half-hour. 'Did you enjoy the theatre?'

'Oh, it was bonny! All those lovely clothes, and the music – and Lena was beautiful!'

Bob said nothing, but Elspeth was aware of his eyes on her as she fetched her coat. 'I'll walk ye home,' he offered.

'I'll manage fine on my own.'

He tried to insist, then lapsed into a huffy silence when she finally told him sharply that she could manage. Rachel accompanied her to the close-mouth. Someone had shattered the gas mantle, and the close behind them was pitch black.

'Don't mind Bob,' Rachel whispered as soon as they left the flat. 'He's tired.'

'How much did he have to drink on the way home?'

'Just the one wee glass, to keep the cold out. Just the one. You'll not say to—'

When Bob spoke his wife's name from just behind her, both women jumped and gasped.

'What're ye whisperin' about?' he wanted to know suspiciously, sliding an arm about Rachel's hips and glaring at Elspeth. In the dim light from the street, he looked menacing, and Elspeth edged towards the pavement as Rachel, chattering nervously, 'I'm comin' – just comin',' was drawn back into the close.

Once out on the pavement Elspeth broke into a run, and raced all the way to Mearns Street as though a pack of devils were at her heels.

*

Despite his mother's open dislike of Lena, Lachlan insisted on bringing her to Mearns Street for the midday meal on Saturday, the day of her final appearance at the King's Theatre. Out of deference to Flora the girl dressed demurely in a plain jersey and skirt, scrubbed her face clean of make-up, and tied her glorious hair back with a ribbon.

'Mrs McDonald, it's lovely to see you again,' she flattered as soon as Lachlan ushered her proudly into the kitchen. Flora murmured something unintelligible.

'And Mr McDonald. Did I not see you in the audience on Thursday night?' Lena asked, shaking Henry's hand.

'What?' Flora barked, while her husband's face drained of colour.

'No, no, lassie, it was never me – I've a union meetin' on Thursday nights.'

'If ye were at yer precious meeting last Thursday, how did the lassie come tae see ye in the theatre?' Flora asked ominously.

'I must have been mistaken,' Lena said before Henry could speak. 'With the lights shining on us it's difficult to see the audience – we just get wee glimpses sometimes.'

'But ye saw Henry clear enough.'

'I thought I saw someone like him. But now I look at you, Mr McDonald, the man was nothing like you at all. It was a right noisy audience that night—' Lena chattered on until Flora finally turned back to her cooking. Henry, relaxing visibly behind her back, winked at Lena, who winked back.

She did her best to dampen down her natural vitality during her short visit, but even so Flora's disapproval hung in the air like the smell of burned cabbage. She studiously ignored the angry looks Lachlan gave her from time to time, and by the time he and Lena left for the Saturday matinée his face was tight with suppressed rage.

Elspeth walked downstairs with them. 'Pay no heed to Aunt Flora, Lena, you know what she's like.'

'Stop makin' excuses for her, Ellie,' Lachlan burst out. 'She'd no right to be so cold!'

'Ach, don't fret, she doesnae bother me,' Lena assured him, then hugged Elspeth. 'Mebbe next time I'm back in Greenock you'll be a married woman with a bundle of weans round your knees.'

'And you'll be the top of the bill.'

'I will that,' Lena said, and left for the theatre, Lachlan in attendance.

Upstairs, Flora was already washing the dishes vigorously, as though trying to erase every sign of the recent visitor. 'Thank goodness the week's over,' she said as soon as Elspeth went into the kitchen. 'She'll be out of the town tomorrow and we can get back tae normal.'

Lachlan hadn't returned from the theatre by the time they went to bed that night.

'They'll be clearin' everythin' away, ready tae move on tomorrow,' Henry said placidly when Flora looked at the clock for the hundredth time. 'Mebbe havin' a bit of a party. He'll come home when he's ready.'

Elspeth was roused some time later by the sound of the outer door closing softly, and when she slid back into sleep a few minutes later Lachlan was still moving about his room.

When he came into the kitchen the next morning, shaved and dressed in his best clothes, Henry raised his brows.

'I thought ye'd be too tired tae go tae the church today.' The McDonalds weren't regular churchgoers, but since recovering from the effects of his shell shock Lachlan had taken to attending the Sunday service almost every week.

'No, I'm—' Lachlan hesitated, then said, looking at his mother, 'I'm off to Ayr, with the company. I've taken up a position with them.'

Henry, still tousled from a night's sleep, his unshaven chin black with stubble, gaped, while Elspeth almost dropped the

311

large teapot she was carrying from the cooker to the table.

'Don't be stupid,' Flora said crisply. 'Ye've got a good job here. There'll be no goin' off tae Ayr or anywhere else.'

'Mam, the train leaves in an hour's time and I'll be on it. I'd have told you two days ago, when they first asked me, but I knew you'd only start on at me to turn it down, so I kept my mouth shut.'

Flora spun away from the cooker, porridge ladle in hand. 'It's her – that woman. I knew she'd try tae entice ye away from us!'

'It's not Lena, Mam, not altogether.' Although he had had very little sleep Lachlan looked rested and confident. It was clear to Elspeth, at any rate, that he meant what he said and wouldn't be swayed from the path he had decided to take. 'Mebbe she's part of it, but it's mostly the work. I've enjoyed this week, and I like the thought of the travellin', too.'

'Ye're not goin'!'

'I am. I'll write to you, every week, and I'll send what I can afford—'

'Ye're not goin'!' his mother repeated, dropping the ladle, oblivious of the porridge spraying from it. She advanced on Lachlan and caught at the lapels of his coat. 'D'ye hear me? Ye're not goin' – I won't let ye go!'

Her voice began to rise, out of control. Henry pushed his chair back and got up, taking his wife by the shoulders. 'Flora, sit down and let's talk about it.'

She ignored him, and Lachlan himself had to loosen her grip on his coat, finger by finger. 'Mam, will you listen to me, just for once? I want to do this. I want to get on with my life!'

'He's got the right tae dae as he pleases, Flora.' Henry's voice was gruff as he drew his wife back against his own body, wrapping his arms about her in an attempt to confine her struggles. 'I don't want tae see him go any more than you, but it's his decision and we have tae abide by it.'

'We don't have tae do anythin' of the sort! She'll desert ye when she's done with ye, d'ye not have the sense tae realise that?' Flora spat the words at her son. 'She'll laugh at ye an' send ye crawlin' back home!'

'I told you, Mam, it's not Lena I'm doing this for, it's me.' Lachlan's face was pale but determined. 'Mebbe we'll end up together, mebbe we'll part, but that doesnae matter. What matters is me doin' what I want to do.'

'Ye've already got a job here! And ye've got family, and a home!'

'Ye'll tell Mr Brodie for me, Elspeth? Explain things tae him?' Lachlan said, and she nodded.

'I will. Write to us.'

'Every week.' He hugged her tightly, then glanced at his father.

'I've packed my clothes, they're waitin' at the door.'

Henry was still holding Flora. 'Best just go now, lad. And I hope everythin' goes right for ye.'

'It will, I'll see tae that,' Lachlan said, then, with a faint tremor in his voice, 'Take care of Mam for me.'

He went without a backward glance. Flora, fighting hard against her husband's iron arms, screamed out her son's name, but there was no answer.

The outer door closed, and Lachlan had gone.

31

Pausing on the landing to shift the weighted shopping bag from one hand to the other, Flora McDonald cast a sidelong glance at the smooth brown hair lying against Elspeth's cheek.

'Every time I look at ye I think ye're a stranger.' Her voice was heavy with disapproval. 'I don't know why ye did it – ye'd such bonny hair. Thinkin' of it on someone else's head gives me the shivers. It's like wearin' someone else's dentures.'

'There's plenty that do that, Aunt Flora.' Since taking over Mr Monteith's pawn shop books, Elspeth had seen and heard of many things.

'Aye, well, nob'dy in my family's ever done it, or ever will!'

'The braid was too heavy, and it took so much looking after,' Elspeth explained for the umpteenth time, 'And the money I got for selling it came in useful.'

'Ye'll be sellin' yer soul next.' Flora gave her familiar, last-word sniff, a sniff that indicated that Flora McDonald knew best and there was no sense in further discussion, then set off up the final flight.

When the shopping had been unpacked and stored away, Elspeth went into her own small room to change from her everyday skirt and blouse into a lemon cotton dress with brown trim on the crossover bodice and on the cuffs, for she was calling on a prospective client that afternoon. Glancing in the mirror as she fluffed out her bobbed hair she decided that whatever Flora might say, she herself liked the new style. It made her look older, more like the professional woman she had become.

Returning to the kitchen, she found Flora, who always made tea her priority after being out, filling two cups from the teapot.

'Aunt Flora, I've not got much time—'

'Time enough for a cup of tea and a scone.' It was waiting on a plate, already buttered. 'Ye don't eat enough these days. Too eager tae look smart for yer precious clients' – Flora said the word with contempt – 'and that Forbes Cameron.'

The accusation was unjustified. Elspeth's weight and shape were the same as two years before, when she had worked in Brodie's sewing room. It was true that the clothes she wore now were more fashionable and flattered her slim figure, but there was no sense in explaining that to Flora, for Elspeth knew very well that there was another reason behind the woman's carping.

After years of dominating her family, Flora McDonald had lost her main purpose in life now that they had all flown the nest, and was finding it very hard to come to terms with the situation she now found herself in.

Lachlan had been gone for six months, and despite his mother's dire predictions at the time, the letters that arrived every week were written by a man who had finally found his proper place in life, and was supremely happy. Flora always left it to Henry to open the letters, and looked as though she was sucking lemons as he proudly read each one aloud.

'You'd think she'd be pleased for Lachlan,' Elspeth had said to Rachel, who replied flatly, 'I sometimes think Mam can only be pleased for folk if they're doing what she wants them to do.'

Mattie and Kenneth had married at Easter, and had settled in Glasgow, where Kenneth was working in the Southern General Hospital. Thomas still drove himself on relentlessly, and had done so well that Forbes Cameron had made him his partner and there was talk of buying another garage. He had long since cut his mother's apron strings, and even Rachel's visits weren't so frequent now that she had her sewing to occupy her time.

Only Elspeth, the child Flora had taken in and never loved, remained. As she sat down at the table she flicked a swift glance at the clock on the mantel shelf. She and Peggy and Kirsty organised their work round the needs of their clients and their own domestic duties, each taking time off in turn when the office was quiet. Elspeth saw to it that the other two were always free on Saturday afternoons and Sundays, but she herself often worked at the weekends, enjoying the peace and quiet of the office when nobody else was there.

As she glanced at the clock again, someone knocked on the outer door. Flora, tutting, put her hands flat on the table and started to lever herself up. 'That'll be Annie from across the landing. That nose of hers can smell fresh-made tea through stone walls.'

Elspeth was already on her feet. 'I'll go.'

As she opened the door her eyes moved to the spot where she expected to find wee fat Mrs McGlashan's face, and saw instead the buttons on a smart grey morning coat. Startled, she lifted her gaze and saw a tall, elegantly dressed man in the act of raising his bowler hat.

'Good afternoon, is Mrs McDonald—' His voice faltered and his polite smile faded as their eyes met. Elspeth's knees suddenly started to tremble, forcing her to tighten her grip on the edge of the door in order to stay upright. The man was a stranger to her, and yet she recognised him after just one glance at the clear blue eyes set in a handsome, middle-aged face. She knew those eyes so well; she should, for she saw them every time she looked into a mirror.

'Elspeth,' Flora said impatiently from behind her, 'there's a terrible draught comin' intae the house. Who is it?'

The man on the landing tore his gaze from Elspeth's face to look beyond her shoulder. 'Good afternoon, Flora,' he said through pale lips, and Flora's hand clutched at Elspeth's arm, her fingers digging in painfully.

'Oh my God!' Her voice came out in a strange croak. 'You?'

'Yes, it's me.'

'What d'ye want?'

'I've come to see my daughter,' he said, then, throwing a glance over his shoulder as Mrs McGlashan's door gave a slight creak, 'Would it not be better if I came in?'

'I thought you were still a child,' Duncan Crombie said in the kitchen a few minutes later. 'Time passes so quickly.'

'Aye, 'specially when ye've turned yer back on yer responsibilities,' Flora said harshly. She hadn't mentioned the cup of tea that was always offered to visitors as soon as they stepped into any West of Scotland home. Instead, she sat on the edge of an upright chair, her face pinched, her hands clasped tightly in her lap.

'I'm not proud of what I did, Flora.' His voice was pleasant to the ear, his accent anglicised Scots. 'I can only say in my own defence that I was very young – mebbe too young to face up to my responsibilities.'

Although he was answering Flora, he spoke directly across the table to Elspeth. Since his arrival they had been unable to take their eyes off each other. 'And Maisie's parents didn't make things any easier. They were against me from the first.'

'With good reason – look what ye did tae her,' Flora said bitterly, and he flinched.

'Aunt Flora—' Elspeth, embarrassed, put a hand on the woman's arm but it was twitched off.

'This is my house, I'll say what I please!'

'You never liked me either, did you, Flora? Between you and Maisie's mother we never had a chance.'

'I didnae trust ye, and I was proved right – ye cannae deny that.'

He shrugged, then got to his feet and reached for his hat

and cane. 'I'd best go. I've no wish to upset anyone.' Dipping into a breast pocket he removed a small flat case and opened it to extract a slip of pasteboard. 'Here's my card, Elspeth. The address of my hotel's on the back. I hope you'll call on me there.' Then, as Flora got to her feet, clearly determined not to let him have a moment alone with Elspeth, 'I'll see myself out.'

'Let me see that wee bit of paper,' Flora demanded as soon as the outer door closed behind him.

Elspeth, knowing that it would be thrown into the fire immediately, curled her fingers about the card. 'It's mine, Aunt Flora.'

'Ye're surely no' goin' tae see him?'

'I have to. I can't just let him walk out of my life again.'

'Of course ye can, and ye must, if ye've got any sense at all. That man's no use tae anyone, you take my word for it. He's a sleekit, deceitful devil – look what he did tae yer poor wee mother!'

'He meant a lot to her, once.'

'Aye – and she died hatin' him. She'd no' want ye tae have anythin' tae dae with him!' Flora's eyes were slits, her lips drawn back in a snarl. Elspeth jumped up, suddenly desperate to get out of the place. 'I must go, I'm late as it is.'

'If ye see that man again ye'll be turnin' yer back on me and all I've done for ye.' Flora followed her out on to the landing to throw the words at her departing back, then, as Elspeth started down the stairs, she leaned over the wrought-iron railing that edged the landing. 'I'm tellin' ye,' she called down as Elspeth started down the stairs, 'ye'll be turnin' against me if ye as much as set eyes on him!'

Thomas McDonald, leaning against the door of the car he had been working on, took a large swallow of tea from the mug Elspeth had brought him, then wiped the back of his hand across his mouth. 'So – what are you going to do?'

'I don't know. What d'you think would be best?'

'You're a woman, Ellie, not a bairn,' he said implacably. 'You have to make your own decisions.'

She clenched her fists, longing to batter them on his chest. 'Thomas, this is important – help me!'

He emptied the mug and handed it over before turning back to the car that stood with bonnet raised, like a fledgling waiting in the nest to be fed by the parent bird. 'Don't bring me or anyone else into it, Ellie.' He tossed the words over his shoulder, his hands already on the engine. 'I've told you, it's your decision.'

Going back into the house, she met Rachel settling little Pearl in her perambulator while Mary and Sandra, Kirsty's little girl, bounded around the hall like little rubber balls.

'We're going to the park,' Mary announced, rushing to hug Elspeth's knees as she always did.

'Mind your Aunt Elspeth's nice dress,' Rachel ordered, tucking a blanket round the baby's waist.

'It's only a dress, and I've got my smock on anyway.' Rachel had made loose smocks for herself and the typists to wear over their clothes as a protection against oil and grime. With the garage yard so close, they frequently got stains on their clothes.

'I'd best get this lot out of your way. We'll be back by the time Kirsty's ready to go home.'

Rachel had been working for Elspeth for the past two months, ever since Kirsty, her face white with misery, had handed in her notice.

'I don't want to leave, for I've loved working with you, but it's the wee one.'

Sandra, a toddler with dark curly hair and a dimpled smile, was the reason why Kirsty had been unable to apply for full-time work after completing her typing course. Deserted by the child's father before Sandra was born, Kirsty had refused to consider giving her baby up for adoption, and the two of them lived with Kirsty's parents. When Elspeth had first set up her agency nine months before, Kirsty's mother, delighted at her daughter finally getting the chance to earn her own living, had agreed to care for the little girl.

But the woman had recently had a bad bout of pleurisy, and as there was nobody else to care for Sandra, Kirsty had no option but to leave.

Elspeth, distressed at losing a good worker as well as a friend, had had the idea of turning the room she had intended one day as a second office into a nursery, and asking Rachel to spend time at the garage every day, caring for Sandra and her own two.

'I'd pay you,' she told Rachel. 'And it would only be for the afternoons, because Kirsty doesn't work in the mornings.'

'Folk don't get paid to look after bairns,' Rachel protested.

'Nannies and nurserymaids do.'

'That's different. Anyway, why should you put out more money just for the one wee girl? Would it not be easier just to let Kirsty go and find someone else?'

'Kirsty's my friend,' Elspeth said firmly, 'and she's a good worker. She needs the little I can afford to pay her.'

Rachel's eyes brightened, and a touch of colour came to her pale face. 'It's a bonny room, right enough, and there's so much space for the bairns to play.'

'What about Bob? What would he say about it?' He had been getting moodier lately, and had lost his job after arguing with the foreman. Henry had managed to find a place for him in the shipyard where he himself worked. Elspeth didn't want to cause even more trouble for Rachel by crossing Bob.

'He'll not care as long as his dinner's on the table when he comes home from work – if he comes home instead of going to the public house,' Rachel added with contempt.

Elspeth had scoured the second-hand shops and pawn shops for furniture for the empty room, gaining two new clients in the process, and Sandra had quickly settled down with Rachel, who loved children and got a lot of pleasure herself out of the new arrangement.

'It's such an easy room to keep nice,' she told Elspeth. 'Not like home, where everything's packed in like sardines in a tin. It minds me of the times we had, you and me and Mattie, playing at wee houses.'

She insisted on taking over responsibility for cleaning the whole upper floor, and keeping everyone – Thomas and his staff as well as the typists – supplied with tea. She organised the kitchen and even baked scones occasionally in the large old cooker, brushing Thomas's mild grumbles aside.

'This is a garage, not a restaurant,' he pointed out when the first plate of scones, light as feathers and smelling delicious, came from the oven.

'I've not set foot in your yard, nor do I intend to,' Rachel retorted, her face flushed with the heat, her curly fair hair escaping in wisps from the pins that were supposed to keep it in place. 'But there's surely no harm in a wee bit of baking now and then.'

'No harm at all,' Joe agreed enthusiastically, his voice muffled by a mouthful of scone. 'I've never tasted anythin' as good as this!'

Rachel slapped at Thomas's hand as it reached out towards the plate. 'Wash that first – I'm not having good food smothered in oil before it gets to your mouth.'

He gave her an exasperated look tinged with amusement, and did as he was told. From then on, Rachel ruled the kitchen. She had blossomed since starting work, Elspeth thought now as she helped her to lift the perambulator down the front steps, though she still tended to keep her sleeves rolled down, to hide her forearms.

Elspeth saw the little group off, then, glancing up to make sure that Rachel's back was turned, rubbed at an imaginary speck of dirt on the nameplate, 'Bremner Office Agency, First Floor', with a corner of her smock. Rachel polished the plate every day, but now and again Elspeth liked to find an excuse to touch it, just to make sure that it was real, and not a dream.

Later, she tried to concentrate on the long list she was typing, the rattle of Peggy's and Kirsty's typewriters providing a pleasant background as she painstakingly transferred scribbled notes on crumpled scraps of paper into neat, clear columns on a fresh white sheet. But her mind kept returning to Duncan Crombie. Discovering that she had typed 'father' on the list instead of 'feather', she ripped the half-finished page free with an exclamation of disgust.

'Something wrong?' Peggy asked cheerfully.

'I wasn't concentrating properly.' Elspeth glanced at the clock and pushed her chair back. 'It'll have to wait until later, I'm due to call in at that new bookseller's soon.'

As it happened, the bookseller's shop was almost directly across the road from the hotel where Duncan Crombie was staying. From where she stood explaining the services the agency offered, Elspeth could see the corner of the building; by the time the business meeting had come to a mutually satisfying conclusion her mind was made up.

When she left the shop, she crossed the road and stepped into the hotel.

32

'You're so like Maisie,' Duncan Crombie marvelled an hour later, as they faced each other across a small tea table in the hotel lounge.

'But I've got your eyes.'

He smiled. 'You have indeed. Maisie's were like trees in the autumn, golden brown – something like the colour of your own hair.' His face softened with memories. 'They were long-lashed and always laughing. She was so unlike her parents that I used to tell her she must have been a changeling, left in her crib by the little folk.' Then, returning to the present, 'I understand that her parents have both died.'

'My grandmother died two years ago. She'd been' – Elspeth hesitated, then said carefully, reluctant to entrust Celia Bremner's bitter betrayal to this man who was her own flesh and blood, yet a complete stranger – 'on her own for years, since I was very small. I never knew my grandfather.'

'I liked him well enough, but his wife ruled the roost,' Crombie recalled. 'Poor man, he must have been stifled, living with that woman year in and year out. As for me – Maisie's mother was convinced that I'd never come to anything. She wanted better for her daughter. I don't think anyone other than royalty would have pleased her.'

Two middle-aged women passing their table glanced back at him with interest. He was still a good-looking man; in his youth he must have been very handsome. Elspeth could understand why her young mother had fallen in love with him.

'Tell me about my mother. There was nothing of hers in Grandmother's flat, not even a picture.'

He looked down at his cup, taking the teaspoon from the saucer and stirring his cooling tea slowly. 'She was beautiful, and loving, and I treated her badly. I was an orphan, living with my uncle, a man with no time for human weakness. I took fright when she told me she was carrying my child, and I ran away. My uncle had apprenticed me to a legal office, and I wasn't earning enough to keep the two of us. I couldn't face him – or Maisie's parents.'

He put the spoon down and took a sip of tea. 'I thought that if I was out of the way her mother and father would help her. If I'd only known how wrong I was!'

They talked the afternoon away without noticing time passing. Crombie told of his life in England, where he had found a position in another lawyer's office, working his way up and eventually marrying his employer's daughter.

'My wife's health broke down and we moved to the Isle of Man. I've been very lonely since she died a year ago, and finally I thought of trying to discover what had happened to Maisie and to our child. I'd always assumed that she had married, and that you had probably been raised by her husband as his own. I knew that I'd already caused her great unhappiness – I didn't want to do so again. Then I discovered that she died all those years ago, and that you'd been raised by Flora and her husband.'

His mouth twisted wryly. 'Flora never had any time for me either, because I worked in an office. In her opinion the only real men are those who work with their hands.'

'She was opposed to me taking up office work.' Elspeth told him about her struggle to achieve her ambitions, and he listened with interest.

'I'd like to see this office of yours.'

'You will, on Monday,' she promised, then, her heart

quickening at the thought of half-brothers and sisters, 'Did you and your wife have a family?'

To her disappointment he shook his head. 'We would have liked children, but there were none – until now.' He reached out and covered her hand briefly with his, his eyes sparkling. 'And now I have a beautiful daughter – I can't believe that we're finally together.'

Smiling at him, Elspeth relished the thought of introducing this man to people with the words, 'This is my father.'

At last she belonged to someone who was truly her own flesh and blood.

Everyone who met Duncan Crombie took a liking to him, apart from Flora and, to Elspeth's surprise, Forbes.

'I hope he doesn't intend to try to interfere with your life.' He took her hands in his. 'You've got your own business, and folk who cared for you long before he came along. He's left it too late to start making demands on you.'

'For goodness' sake, Forbes, he has no intention of making demands. Even if he did I wouldn't give in to them.'

She had cause to remember his words a short week later, when Duncan Crombie rented a small but comfortable house in Greenock, hired a housekeeper, and asked Elspeth to live there with him.

'We've been apart for so long, my dear, and now I want to be with my daughter. We need to get to know each other.'

When she refused, as gently as possible, hurt flooded into his expressive face. She tried to explain, choosing her words carefully in order to avoid causing further pain. 'I've just begun to control my own life. I need to be free at the moment to get the business established.'

'But you know I would never stand in your way! I'm very proud of what you've achieved already.'

'I know you are, but in any case I can't leave Aunt Flora and Uncle Henry just now.'

'Now that,' he said explosively, 'is ridiculous! You've just been talking about controlling your own life, and now you tell me that you can't live where you choose.'

'Their own family's gone now and I know that Aunt Flora's missing them. If I left I'd feel that I was deserting the two of them.'

'You're too soft, Elspeth. How d'you expect to run a successful business when you're worried about hurting people?'

They were in the drawing room of his new home, facing each other across the fireplace after enjoying an excellent meal.

'Aunt Flora's not a client. I owe a great deal to her, and caring about her feelings is entirely different from doing business.'

He bit his lip. 'You're right, and I apologise. It's just that—' He got up and paced the floor for a moment, then turned. 'We've lost so much time, you and I.'

'It may take more time for us to get to know each other.' With an effort, she managed to rise fairly gracefully from the deep, soft armchair. 'I must go. Give me a little while yet.'

He put his hands on her shoulders and kissed her forehead. 'I won't mention the matter again. I'm just fortunate to have found you at all.'

As the summer passed, Duncan Crombie moved with ease into the town's social life, drawing Elspeth with him. Without quite knowing how it had happened, she found herself attending concerts and soirées and dinner parties, even acting as his hostess when he invited people to his new home.

She gained a few more clients at these social occasions, for Duncan, proud of his new-found daughter, bragged to all and sundry about her talents as a businesswoman.

Once, when the two of them attended a performance by the Carl Rosa Opera Company at the King's Theatre with Forbes and his parents, she came face to face with James Brodie and his wife.

326

The store owner looked at her, puzzled, as they were introduced. 'I've met you before, Miss Bremner.'

'I used to work in Brodie's sewing room, and did some typing in the accounts office when Theresa McCabe was ill.'

His jaw dropped. 'Good heavens, so you did. And you left because you didn't get the position when it fell vacant. I always regretted that – I felt that we had let you down.'

'On the contrary, I'm grateful to you. I set up my own agency after I left Brodie's,' she explained as the puzzled look came back. 'And the bonus you paid me for doing your typing came in useful.'

'I'm very glad to hear it, and to see you looking so prosperous.'

Mrs Brodie, an elegant woman, had been studying Elspeth with interest, taking in her smooth, shining cap of hair and her elegant, simply cut crimson dress.

'Tell me, Miss Bremner,' she asked carefully, 'did you buy your gown in Glasgow?'

'I made it myself.' She had bought the material only the day before, and had persuaded Flora to let her use her old heavy sewing machine. With Rachel's help she had made the gown in an evening.

The woman's eyebrows rose. 'To your own design?'

'I copied it from a sketch in a magazine.'

'Indeed?' Envy flickered across Mrs Brodie's face. 'You have more than one talent,' she observed, and Duncan and Forbes, flanking Elspeth, both glowed with pride.

'You can look better in a home-made gown than all the other women in the clothes that cost them a fortune,' Duncan murmured as they left the Brodies and returned to their seats for the second part of the opera.

Hurrying along Hamilton Street with a thick envelope of completed work under her arm, Elspeth noticed a 'For Sale' sign on the opposite side of the street. She hesitated, then crossed over during a break in the traffic to look more closely at the property – a double-fronted shop. Pressing her nose against the glass and holding the bulky envelope up to block the reflection from the street behind, she made out a spacious interior with a counter, and a door in the rear wall. Further investigation through the close by the side of the shop revealed a walled back yard.

Elspeth returned to the street and took another look at the empty property. Then, thinking hard, she went on her way.

During dinner that evening at the Camerons' – a frequent occurrence, since Mrs Cameron had taken to Duncan from their first meeting – Elspeth announced that she was thinking of moving the agency to new premises. She could tell by the way his brows drew together that Forbes disapproved.

'There would be more space for us in that shop than at the garage,' she hurried on before he had a chance to object. 'I was asked only a few weeks ago to supply a temporary typist to work in an office in Port Glasgow, but none of the three of us can be spared for that sort of thing, and I've not got the space to bring anyone else in.'

'That's because you gave the extra room over to a child minder,' Forbes pointed out curtly.

'If I hadn't done that I would've lost Kirsty, and she's a good worker. Now that I've got Rachel I could mebbe employ another young mother looking for part-time work. I've been thinking of going back to letter-writing as well – I'm sure there's still a demand for that. It would help to be nearer the centre of the town, too. As things are, the three of us have to walk quite a distance each time we deliver work to our customers. If I took over that ground-floor shop the clients could come to us.'

'I think it's a good idea,' Duncan Crombie said. 'Perhaps it's time for you to expand your business.'

She turned to him gratefully. 'The shop itself would make

a good-sized office and I'd not need to do much more than have it painted. The big windows would give us more light – I'd put some net curtaining over them to prevent folk gawping in at us from the pavement. And there's a back room with a cooker and a sink.'

'You sound as though you've already decided.' Forbes sounded hurt, and she turned to him apologetically.

'I know you've done a lot to the old house for my sake, Forbes, but you did say at the beginning that if I failed you could let the upper floor out to someone else.'

'If you ask me, it's too early for you to consider moving, Elspeth. You should harvest your resources for at least a year before making changes.'

'I don't agree,' Duncan Crombie said at once. 'There's nobody else in the area with a typing agency. If Elspeth expands now folk'll take that as an indication that she's doing well. Success builds on success – you should know that as well as I do.'

Forbes said nothing, but looking from his closed face to her father's bland, handsome features, Elspeth felt, not for the first time, like a bone being fought over by two dogs. The coolness between the two men and the way they tended to vie for her attention made her uneasy. She was quite sure that if Forbes had shown enthusiasm for her new plans, her father would then have opposed them.

On the following afternoon Duncan Crombie arrived at the garage when Elspeth was working on her own. He took a turn about the room, stared out of the window for a few minutes, then said, 'I've had a look at that property you mentioned last night.'

She felt a tingle of annoyance at his interference, but curbed it, asking mildly, 'What do you think of it?'

'I notice that there's a small upstairs flat included. Are you thinking of living there?'

She was, but knowing of Duncan's desire to have her living

under his roof, she avoided a direct answer to his question, 'If I take on the property, Rachel'll need somewhere to care for the children.'

'Ah.' There was relief in his voice. 'You don't want to pay too much attention to what young Cameron says, Elspeth. He's never had to worry about money. It's folk like you and me who've pulled themselves up by their bootstraps who know when to take our chances. What d'you plan to do about financing the move?'

'I've already seen the bank manager and I think I can get a loan large enough to set up the place and compensate Forbes for the move. He let me have these rooms for a low rent for the first year, and I'd like to reimburse him for that if I leave,' she explained as her father gave her a questioning look.

'I don't see why you should, if he made the offer of his own free will.'

'I'd prefer to set things straight. After all, he was very kind to me when I first decided to start the agency. I could never have done it without his help.'

'I'm sure,' Crombie said drily, 'that he had his reasons. The man's besotted with you, Elspeth, you must know that. It would only be natural for him to want to help you and place you under an obligation so that he could turn things to his own advantage.'

She felt herself tense with anger. Why did her father and Forbes always have to use her as an excuse to criticise each other? Why couldn't they be more like Thomas, who believed in giving others the right to do as they pleased, and had merely said when told of her new plans, 'You could do well with anything you tackled, Ellie. You've got the courage to fight your own battles.'

'I think you're being unnecessarily hard on Forbes,' she said. 'He's a good friend, and I'm very fond of him.'

'Fond enough to agree to marry him? That's what he's after, my dear. Make no mistake about it.'

'As to that, he hasn't proposed marriage – and if he does,' she said, letting a little of her growing irritation reveal itself, 'I'll be the one to decide what to say.'

He lifted his hands in swift apology. 'Of course you will. Forgive me if I'm interfering, my dear. I'm still learning how to be a father. In any case, I didn't come here to criticise Cameron. I came to say that I'd like to give you a personal loan for the new premises, instead of you having to go cap in hand to the bank. My terms would be more advantageous.'

'I can't let you risk your own money. What if something went wrong?'

'It won't. I have faith in you, and I want to show it in more than words. Please consider it, at least.'

Forbes, Elspeth thought, might say that now it was the older man who wanted to place her under an obligation. On the other hand, she had already hurt her father's feelings by turning down his invitation to move into his home. She owed him something.

'I accept. Thank you,' she said at last, and his face lit up.

'I'm so glad, my dear! I wish your mother could have known that we're together at last. It would have made her happy, I'm sure.'

Elspeth and Forbes almost fell out over her decision to lease the shop and the flat above with a loan from Duncan Crombie.

'You should have let me lend you the money!' he argued, his lower lip pushed out like a sulky child's.

'You've done more than enough for me as it is.'

'And how d'you repay me? By moving out of the garage house.'

They were down on the beach, still one of Elspeth's favourite places. She sat on a rock, while Forbes, sprawling on the ground, threw pebbles into the water, one after another. He had none of Thomas's expertise, she noticed, but on the other hand Forbes wasn't attempting to skim the stones across the water's surface, he was hurling them as though trying to punish the waves, which took no notice, but continued to break in lacy froth on the beach, absorbing the thrown pebbles effortlessly.

'I need more space.'

'I could have given you the other downstairs room.'

'You need it as an office – and I'd not put Thomas out of the only home he has.'

He tossed a final stone and sat up, linking his hands round his knees. 'Why expand the business anyway? You've proved your point – you've shown everyone that you can do it. Isn't that enough?'

'No, it's not. It's more important to me than that – it's my future.'

'I'm your future.' Forbes suddenly twisted round on to his knees, reaching out to take her hand. 'Marry me, Elspeth.'

'Forbes—'

'I'm serious. I want you to be my wife.'

She hadn't been prepared for such a sudden proposal. 'I'm too young for marriage,' she protested weakly.

'You're almost nineteen, the same age my mama was when I was born.'

'But I don't want to marry anyone just yet,' she said in a panic. Despite himself, he started to laugh, then gave a grimace of pain.

'Ouch! I wish I'd picked a better place to propose.' He got to his feet and bent to rub at his knees. 'I'm crippled – and you don't even have the decency to say yes and make it all worth the suffering.'

She rose and put a hand on his arm. 'I'm sorry, Forbes, but I really and truly don't want to think of marriage just now. Not yet.'

'It's not Crombie, is it? Is he turning you against the idea of marrying me?'

'Of course not!'

'He doesn't approve of me. I don't think he'd approve of any man who might come between you and him.'

Elspeth thought fleetingly of her father's comment that only royalty would have met with Celia Bremner's approval as far as her daughter was concerned. 'You're wrong, Forbes. I'm not the sort of spineless creature who would allow anyone to dominate her.'

'I know – that's why I love you, and why I'm going to keep on proposing until you say yes.' Then, as they turned together to walk back to where the car stood, 'You don't really know much about him, do you?'

'I know that he's my father, and he's a good man.'

'A wealthy man, too – yet he came from nothing. What d'you know about the way he earned his money?'

'He earned it honestly!' she snapped, breaking free of him and striding ahead to the road.

Hours later, lying in bed and staring up at the pattern thrown on the bedroom ceiling by the moonlight, she tried to understand why she hadn't accepted his proposal. Was it because of her father's attitude towards Forbes? she wondered, then decided that the reason lay in herself. She liked Forbes very much, and took great pleasure in their shared caresses. But surely there should be more than just a sense of pleasure between two people who genuinely loved each other?

On the following morning Rachel and her daughters were late arriving at the office. The children were unusually subdued when they got there, while Rachel, who claimed to have toothache, had tied a scarf over her head, half obscuring her face.

Once she had given her foster sister time to settle the children, Elspeth left her typewriter and went down to the yard. Thomas, in his dungarees, was working on a car and reluctant to leave it.

'If it's something that needs fixing upstairs, get one of the other men to see to it.'

'I doubt if you'd want any of the men to see to this problem,' she persisted, and finally, grumbling, he wiped his hands with a rag and followed her into the house and upstairs.

Leaving him in the corridor, she put her head round the playroom door and asked Rachel to come outside. When the other girl joined them her face was still wrapped in the scarf. At sight of Thomas she ducked away and tried to go back into the room, but Elspeth was too quick for her. She caught at the scarf and it fell away to reveal a livid black bruise covering most of the side of Rachel's face and puffing the tender flesh beneath one eye.

Thomas's breath caught in his throat. 'Good God, Rachel, what's happened to you?'

'I fell against a door.' His sister tried to turn her injured cheek into the shadows, but he forestalled her, putting one hand beneath her chin and turning her head so that the light from the window at the end of the hall showed up the ugly bruise.

'I think she fell against Bob's fist, and more than once by the look of it,' Elspeth told Thomas.

'Bob?' His voice cracked with disbelief. 'Did Bob do this to you?'

'He's been ill-treating her for a long time, but she wouldn't let me tell anyone.'

'You promised you wouldn't!' Rachel accused Elspeth, tears glistening in her eyes.

'I know I did, but I've held my tongue long enough, and so have you. He's never hurt you as badly as this, Rachel – what d'you think his next step'll be? You could end up in the hospital, or in a graveyard. And what about the bairns? When'll he start on them?'

'He won't – and he'll never touch my sister again,' Thomas said thickly, releasing Rachel and moving towards the stairs.

'Thomas!' She threw herself after him, clutching at the banisters. 'Where are you going?'

'To see Bob,' he said from the landing. 'He's not going to get away with what he's done!'

'No – please! Thomas!' Rachel tried to follow him, but Elspeth held her back.

'Rachel, he can't mark you like that and think that nobody'll see it. Sit down.' As Rachel's knees sagged, Elspeth eased her on to the top step and wrapped her arms about the banisters. 'I'll be back in a minute.'

She put her head round the office door and asked Kirsty to keep an eye on the children for a while. 'Rachel's toothache's worse and I'm going to make some tea for her,' she explained, then helped Rachel downstairs.

As there was a risk of Joe or the other men coming into the

kitchen and finding them, she led the distraught girl into the downstairs room that had once been the garage office, and was now Thomas's home.

'He'll not mind us sitting in here, I'm sure.' She settled Rachel in a chair and went to the kitchen, returning a few minutes later with two cups of strong tea.

'Bob'll kill me for this,' the girl said as Elspeth put a cup into her hand and folded the cold fingers of her other hand round it to hold it steady. Her voice was flat and listless and eerily certain of the truth of the words.

'He'll not.' Elspeth leaned forward and put her own hands round Rachel's. 'We'll see to that – Thomas and me.'

'I'm his wife, you can't stop him.'

'Yes we can. For a start, you're not going back to that house.'

'I have to – where else can I go? I'm not having my bairns sleeping in the gutter or the poors' hospital.'

'Aunt Flora and Uncle Henry'll take you in.'

Rachel laughed bleakly, then winced at the pain in her face. 'Mam? She's told me often enough that a woman's place is with her man, no matter what happens.'

'Uncle Henry wouldn't agree with that.'

'He's got little choice,' Rachel said wryly. 'I'll not be the cause of trouble between them – and I'll not live where I'm not wanted.'

She was right. If Flora McDonald was overruled, and forced to take Rachel and the children in, she would make their lives miserable. Elspeth thought briefly of her father, who had room enough in his rented house, but she couldn't see him agreeing to having two children he didn't know running round the place.

Searching for a solution, she glanced around the room Thomas had been living in for several months. It was immaculate and sparsely furnished, with nothing out of place. The chairs she and Rachel sat in flanked the fireplace, and the sagging old *chaise-longue* that she and Thomas had sat on, holding each other, on the night of Aileen's death had been replaced by a sturdier couch that acted as a seat by day and Thomas's bed by night. A marble-topped washstand in one corner of the room held a large basin and ewer, and a curtain had been hung across one corner as a makeshift wardrobe. The only other pieces of furniture in the room were a chest of drawers with a brush and comb and mirror on top, and a small bookcase.

The house had been designed and built to hold large, heavy Victorian furniture, and Thomas's few possessions scarcely began to use the available floor space. As a result, the room had a barren, cheerless air about it. Every time she went into it Elspeth longed to make it more comfortable, but knew that Thomas would resist such attempts. Since becoming a widower he had had no time for comfort and pleasure.

She sighed, cast a glance at Rachel, who was sipping her tea, then looked up at the ceiling and found the answer to their problems.

'You could live here, Rachel, you and the girls – in the playroom. It's big enough for the three of you, and there's the bathroom – and the kitchen downstairs, and Thomas here at nights, so you'd not be alone.' Now that the idea had occurred to her, Elspeth could see no barrier to it. 'We'll get some furniture easily enough, from second-hand shops. Mr Monteith might be able to help us, and some of my other clients.'

'It wouldn't work,' Rachel said, but there was a faint gleam of hope in her eyes. 'Thomas wouldn't agree – and what about Mr Cameron? It's his house.'

'Leave them to me. We could get something arranged today, then you'd not have to go back to Bob at all. And,' Elspeth added, regretfully relinquishing her secret hopes of moving out of Mearns Street, 'there's the flat above the shop. That'd be ideal for you once I move the office from here.' She got to her feet. 'Finish your tea and we'll see what we can do.'

*

Thomas was working in the yard when they returned, and at sight of him Rachel gave a squeal of horror.

'What happened to your mouth?'

Hampered by a cut lip and a blue knot on his jaw, he gave her a lopsided grin. 'I went to the shipyard and made it clear to Bob Cochran that the McDonalds don't take kindly to their womenfolk being ill-treated.' He looked at his bruised knuckles thoughtfully, then added, 'It took a bit of explaining, but I think he understood what I was trying to tell him.'

'You hit Bob?' Her eyes were dark with horror.

'It's the only language a man like that understands, Rachel. Don't fret – I'll mend, and so will he, for I let him off lightly.'

'And he'll not be able to take it out on you or the children, for you're not going back to the flat,' Elspeth put in, and explained to Thomas about the upstairs room.

He nodded. 'It's the best way, and I'll be here during the night to look after them. You'd mebbe better ask Mr Cameron's permission, though, since it's his property.'

'I've already done that, and he's agreed.'

Thomas gave her a look that Granjan would have described as 'old-fashioned'.

'He'd not deny you anything, would he?'

She flushed, but refused to rise to the bait. 'And I've arranged for some bits of furniture to be delivered, to tide Rachel over.'

'Bob'll not like this,' Rachel moaned. 'He'll mebbe come after us and make us go home.'

'He'll do nothing of the sort. Da was there when I went to the yard, and if I hadnae seen to Bob, he would've. He'll not let the man bother you again,' Thomas assured her.

'But my clothes, and all the bairns' things – they're still at the house.'

'Elspeth and me'll go down with you this evening to collect them. There'll be no more trouble, Rachel, I promise you. Men like Bob Cochran are cowards. They only hurt folk that

338

can't hit back. Now that me and Da know about him, he'll keep well away from you.'

In spite of all their reassurances, Rachel was shaking with fear as the three of them walked to the flat that evening, and Elspeth herself, remembering the way Bob had looked at her in January when she had cared for the children while he and Rachel went to see Lena at the theatre, felt her stomach clenching as her foster sister turned the key in the door.

Thomas went in first, and the two girls stood quaking in the close, clutching at each other and ready to flee if necessary, until he reappeared, grim-faced.

'He's not here, but the place is in a bit of a mess, Rachel.'

'How can it be? I always clean it before I go to the gar—' Rachel, who had pushed past him as she spoke, stopped short, a hand flying to her mouth. Following close behind, Elspeth saw that the kitchen looked as though a whirlwind had passed through it, with drawers thrown to the floor, the curtains ripped from the window, and plates smashed. Clothes and the few toys that Mary and Pearl owned had been strewn everywhere, and a pretty little wall mirror, a wedding gift from Granjan, had been torn down and smashed.

Rachel fell to her knees, trying to gather everything up at once. 'Look at Mary's bonny wee dress that I made just last week!' She held it up to show them the great jagged rip where the skirt was almost torn away from the carefully smocked bodice. 'And Pearl's dolly—' The head had been wrenched off, and lay in a corner, half under a torn fragment of cloth that Elspeth recognised as part of Rachel's favourite skirt.

She knelt and took the other girl into her arms. 'Don't fret, Rachel, it'll all mend.'

Above their heads Thomas said grimly, 'We'd best just gather the lot up and take it all out of here. Then he can live on his lone in the pigsty he's created.'

34

They had to support Rachel between them back to Mearns Street, where Flora, tight-lipped, was looking after the children. To Elspeth's relief the little girls were sound asleep in the darkness of the curtained wall-bed, and were spared the sight of their mother's distress.

Granjan had arrived, and she immediately gathered Rachel into her plump arms and rocked her while Thomas upended the sack he carried and let the debris of Rachel's married life spill out on to the kitchen floor.

'There, there, pet, don't fret yersel', we're all here tae put everythin' right,' Janet Docherty soothed, while Henry, his shirtsleeves rolled up and his braces dangling round his hips, chimed in with, 'As tae that blaggard Bob Cochran, don't give him another thought, for he'll have more sense than tae come near ye after the lesson our Thomas taught him. By God, but it's been many a year since the yard saw such a fight!' He slapped his son on the back. 'Ye went at him as if he was responsible for all the ills o' the world.'

'He's been responsible for enough of them,' Thomas said shortly, his eyes on his sister.

'I didnae know ye were so handy with yer fists—'

'Bein' able tae hit a man hard's nothin' tae be proud of,' Flora broke in. 'And we'll have no more talk of fightin' in my kitchen. Elspeth, make some tea. Rachel, wash yer face and help me tae sort out this mess that's been dumped on my clean floor.'

Henry prudently took his son out for a drink while the womenfolk sifted through the pile of toys and clothing that Thomas had brought from Rachel's flat.

On closer inspection, the damage wasn't as bad as they had first thought. In the throes of his mindless rage, Bob hadn't taken the time to destroy each item individually, so quite a few of the garments and toys had simply been thrown down and were still intact. Some were repairable, and only a small percentage was beyond redemption. The four women settled down with needle and thread, putting things to rights.

'I'm sorry, Mam,' Rachel said meekly as they stitched.

'Sorry doesnae pay for food tae put intae yer bairns' bellies and clothes on their backs. It's menfolk that dae that.' Flora's voice was hard and unforgiving, and Elspeth felt sudden anger against her. Not once had the woman comforted her distraught, bruised daughter.

'If this is what Bob does to his children's clothes,' she held up the tiny skirt she was trying to mend, 'his children are better off without him.'

'And what dae you know about husbands – or fathers, come to that?' Flora asked crushingly.

'I know that Rachel would be better off earning her own money. At least she'd get the use of it, instead of seeing it all go in drink.'

Bright spots of colour flamed on Flora's cheekbones. She had been proud of Bob's teetotal background when he and Rachel first married, and had bragged about it to the neighbours. Now she would have to eat humble pie, something that Flora McDonald hated doing. 'Ye think our Rachel's goin' tae manage on the few pence ye hand over tae her every week like Lady Muck?'

'It's not just what I earn at the garage, Mam.' Rachel rushed to Elspeth's defence. 'There's the money in the—' She caught Elspeth's warning glance and subsided.

'What money?' Flora asked at once. 'What're ye talkin' about?'

The two young women exchanged glances, then Rachel said carefully, 'I've been doing sewing for folk, and Elspeth put the money I earned into the bank for me.'

'Bank?' Flora spoke as though her daughter had just admitted that she had been working in a brothel. 'What are ye doin', havin' truck with banks?'

'It was the only way to keep Bob from taking it, Aunt Flora.'

To Elspeth's relief, the menfolk returned just then, Henry jovial and Thomas his usual quiet, controlled self. The children were coaxed awake and tucked into their coats, and while Henry set off to walk Granjan home, Elspeth accompanied the others to the garage to settle Rachel and the children into the playroom.

'I'm sorry, Mam,' Rachel said timidly as she was about to leave.

'Sorry?' Thomas echoed. 'It's not your fault that Bob Cochran turned out to be such a poor excuse for a man.'

Flora's face was still stony. 'What's done can't be undone,' she said enigmatically.

Thomas carried Mary, the older and heavier of the two little girls, while Elspeth hoisted Pearl's solid, warm little body into her arms and Rachel carried the sack with the salvaged clothes and toys. They walked uphill through the darkness in silence, past the lit windows of tenements. Pearl, light enough when they first set out, seemed to grow heavier with each uphill step. Her head rested on Elspeth's shoulder and her breath was hot and tickly. Elspeth longed to shift her burden to her other arm, but didn't dare for fear of wakening the little girl, who had fallen asleep again.

'Are you managing?' Thomas asked as they neared the garage.

'I'm fine.'

'I hope Bob's not come after us,' Rachel said nervously.

'He's got other things on his mind. It's not just the hiding he got from me – now that Da knows what he's been doing to you, he'll be keeping a close eye on Mr Bob Cochran too,' Thomas told her confidently.

After the day's turmoil it was soothing to be out in the night. Thomas walked between Elspeth and Rachel, and the three of them had fallen into step, their shoes tapping down on the pavement to the same beat. Now and again their arms touched and Elspeth took comfort from Thomas's reassuring nearness.

Despite the fact that the furniture had been acquired so hurriedly, the playroom looked quite comfortable. Joe had set a fire in the grate, and when Thomas put a match to it, the flames took hold at once. Elspeth drew the curtains as Rachel turned slowly, wide-eyed, to take everything in.

'It looks so – cosy!'

They helped her to tuck the children into bed, then left her. 'I'll walk you back home,' Thomas said as they reached the front door.

'And leave Rachel and the bairns here on their own? You'll do nothing of the sort – you know that she's nervous in case Bob's around.'

'Him? He'll be licking his wounds in some public house.'

'Did you really give him a thrashing?'

'Not as bad as Da says, and not as bad as he deserved.' His jaw tightened. 'I could have killed him, Ellie, and I wanted to. I wanted to just keep on hitting until there was nothing left of him but I held back because I knew it wasn't just Bob Cochran I was lashing out at, it was Ian Bruce as well. I've been needin' to hurt someone for a long time, and today I got my chance.'

'Mebbe now that you've got it out of your system you'll be able to get on with your life.'

Although he didn't move she sensed his instant withdrawal. 'I'm fine as I am.'

343

'You should take some time off.'

He gave her a level look from beneath his brows. 'What would I do with it?'

'Go further down the river and sit on the beach, or walk up over the braes to Loch Thom. I'll come with you, if you like.'

He smiled slightly. 'You've already got your hands full with Mr Cameron.'

She poked him in the ribs. 'Do you want another punch in the mouth?'

His smile widened to a grin, then he was serious again. 'Mam didn't have much to say for herself tonight, did she? I thought she'd have been ranting on about Bob.'

'She already knew about him,' Elspeth said, then, as he looked puzzled, 'Bob's been ill-treating Rachel since Mary was small.'

'And Mam knew? Why didn't she say anything?'

'She didn't want to admit that Rachel had made a bad marriage.'

The anger was back in his face and his voice. 'She stood by and let her own daughter suffer just because she didn't want the neighbours to talk? I'll never understand that woman!'

'There are a lot of folk like her in Greenock – probably in the rest of the world too.'

'Aye – folk that let everything crumble about their ears just so's they can go on pretending everything's fine.' His voice was thick with contempt.

'I'll have to go, it's getting late.'

'What'll happen to Rachel when you move?'

'She'll live in the wee flat above the shop.'

'I thought you'd want that for yourself.'

'I was thinking about it, but Rachel's need's greater than mine.'

Thomas ran a hand through his fair hair. 'She's my sister, and it should be my place to find somewhere for her to live – especially after the way Mam turned her back when Rachel needed her most.'

'She's my sister too, and you're doing enough. She can sleep safely at night knowing that you're downstairs.'

He tried again to insist on walking back to Mearns Street with her, but she was adamant.

'Rachel needs to know that you're downstairs and she's not alone in the house. I can look after myself.'

'I never doubted that, but even so—'

'I mean it. I'll be home in five minutes.'

He gave a resigned shrug and reached for the front door latch. Elspeth too had begun to reach for it, but Thomas was swifter, and as her hand landed on his knuckles he winced slightly.

'Let me see—' She took his hand and turned it over, palm on palm, drawing him towards the glow of the gas mantle. His knuckles were bruised and torn and painful-looking.

'I'll find something to put on them,' she said, but Thomas put a hand on her shoulder as she began to lead him to the kitchen, where she had gathered together a box of ointments and salves to treat any cuts or bruises the men might suffer during their workday.

'Don't fuss, it'll be healed by the morning.'

She glared up at him, exasperated. 'You're such a difficult man to help.'

'And you care too much about folk.'

'Only some folk,' Elspeth said. His hand was warm against hers and his other hand still gripped her shoulder. As she looked up at him she saw that the dim light from the gas mantles touched the ends of his rumpled fair hair and his eyelashes with pale gold and cast shadows over his face, emphasising its strong planes and angles. His hazel eyes glowed, and she could smell a hint of the drink he had had earlier on his breath, mingled with the fresh outdoor air on his clothes. She felt slightly dizzy and confused.

'Only special folk,' she heard herself say, then the words died away into silence. Something was happening; it was as if the hallway where they stood was changing, becoming a magic place she had never been in before. Thomas, and her feelings towards him, were also changing.

Suddenly embarrassed in his presence, she dipped her head and found herself looking at the square, strong hand still resting on her own. Although he scrubbed his hands thoroughly after each day's work his trade was etched on them in a faint, permanent tracery of oil around the knuckles and dark shadowing beneath the fingernails, cut short and straight across. The sight of his bruised, painful knuckles struck her to the heart; she laid the palm of her other hand gently over the broken skin as though trying by touch to make him whole again.

The hand on her shoulder moved, the fingers landing lightly on her neck, just below the smooth line of her bobbed hair. The unexpected caress sent a blaze of warmth through her. His thumb moved across her cheek so gently that she scarcely felt it, to touch the corner of her mouth. Giving way to impulse, she turned her head so that her lips brushed the hollow of his palm, tasting the faint mixture of oil and soap that was Thomas's physical signature.

She heard him make a tiny sound in his throat, and as if it was a signal she had been waiting for all her life, she let herself sway towards him. His arms received her, closing round her, gathering her body against his.

She lifted her face, seeking and welcoming his mouth with parted lips. His hair was soft and springy beneath her hands, his kisses urgent, his arms strong and possessive. This was surely what loving felt like. It was far greater than the mere pleasure she knew with Forbes; it was a fierce hunger that, for her, could only be sated by one man. And at last she had found him.

When they drew back from each other she looked up into

his eyes and for just one fleeting moment saw what she had been confidently looking for. Then it was gone. His lids dropped to hood his eyes, his face went blank, his hands put her gently but firmly away from him.

'You'd best go, Elspeth.'

'Go? How can I just go after what's happened?'

'Because it should never have happened. I – forgot myself.'

'It seems to me that we've just found ourselves.' She couldn't believe that he was sending her away. 'Thomas—' She put a hand on his arm, which was hard and unyielding. 'You've been alone for almost two years now. That's long enough.'

'Long enough to realise that happiness has to be paid for, and the price is too high. I'll not walk that road again.'

'Do my feelings not mean anything to you?'

'They mean a great deal – too much for me to let you throw yourself away on me. I failed Aileen and I couldn't bear to fail you too.'

'You didn't fail Aileen – she loved you, and you never let her down.'

'Talk sense, Ellie,' he blazed down at her. 'I took her away from all she'd ever known and put her into a – a box! If I hadn't let her down she'd never have been in that car. She'd be alive today!'

There was no reasoning with him, she thought in despair. No way of convincing him that the blame for Aileen's death shouldn't be lying on his conscience. 'So you're going to punish yourself – and me – for the rest of our lives over what happened to Aileen?'

'You'll thank me, one day. Leave it, Ellie,' he ordered as she began to protest. 'I'll not discuss it again. Are you certain that you don't want me to walk down with you?'

She did, so much. She wanted to be alone with him in the dark night, just the two of them, but she knew by the set of his jaw and the steely note in his voice that he meant what he had

347

said. She had found him and lost him in the space of five minutes.

All that was left to her now was her dignity – tattered, but still there. She gathered it around herself like a shield. 'I'll manage fine,' she said, and stepped out on to the pavement, feeling more alone than ever before.

35

When Elspeth told Joe about what had happened to Rachel he made no secret of his disgust and anger.

'How can anyone treat a bonny wee family like that so badly?'

'There are plenty around like Bob Cochran.'

'I hope I never come across them.' His big fists clenched. 'I'm glad tae hear that Thomas taught the man a thing or two.'

'You'll not say a word in front of Rachel? She's so ashamed of what's happened.'

'What's she got tae be ashamed about?' Joe demanded to know. 'We're all responsible for our own sins, but not for other folk's. Ye neednae fear, lassie, she'll no' hear a word about it from me. Mind you, I thought there was somethin' goin' on. The bairns were too quiet at times – wee ones shouldnae ever look worried, but there were days when Mary and Pearl seemed tae have the cares of the world on their wee shoulders. I can see the difference in them already.'

'Now you come to mention it, so can I. Why didn't I notice it before?'

'You were too close tae them,' he told her. 'We tend tae see what we expect tae see, an' it never occurs tae us tae take a fresh look at folk now and again.'

'I wish I had your understanding, Joe.'

'I learned the hard way.' His face took on a grim look. 'I lost a mate once, at sea. He deliberately put himself overboard,

349

with his pockets weighted down so's we couldnae save him. A right cheery fellow he was, tae. It wasnae until he died that I discovered that he'd been nursin' all sorts of problems and never sayin' a word. I never forgave mysel' for not seein' the truth and doin' somethin' about it in time tae save him. How's Ra – yer sister goin' tae manage?'

'There's the wee bit I pay her, and she'll not be without a roof over her head. She does sewing for people, and that'll help.'

'I'll pass the word around our street,' said Joe. 'She'll probably be glad of some extra work.'

They were in the kitchen. The other mechanics had returned to the yard, but Elspeth had kept Joe back to tell him about Rachel. Now he glanced out of the window and moved away from the sink, where he had been rinsing his cup.

'There's the gaffer – I'd best get back tae work.'

A sense of loss swept over Elspeth as she stood by the window, watching Thomas stride across the yard and disappear into the garage. The night before he had talked of the heavy price he had to pay for Aileen's death, and now Elspeth felt that she herself was paying for the few moments she had spent in his arms. The closeness they had always shared had vanished, possibly for ever. She didn't know whether the ache of bereavement in her heart was due to losing the old Thomas, a dear and trusted friend, or the Thomas she had just discovered and known so briefly. The only thing she was certain of was that the pain of her loss was more than she could bear.

Drearily, dragging her feet, she went back upstairs and tried to get on with her work.

In the afternoon she walked down to Hamilton Street, where she had arranged to meet a local painter to discuss work to be carried out on her new premises.

It took an hour to agree on colours and terms for the work on the flat as well as the office; Elspeth had been looking forward to the task of redecorating the former dress shop to suit her own tastes, but now that the moment had come, she found herself unable to concentrate, and ended up agreeing to the painter's suggestions.

'Aye, ye've got yersel' a nice wee property here,' he said as they returned downstairs after going through the flat. 'Well placed, too.'

'Yes.' Elspeth looked round the spacious area that was to be the office, and wondered if she had done the right thing in renting it. She suddenly realised that the painter was looking at her as though expecting an answer to some question.

'Did you say something?'

'Twice, lassie. I wanted tae know about your name above the door.'

She looked at him blankly for a moment, then remembered that that had been one of the first things she had written at the top of her list – a list she had left lying on her desk at the garage.

'I'd forgotten about that.'

'I thought ye had,' the man said drily. 'Now – what sort of letterin', and what d'ye want it tae say?'

All the pleasure had gone out of the move, Elspeth thought when the man had departed after agreeing to start work the following day, and to call in someone he knew to put the back yard to rights. Rachel and the little girls would be happy in the snug flat, Kirsty and Peggy would enjoy the spaciousness of their new workplace, and now there would be room for another desk and another typist. Thanks to her father's generosity she had a loan large enough to accommodate her plans for expansion.

She looked out at the busy street, so unlike the quiet area where the garage was located, and knew why she had suddenly lost interest in the move. In Hamilton Street she might go for days or even weeks without seeing Thomas. She would have no reason to go to the garage, and that would probably suit him, for he hadn't as much as glanced at her since the previous night.

A church clock chimed as she was locking the door. She had stayed longer than she had intended, and it was too late to return to the garage. She might as well go back to Mearns Street.

Flora was crashing pots about in the kitchen, her features gathered into a tight knot, her body almost throwing off sparks. As soon as Elspeth went in, the woman rounded on her.

'You've got a nerve, walkin' in here as if ye owned the place!'

'What?'

'Don't play the innocent with me, miss. I can see through ye, even if others can't – breakin' up our Rachel's marriage and makin' her the laughin' stock of the town!'

'Aunt Flora, you saw the mess her face was in. Everyone saw it. You surely don't want her to stay with a man who'd treat her like that?'

'A marriage should only concern the two folk that's wed tae each other. "For better or for worse." Rachel made the vows, and it's her duty tae keep them.'

'Bob made vows as well. He vowed to care for her,' Elspeth pointed out, and her aunt glared.

'Bob Cochran was a decent enough man when our Rachel married him. If anythin's gone wrong between them she's tae blame as much as him.'

'Bob Cochran,' said Elspeth clearly, 'is a weakling who needs drink and a woman to bully before he can pretend to be a man.'

'Ye know an awful lot for someone who couldnae even keep her own sweetheart. Ye've never forgiven our Mattie for takin' Kenneth away from ye, have ye? Ye've been spoilin' tae cause trouble in this family ever since.'

'Aunt Flora, that's not true and you know it. I've never wished Mattie and Kenneth anything but well.'

Flora had worked herself up into a frenzy. 'Sniffin' round

that Forbes Cameron just because he's got money! I don't know what yer mother would say if she could see what ye've turned intae! She was an angel, and God knows I did my best tae raise ye tae be like her, but it's been an uphill battle all these years. And how dae ye show yer gratitude for all me and Henry's done for ye? Ye talk Rachel intae makin' fools of us in front of the whole town!'

'I'm grateful to you for taking me in, and I've always done my best to please you, Aunt Flora. But I've always known that you didn't want me.'

'That's what I mean – ingratitude!' Flora shrieked, her rage going out of control. 'It's that wastrel of a father of yours – he's turned yer head altogether since he's come here. Not that it was hard tae dae, for ye've always been his daughter, rotten tae the core!'

Years of resentment had broken through, and now her hatred filled the room, pushing against the walls and stifling the breath in Elspeth's lungs, so that she could only stare at the older woman in stunned silence.

'An' look at what's happened tae our Lachlan, runnin' off after that whore that flaunts hersel' on the stage for all tae see – it was you that encouraged him, and you that got the two of them together—'

At last Elspeth found the energy to turn and stumble from the room. Ranting on, Flora followed. Elspeth shut the bedroom door on the older woman's crimson face, then pushed the one and only chair beneath the door handle which twisted back and forth. Thwarted, Flora McDonald banged on the closed door, screaming abuse, the words running into each other. As Elspeth began to gather up her belongings with shaking hands and push them into the battered old case which one of the boys had used when they went off to the army, she heard the outer door open, then Henry asking, 'Flora? What's amiss?'

To Elspeth's relief Flora McDonald stopped banging on the

door. 'She's amiss – that ungrateful besom I took in when nobody else wanted her!' One single blow on the door made Elspeth jump nervously. 'Get her out of my house – tell her tae go!'

'Who are ye talkin' about? What besom?'

'That daughter of Satan that's destroyed my family,' Flora screamed.

There was a tentative tap on the door. 'Hullo?'

Elspeth's knees were shaking. She leaned against the door panels. 'Uncle Henry—'

'Don't you talk tae her!'

There was the sound of a scuffle, then Flora started to cry with loud, harsh tearing sobs. Beneath the noise, Elspeth heard Henry murmuring soothingly and coaxing her along to the kitchen. The door closed but Elspeth waited, afraid to venture out in case Flora came back.

Five minutes later knuckles tapped gently on the door. 'Ellie?' Henry McDonald whispered. 'Let me in, hen.' She had never been so glad to see his sturdy, stolid bulk. His hair was tousled, his face almost grey. 'Are ye all right, lass?'

'I'm fine,' she told him through chattering teeth. 'How's Aunt Flora?'

'I've never seen her like this – but I knew somethin' was comin' on her, for she's not been hersel' for a while. She's quietened down now.' His eyes fell on the bag in her arms. 'Ye're leavin'?'

'I can't stay here, can I?'

'Where'll ye go?'

If the quarrel had happened a few days earlier she would have gone straight to Thomas, but now that avenue of escape was closed. Nor could she involve Granjan – that would only force the old woman to take sides between her daughter and Elspeth.

'My father's got a spare room I can use. What'll you do?'

'I'll send a neighbour's bairn tae fetch Flora's ma. She'll

know what's best.' As Elspeth opened the main door he put a hand on her shoulder. 'Take care, lass.'

'It's you that needs to do that, Uncle Henry.'

'I'll be fine – and so will she,' he said sturdily.

Duncan Crombie himself opened the door, his eyebrows rising as he saw his daughter standing in the tiny porch, a battered old suitcase clutched in both arms, her face white as a sheet.

'My dear girl, what's happened?'

'I've come to live with you,' said Elspeth, and burst into tears.

Although her father and his housekeeper did all they could to make Elspeth feel at home, she found it hard to settle down. Her new room was bright and spacious and comfortable, but she couldn't forget that if things had gone as she had originally planned she would have been able to live alone in the flat above the shop. Now that the flat was earmarked for Rachel and her children, Elspeth had no option but to stay with her father for the time being, much to his delight.

After her outburst, Flora had alarmed the entire family by taking to her bed for the first time in her life. Janet Docherty moved into Elspeth's former bedroom to nurse her daughter, who lay flat on her back in the wall-bed, staring at the ceiling and taking no interest in life.

The doctor was called in and prescribed an iron tonic to build up her strength, and the removal of all her remaining teeth.

'He says they might be poisonin' her system,' Janet reported to Elspeth. 'But our Flora just gave him one of her looks, then shut her mouth tight and stared back at the ceiling. It'll take a better man than Dr McKee tae open that mouth and take the teeth from it.'

Lachlan, who was working near Glasgow that week, was contacted, and travelled to Greenock with Kenneth and Mattie for a family consultation. He bounded into Thomas's garage room and gave Rachel and Elspeth hugs that almost crushed them.

'It's good to see you both again – and to see Greenock, though I've got no regrets about leaving the place.' He had put on weight, most of it muscle, and had regained all his pre-war vigour, but now it was tempered with maturity and a purposeful air. Studying him, Elspeth saw that Lachlan looked as though he fitted perfectly into his own skin and his own personality, with none of the boneless gawkiness of his youth, or the heartbreaking timidity the war had stamped on him.

'Is Lena with you?'

'She wasn't able to get away – she's almost top of the bill now,' he reported proudly. 'I can only stay for two days myself, for we're moving to Edinburgh at the weekend and I'll be needed.'

'Have you seen Mam?' Rachel asked anxiously.

'We all went straight to the house from the station.' Mattie, bulky in the sixth month of pregnancy, cast an envious sidelong glance at Elspeth's royal-blue hip-length jacket over a slim-fitting cream dress.

The excitement and pleasure vanished from Lachlan's face, leaving it still and shadowed. 'Poor wee Mam – I never thought to see her looking so pathetic and helpless, lying in her bed in the middle of the day.'

Henry and Janet arrived just then, having left Flora in a neighbour's care so that they could join in the family conference, and the excitement of meeting up again abated as they settled down to discuss the reason for their gathering.

Rachel had taken her mother's illness badly. 'It's my fault,' she told the others wretchedly. 'It's me leaving Bob and defying her when she told me to go back to him that did it.'

'From what I hear, you did the right thing,' Lachlan said at once, while Mattie chimed in, 'The only thing. No man should be allowed to strike his own wife!'

Henry, his normally cheerful face suddenly old, put an arm about his elder daughter's shoulders. 'It's not your fault, hen. Ye were quite right tae leave him. If I'd only known about this sooner ye'd have left him long since.' He looked around the group. 'Bob's goin' from bad tae worse, drinkin' most of the time. If he doesnae watch out he'll be turned off from his job. I've tried tae get him tae see sense, but there's no talkin' tae him.'

'If anyone's to blame for Aunt Flora's condition it's me,' Elspeth pointed out. 'I'm the one she quarrelled with just before she fell ill.'

She found an unexpected ally in Thomas. 'I'd say that it's her own temper that's finally turned in on her. Mam's always been used to ruling our lives, and now that we've grown and gone our own ways she misses being able to dominate us. She's brought this on herself.'

'Thomas!' Mattie was shocked. 'It's your own mother you're talking about!'

'I know, but I'm only speaking my mind.' His glance at his father was half apologetic, half defiant. 'This is mebbe hard for you to hear, Da, but it's the way I see it.'

Henry nodded his grey head. 'I cannae deny that yer mam has a temper. It's somethin' I've always accepted, for it's just part of the way she is. It's mebbe the only way she has of showin' she cares. But I know it was hard at times on the rest of ye.' He looked round the circle of faces. 'Especially you, Thomas. I'll always regret that, but it's too late now tae do anythin' about it.'

'Far too late,' Thomas agreed, his face suddenly grim with bitter memories. There was an awkward silence, then Kenneth did his best to bring a note of optimism to the meeting.

'As far as I can gather from Dr McKee there's little physically wrong with her. What she needs most is a good rest.'

'I think she's on her way back to her old self already.' The mischievous smile that had been missing for so many years began to break through Lachlan's solemnity. 'She managed to rouse herself enough to tell me that it was time I settled down and got back to the shipyards.'

'Kenneth's right,' Granjan said briskly. 'All she needs is rest and looking after for a wee while. And some plain, nourishing food.'

Henry looked hurt. 'When did I ever deny her the money tae buy good food?'

'It's nothin' tae do with that,' his mother-in-law told him briskly. 'Women who raise families never eat properly – they're more inclined tae feed themselves from what's left on other folk's plates. They're like rubbish tips, but it's all part of bein' a wife and mother.'

'Are you all right, Da?' Thomas suddenly asked, reaching across the table to put a hand on his father's arm. 'There's nothing to worry about. Kenneth's right – she needs a rest, and once she's had that she'll be right as rain.'

'I know that. Don't worry about us, laddie, ye've got enough tae do with keeping this place goin'.' Henry looked at those who had been away for a while, and added proudly, 'Our Thomas has done a grand job. He'll be owner of his own garage afore he's finished.'

After that, the business over and everyone more at ease about Flora, they settled down to the serious work of catching up on each other's news.

Tomorrow, far too soon, Lachlan and Mattie and Kenneth would return to their own lives, but they would all, those who left and those who stayed, retain a little of the rekindled warmth of their relationships with each other, Elspeth thought, looking at their animated faces.

Flora McDonald's breakdown had served one very useful purpose – it had brought her family together again.

36

Two days after Lachlan and Kenneth and Mattie left Greenock, a horse-drawn wagon clattered to a standstill in front of the garage house to be loaded with furniture for Hamilton Street.

'I never realised we'd gathered up so much stuff,' Peggy lamented, opening yet another drawer to find it filled with papers and notebooks.

'Folk are like magpies,' Kirsty told her. 'Put it all into different boxes, so that it doesn't get mixed up.'

With Thomas's permission, Joe was pressed into carrying boxes downstairs to the waiting cart. Kirsty's daughter and Rachel's little girls, excited by all the activity, tried to accompany him, weaving dangerously round his legs, and Rachel was forced to round them up and remove them from under his feet.

'They're no trouble,' Joe assured her breathlessly, staggering out of the office under the weight of a pile of boxes. 'I'm just worried about their own safety, for I'd not like tae see them trip and fall down the stairs.'

'If you ask me,' Peggy remarked to Elspeth when Joe and Rachel were both safely out of the way, 'Joe's got a fancy for your Rachel – and she likes him too.' She tossed her head. 'After what she's been through she's entitled to some happiness with someone else.'

'But she's married. D'you mean she should get a divorce?'

Kirsty asked, wide-eyed. Not many people in Greenock got divorced.

'She's still young, and Joe's a good man. He dotes on those bairns too—' Kirsty swiftly changed the subject as Rachel returned, her eyes shining with excited anticipation. Even with her hair tied up in a scarf she looked pretty, Elspeth thought. It was understandable that Joe was attracted to her. And Peggy was right – surely Rachel deserved some happiness after what she'd been through. Mebbe a divorce wasn't out of the question.

Carrying down a box filled with pens and pencils and ink bottles and paper a few moments later she almost bumped into Thomas, who was ushering out a client.

'I'll take these.'

'I can manage. You don't want to get your good suit all dusty,' she pointed out, but he took the box from her arms.

As he stowed it on the wagon, she lingered in the doorway, using her handkerchief to remove a slight smear from the brass plate, which was to be unscrewed in the morning. There was no need for it in Hamilton Street, where her name was painted above the door, but she intended to keep it safe forever.

'A car sale?' she asked as Thomas returned.

'I hope so. How's the move going?'

'We'll finish it tomorrow.'

'The place'll be quiet without the lot of you running in and out.'

'I wish we weren't going, Thomas,' Elspeth said impulsively, and for a brief moment their eyes met. Then his were veiled.

'I think it's for the best,' he said quietly.

'I don't—'

He held a hand up. 'Ellie, I don't want to lose your friendship. Leave it at that,' he said, and after a long, difficult moment she bit back the rebellious words flooding to her lips and nodded.

'Neither do I.'

Then they went their separate ways, Thomas to his room to change into his working clothes, Elspeth to climb the stairs, the now-familiar ache, lodged uncomfortably somewhere near her heart, worse than ever.

The opening of the new office was marked with a party on the premises, followed in the evening by a dinner held in Elspeth's honour by Forbes' parents, and attended by Duncan and several of the area's businessmen.

'Forbes and his father thought of inviting them for your benefit, my dear,' Mrs Cameron murmured confidentially as she led Elspeth to a bedroom to take off her coat and brush her hair. 'They're all influential people – they may well bring business your way.'

'I hope so.' Elspeth sat down at the dressing table and studied her face critically. She had learned to use make-up discreetly – a very thin film of powder, a touch of pale pink lipstick to highlight her mouth.

'That's such a pretty dress. I like periwinkle blue – and it matches your eyes perfectly. I can't tell you how pleased my husband and I are about you and Forbes, my dear,' Mrs Cameron went on. 'Every mother likes to see her son settled.' Then, with an arch twinkle in her eyes, she added, 'As you'll find out for yourself one day.'

'Forbes and I are good friends, Mrs Cameron, nothing more.'

'There I go again, jumping to conclusions! I know nothing's been decided, Elspeth, but perhaps one day . . .?'

Elspeth smiled and murmured something noncommittal as she ran a comb through her hair, which now clung to the shape of her head and fell in soft feathers round her face.

As she and her hostess walked into the drawing room, Forbes came forward to meet them, his eyes signalling his approval of her simple tubular dress and its silver lace over-bodice.

361

'The best-dressed woman in the room,' he murmured. 'And without doubt the most successful. Come and meet everyone.'

The dinner was superb, but only part of Elspeth's mind was on the food she ate and the conversation around her. The other part was looking ahead to the following day, the first in the new office. She had advertised for another typist, and hoped that there would be at least a few applications.

While listening with apparent interest to someone enthusing over a play that had recently been staged in Greenock, she ran over the list of things that had been done that day. Everything was in order for the morning, and Rachel and the children were comfortably settled in their new home. As the dinner party prevented Elspeth herself from looking in on them that evening, Joe had promised to call on his way home from the garage to make sure that they had everything they needed. Not that Hamilton Street was on his way, but that wouldn't worry Joe, who lived alone and had little to go home to.

She glanced up the length of the table and saw her father talking animatedly to an attractive woman by his side, who hung on his every word. Duncan Crombie adored social events. He had so much energy and such enthusiasm for life that sometimes Elspeth wondered how long it would be before he tired of Greenock and wanted to move on. He had indicated to her several times his desire to travel, suggesting that she should accompany him.

'See something of the world before you settle down,' he had advised.

'I have settled down. I'm quite content here.'

'Nonsense,' he had retorted. 'How can you know you're settled until you've tried other places and met other people?'

Once, he had spoken like that in front of Forbes, who had flown into a panic in case Elspeth gave in to her father and went off with him. The gulf between the two men was gradually widening, and Elspeth was uncomfortably aware that she herself stood in the middle, courted by both of them.

After the meal the guests roamed the downstairs rooms freely, their voices rising and falling. Forbes escorted Elspeth round the drawing room to make what he called useful introductions.

The warmth and the wine she had had during dinner, coupled with the day's excitement, had made her sleepy. The curtains hadn't yet been drawn over the long drawing room windows and it was dark outside, the glass reflecting movement and colour from within the room. She smothered a yawn and glanced at a clock. It was almost ten o'clock. In another hour, she decided, she would make her excuses and leave.

Forbes was making his way over to her, a prosperous-looking man by his side. Elspeth pinned a polite smile to her lips, but before the two men reached her a maidservant touched Forbes on the arm, murmuring to him. He halted, frowned, asked a question. The woman shook her head and pointed to the hallway, and with a brief word to his companion Forbes turned away.

Elspeth followed, her curiosity roused. At sight of the police constable standing in the hall her blood froze and memories of the night the policeman had called at Mearns Street to tell them that Thomas had been beaten unconscious flooded her mind. This constable, like the other, looked solemn and carried his high helmet beneath one arm. She hurried across the carpet and caught at Forbes' elbow.

'What's happened?'

His face was dazed with disbelief. 'This fellow says the garage is on fire—'

'Thomas! Is Thomas there? Is he all right?' She let Forbes go and clutched at the policeman, who shook his head.

'I don't know any names, miss, but I b'lieve there was someone found on the premises.'

'I must go,' Forbes said. The maidservant was already on her way back from the cloakroom with his coat. 'Tell my parents that—'

363

'I'm coming with you.'

'Elspeth, you can't do anything to help!'

She was already running to the cloakroom, for there was no time to go upstairs to fetch her own coat. She took the nearest garment from its hook and struggled into it as she hurried outside. Forbes was already getting into his car while the policeman pedalled off down the driveway on his bicycle. Hampered a little by the borrowed coat, which was far too large for her and smelled of cigars, Elspeth reached the car and climbed in just as the engine roared into life.

A cloud of oily smoke shot through with streaks of fire hung above the garage. The red glow of flames nearer ground level flickered and danced over the street and the buildings beyond. A fair-sized crowd had gathered, and a fire wagon stood at the kerb.

'The house is standing – it's the garage itself that's burning,' Elspeth heard Forbes say as the car came to a standstill. She threw herself from it and pushed through the gawping people, her muscles and bones strangely lethargic, as though she was struggling through deep water.

'You can't come any closer, miss.' A policeman barred her way. 'It's too dangerous.'

'I'm the owner,' Forbes said breathlessly from her side.

'In that case, follow me, sir.' The man turned, and Elspeth hooked a hand into Forbes' coat pocket to make sure that she wouldn't be left behind. His own hand slid into the pocket to close over hers.

'It'll be all right,' she heard him say reassuringly, but in the red glow from the flames she saw that he was as apprehensive as she was.

They were led across the road to where a group of men huddled together a safe distance from the blaze. Elspeth glimpsed a fireman, axe in hand, running round the side of the house, and others handling a hose. From this vantage point she could also see an ambulance wagon waiting further down the street, well away from the conflagration.

'I'm afraid we're not going to be able to save your garage, sir, or any of the vehicles in it,' someone was saying to Forbes, 'not with all that petrol about. But the house is all right and the fire's beginning to come under control.'

'Damn the garage, man, my manager was in the house,' Forbes said impatiently. 'Is he safe?'

'My men searched the house, but there wasn't anyone there. They've found two men in the garage, though. I can't tell you yet what condition they're in. The medical people are with them now.'

Fear caught at Elspeth's throat and her grip on Forbes' hand tightened. 'Two?' she heard him ask, then his face, stained crimson by the flames, as though covered with blood, swung round towards her. 'Who—?'

'Joe.' To her own ears her voice sounded strange, as though someone else was speaking. 'He must have stayed later than he meant.'

'Oh my God!' Forbes said, just as a group of men appeared through the smoke, two stretchers being handled among them.

'Thomas!' Elspeth tried to run across the street, but some-one held her back. 'Best to leave them to get on with their work, miss,' a voice told her, while Forbes said swiftly, 'We'll go to the hospital.'

As she followed him back to the car she realised that the fingers of one hand were scrabbling at the lapel of the thick leather coat she had dragged on during her rush from the Camerons' house. For a moment she couldn't understand why, then she remembered the pebble brooch, pinned to the collar of her own coat.

She had been trying to clutch at it for comfort, as she always did in moments of stress. But this time, the brooch wasn't there to reassure her that all would be well.

*

365

It turned out that when the fire started Joe was sitting in the flat above the Hamilton Street office, chatting comfortably to Rachel. Thomas McDonald, found in the yard where the blast from an explosion within the workshop had thrown him, had been badly burned. Bob Cochran, inside the workshop at the time, had died when it blew up.

Elspeth would gladly have spent all her time sitting by Thomas's bed in the hospital, but Flora, who had recovered with startling suddenness on hearing that one of her own had been hurt, was there each time Elspeth went into the ward, straight-backed and stony-faced in an upright chair. Uncomfortable in her presence, Elspeth was forced to cut her own visits back. There was plenty for her to do, but she went about all her tasks feeling as though she had been split into two people. One of them was in the hospital with Thomas, the other dealt with the office and with Rachel, shattered by sudden widowhood. Mrs Cameron, who loved children and had told Elspeth frequently that although she herself had not been blessed with the large family she had desired, she hoped to have a lot of grandchildren, took Mary and Pearl over to let Rachel cope with the suddenness of Bob's death.

'I never thought he'd – mebbe if I'd stayed,' she said to Elspeth and Granjan, her face blotched with tears. 'I should never have left him!'

'It was the only thing ye could have done, lassie,' Janet Docherty told her. 'Ye've heard what the polis said – the man was so drunk that he didnae know what he was doin'. An' he'd just been turned away from the shipyard. Ye might as well say that they were tae blame for takin' his work away from him. If that had happened, an' you were still with him, there's no knowing what he'd have done tae ye.' She shivered, holding Rachel close. 'It might be you and the bairns bein' buried at the end of the week, and not Bob, God rest him.'

Bob's drunken rage and his thirst for revenge had centred instead on Thomas, who had given him such a humiliating beating at the shipyard. Venturing into the ward on the day after Bob's funeral, Elspeth was startled to see Thomas's bed unattended, the bedside chair empty. He was lying back on the pillows, eyes closed, bandaged hands lying limply on the bedspread. She perched on the edge of the chair supplied for visitors, anxious not to disturb him. When he was first taken in almost all of his face had been swathed in bandages; now, only one side was covered, and the bandages had been removed from his neck and chest, revealing red but healing skin.

It was the first chance she had had to study him, and now her eyes devoured him as though trying to imprint the memory of him forever in her mind. His fair curly hair had, amazingly, been spared by the flames though his lashes and part of his eyebrows had been burned off, giving what could be seen of his face a strangely naked look.

With a twist of the heart she recalled the night he had kissed her in the garage house. Gaslight from the street outside had caught the tips of his lashes then, making them sparkle with gold light.

In repose he looked vulnerable against the crisp white of the hospital pillows. She desperately wanted to touch him, to brush her fingertips or, better still, her lips over his sleeping face, but she held the yearning in check. Which was just as well, since she found, on transferring her gaze from his mouth to his eyes, that they, in turn, were studying her.

'Did I wake you?'

'I wasn't asleep. I heard you coming and I thought it was Mam. She sits and stares and won't answer any questions. I'll be glad to get out of here.'

'When'll that be?'

'Next week, they say. I'll mebbe have a bit of scarring on my face and on the back of my hands, but I'll be fine.' A shadow came into his eyes. 'It was Bob's funeral yesterday, wasn't it?'

'Yes.' It had been a sorry affair, with only Rachel and Forbes and herself sharing the graveside with Bob's parents and his sister and brother-in-law. There had been no gathering afterwards; each group had gone silently away, with nothing to say to the other.

'How's Rachel?'

'She's taken Bob's death badly. Granjan's been staying with her.'

'It's a terrible thing to say about a man who's dead, but she's better off with him out of her life once and for all.'

'What happened?'

He wrinkled his brow. 'I don't mind much about it – I was in my room and I heard a noise round the back. When I went into the workshop Bob was splashing petrol around the place. I went for him, and he threw the can at me and knocked me off my feet. I must have hit my head when I fell, for the next thing I knew there was fire all round and someone was dragging me along the ground.' He shook his head. 'You'd have thought the man would at least have had the sense to get clear before he started the fire.'

'He was very drunk, seemingly. Mebbe he didn't know what was happening.'

'If so, it would be for the best, poor creature.'

She shivered, and changed the subject. 'Forbes says he's going ahead and buying that other garage he's thinking of, and you'll manage it.'

'Aye, I know. He looked in this morning to tell me.'

She began to say something else, but the words seemed to clump together into a large ball that stuck in her throat. Thomas's face misted then shimmered.

'What's amiss? Is there something they haven't told me yet?'

She swiped at her eyes with one hand. 'It's you. You could have died.'

'But I didn't.'

'You could have! And then I'd not have had the chance to tell you—'

'Ellie,' he said wearily. 'Nothing's changed, and nothing will change.'

'Of course things have changed.' Tears gave way to anger. 'Everything's changed. You almost died! Does that not make you give some thought to your future – our future?'

'My future lies in getting another garage started. Yours is with your agency, and mebbe with Forbes Cameron.' For a moment their eyes locked and to her despair she saw the same stubborn determination in his as before. Then his gaze slid past her and he gave a muffled groan then went limp, his lids closing as Flora McDonald arrived at the other side of the bed.

'I thought you'd be busy with yer fancy new office.'

'I just looked in. He's sleeping.'

'He's always sleepin',' Flora said with a sniff. 'It's this place – it doesnae agree with him.'

She looked pointedly at the chair, and Elspeth relinquished it and left.

37

To Flora's annoyance Thomas refused to convalesce at Mearns Street when he was discharged from hospital. He went straight back to his own home, beside the blackened ruins of the garage he had worked so hard to build up, and he and Forbes immediately became absorbed in plans for the new garage, on the shore road between Greenock and Port Glasgow.

Elspeth rarely saw him. She too had thrown herself into her work, taking on another typist earmarked for temporary work in offices. Her belief that the agency would do well in the heart of the town proved to be correct and her decision to return to letter-writing brought in a fairly steady stream of clients. Peggy, a good letter-writer, shared the task with her.

The rivalry between Forbes Cameron and Duncan Crombie continued as Duncan became increasingly bored with life in Greenock, and pressed Elspeth to sell the business and travel with him.

'Can't you see what he's up to, Elspeth?' Forbes asked. 'He wants you all to himself, and he doesn't care what sort of sacrifice you might have to make. You wouldn't be allowed to be your own person.'

'And could I be my own person if I stayed here and married you?' she asked drily, and he flushed.

'That's different – you know that I'd do anything to make you happy. And you've known me longer – I'm not a fly-by-night who's scarcely been here long enough to take my hat off.'

Often in the evenings she escaped from them both to Granjan's placid little flat, where there were no demands made on her other than making toast or buttering hot home-made pancakes. A month after the fire she found Thomas there one evening; the skin on one side of his face was still red and tender-looking and although the backs of his hands would always be scarred he had retained full use of them.

He didn't stay for long after she arrived. 'He's lookin' well, our Thomas,' Janet said as she returned from seeing him out. 'Havin' that new garage tae hold his interest has helped.'

Elspeth, staring into the fire and wrapped in her own thoughts, said nothing, and Janet lowered herself into her chair with a grunt of relief, turning her skirts back to let the fire warm her knees.

'The nights are fair drawin' in – the bairns'll be round the doors lookin' for their Hallowe'en next week.' Then, with a sidelong look, 'When are ye goin' tae stop pinin' for the man, lassie, an' do somethin' about it?'

'What?' Elspeth was startled out of her reverie. 'D'you mean Forbes?'

Janet Docherty tutted. 'Of course not! Oh, he's a nice enough laddie, but he's not for you. I'm talkin' about Thomas – an' don't try tae tell me I'm haverin', for I've seen the way of it ever since he came back from the army.'

'That's nonsense!'

'I mebbe talk a lot of rubbish at times, but never nonsense. I did think when he met Aileen, rest her soul, that that was an end tae it for you and him, but as it turned out I was wrong there.'

'Thomas has told me that he won't marry again. He means it.'

'So ye've discussed it?'

'No, we—' Elspeth stopped short and felt her face warm. She knew that it wasn't caused by the fire.

'He always was stubborn. So are you – that's what makes

371

the two of ye so suited.' Janet Docherty leaned across the rag rug and put a swollen-veined, work-roughened hand on Elspeth's knee. 'But it seems tae me that you've been short on yer usual stubbornness over this business. Lassie, if something's worth the havin', it's worth fightin' for.'

'I've tried.'

'Tuts – if ye havenae won it means ye've no' tried all that hard. You're the only person that can get ye what ye want. Nob'dy'll dae it for ye.'

Elspeth stared into the flames. 'Mebbe I'd be as well marrying Forbes, or giving in to my father and going away from here.'

'Have I not already told ye that he's no' the right one for ye? Oh, he'd make ye happy enough, and so would Duncan Crombie, for they both care for ye in their own ways and they've both got the money tae spend on ye. But will either one of them bring ye contentment? That's what ye've got tae ask yersel'. Contentment's gettin' what's right for ye, no' just gettin' by.'

Elspeth snuggled into her warm coat and watched the moonlight tracing a path across the dark, almost still river. On the opposite shore, houses and streetlights looked like jewels strewn over the black velvet of the hills. It was a clear, cold night in early December, and Forbes was driving her home along the coast road after an evening spent with friends of his.

As they drew up at the house and she moved to open the door he put a hand out to stop her. 'Let's just sit here for a minute.'

'D'you not want to come in for a cup of tea? My father'll be expecting us.'

'I want to say something, and it's not for his ears.'

Her stomach fluttered, then tensed. She had been expecting another marriage proposal from him, but had thought that he would choose Christmas or possibly the New Year. She hadn't been prepared for it to be so soon.

He sensed the slight withdrawal. 'What's the matter? Are you cold? There's a rug in the back. Or, even better—' He drew her towards him and kissed her, his mouth moving gently on hers, the moustache he had recently grown rough on her upper lip. The scent of the hair oil he used mingled with cigarette smoke and the car's leather upholstery to produce a familiar, pleasant, essentially secure aroma. Security, Elspeth thought, could be very important. Not that Granjan would agree.

When they finally drew apart he shifted slightly in his seat, clearing his throat and staring out through the windscreen. 'Elspeth, I've – heard something about your father.'

'Heard?'

'If you must know, I've been making enquiries. I know I'd no business to do so,' he added hurriedly as she started to speak. 'But he's only just come into your life and I felt it was right that somebody should look after your interests. I discussed it with my father, and he agreed.'

'But you didn't discuss it with me.' She was furious with him for interfering, and for broaching the subject in a voice so serious that it caused her flesh to cringe with apprehension and anxiety.

'You're still very young—'

'I'm old enough to run my own business, old enough to look after my own life!'

'D'you want to hear what I have to say?'

She didn't. She wanted to get out of the car and walk away from him and from Greenock and from everyone. She wanted to put her head under the blankets then wake up to find that the world had been set to rights. She reached up to touch the pebble brooch; she wanted to go back to the day Thomas had given it to her, the day of her thirteenth birthday dumpling.

Instead, reluctantly, she listened to what Forbes had to say, then crept quietly into the hall in the vain hope that Duncan Crombie might have decided, for once, not to stay up for her return.

He appeared from the drawing room as she eased the front door shut. 'Is young Cameron not with you?'

'Not tonight.'

'Come and tell me all about your evening.'

'I'd rather just go to bed. I've got a bit of a headache.' It wasn't a lie; there was a tight metal band round her temples.

'Do you want something for it?'

'I just need my bed.'

'Elspeth,' Duncan Crombie asked with an edge to his voice as she started to climb the stairs, 'Cameron hasn't upset you, has he?'

'No, I'm just tired. Goodnight.' She escaped to the privacy of her room, closing the door with relief. She had a great deal to think about before morning.

Crombie's handsome face wore a worried frown when the two of them met at the breakfast table.

'You don't look at all well. You'd better go back to bed and I'll call a doctor.'

'I'm fine, please don't fuss.'

He looked more closely, and his face darkened. 'Cameron did upset you last night. What happened?'

Elspeth poured herself a cup of tea with a steady hand. 'He asked me to marry him.' Then, as his eyes went blank, 'And I turned him down, once and for all, because he told me that he'd been making enquiries about you.'

'He did what? The young pup!' he exploded, half rising from the table.

'Sit down please, Father.'

He did as she asked. 'What did he tell you?'

'That when your uncle died six months after you went away he left you quite a lot of money in spite of what happened between you and my mother. In fact, it was because you went away – because you did as he told you – that he kept you in his will. Forbes says' – she set the teapot down gently –

'that you inherited enough to support my mother and me. But in spite of that you didn't come back to Greenock.'

The colour drained from his face and the piece of toast he was about to butter was put back on to his plate. 'I – I wrote to Maisie, at her parents' home, asking her to come to England. When she didn't reply I thought—'

'You must have known that her mother would intercept the letter and probably destroy it. You should have come back for her.' Elspeth fisted her hands on the table. 'For us.'

'I – you have to understand that I was very young, Elspeth, younger than you are now. I had no way of knowing if Maisie would take me back. I had no choice but to leave – my uncle held the purse strings, and he arranged the job in England for me with a lawyer he knew.' He swallowed hard, then went on, 'I don't suppose Cameron told you that my uncle had already arranged with the lawyer to buy a junior partnership for me once I'd served my time. The money left to me in his will was part of the arrangement. If I'd returned to Greenock I would have lost it all. I still wouldn't have been able to support you and Maisie.'

'So you put yourself first and kept the money, and left my mother to cope as best she could.'

'I told you – I thought that her parents would look after her – and you – if I was out of the way. And I did come back to look for you, to atone for what I'd done to the two of you all those years ago.'

He leaned across the table earnestly. 'Elspeth, we've only just found each other. Now's the time for us to start again, together. Don't let Cameron's mischief-making come between us – that's what he wants. Once he gets me out of your life, he'll marry you. That's what he plans. You deserve better than him, my dear. Sell the agency and come away with me.'

Elspeth had been making a pretence of drinking her tea. Now she put the cup down gently and got to her feet. 'I'm not my mother. She's dead, and nothing you can do for me will make up for the wrong you did her.'

'Elspeth—'

'I'll come and collect my things when I've found somewhere to stay,' she said steadily from the doorway. 'As for the loan you made me to rent the shop and the flat—'

All his confident charm had gone. He looked old and defeated. It would have been easy to pity him, but Elspeth knew of the dangers that lay in that direction. 'I don't want it back!'

'I wasn't going to offer it. I'm going to do as you wanted in the first place and accept it as a gift – for my mother's sake,' she said, and went out of the house without a backward glance.

She attended to her office duties as usual throughout the day, glad that there were no prospective clients to see, and worked on into the evening, until she was sure that Thomas would be home.

He answered the door in shirt and trousers, blinking his surprise. 'What are you doing here?'

'I want to ask a favour.'

'Did you forget your key?' he asked over his shoulder as she followed him into his room.

'I gave it back to Forbes.'

The room was neat and clean, as usual. An empty plate with knife and fork on it stood on the table, together with a mug.

'I was just finishing my dinner,' Thomas said, following her glance. 'D'you want some tea?' He reached for his jacket, hanging over the back of his chair.

'No, I want you to come to my – to Duncan Crombie's house with me to collect my things.'

He paused in the act of slipping one arm into a jacket sleeve. 'You're moving out? Have you found somewhere else to stay?'

'I'm sharing with Rachel and the bairns for the time being.' She told him, in detail, what Forbes had found out about Duncan Crombie, and he heard her out in silence, then said,

'It takes all sorts of folk to make the world, Ellie.'

'I know that, and mebbe one day I'll forgive him for what he did to my mother. But I'll not stay under his roof.'

'What're you going to do? Marry Forbes?'

She looked him in the eye. 'D'you think I should?'

His gaze dropped. 'You could do worse. He'd be able to give you everything you want, not like—' He paused, then said carefully, 'Not like most men in this town.'

'Money's not everything.'

A muscle jumped in Thomas's jaw, just below the livid scar that now bisected one cheek. 'Mebbe not, but it can be very important.'

'Aileen didn't think so, and neither do I. I'm not going to marry Forbes, for I couldn't marry a man who thinks he has the right to pry into other folk's lives. But I can do business with him.' She glanced round the room. The house windows had shattered in the heat from the fire, but they had been replaced, and the old building still stood steady as a rock. 'I'm going to ask him to sell me this place.'

His jaw dropped. 'What on earth—?'

'I need to live somewhere, and I've always liked this house. It should be lived in, properly, by a family. I'm going to see the bank manager tomorrow, then I'll have a word with Forbes. He might be quite glad to get the place off his hands now that he's got a new garage to finance.'

'And what about me?'

'I'd never turn you out on the street. There's room enough for us both, though I'd really like to see this room going back to being a drawing room. I'm sure we could come to some arrangement,' she said sweetly, and understanding began to dawn in his face.

'Ellie, if this is a ploy to force me to—'

'I've no intention of forcing you to do anything, Thomas McDonald, but I've had enough of accepting what other folk say. Granjan told me that if I wanted something badly enough

I should fight for it. And that's what I'm going to do.'

She held his gaze with her own, while her fingers nimbly unfastened the pebble brooch from the lapel of her grey jacket. 'I can never take Aileen's place, but I can give you a different kind of happiness. I want you to think over what I'm saying, and when you get round to admitting that I'm right, I'm going to sell the agency and buy a wee garage where you can look after the motorcars and I can see to your books. We'll mebbe even rebuild this garage, if that's what you want. Here—'

She crossed to where he stood, going up on tiptoe to fasten the brooch to the inside of his lapel, feeling his chest warm and solid beneath her fingers as she did so. 'You can keep it for the next five years if necessary,' she told him, stepping back. 'When you're ready to see sense you don't have to say so, you only have to return the brooch. Now – come and help me to collect my things and take them to Hamilton Street.'

'You're daft, Elspeth Bremner,' he said, as she reached the door.

She smiled at him over her shoulder, and saw his lips twitch in reply.

'I know I am, but I see no reason to change,' she said, and went through the door and out into the dark street, knowing without having to look back that he was just behind her.

She doubted whether it would be another five years before the pebble brooch came back to her, but even if it was, she could afford to wait.

Five years was such a small price to pay for an entire future.